"MICKEY SPILLANE IS TH[...]
OF THE HARD-BOILED MYSTERY."
—*Detecting Men*

> *I snapped the side of the rod across his jaw and laid the flesh open to the bone. I pounded his teeth back into his mouth with the end of the barrel . . . and I took my own damn time about kicking him in the face. He smashed into the door and lay there bubbling. So I kicked him again and he stopped bubbling.*

One Lonely Night

Mike Hammer's on the prowl for international thugs, on the lookout for military secrets, and on the make with a treacherous society doll too tempting for her own good.

The Big Kill

Mike Hammer slugs it out with a two-timing still luscious ex-Hollywood starlet who's using everything she's got to block the trail of a vicious killer.

Kiss Me, Deadly

She was desperate, terrified, and out of her mind. Now she's dead. Acting as an avenging angel, Mike Hammer heads into an underground urban nightmare.

Also available:

The Mike Hammer Collection, Volume 1, featuring:

I, the Jury, My Gun Is Quick, and *Vengeance Is Mine!*
Introduction by Max Allan Collins

Mike Hammer Novels by Mickey Spillane

I, the Jury

My Gun Is Quick

Vengeance Is Mine!

One Lonely Night

The Big Kill

Kiss Me, Deadly

The Girl Hunters

The Snake

The Twisted Thing

The Body Lovers

Survival . . . ZERO!

The Killing Man

Black Alley

MICKEY SPILLANE

THE MIKE HAMMER COLLECTION

VOLUME 2

ONE LONELY NIGHT

THE BIG KILL

KISS ME, DEADLY

NEW AMERICAN LIBRARY

New American Library
Published by New American Library, a division of
Penguin Putnam Inc., 375 Hudson Street,
New York, New York 10014, U.S.A.
Penguin Books Ltd, 27 Wrights Lane,
London W8 5TZ, England
Penguin Books Australia Ltd, Ringwood,
Victoria, Australia
Penguin Books Canada Ltd, 10 Alcorn Avenue,
Toronto, Ontario, Canada M4V 3B2
Penguin Books (N.Z.) Ltd, 182–190 Wairau Road,
Auckland 10, New Zealand

Penguin Books Ltd, Registered Offices:
Harmondsworth, Middlesex, England

Published by New American Library, a division of Penguin Putnam Inc. Previously published in
separate Dutton editions.

First New American Library Printing, September 2001
10 9 8 7 6 5 4 3 2 1

(NAL)   REGISTERED TRADEMARK—MARCA REGISTRADA

LIBRARY OF CONGRESS CATALOGING-IN-PUBLICATION DATA
Spillane, Mickey, 1918–
The Mike Hammer collection / Mickey Spillane.
    p. cm.
Contents: v. 2. One lonely night—The big kill—Kiss me, deadly
ISBN 0-451-20425-5 (alk. paper)
1. Hammer, Mike (Fictitious character)—Fiction.   2. Private investigators—New York (State)—
New York—Fiction.   3. Detective and mystery stories, American.   I. Title.
PS3537.P652 A6 2001
813'.54—dc21   00-052728

Set in Bembo
Designed by Leonard Telesca

Printed in the United States of America

Contents

Introduction

I don't know what the hell Mickey Spillane needs with an introduction. He certainly didn't get one when the first Dutton hardcovers and Signet paperbacks appeared half a century ago. There were no prefatory remarks by the author, no back cover blurbs by admiring colleagues, no pithy extracts from rave reviews. (There may have been some admiring colleagues around, but as I recall, there weren't a whole lot of rave reviews.)

Nobody had to introduce you to Mike Hammer. You picked up a book and opened it, and he introduced himself.

Like this, in *One Lonely Night*:

> Nobody ever walked across the bridge, not on a night like this. The rain was misty enough to be almost fog-like, a cold gray curtain that separated me from the pale ovals of white that were faces locked behind the steamed-up windows of the cars that hissed by. Even the brilliance that was Manhattan by night was reduced to a few sleepy yellow lights off in the distance.
>
> Some place over there I had left my car and started walking, burying my head in the collar of my raincoat, with the night pulled in around me like a blanket. I walked and I smoked and I flipped the spent butts ahead of me and watched them arch to the pavement and fizzle out with one last wink. If there was life behind the windows of the buildings on either side of me, I didn't notice it. The street was mine, all mine. They gave it to me gladly and wondered why I wanted it so nice and all alone.

Or if that's too hard to get into, try *The Big Kill*:

Two drunks with a nickel between them were arguing over what to play on the juke box until a tomato in a dress that was too tight a year ago pushed the key that started off something noisy and hot. One of the drunks wanted to dance and she gave him a shove. So he danced with the other drunk.

She saw me sitting there with my stool tipped back against the cigarette machine and change of a fin on the bar, decided I could afford a wet evening for two and walked over with her hips waving hello.

"You're new around here, ain't ya?"

"Nah. I've been here since six o'clock."

"Buy me a drink?" She crowded in next to me, seeing how much of herself she could plaster against my legs.

"No." It caught her by surprise and she quit rubbing.

"Don't gentlemen usually buy ladies a drink?". . . .

"I'm not a gentleman, kid."

"I ain't a lady either so buy me a drink."

So I bought her a drink . . .

Here's how he does it in *Kiss Me, Deadly*:

All I saw was the dame standing there in the glare of the headlights waving her arms like a huge puppet and the curse I spit out filled the car and my own ears. I wrenched the wheel over, felt the rear end start to slide, brought it out with a splash of power and almost ran up the side of the cliff as the car fishtailed. The brakes bit in, gouging a furrow in the shoulder, then jumped to the pavement and held.

Somehow I had managed a sweeping curve around the babe. For a few seconds she had been living on stolen time because instead of getting out of the way she had tried to stay in the beam of the headlights. I sat there and let myself shake. The butt that had fallen out of my mouth had burned a hole in the leg of my pants and I flipped it out the window. The stink of burned rubber and brake lining hung in the air like smoke and I was thinking of every damn thing I ever wanted to say to a harebrained woman so I could have it ready when I got my hands on her.

That was as far as I got. She was there in the car beside me, the door slammed shut and she said, "Thanks, mister."

You see what I mean? What you want to do now is keep reading, not sit around while some clown explains why what you just read was gripping. I have to write this crap—I'm getting paid, and I have to give the people something for their money—but you don't have to read it, and I don't see why you would want to. Skip past these ill-chosen words of mine, shake hands with Mike Hammer, and enjoy yourself.

Still with me, eh? Oh, well. Have it your own way.

Hammett and Hemingway and plain-spoken, hard-boiled fiction were born in the Prohibition Era in the aftermath of the First World War. Twenty years and another war later, Mickey Spillane wrote a series of books that grabbed a new generation of readers. Spillane was a vet, and it was vets and their kid brothers who constituted his eager audience.

Spillane's books were different, though no one could tell you exactly how. The action was slam-bang, but that was true of pulp fiction written thirty years earlier. His hero was blunt and violent, given to taking the law into his own hands, but no more so than Carroll John Daly's Race Williams, to mention one of many. There was sexual content, too, but it's hard nowadays to imagine that the decorous erotic episodes in these books could have inflamed a generation of adolescent males. There were people who denounced Spillane for writing pornography, and you've got to wonder what they were thinking of.

If I were an academic I could spin out a hundred thousand words in an attempt to explain what makes Spillane Spillane, but I'm not, and we can all be thankful for that. I'll boil it all down to two words:

Comic books.

Before he wrote novels, Mickey Spillane wrote for the comic books. His first prose fiction consisted of a slew of one- and two-page stories for the comics, and his hero, Mike Hammer, was originally intended as a comic-strip hero. The fast cuts, the in-your-face immediacy, and the clear-cut, no-shades-of-gray, good v. evil story lines of the Mike Hammer novels come straight out of the comic-book world.

Mickey Spillane was writing something new—comic books for grown-ups.

The new generation of readers who embraced Spillane had read comic books before they read novels. They were used to the pace, the frame-by-frame rhythm. And they took to Mike Hammer like a duck to a pool of dark red blood shimmering in the sickly yellow light of the streetlamp . . .

Sorry. I got carried away there for a moment.

★ ★ ★

There are a lot of Mickey Spillane stories, and everybody's got a favorite. Here's mine:

Quite a few years ago, several crime novelists were invited to appear for a radio panel discussion of their craft. I wasn't one of them, but Donald E. Westlake was, and it was he who told me the story. Whoever the panelists were, they nattered back and forth until their hour was up, and when they were off the air, Spillane said, "You know what? We never talked about money."

The host winced and steeled himself to explain to the creator of Mike Hammer that there was no money budgeted to pay the panelists. But that wasn't what Mickey was getting at.

"We didn't talk about money," he said, "and money's very important. Let me give you an example. Back when we first moved down to South Carolina, I just relaxed and took it easy for a while, and every now and then it would occur to me that it would be fun to write a story. But I didn't have any ideas. I would take long walks on the beach, I would sit and think, but I could never manage to come up with an idea.

"Then one day I got a call from my accountant. 'Mickey,' he said, 'it's not desperate or anything, but the money's starting to run low. It might be a good idea to generate some income.'

"So I thanked him and hung up the phone, and *bang!* just like that, I started getting ideas!"

—Lawrence Block
Greenwich Village
September 2001

Lawrence Block's novels range from the urban noir of Matthew Scudder (*Everybody Dies*) to the urbane effervescence of Bernie Rhodenbarr (*The Burglar in the Rye*). Other characters include the globe-trotting insomniac Evan Tanner (*Tanner On Ice*) and the introspective assassin Keller (*Hit List*). He has published articles and short fiction in *American Heritage, Redbook, Playboy, GQ,* and *The New York Times,* and he has brought out several collections of short fiction, the most recent being his *Collected Mystery Stories.* Larry is a Grand Master of the Mystery Writers of America and a past president of both MWA and the Private Eye Writers of America. He has won the Edgar and Shamus awards four times each and the Japanese Maltese Falcon award twice, as well as the Nero Wolfe and Philip Marlowe awards. Larry and his wife, Lynne, are enthusiastic New Yorkers and relentless world travelers.

ONE LONELY NIGHT

To Marty

CHAPTER 1

Nobody ever walked across the bridge, not on a night like this. The rain was misty enough to be almost fog-like, a cold gray curtain that separated me from the pale ovals of white that were faces locked behind the steamed-up windows of the cars that hissed by. Even the brilliance that was Manhattan by night was reduced to a few sleepy, yellow lights off in the distance.

Some place over there I had left my car and started walking, burying my head in the collar of my raincoat, with the night pulled in around me like a blanket. I walked and I smoked and I flipped the spent butts ahead of me and watched them arch to the pavement and fizzle out with one last wink. If there was life behind the windows of the buildings on either side of me, I didn't notice it. The street was mine, all mine. They gave it to me gladly and wondered why I wanted it so nice and all alone.

There were others like me, sharing the dark and the solitude, but they huddled in the recessions of the doorways not wanting to share the wet and the cold. I could feel their eyes follow me briefly before they turned inward to their thoughts again.

So I followed the hard concrete footpaths of the city through the towering canyons of the buildings and never noticed when the sheer cliffs of brick and masonry diminished and disappeared altogether, and the footpath led into a ramp then on to the spidery steel skeleton that was the bridge linking two states.

I climbed to the hump in the middle and stood there leaning on the handrail with a butt in my fingers, watching the red and green lights of the boats in the river below. They winked at me and called in low, throaty notes before disappearing into the night.

Like eyes and faces. And voices.

I buried my face in my hands until everything straightened itself out again, wondering what the judge would say if he could see me now. Maybe he'd laugh because I was supposed to be so damn tough, and here I was with hands that wouldn't stand still and an empty feeling inside my chest.

He was only a little judge. He was little and he was old with eyes like two berries on a bush. His hair was pure white and wavy and his skin was loose and wrinkled. But he had a voice like the avenging angel. The dignity and knowledge behind his face gave him the stature of a giant, the poise of Gabriel reading your sins aloud from the Great Book and condemning you to your fate.

He had looked at me with a loathing louder than words, lashing me with his eyes in front of a courtroom filled with people, every empty second another stroke of the steel-tipped whip. His voice, when it did come, was edged with a gentle bitterness that was given only to the righteous.

But it didn't stay righteous long. It changed into disgusted hatred because I was a licensed investigator who knocked off somebody who needed knocking off bad and he couldn't get to me. So I was a murderer by definition and all the law could do was shake its finger at definitions.

Hell, the state would have liquidated the guy anyway . . . maybe he would have pronounced sentence himself. Maybe he thought I should have stayed there and called for the cops when the bastard had a rod in his hand and it was pointing right at my gut.

Yeah, great.

If he had let it stay there it would have been all right. I'd been called a lot of things before. But no, he had to go and strip me naked in front of myself and throw the past in my face when it should have stayed dead and buried forever. He had to go back five years to a time he knew of only secondhand and tell me how it took a war to show me the power of the gun and the obscene pleasure that was brutality and force, the spicy sweetness of murder sanctified by law.

That was me. I could have made it sound better if I'd said it. There in the muck and slime of the jungle, there in the stink that hung over the beaches rising from the bodies of the dead, there in the half-light of too many dusks and dawns laced together with the crisscrossed patterns of bullets, I had gotten a taste of death and found it palatable to the extent that I could never again eat the fruits of a normal civilization.

Goddamn, he wouldn't let me alone! He went on and on cutting me down until I was nothing but scum in the gutter, his fists slamming against the bench as he prophesied a rain of purity that was going to wash me into the sewer with the other scum leaving only the good and the meek to walk in the cleanliness of law and justice.

One day I would die and the world would be benefited by my death. And to the good there was only the perplexing question: Why did I live and breathe now . . . what could possibly be the reason for existence when there was no good in me? None at all.

So he gave me back my soul of toughness, hate and bitterness and let me dress in the armor of cynicism and dismissed me before I could sneer and make the answer I had ready.

He had called the next case up even before I reached the side of the room. It had all the earmarks of a good case, but nobody seemed to be interested. All they watched was me and their eyes were bright with that peculiar kind of horrified disgust that you see in people watching some nasty, fascinating creature in a circus cage.

Only a few of them reflected a little sympathy. Pat was there. He gave me a short wave and a nod that meant everything was okay because I was his friend. But there were things the judge had said that Pat had wanted to say plenty of times too.

Then there was Pete, a reporter too old for the fast beats and just right for the job of picking up human interest items from the lower courts. He waved too, with a grimace that was a combination grin for me and a sneer for the judge. Pete was a cynic too, but he liked my kind of guy. I made bonus stories for him every once in a while.

Velda. Lovely, lovely Velda. She waited for me by the door and when I walked up to her I watched her lips purse into a ripe, momentary kiss. The rows and rows of eyes that had been following me jumped ahead to this vision in a low-cut dress who threw a challenge with every motion of her body. The eyes swept from her black pumps to legs and body and shoulders that were almost too good to be real and staggered when they met a face that was beauty capable of the extremes of every emotion. Her head moved just enough to swirl her black page-boy hair and the look she sent back to all those good people and their white-haired guardian of the law was something to be remembered. For one long second she had the judge's eye and outraged justice flinched before outraged love.

That's right, Velda was mine. It took a long time for me to find out just how much mine she was, much too long. But now I knew and I'd never forget it. She was the only decent thing about me and I was lucky.

She said, "Let's get out of here, Mike. I hate people with little minds."

We went outside the building to the sidewalk and climbed in my car.

She knew I didn't want to talk about it and kept still. When I let her out at her apartment it was dark and starting to rain. Her hand went to mine and squeezed it. "A good drunk and you can forget about it, Mike. Sometimes people are too stupid to be grateful. Call me when you're loaded and I'll come get you."

That was all. She knew me enough to read my mind and didn't care what I thought. If the whole damn world climbed on my back there would still be Velda ready to yank them off and stamp on their faces. I didn't even tell her good-by. I just shut the door and started driving.

No, I didn't get drunk. Twice I looked in the mirror and saw me. I didn't look like me at all. I used to be able to look at myself and grin without giving a damn how ugly it made me look. Now I was looking at myself the same way those people did back there. I was looking at a big guy with an ugly reputation, a guy who had no earthly reason for existing in a decent, normal society. That's what the judge had said.

I was sweating and cold at the same time. Maybe it did happen to me over there. Maybe I did have a taste for death. Maybe I liked it too much to taste anything else. Maybe I was twisted and rotted inside. Maybe I would be washed down the sewer with the rest of all the rottenness sometime. What was stopping it from happening now? Why was I me with some kind of lucky charm around my neck that kept me going when I was better off dead?

That's why I parked the car and started walking in the rain. I didn't want to look in that damn mirror any more. So I walked and smoked and climbed to the hump in the bridge where the boats in the river made faces and spoke to me until I had to bury my face in my hands until everything straightened itself out again.

I was a killer. I was a murderer, legalized. I had no reason for living. Yeah, he said that!

The crazy music that had been in my head ever since I came back from those dusks and dawns started again, a low steady beat overshadowed by the screaming of brassier, shriller instruments that hadn't been invented yet. They shouted and pounded a symphony of madness and destruction while I held my hands over my ears and cursed until they stopped. Only the bells were left, a hundred bells that called for me to come closer to the music, and when I wouldn't come they stopped, one by one, all except one deep, persistent bell with a low, resonant voice. It wouldn't give up. It called me to it, and when I opened my eyes I knew the bell was from a channel marker in the river, calling whenever it swayed with the tide.

It was all right once I knew where it came from. At least it was real. That judge, that damn white-headed son-of-a-bitch got me like this. I wasn't so tough after all. It wouldn't have been so bad . . . but maybe he was right. Maybe he was dead right and I'd never be satisfied until I knew the answer myself. If there was an answer.

I don't know how long I stood there. Time was just the ticking of a watch and a blend of sound from the ramp behind me. At some point after the sixth cigarette the cold mist had turned into a fine snow that licked at my face and clung to my coat. At first it melted into damp patches on the steel and concrete, then took hold and extended itself into a coverlet of white.

Now the last shred of reality was gone completely. The girders became giant trees and the bridge an eerie forest populated by white-capped rubber-tired monsters streaking for the end of the causeway that took them into more friendly surroundings. I leaned back into the shadow of a girder and watched them to get my mind off other things, happy to be part of the peace and quiet of the night.

It came at last, the lessening of tension. The stiffness went out of my fingers and I pulled on a smoke until it caught in my lungs the way I liked it to do. Yeah, I could grin now and watch the faces fade away until they were onto the port and starboard lights of the ships again, and the bell that called me in was only a buoy some place off in the dark.

I ought to get out of it. I ought to take Velda and my office and start up in real estate in some small community where murder and guns and dames didn't happen. Maybe I would, at that. It was wonderful to be able to think straight again. No more crazy mad hatred that tied my insides into knots. No more hunting the scum that stood behind a trigger and shot at the world. That was official police business. The duty of organized law and order. And too slow justice. No more sticks with dirty ends on them either.

That's what the snow and the quiet did for me. It had been a long time since I had felt this good. Maybe the rottenness wasn't there at all and I was a killer only by coincidence. Maybe I didn't like to kill at all.

I stuck another Lucky in my mouth and searched my pockets for matches. Something jerked my head up before I found them and I stood there listening.

The wind blew. The snow hissed to the street. A foghorn sounded. That was all.

I shrugged and tore a match out of the book when I heard it again. A little, annoying sound that didn't belong on the bridge in the peace and quiet. They were soft, irregular sounds that faded when the wind shifted, then came back stronger. Footsteps, muted by the inch or so of snow on the walk.

I would have gotten the butt lit if the feet weren't trying to run with the desperate haste that comes with fatigue. The sound came closer and closer until it was a shadow fifty feet away that turned into a girl wrapped in a coat with a big woolly collar, her hands reaching for the support of a girder and missing.

She fell face down and tried to pull herself up to run again, but she couldn't make it. Her breathing was a long, racking series of sobs that shook her body in a convulsion of despair.

I'd seen fear before, but never like this.

She was only a few steps away and I ran to her, my hands hooking under her arms to lift her to her feet.

Her eyes were like saucers, rimmed with red, overflowing with tears that blurred her pupils. She took one look at me and choked, "Lord . . . no, please!"

"Easy, honey, take it easy," I said. I propped her against the girder and her eyes searched my face through the tears unable to see me clearly. She tried to talk and I stopped her. "No words, kid. There's plenty of time for that later. Just take it easy a minute, nobody's going to hurt you."

As if that stirred something in her mind, her eyes went wide again and she turned her head to stare back down the ramp. I heard it too. Footsteps, only these weren't hurried. They came evenly and softly, as if knowing full well they'd reach their objective in a few seconds.

I felt a snarl ripple across my mouth and my eyes went half shut. Maybe you can smack a dame around all you want and make her life as miserable as hell, but nobody has the right to scare the daylights out of any woman. Not like this.

She trembled so hard I had to put my arm around her shoulder to steady her. I watched her lips trying to speak, the unholy fear spreading into her face as no sound came.

I pulled her away from the girder. "Come on, we'll get this straightened out in a hurry." She was too weak to resist. I held my arm around her and started walking toward the footsteps.

He came out of the wall of white, a short, pudgy guy in a heavy belted ulster. His homburg was set on the side of his head rakishly, and even at this distance I could see the smile on his lips. Both his hands were stuck in his pockets and he walked with a swagger. He wasn't a bit surprised when he saw the two of us. One eyebrow went up a little, but that was all. Oh yes, he had a gun in one pocket.

It was pointing at me.

Nobody had to tell me he was the one. I wouldn't even have to know he had a rod in his hand. The way the kid's body stiffened with the shock of seeing him was enough. My face couldn't have been nice to look at right then, but it didn't bother the guy.

The gun moved in the pocket so I'd know it was a gun.

His voice fitted his body, short and thick. He said, "It is not smart to be a hero. Not smart at all." His thick lips twisted into a smile of mingled satisfaction and conceit. It was so plain in his mind that I could almost hear him speak it. The girl running along, stumbling blindly into the arms of a stranger. Her pleas for help, the guy's ready agreement to protect her, only to look down the barrel of a rod.

It didn't happen like that at all, but that's what he thought. His smile widened and he said harshly, "So now they will find the two of you here tomorrow." His eyes were as cold and as deadly as those of a manta ray.

He was too cocky. All he could see was his own complete mastery of the situation. He should have looked at me a little harder and maybe he would have seen the kind of eyes I had. Maybe he would have known that I was a killer in my own way too, and he would have realized that I knew he was just the type who would go to the trouble of taking the gun out of his pocket instead of ruining a good coat.

I never really gave him a chance. All I moved was my arm and before he had his gun out I had my .45 in my fist with the safety off and the trigger back. I only gave him a second to realize what it was like to die then I blew the expression clean off his face.

He never figured the hero would have a gun, too.

Before I could get it back in the holster the girl gave a lunge and backed up against the railing. Her eyes were clear now. They darted to the mess on the ground, the gun in my hand and the tight lines that made a mask of kill-lust of my face.

She screamed. Good God, how she screamed. She screamed as if I were a monster that had come up out of the pit! She screamed and made words that sounded like, "You . . . one of them . . . no more!"

I saw what she was going to do and tried to grab her, but the brief respite she had was enough to give her the strength she needed. She twisted and slithered over the top of the rail and I felt part of her coat come away in my hand as she tumbled headlong into the white void below the bridge.

Lord, Lord, what happened? My fingers closed over the handrail and I stared down after her. Three hundred feet to the river. The little fool didn't have to do that! She was safe! Nothing could have hurt her, didn't she realize that? I was shouting it at the top of my lungs with nobody but a dead man to hear me. When I pulled away from the rail I was shaking like a leaf.

All because of that fat little bastard stretched out in the snow. I pulled back my foot and kicked what was left of him until he rolled over on his face.

I did it again, I killed somebody else! Now I could stand in the courtroom in front of the man with the white hair and the voice of the Avenging Angel and let him drag my soul out where everybody could see it and slap it with another coat of black paint.

Peace and quiet, it was great! I ought to have my head examined. Or the guy should maybe; his had a hell of a hole in it. The dirty son-of-a-bitch for trying to get away with that. The fat little slob walks right up to me with a rod in his hand figuring to get away with it. The way he strutted you'd think he didn't have a care in the world, yet just like that he was going to kill two people without batting an eye. He got part of what he wanted anyway. The girl was dead. He was the kind of a rat who would have gotten a big laugh out of the papers tomorrow. Maybe he was supposed to be the rain of purity that was going to wash me down the gutter into the sewer with the rest of the scum. Brother, would that have been a laugh.

Okay, if he wanted a laugh, he'd get it. If his ghost could laugh I'd make it real funny for him. It would be so funny that his ghost would be the laughingstock of hell and when mine got there it'd have something to laugh at too. I'm nothing but a stinking no-good killer but I get there first, Judge. I get there first and live to do it again because I have eyes that see and a hand that works without being told and I don't give a damn what you do to my soul because it's so far gone nothing can be done for it! Go to hell yourself, Judge! Get a real belly laugh!

I tore his pockets inside out and stuffed his keys and wallet in my coat. I ripped out every label on his clothes right down to the laundry marks then I kicked the snow off the pavement and rubbed his fingertips against the cold concrete until there weren't any fingertips left. When I was finished he looked like the remains of a scarecrow that had been up too many seasons. I grabbed an arm and a leg and heaved him over the rail, and when I heard a faint splash many seconds later my mouth split into a grin. I kicked the pieces of the cloth and his gun under the rail and let them get lost in the obscurity of the night and the river. I didn't even have to worry about the bullet. It was lying right there in the snow, all flattened out and glistening wetly.

I kicked that over the side too.

Now let them find him. Let them learn who it was and how it happened. Let everybody have a laugh while you're at it!

It was done and I lit a cigarette. The snow still coming down put a new layer over the tracks and the dark stain. It almost covered up the patch of cloth that had come from the girl's coat, but I picked that up and stuck it in with the rest of the stuff.

Now my footsteps were the only sound along the ramp. I walked back to the city telling myself that it was all right, it had to happen that way. I was me and I couldn't have been anything else even if there had been no war. I was all right, the world was wrong. A police car moaned through the pay station and passed me as its siren was dying down to a low whine. I didn't even give it a second thought. They weren't going anywhere, certainly not to the top of the hump because not one car had passed during those few minutes it had happened. Nobody saw me, nobody cared. If they did the hell with 'em.

I reached the streets of the city and turned back for another look at the steel forest that climbed into the sky. No, nobody ever walked across the bridge on a night like this.

Hardly nobody.

CHAPTER 2

I didn't go home that night. I went to my office and sat in the big leather-covered chair behind the desk and drank without getting drunk. I held the .45 in my lap, cleaned and reloaded, watching it, feeling in it an extension of myself. How many people had it sent on the long road? My mind blocked off the thought of the past and I put the gun back in the sling under my arm and slept. I dreamt that the judge with the white hair and eyes like two berries on a bush was pointing at me, ordering me to take the long road myself, and I had the .45 in my hand and my finger worked the trigger. It clicked and wouldn't go off, and with every sharp click a host of devilish voices would take up a dirge of laughter and I threw the gun at him, but it wouldn't leave my hand. It was part of me and it stuck fast.

The key turning in the lock awakened me. Throughout that dream of violent action I hadn't moved an inch, so that when I brought my head up I was looking straight at Velda. She didn't know I was there until she tossed the day's mail on the desk. For a second she froze with startled surprise, then relaxed into a grin.

"You scared the whosis out of me, Mike." She paused and bit her lip. "Aren't you here early?"

"I didn't go home, kid."

"Oh. I thought you might call me. I stayed up pretty late."

"I didn't get drunk, either."

"No?"

"No."

Velda frowned again. She wanted to say something, but during office hours she respected my position. I was the boss and she was my secretary. Very beautiful, of course. I loved her like hell, but she didn't know how much and she was still part of the pay roll. She decided to brighten the office with a smile instead, sorted the things on my desk, and started back to the reception room.

"Velda . . ."

She stopped, her hand on the knob and looked over her shoulder. "Yes, Mike?"

"Come here." I stood up and sat on the edge of the desk tapping a Lucky against my thumbnail. "What kind of a guy am I, kitten?"

Her eyes probed into my brain and touched the discontent. For a moment her smile turned into an animal look I had seen only once before. "Mike . . . that judge was a bastard. You're an all-right guy."

"How do you know?" I stuck the butt between my lips and lit it.

She stood there spraddle-legged with her hands low on her hips like a man, her breasts rising and falling faster than they should, fighting the wispy thinness of the dress. "I could love you a little or I could love you a lot, Mike. Sometimes it's both ways but mostly it's a lot. If you weren't all right I couldn't love you at all. Is that what you wanted me to say?"

"No." I blew out a stream of smoke and looked at the ceiling. "Tell me about myself. Tell me what other people say."

"Why? You know it as well as I do. You read the papers. When you're right you're a hero. When you're wrong you're kill-happy. Why don't you ask the people who count, the ones who really know you? Ask Pat. He thinks you're a good cop. Ask all the worms in the holes, the ones who have reason to stay out of your way. They'll tell you too . . . if you can catch them."

I chucked the butt into the metal basket. "Sure, the worms'll tell me. You know why I can't catch them, Velda? Do you know why they're scared to death to tangle with me? I'll tell you why. They know damn well I'm as bad as they are . . . worse, and I operate legally."

She reached out a hand and ran it over my hair. "Mike, you're too damn big and tough to give a hang what people say. They're only little people with little minds, so forget it."

"There's an awful lot of it."

"Forget it."

"Make me," I said.

She came into my arms with a rush and I held her to me to get warm and let the moist softness of her lips make me forget. I had to push to get her away and I stood there holding her arms, breathing in a picture of what a man's woman should look like. It was a long time before I could manage a grin, but she brought it out of me. There's something a woman does without words that makes a man feel like a man and forget about the things he's been told.

"Did you bring in the paper?"

"It's on my desk."

She followed me when I went out to get it. A tabloid and a full-sized job were there. The tab was opened to a news account of the trial that was one column wide and two inches long. They had my picture, too. The other rag gave me a good spread and a good going over and they didn't have my picture. I could start picking my friends out of the pack now.

Instead of digesting the absorbing piece of news, I scanned the pages for something else. Velda scowled at my concentration and hung over my shoulder. What I was looking for wasn't there. Not a single thing about two bodies in the river.

"Something, Mike?"

I shook my head. "Nope. Just looking for customers."

She didn't believe me. "There are some excellent prospects in the let-ter file if you're interested. They're waiting for your answer."

"How are we fixed, Velda?" I didn't look at her.

I put the paper down and reached in my pocket for a smoke.

"We're solvent. Two accounts paid up yesterday. The money has been banked and there's no bills. Why?"

"Maybe I'll take a vacation."

"From what?"

"From paid jobs. I'm tired of being an employee."

"Think of me."

"I am," I said. "You can take a vacation too if you want to."

She grabbed my elbow and turned me around until I was fencing with her eyes again. "Whatever you're thinking isn't of fun on some beach, Mike."

"It isn't?" I tried to act surprised.

"No." She took the cigarette from my mouth, dragged on it and stuck it back. She never moved her eyes. "Mike, don't play with me, please. Either tell me or don't, but quit making up excuses. What's on your mind?"

My mouth felt tight. "You wouldn't believe it if I told you."

"Yes I would." There was nothing hidden in her answer. No laugh-ter, no scorn. Just absolute belief in me.

"I want to find out about myself, Velda."

She must have known what was coming. I said it quietly, almost softly, and she believed me. "All right, Mike," she said. "If you need me for anything you know where to find me."

I gave her the cigarette and went back to the office. How deep can a woman go to search a man's mind? How can they know without being told when some trival thing can suddenly become so important? What is it that gives them that look as if they know the problem and the answer too, yet hold it back because it's something you have to discover for yourself?

I sat down in the swivel chair again and pulled all the junk out of my pockets: the keys, the wallet and the change. Two of the keys were for a car. One was an ordinary house key, another for a trunk or suitcase, and another for either a tumbler padlock or another house.

If I expected to find anything in the wallet I was mistaken. There were six fives and two singles in the bill compartment, a package of three-cent stamps and a card-calendar in one pocket, and a plain green card with the edges cut off at odd angles in the other pocket. That was all.

That was enough.

The little fat boy didn't have his name in print anywhere. It wasn't a new wallet either. Fat boy didn't want identification. I didn't blame him. What killer would?

Yeah, that was enough to make me sit back and look at the scuffed folder of calfskin and make me think. It would make you think too. Take a look at your own wallet and see what's in it.

I had the stuff spread out on the desk when I remembered the other pocket of my raincoat and pulled out the huge tweed triangle that had come from the girl's coat. I laid it out on my lap with the night before shoved into some corner of my brain and looked at it as though it were just another puzzle, not a souvenir of death.

The cloth had come apart easily. I must have grabbed her at the waist because the section of the coat included the right-hand pocket and part of the lining. I rubbed the fabric through my fingers feeling the soft texture of fine wool, taking in the details of the pattern. More out of curiosity than anything else, I stuck my hand inside the pocket and came up with a crumpled pack of cigarettes.

She didn't even have time for a last smoke, I thought. Even a condemned man gets that. She didn't. She took one look at me and saw my eyes and my face and whatever she saw there yanked a scream from her lungs and the strength to pull her over the rail.

What have I got locked up inside me that comes out at times like that? What good am I alive? Why do I have to be the one to pull the trigger and have my soul torn apart afterwards?

The cigarettes were a mashed ball of paper in my hand, a little wad of paper, cellophane and tinfoil that smelt of tobacco and death. My teeth were locked together and when I looked down at my hand my nail ripped through the paper and I saw the green underneath.

Between the cigarettes and the wrapper was another of those damnable green cards with the edges cut off at odd angles.

Two murders. Two green cards.

It was the same way backwards. Two green cards and two murders.

Which came first, the murders or the cards?

Green for death.

Murder at odd angles. Two murders. Eight odd angles. Yes, two murders. The fat boy got what he was after. Because of him the girl was murdered no matter how. So I got him. I was a murderer like they said, only to me it was different. I was just a killer. I wondered what the law would say and if they'd make that fine difference now. Yeah. I could have been smart about it; I could have done what I did, called the police and let them take over then take the dirty medicine the papers and the judge and the public would have handed me. No, I had to be smart. I had to go and mix it up so much that if those bodies were found and the finger pointed at me all I could expect was a trip on that long road to nowhere.

Was that why I did it . . . because I felt smart? No, that wasn't the reason. I didn't feel smart. I was mad. I was kill-crazy mad at the bastards the boy with the scythe pointed out to me and goddamn mad at all the screwy little minds and the screwy big minds that had the power of telling me off later. They could go to hell, the judge and the jury and all the rest of them! I was getting too sick and disgusted of fighting their battles for them anyway! The boy with the scythe could go to hell with the rest and if he didn't like it he could come after me, personally. I'd love that. I wish there *was* a special agency called Death that could hear what I was thinking and make a try for me. I'd like to take that stinking black shadow and shove his own scythe down his bony throat and disjoint him with a couple of .45's! Come on, bony boy, let's see you do what you can! Get your white-haired judge and your good people tried and true and let's see just how good you are! I think I'm better, see? I think I can handle any one of you, and if you get the idea I'm kidding, then come and get me.

And if you're afraid to come after me, then I'm going after you.

Maybe I'll know what I'm like then. Maybe I'll find out what's going on in my mind and why I keep on living when fat cold-blooded killers and nice warm-blooded killers are down there shaking hands with the devil!

I pulled the green card out of the cigarettes and matched it to the one from the wallet. They fitted—Twins. I put them in my shirt pocket, grabbed my coat and hat and slammed the door after me when I left the office.

At a little after ten I pulled up outside the brick building that was the house of the law. Here was where the invisible processes went on that made cops out of men and murderers out of clues. The car in front of mine was an official sedan that carried the D.A.'s sticker and I smoked a butt right down to the bottom before I decided to try to reach Pat even if the fair-haired boy of the courts was around.

I should have waited a minute longer. I had my hand on the door when he pushed through and it looked like a cold wind hit him in the face. He screwed his mouth up into a snarl, thought better of it and squeezed a smile out.

Strictly an official smile.

He said, "Morning."

I said, "Nice day."

He got in his car and slammed the door so hard it almost fell off. I waved when he drove by. He didn't wave back. The old guy on the elevator took me upstairs and when I walked into Pat's office I was grinning.

Pat started, "Did you . . ."

I answered with a nod. "I did. We met at the gate. What got into the lad, is he sore at me?"

"Sit down, Mike." Pat waved his thumb at the straight-back wooden chair reserved for official offenders about to get a reprimand. "Look, pal, the District Attorney is only an elected official, but that's a mighty big 'only.' You put him over a barrel not so long ago and he isn't going to forget it. He isn't going to forget who your friends are, either."

"Meaning you."

"Meaning me exactly. I'm a Civil Service servant, a Captain of Homicide. I have certain powers of jurisdiction, arrest and influence. He supersedes them. If the D.A. gets his hooks into you just once, you'll have a ring through your nose and I'll be handed the deal of whipping you around the arena just to give him a little satisfaction. Please quit antagonizing the guy for my sake if not for your own. Now what's on your mind?"

Pat leaned back and grinned at me. We were still buddies.

"What's new on the dockets, chum?"

"Nothing," he shrugged. "Life has been nice and dull. I come in at eight and go home at six. I like it."

"Not even a suicide?"

"Not even. Don't tell me you're soliciting work."

"Hardly. I'm on vacation."

Pat got that look. It started behind the pupils where no look was supposed to be. A look that called me a liar and waited to hear the rest of the lie. I had to lie a little myself. "Since you have it so easy, how about taking your own vacation with me? We could have some fun."

The look retreated and disappeared altogether. "Hell, I'd love to, Mike, but we're still scratching trying to catch up on all the details around here. I don't think it's possible." He screwed up his forehead. "Don't you feel so hot?"

"Sure, I feel fine, that's why I want a vacation while I can enjoy it." I slapped my hat back on my head and stood up. "Well, since you won't come I'll hit the road alone. Too bad. Ought to be lots doing."

He rocked his chair forward and took my hand. "Have fun, Mike."

"I will." I gave it a pause, then: "Oh, by the way. I wanted to show you something before I left." I reached in my shirt pocket and took out the two green cards and tossed them on the desk. "Funny, aren't they?"

Pat dropped my hand like it had been hot. Sometimes he gets the damnedest expression on his face you ever saw. He held those cards in his fingers and walked around the desk to close and lock the door. What he said when he sat down makes dirty reading.

"Where'd you get these?" His voice had an edge to it that meant we were close to not being buddies any more.

"I found 'em."

"Nuts. Sit down, damn it." I sat down easy again and lit a smoke. It was hard to keep a grin off my mouth. "Once more, Mike, where'd they come from?"

"I told you I found them."

"Okay, I'll get very simple in my questioning. *Where* did you find them?"

I was getting tired of wearing the grin. I let it do what it wanted to do and I felt the air dry my teeth. "Look, Pat, remember me? I'm your friend. I'm a citizen and I'm a stubborn jerk who doesn't like to answer questions when he doesn't know why. Quit the cop act and ask right. So tell me I handed you a line about a vacation when all I wanted to get was some information. So tell me something you haven't told me before."

"All right, Mike, all right. All I want to know is where you got them."

"I killed a guy and took it off his body."

"Stop being sarcastic."

I must have grinned the dirtiest kind of grin there was. Pat watched me strangely, shook his head impatiently and tossed the cards back on the desk. "Are they so important I can't hear about it, Pat?"

He ran his tongue across his lips. "No, they're not so important in one way. I guess they could be lost easily enough. There're plenty of them in circulation."

"Yeah?"

He nodded briefly and fingered the edge of one. "They're Communist identification cards. One of the new fronts. The Nazi bund that used to operate in this country had cards just like 'em. They were red though. Every so often they change the cuts of the edges to try to trip up any spies. When you get in the meeting hall your card has to match up with a master card."

"Oh, just like a lodge." I picked one up and tucked it in my coat pocket.

He said, "Yeah," sourly.

"Then why all the to-do with the door. We're not in a meeting hall."

Pat smacked the desk with the flat of his hand. "I don't know, Mike. Damn it, if anybody but you came in with a couple of those cards I would have said what they were and that's all. But when it's you I go cold all over and wait for something to happen. I know it won't happen, then it does. Come on, spill it. What's behind them?" He looked tired as hell.

"Nothing, I told you that. They're curious and I found two of them. I'd never seen anything like it before and thought maybe you'd know what they were."

"And I did."

"That's right. Thanks."

I put my hat back on and stood up. He let me get as far as the door. "Mike . . ." He was looking at his hand.

"I'm on vacation now, pal."

He picked up a card and looked at the blank sides of it. "Three days ago a man was murdered. He had one of these things clutched in his hand."

I turned the knob. "I'm still on vacation."

"I just thought I'd tell you. Give you something to think about."

"Swell. I'll turn it over in my mind when I'm stretched out on a beach in Florida."

"We know who killed him."

I let the knob slip through my fingers and tried to sound casual. "Anybody I know?"

"Yes, you and eight million others. His name is Lee Deamer. He's running for State Senator next term."

My breath whistled through my teeth. Lee Deamer, the people's choice. The guy who was scheduled to sweep the state clean. The guy who was kicking the politicians all over the joint. "He's pretty big," I said.

"Very."

"Too big to touch?"

His eyes jumped to mine. "Nobody is that big, Mike. Not even Deamer."

"Then why don't you grab him?"

"Because he didn't do it."

"What a pretty circle *that* is. I had you figured for a brain, Pat. He killed a guy and he didn't do it. That's great logic, especially when it comes from you."

A slow grin started at the corner of his eyes. "When you're on vacation you can think it over, Mike. I'll wrap it up for you, just once. A dead man is found. He has one of these cards in his hand. Three people positively identified the killer. Each one saw him under favorable conditions and was able to give a complete description and identification. They came to the police with the story and we were lucky enough to hush it up.

"Lee Deamer was identified as the killer. He was described right to the scar on his nose, his picture was snapped up the second it was shown and he was identified in person. It's the most open-and-shut case you ever saw, yet we can't touch him because when he was supposed to be pulling a murder he was a mile away talking to a group of prominent citizens. I happened to be among those present."

I kicked the door closed with my foot and stood there. "Hot damn."

"Too hot to handle. Now you know why the D.A. was in such a foul mood."

"Yeah," I agreed. "But it shouldn't be too tough for you, Pat. There's only four things that could have happened."

"Tell me. See if it's what I'm thinking."

"Sure, kid. One: twins. Two: a killer disguised as Deamer. Three: a deliberate frame-up with witnesses paid to make the wrong identification. Four: it was Deamer after all."

"Which do you like, Mike?"

I laughed at his solemn tone. "Beats me, I'm on vacation." I found the knob and pulled it open. "See you when I get back."

"Sure thing, Mike." His eyes narrowed to slits. "If you run across any more cards, tell me about them, will you?"

"Yeah, anything else?"

"Just that one question. Where did you get them?"

"I killed a guy and took it off his dead body."

Pat was swearing softly to himself when I left. Just as the elevator door closed he must have begun to believe me because I heard his door open and he shouted, "Mike . . . damn it, Mike!"

I called the *Globe* office from a hash house down the street. When I asked the switchboard operator if Marty Kooperman had called in yet she plugged into a couple of circuits, asked around and told me he was just about to go to lunch. I passed the word for him to meet me in the lobby if he wanted a free chow and hung up. I wasn't in a hurry. I never knew a reporter yet who would pass up a meal he wasn't paying for.

Marty was there straddling a chair backwards, trying to keep his eyes on two blondes and a luscious redhead who was apparently waiting for someone else. When I tapped him on the shoulder he scowled and whispered, "Hell, I almost had that redhead nailed. Go away."

"Come on, I'll buy you another one," I said.

"I like this one."

The city editor came out of the elevator, said hello to the redhead and they went out together. Marty shrugged. "Okay, let's eat. A lousy political reporter doesn't stand a chance against that."

One of the blondes looked at me and smiled. I winked at her and she winked back. Marty was so disgusted he spit on the polished floor. Some day he'll learn that all you have to do is ask. They'll tell you.

He tried to steer me into a hangout around the corner, but I nixed the idea and kept going up the street to a little bar that put out a good meal without any background noise. When we had a table between us and the orders on the fire, Marty flipped me a cigarette and the angle of his eyebrows told me he was waiting.

"How much about politics do you know, Marty?"

He shook the match out. "More than I can write about."

"Know anything about Lee Deamer?"

His eyebrows came down and he leaned on his elbows. "You're an investigator, Mike. You're the lad with a gun under his coat. Who wants to know about Deamer?"

"Me."

"What for?" His hand was itching to go for the pad and pencil in his pocket.

"Because of something that's no good for a story," I said. "What do you know about him?"

"Hell, there's nothing wrong with him. The guy is going to be the next senator from this state. He packs a big punch and everybody likes him including the opposition. He's strictly a maximum of statesman and a minimum of politician. Deamer has the cleanest record of anybody, probably because he has never been mixed up in politics too much. He is independently wealthy and out of reach as far as bribery goes. He has no use for chiselers or the spoils system, so most of the sharp boys are against him."

"Are you against him, Marty?"

"Not me, feller. I'm a Deamer man through and through. He's what we need these days. Where do you stand?"

"I haven't voted since they dissolved the Whig party."

"Fine citizen you are."

"Yeah."

"Then why the sudden curiosity?"

"Suppose I sort of hinted to you . . . strictly off the record . . . that somebody was after Deamer. Would you give me a hand? It may be another of those things you'll never get to write about."

Marty balled his hands into fists and rubbed his knuckles together. His face wasn't nice to look at. "You're damn right I'll help. I'm just another little guy who's sick of being booted around the block by the bastards that get themselves elected to public office and use that office to push their own wild ideas and line their own pockets. When a good thing comes along those stinking pigs go all out to smear it. Well, not if I can help it, and not if about nine tenths of the people in this burg can help it either. What do you need, kid?"

"Not much. Just a history on Deamer. All his background from as far back as you can go. Bring it right up to date. Pictures too, if you have any."

"I have folders of the stuff."

"Good," I said. Our lunch came up then and we dug into it. Throughout the meal Marty would alternately frown at his plate then glance up at me. I ate and kept my mouth shut. He could come to his own decision. He reached it over the apple pie he had for dessert. I saw his face relax and he let out a satisfied grunt.

"Do you want the stuff now?"

"Any time will do. Stick it in an envelope and send it to my office. I'm not in a hurry."

"Okay." He eyed me carefully. "Can you let me in on the secret?"

I shook my head. "I would if I could, pal. I don't know what the score is yet myself."

"Suppose I keep my ears to the ground. Anything likely to crop up that you could use?"

"I doubt it. Let's say that Deamer is a secondary consideration to what I actually want. Knowing something about him might help both of us."

"I see." He struck a match under the table and held it to a cigarette. "Mike, if there is a news angle, will you let me in on it?"

"I'd be glad to."

"I'm not talking about publishable news."

"No?"

Marty looked through the smoke at me, his eyes bright. "In every man's past there's some dirt. It can be dirt that belongs to the past and not to the present. But it can be dirty enough to use to smear a person, smear him so good that he'll have to retreat from the public gaze. You aren't tied up in politics like I am so you haven't got any idea how really rotten it is. Everybody is out for himself and to hell with the public. Oh, sure, the public has its big heroes, but they do things just to make the people think of them as heroes. Just look what happens whenever Congress or some other organization uncovers some of the filthy tactics behind government . . . the next day or two the boys upstairs release some big news item they've been keeping in reserve and it sweeps the dirt right off the front page and out of your mind.

"Deamer's straight. Because he's straight he's a target. Everybody is after his hide except the people. Don't think it hasn't been tried. I've come across it and so have the others, but we went to the trouble of going down a little deeper than we were expected to and we came across the source of the so-called 'facts.' Because it was stuff that was supposed to come to light during any normal compilation of a man's background the only way it could reach the public without being suspected of smear tactics by the opposition was through the newspapers.

"Well, by tacit agreement we suppressed the stuff. In one way we're targets too because the big boys with the strings know how we feel. Lee Deamer's going to be in there, Mike. He's going to raise all kinds of hell with the corruption we have in our government. He'll smoke out the rats that live on the public and give this country back some of the strength that it had before we were undermined by a lot of pretty talk and pretty faces.

"That's why I want to get the story from you . . . if there is one. I want to hold a conference with the others who feel like I do and come to an honest conclusion. Hell, I don't know why I've become so damn public-spirited. Maybe it's just that I'm tired of taking all the crap that's handed out."

I put a light to my butt and said, "Has there been anything lately on the guy?"

"No. Not for a month, anyway. They're waiting until he gets done stumping the state before they pick him apart."

Pat was right then. The police had kept it quiet, not because they were part of the movement of righteousness, but because they must have suspected a smear job. Deamer couldn't have been in two places at once by any means.

"Okay, Marty. I'll get in touch with you if anything lousy comes up. Do me a favor and keep my name out of any conversation, though, will you?"

"Of course. By the way, that judge handed you a dirty one the other day."

"What the hell, he could be right, you know."

"Sure he could, it's a matter of opinion. He's just a stickler for the letter of the law, the exact science of words. He's the guy that let a jerk off on a smoking-in-the-subway charge. The sign said NO SMOKING ALLOWED, so he claimed it allowed you not to smoke, but didn't say anything about not smoking. Don't give him another thought."

I took a bill from my wallet and handed it to the waiter with a wave that meant to forget the change. Marty looked at his watch and said he had to get back, so we shook hands and left.

The afternoon papers were out and the headlines had to do with the Garden fight the night before. One of the kids was still out like a light. His manager was being indicted for letting him go into the ring with a brain injury.

There wasn't a word about any bodies being found in the river. I threw the paper in a waste barrel and got in my car.

I didn't feel so good. I wasn't sick, but I didn't feel so good. I drove to a parking lot, shoved the car into a corner and took a cab to Times Square and went to a horror movie. The lead feature had an actor with a split personality. One was a man, the other was an ape. When he was an ape he killed people and when he was a man he regretted it. I could imagine how he felt. When I stood it as long as I could I got up and went to a bar.

At five o'clock the evening editions had come out. This time the headlines were a little different. They had found one of the bodies.

Fat boy had been spotted by a ferryboat full of people and the police launch had dragged him out of the drink. He had no identification and no fingerprints. There was a sketch of what he might have looked like before the bullet got him smack in the kisser.

The police attributed it to a gang killing.

Now I was a one-man gang. Great. Just fine. Mike Hammer, Inc. A gang.

CHAPTER 3

The rain. The damned never-ending rain. It turned Manhattan into a city of reflections, a city you saw twice no matter where you looked. It was a slow, easy rain that took awhile to collect on your hat brim before it cascaded down in front of your face. The streets had an oily shine that brought the rain-walkers out, people who went native whenever the sky cried and tore off their hats to let the tears drip through their hair.

I buttoned my coat under my neck and turned the collar up around my ears. It was good walking, but not when you were soaking wet. I took it easy and let the crowd sift past me, everybody in a hurry to get nowhere and wait. I was going south on Broadway, stopping to look in the windows of the closed stores, not too conscious of where my feet were leading me. I passed Thirty-fourth still going south, walked into the Twenties with a stop for a sandwich and coffee, then kept my course until I reached the Square.

That was where my feet led me. Union Square. Green cards and pinched-faced guys arguing desperately in the middle of little groups. Green cards and people listening to the guys. What the hell could they say that was important enough to keep anybody standing in the rain? I grinned down at my feet because they had the sense that should have been in my head. They wanted to know about the kind of people who carried green cards, the kind of people who would listen to guys who carried green cards.

Or girls.

I ambled across the walk into the yellow glare of the lights. There were no soapboxes here, just those little knots of people trying to talk at once and being shouted down by the one in the middle.

A cop went by swinging his night stick. Whenever he passed a group he automatically got a grip on the thing and looked over hopefully.

I heard some of the remarks when he passed. They weren't nice.

Coming toward me a guy who looked like a girl and a girl who looked like a guy altered their course to join one group. The girl got right into things and the guy squealed with pleasure whenever she said something clever.

Maybe there were ten groups, maybe fifteen. If it hadn't been raining there might have been more. Nobody talked about the same thing. Occasionally someone would drop out of one crowd and drift over to another.

But they all had something in common. The same thing you find in a slaughterhouse. The lump of vomit in the center of each crowd was a Judas sheep trying to lead the rest to the ax. Then they'd go back and get more. The sheep were asking for it too. They were a seedy bunch in shapeless clothes, heavy with the smell of the rot they had asked for and gotten. They had a jackal look of discontent and cowardice, a hungry look that said you kill while we loot, then all will be well with the world.

Yeah.

Not all of them were like that, though. Here and there in the crowd was a pin-striped business suit and homburg. An expensive mink was flanked by a girl in a shabby gray cloth job and a guy in a hand-me-down suit with his hands stuck in the pockets.

Just for the hell of it I hung on the edge of the circle and listened. A few latecomers closed in behind me and I had to stand there and hear just why anybody that fought the war was a simple-minded fool, why anybody who tolerated the foreign policy of this country was a Fascist, why anybody who didn't devote his soul and money to the enlightenment of the masses was a traitor to the people.

The goddamn fools who listened agreed with him, too. I was ready to reach out and pluck his head off his shoulders when one of the guys behind me stood on his toes and said, "Why don't you get the hell out of this country if you don't like it?" The guy was a soldier.

I said, "Attaboy, buddy," but it got lost in the rumble from the crowd and the screech the guy let out. The soldier swore back at him and tried to push through the crowd to get at the guy, only two guys in trench coats blocked him.

Lovely, lovely, it was just what I wanted! The soldier went to shove the two guys apart and one gave him an elbow. I was just going to plant a beauty behind his ear when the cop stepped in. He was a good cop, that one. He didn't lift the night stick above his waist. He held it like a lance and when it hit it went in deep right where it took all the sound out of your body. I saw two punks fold up in the middle and one of the boys in the raincoats let out a gasp. The other one stepped back and swore.

The cop said, "Better move on, soldier."

"Ah, I'd like to take that pansy apart. Did you hear what he said?"

"I hear 'em every night, feller," the cop told him. "They got bats in their heads. Come on, it's better to let 'em talk."

"Not when they say those things!"

The cop grinned patiently. "They gotta right to say 'em. You don't *have* to listen, you know."

"I don't give a hoot. They haven't got a right to say those things. Hell, the big mouth probably was too yeller to fight a war and too lazy to take a job. I oughta slam 'im one."

"Uh-huh." The cop steered him out of the crowd. I heard him say, "That's just what they want. It makes heroes of 'em when the papers get it. We still got ways of taking care of 'em, don't worry. Every night this happens and I get in a few licks."

I started grinning and went back to listening. One boy in a trench coat was swearing under his breath. The other was holding on to him. I shifted a little to the side so I could see what I thought I had seen the first time. When the one turned around again I knew I was right the first time.

Both of them were wearing guns under their arms.

Green cards, loud-mouthed bastards, sheep, now guns.

It came together like a dealer sweeping in the cards for shuffling. The game was getting rough. But guns, why guns? This wasn't a fighting game. Who the devil was worth killing in this motley crowd? Why guns here when there was a chance of getting picked up with them?

I pulled back out of the crowd and crossed the walk into the shadows to a bench. A guy sat on the other end of it with a paper over his face, snoring. Fifteen minutes later the rain quit playing around and one by one the crowd pulled away until only a handful was left around the nucleus. For guys who were trying to intimidate the world they certainly were afraid of a little water. All of a sudden the skies opened up and let loose with everything in sight. The guy on the end of the bench jumped up, fighting the paper that wrapped itself around his face. He made a few drunken animal noises, swallowed hard when he saw me watching him and scurried away into the night.

I had to sit through another five minutes of it before I got up. The two men in the trench coats waited until the loose-jointed guy in the black overcoat had a fifty-foot start, then they turned around and followed him. That gave them a good reason for the rods under their arms.

Bodyguards.

Maybe it was the rain that made my guts churn. Maybe it was those words beating against my head, telling me that I was only scum. Maybe it was just me, but suddenly I wanted to grab that guy in the overcoat and slam his teeth down his throat and wait to see what his two boys would do. I'd like to catch them reaching for a gun! I'd like them to move their hands just one inch, then I'd show them what practice could do when it came to snagging a big, fat gun out of a shoulder sling! So I was a sucker for fighting a war. I was a sap for liking my country. I was a jerk for not thinking them a superior breed of lice!

That cop with the round Irish face should have used a knife in their bellies instead of the butt end of a night stick.

I waited until they were blurs in the rain then tagged along in the rear. They were a fine pair, those two, a brace of dillies. I tailed them into the subway and out again in Brooklyn. I was with them when they walked down Coney Island Avenue and beside them when they turned into a store off the avenue and they never knew I was there.

Down at the corner I crossed the street and came back up the other side. One of the boys was still in the doorway playing watchdog. I wanted to know how smart the people were who wanted to run the world. I found out. I cut across the street and walked right up to the guy without making any fuss about it. He gave me a queer look and drew his eyebrows together in a frown, trying to remember where he had seen me before. He was fumbling for words when I pulled out the green card.

He didn't try to match them up. One look was enough and he waved his head at the door. I turned the knob and went in. I'd have to remember to tell Pat about that. They weren't being so careful at all.

When I closed the door I changed my mind. The light went on, just like a refrigerator, and I saw the blackout shades on the windows and door, the felt padding beneath the sill so no light could escape under the door. And the switch. A home-made affair on the side of the door that cut the light when the door opened and threw it back on again when it closed.

The girl at the desk glanced up impatiently and held out her hand for the card. She matched them. She matched them damn carefully, too, and when she handed them back she had sucked hollows into her cheeks trying to think of the right thing to say.

"You're from . . . ?"

"Philly," I supplied. I hoped it was a good answer. It was. She nodded and turned her head toward a door in the back of the anteroom. I had to wait for her to push a button before it opened under my hand.

There were twenty-seven people in the other room. I counted them. They were all very busy. Some of them were at desks clipping things from newspapers and magazines. One guy in a corner was taking pictures of the things they clipped and it came out on microfilm. There was a little group around a map of the city over against one wall, talking too earnestly and too low for me to catch what they were saying.

I saw the other boy in the trench coat. He still had it on and he was sticking close with the guy in the overcoat. Evidently the fellow was some kind of a wheel, checking on activities here and there, offering sharp criticism or curt words of approval.

When I had been there a full five minutes people began to notice me. At first it was just a casual glance from odd spots, then long searching looks that disappeared whenever I looked back. The man in the overcoat licked his lips nervously and smiled in my direction.

I sat down at a table and crossed my legs, a smoke dangling from my mouth. I smoked and I watched, trying to make some sense out of it. Some of them even looked like Commies, the cartoon kind. There were sharp eyes that darted from side to side, too-wise women dazzled by some meager sense of responsibility, smirking students who wore their hair long, tucked behind their heads. A few more came in while I sat and devoted themselves to some unfinished task. But sooner or later their eyes came to mine and shifted away hurriedly when I looked at them.

It became a game, that watching business. I found that if I stared at some punk who was taking his time about doing things he became overly ambitious all of a sudden. I went from one to the other and came at last to the guy in the overcoat.

He was the head man here, no doubt about it. His word was law. At twenty minutes past eleven he started his rounds of the room, pausing here and there to lay a mimeographed sheet on a desk, stopping to emphasize some obscure point.

Finally he had to pass me and for a split second he hesitated, simpered and went on. I got it and played the game to the hilt. I walked to a desk and picked up one of the sheets and read it as I sat on the edge of the desk. The scraggly blonde at the desk couldn't keep her hands from shaking.

I got the picture then. I was reading the orders for the week; I was in on the pipeline from Moscow. It was that easy. I read them all the way through, tossed the sheet down and went back to my chair.

I smiled.

Everybody smiled.

The boy in the trench coat with the gun under his arm came over and said, "You will like some coffee now?" He had an accent I couldn't place.

I smiled again and followed him to the back of the room. I didn't see the door of the place because it was hidden behind the photography equipment.

It led into a tiny conference room that held a table, six chairs and a coffee urn. When the door closed there were seven of us in the room including two dames. Trench Coat got a tray of cups from the closet and set them on the table. For me it was a fight between grinning and stamping somebody's face in. For an after-office-hours coffee deal it certainly was a high-tension deal.

To keep from grinning I shoved another Lucky in my mouth and stuck a light to it. There they were, everyone with a coffee cup, lined up at the urn. Because I took my time with the smoke I had to join the end of the line, and it was a good thing I did. It gave me time enough to get the pitch.

Everybody had been watching me covertly anyway, saying little and satisfied with me keeping my mouth shut. When they took their coffee black and wandered off to the table the two women made a face at the bitter taste. They didn't like black coffee. They weren't used to black coffee. Yet they took black coffee and kept shooting me those sidewise glances.

How simple can people get? Did they take everybody for dummies like themselves? When I drew my cup from the urn Trench Coat stood right behind me and waited. He was the only one that bothered to breathe and he breathed down my neck.

I took my sugar and milk. I took plenty of it. I turned around and lifted my cup in a mock toast and all the jerks started breathing again and the room came to life. The two women went back and got sugar and milk.

The whole play had been a signal setup a kid could have seen through.

Trench Coat smiled happily. "It is very good you are here, comrade. We cannot be too careful, of course."

"Of course." It was the first time I had said anything, but you might have thought I gave the Gettysburg Address. Overcoat came over immediately, his hand reaching out for mine.

"I am Henry Gladow, you know. Certainly you know." His chuckle was nervous and high-pitched. "We had been expecting you, but not so quickly. Of course we realize the party works quickly, but this is almost faith-inspiring! You came with incredible speed. Why, only tonight I picked up the telegram from our messenger uptown announcing your arrival. Incredible."

That was the reason for the bodyguards and the guns. My new chum was receiving party instructions from somebody else. That was why the Trench Coats closed in around the soldier, in case it had been a trap to intercept the message. Real cute, but dumb as hell.

". . . happy to have you inspect our small base of operation, comrade." I turned my attention back to him again and listened politely. "Rarely do we have such an honor. In fact, this is the first time." He turned to Trench Coat, still smiling. "This is my, er, traveling companion, Martin Romberg. Very capable man, you know. And my secretary," he indicated a girl in thick-lensed glasses who was just out of her teens, "Martha Camisole."

He went around the room introducing each one and with every nod I handed out I got back a smile that tried hard to be nice but was too scared to do a good job of it.

We finished the coffee, had another and a smoke before Gladow looked at his watch. I could see damn well he had another question coming up and I let him take his time about asking it. He said, "Er, you are quite satisfied with the operation at this point, comrade? Would you care to inspect our records and documents?"

My scowl was of surprise, but he didn't know that. His eyebrows went up and he smiled craftily. "No, comrade, not written documents. Here, in the base, we have experts who commit the documents . . ." he tapped the side of his head, "here."

"Smart," I grunted. "What happens if they talk?"

He tried to seem overcome with the preposterous. "Very funny, comrade. Quite, er . . . yes. Who is there to make them talk? That is where we have the advantage. In this country force is never used. The so-called third degree has been swept out. Even a truthful statement loses its truth if coercion is even hinted at. The fools, the despicable fools haven't the intelligence to govern a country properly! When the party is in power things will be different, eh, comrade?"

"Much, much different," I said.

Gladow nodded, pleased. "You, er, care to see anything of special importance, comrade?" His voice had a gay tone.

"No, nothing special. Just checking around." I dragged on the butt and blew a cloud of smoke in his face. He didn't seem to mind it.

"Then in your report you will state that everything *is* satisfactory here?"

"Sure, don't give it another thought."

There was more sighing. Some of the fear went out of their eyes. The Camisole kid giggled nervously. "Then may I say again that we have been deeply honored by your visit, comrade," Gladow said. "Since the sudden, untimely death of our former, er, compatriot, we have been more or less uneasy. You understand these things of course. It was gratifying to see that he was not identified with the party in any way. Even the newspapers are stupid in this country."

I had to let my eyes sink to the floor or he would have seen the hate in them. I was an inch away from killing the bastard and he didn't know it. I turned my hand over to look at the time and saw that it was close to midnight. I'd been in the pigsty long enough. I set the empty cup down on the table and walked to the door. The crumbs couldn't even make good coffee.

All but two of the lesser satellites had left, their desks clear of all papers. The guy on the photography rig was stuffing the microfilm in a small file case while a girl burned papers in a metal waste basket. I didn't stop to see who got the film. There was enough of it that was so plain that I didn't need any pictures drawn for me.

Gladow was hoping I'd shake hands, but he got fooled. I kept them both in my pockets because I didn't like to handle snakes, not of their variety.

The outside door slammed shut and I heard some hurried conversation and the girl at the desk say, "Go right in." I was standing by the inside door when she opened it.

I had to make sure I was in the right place by taking a quick look around me. This was supposed to be a Commie setup, a joint for the masses only, not a club for babes in mink coats with hats to match. She was one of those tall, willowy blondes who reached thirty with each year an improvement.

She was almost beautiful, with a body that could take your mind off beauty and put it on other things. She smiled at Gladow as soon as she saw him and gave him her hand.

His voice took on a purr when he kissed it. "Miss Brighton, it is always a pleasure to see you." He straightened up, still smiling. "I didn't expect you to come at this hour."

"I didn't expect you to be here either, Henry. I decided to take the chance anyway. I brought the donations." Her voice was like rubbing your hand on satin. She pulled an envelope out of her pocketbook and handed it to Gladow unconcernedly. Then, for the first time, she saw me.

She squinted her eyes, trying to place me.

I grinned at her. I like to grin at a million bucks.

Ethel Brighton grinned back.

Henry Gladow coughed politely and turned to me. "Miss Brighton is one of our most earnest comrades. She is chiefly responsible for some of our most substantial contributions."

He made no attempt to introduce me. Apparently nobody seemed to care. Especially Ethel Brighton. A quick look flashed between them that brought the scowl back to her face for a brief moment. A shadow on the wall that came from one of the Trench Coats behind me was making furious gestures.

I started to get the willies. It was the damnedest thing I had ever seen. Everybody was acting like at a fraternity initiation and for some reason I was the man of the moment. I took it as long as I could. I said, "I'm going uptown. If you're going back you can come along."

For a dame who had her picture in most of the Sunday supplements every few weeks, she lost her air of sophistication in a hurry. Her cheeks seemed to sink in and she looked to Gladow for approval. Evidently he gave it, for she nodded and said, "My car . . . it's right outside."

I didn't bother to leave any good nights behind me. I went through the receptionist's cubicle and yanked the door open. When Ethel Brighton was out I slammed it shut. Behind me the place was as dark as the vacant hole it was supposed to be.

Without waiting to be asked I slid behind the wheel and held out my hand for the keys. She dropped them in my palm and fidgeted against the cushions. That car . . . it was a beauty. In the daylight it would have been a maroon convertible, but under the street lights it was a mass of mirrors with the chrome reflecting every bulb in the sky.

Ethel said, "Are you from . . . New York?"

"Nope. Philly," I lied.

For some reason I was making her mighty nervous. It wasn't my driving because I was holding it to a steady thirty to keep inside the green lights. I tried another grin. This time she smiled back and worried the fingers of her gloves.

I couldn't get over it, Ethel Brighton a Commie! Her old man would tan her hide no matter how old she was if he ever heard about it. But what the hell, she wasn't the only one with plenty of rocks who got hung up on the red flag. I said, "It hasn't been too easy for you to keep all this under your hat, has it?"

Her hands stopped working the glove. "N-no. I've managed, though."

"Yeah. You've done a good job."

"Thank you."

"Oh, no thanks at all, kid. For people with intelligence it's easy. When you're, er, getting these donations, don't people sorta wonder where it's going?"

She scowled again, puzzled. "I don't think so. I thought that was explained quite fully in my report."

"It was, it was. Don't get me wrong. We have to keep track of things, you know. Situations change." It was a lot of crap to me, but it must have made sense to her way of thinking.

"Usually they're much too busy to listen to my explanations, and anyway, they can deduct the amounts from their income tax."

"They ought to be pretty easy to touch, then."

This time she smiled a little. "They are. They think it's for charity."

"Uh-huh. Suppose your father finds out what you've been doing?"

The way she recoiled you'd think I smacked her. "Oh . . . please, you wouldn't!"

"Take it easy, kid. I'm only supposing."

Even in the dull light of the dash I could see how pale she was. "Daddy would . . . never forgive me. I think . . . he'd send me someplace. He'd disinherit me completely." She shuddered, her hands going back to the glove again. "He'll never know. When he does it will be too late!"

"Your emotions are showing through, kid."

"So would yours if . . . oh . . . oh, I didn't mean . . ." Her expression made a sudden switch from rage to that of fear. It wasn't a nice fear, it was more like that of the girl on the bridge.

I looked over slowly, an angle creeping into the corner of my mind. "I'm not going to bite. Maybe you can't say things back there in front of the others, but sometimes I'm not like them. I can understand problems. I have plenty of my own."

"But you . . . you're . . ."

"I'm what?"

"You know." She bit into her lip, looking at me obliquely.

I nodded as if I did.

"Will you be here long?"

"Maybe," I shrugged. "Why?"

The fear came back. "Really, I wasn't asking pointed questions. Honest I wasn't. I just meant . . . I meant with the . . . other being killed and all, well . . ."

Damn it, she let her sentence trail off as if I was supposed to know everything that went on. What the hell did they take me for anyway? It was the same thing all night!

"I'll be here," I said.

We went over the bridge and picked a path through the late traffic in Manhattan. I went north to Times Square and pulled into the curb. "This is as far as I go, sugar. Thanks for the ride. I'll probably be seeing you again."

Her eyes went wide again. Brother, she could sure do things with those eyes. She gasped, "Seeing me?"

"Sure, why not?"

"But . . . you aren't . . . I never supposed . . ."

"That I might have a personal interest in a woman?" I finished.

"Well, yes."

"I like women, sugar. I always have and always will."

For the first time she smiled a smile she meant. She said, "You aren't a bit like I thought you'd be. Really. I like you. The other . . . agent . . . he was so cold that he scared me."

"I don't scare you?"

"You could . . . but you don't."

I opened the door. "Good night, Ethel."

"Good night." She slid over under the wheel and gunned the motor. I got one last quick smile before she pulled away.

What the hell. That's all I could think of. What the hell. All right, just what the hell was going on? I walked right into a nest of Commies because I flashed a green card and they didn't say a word, not one word. They played damn fool kids' games with me that any jerk could have caught, and bowed and scraped like I was king.

Not once did anyone ask my name.

Read the papers today. See what it says about the Red Menace. See how they play up their sneaking, conniving ways. They're supposed to be clever, bright as hell. They were dumb as horse manure as far as I was concerned. They were a pack of bugs thinking they could outsmart a world. Great. That coffee-urn trick was just great.

I walked down the street to a restaurant that was still open and ordered a plate of ham and eggs.

It was almost two o'clock when I got home. The rain had stopped long ago, but it was still up there, hanging low around the buildings, reluctant to let the city alone. I walked up to my apartment and shoved the key in the lock. My mind kept going back to Gladow, trying to make sense of his words, trying to fit them into a puzzle that had no other parts.

I could remember his speaking about somebody's untimely death. Evidently I was the substitute sent on in his place. But whose death? That sketch in the paper was a lousy one. Fat boy didn't look a bit like that sketch. All right then, who? There was only one other guy with a green card who was dead, the guy Lee Deamer was supposed to have killed.

Him. He's the one, I thought. I was his replacement. But what was I supposed to be?

There was just too much to think about; I was too tired to put my mind to it. You don't kill a fat man and see a girl die because of the look on your face and get involved with a Commie organization all in two days without feeling your mind sink into a soggy ooze that drew it down deeper and deeper until it relaxed of its own accord and you were asleep.

I sat slumped in the chair, the cigarette that had dropped from my fingers had burned a path through the rug at right angles with another. The bell shrilled and shrilled until I thought it would never stop. My arm going out to the phone was an involuntary movement, my voice just happened to be there.

I said hello.

It was Pat and he had to yell at me a half-dozen times before I snapped out of it. I grunted an answer and he said, "Too late for you, Mike?"

"It's four o'clock in the morning. Are you just getting up or just going to bed?"

"Neither. I've been working."

"At this hour?"

"Since six this evening. How's the vacation?"

"I called it off."

"Really now. Just couldn't bear to leave the city, could you? By the way, did you find any more green cards with the ends snipped off?"

The palms of my hands got wet all of a sudden. "No."

"Are you interested in them at all?"

"Cut the comedy, Pat. What're you driving at? It's too damn late for riddles."

"Get over here, Mike," his voice was terse. "My apartment, and make it as fast as you can."

I came awake all at once, shaking the fatigue from my brain. "Okay, Pat," I said, "give me fifteen minutes." I hung up and slipped into my coat.

It was easier to grab a cab than wheel my car out of the garage. I shook the cabbie's shoulder and gave him Pat's address, then settled back against the cushions while we tore across town. We made it with about ten seconds to spare and I gave the cabbie a fin for his trouble.

I looked up at the sky before I went in. The clouds had broken up and let the stars come through. Maybe tomorrow will be nice, I thought. Maybe it will be a nice normal day without all the filth being raked to the top. Maybe. I pushed Pat's bell and the door buzzed almost immediately.

He was waiting outside his apartment when I got off the elevator. "You made it fast, Mike."

"You said to, didn't you?"

"Come on in."

Pat had drinks in a shaker and three glasses on the coffee table. Only one had been used so far. "Expecting company?" I asked him.

"Big company, Mike. Sit down and pour yourself a drink."

I shucked my coat and hat and stuck a Lucky in my mouth. Pat wasn't acting right. You don't go around entertaining anybody at this hour, not even your best friends. Something had etched lines into his face and put a smudge of darkness under each eye. He looked tight as a drumhead. I sat there with a drink in my hand watching Pat trying to figure out what to say.

It came halfway through my drink. "You were right the first time," he said.

I put the glass down and stared at him. "Do it over. I don't get it."

"Twins."

"What?"

"Twins," Pat repeated. "Lee Deamer had a twin brother." He stood there swirling the mixture around in his glass.

"Why tell me? I'm not in the picture."

Pat had his back to me, staring at nothing. I could barely hear his voice. "Don't ask me that, Mike. I don't know why I'm telling you when it's official business, but I am. In one way we're both alike. We're cops. Sometimes I find myself waiting to know what you'd do in a situation before I do it myself. Screwy, isn't it?"

"Pretty screwy."

"I told you once before that you have a feeling for things that I haven't got. You don't have a hundred bosses and a lot of sidelines to mess you up once you get started on a case. You're a ruthless bastard and sometimes it helps."

"So?"

"So now I find myself in one of those situations. I'm a practical cop with a lot of training and experience, but I'm in something that has a personal meaning to me too and I'm afraid of tackling it alone."

"You don't want advice from me, chum. I'm mud, and whatever I touch gets smeared with it. I don't mind dirtying myself, but I don't want any of it to rub off on to you."

"It won't, don't worry. That's why you're here now. You think I was taken in by that vacation line? Hell. You have another bug up your behind. It has to do with those green cards and don't try to talk your way out of it."

He spun around, his face taut. "Where'd you get them, Mike?"

I ignored the question. "Tell me, Pat. Tell me the story."

He threw the drink down and filled the glass again. "Lee Deamer . . . how much do you know about him?"

"Only that he's the up-and-coming champ. I don't know him personally."

"I do, Mike. I know the guy and I like him. Goddamn it, Mike, if he gets squeezed out in this state, this country will lose one of its greatest assets! We can't afford to have Deamer go under!"

"I've heard that story before, Pat," I said, "a political reporter gave it to me in detail."

Pat reached for a cigarette and laid it in his lips. The tip of the flame from the lighter wavered when he held it up. "I hope it made an impression. This country is too fine to be kicked around. Deamer is the man to stop it if he can get that far.

"Politics never interested you much, Mike. You know how it starts in the wards and works itself right up to the nation. I get a chance to see just how dirty and corrupt politics can be. You should put yourself in my shoes for a while and you'd know how I feel. I get word to lay off one thing or another . . . or else. I get word that if I do or don't do a certain thing I'll be handed a fat little present. You'd think people would respect the police, but they don't. They try to use the department to push their own lousy schemes and it happens more often than you'd imagine."

"And you, Pat, what did you do?" I leaned forward in my chair, waiting.

"I told them to go to hell. They can't touch an honest man until he makes a mistake. Then they hang him for it."

"Any mistakes yet?"

Two streams of smoke spiraled from his nostrils. "Not yet, kid. They're waiting though. I'm fed up with the tension. You can feel it in the air, like being inside a storage battery. Call me a reformer if you want to, but I'd love to see a little decency for a change. That's why I'm afraid for Deamer."

"Yeah, you were telling me about him."

"Twins. You were right, Mike. Lee Deamer was at that meeting the night he was allegedly seen killing this Charlie Moffit. He was talking to groups around the room. I was there."

I stamped the butt out in a tray and lit another. "You mean it was as simple as that . . . Lee Deamer had a twin brother?"

Pat nodded. "As simple as that."

"Then why the secrecy? Lee isn't exactly responsible for what his brother does. Even a blast in the papers couldn't smear him for that, could it?"

"No . . . not if that was all there was to it."

"Then . . ."

Pat slammed the glass down impatiently. "The brother's name was Oscar Deamer. He was an escaped inmate of a sanitarium where he was undergoing psychiatric treatment. Let that come out and Lee is finished."

I let out a slow whistle. "Who else knows about this, Pat?"

"Just you. It was too big. I couldn't keep it to myself. Lee called me tonight and said he wanted to see me. We met in a bar and he told me the story. Oscar arrived in town and told Lee that he was going to settle things for him. He demanded money to keep quiet. Lee thinks that Oscar deliberately killed this Charlie Moffit hoping to be identified as Lee, knowing that Lee wouldn't dare reveal that he had a lunatic for a brother."

"So Lee wouldn't pay off and he got the treatment."

"It looks that way."

"Hell, this Oscar could have figured Lee would have an alibi and couldn't be touched. It was just a sample, something to get him entangled. That doesn't make him much of a loony if he can think like that."

"Anybody who can kill like that is crazy, Mike."

"Yeah, I guess so."

Before he could answer me, the bell rang, two short burps and Pat got up to push the buzzer. "Lee?" I asked.

Pat nodded. "He wanted more time to think about it. I told him I'd be at home. It has him nearly crazy himself." He went to the door and stood there holding it open as he had done for me. It was so still that I heard the elevator humming in its well, the sound of the doors opening and the slow, heavy feet of a person carrying a too-heavy weight.

I stood up myself and shook hands with Lee Deamer. He wasn't big like I had expected. There was nothing outstanding about his appearance except that he looked like a schoolteacher, a very tired, middle-aged Mr. Chips.

Pat said, "This is Mike Hammer, Lee. He's a very special, capable friend of mine."

His handshake was firm, but his eyes were too tired to take me in all at once. He said to Pat very softly, "He knows?"

"He knows, Lee. He can be trusted."

I had a good look at warm gray eyes then. His hand tightened just a little around mine. "It's nice to find people that can be trusted."

I grinned my thanks and Pat pulled up a chair. Lee Deamer took the drink Pat offered him and settled back against the cushions, rubbing his hand across his face. He took a sip of the highball, then pulled a cigar from his pocket and pared the end off with a tiny knife on his watch chain.

"Oscar hasn't called back," he said dully. "I don't know what to do." He looked first at Pat, then to me. "Are you a policeman, Mr. Hammer?"

"Just call me Mike. No, I'm not a city cop. I have a Private Operator's ticket and that's all."

"Mike's been in on a lot of big stuff, Lee," Pat cut in. "He knows his way around."

"I see." He was talking to me again. "I suppose Pat told you that so far this whole affair has been kept quiet?" I nodded and he went on. "I hope it can stay that way, though if it must come out, it must. I'm leaving it all to the discretion of Pat here. I—well, I'm really stumped. So much has happened in so short a time I hardly know where I'm at."

"Can I hear it from the beginning?" I asked.

Lee Deamer bobbed his head slowly. "Oscar and I were born in Townley, Nebraska. Although we were twins, we were worlds apart. In my younger days I thought it was because we were just separate person-alities, but the truth was . . . Oscar was demented. He was a sadistic sort of person, very sly and cunning. He hated me. Yes, he hated me, his own brother. In fact, Oscar seemed to hate everyone. He was in trouble from the moment he ran off from home until he came back, then he found more trouble in our own state. He was finally committed to an institution.

"Shortly after Oscar was committed I left Nebraska and settled in New York. I did rather well in business and became active in politics. Oscar was more or less forgotten. Then I learned that he had escaped from the institution. I never heard from him again until he called me last week."

"That's all?"

"What else can there be, Mike? Oscar probably read about me in the papers and trailed me here. He knew what it would mean if I was known to have a brother who wasn't quite . . . well, normal. He made a demand for money and told me he'd have it one way or another."

Pat reached for the shaker and filled the glasses again. I held mine out and our eyes met. He answered my question before I could ask it. "Lee was afraid to mention Oscar, even when he was identified as the killer of Moffit. You can understand why, can't you?"

"Now I can," I said.

"Even the fact that Lee *was* identified, although wrongly, would have made good copy. However, the cop on the beat brought the witnesses in before they could speak to the papers and the whole thing was such an obvious mistake that nobody dared take the chance of making it public."

"Where are the witnesses now?"

"We have them under surveillance. They've been instructed to keep quiet about it. We checked into their backgrounds and found that all of them were upright citizens, plain, ordinary people who were as be-fuddled as we were about the whole thing. Fortunately, we were able to secure their promise of silence by proving to them where Lee was that night. They don't understand it, but they were willing to go along with us in the cause of justice."

I grunted and pulled on the cigarette. "I don't like it."

Both of them looked at me quickly. "Hell, Pat, you ought to smell the angle as well as I do."

"You tell me, Mike."

"Oscar served his warning," I said. "He'll make another stab at it. You can trap him easily enough and you know it."

"That's right. It leaves one thing wide open, too."

"Sure it does. You'll have another Lee Deamer in print and pictures, this one up for a murder rap which he will skip because he's nuts." Lee winced at the word but kept still.

"That's why I wanted you here," Pat told me.

"Fine. What good am I?"

The ice rattled against the side of his glass. Pat tried to keep his voice calm. "You aren't official, Mike. My mind works with the book. I know what I should do and I can't think of anything else."

"You mean you want me to tell you that Oscar should be run down and quietly spirited away?"

"That's right."

"And I'm the boy who could do it?"

"Right again." He took a long swallow from the glass and set it on the table.

"What happens if it doesn't work out? To you, I mean."

"I'll be looking for a job for not playing it properly."

"Gentlemen, gentlemen." Lee Deamer ran his hand through his hair nervously. "I-I can't let you do it. I can't let you jeopardize your positions. It isn't fair. The best thing is to let it come to light and let the public decide."

"Don't be jerky!" I spat out. Lee looked at me, but I wasn't seeing him. I was seeing Marty and Pat, hearing them say the same thing . . . and I was hearing that judge again.

There were two hot spaces where my eyes should have been. "I'll take care of it," I said. "I'll need all the help I can get." I looked at Pat. He nodded. "Just one thing, Pat. I'm not doing this because I'm a patriot, see? I'm doing it because I'm curious and because of it I'll be on my toes. I'm curious as hell about something else and not about right and wrong and what the public thinks."

My teeth were showing through my words and Pat had that look again. "Why, Mike?"

"Three green cards with the edges cut off, kid. I'm curious as hell about three green cards. There's more to them than you think."

I said good night and left them sitting there. I could hear the judge laughing at me. It wasn't a nice laugh. It had a nasty sound. Thirteen steps and thirteen loops that made the knot in the rope. Were there thirteen thousand volts in the chair too? Maybe I'd find out the hard way.

CHAPTER 4

I slept for two hours before Velda called me. I told her I wouldn't be in for a good long while, and if anything important came up she could call, but unless it was a matter of life or death, either hers or mine, to leave me be.

Nothing came up and I slept once around the clock. It was five minutes to six when my eyes opened by themselves and didn't feel hot any more. While I showered and shaved I stuck a frozen steak under the broiler and ate in my shorts, still damp.

It was a good steak; I was hungry. I wanted to finish it but I never got the time. The phone rang and kept on ringing until I kicked the door shut so I wouldn't hear it. That didn't stop the phone. It went on like that for a full five minutes, demanding that I answer it. I threw down my knife with a curse and walked inside.

"What is it?" I yelled.

"It took you long enough to wake up, damn it!"

"Oh, Pat. I wasn't asleep. What's up this time?"

"It happened like we figured. Oscar made the contact. He called Lee and wants to see him tonight. Lee made an appointment to be at his apartment at eight."

"Yeah?"

"Lee called me immediately. Look, Mike, we'll have to go this alone, just the three of us. I don't want to trust anybody else."

The damp on my body seemed to turn to ice. I was cold all over, cold enough to shake just a little. "Where'll I meet you, Pat?"

"Better make it at my place. Oscar lives over on the East Side." He rattled off the address and I jotted it down. "I told Lee to go ahead and keep his appointment. We'll be right behind him. Lee is taking the subway up and we'll pick him up at the kiosk. Got that?"

"I got it. I'll be over in a little while."

We both stood waiting for the other to hang up. Finally, "Mike. . . ."

"What?"

"You sure about this?"

"I'm sure." I set the receiver back in its cradle and stared at it. I was sure, all right, sure to come up with the dirty end of the stick. The dam would open and let the clean water through and they could pick me out of the sewer.

I pulled on my clothes halfheartedly. I thought of the steak in the kitchen and decided I didn't want any more of it. For a while I stood in front of the mirror looking at myself, trying to decide whether or not I should wear the artillery. Habit won and I buckled on the sling after checking the load in the clip. When I buttoned up the coat I took the box from the closet shelf that held the two spare barrels and the extra shells, scooped up a handful of loose .45's and dropped them in my pocket. If I was going to do it I might as well do it right.

Velda had just gotten in when I called her. I said, "Did you eat yet, kitten?"

"I grabbed a light bite downtown. Why, are you taking me out?"

"Yeah, but not to supper. It's business. I'll be right over. Tell you about it then."

She said all right, kissed me over the phone and hung up. I stuck my hat on, picked up another deck of Luckies and went downstairs where I whistled for a cab.

I don't know how I looked when she opened the door. She started to smile then dropped it like a hot rivet to catch her lower lip between her teeth. Velda's so tall I didn't have to bend down far to kiss her on the cheek. It was nice standing there real close to her. She was perfume and beauty and all the good things of life.

She said, "Come into the bedroom, Mike. You can tell me while I'm getting dressed."

"I can talk from out here."

Velda turned around, a grin in her eyes. "You *have* been in a woman's bedroom before, haven't you?"

"Not yours."

"I'm inviting you in to talk. Just talk."

I faked a punch at her jaw. "I'm just afraid of myself, kid. You and a bedroom could be too much. I'm saving you for something special."

"Will it cost three dollars and can you frame it?"

I laughed for an answer and went in after her. She pointed to a satin-covered boudoir chair and went behind a screen. She came out in a black wool skirt and a white blouse. God, but she was lovely.

When she sat down in front of the vanity table and started to brush her hair I caught her eyes in the mirror. They reflected the trouble that was in mine. "Now tell me, Mike."

I told her. I gave her everything Pat gave me and watched her face.

She finished with the brush and put it down. Her hand was shaking. "They want a lot of you, don't they?"

"Maybe they want too much." I pulled out a cigarette and lit one. "Velda, what does this Lee Deamer mean to you?"

This time she wouldn't meet my eyes. She spaced her words carefully. "He means a lot, Mike. Would you be mad if I said that perhaps they weren't asking too much?"

"No . . . not if you think not. Okay, kid. I'll play the hand out and see what I can do with a kill-crazy maniac. Get your coat on."

"Mike . . . you haven't told me all of it yet."

She was at it again, looking through me into my mind. "I know it."

"Are you going to?"

"Not now. Maybe later."

She stood up, a statuesque creature that had no equal, her hair a black frame for her face. "Mike, you're a bastard. You're in trouble up to your ears and you won't let anybody help you. Why do you always have to play it alone?"

"Because I'm me."

"And I'm me too, Mike. I *want* to help. Can you understand that?"

"Yes, I understand, but this isn't another case. It's more than that and I don't want to talk about it."

She came to me then, resting her hands on my shoulders. "Mike, if you *do* need me . . . ever, will you ask me to help?"

"I'll ask you."

Her mouth was full and ripe, warm with life and sparkling with a delicious wetness. I pulled her in close and tasted the fire that smoldered inside her, felt her body mold itself to mine, eager and excited.

My fingers ran into her hair and pulled her mouth away. "No more of it, Velda. Not now."

"Some day, Mike."

"Some day. Get your coat on." I shoved her away roughly, reluctant to let her go. She opened the closet and took the jacket that matched the skirt from a hanger and slipped into it. Over her shoulder she slung a shoulderstrap bag, and when it nudged the side of the dresser the gun in it made a dull clunk.

"I'm ready, Mike."

I pushed the slip of paper with Oscar's address on it into her hand. "Here's the place where he's holed up. The subway is a half-block away from the place. You go directly there and look the joint over. I don't know why, but there's something about it I don't like. We're going to tag after Lee when he goes in, but I want somebody covering the place while we're there.

"Remember, it's a rough neighborhood, so be on your toes. We don't want any extra trouble. If you spot anything that doesn't seem to be on the square, walk over to the subway kiosk and meet us. You'll have about a half-hour to look around. Be careful."

"Don't worry about me." She pulled on her gloves, a smile playing with her mouth. Hell, I wasn't going to worry about her. That rod in her bag wasn't there for ballast.

I dropped her at the subway and waited on the curb until a cab cruised by.

Pat was standing under the canopy of his apartment building when I got there. He had a cigarette cupped in the palm of his hand and dragged on it nervously. I yelled at him from the taxi and he crossed the street and got in.

It was seven-fifteen.

At ten minutes to eight we paid off the cab and walked the half-block to the kiosk. We were still fifty feet away when Lee Deamer came up. He looked neither to the right nor left, walking straight ahead as if he lived there. Pat nudged me with his elbow and I grunted an acknowledgment.

I waited to see if Velda would show, but there wasn't a sign of her.

Twice Lee stopped to look at house numbers. The third time he paused in front of an old brick building, his head going to the dim light behind the shades in the downstairs room. Briefly, he cast a quick glance behind him, then went up the three steps and disappeared into the shadowy well of the doorway.

Thirty seconds, that's all he got. Both of us were counting under our breaths, hugging the shadows of the building. The street boasted a lone light a hundred yards away, a wan, yellow eye that seemed to search for us with eerie tendrils, determined to pull us into its glare. Somewhere a voice cursed. A baby squealed and stopped abruptly. The street was too damn deserted. It should have been running with kids or something.

Maybe the one light scared them off. Maybe they had a better place to hang out than a side street in nowhere.

We hit the thirty count at the same time, but too late. A door slammed above our heads and we could hear feet pounding on boards, diminishing with every step. A voice half sobbed something unintelligible and we flew up those stairs and tugged at a door that wouldn't give. Pat hit it with his shoulder, ramming it open.

Lee was standing in the doorway, hanging on to the sill, his mouth agape. He was pointing down the hall. "He ran . . . he ran. He looked out the window . . . and he ran!"

Pat muttered, "Damn . . . we can't let him get away!" I was ahead of him, my hands probing the darkness. I felt the wall give way to the inky blackness that was the night behind an open door and stumbled down the steps.

That was when I heard Velda's voice rise in a tense, "Mike . . . MIKE!"

"Over here, Pat. There's a gate in the wall. Get a light on!"

Pat swore again, yelling that he had lost it. I didn't wait. I made the gate and picked my way through the litter in the alley that ran behind the buildings. My .45 was in my hand, ready to be used. Velda yelled again and I followed her voice to the end of the alley.

When I came to the street through the two-foot space that separated the buildings I couldn't have found anybody, because the street was a funnel of people running to the subway kiosk. They ran and yelled back over their shoulders and I knew that whatever it was had happened down there and I was afraid to look. If anything happened to Velda I'd tear the guts out of some son-of-a-bitch! I'd nail him to a wall and take his skin off him in inch-wide strips!

A colored fellow in a porter's outfit came up bucking the crowd yelling for someone to get a doctor. That was all I needed. I made a path through that mob pouring through the exit gates into the station and battled my way up to the front.

Velda was all right. She was perfectly all right and I could quit shaking and let the sweat turn warm again. I shoved the gun back under my arm and walked over to her with a sad attempt of trying to look normal.

The train was almost all the way in the station. Not quite. It had to jam on the brakes too fast to make the marker farther down the platform. The driver and two trainmen were standing in front of the lead car poking at a bloody mess that was sticking out under the wheels. The driver said, "He's dead as hell. He won't need an ambulance."

Velda saw me out of the corner of her eye. I eased up to her, my breath still coming hard. "Deamer?"

She nodded.

I heard Pat busting through the crowd and saw Lee at his heels. "Beat it, kid. I'll call you later." She stepped back and the curious crowd surged around her to fill the spot. She was gone before Pat reached me.

His pants were torn and he had a dirty black smear across his cheek. He took about two minutes to get the crowd back from the edge and when a cop from the beat upstairs came through the gang was herded back to the exits like cattle, all bawling to be in on the blood.

Pat wiped his hand across his face. "What the hell happened?"

"I don't know, but I think that's our boy down there. Bring Lee over."

The trainmen were tugging the remains out. One said, "He ain't got much face left," then he puked all over the third rail.

Lee Deamer looked over the side and turned white. "My God!"

Pat steadied him with an arm around his waist. They had most of the corpse out from under the train now. "That him?" Pat asked.

Lee nodded dumbly. I could see his throat working hard.

Two more cops from the local precinct sauntered over. Pat shoved his badge out and told them to take over, then motioned me to bring Lee back to one of the benches. He folded up in one like a limp sack and buried his face in his hands. What the hell could I say? So the guy was a loony, but he was still his brother. While Pat went back to talk to the trainmen I stood there and listened to him sob.

We put Lee in a cab outside before I had a chance to say anything. The street was mobbed now, the people crowding around the ambulance waiting to see what was going in on the stretcher. They were disappointed when a wicker basket came up and was shoved into a morgue wagon instead. A kid pointed to the blood dripping from one corner and a woman fainted. Nice.

I watched the wagon pull away and reached for a butt. I needed one bad. "It was an easy way out," I said. "What did the driver say?"

Pat took a cigarette from my pack. "He didn't see him. He thinks the guy must have been hiding behind a pillar then jumped out in front of the car. He sure was messed up."

"I don't know whether to be relieved or not."

"It's a relief to me, Mike. He's dead and his name will get published but who will connect him with Lee? The trouble's over."

"He have anything on him?"

Pat stuck his hand in his pocket and pulled out some stuff. Under the light it looked as if it had been stained with ink. Sticky ink. "Here's a train ticket from Chicago. It's in a bus envelope so he must have taken a bus as far as Chi then switched to rail." It was dated the 15th, a Friday.

I turned the envelope over and saw DEAMER printed across the back with a couple of schedule notations in pencil. There was another envelope with the stuff. It had been torn in half and used for a memo sheet, but the name Deamer, part of an address in Nebraska and a Nebraska postage mark were still visible. It was dated over a month ago. The rest of the stuff was some small change, two crumpled bills and a skeleton key for a door lock.

It was as nice an answer as we could have hoped for and I didn't like it. "What's the matter now?" Pat queried.

"I don't know. It stinks."

"You're teed off because you were done out of a kill."

"Aw, shaddup, will you!"

"Then what's so lousy about it?"

"How the hell do I know? Can't I not like something without having to explain about it?"

"Not with me you can't, pal. I stuck my neck out when I invited you in."

I sucked in on the cigarette. It was cold standing there and I turned my collar up. "Get a complete identification on that corpse, Pat. Then maybe I can tell you why I think it stinks."

"Don't worry, I intend to. I'm not taking any chances of having him laughing at us from somewhere. It would be like the crazy bastard to push someone else under that train to sidetrack us."

"Would he have time to jam that stuff in his pockets too?" I flipped my thumb at the papers Pat was holding.

"He could have. Just the same, we'll be sure. Lee has both their birth certificates and a medical certificate on Oscar that has his full description. It won't take long to find out if that's him or not."

"Let me know what you find."

"I'll call you tomorrow. I wish I knew how the devil he spotted us. I nearly killed myself in that damn alley. I thought I heard somebody yelling for you, too."

"Couldn't have been."

"Guess not. Well, I'll see you tomorrow?"

"Uh-huh." I took a last pull on the butt and tossed it at the curb. Pat went back into the station and I could hear his heels clicking on the steps.

The street was more deserted now than ever. All that was left was the one yellow light. It seemed to wink at me. I walked toward it and went up the three steps into the building. The door was still standing open, enough light from the front room seeping into the hall so I could find my way.

It wasn't much of a place, just a room. There was a chair, a closet, a single bed and a washstand. The suitcase on the bed was half filled with well-worn clothes, but I couldn't tell whether it was being packed or unpacked. I poked through the stuff and found another dollar bill stuffed in the cloth lining. Twenty pages of a mail-order catalog were under everything. Part of them showed sporting goods including all sorts of guns. The others pictured automobile accessories. Which part was used? Did he buy a gun or a tire? Why? Where?

I pulled out the shirts and shook them open, looking for any identifying marks. One had DEA for a laundry tag next to the label, the others had nothing so he must have done his own wash.

That was all there was to it.

Nothing.

I could breathe a little easier and tell Marty Kooperman that his boy was okay and nothing could hurt him now. Pat would be satisfied, the cops would be satisfied and everything was hunky-dory. I was the only one who still had a bug up my tail. It was a great big bug and it was kicking up a fuss. I was a hell of a way from being satisfied.

This wasn't what I was after, that's why. This didn't have to do with three green cards except that the dead man had killed a guy who carried one. What was his name . . . Moffit, Charlie Moffit. Was he dead because of a fluke or was there more to it?

I kicked at the edge of the bed in disgust and took one last look around. Pat would be here next. He'd find prints and check them against the corpse in his usual methodical way. If there was anything to be found, he'd find it and I could get it from him.

It had only been a few hours since I climbed out of the sack, but for some reason I was more tired than ever. Too much of a letdown, I guessed. You can't prime yourself for something to happen and feel right when it doesn't come off. The skin of my face felt tight and drawn, pulling away from my eyes. My back still crawled when I thought of the alley and that thing under the train.

I went into a shabby drugstore and called Velda's home. She wasn't there. I tried the office and she was. I told her to meet me in the bar downstairs and walked outside again, looking for a cab. The one that came along had a driver who had all the information about the accident in the subway secondhand and insisted on giving me a detailed account of all the gruesome details. I was glad to pay him off and get out of there.

Velda was sitting in a back booth with a Manhattan in front of her. Two guys at the bar had swung halfway around on their stools and were trying out their best leers. One said something dirty and the other laughed. Tony walked down behind the bar, but he saw me come in and stopped. The guy with the dirty mouth said something else, slid off his stool and walked over to Velda.

He set his drink down and leaned on her table, mouthing a few obscenities. Velda moved too fast for him. I saw her arm fly out, knock away the support of his hand and his face went into the table. She gave him the drink right in the eyes, glass and all.

The guy screamed, "You dirty little . . ." then she laid the heavy glass ash tray across his temple and he had it. He went down on his knees, his head almost on the floor. The other guy almost choked. He slammed his drink down and came off his stool with a rush. I let him go about two feet before I snagged the back of his coat collar with a jerk that put him right on his skinny behind.

Tony laughed and leaned on the bar.

I wasn't laughing. The one on the floor turned his head and I saw a pinched weasel face with eyes that had quick death in them. Those eyes crawled over me from top to bottom, over to Velda and back again. "A big tough guy," he said. "A big wise guy."

As if a spring exploded inside him, he came up off the floor with a knife in his hand, blade up.

A .45 can make an awful nasty sound in a quiet room when you pull the hammer back. It's just a little tiny click, but it can stop a dozen guys when they hear it. Weasel Face couldn't take his eyes off it. I let him have a good look and smashed it across his nose.

The knife hit the floor and broke when I stepped on it. Tony laughed again. I grabbed the guy by the neck and hauled him to his feet so I could drag the cold sharp metal of the rod across his face until he was a bright red mask mumbling for me to stop.

Tony helped me throw them in the street outside. He said, "They never learn, do they, Mike? Because there's two of 'em and they got a shiv they're the toughest mugs in the world. It ain't nice to get took, by a woman, neither. They never learn."

"They learn, Tony. For about ten seconds they're the smartest people in the world. But then it's always too late. After ten seconds they're dead. They only learn when they finally catch a slug where it hurts."

I walked back to the booth and sat down opposite Velda. Tony brought her another Manhattan and me a beer. "Very good," I said.

"Thanks. I knew you were watching."

She lit a cigarette and her hands were steadier than mine. "You were too rough on him."

"Nuts, he had a knife. I have an allergy against getting cut." I drained off half of the beer and laid it down on the table where I made patterns with the wet bottom. "Tell me about tonight."

Velda started to tear matches out of the book without lighting them. "I got there about seven-thirty. A light was on in the front window. Twice I saw somebody pull aside the corner of the shade and look out. A car went around the block twice, and both times it slowed down a little in front of the house. When it left I tried the door, but it was locked so I went next door and tried that one. It was locked too, but there was a cellar way under the stairs and I went down there. Just as I was going down the steps I saw a man coming up the block and I thought it might be Deamer.

"I had to take the chance that it was and that you were behind him. The cellar door was open and led through to the back yard. I was trying to crawl over a mound of boxes when I heard somebody in the back yard. I don't know how long it took me to get out there, possibly two minutes. Anyway, I heard a yell and somebody came out the door of the next house. I got through into the back alley and heard him running. He went too fast for me and I started yelling for you."

"That was Oscar Deamer, all right. He saw us coming and beat it."

"Maybe."

"What do you mean . . . 'maybe'?"

"I think there were two people in that alley ahead of me."

"Two people?" My voice had an edge to it. "Did you see them?"

"No."

"Then how do you know?"

"I don't. I just think so."

I finished the beer and waved to Tony. He brought another. Velda hadn't touched her drink yet. "Something made you think that. What was it?"

She shrugged, frowning at her glass, trying to force her mind back to that brief interval. "When I was in that cellar I thought I heard somebody in the other yard. There was a flock of cats around and I thought at the time that I was hearing them."

"Go on."

"Then when I was running after him I fell and while I lay there it didn't sound like just one person going down that alley."

"One person could sound like ten if they hit any of the junk we hit. It makes a hell of a racket."

"Maybe I'm wrong, Mike. I thought there could have been someone else and I wanted you to know about it."

"What the hell, it doesn't matter too much now anyway. The guy is dead and that should end it. Lee Deamer can go ahead and reform all he wants to now. He hasn't got a thing to worry about. As far as two people in that alley . . . well, you saw what the place was like. Nobody lives there unless he has to. They're the kind of people who scare easily, and if Lee started running somebody else could have too. Did you see him go down the subway?"

"No, he was gone when I got there, but two kids were staring down the steps and waving to another kid to come over. I took the chance that he went down and followed. The train was skidding to a stop when I reached the platform and I didn't have to be told why. When you scooted me away I looked for those kids in the crowd upstairs but they weren't around."

I hoisted my glass, turned it around in my hand and finished it. Velda downed her Manhattan and slipped her arms into her coat. "What now, Mike?"

"You go home, kid," I told her. "I'm going to take me a nice long walk."

We said good night to Tony and left. The two guys we had thrown in the street were gone. Velda grinned. "Am I safe?"

"Hell yes!"

I waved a taxi over, kissed her good night and walked off.

My heels rapped the sidewalk, a steady tap-tap that kept time with my thoughts. They reminded me of another walk I took, one that led to a bridge, and still another one that led into a deserted store that came equipped with blackout curtains, light switches on the door and coffee urns.

There lay the story behind the green cards. There was where I could find out why I had to kill a guy who had one, and see a girl die because she couldn't stand the look on my face. That was what I wanted to know . . . why it was me who was picked to pull the trigger.

I turned into a candy store and pulled the telephone directories from the rack. I found the Park Avenue Brightons and dialed the number.

Three rings later a somber voice said, "Mr. Brighton's residence."

I got right to the point. "Is Ethel there?"

"Who shall I say is calling, sir?"

"You don't. Just put her on."

"I'm sorry, sir, but . . ."

"Oh, shut up and put her on."

There was a shocked silence and a clatter as the phone was laid on a table. Off in the distance I heard the mutter of voices, then feet coming across the room. The phone clattered again, and, "Yes?"

"Hello, Ethel," I said. "I drove your car into Times Square last night. Remember?"

"Oh! Oh, but . . ." Her voice dropped almost to a whisper. "Please, I can't talk to you here. What is . . ."

"You can talk to me outside, kid. I'll be standing on your street corner in about fifteen minutes. The northeast corner. Pick me up there."

"I-I can't. Honestly . . . oh, please . . ." There was panic in her voice, a tone that held more than fear.

I said, "You'd better, baby." That was enough. I hung up and started walking toward Park Avenue. If I could read a voice right she'd be there.

She was. I saw her while I was still a half-block away, crossing nervously back and forth, trying to seem busy. I came up behind her and said hello. For a moment she went rigid, held by the panic that I had sensed in her voice.

"Scared?"

"No—of course not." The hell she wasn't! Her chin was wobbling and she couldn't hold her hands still. This time I was barely smiling and dames don't usually go to pieces when I do that.

I hooked my arm through hers and steered her west where there were lights and people. Sometimes the combination is good for the soul. It makes you want to talk and laugh and be part of the grand parade.

It didn't have that effect on her.

The smile might have been pasted on her face. When she wasn't looking straight ahead her eyes darted to me and back again. We went off Broadway and into a bar that had one empty end and one full end because the television wasn't centered. The lights were down low and nobody paid any attention to us on the empty end except the bartender, and he was more interested in watching the wrestling than hustling up drinks for us.

Ethel ordered an Old Fashioned and I had a beer. She held the fingers of her one hand tightly around the glass and worked a cigarette with the other. There was nothing behind the bar to see, but she stared there anyway. I had to give up carrying the conversation. When I did and sat there as quietly as she did the knuckles of her fingers went white.

She couldn't keep this up long. I took a lungful of smoke and let it come out with my words. "Ethel . . ." She jerked, startled. "What's there about me that has you up a tree?"

She wet her lips. "Really, there's . . . there's nothing."

"You never even asked me my name."

That brought her head up. Her eyes got wide and stared at the wall. "I . . . I'm not concerned with names."

"I am."

"But you . . . I'm . . . please, what have I done? Haven't I been faithful? Must you go on. . . ." She had kept it up too long. The panic couldn't stay. It left with a rush and a pleading tone took its place. There were tears in her eyes now, tears she tried hard to hold back and being a woman, couldn't. They flooded her eyelids and ran down her cheeks.

"Ethel . . . quit being scared of me. Look in a mirror and you'll know why I called you tonight. You aren't the kind of woman a guy can see and forget. You're too damned serious."

Dames, they can louse me up every time. The tears stopped as abruptly as they came and her mouth froze in indignation. This time she was able to look at my eyes clearly. "We have to be serious. You, of all people, should know that!"

This was better. The words were her own, what was inside her and not words that I put there. "Not all the time," I grinned.

"All the time!" she said. I grinned at her and she returned it with a frown.

"You'll do, kid."

"I can't understand you." She hesitated, then a smile blossomed and grew. She was lovely when she smiled. "You were testing me," she demanded.

"Something like that."

"But . . . why?"

"I need some help. I can't take just anybody, you know." It was true. I did need help, plenty of it too.

"You mean . . . you want me to help you . . . find out who . . . who did it?"

Cripes, how I wanted her to open up. I wasn't in the mood for more of those damn silly games and yet I had to play them. "That's right."

It must have pleased her. I saw the fingers loosen up around the glass and she tasted the drink for the first time. "Could I ask a question?"

"Sure, go ahead."

"Why did you choose me?"

"I'm attracted to beauty."

"But my record . . ."

"I was attracted to that too. Being beautiful helped."

"I'm not beautiful." She was asking for more. I gave it to her.

"All I can see are your face and hands. They're beautiful, but I bet the rest of you is just as beautiful, the part I can't see."

It was too dark to tell if she had the grace to blush or not. She wet her lips again, parting them in a small smile. "Would you?"

"What?"

"Like to see the rest of me." No, she couldn't have blushed.

I laughed at her, a slow laugh that brought her head around and showed me the glitter in her eyes. "Yeah, Ethel, I want to. And I will when I want to just a little more."

Her breath came so sharply that her coat fell open and I could see the pulse in her throat. "It's warm here. Can we . . . leave?"

Neither of us bothered to finish our drinks.

She was laughing now, with her mouth and her eyes. I held her hand and felt the warm pressure of her fingers, the stilted reserve draining out of her at every step. Ethel led the way, not me. We walked toward her place almost as if we were in a hurry, out to enjoy the evening.

"Supposing your father . . . or somebody you know should come along," I suggested.

She shrugged defiantly. "Let them. You know how I feel." She held her head high, the smile crooked across her lips. "There's not one of them I care for. Any feeling I've had for my family disappeared several years ago."

"Then you haven't any feeling left for anyone?"

"I have! Oh, yes I have." Her eyes swung up to mine, half closed, revealing a sensuous glitter. "For the moment it's you."

"And other times?"

"I don't have to tell *you* that. There's no need to test me any longer."

A few doors from her building she stopped me. Her convertible was squatting there at the curb. The cars in front and behind had parking tickets on the windshield wiper. Hers bore only a club insignia.

"I'll drive this time," she said.

We got in and drove. It rained a little and it snowed a little, then, abruptly, it was clear and the stars came in full and bright, framed in the hole in the sky. The radio was a chant of pleasure, snatching the wild symphonic music from the air and offering us orchestra seats though we were far beyond the city, hugging the curves of the Hudson.

When we stopped it was to turn off the highway to a winding mac-adam road that led beneath the overhanging branches of evergreens. The cottage nestled on top of a bluff smiling down at the world. Ethel took my hand, led me inside to the plush little playhouse that was her own special retreat and lit the heavy wax candles that hung in brass hold-ers from the ceiling.

I had to admire the exquisite simplicity of the place. It proclaimed wealth, but in the most humble fashion. Somebody had done a good job of decorating. Ethel pointed to the little bar that was set in the corner of the log cabin. "Drinks are there. Would you care to make us one . . . Then start the fire? The fireplace has been laid up."

I nodded, watched her leave the room, then opened the doors of the liquor cabinet. Only the best, the very best. I picked out the best of the best and poured two straight, not wanting to spoil it with any mixer, sipped mine then drank it down. I had a refill and stared at it.

A Commie. She was a jerky Red. She owned all the trimmings and she was still a Red. What the hell was she hoping for, a government order to share it all with the masses? Yeah. A joint like this would suddenly as-sume a new owner under a new regime. A fat little general, a ranking se-cret policeman, somebody. Sure, it's great to be a Commie . . . as long as you're top dog. Who the hell was supposed to be fooled by all the crap?

Yet Ethel fell for it. I shook my head at the stupid asses that are left in this world and threw a match into the fireplace. It blazed up and licked at the logs on the andirons.

Ethel came out of the other room wearing her fur coat. Her hair looked different. It seemed softer. "Cold?"

"In there it is. I'll be warm in a moment."

I handed her the glass and we touched the rims. Her eyes were bright, hot.

We had three or four more and the bottom was showing in the bot-tle. Maybe it was more than three or four. I wanted to ask her some questions. I wanted the right answers and I didn't want her to think about them beforehand. I wanted her just a little bit drunk.

I had to fumble with the catch to get the liquor cabinet open. There was more of the best of the best in the back and I dragged it out. Ethel found the switch on a built-in phonograph and stacked on a handful of records.

The fireplace was a leaping, dancing thing that threw shadows across the room and touched everything with a weird, demoniac light. Ethel came to me, holding her arms open to dance. I wanted to dance, but there were parts of me trying to do other things.

Ethel laughed. "You're drunk."

"I am like hell." It wasn't exactly the truth.

"Well *I'm* drunk. I'm very, very drunk and I love it!" She threw her arms up and spun around. I had to catch her. "Ooh, I want to sit down. Let's sit down and enjoy the fire."

She pulled away and danced to the sofa, her hands reaching out for the black bearskin rug that was draped over the back of it. She threw it on the floor in front of the fire and turned around. "Come on over. Sit down."

"You'll roast in that coat," I said.

"I won't." She smiled slyly and flipped open the buttons that held it together. She shrugged the shoulders off first, letting it fall to her waist, then swept it off and threw it aside.

Ethel didn't have anything on. Only her shoes. She kicked them off too and sank to the softness of the bearskin, a beautiful naked creature of soft round flesh and lustrous hair that changed color with each leap of the vivid red flame behind her.

It was much too warm then for a jacket. I heard mine hit a chair and slide off. My wallet fell out of the pocket and I didn't care. The sling on my gun rack wouldn't come loose and I broke it.

She shouldn't have done it. Damn it, she shouldn't have done it! I wanted to ask her some questions.

Now I forgot what I wanted to ask her.

My fingers hurt and she didn't care. Her lips were bright red, wet. They parted slowly and her tongue flicked out over her teeth inviting me to come closer. Her mouth was a hungry thing demanding to be tasted. The warmth that seemed to come from the flames was a radiation that flowed from the sleek length of her legs and nestled in the hollow of her stomach a moment before rising over the convex beauty of her breasts. She held her arms out invitingly and took me in them.

I came awake with the dawn, my throat dry and my mind groping to make sense out of what had happened. Ethel was still there, lying curled on her side up against me. Sometime during the night the fire had gone down and she had gotten up to get a blanket and throw it over us.

Somehow I got to my feet without waking her up. I pulled on my clothes, found my gun sling and my jacket on the floor. I remembered my wallet and felt around for it, getting mad when I didn't find it. I sat on the arm of the sofa and shook my head to clear out the spiders. Bending over didn't do me much good. The next time I used my foot and scooped it out from under the end table where I must have kicked it in getting dressed.

Ethel Brighton was asleep and smiling when I left. It was a good night, but not at all what I had come for. She giggled and wrapped her arms around the blankets. Maybe Ethel would quit being mad at the world now.

I climbed into my raincoat and walked out, looking up once at the sky overhead. The clouds had closed in again, but they were thinner and it was warmer than it had been.

It took twenty minutes to reach the highway and I had to wait another twenty before a truck came along and gave me a lift into town. I treated him to breakfast and we talked about the war. He agreed that it hadn't been a bad war. He had gotten nicked too, and it gave him a good excuse to cop a day off now and then.

I called Pat about ten o'clock. He gave me a fast hello, then: "Can you come up, Mike? I have something interesting."

"About last night?"

"That's right."

"I'll be up in five minutes. Stick around."

Headquarters was right up the street and I stepped it up. The D.A. was coming out of the building again. This time he didn't see me. When I rapped on Pat's door he yelled to come in and I pushed the knob.

Pat said, "Where the hell have you been?" He was grinning.

"No place." I grinned back.

"If what I suspect goes on between you and Velda, then you better get that lipstick off your face and shave."

"That bad?"

"I can smell whisky from here too."

"Velda won't like that," I said.

"No dame in love with a dope does," Pat laughed. "Park it, Mike. I have news for you." He opened his desk drawer and hauled out a large manila envelope that had CONFIDENTIAL printed across the back.

When he was draped across the arm of the chair he handed a fingerprint photostat to me. "I took these off the corpse last night."

"You don't waste time, pal."

"Couldn't afford to." He dug in the envelope and brought out a three-page document that was clipped together. It had a hospital masthead I didn't catch because Pat turned it over and showed me the fingerprints on the back. "These are Oscar Deamer's too. This is his medical case history that Lee was holding."

I didn't need to be an expert to see that they matched. "Same guy all right," I remarked.

"No doubt about it. Want to look at the report?"

"Ah, I couldn't wade through all that medical baloney. What's it say?"

"In brief, that Oscar Deamer was a dangerous neurotic, paranoiac and a few other psychiatric big words."

"Congenital?"

Pat saw what I was thinking. "No, as a matter of fact. So rest easy that no family insanity could be passed on to Lee. It seems that Oscar had an accident when he was a child. A serious skull fracture that somehow led to his condition."

"Any repercussions? Papers get any of it?" I handed the sheets back to Pat and he tucked them away.

"None at all, luckily. We were on tenterhooks for a while, but none of the newsboys connected the names. There was one fortunate aspect to the death of Oscar . . . his face wasn't recognizable. If the reporters had seen him there wouldn't have been a chance of covering up, and would some politicians like to have gotten that!"

I pulled a Lucky from my pack and tapped it on the arm of the chair. "What was the medical examiner's opinion?"

"Hell, suicide without a doubt. Oscar got scared, that's all. He tried to run knowing he was trapped. I guess he knew he'd go back to the sanitarium if he was caught . . . if he didn't stand a murder trial for Moffit's murder, and he couldn't take it."

Pat snapped his lighter open and fired my butt. "I guess that washes it up then," I said.

"For us . . . yes. For you, no."

I raised my eyebrows and looked at him quizzically.

"I saw Lee before I came to work. He called," Pat explained. "When he spoke to Oscar over the phone Oscar hinted at something. He seems to think that Oscar might have done other things than try to have him identified for a murder he didn't do. Anyway, I told him you had some unusual interest in the whole affair that you didn't want to speak about, even to me. He quizzed me about you, I told all and now he wants to see you."

"I'm to run down anything left behind?"

"I imagine so. At any rate, you'll get a fat fee out of it instead of kicking around for free."

"I don't mind. I'm on vacation anyway."

"Nuts. Stop handing me the same old thing. Think of something different. I'd give a lot to know what you have on your mind."

"You sure would, Pat." Perhaps it was the way I said it. Pat went into a piece of police steel. The cords in his neck stuck out like little fingers and his lips were just a straight, thin line.

"I've never known you to hang your hat on anything but murder, Mike."

"True, ain't it." My voice was flat as his.

"Mike, after the way I've been pitching with you, if you get in another smear you'll be taking me with you."

"I won't get smeared."

"Mike, you bastard, you have a murder tucked away somewhere."

"Sure, two of 'em. Try again."

He let his eyes relax and forced a grin. "If there were any recent kills on the pad I'd go over them one by one and scour your hide until you told me which one it was."

"You mean," I said sarcastically, "that the Finest haven't got one single unsolved murder on their hands?"

Pat got red and squirmed. "Not recently."

"What about that laddie you hauled out of the drink?"

He scowled as he remembered. "Oh, that gang job. Body still unidentified and we're tracking down his dental work. No prints on file."

"Think you'll tag him?"

"It ought to be easy. That bridgework was unusual. One false tooth was made of stainless steel. Never heard of that before."

The bells started in my head again. Bells, drums, the whole damn works. The cigarette dropped out of my fingers and I bent to pick it up, hoping the blood pounding in my veins would pound out the crazy music.

It did. That maddening blast of silent sound went away. Slowly.

Maybe Pat never heard of stainless-steel teeth before, but I had.

I said, "Is Lee expecting me?"

"I told him you'd be over some time this morning."

"Okay." I stood up and shoved my hat on. "One other thing, what about the guy Oscar bumped?"

"Charlie Moffit?"

"Yeah."

"Age thirty-four, light skin, dark hair. He had a scar over one eye. During the war he was 4-F. No criminal record and not much known about him. He lived in a room on Ninety-first Street, the same one he's had for a year. He worked in a pie factory."

"Where?"

"A pie factory," Pat repeated, "where they make pies. Mother Switcher's Pie Shoppe. You can find it in the directory."

"Was that card all the identification he had on him?"

"No, he had a driver's license and a few other things. During the scuffle one pocket of his coat was torn out, but I doubt if he would have carried anything there anyway. Now, Mike, . . . why?"

"The green cards, remember?"

"Hell, quit worrying about the Reds. We have agencies who can handle them."

I looked past Pat outside into the morning. "How many Commies are there floating around, Pat?"

"Couple hundred thousand, I think," he said.

"How many men have we got in those agencies you mentioned?"

"Oh . . . maybe a few hundred. What's that got to do with it?"

"Nothing . . . just that that's the reason I'm worried."

"Forget it. Let me know how you make out with Lee."

"Sure."

"And Mike . . . be discreet as hell about this, will you? Everybody with a press card knows your reputation and if you're spotted tagging around Lee there might be some questions asked that will be hard to answer."

"I'll wear a disguise," I said.

Lee Deamer's office was on the third floor of a modest building just off Fifth Avenue. There was nothing pretentious about the place aside from the switchboard operator. She was special. She had one of those faces that belonged in a chorus and a body she was making more effort to show than to conceal. I heard her voice and it was beautiful. But she was chewing gum like a cow and that took away any sign of pretentiousness she might have had.

There was a small anteroom that led to another office where two stenos were busy over typewriters. One wall of that room was all glass with a speaking partition built in at waist level. I had to lean down to my belt buckle to talk and gave it up as a bad job. The girl behind it laughed pleasantly and came out the door to see me.

She was a well-tailored woman in her early thirties, nice to look at and speak to. She wore an emerald ring that looked a generation older than she was. She smiled and said, "Good morning, can I do something for you?"

I remembered to be polite. "I'd like to see Mr. Deamer, please."

"Is he expecting you?"

"He sent word for me to come up."

"I see." She tapped her teeth with a pencil and frowned. "Are you in a hurry?"

"Not particularly, but I think Mr. Deamer is."

"Oh, well . . . the doctor is inside with him. He may be there awhile, so . . ."

"Doctor?" I interrupted.

The girl nodded, a worried little look tugging at her eyes. "He seemed to be quite upset this morning and I called in the doctor. Mr. Deamer hasn't been too well since he had that attack awhile back."

"What kind of attack?"

"Heart. He had a telephone call one day that agitated him terribly. I was about to suggest that he go home and at that moment, he collapsed. I . . . I was awfully frightened. You see, it had never happened before, and . . ."

"What did the doctor say?"

"Apparently it wasn't a severe attack. Mr. Deamer was instructed to take it easy, but for a man of his energy it's hard to do."

"You say he had a phone call? That did it?"

"I'm sure it did. At first I thought it was the excitement of watching the Legion parade down the avenue, but Ann told me it happened right after the call came in."

Oscar's call must have hit him harder than either Pat or I thought. Lee wasn't a young man any more, a thing like that could raise a lot of hell with a guy's ticker. I was about to say something when the doctor came out of the office. He was a little guy with a white goatee out of another era.

He nodded to us both, but turned his smile on the girl. "I'm sure he'll be fine. I left a prescription. See that it's filled at once, please?"

"Thank you, I will. Is it all right for him to have visitors?"

"Certainly. Apparently he has been thinking of something that disturbed him and had a slight relapse. Nothing to worry about as long as he takes it easy. Good day."

We said so long and she turned to me with another smile, bigger this time. "I guess you can go ahead in then. But please . . . don't excite him."

I grinned and said I wouldn't. Her smile made her prettier. I pushed through the door, passed the steno and knocked on the door with Deamer's name on it.

He rose to greet me but I waved him down. His face was a little flushed and his breathing fast. "Feeling better now? I saw the doctor when he came out."

"Much better, Mike. I had to fabricate a story to tell him . . . I couldn't tell the truth."

I sat in the chair next to his and he pushed a box of cigars toward me. I said no and took out a Lucky instead. "Best to keep things to yourself. One word and the papers'll have it on page one. Pat said you wanted to see me."

Lee sat back and wiped his face with a damp handkerchief. "Yes, Mike. He told me you were interested somehow."

"I am."

"Are you one of my . . . political advocates?"

"Frankly, I don't know a hoot about politics except that it's a dirty game from any angle."

"I hope to do something about that. I hope I can, Mike, I sincerely hope I can. Now I'm afraid."

"The heart?"

He nodded. "It happened after Oscar called. I never suspected that I have a . . . condition. I'm afraid now the voters must be told. It wouldn't be fair to elect a man not physically capable of carrying out the duties of his office." He smiled wistfully, sadly. I felt sorry for the old boy.

"Anyway, I'm not concerned with the politics of the affair."

"Really? But what . . ."

"Just a loose end, Lee. They bother me."

"I see. I don't understand, but I see . . . if you can make sense of that."

I waved the smoke away from in front of him. "I know what you mean. Now about why you wanted to see me. Pat gave me part of it already, enough so I can see the rest."

"Yes. You see, Oscar intimated that no matter what happened, he was going to see to it that I was broken, completely broken. He mentioned some documents he had prepared."

I crushed the butt out and looked at him. "What kind of documents?"

Lee shook his head slowly. "The only possible thing he could compound would be our relationship as brothers. How, I don't know, because I have all the family papers. But if he could establish that I was the brother of a man committed to a mental institution, it would be a powerful weapon in the hands of the opposition."

"There's nothing else," I asked, "that could stick you?"

He spread his hands apart in appeal. "If there was it would have been brought to light long ago. No, I've never been in jail or in trouble of any sort. I'm afraid that my attention to business precluded any trouble."

"Uh-huh. How come this awful hatred?"

"I don't know, actually. As I told Pat and you previously, it may have been a matter of ideals, or because though we were twins, we weren't at all alike. Oscar was almost, well . . . sadistic in his ways. We had little to do with each other. As younger men I became established in business while Oscar got into all sorts of scrapes. I've tried to help him, but he wouldn't accept help from me at all. He hated me fiercely. I'm inclined to believe that this time Oscar had intended to bleed me for all the money he could, then make trouble for me anyway."

"You were lucky you took the attitude you did. You can't pay off, it only makes matters worse."

"I don't know, Mike; as much as he hated me I certainly didn't want that to happen to him."

"He's better off."

"Perhaps."

I reached for another cigarette. "You want me to find out what he left then, that's it."

"If there is anything to be found, yes."

When I filled my lungs with smoke I let it go slowly, watching it swirl up toward the ceiling. "Lee," I said, "you don't know me so I'll tell you something. I hate phonies. Suppose I *do* find something that ties you up into a nice little ball. Something real juicy. What do you think I should do with it?"

It wasn't the reaction I expected. He leaned forward across the desk with his fingers interlocked. His face was a study in emotions. "Mike," he said in a voice that had the crisp clarity of static electricity, "if you do, I charge you to make it public at once. Is that clear?"

I grinned and stood up. "Okay, Lee. I'm glad you said that." I reached out my hand and he took it warmly. I've seen evangelists with faces like that, unswerving, devoted to their duty. We looked at each other then he opened his desk drawer and brought out a lovely sheaf of green paper. They had big, beautiful numbers in the corners.

"Here is a thousand dollars, Mike. Shall we call it a retainer?"

I took the bills and folded them tenderly away. "Let's call it payment in full. You'll get your money's worth."

"I'm sure of it. If you need any additional information, call on me."

"Right. Want a receipt?"

"No need of it. I'm sure your word is good enough."

"Thanks. I'll send you a report if anything turns up." I flipped a card out of my pocket and laid it on his desk. "In case you want to call me. The bottom one is my home phone. It's unlisted."

We shook hands again and he walked me to the door. On the way out the cud-chewing switchboard sugar smiled between chomps then went back to her magazine. The receptionist said so long and I waved back.

Before I went to the office I grabbed a quick shave, a trim around the ears and took a shower that scraped the hide off me along with the traces of Ethel's perfume. I changed my shirt and suit but kept old Betsy in place under my arm.

Velda was working at the filing cabinet when I breezed in with a snappy hello and a grin that said I had money in my pocket. I got a quick once-over for lipstick stains, whisky aromas and what not, passed and threw the stack of bills on the desk.

"Bank it, kid."

"Mike! What did *you* do?"

"Lee Deamer. We're employed." I gave it to her in short order and she listened blankly.

When I finished she said, "You'll never find a thing, Mike. I know you won't. You shouldn't have taken it."

"You're wrong, chick. It wasn't stealing. If Oscar left anything that will tie Lee up wouldn't you want me to get it?"

"Oh, Mike, you must! How long do we have to put up with the slime they call politics? Lee Deamer is the only one . . . the only one we can look to. Please, Mike, you *can't* let anything happen to him!"

I couldn't take the fear in her voice. I opened my arms out and she stepped into them. "Nobody will hurt the little guy, Velda. If there's anything I'll get it. Stop sniffling."

"I can't. It's all so nasty. You never stop to think what goes on in this country, but I do."

"Seems to me that I helped fight a war, didn't I?"

"You shouldn't have let it stop there. That's the matter with things. People forget, even the ones who *shouldn't* forget! They let others come walking in and run things any way they please, and what are they after— the welfare of the people they represent? Not a bit. All they want is to line their own pockets. Lee isn't like that, Mike. He isn't strong like the others, and he isn't smart politically. All he has to offer is his honesty and that isn't much."

"The hell it isn't. He's made a pretty big splash in this state."

"I know, and it has to stick, Mike. Do you understand?"

"I understand."

"Promise me you'll help him, Mike, promise me your word."

Her face turned up to mine, drawn yet eager to hear. "I promise," I said softly. "I'll never go back on a promise to you, nor to myself."

It made her feel better in a hurry. The tears stopped and the sniffling died away. We had a laugh over it, but behind the laughter there was a dead seriousness. The gun under my arm felt heavy.

I said, "I have a job for you. Get me a background on Charlie Moffit. He's the one Oscar Deamer bumped."

Velda stopped her filing. "Yes, I know."

"Go to his home and his job. See what kind of a guy he was. Pat didn't mention a family so he probably didn't have any. Take what cash you need to cover expenses."

She shoved the drawer in and fingered the bills on the desk. "How soon?"

"I want it by tonight if you can. If not, tomorrow will do."

I could see her curiosity coming out, but there are times when I want to keep things to myself and this was one of them. She knew it and stayed curious without asking questions.

Before she slipped the bills inside the bank book I took out two hundred in fifties. She didn't say anything then, either, but she smelt a toot coming up and I had to kiss the tip of her nose to get the scowl off her puss.

As soon as Velda left I picked up the phone and dialed Ethel Brighton's number. The flunky recognized my voice from last night and was a little more polite. He told me Ethel hadn't come in yet and hung up almost as hard as he could but not quite.

I tapped out a brief history of the case for the records, stuck it in the file and called again. Ethel had just gotten in. She grabbed the phone and made music in it, not giving a damn who heard her. "You beast. You walked right out of the cave and left me to the wolves."

"That bearskin would scare them away. You looked nice wrapped up in it."

"You liked . . . all of me, then. The parts you could see?"

"All of you, Ethel. Soft and sweet."

"We'll have to go back."

"Maybe," I said.

"Please," softly whispered.

I changed the subject. "Busy today?"

"Very busy. I have a few people to see. They promised me sizable . . . donations. Tonight I have to deliver them to Com . . . Henry Gladow."

"Yeah. Suppose I go with you?"

"If *you* think it's all right I'm sure no one will object."

"Why me?" That was one of the questions I wanted an answer to.

She didn't tell me. "Come now," she said. "Supposing I meet you in the Oboe Club at seven. Will that do?"

"Fine, Ethel. I'll save a table so we can eat."

She said so long with a pleasant laugh and waited for me to hang up. I did, then sat there with a cigarette in my fingers trying to think. The light hitting the wall broke around something on the desk making two little bright spots against the pale green.

Like two berries on a bush. The judge's eyes. They looked at me.

Something happened to the light and the eyes disappeared. I picked the phone up again and called the *Globe*. Marty was just going out on a story but had time to talk to me. I asked him, "Remember the Brighton family? Park Avenue stuff."

"Sure, Mike. That's social, but I know a little about them. Why?"

"Ethel Brighton's on the outs with her father. Did it ever make the papers?"

I heard him chuckle a second. "Getting tony, aren't you, kid? Well, part of the story was in the papers some time ago. It seems that Ethel Brighton publicly announced her engagement to a certain young man. Shortly afterwards the engagement was broken."

"Is that all?"

"Nope," he grunted, "the best is yet to come. A little prying by our diligent Miss Carpenter who writes the social chatter uncovered an interesting phase that was handled just as interestingly. The young man in question was a down-and-out artist who made speeches for the Communist Party and was quite willing to become a capitalist by marriage. He was a conscientious objector during the war though he probably could have made 4-F without trouble. The old man raised the roof but there was nothing he could do. When he threatened to cut Ethel off without a cent she said she'd marry him anyway.

"So the old man connived. He worked it so that he'd give his blessing so long as the guy enlisted in the army. They needed men bad so they took him and as soon as he was out of training camp he was shipped overseas. He was killed in action, though the truth was that he went AWOL during a battle and deserved what he got. Later Ethel found out that her father was responsible for everything but the guy's getting knocked off and he had hoped for that too. She had a couple of rows with him in public, then it died down to where they just never spoke."

"Nice girl," I mused.

"Lovely to look at anyway."

"You'll never know. Well, thanks, pal."

He stopped me before I could hang up. "Is this part of what you were driving at the other day . . . something to do with Lee Deamer?" His voice had a rasp.

"Not this," I said. "It's personal."

"Oh, well call me any time, Mike." He sounded relieved.

And so the saga of one Ethel Brighton. Nice girl turned dimwit because her old man did her out of a marriage. She was lucky and didn't know it.

I looked at my watch, remembered that I had meant to buy Velda lunch and forgot, then went downstairs and ate by myself. When I finished the dessert I sat back with a cigarette and tried to think of what it was that fought like the hammers of hell to come through my mind. Something was eating its way out and I couldn't help it. I gave up finally and paid my check. There was a movie poster behind the register advertising the latest show at the house a block over, so I ambled over and plunked in a seat before the show started. It wasn't good enough to keep me awake. I was on the second time around when I glanced at the time and hustled into the street.

The Oboe Club had been just another second-rate saloon on a side street until a wandering reporter happened in and mentioned it in his column as a good place to relax if you liked solitude and quiet. The next day it became a first-rate nightclub where you could find anything but solitude and quiet. Advertising helped plenty.

I knew the headwaiter to nod to and it was still early enough to get a table without any green passing between handshakes. The bar was lined with the usual after-office crowd having one for the road. There wasn't anyone to speak to, so I sat at the table and ordered a highball. I was on my fourth when Ethel Brighton came in, preceded by the headwaiter and a few lesser luminaries.

He bowed her into her seat, then bowed himself out. The other one helped her adjust her coat over the back of the chair. "Eat?" I asked.

"I'll have a highball first. Like yours." I signaled the waiter and called for a couple more.

"How'd the donations come?"

"Fine," she said, "even better than I expected. The best part is, there's more where that came from."

"The party will be proud of you." She looked up from her drink with a nervous little smile.

"I . . . hope so."

"They should. You've brought in a lot of mazuma."

"One must do all one can." Her voice was a flat drone, almost machine-like. She picked up her glass and took a long pull. The waiter came and took our orders, leaving another highball with us.

I caught her attention and got back on the subject. "Do you ever wonder where it all goes to?"

"You mean . . . the money?" I nodded between bites. "Why . . . no.

It isn't for me to think about those things. I only do as I'm told." She licked her lips nervously and went back to her plate.

I prodded her again. "I'd be curious if I were in your shoes. Give a guess, anyway."

This time there was nothing but fear in her face. It tugged at her eyes and mouth, and made her fork rattle against the china. "Please . . ."

"You don't have to be afraid of me, Ethel. I'm not entirely like the others. You should know that."

The fear was still there, but something else overshadowed it. "I can't understand you . . . you're different. It's well. . . ."

"About the money, give a guess. Nobody should be entirely ignorant of party affairs. After all, isn't that the principle of the thing . . . everybody for everybody? Then you'd have to know everything about everybody to be able to really do the party justice."

"That's true." She squinted and a smile parted her lips. "I see what you mean. Well, I'd guess that most of the money goes to foster the schools we operate . . . and for propaganda, of course. Then there are a lot of small things that come up like office expenses here and there."

"Pretty good so far. Anything else?"

"I'm not too well informed on the business side of it so that's about as far as I can go."

"What does Gladow do for a living?"

"Isn't he a clerk in a department store?"

I nodded as if I had known all along. "Ever see his car?"

Ethel frowned again. "Yes. He has a new Packard, why?"

"Ever see his house?"

"I've been there twice," she said. "It's a big place up in Yonkers."

"And all that on a department store clerk's salary."

Her face went positively white. She had to swallow hard to get her drink down and refused to meet my eyes until I told her to look at me. She did, but hesitantly. Ethel Brighton was scared silly . . . of me. I grinned but it was lost. I talked and it went over her head. She gave all the right answers and even a laugh at one of my jokes, but Ethel was scared and she wasn't coming out of it too quickly.

She took the cigarette I offered her. The tip shook when she bent into the flame of my lighter. "What time do you have to be there?" I asked.

"Nine o'clock. There's . . . a meeting."

"We'd better go then. It'll take time getting over to Brooklyn."

"All right."

The waiter came over and took away a ten spot for his trouble while the headboy saw us to the door. Half the bar turned around to look at Ethel as she brushed by. I got a couple of glances that said I was a lucky guy to have all that mink on my arm. Real lucky.

We had to call the parking lot to get her car brought over then drove the guy back again. It was a quarter after eight before we pointed the car toward the borough across the stream. Ethel was behind the wheel, driving with a fixed intensity. She wouldn't talk unless I said something that required an answer. After a while it got tiresome so I turned on the radio and slumped back against the seat with my hat down over my eyes.

Only then did she seem to ease up. Twice I caught her head turning my way, but I couldn't see her eyes nor read the expression on her face. Fear. It was always there. Communism and Fear. Green Cards and Fear. Terror on the face of the girl on the bridge; stark, unreasoning fear when she looked at my face. Fear so bad it threw her over the rail to her death.

I'd have to remember to ask Pat about that, I thought. The body had to come up sometime.

The street was the same as before, dark, smelly, unaware of the tumor it was breeding in its belly. Trench Coat was standing outside the door seemingly enjoying the night. Past appearance didn't count. You showed your card and went in the door and showed it again. There was the same girl behind the desk and she made more of me than the card I held. Her voice was a nervous squeak and she couldn't sit still. Deliberately, I shot her the meanest grin I could dig up, letting her see my face when I pulled my lip back over my teeth. She didn't like it. Whatever it was scared her, too.

Henry Gladow was a jittery little man. He frittered around the room, stopped when he saw us and came over with a rush. "Good evening, good evening, comrades." He spoke directly to me. "I am happy to see you again, comrade. It is an honor."

It had been an honor before, too.

"There is news?" I screwed my eyebrows together and he pulled back, searching for words until he found them. "Of course. I am merely being inquisitive. Ha, ha. We are all so very concerned, you know."

"I know," I said.

Ethel handed him another of those envelopes and excused herself. I watched her walk to a table and take a seat next to two students where she began to correct some mimeographed sheets. "Wonderful worker,

Miss Brighton," Gladow smiled. "You would scarcely think that she represents all that we hate."

I made an unintelligible answer.

"You are staying for the meeting?" he asked me.

"Yeah, I want to poke around a little."

This time he edged close to me, looking around to see if there was anyone close enough to hear. "Comrade, if I am not getting too inquisitive again, is there a possibility that . . . the person could be here?"

There it was again. Just what I wanted to know and I didn't dare ask the question. It was going to take some pretty careful handling. "It's possible," I said tentatively.

He was aghast. "Comrade! It is unthinkable!" He reflected a moment then: "Yet it had to come from somewhere. I simply can't understand it. Everything is so carefully screened, every member so carefully selected that it seems impossible for there to be a leak anywhere. And those filthy warmongers, doing a thing like that . . . so cold-blooded! It is simply incredible. How I wish the party was in power at this moment. Why, the one who did that would be uncovered before the sun could set!"

Gladow cursed through his teeth and pounded a puny, carefully tended fist into his palm. "Don't worry," I said slowly.

It took ten seconds for my words to sink in. Gladow's little eyes narrowed in pleasure like a hog seeing a trough full of slops. The underside of his top lip showed when he smiled. "No, comrade. I won't worry. The party is too clever to let a direct representative's death go unpunished. No, I won't worry because I realize that the punishment that comes will more than equal the crime." He beamed at me fatuously. "I am happy to realize that the higher echelon has sent a man of your capacity, comrade."

I didn't even thank him. I was thinking and this time the words made sense. They made more than sense . . . they made murder! Only death is cold-blooded, and who was dead? Three people. One hadn't been found. One was found and not identified, even by a lousy sketch. The other was dead and identified. He was cold-bloodedly murdered and he was a direct representative of the party and I was the guy looking for his killer.

Good Lord, the insane bastards thought I was an M.V.D. man!

My hands started to shake and I kept them in my pockets. And who was the dead man but Charlie Moffit! My predecessor. A goddamned Commie gestapo man. A hatchetman, a torpedo, a lot of things you want to call him. Lee ought to be proud of his brother, damn proud. All by himself he went out and he knocked off a skunk.

But I was the prize, I was the M.V.D. guy that came to take his place and run the killer down. Oh, brother! No wonder the jerks were afraid of me! No wonder they didn't ask my name! No wonder I was supposed to know it all.

I felt a grin trying to pull my mouth out of shape because so much of it was funny. They thought they were clever as hell and here I was right in the middle of things with an *in* that couldn't be better. Any good Red would give his shirt to be where I was right this minute.

Everything started to come out right then, even the screwy test they put me through. A small-time setup like this was hardly worth the direct attention of a Moscow man unless something was wrong, so I had to prove myself.

Smart? Sure, just like road apples that happen behind horses.

Now I knew and now I could play the game. I could be one of the boys and show them some fun. There were going to be a lot of broken backs around town before I got done.

There was only one catch I could think of. Someplace was another M.V.D. laddie, a real one. I'd have to be careful of him. At least careful that he didn't see me first, because when I met up with that stinkpot I was going to split him right down the middle with a .45!

I had been down too deep in my thoughts to catch the arrival of the party that came in behind me. I heard Gladow extending a welcome that wasn't handed out to just everybody. When I turned around to look I saw one little fat man, one big fat man and a guy who was in the newspapers every so often. His name was General Osilov and he was attached to the Russian Embassy in Washington. The big and little fat men were his aides and they did all the smiling. If anything went on in the head of the bald-headed general it didn't show in his flat, wide face.

Whatever it was Henry Gladow said swung the three heads in my direction. Two swung back again fast leaving only the general staring at me. It was a stare-down that I won. The general coughed without covering his mouth and stuck his hands in the pockets of his suitcoat. None of them seemed anxious to make my acquaintance.

From then on there was a steady flow of traffic in through the door. They came singly and in pairs, spaced about five minutes apart. Before the hour was out the place was packed. It was filled with the kind of people you'd expect to find there and it would hit you that when the cartoonists did a caricature of a pack of shabby Reds lurking in the shadow of democracy they did a good job.

A few of them dragged out seats and the meeting was on. I saw Ethel Brighton slide into the last chair in the last row and waited until she was settled before I sat down beside her. She smiled, let that brief look of fear mask her face, then turned her head to the front. When I put my hand over hers I felt it tremble.

Gladow spoke. The aides spoke. Then the general spoke. He pulled his tux jacket down when he rose and glared at the audience. I had to sit there and listen to it. It was propaganda right off the latest Moscow cable and it turned me inside out. I wanted to feel the butt of an M-1 against my shoulder pointing at those bastards up there on the rostrum and feel the pleasant impact as it spit slugs into their guts.

Sure, you can sit down at night and read about the hogwash they hand out. Maybe you're fairly intelligent and can laugh at it. Believe me, it isn't funny. They use the very thing we build up, our own government and our own laws, to undermine the things we want.

It wasn't a very complicated speech the general made. It was plain, bitter poison and they cheered him noiselessly. He was making plain one thing. There were still too many people who didn't go for Communism and not enough who did and he gave a plan of organization that had worked in a dozen countries already. One armed Communist was worth twenty capitalists without guns. It was Hitler all over again. A powerful Communist government already formed would be there to take over when the big upset came, and according to him it was coming soon. Here, and he swept the room with his arm, was one phase of that government ready to go into action.

I didn't hear the rest of it. I sat there fiddling with my fingernails because I was getting ready to bust loose and spoil their plans. If I let any more words go in my ears there was going to be blood on the floor and it wasn't time for that yet. I caught snatches of things that went on, repeated intimations of how the top men were already in the core of the present government eating its vitals out so the upset would be an easy one.

For a long time I sat there working up more hatred than I had ever had at any time and I wasn't conscious of how tightly Ethel Brighton was squeezing my hand. When I looked at her tears were running down her face. That's the kind of thing the general and his party could do to decent people.

I took a long look at him, making sure that I wouldn't forget his face, because some day he'd be passing a dark alley or forget to lock his door when he went to bed. That's when he'd catch it. And I didn't want to get tagged for it either. That would be like getting the chair for squashing a spider.

The meeting ended with handshakes all around. The audience lined up along the walls taking handfuls of booklets and printed sheets to distribute later, then grouped in bunches around the room talking things over in excited murmurs. Henry Gladow and Martin Romberg were up on the rostrum having their own conference. The general said something to Henry and he must have ordered his bodyguard down into the crowd to look for his trench coat or something. Martin Romberg looked hurt. Tough.

While the seats were folded and stacked I lost track of Ethel. I saw her a few minutes later coming from the washroom and she looked a little better. She had a smile for me this time, a big one. I would have made something of it if a pimply-faced kid about twenty didn't come crawling over and tell me that the general wanted to know if I had time to speak to him.

Rather than answer I picked a hole in the crowd that had started to head for the door and walked up to the rostrum. The general stood alone, his hands behind his back. He nodded briefly and said something in a guttural tongue.

I let my eyes slide to the few who remained near by. There wasn't any respect in my tone when I said, "English. You know better than that."

The general paled a little and his mouth worked. "Yes . . . yes. I didn't expect to find anyone here. Do you have a report for me?"

I shook a cigarette out of the pack and stuck it in my mouth. "When I have you'll know about it."

His head bobbed anxiously and I knew I had the bull on him. Even a general had to be leery of the M.V.D. That made it nice for me. "Of course. But there should be some word to bring back to the committee."

"Then tell 'em things are looking up. It won't be long."

The general's hands came out in front where he squeezed them happily. "Then you *do* have word! The courier . . . he did have the documents? You know where they are?"

I didn't say a word. All I did was look at him and he got that same look on his face as the others had. He was thinking what I thought he was thinking, that he had taken me for granted and it was his mistake and one word to the right sources and he'd feel the ax.

He tried his first smile. "It is very all right, you know. Comrade Gladow told me."

I dragged on the cigarette and blew it in his face wishing it was some mustard gas. "You'll know soon enough," I said. I left him standing there and walked back to Ethel. She was slipping into her mink and nobody seemed to care a hoot what she wore.

"Going home?"

"Yes . . . are you?"

"I don't mind."

One of the men paused to have a word with her before she left. She excused herself to talk to him and I used the time to look around and be sure there weren't any faces there that I'd ever forget. When the time came I wanted to be able to put the finger on them and put it on good.

Maybe it was the way I stared at the babe from the desk at the door or maybe it was because I looked at her too long. Her lashes made like bird's wings for a second and everything in the room seemed to get interesting all of a sudden. Her eyes jerked around but kept coming back to mine and each time there was a little more of a blush crowding her hairline.

I kept my grin hidden because she thought I was on the make. It could have been pathetic if it wasn't so damn funny. She wasn't the kind of woman a guy would bother with if there was anything else around. Strictly the last resort type. From the way she wore her clothes you couldn't tell what was underneath and suspected probably nothing. Her face looked like nature had been tired when it made it and whatever she did to her hair certainly didn't improve things any.

Plain was the word. Stuffy was the type. And here she thought a man saw something interesting in her.

I guessed that all women were born with some conceit in them so I put on a sort of smile and walked over to her casually. A little flattery could make a woman useful sometimes.

I held out my deck of butts. "Smoke?"

It must have been her first cigarette. She choked on it, but came up smiling. "Thank you."

I said, "You've, er . . . belonged some time, Miss . . ."

"Linda Holbright." She got real fluttery then. "Oh, yes, for years, you know. And I . . . try to do anything I can for the party."

"Good, good," I said. "You seem to be . . . very capable. Pretty, too."

Her first blush had been nothing. This one went right down to her shoes. Her eyes got big and blue and round and gave me the damnedest look you ever saw. Just for the hell of it I gave one back with a punch in it. What she made of it stopped her from breathing for a second.

I heard Ethel finish her little conversation behind me and I said, "Good night, Linda. I'll see you soon." I gave her that look again. "Real soon."

Her voice sounded a little bit strained. "I . . . meant to ask you. If there is anything . . . important you should know . . . where can I reach you?"

I ripped the back off a book of matches and wrote down my address. "Here it is. Apartment 5B."

Ethel was waiting for me, so I said good night again and started for the door behind the mink coat. It made nice wiggles when she walked. I liked that.

I let her go out first then followed her. The street was empty enough so you wouldn't think anything unusual about the few couples who were making their way to the subways. Trench Coat was still at the door holding a cigarette in his mouth. His belt was too tight and the gun showed underneath. One day a cop would spot that and there'd be more trouble.

Yeah, they sure were smart.

Going back was better than going down. This time Ethel turned into a vivid conversationalist, commenting on everything she saw. I tried to get in a remark about the meeting and she brushed it off with some fast talk. I let her get it out of her system, sitting there with my mouth shut, grinning at the right places and chiming in with a grunt whenever she laughed.

About a block from my apartment I pointed to the corner and said, "I'll get off under the light, kid."

She edged into the curb and stopped. "Good night, then," she smiled. "I hope you enjoyed the meeting."

"As a matter of fact, I thought they stunk." Ethel's mouth dropped open. I kissed it and she closed it, fast. "Do you know what I'd do if I were you, Ethel?"

She shook her head, watching me strangely.

"I'd go back to being a woman and less of a dabbler in politics."

This time her eyes and mouth came open together. I kissed her again before she could get it shut. She looked at me as if I were a puzzle that couldn't be solved and let out a short, sharp laugh that had real pleasure in it.

"Aren't you a bit curious about my name, Ethel?"

Her face went soft. "Only for my own sake."

"It's Mike. Mike Hammer and it's a good name to remember."

"Mike . . ." very softly. "After last night . . . how could I forget?"

I grinned at her and opened the door. "Will I be seeing you again?"
"Do you want to?"
"Very much."
"Then you'll be seeing me again. You know where I live."
I couldn't forget her, either. On that bearskin rug with the fire be-
hind her she was something a man never forgets. I stuck my hands in my
pockets and started to whistle my way down the street.

I got as far as the door next to mine when the sedan across the street
came to life. If the guy at the wheel hadn't let the clutch out so fast I
wouldn't have looked up and seen the snout of the rifle that hung out
the back window. What happened then came in a blur of motion and
a mad blasting of sound. The long streak of flame from the rifle, the
screaming of the ricocheted slug, the howl of the car engine. I dived flat
out. Rolling before I hit the concrete, my hand pulling the gun out, my
thumb grabbing for the hammer. The rifle barked again and gouged a
hunk out of the sidewalk in front of my face, but by that time the .45 in
my hand was bucking out the bullets as fast as my finger could pull the
trigger, and in the light of the street lamp overhead I saw the dimples
pop into the back of the car and the rear window spiderweb suddenly
and smash to the ground. Somebody in the car screamed like a banshee
gone mad and there were no more shots. Around me the windows were
slamming up before the car had made the turn at the corner.

I kept saying it over and over to myself. "Those goddamned bastards.
They got wise! Those goddamn bastards!"

A woman shrieked from a window that somebody was dead and
when I looked up I saw she was pointing to me. When I climbed back
on my feet she shrieked again and fell away from the window.

It hadn't been a full twenty seconds since that car had started up, and
a police car was wheeling around the corner. The driver slammed on the
brakes and the two of them came out with Police Specials in their
hands, both of them pointed at me. I was trying to shove a fresh load
into the clip when the cop snarled, "Drop that gun, damn it!"

I wasn't doing any arguing with them. I tossed the gun so it landed
on my foot then shoved it away gently. The other cop picked it up. Before they told me to, I put my hands on my head and stood there while
they flashed the beam of light in my face.

"There's a ticket for that rod in my wallet along with a Private Operator's license."

The cop didn't lose any time frisking me for another rod before
yanking my wallet out. He had a skeptical look on his face until he saw

the ticket. "Okay, put 'em down," he said. I dropped my hands and reached for my .45. "I didn't say to pick that up yet," he added. I let it stay there. The cop who drove the buggy looked the ticket over then looked at me. He said something to his partner and motioned for me to get the gun.

"All clear?" I blew the dust off old Betsy and stowed it away. A crowd was beginning to collect and one of the cops started to herd them away.

"What happened?" He wasn't a man of many words.

"There you got me, feller. I was on my way home when the shooting started. Either it's the old yarn of mistaken identity which isn't too probable or somebody whom I thought was a friend, isn't."

"Maybe you better come with us."

"Sure, but in the meantime a black Buick sedan with no back window and a few bullets in its behind is making tracks to the nearest garage. I think I got one of the guys in the car and you can start checking the doctors."

The cop peered at me under his visor and took my word for it. The call went out on the police wires without any more talk. They were all for dragging me with them until I had a call put in to Pat and his answer relayed back to the squad car. Pat told them I was available at any time and they gave me the green light through the crowd.

I got a lot of unfriendly looks that night.

When I stood in front of my door with the key in my hand it hit me just like that. My little love scene with Ethel Brighton had had repercussions. My wallet on the floor. It wasn't in the same place in the morning. When she had gotten up for that blanket she had seen it, and my P.I. card in the holder. Tonight she passed the word.

I was lucky to get out of there with a whole skin.

Ethel, I thought, you're a cute little devil. You looked so nice in your bare skin with the fire behind you. Maybe I'll see you stripped again. Soon. When I do I'm going to take my belt off and lash your butt like it should have been lashed when you first broke into this game.

In fact, I looked forward to doing it.

CHAPTER 6

I finished a quart bottle of beer before calling Velda. I got her at home and asked her what she'd found. She said, "There wasn't much *to* find, Mike. His landlady said he was on the quiet side because he was too stupid to talk. He never complained about a thing and in all the time he was living there he never once had company."

No, he wouldn't talk too much if he was an M.V.D. agent. And he wouldn't have company for that matter, either. His kind of company was met at night and in the dark recesses of a building somewhere.

"Did you try the pie factory where he worked?"

"I did but I didn't get anywhere. The last few months he had been on deliveries and most of the guys who knew him were out selling pies. The manager told me he was a stupid egg who had to write everything down in order to remember it, but he did his job fairly well. The only driver I did see said something nasty when I mentioned Moffit and tried to date me."

The boy put on a good act. People aren't likely to get too friendly with somebody who's pretty stupid. I said. "When do the drivers leave the plant?"

"Eight A.M., Mike. Are you going back?"

"I think I'd better. Supposing you come along with me. I'll meet you on the street in front of the office about seven and that'll give us time to get over there and see some of them."

"Mike . . . what's so important about Charlie Moffit?"

"I'll tell you tomorrow."

Velda grunted her displeasure and said good night. I had hardly hung up when I heard the feet in the hall and my doorbell started to yammer. Just in case, I yanked the .45 out and dropped it in my pocket where I could keep my hand around it.

The gun wasn't necessary at all. It was the boys from the papers, four of them. Three were on the police beat and the fourth was Marty Kooperman. He wore a faint, sardonic smile that was ready to disbelieve any lie I told.

"Well, the Fourth Estate. Come on in and don't stay too long." I threw the door open.

Bill Cowan of the *News* grinned and pointed to my pocket. "Nice way to greet old friends, Mike."

"Isn't it. Come on in."

They made a straight line for the refrigerator, found it empty, but uncovered a fresh bottle of whisky that I had been saving and helped themselves. All but Marty. He closed the door himself and stood behind me.

"We hear you got shot at, Mike."

"You heard right, friend. They missed."

"I'm thinking that I could say 'too bad' and mean it."

"What's your bitch, Marty! I've been shot at before. How come you're on the police run?"

"I'm not. I came along for the ride when I heard what happened." He paused. "Mike . . . for once come clean. Has this got to do with Lee Deamer?"

The boys in the kitchen were banging their first drinks down. I had that much time at least. I said, "Marty, don't worry about your idol. Let's say that this happened as a result of my poking into something that I *thought* was connected with Deamer. He doesn't figure into it in any way."

Marty took in a breath and let it out slowly. He twisted his hat in his hands then flipped it on the coat rack. "Okay, Mike, I'll take your word for it."

"Suppose it had to do with Lee, what then, chum?"

His lips tightened over a soft voice. "We'd have to know. They're out to get Lee any way they can and there aren't many of us who can stop them."

I scowled at him. "Who's us?"

"Your Fourth Estate, Mike. Your neighbors. Maybe even you if you knew what we knew."

That was all we had time for. The boys came charging back with fresh drinks and pencils ready. I led them inside to the living room and sat down. "Shoot, laddies. What's on your mind?"

"The shooting, Mike. Good news item, ya know."

"Yeah, great news. Tomorrow the public gets my picture and another lurid account of how that Hammer character conducts a private war on a public thoroughfare and I'll get an eviction notice from my landlord and a sudden lack of clients."

Bill laughed and polished his drink off. "Just the same, it's news. We got some of it from headquarters but we want the story straight from you. Hell, man, look how lucky you are. You get to tell your side of it while the others can't say a word. Come on, give."

"Sure, I'll give." I lit up a Lucky and took a deep drag on it. "I was walking home and . . ."

"Where were you?"

"Movies. So just as I . . ."

"What movie?"

I showed him my teeth in a lopsided grin. That was an easy one. "Laurance Theatre. Bum show."

Marty showed me his teeth back. "What was playing, Mike? He was the only one not ready to take notes.

I started in on as much of the picture as I had seen and he stopped me with his hand. "That's enough. I saw it myself. Incidentally, have you still got your stub?"

Marty should have been a cop. He knows damn well that most men have an unconscious habit of dropping the things in their pockets. I pulled out an assortment and handed him one. He took it while the other boys watched, wondering what the hell it was all about. He picked up the phone, called the theatre and gave them the number on the ticket, asking if it had been sold that day. They said it had been and Marty hung up sheepishly. I let go my breath, glad that he hadn't asked what time. He wasn't such a good detective after all.

"Go on," he said.

"That's all. I was coming home when the punks in the car started to blast. I didn't get a look at any of 'em."

Bill said, "You on a case now?"

"If I was I wouldn't say so anyhow. What else?"

One of the boys from a tabloid wrinkled his nose at my story. "Come on, Mike, break down. Nobody took a shot at you without a reason."

"Look, pal, I have more enemies than I have friends. The kind of enemies I make go around loaded. Take a check on most known criminals and you'll find people who don't like me."

"In other words, we don't get a story," Bill said.

"In other words," I told him, ". . . yes. Want another drink?"

At least that was satisfactory. When they had the bottom of the bottle showing I whistled to stop their jabbering and got them together so I could get in a last word. "Don't any of you guys try tagging me around hoping for a lead about this. I'm not taking anything without paying it back. If a story crops up I'll let you in on it, meantime stick to chasing ambulances."

"Aw, Mike."

"No, 'Aw,' pally. I'm not kidding around about it, so stay out of my way."

As long as the bottle was empty and I wouldn't give with a yarn, they decided that there wasn't much sense in sticking around. They went out the door in a bunch with Marty trailing along in the rear. He said so long ruefully, his eyes warning me to be careful.

I spread the slats of the blinds apart and watched them all climb into a beat-up coupé and when I was sure they were gone for the night I took off my clothes and climbed into the shower.

I took a hot and a cold, brushed my teeth, started to put away my tools and the bell rang again. I damned a few things in general and the Fourth Estate in particular for not making sure all the boys were there when they started their inquisition. Probably a lone reporter who got the flash late and wanted to know all about it. I wrapped a towel around my lower half and made wet tracks from the bathroom to the front door.

She stood there in the dim light of the hall not knowing whether to be startled, surprised or shocked. I said, "Goddamn!"

She smiled hesitantly until I told her to come in and made a quick trip back for a bathrobe. Something had happened to Linda Holbright since the last time I had seen her and I didn't want to stand there in a towel while I found out what it was.

When I got back to the living room she was sitting in the big chair with her coat thrown over the back. This time she didn't have on a sack suit and you knew what was underneath it. It wasn't "probably nothing" either. It was a whole lot of something that showed and she wasn't making any bones about it. The angles seemed to be gone from her face and her hair was different. Before it was hair. Now it was a smooth wavy mass that trailed across her shoulders. She still wasn't pretty, but a guy didn't give a damn about that when there was a body like hers under her face.

Because of a smile she had gone to a hell of a lot of trouble. She must have taken her one asset to a perfectionist and let him build a dress around it. I think it was a dress. Paint would have done the same thing.

There wasn't anything on underneath to spoil the effect and that showed. She was excited as hell and that showed too.

I was thinking that it could be very nice if she had only come a little sooner before I knew that Ethel had told what she had found in my wallet. Linda smiled at me tentatively as I sat down opposite her and lit up a smoke. I smiled back and started thinking again. This time there was a different answer. Maybe they were playing real cute and sent her in for the kicker. Maybe they had figured that their little shooting deal might get messed up and sent her around to get the score on me.

It made nice thinking because that was the way they worked and I didn't feel sorry for her any more. I got up and moved to the couch and told her to come over. I made her a drink and it must have been her first drink because she choked on it.

I kissed her and it must have been her first kiss, but she didn't choke on it. She grabbed me like the devil was inside her, bit me twice on the neck then pushed back to look at me to be sure this was happening to her.

There was no softness to her body. It was tense with the pain that was pleasure, oddly resilient under my hands. She closed her eyes, smothering the leaping fire to glowing coals. She fought to open them halfway and when she saw that I had been burnt by their flame she smiled a twisted smile as if she was laughing at herself.

If she was going to, she should have asked me then. Any woman should know when a man is nothing but a man and when he'll promise or tell anything. I knew all those things too and it didn't do me any good because I was still a man.

She asked nothing. She said, "This . . . is the first time . . . I ever . . ." and stopped there with the words choking to a hoarse whisper in her throat. She made me feel like a goddamn heel. She hadn't known about Ethel's little stunt because she had been too busy getting prettied up for me.

I was going to make her put her coat on and tell her to get the hell out of there and learn more about being a woman before she tried to act like one. I would have done just that until I thought a little further and remembered that she was new to the game and didn't know when to ask the questions but figured on trying anyway. So I didn't say a damn thing.

Her hand did something at her back and the dress that looked like paint peeled off like paint with a deliberate slowness that made me go warm all over.

And she still asked nothing except to be shown how to be a woman.

She wouldn't let me go to the door with her later. She wanted to be part of the darkness and alone. Her feet were a soft whisper against the carpet and the closing of the door an almost inaudible click.

I made myself a drink, had half of it and threw the rest away. I had been right the first time and went back to feeling like a heel. Then it occurred to me that now that she had a little taste of life maybe she'd go out and seek some different company for a change.

I stopped feeling like a heel, made another drink, finished it and went to bed.

The alarm woke me up at six, giving me time to shower and shave before getting dressed. I grabbed a plate of bacon and eggs in a diner around the corner then hopped in my car and drove downtown to pick up Velda. She was standing in front of the building tucked inside a dark gray business suit, holding her coat open with her hand on her hip.

A newsboy was having trouble trying to watch her and hawk his editions too. I pulled in at the curb and tooted the horn. "Let's go, sugar."

When she climbed in next to me the newsboy sighed. "Early, isn't it?" she grinned.

"Too damned."

"You were going to tell me something today, Mike."

"I didn't say when."

"One of those deals. You're a fine one." She turned her head and looked out the window.

I tugged at her arm and made her look back at me. "I'm sorry, Velda. It doesn't make nice conversation. I'll give it to you all at once when we get back. It's important to me not to talk about it right now. Mind?"

Maybe she saw the seriousness in my eyes. She smiled and said all right, then turned on the radio so we could have some music on our way across the bridge to Brooklyn where Mother Switcher had her pie factory.

Mother Switcher turned out to be a short, squat guy with long handlebar whiskers and eyebrows that went up and down like window shades. I asked him if I could speak to a few of his drivers and he said, "If you're a union organizer it's no good. All my boys already belong to a union and get paid better'n union wages besides."

I said I was no organizer. "So what is it then?"

"I want to find out about a guy named Moffit. He worked for you."

"That dope! He owe you money?"

"Not exactly."

"Sure. Go talk to the boys, only don't stop their work."

I said thanks and took Velda with me when I went around behind the building where the trucks were lined up for their quota of pies. We waited until the first truck was filled then buttonholed the driver. He gave Velda a big smile and tipped his cap.

She took it from there. "You knew Charlie Moffit, didn't you?"

"Yeah, sure, lady. What's he done now, crawled out of his grave?"

"I imagine he's still there, but tell me, what was he like?"

The guy frowned and looked at me for the first time. "I don't get it," he grunted.

I flashed my buzzer. So did Velda. "Now I get it," he said. "Was he in trouble?"

"That's what we want to find out. What was he like?"

He leaned against his truck and chewed on a match. "Well, I'll tell ya. Charlie was a queer duck." He tapped his head and made a screwy face. "Not all there, ya know. We were forever playing all kinds of gags on him. The dope would fall for 'em too. He was always losing something. Once it was his change bag and once it was a whole load of pies. He said some kids got him in a ball game and while he played they swiped his pies. Ever hear of anything like that?"

"No, I didn't," Velda laughed.

"That wasn't all, either. He was a mean bast . . . son-of-a-gun. Once we caught him trying to set fire to a cat. One of the boys slugged him."

It didn't sound right, that picture of Charlie Moffit. I was thinking while Velda popped the questions. Some of the other men came over and added a little something that distorted the picture even more. Charlie liked women and booze. Charlie molested kids in the street. Charlie was real bright for long periods then he'd get drunk and seem to fall into a conscious coma when he'd act like a kid. He wasn't right in his dome. He had rocks in his head. He sure liked the women, though.

I took Velda out of there and started back to Manhattan, my head aching from thoughts that were too big for it. I had to squint to watch the traffic and hunch over the wheel to be sure I knew where I was going. Away in the back of my mind that devilish unseen conductor was warming up his orchestra for another of those wild symphonies. I must be mad, I thought, I must be mad. I don't think like I used to. The little things won't come through any more and it was the little things falling into place that made big things.

My mind rambled on until Velda said, "We're here."

The attendant was waving me into the parking lot. I took my ticket and handed him the keys while she flagged a cab. All the way to the office I sat with my eyes closed and kept the curtains down on the orchestra that was trying so hard to play. Whoever was at the drums wouldn't give up. He kept up a steady beat, thumping his drum with a muted stick, trying to make me open the curtain.

Velda brought out the bottle and handed it to me. I stared at the glass, filled it and drank it down. She offered me another and I shook my head. I had to sit down. I wanted to sit down and pull something over my head to shut out the light and the sound.

"Mike." Velda ran her fingers through my hair.

"What is it, kid?" My voice didn't sound right.

"If you tell me I might be able to help you." I opened my eyes and looked at her. She had her coat off and her breasts rose high against the folds of the blouse. She pulled up the big chair and sat down, her legs flashing in the light that streamed through the window. They were beautiful legs, long, alive with smooth muscles that played through the tight fabric of her dress as she moved. It was so easy to love that woman. I ought to try it more often. It was mine whenever I wanted it.

I closed my eyes again.

There wasn't any answer or any special way to tell her. I sat there with my eyes closed and gave it to her as it happened, bit by bit. I told her how I killed on the bridge. I told her about Marty and almost all about Ethel. I told her everything that happened and waited to see what she would say.

A minute went by. I opened my eyes and saw that Velda was watching me and there was no shame, no terror in her face. She believed in me. She said, "It doesn't make sense, Mike."

"It doesn't at that," I said tiredly. "There's a flaw in it that I can see. Do you see it too?"

"Yes. Charlie Moffit."

"That's right. The man with a present and no past. Nobody knows him or knows where he comes from. He's just a present."

"Almost ideal for an M.V.D. operative."

"That's right again. Almost. Where's the flaw?"

Velda's fingers made a little tap-tap against the arm of the chair. "The act was too nearly perfect. It was too good to be anything but true."

"Roger. Charlie Moffit was anything but M.V.D. I thought those Reds were figuring me to be the man who took his place. I was wrong. I was impersonating the wrong dead man. The boy on the bridge was M.V.D. Pat handed it to me on a platter but I let it slip by. His only identifiable mark was his bridge-work because he had a stainless-steel tooth.

There's only one country where they use stainless steel for teeth . . . the U.S.S.R. Fat boy was an imported killer, a checkrein on other agents in this country. Do you know how they knew he was dead?"

"Not from the sketch in the papers. He didn't have any fingerprints, either."

"They wouldn't have found them if he did. I forgot to tell you, but I wore his fingertips to the bone on the concrete before I threw him over."

Velda bit her lip and shuddered. She said "Mike!" too softly.

"No, the reason they knew he was dead was because he dropped out of sight. I don't think they got the connection until later when some smart apple started to check the unidentified bodies in the morgue. Pat said they sent dental charts out. One of those that received them could have recognized what that stainless-steel tooth meant and there it was."

"But they knew he was dead the next night . . . or so you supposed."

"Uh-huh. Fat boy didn't check in. They must have a system for those things. There was only one answer if he didn't check in. He was dead. The dental charts only verified it."

"What must they think? Why . . ."

I kept my voice low so I wouldn't get boiling mad again. "They think it was a dirty democratic conspiracy. It was all too secret to be normal. They think it was our government playing them dirty. They're the only ones who are supposed to be able to kick you under the table."

Velda said something dirty and she wasn't smiling.

I went on: "The other night there was a new note in the party. Something happened to a courier of theirs, something about documents. They are missing. The party is very upset, the poor devils."

Velda came up out of her seat, her face tight as a drumhead. "They're at it again, Mike. Government documents and double-dealing. Damn it, Mike, why do these things have to happen?"

"They happen because we're soft. We're honorable."

"Did they say what they were?"

"No. I gathered they were pretty important."

"They must be."

"Velda, there's a lot of things that are important that we give away for free. Do you know what they were doing one night? They had a pile of technical journals and flying mags you can pick up on any newsstand. They were photographing the stuff onto microfilm for shipment back. A good intelligence man can pick out a lot of data from photos. They take a bit here and a bit there until the picture is complete and bingo, they have something we're trying to keep under the hat."

"But documents, Mike. That's government stuff! That's something the F.B.I. should know about."

"I know, I know. Maybe they do. Maybe they know they're missing and suspect where they've gone. Maybe they don't know because the documents were photostats. They're gone and that's what counts. I'm in a muddle because they found me out and now I can't do any more snooping. They'll be looking for me with a vengeance now. They tried to kill me last night and . . ."

"Mike!"

"Oh, you didn't hear about that. You should read the papers. There's six lines about it on page four. They didn't even print my picture. Yeah, they know me now and it's every man for himself. The next time I'll start the shooting and I won't miss."

Velda had her hand over her mouth, her teeth clamped on a finger-nail. "God, you get into some of the most horrible scrapes! I do wish you'd be careful." Her eyes got a little wet and she got mad at herself. "You won't tell anybody anything and you won't ask for help when you need it most. Mike . . . please . . . there are times when you have to let somebody else in on things."

I could feel my lip curling. "Sure, Velda, sure. I'll tell everybody that I go around killing people just like that. It's easy to say, but I'm the guy who's supposed to be a menace to society. Hell, I'll take it my way and the public can lump it."

She wiped away a tear that was feeling its way down her cheek. "He shouldn't have done that to you, Mike."

"Who?"

"The judge."

I swore violently and my voice was hoarse.

"Are you . . . going to keep looking?"

I nodded my head. "Indirectly, yes. I'm still on a case for Lee Deamer."

Velda's head snapped up. "Mike . . . that's it!"

"What?"

"The documents! Charlie Moffit was the courier they spoke about! He was carrying those documents the night Oscar attacked and killed him! Oscar must have taken them from him."

"Damn!" The word exploded out of me. Of course, of course! the pocket that was ripped out of his coat! I shot Velda a grin that had "thanks" written on it. "It comes clear, kid, real clear. Oscar came to town to bleed Lee and he wouldn't bleed. So he goes out and kills a guy hoping to be identified as Lee, knowing damn well Lee would have an alibi and it would just make sensational reading for the public. He figured that would bring Lee to heel when he asked for money again. The gimmick came when he killed the guy. The papers must have stuck out of his pocket and Oscar grabbed them. When he realized what they were he saw the ideal way to bring Lee around. That's what he hinted at to Lee over the phone. If Lee brought in the cops and anything happened to him, the presence of those papers was to be attributed to Lee."

Velda was white, dead-white and her breathing came too fast. "It's rotten, Mike. Good heavens, if it ever gets out . . ."

"Yeah, Lee is finished even if he *can* prove himself innocent."

"Oh, no!"

"Beautiful. No matter what happens the Commies win. If they get the documents they probably have something juicy for cruddy Uncle Joe. If they don't and somebody else finds them, their worst enemy is yanked off their necks."

"Mike . . . it can't happen!"

"Now do I go it alone, Velda? Now do I take it by myself?"

"Yes. You . . . and me. The bastards. The dirty, filthy Red bastards!" They should see her now, I was thinking. Gladow, the general, the boys in the Kremlin should see her now and they'd know what they were getting into. They'd see the face of beauty that had a kill-lust in every beautiful line and they'd stick inside their cold, walled-in city and shake in their shoes!

"When do we start, Mike?"

"Tonight. Be here at nine sharp. We'll see if we can find what Oscar did with those papers." She sat back in the chair and stared at the wall.

I picked up the phone and dialed Pat's number. He came on with, "Homicide, Captain Chambers speaking."

"Mike, pal. Any new corpses today?"

"Not yet. You didn't shoot straight enough. When are you coming in to explain about last night? I went to bat for you and I want a report and not a lot of subterfuge."

"I'm practically on my way now. I'll drop by your office and pick you up for lunch."

"Okay. Make it snappy."

I said I would and cradled the receiver. Velda was waiting for orders.

"Stay here," I told her. "I have to see Pat and I'll call you when I'm finished. In case I don't call or come back, be here at nine."

"That's all?"

"That's all," I repeated. I tried to look stern like a boss should, but she grinned and spoiled it. I had to kiss her good-by before she'd let me go. "There's no telling if I'll see you alive again," she laughed. Then she slapped her hand over her mouth and her eyes went wide. "What am I saying?"

"I still have a couple of lives left, kid. I'll save one for you, so don't worry." I grinned again and went out the door.

Downstairs I got tired of waiting for a cab so I walked the half mile to the lot. A car in the city could be a pain in the butt sometimes. But what the hell, it was a nice day for a change and the air felt fairly fresh if a bus or something didn't go by.

I picked up my keys when I handed over the ticket and found my heap. I was in second and heading toward the gate when I saw that the boy had cleaned off my windows, and jammed on my brakes to flip him a quarter. That two-bits saved my skin. The truck that had been idling up the street had jumped ahead to intercept me broadside, saw I was stopping and tried to get me by swerving onto the driveway and off again.

Metal being ripped out by the roots set up a shriek and the car leaped ahead before there was a nasty snap that disengaged it from the body of the truck. I let out a string of curses because the jolt had wedged me up against the wheel and I couldn't get my rod out. By the time I was back in the seat the truck was lost in the traffic.

The attendant yanked the door open, his face ashen. "Gawd, mister, you hurt?"

"No, not this time."

"Them crazy fools! Gawd, they coulda killed ya!" His teeth started to chatter violently.

"They sure coulda." I got out of the car and walked around the front. One side of the bumper had been ripped clear off the frame and stuck out like an oversize L.

"Boy, that was close, awright. I seen 'em come up the street but I never give 'em a thought. Them crazy fools musta been fooling around the cab and hit the gas. They never stopped. You want I should call a cop?"

I kicked the bumper and it all but fell loose. "Forget it. They got away by now. Think you can get this bumper off?"

"Sure, I got some tools. Only two bolts holding it on anyway."

"Okay, take it off and pick one up for this model at a garage some-where. I'll fix you up for your trouble."

He said, "Yessir, mister. Sure," and ran after his tools. I sat on the fender and smoked a cigarette until he finished then passed him two bucks and told him not to forget a new bumper. He said he wouldn't forget.

When I pulled away I looked up and down the one-way street just to be sure. It happened twice. I said it wouldn't but it happened again any-way. They must have had a tail on me when I came out of the office and saw a beautiful chance to nail me cold. That truck would have made hash of me if it had connected right.

They were going to all kinds of trouble, weren't they? That made me important. You have to be important if you were better off dead. The judge should like that.

Pat was sitting with his back to the door looking out the window at the city when I came in. He swung around in his chair and nodded hello. I pulled a chair up and sat down with my feet propped up on his desk. "I'm all set, Captain. Where are the bright lights?"

"Cut it out, Mike. Start talking."

"Pat, so help me, you know almost everything right now."

"Almost. Give me the rest."

"They tried again a little while ago. This time it was a truck and not bullets."

The pencil in Pat's hand tapped the desk. "Mike, I'm not a complete fool. I play along with you because we're friends, but I'm a cop, I've been a cop a long time, and I know my business. You're not telling me people are shooting you up in the streets without a reason."

"Hell, they gotta have a reason?"

"Do you know what it is?" He was drawing to the end of his patience.

I took my feet off the desk and leaned toward him. "We've been through this before, Pat. I'm not a complete fool either. In your mind every crime belongs to the police, but there are times when an apparent crime is a personal affront and it isn't very satisfying not to take care of it yourself. That's how I feel about it."

"So you know then."

"I think I know. There's nothing you can do about it so quit being a cop and let's get back to being friends."

Pat tried to grin, but didn't put it over too well. "Are you straightened out with Lee?"

My feet went up on the desk again. "He gave me a tidy sum to poke around. I'm busy at it."

"Good, Mike. Be sure you make a clean sweep." He dropped his head and passed his hand over his hair. "Been reading the papers lately?"

"Not too much. I noticed one thing . . . they're pulling for Deamer in nearly every editorial column. One sheet reprints all his speeches."

"He's giving another tonight. You should go hear him."

"I'll leave that stuff up to you, chum. There's too much dribble and not enough pep talk at those meetings."

"The devil there isn't! Take the last one I was at. We had supper with the customary speeches afterward, but it was the small talk later that counted. Lee Deamer made the rounds speaking to small groups and he gave them the real stuff. It was easier for him to talk that way. Most of us had never met him until that time, but when he spoke we were sold completely. We have to have that guy in, Mike. No two ways about it. He's strong. He can't be pushed or bullied. You wouldn't know it to look at him, but he's the strength that this nation will be relying on some day."

"That was the same night Oscar pulled the stops out, wasn't it?"

"That's right. That's why we didn't want any of it to reach the public. Even a lie can be told to give the people the wrong impression."

"You've sure gotten a big interest in politics, Pat."

"Hell, why not? I'll be glad to go back to being a cop again instead of a tool in some politician's workshop. Lee gave a talk over the radio last night. You know what he said?"

I said no. I had been too busy to listen.

"He's brought some of his business sense into politics. He sat down with an adding machine and figured things up. He wanted to know why it cost the state ten million for it to have a job done when any private contractor could do it for six. He quoted names and places and figures and told the public that if he was elected his first order would be to sign warrants of arrest for certain political joes who are draining the state dry."

"And?"

Pat looked at the desk and glared. "And today I heard that the big push comes soon. Lee has to be smeared any way at all."

"It won't happen, Pat."

I shouldn't have used that tone. His head jerked up and his eyes were tiny bright spots watching me from tight folds of skin. His hand closed into a fist slowly and tightened until the cords bulged out. "You know something, Mike, by God, you know something!"

"I do?" I couldn't make it sound funny.

Pat was ready to split wide open. "Mike, you're in on it. Damn it, you went and found something. Oh, I know you . . . no talking until you're ready, but this isn't a murder that involved only a handful of people . . . this is something that takes in a whole population and you better not tip the apples over."

He stood up, his hands on the edge of the desk for support. He spat the words out between his teeth and meant every one. "We've been friends, Mike. You and I have been in and out of a lot of things together and I've always valued your friendship. And your judgment. Just remember this, if I'm guessing right and you're in on something that might hurt Lee and won't talk about it, and if that something *does* hurt Lee, then we can forget about being friends. Is that clear?"

"That's clear, Pat. Would it make you feel better if I told you that your line of reasoning is a little off? You're getting teed off at me when you ought to be teeing off on some of the goddamn Commies we got loose in this city."

His face had a shrewd set to it. "So they're part of it too." Muscles stuck out in lumps along his jaws. Let him think how he liked.

"Nothing will happen to Lee," I said. "At least nothing that I'm concerned with." This time I got some conviction in my voice. Pat stopped glaring and sat down.

He didn't forget the subject. "You still have those green cards on your mind?"

"Yeah, I have. I don't like what they mean, and you shouldn't either."

"I hate everything they stand for. I'm sorry we have to tolerate it. We ought to do what they would have done a hundred years ago."

"Stop talking nonsense. You're in America now."

"Sure I am, and I want to stay here. If you want a democracy you have to fight for it. Why not now before it's too late? That's the trouble, we're getting soft. They push us all around the block and we let them get away with it!"

"Calm down, will you." I hadn't realized that I was banging on his desk until he rapped my knuckles. I sat down.

"What did you do about Oscar?" I asked.

"What could we do? Nothing. It's over, finished."

"And his personal effects?"

"We went through them and there was nothing to be found. I posted a man to check his place in case any mail came in. I had the idea that Oscar might have mailed something to himself. I took the man off today when nothing showed."

I had to struggle to hold my face straight. Pat had the place watched! Neat, very neat. If we weren't the only ones who wanted to go through that apartment then we wouldn't be going in on a cold deal. Nobody else could have gotten there either!

I reached for a butt and lit it. "Let's go out to eat, Pat."

He grabbed his coat off the rack and locked the door to the office. On the way out I thought of something I should have thought of before and had him open it up again. I picked up the phone and called the office. Velda answered with a silky hello.

I said, "Mike, honey. Look, have you emptied the waste basket by my desk yet?"

"No, there wasn't anything to empty."

"Go look if there's a cigarette pack there. Don't touch it."

She dropped the phone and I heard her heels clicking along the floor. In a moment she was back. "It's there, Mike."

"Swell. Take it out of there without touching it if you can. Put it in a box and have a boy run it down to Pat right away."

Pat watched me curiously. When I hung up he said, "What is it?"

"An almost empty pack of butts. Do me a favor and lift the prints off it. You'll find a lot of mine on them and if I'm lucky you'll find some others too."

"Whose?"

"Hell, how do I know? That's why I want you to get the prints. I need an identification. That is, if we're still friends."

"Still friends, Mike," he grinned. I socked him on the arm and started for the door again.

CHAPTER 7

That night the nation got the report on the 6:15 P.M. news broadcast. There had been a leak in the State Department and the cat was out of the bag. It seemed that we had had a secret. Somebody else was in on it now. The latest development in the process for the annihilation of man had been stolen. Supposedly secret files had been rifled and indications pointed to the duplication of the secret papers. The F.B.I. was making every effort to track down the guilty parties.

I threw my cigarette against the wall and started swearing until I ran out of words. Then I started over again. The commentator droned on repeating what he had already said and I felt like screaming at him to tell the world who took those damn papers. Tell 'em it was the same outfit who tried to make a mockery of our courts and who squirmed into the government and tried to bring it down around our necks. Tell everybody who did it. You know you want to say it; what are you afraid of?

There wasn't any doubt of it now, those documents the general had been so anxious to get hold of were the ones we were looking for ourselves! My guts were all knotted up in a ball and my head felt like a machine shop was going on inside it. Here I had the whole lousy situation right in my hands and I had to keep it there.

Me. Mike Hammer. I was up in the big leagues now. No more plain and simple murders. I was playing ball with the big boys and they played rough. The end justified the means, that was their theory. Lie, steal, kill, do anything that was necessary to push a political philosophy that would enslave the world if we let it. Great!

Nice picture, Judge, a beautiful picture of a world in flames. You must be one of the normal people who get the trembles when they read the papers. A philosophy like that must give you the willies. What are you thinking now . . . how that same secret that was stolen might be the cause of your death? And what would you say if you knew that I was the only one who might be able to stop it in time? Okay, Judge, sit your fanny in a chair and relax. I have a little philosophy of my own. Like you said, it's as bad as theirs. I don't give a damn for a human life any more, even my own. Want to hear that philosophy? It's simple enough. Go after the big boys. Oh, don't arrest them, don't treat them to the dignity of the democratic process of courts and law . . . do the same thing to them that they'd do to you! Treat 'em to the unglorious taste of sudden death. Get the big boys and show them the long road to nowhere and then one of those stinking little people with little minds will want to get big. Death is funny, Judge, people are afraid of it. Kill 'em left and right, show 'em that we aren't so soft after all. Kill, kill, kill, kill! They'll keep away from us then!

Hell, it was no use trying to smoke. I'd light up a butt and take a drag then throw it away because my fingers weren't steady enough to hold it. I went inside to the bedroom and took my .45 off the top of the dresser to clean it for the second time. It felt good, feeling the cold butt setting up against the palm of my hand. The deadly noses of the slugs showing in the clip looked so nice and efficient.

They liked to play dirty, I was thinking. Let's make it real dirty. I thumbed the slugs out, laying them in a neat row, then took a penknife and clipped the ends off the noses. That was real dirty. They wouldn't make too much of a hole where they went in, but the hole on the other side would be a beaut. You could stick your head in and look around without getting blood on your ears. I put the gun together, shoved the slugs back in the clip and strapped on the sling. I was ready.

It was a night to give you the meemies. Something happened to the sky and a slow, sticky fog was rolling in from the river. The cold was penetrating, indecisive as to whether to stay winter or turn into spring. I turned the collar of my coat up around my ears and started walking down the street. I didn't lose myself in any thoughts this time. My eyes looked straight ahead, but they saw behind me and to either side. They picked up figures hurrying to wherever it was they were going, and the twin yellow eyes of the cars that rolled in the street, boring holes in the fog. My ears picked up footsteps, timed their pace and direction, then discarded them for other sounds.

I was waiting for them to try again.

When I reached the corner I crossed over to my car, passed it, then walked back again. I opened the door, felt for the handle that unlocked the hood and took a quick check of the engine. I wasn't in the mood to get myself blown all over the neighborhood when I started the car. The engine was clean. So was the rest of the heap.

A car came by and I drew out behind it, getting in line to start the jaunt downtown to the office. The fog was thicker there and the traffic thinner. The subways were getting a big play. I found a place to park right outside the office and scraped my wheels against the curb then cut the engine. I sat there until a quarter to nine trying to smoke my way through a deck of Luckies. I still had a few to go when I went inside, put my name in the night register and had the elevator operator haul me up to my office floor.

At exactly nine P.M. a key turned in the lock and Velda came in. I swung my feet off the desk and walked out to the outside office and said hello. She smiled, but her heart wasn't in it. "Did you catch the news broadcast, kid?"

Her lips peeled back. "I heard it. I didn't like it."

"Neither did I, Velda. We have to get them back."

She opened her coat and perched on the edge of the desk. Her eyes were on the floor, staring at a spot on the carpet. She wasn't just a woman now. An aura of the jungle hung around her, turning her into a female animal scenting a game run and anxious to be in on the kill. "It can't stop there, Mike."

I dropped my butt and ground it into the carpet. "No, it can't." I knew what she was thinking and didn't like it.

"The papers aren't all. As far as they can go is to checkmate us. They'll try again."

"Will they?"

Her eyes moved up to meet mine, but that was all. "We can stop them, Mike."

"I can, sugar. Not you. I'm not shoving you into any front lines."

Her eyes still held mine. "There's somebody in this country who directs operations for them. It isn't anyone we know or the F.B.I. knows or the party knows. It's somebody who can go and come like anybody else and not be interfered with. There are others who take orders and are equally dangerous because they represent the top of the chain of command and can back up their orders with force if necessary. How long will it take us to get them all, the known and the unknown?"

"It might take *me* a long time. Me, I said."

"There's a better way, Mike. We can get all those we know and any we suspect and the rest will run. They'll get the hell out of here and be afraid to come back."

It was almost funny, the way her reasoning followed mine. "Just me, Velda," I said.

Her head came up slowly and all I could think of was a big cat, a great big, luxurious cat leaning against the desk. A cat with gleaming black hair darker than the night and a hidden body of smooth skin that covered a wealth of rippling, deadly muscles that were poised for the kill. The desk light made her teeth an even row of merciless ivory, ready to rip and tear. She was still grinning, but a cat looks like it's grinning until you see its ears laid flat back against its head.

"Mike, there are men and women in this country. They made it together even when it was worse than now. Women learned how to shoot and shoot straight. They learned fast, and knew how to use a gun or a knife and use it right when the time came. I said we'd do it together. Either that or I take the whole thing to Pat."

I waited a long minute before I said, "Okay, it's us. I want it that way anyhow."

Velda slid off the desk and reached for my hand. I squeezed it hard, happy as hell I had the sense to realize that I knew what I wanted at last. She said it very simply. "I love you, Mike."

I had her in my arms, searched for her mouth and found it, a warm mouth with full, ripe lips that burned into my soul as they fused with mine. I tasted the love she offered and gave it back with all I had to give, crushing her until her breath came in short, quick jerks.

I held her face in my hands and kissed her eyes and her cheeks, listened to her moan softly and press herself closer and closer. I was lucky as hell and I knew it.

She opened her eyes when I held her off. I dropped my hand in my pocket and took out the box that I had picked up that afternoon. When I pressed the button the lid flew up and the sapphire threw back a perfect star. My fingers felt big and clumsy when I took it out and slipped it over her finger.

You don't have to speak at a time like that. Everything has been said and if anything remains it's written there in a silent promise your heart makes and that's all there is to it. Velda looked at it with a strange wonder for a long time before she kissed me again.

It was better than the last time.

It told her everything she wanted to know and no matter what happened now nothing would ever change.

"We have to go," I said.

She snapped out the lights while I waited at the door and we went down the elevator together. The watchman gave me the okay sign, so I knew nobody had been near my car while I was gone. When we were back in the fog I told her about Pat's having kept a man on Oscar's house and she picked it right up.

"Maybe . . . maybe we'll be the first."

"I'm hoping that," I said.

"What will they look like?"

"I don't know. If Moffit had them in his pocket, then they were in a package or an envelope big enough to fit in there. It may be that we're barking up the wrong tree. They might have been on microfilm."

"Let's hope we're right."

About two blocks away I ran the car in between a couple of parked trucks and waved her out. "We're taking the long way around this time."

"Through the alley?"

"Uh-huh. I don't like the idea of using the front door. When we reach the opening between the buildings duck in and keep on going."

Velda felt for my hand and held on to it. For all the world we might have been just a couple of dopes out for a walk. The fog was a white tube all around us, but it could be hiding a lot of things beside us. We crossed the street, came up around the subway kiosk and walked in the protection of the wall, the two of us searching for the narrow passageway that led behind the buildings.

As it was, we almost passed it. I stepped in holding Velda's hand and the darkness swallowed us up. For two or three minutes we stood there letting our eyes accustom themselves to this deeper gloom, then edged forward slowly, picking our way through the trash that had accumulated over the years. Animals and people had made a barely perceptible path through the center of the litter and we followed it until we stood behind the building and could feel our way along the alley by sticking close to the rotted planking that formed the wall of the yards behind the houses.

Velda was fishing in her handbag and I told her, "No lights. Just keep looking for a pile of bottles. There's a door in the wall behind it and that's the place."

I tried to judge the distance from that other night and found little to remember. Soft furry things would squeal and run across our feet whenever we disturbed the junk lying around. Tiny pairs of eyes would glare at us balefully and retreat when we came closer. A cat moved in the darkness and trapped a pair of eyes that had been paying too much attention to us and the jungle echoed with a mad death cry.

Velda tugged my hand and pointed to the ground. "Here're the bottles, Mike." She dropped my hand to walk around them. "The door is still open."

I pushed her through into the yard and we held still, taking in the black shadow of the building. The back door still swung open on one hinge. How many people lived here, I thought. How long ago was it when this dirty pile of brick and mortar was a home besides being a house? I went up the short flight of steps and took the flashlight from my pocket.

Velda flashed hers on the wall beside the door, illuminating a printed square of cardboard tacked to the framework. It read, THIS BUILDING HAS BEEN CONDEMNED FOR OCCUPANCY. A paragraph explained why and a rubber stamp signature made it official.

Ha.

The air had a musty odor of decay that collected in the long hall and clung to the walls. There was a door that led to the cellar, but the stairs were impenetrable, piled high with an unbelievable collection of scrap. Velda opened the door to the room that faced the backyard and threw her spot around the walls. I looked in over her shoulder and saw a black, charred mass and the remains of some furniture. It must have been a year or more since that room had started to burn, and nobody had been in it since. It was amazing to me that the house still stood.

Halfway down the hall there was a doorframe but no door and the room was stacked with old bedframes, a few mattresses left to the fleas and nothing worth stealing. The next room was, or had been, Oscar's. I had my hand on the knob when Velda grabbed me and we froze there.

From somewhere in the upper recesses of the house came a harsh, racking cough and the sound of someone vomiting.

I heard Velda take a deep breath of relief. "Drunk," she said.

"Yeah." I went back to the door. A plain skeleton key unlocked it and we stepped inside, locking it again behind us. Velda went to the windows, and tucked the shade in so there would be no chance of our lights being seen from the outside. Then we started to take that room apart.

Oscar's effects were collecting dust in the police storeroom, but it was unlikely that they had been in his bag or among his clothes. If they had been I would have found them the first time. We peeled the covers off the bed, found nothing and put them back. We felt in the corners and under things. I even tore the molding off the wall and shoved my hand behind it. There was nothing there, either.

Velda was working her way along the rear wall. She called softly, "Mike, come here a minute."

I followed the track of light to where she was fiddling with some aged draperies that had been tacked to the wall in a vain attempt to give a tapestry effect. She had one side pulled away and was pointing to it. "There used to be a door here. It led to that storeroom on the other side."

"Umm. This house was a one-family job at one time."

"Do you suppose. . . ."

"That it's in there?" I finished. She nodded. "We better look. This room is as bare as a baby's spanked tail."

The two of us wormed out into the hall and shut the door. Velda led the way with her light and took a cautious step over the sill into the room beyond. From upstairs the coughing came again. I banged my shin against an iron bedpost and swore softly.

It only took ten minutes to go over that room, but it was long enough to see that nothing had been put in or taken out in months. A layer of dust covered everything; the junk was attached to the walls with thousands of spiderwebs. The only prints in the grime on the floor were those we had made ourselves.

I hated to say it; Velda hated to hear it. "Not a damn thing. Oscar never had those papers."

"Oh, Mike!" There was a sob in her voice.

"Come on, kid, we're only wasting time now."

The flashlight hung in her hand, the penny-sized beam a small, lonely spot on the floor, listlessly trying to add a bit of brightness to a night that was darker than ever now.

"All right, Mike," she said. "There must be other places for it to be."

The guy upstairs coughed again. We would have paid no attention to him except that we heard the thump of his feet hitting the floor then the heavy thud as he fell. The guy started cursing then was still.

It wasn't a conscious thing that held us back; we just stood there and listened, not scared, not worried, just curious and cautious. If we hadn't stopped where we were at the moment we did we would have walked right into the mouth of hell.

The front door opened and for a brief interval the Trench Coats were dimly silhouetted against the gray of the fog outside. Then the door closed and they were inside, motionless against the wall.

I did two things fast. I grabbed Velda and pulled out the .45.

Why did I breathe so fast? I hadn't done a thing and yet I wanted to pant my lungs out. They were on fire, my throat was on fire, my brain was on fire. The gun that I used to be able to hold so still was shaking hard and Velda felt it too. She slid her hand over mine, the one that squeezed her arm so hard it must have hurt, and I felt some of the tension leave me.

Velda wasn't shaking at all. Trench Coats moved and I heard a whispered voice. Something Velda did made a metallic snap. My brain was telling me that now it had come, the moment I had waited for. Trench Coats. Gladow and Company. The hammer and sickle backed up with guns. The general's boys.

They came for me! Even in the fog they had managed to follow me here and now they were ready to try again. *The third time they won't miss.* That was the common superstition, wasn't it? It was to be at close quarters and a crossfire with me in the middle.

I could feel my teeth grinding together. A hot wave of hate, so violent that it shook me from top to bottom, swept through my body. Who the hell were they supposed to be? Did they expect to come in and find me with my back to the door? Was I supposed to be another sap . . . the kind of guy who'd give people like them the old fighting chance . . . a gesture of sportsmanship? I should take a chance on dying like that?

They went in the room then, softly, but not so softly that my ears couldn't follow every step they took. I could hear their breathing coming hard, the scuff of leather against wood. I even heard the catch of the flashlight when it snapped on.

Very slowly I jacked the hammer of the .45 back. My hand told Velda to stay there. Just stay there and shut up. I bent down and unlaced my shoes, stepped out of them and into the hall. I lay on my stomach looking into the room, the .45 propped on my forearm. The light of the flash made a circuit of the wall then stopped on the draperies that covered up the opening to the other room. Trench Coat who didn't have a flash stepped forward to pull the drapes down.

And Velda was in there waiting for me.

I said, "Looking for me, Martin?" The sudden shift of the flash and the lance of flame that spit from his gun came at the same time. I heard the bullets smack the wall over my head. He fired at the door where my belly should have been, mouthing guttural, obscene curses.

Then I shot him. I aimed a little below and inside the red eye of his gun barrel and over the blast of the .45 I heard his breath leave him in a wheezing shriek that died in a bubble of blood that came to his mouth. His rod went off once, a bullet ripped into the floor, and Trench Coat dropped.

The other one didn't stay in the room. I heard cloth rip, feet stumble and a heavy body slam against the wood. The other killer had gone into the room with Velda!

I was on my feet trying to decide. I had to decide! Good God, I had to get him before he saw her. If I went in through either door he'd get me and I had to go! I could feel him waiting for me, the darkness screening him completely. He knew I'd come and he knew he'd get me.

I walked toward the door. I didn't bother trying to be quiet.

I stepped into the doorway.

The crack of the gun was a flat noise that echoed once and was gone. There was no streak of flame, only that sudden, sharp sound and a peculiar hiss that seemed out of place. I felt no shock, no pain, only a sudden tensing of the muscles and a stillness that was nearly audible.

I must have caught it, I thought. It wasn't like this before. The last time it hurt. I tried to raise my hand and it came up slowly, effortlessly. In the room a gun clattered on the bare planking and was followed immediately by a soft thunk.

She seemed far away, so far away. "Mike?"

I couldn't get the breath out of my lungs at first. "You . . . all right, Velda?"

"I killed him, Mike."

Dear God, what was there to say? I reached for her and folded her against my chest feeling her sob softly. I grabbed her flash and threw it on Trench Coat. Martin Romberg lay on his face with a hole in his back. She must have held it right against his spine when she pulled the trigger. That's why I didn't see the flash.

I straightened Velda up and pulled her toward the door. "Come on. We can't stay here." I found my shoes and yanked them on without bothering to tie them.

It was easier going out. It always is. The fog was still there, rolling in over the walls, sifting down between the buildings. Our eyes, so long in the dark, could see things that were hidden before and we raced down that back alley heading for that narrow slit a block away from the house.

The curious had already started their pilgrimage toward the sound of the shooting. A police car whined through the night, its light a blinking eye that cleared the way. We lost ourselves in the throng, came out of it and found the car. Two more police cars passed us as we started to cut back to the land of the living on the other side of town.

Velda sat stiff and straight staring out the window. When I looked down she still held the gun in her hand. I took it away from her and laid it on the seat. "You can file another notch on it, kid. That makes two."

I gave it to her brutally hoping it might snap her out of it. She turned her head and I saw that her mouth had taken on a smile. She picked up that nasty little .32 automatic and dropped it in her handbag. The snap catch made the same metallic sound that I had heard back there in the room. "My conscience doesn't hurt me, Mike," she said softly.

I patted her hand.

"I was afraid I wouldn't be quick enough. He never saw me. He stood in the center of the room covering both entrances and I knew what he was waiting for and I knew you'd come after him. He would have killed you, Mike."

"I know, honey."

"He was standing close enough so I could reach out and put my gun right against him." Her lips tightened. "Is this how . . . you feel, Mike? Is it all right for me to feel like this? Not having a sensation of guilt?"

"I feel happy."

"So do I. Perhaps I shouldn't, Mike. Maybe I should feel ashamed and sinful, but I don't. I'm glad I shot him. I'm glad I had the chance to do it and not you. I wanted to, do you understand that?"

"I understand completely. I know how you feel because it's how I feel. There's no shame or sin in killing a killer. David did it when he knocked off Goliath. Saul did it when he slew his tens of thousands. There's no shame to killing an evil thing. As long as you have to live with the fact you might as well enjoy it."

This time Velda laughed easily. My mind turned to the judge and I could picture his face, disappointed and angry that my time still hadn't come. And we had the best alibi in the world. Self-defense. We had a gun license and they didn't. If it reached us we were still clear.

Velda said, "They were there after the same thing, weren't they?"

"What?"

She repeated it. I slammed the wheel with my hand and said something I shouldn't have. Velda looked at me, her forehead furrowed. "They were . . . weren't they?"

I shook my head in disgust at myself. "What a sap I am. Of course they were! I thought they were after me again and they were searching for those damn documents!"

"Mike! But how would they know? The papers never carried any news of Charlie Moffit's murder. They reported it, but that was all. How could they know?"

"The same way the public knew the documents were stolen. Look, it's been a good time since he was knocked off. Just about long enough for somebody to get a loose tongue and spill something. That's how they knew . . . there was a leak. Somebody said something they shouldn't have!"

"The witnessess. They'd be the ones. Didn't Pat say they were warned to keep quiet about it?"

" 'Advised' is the word," I said. "That doesn't make them liable to any official action. Damn it, why can't people keep their big mouths shut!"

Velda fidgeted in her seat. "It was too big to keep, Mike. You don't witness a murder and just forget about it."

"Ah, maybe you're right. Maybe I give people credit for having more sense than they actually have. Hell, the leak could just as well have come out of police headquarters too. It's too late now to worry about it. The damage is done."

Velda lost herself in her thoughts for a good five minutes. I stayed hunched over the wheel trying to see through the fog. "It wasn't there, Mike. If it wasn't there then it has to be somewhere else."

"Yeah."

"You looked around the place right after Oscar died. It wasn't among his things. The police must have looked too. Then we looked again. Do you think it could possibly be that Oscar didn't have them?"

"What else is there to think? Either that or he hid them outside his room."

"Doubtful, Mike. Remember one thing, if Oscar showed himself anywhere he would have been mistaken for Lee. He couldn't have done much fooling around."

I had to grin because the girl who was wearing my ring was so smart I began to feel foolish around her. I did pretty good for myself. I picked a woman who could shoot a guy just like that and still think straight. "Go on, Velda."

"So maybe Oscar never got those documents. Charlie's ripped pocket just happened when he fell. If Charlie was the courier, and if the documents he was carrying are missing, then Charlie must have them tucked away somewhere. Remember what the men at the pie factory said . . . that he was dopey for certain periods of time? He was forgetful? Couldn't he have. . . ."

I stopped her and took it from there myself. She had tapped it right on the nose.

"When, Mike?"

I glanced at her quickly. "When what?"

"When do we go through his apartment?"

She was asking for more! Once in a night wasn't enough. "Not now," I told her. "Tomorrow's another day. Our dead friends won't be making a report tonight and the party won't be too anxious to make any more quick moves until they figure this one out first. We have time, plenty of time."

"No we don't."

I convinced her that we had by talking my head off all the way up to her apartment. When I let her out I only had one more thing to say. She waited, knowing well enough what was coming. "In case anyone asks, I was with you in your place all night, understand?"

"Can't we partially tell the truth?"

"Nope, we're engaged."

"Oh. Now I have to wait some more."

"Not long, kid, not too long. When this is all finished there'll be time for other things."

"I can wait."

"Good. Now hop upstairs and get to bed, but first, take that gun of yours and hide it somewhere. Put it where it can't be found until I tell you to take it out."

She leaned over and kissed me, a soft, light kiss that left my mouth tingling with the thought of what lay behind this girl who could be so completely lovable and so completely deadly. There were fires burning in her eyes that nothing could ever quench, but they asked me to try . . . to try hard.

I looked at her legs as she got out of the car and decided that I'd never see enough of them. They had been there all the time, mine any time I had wanted to ask and until now I never had the sense to ask. I had been stupid, all right. I was much smarter now. I waited until she was in the door before I turned the car around and crawled back to my own place.

It was late and I was tired. There had been too much in this one night again, I thought to myself. You get wound up like a watch spring, tighter and tighter until the limit is reached and you let go with a bang that leaves you empty and gasping.

When I locked the door I went directly to the closet and took down the box of parts and shells for the gun. I laid them out on the kitchen table and took the .45 apart piece by piece, cleaning and oiling every bit of it. I unwrapped the new barrel and put it in place, throwing the rest of the gun together around it. On second thought I changed the firing pin too. A microscope could pick up a lot of details from empty shell cases.

It took a half-hour to get the gun ready to go again. I shoved the old barrel and pin in a quart beer can, stuffed in some paper to keep it from rattling and dumped the works down the incinerator.

I was feeling pretty good when I crawled into the sack. Now let's see what would happen.

The alarm was about to give up when I finally woke up. There was nothing I wanted more than staying in bed, but I forced myself into a sitting position, fought a brief battle with the sheets and got my feet on the floor. A cold shower took the sleep out of my eyes and a plate of bacon and eggs put some life into my body.

I dressed and called Velda. She wasn't at home so I tried the office. She was there. I said, "How the devil do you do it?"

She laughed and came right back at me. "I'm still a working girl, Mike. Office hours are from eight to five, remember?"

"Any customers?"

"Nope."

"Any bills?"

"Nope."

"Love me?"

"Yup. Love me?"

"Yup. What a conversation. Any calls?"

"Yup. Pat called. He wants to see you. Lee Deamer called. He wants to see you, too."

I brightened up fast. "If they call back, tell them I'll check in. How about the papers?"

"Headlines, Mike. Big black headlines. It seems that a couple of rival gangs met up with each other in an old building over on the East Side. They forgot to carry their dead off when the battle was finished."

"Don't sound so smug. Did Pat mention anything about it?"

"No, but he will. He was pretty edgy with me."

"Okay, give him my love. I'll see you shortly." I hung up and laid out my working suit for the day. When I finished dressing I looked out the window and swore to myself. The fog was gone, but a drizzle had come in on its heels and the people on the street were bundled into coats trying to keep warm. The winter was dying a hard death.

On the way to the office I stopped off at a saloon and saw a friend of mine. I told him I wanted an unlicensed automatic of a certain make and .32 caliber, one that hadn't done anything except decorate somebody's dresser drawer since it was bought. My friend went to the phone and made two calls. He came back, told me to wait a few minutes, served a few customers at the bar, then went into the kitchen in the rear and I heard his voice arguing for a while. He came back with a package in his hand and said, "Twenty bucks, Mike."

I peeled off twenty, took the gun apart and removed the barrel and the pin. The rest I told my friend to dump in with his trash, thanked him and left. I stopped off at the office long enough to hand the two parts to Velda and tell her to slip them in her gun during her lunch hour. Then I went down to see Pat.

As Velda said, he wasn't happy. He said, "Hell, Mike," but his eyes raked me up and down. "Sit," he said.

I sat down and picked the paper off his desk. The headlines were big and black. There was a picture of the outside of the house with an interior shot in the middle section with white dotted lines to indicate where the bodies had been found. "Real trouble, huh, Pat?"

"Yeah, I thought maybe you could explain some of it."

"Don't be silly."

"Been shooting your gun lately?"

"Yesterday, as a matter of fact. I fired one into some waste right in my own apartment to check the ejector action. Why?"

"A paraffin test is out of order then. Mind if I see your gun?"

I said no and handed it over. Pat pressed a button on his desk and one of the technicians came in. Pat handed him the gun. "Get me a photograph of one of the slugs, Art."

"You're assuming a lot, aren't you, Pat?"

"I think so. Want to talk about it?"

"No, wait until you get your photograph."

He sat back and smiled and I read the papers. The two men were identified as Martin Romberg and Harold Valleck. They were good and dead. Both had prison records for various crimes and were suspected of being killed in a gang brawl. The police were expecting early developments in the crime. The reporters didn't have much to go on.

Art came back before I finished the funnies and handed Pat an enlarged sheet that was covered with angle shots of the slug. He laid the gun on the desk. Pat smiled again and pulled another sheet from his desk drawer. There wasn't anything funny about the way he smiled. I looked at him with a frown covering up the grin that was trying to break through, lit a butt and went back to the paper and finished the funnies.

Pat said, "You're too smart to be dumb, Mike. That or you're clean and I'm stupid as hell." His face looked empty.

I had a nice speech all ready to take him down a peg or two when I realized that he was on the spot. "You mean they were supposed to match, is that it?"

He nodded. "Something like that. A .45 killed one of them. There were only three of us who knew about Oscar's being there."

"Were they after Oscar or just there?"

"Hell, I don't know, Mike. Murder isn't uncommon in that neighborhood. Ordinarily I wouldn't give a hoot about it, but this isn't an ordinary thing. I feel about as effective as a clam right now."

"What for? Cripes, you can't help yourself if somebody gets shot. The place was empty. It was a good place for a hideout. Maybe those two eggs were holed up in there when they got caught up with."

Pat leaned back and rubbed his hands across his eyes. "Look, Mike, I'm not too dumb. Anybody can change barrels in a gun. I'll bet you the shell cases won't match your pin either."

"How'd you guess?"

"You're treating me like a kid now, feller. You're the one who's forgetting that we're friends. I know you like a book and I don't want to tear any pages out of that book because if I do I'm afraid of what the ending will be like. I know it was you, I don't know who handled the .32, I'm scared to ask questions and I hate to have you lie to me. Little lies I don't like."

I folded the paper and put it back on his desk. Pat wouldn't look at me. "Why the finger pointing at me, Pat?"

"Nuts. Just plain nuts. You should know why."

"I don't."

"One of those boys had a green Commie card on him. Now do you know why?"

"Yeah," I said. I had forgotten all about that. I lifted the cigarette and dragged the smoke down into my chest. "Now what?"

"I want to know what you're after. I want to know everything, Mike. Whenever I think about things I get cold all over and want to smash things. You've been playing cute and there's no way I can touch you. I have to absorb myself in police work and routine detail when I know I'm on the outside hoping for a look in."

"That's the trouble with the police. They have to wait until something happens. A crime has to be committed before they can make a move."

Pat watched me thoughtfully, his hands locked behind his head. "Things have happened."

"Roger, but, as you stated, they have been played very cute."

"I'm still on the outside looking in."

I snubbed the butt out and stared at the shreds of tobacco hanging out the end. "Pat . . . more things are going to happen. I know you like a book, too, but there's something else I have to know."

"Go on."

"How far can I trust you?"

"It depends on a lot of things. Never forget that I'm still a cop."

"You're still a plain citizen who likes his country and likes to see it stay the way it is, aren't you?"

"Naturally."

"All right. You're all snagged up in the ritual of written law and order. You have to follow the rules and play it square. There's a weight around your neck and you know it. If I told you what I knew you'd bust a gut trying to get something done that couldn't be done and the rats would get out of the trap.

"I'm only one guy, Pat, but I'm quite a guy and you know it. I make my own rules as I go along and I don't have to account to anybody. There's something big being kicked around and it's exactly as you said . . . it's bigger than you or me or anybody and I'm the only one who can handle it. Don't go handing me the stuff about the agencies that are equipped to handle every conceivable detail of this and that. I'm not messing with detail . . . I'm messing with people and letting them see that I'm nobody to mess with and there are a lot more like me if you want to look for them.

"What's going on isn't a case for the crime laboratory and it isn't a case for the police. The whole thing is in the hands of the people, only they don't know it yet. I'm going to show it to them because I'm the only one who has the whole works wrapped up tight trying to bring it together so we can see what it is. You can stop worrying about your law and your order and about Lee Deamer, because when I'm finished Lee can win his election and go ahead and wipe out the corruption without ever knowing that he had a greater enemy than crime plain and simple."

I picked up my gun and stuck it in the sling. Pat hadn't moved. His head bobbed slightly when I said so long, but that was all.

I was still seeing the tired smile on Pat's face, telling me that he

understood and to go ahead, when I called Lee Deamer's office. His secretary told me that he was speaking at a luncheon of U.N. delegates in a
midtown hotel and had already left. I got the name of the hotel, thanked
her and hung up.

He must be getting anxious and I didn't blame him a bit. It was a little before noon, so I hopped in the heap and tooled it up Broadway and
angled over to the hotel where it cost me a buck to park in an unloading
zone with a guy to cover for me.

The clerk at the desk directed me to the hall where the luncheon was
to be held and had hardly finished before I saw Lee come in the door.
He swung a brief case at his side and one of the girls from his office
trailed behind him carrying another. Before I could reach him a swarm
of reporters came out of nowhere and took down his remarks while the
photogs snapped his picture.

A covey of important-looking joes stood on the outside of the circle
impatient to speak to Deamer, yet unwilling to offend the press by breaking up the party. It was Lee himself who told the boys to see him after
the luncheon and walked through their midst. He had spotted me leaning against the desk and went directly into the manager's office. That little man went in after him, came out in a minute and scanned the desk. I
didn't have to be told that he was looking for me.

I nodded and strode in as casually as I could. The manager smiled at
me, then took up a position near the door to give us a few minutes in
private. Lee Deamer was sitting in a leather-covered chair next to the
desk and his face was a study in anxiety.

"Hello, Lee."

"Mike, how are you? I've been worried sick ever since I saw the papers this morning."

I offered him a butt and he shook his head. "There's nothing to
worry about, Lee. Everything is fine."

"But last night. I . . . you mean you weren't connected with the do-
ings in Oscar's place?" I grinned and lit the smoke.

"I don't know what to think. I called Captain Chambers and he led
me to believe that he thought the same thing."

"He did. I talked him out of it." I raked another chair up with my
foot and sat down. Murder is murder. It can be legal and it can't. No
matter what it is it's still murder and the less people know about it the
better. I said, "I went through Oscar's place right after the accident. Pat
went through it himself. Later I took another check and I'm satisfied

that if Oscar *did* leave any incriminating junk lying around, he didn't leave it in his room."

Lee sighed, relieved. "I'm glad to hear that, Mike, but I'm more than glad to hear that you didn't have anything to do with those . . . deaths. It's ugly."

"Murder is always ugly."

"Then there's nothing further to be said, I imagine. That takes a great load off my mind. Truly, Mike, I was terribly worried."

"I should think so. Well, keep your mind at rest. I'm going to back-track on Oscar a little bit and see what comes up. It's still my opinion that he was bluffing. It's not the easiest thing in the world to frame somebody who can't be framed. If anything comes up I'll let you know, meanwhile, no news is good news, so they say."

"Fine, Mike, I'll leave everything to you. Captain Chambers will co-operate as he sees possible. I want nothing hanging over my head. If it becomes necessary I would rather the public knew about my relation-ship with Oscar and the facts of the case before the election."

"Forget that stuff," I told him brusquely, "there's plenty the public shouldn't know. If you went into George Washington's background you'd probably kick up a lot of dirt too. You're the one that counts, not Oscar. Remember that."

I put the chair back in place and doused the butt in a flower pot. I told Lee to give me a few minutes before he left, said so long and took off. Lee looked ten years younger than he had when he came in. I liked that guy.

There was a public phone in the lobby and I called Velda to ask her if she had switched parts in her gun. She said she had, then told me Pat had just been on the wire. I said, "But I just saw him a little while ago."

"I know, but he told me to have you contact him right away if I could reach you."

"Okay, I'll call him back. Look, I'll probably be out most of the day, so I'll pick you up sometime tonight at your place."

"Charlie Moffit?"

"Yeah, we'll take in his joint."

"I'll be ready, Mike."

I hung up, threw in another nickel and spun Pat's number when I got the dial tone. The last time I had seen him he looked tired. This time his voice was dancing.

Like on hot coals.

"Pat, feller, why the sudden rush?"

"I'll tell you later. Get your tail down here chop-chop. I have things to talk over with you. Privately."

"Am I in trouble?"

"There's a damn good chance that you'll be in jail if you don't hurry."

"Get off my back, Pat. Get a table in Louie's and I'll be down for lunch. The check is yours this time."

"I'll give you fifteen minutes."

I made it just in time. Louie was behind the bar and thumbed me toward the booths in the rear. Pat was in the last one on the aisle sucking on a cigarette as hard as he could.

Did you ever see a guy who was burned up at his wife? He was like a bomb trying hard to go off and couldn't because the powder was wet. That's what Pat reminded me of. Police efficiency was leaking out his ears and his usual suavity hung on him like a bag. If you could call those narrow slits eyes then you could say he was looking at me with intent to kill.

I walked back to the bar and had Louie make me up a drink before the session started.

He waited until I was comfortable against the back of the booth and started on my drink before he yanked an envelope out of his pocket and flipped it across the table at me. I slid the contents out and looked at him.

They were photographs of fingerprints. Most were mine.

Four weren't.

Attached to the four that weren't was a typewritten sheet, single spaced and carefully paragraphed. "They came off that cigarette pack," Pat said.

I nodded and read through the report.

Her name was Paula Riis. She was thirty-four years old, a college grad, a trained nurse and a former employee in a large Western insane asylum. Since it was a state job her prints were on file there and in Washington.

Pat let me stuff the sheets back in the envelope before he spoke. I hardly heard him say unnecessarily, "She worked in the same place that Oscar had been assigned to." A cloud of smoke circled his head again.

The music started in my head. It was different this time. It wasn't loud and it had a definite tune and rhythm. It was soft, melodious music that tried to lullaby me into drowsiness with subtle tones. It tried to keep me from thinking and I fought it back into the obscurity from which it came.

I looked at his eyes and I looked deep into twin fires that had a maddening desire to make me talk and talk fast. "What, Pat?"

"Where is she?" His voice sounded queer.

I said, "She's dead. She committed suicide by jumping off a bridge into the river. She's dead as hell."

"I don't believe you, Mike."

"That's tough. That's just too damn bad because you have to believe me. You can scour the city or the country from now to doomsday and you won't find her unless you dredge the river and by now maybe even that's too late. She's out at sea somewhere. So what?"

"I'm asking the same thing. So what, Mike? She isn't an accident, a freak coincidence that you can explain off. I want to know why and how. This thing is too big for you to have alone. You'd better start talking or I'm going to have to think one thing. You aren't the Mike Hammer I knew once. You used to have sense enough to realize that the police are set up to handle these things. You used to know that we weren't a bunch of saps. If you still want to keep still then I'm going to think those things and the friendship I had for a certain guy is ended because that guy isn't the same guy any more."

That was it. He had me and he was right. I took another sip of the drink and made circles with the wet bottom on the table.

"Her name was Paula. Like I said, she's dead. Remember when I came to you with those green cards, Pat? I took them from her. I was walking across the bridge one night when this kid was going into her dutch act. I tried to stop her. All I got was the pocket of her coat where she had the pack of butts and the cards.

"It made me mad because she jumped. I had just been dragged over the coals by that damned judge and I was feeling sour enough not to report the thing. Just the same, I wanted to know what the cards meant. When I found out she was a Commie, and that Charlie Moffit was a Commie I got interested. I couldn't help it.

"Now the picture is starting to take form. I think you've put it together already. Oscar was insane. He had to be. He and that nurse planned an escape and probably went into hiding in their little love nest a long time ago. When money became scarce they saw a way to get some through using Oscar's physical similarity to Lee.

"The first thing that happened was that Oscar killed a guy, a Commie. Now: either he took those cards off Moffit's body for some reason, or he and this Paula Riis actually were Commies themselves. Anyway when Oscar killed Moffit, Paula realized that the guy was more insane than she thought and got scared. She was afraid to do anything about it so she went over the bridge."

It was a wonderful story. It made a lot of sense. The two people that could spoil it were dead. It made a lot of sense without telling about the fat boy on the bridge and setting myself up for a murder charge.

Pat was on the last of his smokes. The dead butts littered the table and his coat was covered with ashes. The fires in his eyes had gone down . . . a little anyway. "Very neat, Mike. It fits like a glove. I'm wondering what it would fit like if there was more to it that you didn't tell me."

"Now you're getting nasty," I said.

"No, just careful. If it's the way you told it the issue's dead. If it isn't there will be a lot of hell coming your way."

"I've seen my share," I grunted.

"You'll see a lot more. I'm going to get some people on this job to poke around. There're other friends of mine and though it won't be official it will be a thorough job. These boys carry little gold badges with three words you can condense to F.B.I. I hope you're right, Mike. I hope you aren't giving me the business."

I grinned at him. "The only one who can get shafted is me. You . . . hell, you're worried about Lee. I told you I wouldn't line him up for a smear. He's my client and I'm mighty particular about clients. Let's order some lunch and forget about it."

Pat reached for the menu. The fires were still in his eyes.

CHAPTER 8

I left Pat at two o'clock and picked up a paper on the corner. The headlines had turned back to the cold war and the spy trials going on in New York and Washington. I read the sheet through and tossed it in a basket then got in my car.

I made a turn at the corner and cut over to an express street to head back to my place when I noticed the blue coupé behind me. The last time I had seen it it had been parked across from mine outside Pat's office. I turned off the avenue and went down a block to the next avenue and paralleled my course. The blue coupé stuck with me.

When I tried the same thing again it happened all over This time I picked out a one-way street, crept along it behind a truck until I saw room enough at the curb to park the car. I went into the space head first and sat there at the wheel waiting. The coupé had no choice, it had to pass me.

The driver was a young kid in a pork-pie hat and he didn't give me a glance. There was a chance that I could be wrong, but just for the hell of it I jotted down his license number as he went by and swung out behind him. Only once did I see his eyes looking into his mirror, and that was when he turned on Broadway. I stuck with him a way to see what he'd do.

Five minutes later I gave it up as a bad job. He wasn't going anywhere. I made a left turn and he kept going straight ahead. I scowled at my reflection in the dirty windshield.

I was getting the jumps, I thought. I never used to get like that. Maybe Pat had put his finger on it . . . I'd changed.

When I stopped for the red light I saw the headlines on the papers laid out on a stand. More about the trials and the cold war. Politics. I felt like an ignorant bastard for not knowing what it was all about. There's no time like the present then. I swung the wheel and cut back in the other direction. I parked the car and walked up to the gray stone building where the pickets carried banners protesting the persecution of the "citizens" inside.

One of the punks carrying a placard was at the meeting in Brooklyn the other night. I crossed the line by shoving him almost on his fanny. An attendant carried my note in to Marty Kooperman and he came out to lead me back to the press seats.

Hell, you read the papers, you know what went on in there. It made me as sick to watch it as it did you to read about it. Those damned Reds pulled every trick they knew to get the case thrown out of court. They were a scurvy bunch of lice who tried to turn the court into a burlesque show.

But there was a calm patience in this judge and jury, and in the spectators too that told you what the outcome would be. Oh, the defendants didn't see it. They were too cocksure of themselves. They were The Party. They were Powerful. They represented the People.

They should have turned around and seen the faces of the people. They would have had their pants scared off. All at once I felt good. I felt swell!

Then I saw the two guys in the second row. They were dressed in ordinary business suits and they looked too damn smug. They were the boys who came in with General Osilov that night. I sat through two more hours of it before the judge broke it up for the day. The press boys made a beeline for the phones and the crowd started to scramble for the doors.

A lot of the people covered it up, but I had time to see the general's aides pass a fat brief case to another guy who saw that it reached one of the defendants.

All I could think of was the nerve they had, the gall of them to come into a court of law and directly confirm their relationship with a group accused of a crime against the people. Maybe that's why they could get ahead so fast. They were brazen. That brief case would hold one thing. Money. Cash in bills. Dough to support the trial and the accompanying propaganda.

Nuts.

I waited until they went through the doors and stayed on their heels. At least they had the sense not to come in an official car; that would have been overdoing it. They walked down a block, waved a cab to the curb and climbed in. By that time I was in a cab myself and right behind them. One nice thing about taking a taxi in New York. There're so many cabs you can't tell if you're being followed or not.

The one in front of us pulled to a stop in front of the hotel I had left not so long before. I paid off my driver and tagged after them into the lobby. The place was still jammed with reporters and the usual collection of the curious. General Osilov was standing off in a corner explaining things to four reporters through an interpreter. The two went directly up to him, interrupted and shook his hand as if they hadn't seen him in years. It was all very clubby.

The girl at the newsstand was bored. I bought a pack of Luckies and held out my hand for the change. "What's the Russky doing?"

"Him? He was a speaker at the luncheon upstairs. You should have heard him. They piped all the speeches into the lobby over the loudspeaker and he had to be translated every other sentence."

Sure, he couldn't speak English. Like hell!

I said, "Anything important come out?"

She handed me my change. "Nah, same old drivel every time. All except Lee Deamer. He jumped on that Cossack for a dozen things and called him every name that could sneak by in print. You should have heard the way the people in the lobby cheered. Gosh, the manager was fit to be tied. He tried to quiet them down, but they wouldn't shut up."

Good going, Lee. You tear the bastards apart in public and I'll do it in private. Just be careful, they're like poisonous snakes . . . quiet, stealthy and deadly. Be careful, for Pete's sake!

I opened the Luckies and shook one out. I hung it in my mouth and fumbled for a match. A hand draped with mink held a flame up to it and a voice said, "Light, mister?"

It was a silly notion, but I wondered if I could be contaminated by the fire. I said, "Hello, Ethel," and took the light.

There was something different about her face. I didn't know what it was, but it wasn't the same any more. Fine, nearly invisible lines drew it tight, giving an Oriental slant to her eyes. The mouth that had kissed so nice and spoke the word that put the finger on me seemed to be set too firm. It pulled the curve of her lips out of shape.

She had a lesson coming to her, this one. Bare skin and a leather belt. Either she was playing it bold or she didn't think I had guessed. Maybe she thought she couldn't have made it out the door without my seeing her and decided to make the first move herself. Whatever her reason, I couldn't read it in her voice or her face.

I was going to ask her what she was doing here and I saw why. The reputable Mr. Brighton of Park Avenue and Big Business was holding court next to a fluted column. A lone reporter was taking notes. A couple of big boys whose faces I recognized from newspapers were listening intently, adding a word now and then. They all smiled but two.

The sour pusses were General Osilov and his interpreter. The little guy beside the general talked fast and gesticulated freely, but the general was catching it all as it came straight from Brighton himself.

A couple hundred words later Ethel's old man said something and they all laughed, even the general. They shook hands and split up into new groups that were forming every time a discussion got started.

I took Ethel's arm and started for the door. "It's been a long time, kid. I've missed you."

She tried a smile and it didn't look good on her. "I've missed you too, Mike. I halfway expected you to call me."

"Well, you know how things are."

"Yes, I know." I threw my eyes over her face, but she was expressionless.

"Were you at the luncheon?" I asked.

"Oh . . ." she came out of it with a start. "No, I stayed in the lobby. Father was one of the speakers, you know."

"Really? No need for you to stick around, is there?"

"Oh no, none at all. I can . . . oh, Mike, just a moment. I forgot something, do you mind?"

We paused at the door and she glanced back over her shoulder. I turned her around and walked back. "Want me to go with you?"

"No, I'll be right back. Wait for me, will you?"

I watched her go and the girl at the counter smiled. I said, "There's a ten in it if you see what she does, sister." She was out of there like a shot and closed up on Ethel. I stood by the stand smoking, looking at the mirrors scattered around the walls. I could see myself in a half dozen of them. If Ethel watched to see whether or not I moved she must have been satisfied.

She was gone less than a minute. Her face looked tighter than ever.

I walked up to meet her and the girl scrambled behind her counter. I took out a dime, flipped it in my hand and went over and got a pack of gum. While the girl gave me my nickel change I dropped the ten on the counter. "She spoke to a couple of guys back in the hall. Nothing else. They were young."

I took my gum pack and offered Ethel a piece. She said she didn't want any. No wonder she looked so damned grim. She had fingered me again. Naked skin and ten extra lashes. She was going to be a sorry girl.

When we got in the cab two boys in almost identical blue suits opened the doors of a black Chevy sedan and came out behind us. I didn't look around again until we had reached the lot where I left my car. The black Chevy was down the street. Ethel kept up a running conversation that gave me a chance to look at her, and back over my shoulder occasionally.

If I had been paying any attention I would have gotten what she was driving at. She kept hinting for me to take her up to my place. MAN MURDERED IN OWN APARTMENT. More nice headlines. I ignored her hints and cruised around Manhattan with the black sedan always a few hundred feet behind.

Dusk came early. It drove in with the fog that seemed to like this town, a gray blind that reduced visibility to a minimum. I said to her, "Can we go back to your cabin, kid? It was pretty nice there."

I might have been mistaken, but I thought I saw the glint of tears. "It *was* nice there, wasn't it?"

"It was you, not the cabin, Ethel."

I wasn't mistaken, the tears were there. She dropped her eyes and stared at her hands. "I had forgotten . . . what it was like to live." She paused, then: "Mike . . ."

"What?"

"Nothing. We can go to the cabin if you'd like to."

The Chevy behind us pulled around a car and clung a little closer. I loosened the .45 with my forearm and a shrug. The dusk deepened to dark and it was easy to watch the lights in the mirror. They sat there, glowering, watching, waiting for the right moment to come.

How would it be? Ethel wanted it in my apartment. Why? So she would be out of the line of fire? Now what? They'd draw alongside and open up and they wouldn't give a hoot whether they got the both of us or not. It was a question of whether I was important enough to kill at the same time sacrificing a good Party worker. Hell, there were always suckers who could rake in the dough for them. Those two headlights behind me trying to act casual said that.

We were out of the city on a wide open road that wound into the dark like a beckoning finger. The houses thinned out and there were fewer roads intersecting the main drag.

Any time now, I thought. It can happen any time. The .45 was right where I could get at it in a hurry and I was ready to haul the wheel right into them. The lights behind me flicked on bright, back to dim and on bright again, a signal they were going to pass.

I signaled an okay with my lights and gripped the wheel. The lights came closer.

I didn't watch the mirror. I had my eyes going between the road and the lightbeams on the outside lane that got brighter as they came closer when all of a sudden the beams swerved and weren't there any more. When I looked they were going in a crazy rolling pattern end over end into the field alongside the road.

I half whispered, "Cripes!" and slammed on the brakes. A handful of cars shot by the accident and began to pull in to a stop in front of me.

Ethel was rigid in her seat, her hands pushing her away from the windshield where the quick stop had thrown her. "Mike! What . . ."

I yanked the emergency up. "Stay here. A car went over behind us."

She gasped and said something I didn't catch because I was out and running back toward the car. It was upside down and both doors were open. The horn blasted, a man screamed and the lights still punched holes in the night. I was the first one there, a hundred yards ahead of anyone else.

I had time to see the tommy gun on the grass and the wallet inside the car. So that was it. That was how it was to be pulled off. One quick blast from a chatter gun that would sweep my car and it was all over. Somebody groaned in the darkness and I didn't bother to see who it was. They deserved everything they got. I grabbed that tommy gun and the wallet and ducked behind the car in the darkness and ran back down the road. The others had just reached the wreck and were hollering for somebody to get a doctor.

Ethel screamed when I threw the trunk open and I yelled for her to shut up. I tossed the tommy gun on the spare tire and shut the lid. There were more cars coasting up, threading through the jam along the road. A siren screamed its way up and two state cops started the procession moving again. I joined the line and got away from there.

"Who was it, Mike? What happened back there?"

"Just an accident," I grinned. "A couple of guys were going too fast and they rolled over."

"Were they . . . hurt?"

"I didn't stay to look. They weren't dead . . . yet." I grinned again and her face tightened. She looked at me with an intense loathing and the tears started again.

"Don't worry, baby. Don't be so damn soft-hearted. You know what the Party policies are. You have to be cold and hard. You aren't forgetting, are you?"

The "no" came through her teeth.

"Hell, the ground was soft and the car wasn't banged up much. They were probably just knocked out. You know, you have to get over being squeamish about such things."

Ethel shifted in her seat and wouldn't look at me again. We came to the drive and the trees that hung over it. We pulled up to the front of the cabin that nestled on the bluff atop the river and sat there in the dark watching the lights of the river boats.

Red and green eyes. No, they were boats. From far away came a dull booming, like a giant kettledrum. I had heard it once before, calling that way. It was only a channel marker, only a steel bell on a float that clanged when the tide and the waves swung it. I felt a shudder cross my shoulders and I said, "Shall we go in?"

She answered by opening the door. I went into the cabin behind her.

I closed the door and reached behind my back and turned the key in the lock. Ethel heard the ominous click and stopped. She looked over her shoulder at me once, smiled and went on. I watched her throw her mink on the sofa then put a match to the tapers in the holders.

She thought it was a love nest. We were locked in against the world where we could practice the human frailties without interruption. She thought I didn't know and was going to give her all for the Party so as not to arouse my suspicions. She was crying softly as if the sudden passion was too much for her.

I put the key in my pocket and crossed the room to where she was and put my hands on her shoulders. She spun around, her hands locking behind my waist, her mouth reaching up for mine. I kissed her with a brutal force she'd remember and while I kissed her my fingers hooked in the fabric of her dress.

She ripped her mouth away from mine and pressed it against my cheek. She was crying hard and she said, "I love you, Mike. I never wanted to love again and I did. I love you." It was so low I hardly heard it.

My teeth were showing in a grin. I raised my hand until it was against her breast and pushed. Ethel staggered back a step and I yanked with the hand that held her dress and it came off in one piece with a quick loud tear, leaving her gasping and hurt with vivid red marks on her skin where the fabric had twisted and caught.

She gasped, pressed the back of her hand to her mouth and looked at me through eyes wide with fear. "Mike . . . you didn't have to . . ."

"Shut up." I took a step forward and she backed off, slowly, slowly, until the wall was at her back and she could retreat no more. "Am I going to rip 'em right off your hide, Ethel?"

Her head shook, unbelieving what was happening to her. It only lasted a moment, and her hands that trembled so bent up behind her back and the bra fell away and landed at her feet. Her eyes were on mine as she slid her hands inside the fragile silk of the shorts and pushed them down.

When she stepped out of them I slid my belt off and let it dangle from my hand. I watched her face. I saw the gamut of emotions flash by in swift succession, leaving a startled expression of pure animal terror.

"Maybe you should know why you're getting this, Ethel. It's something you should have gotten a long time ago. Your father should have given it to you when you started fooling around with one of those Commie bastards who was after the dough you could throw his way instead of yourself. I'm going to lace the hell out of you and you can scream all you want, and nobody will be around to hear you but me and that's what I want to hear.

"You put the finger on me twice now. You fingered me when you saw the badge inside my wallet and the Party put a man on my back. They put a lot of men, I guess. Two of 'em are dead already. It didn't go so good and you saw a chance to finger me again in the lobby back there. What did you expect for it, a promotion or something?"

I started to swing the belt back and forth very gently. Ethel pressed against the wall, her face a pale oval. "Mike . . . it wasn't . . ."

"Keep quiet," I said.

A naked woman and a leather belt. I looked at her, so bare and so pretty, hands pressed for support against the paneling, legs spread apart to hold a precarious balance, a flat stomach hollowed under the fear that burned her body a faint pink, lovely smooth breasts, firm with terrible excitement, rising and falling with every gasping breath. A gorgeous woman who had been touched by the hand of the devil.

I raised the belt and swung it and heard the sharp crack of the leather against her thighs and her scream and that horrible blasting roar all at once. Her body twisted and fell while I was running for the window with the .45 in my hand pumping slugs into the night and shouting at the top of my voice.

And there in the darkness I heard a body crashing through the brush, running for the road. I ran to the door that I had locked myself and cursed my own stupidity while I fumbled for the key in my pocket.

The door came open, but there was only silence outside, a dead, empty silence. I jammed a fresh clip into the gun and held it steady, deliberately standing outlined in the light of the door asking to be made a target.

I heard it again, the heavy pounding of feet going away. They were too far to catch. When they stopped a motor roared into life and he was gone. My hands had the shakes again and I had to drop the rod back in the sling. The prints of his feet were in the grass, winding around the house. I followed them to the window and bent over to pick up the hat.

A pork-pie hat. It had a U-shaped nick taken out of the crown. The boy in the blue Chevy. Mr. M.V.D. himself, a guy who looked like a schoolboy and could pass in a crowd for anything but what he was. I grinned because he was one thing he shouldn't have been, a lousy shot. I was duck soup there in that room with my back toward him and he missed. Maybe I was supposed to be his first corpse and he got nervous. Yeah. I turned and looked in the window.

Ethel was still on the floor and a trickle of red drained from her body.

I ran back to her, stumbling over things in the darkness. I turned her over and saw the hole under her shoulder, a tiny blue thing that oozed blood slowly and was beginning to swell at the edges.

I said, "Ethel . . . Ethel honey!"

Her eyes came open and she looked tired, so tired. "It . . . doesn't hurt, Mike."

"I know. It won't for a while. Ethel . . . I'm sorry. God, I feel awful."

"Mike . . . don't."

She closed her eyes when I ran my hand over her cheek. "You said . . . a badge, Mike. You're not one of them, are you?"

"No. I'm a cop."

"I'm . . . glad. After . . . I met you I saw . . . the truth, Mike. I knew . . . I had been a fool."

"No more talking, Ethel. I'm going for a doctor. Don't talk."

She found my hand and hung on. "Let me, Mike . . . please. Will I die?"

"I don't know, Ethel. Let me go for a doctor."

"No . . . I want to tell you . . . I loved you. I'm glad it happened. I had to love somebody . . . else."

I forced her fingers off my hand and pushed her arm away gently. There was a phone on the bar and I lifted it to my ear. I dialed the operator and had a hard time keeping my voice level. I said I wanted a doctor and wanted one quick. She told me to wait and connected me with a crisp voice that sounded steady and alert. I told him where we were and to get here fast. He said he would hurry and broke the connection.

I knelt beside her and stroked her hair until her eyes came open, silently protesting the pain that had started. Her shoulder twitched once and the blood started again. I tried to be gentle. I got my arms under her and carried her to the couch. The wound was a deeper blue and I prayed that there was no internal hemorrhage.

I sat beside her holding her hand. I cursed everything and everybody. I prayed a little and I swore again. I had thoughts that tried to drive me mad.

It was a long while before I realized that she was looking at me. She struggled to find words, her mind clouding from the shock of the bullet. I let her talk and heard her say, "I'm not . . . one of them any more. I told . . . everything . . . I told . . ."

Her eyes had a glazed look. "Please don't try to talk, kid, please."

She never heard me. Her lips parted, moved. "I never . . . told them about you . . . Mike. I never saw . . . your badge. Tonight . . . those men . . ." It was too much for her. She closed her eyes and was still, only the cover I had thrown over her moved enough to tell that she was still alive.

I never heard the doctor come in. He was a tall man with a face that had looked on much of the world. He stepped past me and leaned over her, his hand opening the bag he carried. I sat and waited, smoking one cigarette after another. The air reeked with a sharp chemical smell and the doctor was a tall shadow passing back and forth across my line of vision, doing things I wasn't aware of, desperate in his haste.

His voice came at me several times before I answered him. He said, "She will need an ambulance."

I came out of the chair and went to the phone. The operator said she would call and I hung up. I turned around. "How is she, doc?"

"We won't know for a while yet. There's a slight chance that she'll pull through." His whole body expressed what he felt. Disgust. Anger. His voice had a demanding, exasperated tone. "What happened?"

Perhaps it was the sharpness of his question that startled me into a logical line of reasoning. There was a sudden clarity about the whole thing I hadn't noticed before I heard Ethel telling me that she had pulled out of the Party and it left me with an answer that said this time it wasn't me they were after . . . it was her . . . and Pork-Pie *had* been a good shot. He would have been a dead shot, only Ethel had twisted when I laid the strap across her and the bullet that was intended for her heart had missed by a fraction and might give her life back to her.

The soft kill-music that I always hear at the wrong times took up a beat and was joined by a multitude of ghostly instruments that plucked at my mind to drive away any reason that I had left.

I walked to the doctor and stared at his eyes so he could see that I had looked on the world too, and could see the despair, the lust, the same dirty thoughts that he had seen in so many others and said, "Do you know who I am, doctor?"

He looked long this time, searching me. "Your face is familiar."

"It should be, doctor. You've seen it in the papers. You've read about it many times. It's been described a hundred different ways and there's always that reference to a certain kill-look that I have. My name is Mike Hammer. I'm a private detective. I've killed a lot of people."

He knew me then; his eyes asked if I were trying to buy his silence with the price of death. "Did you do that to her too?"

"No, doctor. Somebody else did that, and for it that somebody is going to die a thousand times. It wasn't just one person who wanted that girl dead. One person ordered it, but many demanded it. I'm not going to tell you the story of what lies behind this, but I will tell you one thing. It's so damned important that it touches your life and mine and the lives of everyone in this country and unless you want to see the same thing happen again and again you'll have to hold up your report.

"You know who I am and I can show you my papers so there will never be any trouble in finding me if you think it should be done. But listen . . . if ever you believed anything, believe this . . . if I get connected with this I'll be tied up in that crazy web of police detail and a lot of other people will die. Do you understand me?"

"No." Just like that, no. I tried to keep from grabbing his neck in my hands and forcing my words down his throat. My face went wild and I couldn't control it. The doctor didn't scare, he just stood there and watched me make myself keep from killing him too.

"Perhaps I do after all." His face became sober and stern. I swallowed hard with the relief I felt. "I don't understand it at all," he said. "I'll never understand these things. I do know this though, a powerful influence motivates murder. It is never simple enough to understand. I can't understand war, either. I'll do what I can, Mr. Hammer. I do have a good understanding of people and I think that you are telling me a truth that could have some very unpleasant aspects, whatever they are."

I squeezed his hand hard and got out of there. So much to be done, I thought, so much that's still left to do. My watch said it was after ten and Velda would be waiting. Tonight we had a mission planned and after that another and another until we found the ending.

I touched the starter and the engine caught with a roar. The night had sped by and there never was enough time to do what I wanted. First Pork-Pie Hat, then those men, then Ethel. I stopped and retraced my thoughts. Ethel and those men. She was going to tell me about them; she almost did. I reached in my pocket and took out the wallet.

The card was behind some others in one of the pockets. It was an official card with all the works. The words I saw stood out as though they were written in flame. FEDERAL BUREAU OF INVESTIGATION. Good Lord, Ethel had fingered me to the F.B.I.! She had turned on the Party and even on me! Now it *was* clear . . . Those two Feds had tailed me hoping to be led to my apartment and perhaps a secret cache of papers that could lead to those missing documents! They tailed me but they in turn were being tailed by somebody else who knew what had happened. Pork-Pit Hat ran them off the road and came after us with the intention of killing Ethel before she could spill anything else she knew!

I let the music in my head play. I laughed at it and it played harder than ever, but this time I didn't fight it. I sat back and laughed, enjoying the symphony of madness and cheered when it was done. So I *was* mad. I *was* a killer and I *was* looking forward to killing again. I wanted them all, every one of them from bottom to top and especially the one at the top even if I had to go to the Kremlin to do it. The time for that wouldn't be now . . . I'd only get a little way up the ladder if one of the rungs didn't break first and throw me to my death.

But some day, maybe, some day I'd stand on the steps of the Kremlin with a gun in my fist and I'd yell for them to come out and if they wouldn't I'd go in and get them and when I had them lined up against the wall I'd start shooting until all I had left was a row of corpses that bled on the cold floors and in whose thick red blood would be the promise of a peace that would stick for more generations than I'd live to see.

The music gave up in a thunder of drums and I racked my wheels against the curb outside Velda's apartment house. I looked up at her floor when I got out and saw the lights on and I knew she was ready and waiting.

I went on in.

She said hello and knew that something was wrong with me. "What happened, Mike?"

I couldn't tell her the whole thing. I said simply, "They tried again."

Her eyes narrowed down and glinted at me. They asked the question.

I said, "They got away again, too."

"It's getting deeper, isn't it?"

"It'll go deeper before we're through. Get your coat on."

Velda went inside and reappeared with her coat on and her handbag slung over her shoulder. It swung slowly under the weight of the gun. "Let's go, Mike."

We went downstairs to the car and started driving. Broadway was a madhouse of traffic that weaved and screamed, stopped for red lights and jumped away at the green. I let the flow take me past the artificial day-light of the marquees and the signs and into the dusk of uptown. When we came to the street Velda pointed and I turned up it, parking in the middle of the block under a street light.

Here was the edge of Harlem, that strange no-man's-land where the white mixed with the black and the languages overflowed into each other like that of the horde around the Tower of Babel. There were strange, foreign smells of cooking and too many people in too few rooms. There were the hostile eyes of children who became suddenly silent as you passed.

Velda stopped before an old sandstone building. "This is it."

I took her arm and went up the stairs. In the vestibule I struck a match and held it before the name plates on the mailboxes. Most were scrawled in childish writing on the backs of match books. One was an aluminum stamp and it read C. C. LOPEX, SUPT.

I pushed the button. There was no answering buzz of the door. In-stead, a face showed through the dirty glass and the door was pulled open by a guy who only came up to my chest. He smoked a smelly cigar and reeked of cheap whisky. He was a hunchback. He said, "Whatta ya want?"

He saw the ten bucks I had folded in my fingers and got a greedy look on his face. "There ain't but one empty room and ya won't like that. Ya can use my place. For a tenner ya can stay all night."

Velda raised her eyebrows at that. I shook my head. "We'll take the empty."

"Sure, go ahead. Ya coulda done whatcha wanted in my place but if ya want the empty go ahead. Ya won't like it, though."

I gave him the ten and he gave me the key, telling me where the room was. He leered and looked somewhat dissatisfied because he wouldn't be able to sneak a look on something he probably never had himself. Velda started up the stairs using her flashlight to pick out the snags in the steps.

The room faced on a dark corridor that was hung heavy with the smell of age and decay. I put the key in the lock and shoved the door open. Velda found the lone bulb that dangled from the ceiling and pulled the cord to throw a dull yellow light in the room. I closed the door and locked it.

Nobody had to tell us what had happened. Somebody had been here before us. The police had impounded Charlie Moffit's personal belongings, but they hadn't ripped the room up doing it. The skinny mattress lay in the center of the floor ripped to shreds. The hollow posts of the bed had been disemboweled and lay on the springs. What had been a rug at one time lay in a heap in the corner under the pile of empty dresser drawers.

"We're too late again, Mike."

"No we're not." I was grinning and Velda grinned too. "The search didn't stop anywhere. If they found it we could have seen where they stopped looking. They tore the place apart and never came to the end. It never was here."

I kicked at the papers on the floor, old sheets from weeks back. There was a note pad with pencil sketches of girls doing things they shouldn't. We roamed around the room poking into the remains, doing nothing but looking out of curiosity. Velda found a box of junk that had been spilled under the dresser, penny curios from some arcade.

There was no place else to look that hadn't already been searched. I took the dresser drawers off the rug and laid them out. They were lined with newspapers and had a few odds and ends rolling on the bottoms. There was part of a fountain pen and a broken harmonica. Velda found a few pictures of girls in next to nothing that had been cut from a magazine.

Then I found the photographs. They were between the paper lining and the side of the drawer. One was of two people, too fuzzy to identify. The other was that of a girl and had "To Charlie, with love from P." written on the bottom. I held it in my hand and looked at the face of Paula Riis. She was smiling. She was happy. She was the girl that had jumped off the bridge and was dead. I stared at her face that smiled back at me as if there never had been anything to worry about.

Velda peered over my shoulder, took the picture from me and held it under the light. "Who is she, Mike?"

"Paula Riis," I said finally. "The nurse. Charlie Moffit's girl friend. Oscar Deamer's nurse and the girl who chose to die rather than look at my face. The girl who started it all and left it hanging in mid-air while people died and killed."

I took out a cigarette and gave her one. "I had it figured wrong. I gave Pat a bum steer, then when I thought it over I got to thinking that maybe I told the truth after all. I thought that Paula and Oscar planned his escape and Oscar killed a guy . . . just any guy . . . in order to squeeze Lee. Now it seems that it wasn't just any guy that Oscar killed. It wasn't an accident. Oscar killed him for a very good reason."

"Mike . . . could it be a case of jealousy? Could Oscar have been jealous because Paula played up to Charlie?"

I dragged the smoke down, held it and let it go into the light. "I wish it happened that simply. I wish it did, sugar. I started out with a couple of green cards and took it from there. I thought I had a coincidental connection but now it looks like it wasn't so damn coincidental after all. We have too many dead people carrying those green cards."

"The answer, Mike . . . what can it be?"

I stared at the wall thoughtfully. "I'm wondering that too. I think it lies out West in an asylum for the insane. Tomorrow I want you to take the first plane out and start digging."

"For what?"

"For anything you can find. Think up the questions and look for the answers. The part we're looking for may be there and it may be here, but we haven't the time to look together. You'll have to go out alone while I plod along this end of the track."

"Mike . . . you'll be careful, won't you?"

"Very careful. Velda. I won't ask questions if I think a gun will do the job quicker. This time I'm going to live up to my reputation. I've been thinking some things I don't like and to satisfy myself I'm going to find out whether or not they're true."

"Supposing they make another try for you?"

"Oh, they will, they will. In fact, they have to. From now on I'll be sleeping with my gun in my fist and my eyes open. They'll make the play again because I know enough and think too much. I might run into a conclusion that will split things wide open. They'll be looking for me and possibly you because they know there were two guns that killed those boys in Oscar's room. They'll know I wasn't alone and they may think of you.

"I'll have to keep my apartment and the office covered while I'm away. They'll get around it somehow, but I'll try anyway."

Velda took my shoulder and made me look at her. "You aren't send-ing me out West just so I won't be there if there's trouble, are you?"

"No, I wouldn't do that to you. I know how much it means to be in on a thing like this."

She knew I was telling the truth for a change and dropped her hand into mine. "I'll do a good job, Mike. When I get back I won't take any chance on their finding any information I have. I'll tuck it in that trick wall lamp in the office so you can get to it without waking me from the sleep I'll probably need."

I pulled the cord and the light did a slow fade-out. Velda held her flash on the floor and stared down the corridor. A little brown face peeked out of a door and withdrew when she threw the spot on it. We held on to the banister and went down the steps that announced our de-scent with sharp squeals and groans.

The hunchback opened his door at the foot of the landing and took the key back. "That was quick," he said. "Pretty quick for your age. Thought ya'd take longer."

I wanted to rap him in the puss, only that would have shut him up when I had a question to ask him. "We woulda stayed only the room was a mess. Who was in there before us?"

"Some guy died who lived there."

"Yeah, but who was in there next?"

"Young kid. Said he wanted a bunk for a night. Guess he was hot or something. He gimme a ten too, plus a five for the room. Yeah, I re-member him 'counta he wore a nice topcoat and one of them flat pork-pie hats. Sure woulda like to get that topcoat."

I pushed Velda outside and down to the car. The M.V.D. had been there. No wonder the search was so complete. He looked and never looked hard enough. In his hurry to find some documents he over-looked the very thing that might have told him where they were.

I drove Velda home and went up for coffee. We talked and we smoked. I laughed at the way she looked at the ring on her finger and told her the next thing she knew there'd be a diamond to match. Her eyes sparkled brighter than the stone.

"When will it be, Mike?" Her voice was a velvet glove that caressed every inch of me.

I squirmed a little bit and managed a sick grin. "Oh, soon. Let's not go too fast, kid."

The devil came into her eyes and she pushed away from the table. I had another smoke and finished it. I started on another when she called me. When I went into the living room she was standing by the light in a gown that was nothing at all, nothing at all. I could see through it and saw things I thought existed only in a dream and the sweat popped out on my forehead and left me feeling shaky all over.

Her body was a milky flow of curves under the translucent gown and when she moved the static current of flesh against sheer cloth made it cling to her in a way that made me hold my breath to fight against the temptation I could feel tugging at my body. The inky blackness of the hair falling around her shoulders made her look taller, and the gown shrouded what was yet to come and was there for me alone.

"For our wedding night, Mike," she said. "When will it be?"

I said, "We're . . . only engaged to be engaged, you know."

I didn't dare move when she came to me. She raised herself on her toes to kiss me with a tongue of fire, then walked back to the light and turned around. I could see through that damned gown as though it weren't there at all.

She knew I'd never be able to wait long after that.

I stumbled out of the room and down to my car. I sat there awhile thinking of nothing but Velda and the brief glimpse of heaven she had showed me. I tried thinking about something else and it didn't work.

I couldn't get her out of my mind.

CHAPTER 9

I slept with a dream that night. It was a dream of nice things and other things that weren't so nice. There were a lot of people in the dream and not all of them were alive. There were faces from the past that mingled with those of the present, drawn silent faces turned toward me to see when I would become one of them, floating in that limbo of nonexistence.

I saw the bridge again, and two people die while the stern face of the judge looked on disapproving, uttering solemn words of condemnation. I saw flashes of fire, and men fall. I saw Ethel hovering between the void that separates life from death, teetering into the black while I screamed for her not to and tried to run to catch her, only to have my feet turn into stumps that grew from the very soil.

There were others too, bodies of dead men without faces, waiting for me to add that one missing part, to identify them with their brother dead in one sweeping blast of gunfire. I was there with them. They didn't want me because I wasn't dead, and the living didn't want me either. They couldn't figure out why I was still alive when I dwelt in the land of the dead men.

Only Velda wanted me. I could see her hovering above the others, trailing the gown of transparent fabric, her finger beckoning me to come with her where nothing would matter but the two of us.

The dead pushed me out and the living pushed me back. I tried to get up to Velda and I couldn't reach her. I screamed once for them all to shut up before there was only the land of the dead and none of the living.

Then I woke up. My head throbbed and the shout was still caught in my throat. My tongue felt thick and there was an ache across my shoulders. I staggered into the bathroom where I could duck myself under a cold shower whose stinging chill would wash away the dream.

I glanced at the clock, seeing that the morning had come and gone, leaving me only the afternoon and night. I picked up the phone, asked for long distance, then had myself connected with the hospital outside the city. I hung on for ten minutes waiting for the doctor, told him who I was when he came on and asked him how she was.

The doctor held his hand over the receiver and his voice was a slight mumble of sound. Then: "Yes, Mr. Hammer, I can talk now. The patient has passed the crisis and in my opinion she will live."

"Has she talked, doc?"

"She was conscious a few minutes but she said nothing, nothing at all. There are quite a few people waiting to hear her words." I sensed the change in his voice. "They are police, Mr. Hammer . . . and Federal men."

"I figured they'd be there. Have you said anything?"

"No. I rather believe that you told me the truth, especially since seeing those Federal men. I told them I received an anonymous call to go to the cabin and when I did I found her."

"Good. I can say thanks but it won't mean much. Give me three days and you can say what you like if it hasn't already been explained."

"I understand."

"Is Mr. Brighton there?"

"He has been here since the girl was identified. He seems considerably upset. We had to give him a sedative."

"Just how upset is he?"

"Enough to justify medical attention . . . which he won't have."

"I see. All right, doctor, I'll call you again. Let me have those three days."

"Three days, Mr. Hammer. You may have less. Those Federal men are viewing me somewhat suspiciously." We said our good-bys and hung up. Then I went out and ate breakfast.

I got dressed and went straight to the office. Velda had left a note in her typewriter saying that she had taken the morning plane out and for me to be careful. I pulled the sheet out of the roller and tore it up. There was no mail to look at so I gave Pat a ring and caught him just as he was coming in from lunch.

He said, "Hello, Mike. What's new?"

If I told him he would have cut my throat. "Nothing much. I wanted to speak to somebody so I called. What're you doing?"

"Right now I have to go downtown. I have to see the medical examiner and he's out on a case. A suicide, I think. I'm going to meet him there and if you feel like coming along you're welcome."

"Well, I don't feel like it, but I will. Be down in a few minutes. We'll use my car."

"Okay, but shake it up."

I dumped a pack of Luckies out of the carton in my desk and shoved it in my pocket, went downstairs and took off for Pat's. He was waiting for me on the curb, talking earnestly to a couple of uniformed cops. He waved, made a final point to the cops and crossed the street.

"Somebody steal your marbles, Mike? You don't look happy."

"I'm not. I didn't get but eleven hours' sleep."

"Gosh, you poor guy. That must hurt. If you can keep awake, drive down to the foot of Third Avenue. How're you making out with Lee?"

"I'll have a definite report for him in a couple of days."

"Negative?"

I shrugged.

Pat looked at me querulously. "That's a hell of a note. What else could it be?"

"Positive."

Pat got mad. "Do you think Oscar left something behind him, Mike? By damn, if he did I want to know about it!"

"Simmer down. I'm checking every angle I know of and when my report is made you'll be able to depend on its answer. If Oscar left one thing that could frame Lee I'll be sure nobody sees it who shouldn't see it. That's the angle I'm worried about. A smear on Lee now will be fatal . . . and Pat, there's a lot of wrong guys out to smear him. If you only knew."

"I will know soon, sonny boy. I've already had a few initial reports myself and it seems that your name has cropped up pretty frequently."

"I get around," I said.

"Yeah." He relaxed into a silence he didn't break until I saw the morgue wagon and a prowl ahead of me. "Here's the place. Stop behind the car."

We hopped out and one of the cops saluted Pat and told him the medical examiner was still upstairs. Pat lugged his brief case along and met him on the stairs. I stood in the background while they rambled along about something and Pat handed him a manila folder. The M.E. tucked it under his arm and said he'd take care of it.

Pat waved his thumb toward the top of the stairs. "What is it this time?"

"Another suicide. Lieutenant Barner is on the case. Some old duck took the gas pipe. They're always doing it in this neighborhood. Go up and take a look."

"I see enough of that stuff. Let Barner handle it."

He would have followed the M.E. down the stairs if I hadn't been curious enough to step up to the landing and peer in the door. Pat came up behind me and laughed. "Curious?"

"Can't help it."

"Sure. Then let's go in and see somebody who died by their own hand instead of yours."

"That's not funny, pal. Can it." Pat laughed again and walked in.

The guy was a middle-aged average man. He had a shock of white hair and a peculiar expression and color that come from breathing too much gas. He stunk of whisky and lay in a heap on the floor with his head partially propped up against the cushioned leg of a chair.

Barner was slipping into his coat. "Damn good thing there wasn't a pilot light on that stove. Would have blown the block to bits."

Pat knelt down and took a close look at the body. "How long has he been dead?"

"Few hours, at least. There hasn't been anybody home in this building all morning. The landlady came in around noon and smelt the gas. The door was closed, but not locked, and she smashed a couple of windows out and called a doctor. There wasn't anything he could do so he called us."

"Any note?"

"Nah. The guy was tanked up. He probably got disgusted with himself and turned on the gas. He used to be an actor. Name's Jenkins, Harvey Robinson Jenkins. The landlady said he was pretty good about thirty years ago, a regular matinee idol. He dropped into character parts, got wiped out when vaudeville went out and picked up a few bucks working in small road shows now and then."

I looked around the room and took stock of his things. There was a good leather chair by the window and a new floor lamp, but the rest of the furnishings had lost their shape and luster with age. There were two rooms, a combination sitting-room-bedroom and a kitchenette. A stack of old theater posters were neatly stacked behind the bed and a new military kit decorated the top of the dresser. The kitchen was big enough to hold one person at a time. A faint odor of gas still hung up high and clung to the curtains. The refrigerator didn't work, but then it didn't have to because it was empty. A jar of jam was on the table next to an empty bottle of whisky. There were a dozen other empties under the table in a cardboard carton.

So this is death. This is the way people die if you don't help them. He was on the long road and glad of it. Too bad he had to leave his most prized possessions behind. The make-up kit was old and battered, but it was clean, unlike everything else, and the tubes and jars inside it were all neatly arranged and labeled. The mirror fastened to the back of the lid was polished clear by a careful hand. I could picture the little guy sitting there night after night playing all the great roles of history, seeing his hand transform him to the glories of his youth.

They were taking the body out in the basket when the landlady came in to see that that was all they took out. Barner said so long and left us watching the procession down the stairs. The landlady was a chubby woman whose scraggly hair fell down past her ears. Her hands were calloused and red from work and she kept rubbing them together as though they were cold.

She turned to me, clucking through her teeth. "There you see the evil of drink, young man. I lost me two husbands that way and now I lose a boarder."

"Tough. Did he owe you any money?"

"No, not one red cent. Oh, he was an honorable one was Mr. Jenkins. Lived here over three years he did but always paid his rent somehow. Too bad he got that inheritance. It was too much for him who never had any real money. He spent it all on drink and now look at him."

"Yeah."

"Well, I warned him, you can't say I didn't try. He was always making those speeches like an actor does and he told me that drink was food for the soul. Food for the soul! He never went hungry then."

Pat grunted, anxious to leave. "Let that be a lesson to you, Mike." He looked at the landlady pointedly. "How long was he on that binge?"

"Oh, for quite a while. Let me see, the letter with the money came a week after the Legion Parade. That was a Wednesday, the 13th. Yes, that's it, a week later he got the money. He paid me the three months he owed me and for two more months in advance, then he started drinking. I never did see a man drink so much. Every night he'd get carried in still mumbling one of them silly parts of his and messing up my floor."

Pat nodded thoughtfully. "See, Mike, that's what you're heading for. An untimely end."

"Nuts, I don't drink that much. Anyway, I'll shoot myself before I try to get charged up on gas. Come on, let's get out of here."

The landlady showed us to the door and watched from the stoop as we pulled away. I hunched behind the wheel when I began thinking of the old coot who took the easy way out.

I thought about it for a long time.

I let Pat out at his office, found a saloon that was half empty and perched on a stool where I could think about it some more. The rows of whisky bottles behind the bar gleamed with reflected light. They were like women. Bait. They lured you in where you forgot what you were doing then sprang the trap and kicked you out.

The bartender filled my glass again, scooping up the rest of my change. I watched myself in the back mirror, wondering if I was as ugly to others as I was to myself. I grinned and the bartender scowled my way. I scowled and the bartender started grinning because my scowl isn't as pretty as most. I swirled the drink around in my glass, slopping it over the top so I could make patterns on the bar.

I made rings, ovals, faces, then overlaid the whole picture with a bridge that towered high at both ends. I stared at the hump in the middle and drained the glass in a hurry to get my mind off it.

A lot of it had fallen into place, piece by piece. Things I didn't see before were suddenly clear. It was a gigantic puzzle that only started here in Manhattan . . . the rest of it reached down to Washington, across to San Francisco, then on across the ocean. And onward still until it encompassed the world and came back to where it started.

It was a picture of hate, terror and death that had no equal in history and it was here with us now. I was the only one who could see it. There were still parts of the puzzle missing, but it had a broad, recognizable outline now. I could make up parts that would fit, but that wouldn't do. *I had to know. I had to be sure!*

This time I wasn't dealing in murder, I was dealing in war!

It was a curious puzzle that had two solutions. Every part could fit in different places, fooling you into thinking you had it. They were clever, I thought. They were clever, crafty, cunning, anything you wanted to call it.

They had a slogan that the end justified the means.

They would kill to accomplish a purpose.

They would wreck everything to gain their ends, even if they had to build again on the wreckage.

They were here and they were smart as hell. Even the Nazis were like schoolchildren as compared to them.

But that was the catch. They were smart . . . for them! I could laugh now and think rings around them all because I was smarter than the best they could offer. Torture, Death, and Lies were their brothers, but I had dealt with those triplets many times myself. They weren't strangers to me. I gave them my orders and they took them because they had to.

I was a ruthless bastard with a twisted mind who could look on death and find it pleasant. I could break an arm or smash in a face because it was easier that way than asking questions. I could out-fox the fox with a line of reasoning that laughed at the truth because I was the worst of the lot and never did deserve to live. That's what that damned judge thought anyway.

This time I got back in the car and drove over to the building that had the radio antenna projecting up from the roof. There were two police cars parked in front of it and I nodded to the drivers. For once I was glad to have been seen around so much with Pat. I went in and leaned on the railing that separated the room and waited until the cop in the faded alpaca coat and the eyeshade came over to me.

He nodded too.

I said, "Hello, George. I need a favor done."

"Sure, Mike. That is, if I can do it."

"You keep a record of incoming calls, don't you?"

"Yeah, why?"

"Look one up for me. A few days ago a New York prowl car crossed the George Washington bridge." I gave him the date and the approximate time. "See if it was on a call."

He went back to a stall where he rummaged around in a filing cabinet. When he returned he carried a sheet, reading from it. He looked up and raised his eyeshade farther on his forehead. "Here it is. Unidentified girl called and asked to have a police car meet her. I think I remember this one. She was in a hurry and instead of giving her address she said on the walk of the bridge. A car was dispatched to see what went on and called in that it was a wild-goose chase."

"That's all?"

"Yeah. Anything to it?"

"I don't know yet. Thanks a lot, George."

"Sure, Mike, any time. So long."

I went out and sat in the car with a cigarette drooping from my lips. Unidentified girl. That car on the bridge wasn't there by chance. I had just missed things. Too bad, too damn bad in one way that the boys in the car had gotten there late. The weather, no doubt. Then again it was lucky they didn't make it.

The engine came to life under my feet and I drove away from the curb. I took the notebook from my pocket and thumbed the pages while I was stalled in traffic, picking up Paula Riis's address from the jumble of notes. I hoped I had it right, because I had jotted it down after coming from Pat's the time he had thrown her identity at me.

It was a number in the upper Forties just off Eighth Avenue, a four-story affair with three apartments above a shoddy beauty parlor that took up the first floor. A sedan with United States Post Office Department inscribed on the door was double parked outside it. I found a place to leave my heap and got back just as two men came down the stairs and got into the car. I had seen the taller guy before; he was a postal inspector.

A dark, swarthy woman stood in the door with her hands on chunky hips muttering to herself. I took the steps two at a time and said hello to her.

She looked me up and down first. "Now what you want? You not from Post Office."

I looked past her shoulder into the vestibule and knew why those men had been here. A good-sized rectangle had been torn out of the wall. The mailbox that had been there had been ripped out by the roots and the marks of the crowbar that did it still showed in the shattered lath and plaster.

I got that cold feeling again, of being just a little bit too late. I palmed my buzzer and held it out where she could see it.

"Oh, you the police. You come about the room. Whassa matter with other police? He see everything. These crooks! When that girl comes back she be one mad cookie, you bet!"

"That's right, I came about the room. Where is it?"

"Upstairs, what's left of it. Now there's nothing but junk. Thassall, just junk. Go look."

I went and looked. I saw the same thing that had happened to Charlie Moffit's room. This was a little worse because there was more to it. I cursed softly and backed out of the room. I cursed because I was pleased that the room *was* like Charlie Moffit's room, a room ripped apart by a search that didn't have an end. They were still looking. They tore the room up then stole the mailbox because they thought that Charlie had mailed his girl friend the stuff.

Then I stopped cursing because I knew then that they did have it after all. Charlie mailed the stuff and it lay in the mailbox because she was dead. They couldn't get it out so they took the whole works. This time I cursed because I was mad, mad as hell.

I made a circuit of the room, kicking at the pieces with a frenzied futility. Clothes that had been ripped apart at the seams were everywhere. The furniture was broken, disemboweled and scattered across the floor. The bottom had been taken out of the phone and lay beneath the stand by the window. I picked it up, turned it over then chucked it away.

They had come in through the window and gouged hunks out of the sill when they pried up the sash. I threw it up and looked around, saying damn to myself because it had been so easy. There was an overturned ash can on the ground below. They had stepped on that, then on to the roof of the extension below and right into the room.

Too bad Mr. M.V.D. couldn't have tripped over the phone line and broken his lousy neck. I picked up the strand of wire that ran out the window to the pole and switched it out of the way. It was slack, too damn slack. I saw why in a minute. The insulator that had held it to the wall had been pulled out. I climbed out on the roof and ran my hand along the wire and the answer was in the slit that was in the insulation.

Somebody had a tap on that wire and when they pulled it off they yanked too hard and it came right off the wall. Damn! Damn it all to hell and back again! I climbed back in the room and slammed the window shut, still swearing to myself.

The woman still stood in the doorway. "You see, you see?" Her voice went higher on each word. "These damn crooks. Nobody is safe. What for are the police? What that girl going to say, eh? You know! She give me hell, you betcha. She was all paid up, too. Now whatcha think?"

"Don't get excited. Whoever searched her room took the mailbox too. They were looking for a letter."

She made a sour mouth. "Huh. They don't get it, I tell you that, for sure. She's a lose her key a month ago and I always get her mail personal. The postman he's give it to me every day and I take it inside."

My heart hammered against my ribs and I heard it send the blood driving into my head. I licked my lips to get the words out. "Maybe I better take it all along then. She can call for it when she returns."

She squinted, then bobbed her head. "That is good. I don't have to worry no more about it. From now on till I get a new mailbox I have to take everybody's mail anyhow. Come inside, I give it to you."

We went into the beauty parlor on the first floor and I waited with my hat in my hand. She came back with a handful of envelopes and one of them was a heavy job stuffed so full the flap had torn a little. I thanked her and left.

Just like that.

How simple could it get?

The murder and the wreckage that had been caused by this one fat envelope, and she drops it in my hand just like that. No trouble. No sneaking around with a gun in your hand. No tight spots that left you shaken and trembling. She hands it to me and I take it and leave.

Isn't that the way life is? You fight and struggle to get something and suddenly you're there at the end and there's nothing left to fight for any longer.

I threw the works in the glove compartment and drove back to my office. From force of habit I locked the door before I sat down to see what it was all about. There were nine letters and the big one. Of the nine three were bills, four were from female friends and had nothing to say, one was an answer to a letter she sent an employment agency and the other enclosed a Communist Party pamphlet. I threw it in the waste basket and opened the main one.

They were photostats, ten in all, both negatives and positives, on extra thin paper. They were photos of a maze of symbols, diagrams and meaningless words, but there was something about them that practically cried out their extreme importance. They weren't for a mind like mine and I knew it.

I folded them up into a compact square and took them to the lamp on the wall. It was a tricky little job that came apart in the middle and had been given to me by a friend who dabbled in magic. At one time a bird flew out of the hidden compartment when you snapped the light on and scared the hell out of you. I stuck the photostats in there and shut it again.

There was an inch of sherry left on the bottom of the bottle in my desk and I put the mouth to my lips.

It was almost over. I had come to the pause before the end. There was little left to do but sort the parts and make sure I had them straight. I sat down again, pulling the phone over in front of me. I dialed headquarters and asked for Pat.

He had left for the weekend.

The next time I dialed Lee Deamer's office. The blonde at the switchboard was still chewing gum and threw the connection over to his secretary. She said, "I'm sorry, but Mr. Deamer has left for Washington."

"This is Mike Hammer. I was there once before. I'd like to get a call in to him."

"Oh, yes, Mr. Hammer. He's registered at the Lafayette. You can call him there. However, you had better call before six because he's speaking at a dinner meeting tonight."

"I'll call him now, and thanks."

I got long distance, gave the number and she told me the lines were all busy and I would have to wait. I hung up and went to the filing cabinet where I had the remains of another bottle of sherry stashed away. There was a box of paper cups with it and I put the makings on my desk and settled back to enjoy the wait.

After the third half-cup of sherry I snapped the radio on and caught the broadcast. The boy with the golden voice was snapping out the patter in a tone so excited that he must have been holding on to the mike to stay on his feet. It was all about the stolen documents. Suspicions were many and clues were nil. The F.B.I. had every available man on the case and the police of every community had pledged to help in every way.

He went off and a serious-voiced commentator took his place. He told the nation of the calamity that had befallen it. The secret of our newest, most powerful weapon was now, most likely, in the hands of agents of an unfriendly power. He told of the destruction that could be wrought, hinted at the continuance of the cold war with an aftermath of a hotter one. He spoke and his voice trembled with the rage and fear he tried so hard to control.

Fifteen minutes later another commentator came on with a special bulletin that told of all ports being watched, the roundup of suspected aliens. The thing that caused the roundup was still as big a mystery as ever, but the search had turned up a lot of minor things that never would have been noticed. A government clerk was being held incommunicado. A big shot labor leader had hanged himself. A group of Communists had staged a demonstration in Brooklyn with the usual scream of persecution and had broken some windows. Twenty of them were in the clink.

I sat back and laughed and laughed. The world was in an uproar when the stuff was safe as hell not five feet away from me. The guardians of our government were jumping through hoops because the people demanded to know why the most heavily guarded secret we ever had could be swiped so easily. There were shake-ups from the top to bottom and the rats were scurrying for cover, pleading for mercy. Investigations were turning up Reds in the damnedest spots imaginable and the senators and congressmen who recommended them for the posts were on the hot spots in their bailiwicks. Two had already sent in resignations.

Oh, it was great. Something was getting done that should have been done years ago. The heat was on and the fire was burning a lot of pants. The music I had on the radio was interrupted every five minutes now with special newscasts that said the people were getting control of the situation at last.

Of the people, for the people, by the people. We weren't so soft after all. We got pushed too far once too often and the backs were up and teeth bared.

What were the Commies doing! They must be going around in circles. The thing that would have tipped the balance back to them again had been in their hands and they'd dropped it. Was the M.V.D. out taking care of those who had been negligent? Probably. Very probably. Pork-Pie Hat would have himself a field day. They were the only ones who knew where those documents *weren't*. Our own government knew where they started to go and still thought they were in their hands. I was the only one who knew where they *were*.

Not five feet away. Safe as pie, I thought.

The phone rang and I picked it up. The operator said, "I have your party, sir."

I said thanks, waited for the connection and heard Lee saying, "Hello, hello . . ."

"Mike Hammer, Lee."

"Yes, Mike, how are you?"

"Fine. I hear Washington is in an uproar."

"Quite. You can't imagine what it's like. They tell me the hall is filled to the rafters already, waiting to hear the speeches. I've never seen so many reporters in my life."

"Going to give 'em hell tonight?"

"I'll do my best. I have an important topic to discuss. Was there something special you wanted, Mike?"

"Yeah, sort of. I just wanted to tell you that I found it."

"It?"

"What Oscar left behind. I found it."

His voice held a bitter ring. "I knew it, I knew it! I knew he'd do something like that. Mike . . . is it bad?"

"Oh no. In fact it's pretty good. Yeah, pretty good."

He paused, and when he spoke again he sounded tired. "Remember what I told you, Mike. It's in your hands. Authenticate what you found, and if you believe that it would be better to publish the facts, then make them public."

I laughed lightly. "Not this, Lee. It isn't something you can print in a paper. It isn't anything that you nor Pat nor I expected to find. It doesn't tie you into a damn thing so you can blast 'em tonight and make it good because what I have can push you right up there where you can do a good housecleaning job."

The surprise and pleasure showed in his voice. "That *is* fine news, Mike. When can I see it?"

"When will you be back in New York?"

"Not before Monday night."

"It'll keep. I'll see you then."

I pushed the phone back across the desk and started working on the remainder of the sherry. I finished it in a half-hour and closed up the office. It was Saturday night and time to play. I had to wait until Velda came back before I made my decision. I ambled up Broadway and turned into a bar for a drink. The place was packed and noisy, except when the news bulletin came on. At seven o'clock they turned on the TV and all heads angled to watch it. They were relaying in the pics of the dinner in Washington that was to be followed by the speeches. The screen was blurred, but the sound was loud and clear.

I had a good chance to watch Mr. and Mrs. Average People take in the political situation and I felt good all over again. It was no time to come up with the documents. Not yet. Let the fire stay on full for a while. Let it scorch and purify while it could.

The bartender filled my glass and I leaned forward on my elbows to hear Lee when he spoke.

He gave them a taste of hell. He used names and quotations and pointed to the big whiskers in the Kremlin as the brother of the devil. He threw the challenge in the faces of the people and they accepted it with cheers and applause that rocked the building.

I shouted the way I felt louder than anybody and had another drink.

At midnight I walked back to my car and drove home slowly, my mind miles away from my body. Twice I patted the .45 under my arm and out of force of habit I kept a constant check on the cars behind me.

I put the car in the garage, told the attendant to service it fully and went out the side door that led to the street. When I looked both ways and was satisfied that I wasn't going to run into another ambush I stepped out to the sidewalk and walked to my building.

Before I went upstairs I checked the little panel of lights behind the desk in the lobby. It was a burglar alarm and one of the lights was connected to the windows and doors in my apartment. They were all blank so I took the stairs up and shoved the key in the lock.

For safety's sake I went through the place and found it as empty as when I left it. Maybe Pork-Pie was afraid of a trap. Maybe he was waiting to get me on the street. He and the others had the best reason in the world to get me now. It wouldn't be too long before they figured out where the documents went to, and that was the moment I was hoping for.

I wanted them, every one of the bastards. I wanted them all to myself so I could show the sons-of-bitches what happened when they tried to play rough with somebody who likes that game himself!

The late news broadcast was on and I listened for further developments. There weren't any. I shoved the .45 under my pillow and rolled into the sack.

CHAPTER 10

I slept all day Sunday. At six-fifteen P.M. I got up to answer the persistent ringing of my doorbell and a Western Union messenger handed me a telegram. He got a buck for his persistence and I went into the living room where I opened it up.

The telegram was from Velda. It was very brief, saying the mission was accomplished and she was carrying the papers out on the first plane. I folded the yellow sheet and stuck it in the pocket of my coat that was draped on the back of the chair.

I had a combination meal, sent down for the papers and read them in bed. When I finished I slept again and didn't wake up until twelve hours later. The rain was beating against the windows with a hundred tiny fingers and the street was drenched with an overflow too great to be carried off by the sewers at the end of the block.

For a few minutes I stood at the window and looked out into the murk of the morning, not aware of the people that scurried by on the sidewalks below, or of the cars whose tires made swishing sounds on the wet pavement. Across the street, the front of the building there wavered as the water ran down the glass, assuming the shape of a face molded by ghostly hands. The face had eyes like two berries on a bush and they turned their stare on me.

This is it, Judge. Here is your rain of purity. You're a better forecaster than I thought. Now, of all times, it should rain. Cold, clear rain that was washing away the scum and the filth and pulling it into the sewer. It's here and you're waiting for me to step out into it and be washed away, aren't you? I could play it safe and stay where I am, but you know I won't. I'm me, Mike Hammer, and I'll be true to form. I'll go down with the rest of the scum.

Sure, Judge, I'll die. I've been so close to death that this time the scythe can't miss me. I've dodged too often, now I've lost the quick-step timing I had that made me duck in time. You noticed it and Pat noticed it . . . I've changed, and now I notice it myself. I don't care any more.

The hell of it is, Judge . . . your question won't get answered. You'll never know why I was endowed with the ability to think and move fast enough to keep away from the man with the reaper. I kept breaking his hour-glass and dulling his blade and he couldn't do a thing about it.

Your rain of purity has come, and out there in it is the grim specter who is de-termined that this time he will not miss. He'll raise his vicious scythe and swing at me with all the fury of his madness and I'll go down, but that one wild swing will take along a lot of others before it cuts me in half.

Sorry, Judge, so sorry you'll never know the answer. I was curious myself. I wanted to know the answer too. It's been puzzling me a long, long time.

I showered and dressed, packing the automatic away in the oiled leather holster under my arm. When I finished I called long distance and was connected with the hospital. Again I was lucky and got the doctor while he was there. I told him my name and that was enough.

"Miss Brighton is out of danger," he said. "For some reason she is under police guard."

"Studious young men?"

"Yes."

"How about her father?"

"He visits her daily. His own doctor is prescribing for her."

"I see. My time is up, you know. You can talk if you like."

"For some reason I prefer not to, Mr. Hammer. I still don't under-stand, but I still believe that there is more to this than I can see. Miss Brighton asked me if you had called and I repeated our conversation. She has taken the same attitude of silence."

"Thanks, doc. It's going to be rough when it starts, but thanks. Tell Miss Brighton I was asking for her."

"I will. Good day."

I put the phone back and shrugged into my raincoat. Downstairs I got my car out of the garage and backed out into the rain. The wind-shield wipers were little demons working furiously, fighting to keep me from being purified. I drove downtown hoping to see Pat, but he had called in that his car was stuck somewhere along the highway and he might not make it in at all.

The morning went by without my noticing its passing. When my stomach tightened I went in and had lunch. I bought a paper and parked the car to read it through. The headlines hadn't changed much. There were pages devoted to the new aspect of the cold war; pages given to the coming election, pages that told of the shake-up in Washington, and of the greater shake-up promised by the candidates running for election.

Lee had given 'em hell, all right. The editorial quoted excerpts from his speech and carried a two-column cut of him shaking his fist at the jackals who were seeking the protection of the same government they had tried to tear down. There was another Communist demonstration, only this one was broken up by an outraged populace and ten of the Reds had landed in the hospital. The rest were sweeping out corridors in the city jail.

The rain let up, but it was only taking a breather before it came down even harder. I took advantage of the momentary lull to duck into a drugstore and put in a call to Lee's office. His secretary told me that he wasn't expected in until evening and I thanked her. I bought a fresh pack of Luckies and went back to the car and sat. I watched the rain and timed my thoughts to its intensity.

I took all the parts and let them drop, watching to see how they fit in place. They were all there now, every one. I could go out any time and show that picture around and anybody could tell that it was a big red flag with a star and a hammer and sickle. I could show it to them but I'd have to have the last piece of proof I needed and I'd have that when Velda got back. I went over it time after time until I was satisfied, then I reached for a butt.

There was only one left. I had just bought a pack and there was only one left. My watch was a round little face that laughed at me for thinking the afternoon away and I stared at it, amazed that the night had shifted in around the rain and I hadn't noticed it. I got out and went back to the same drugstore and looked up the number of the terminal.

A sugar-coated voice said that all the planes were on schedule despite the rain and the last one from the Midwest had landed at two o'clock. I smacked my hand against my head for letting time get away from me and called the office. Velda didn't answer so I hung up. I was about to call her apartment when I remembered that she'd probably be plenty tired and curled up in the sack, but she said she'd leave anything she had in the lamp if I wasn't in the office when she got in.

I started the car up and the wipers went back into action. The rain of purity was starting to give up and here I was still warm and dry. For how long?

The lights were on in the office and I practically ran in. I yelled, "Hey, Velda!" The smile I had ready died away because she wasn't there.

She *had* been there, though. I smelled the faintest trace of the perfume she used. I went right to the lamp and opened the little compartment. She had laid it right on top of the other stuff for me.

I pulled it out and spread it across my desk, feeling the grin come back slowly as I read the first few lines.

It was done. Finished. I had it all ready to wrap up nice and legal now. I could call Pat and the studious-looking boys with the F.B.I. badges and drop it in their laps. I could sit back in a ringside seat and watch the whole show and laugh at the judge because this time I was free and clear, with my hands clean of somebody's blood. The story would come out and I'd be a hero. The next time I stepped into that court of law and faced the little judge his voice would be quiet and his words more carefully chosen because I was able to prove to the world that I wasn't a bloodthirsty kill-happy bastard with a mind warped by a war of too many dawns and dusks laced by the crisscrossed patterns of bullets. I was a normal guy with normal instincts and maybe a temper that got a little out of hand at times, but was still under control when I wanted it that way.

Hell, Pat should be back now. I'll let him get the credit for it. He won't like it, but he'll have to do it. I reached for the phone.

That's when I saw the little white square of cardboard that had been sitting there in front of me all the time. I picked it up, scowling at the brief typewritten message. CALL LO 3-8099 AT EXACTLY NINE P.M. That was all. The other side was blank.

I didn't get it. Velda was the only one to have been here and she would have left more of an explanation, at least. Besides, we had memo pads for stuff like this. I frowned again and threw it back on the desk. It was ten to eight now. Hell, I wasn't going to wait another hour. I dialed the number and heard the phone ring a dozen times before I hung up.

A nasty taste was in my mouth. My shoulders kept hunching up under my coat as if I were cold. I went to the outer office to see if she had left a note in her desk typewriter and found nothing.

It wasn't right. Not at a moment like this. Nothing else could come up now. Hell, I was on my way to being a hero. The door of the washroom was standing open a little and I went to close it. The light from the lamp on the wall darted in the crack and bounced back at me with bright sparkle. I shoved the door open and every muscle in my body pulled tight as a bowstring and my breath caught in my throat.

There beside the faucet was Velda's ring . . . the sapphire ring I had given her and her wrist watch!

Velda wasn't here but her ring was and no girl is going to go off

and forget her ring! No girl will wash her hands and not dry them, either . . . But Velda apparently had, for there was no crumpled paper
towel in the basket under the sink!

Somehow I staggered back to my chair and sat down, the awful realization of it hitting me hard. I buried my face in my hands and said,
"Oh, God . . . oh, God!" I knew what had happened now . . . *they* had
her! They walked in on her and took her away.

I thought I was clever. I thought they'd try for me. But they *were* clever
when the chips were down and now they had something they could
trade. That's what they'd say . . . trade. Ha, that was a laugh. They'd take
the documents and when I asked them to give her back I'd get a belly full
of slugs. Nice trade. A stupid ass like me ought to get shot anyway.

Goddamn 'em anyway! Why couldn't they act like men and fight
with me! Why did they have to pick on women! The dirty yellow bastards were afraid to tangle with me so they decided to do it the easy way.
They knew the score, they knew I'd have to play ball. They seemed to
know a lot of things.

All right, you conniving little punks, I'll play ball, but I'm going to
make up a lot of rules you never heard of. You think I'm cornered and
it'll be a soft touch. Well, you won't be playing with a guy who's a hero.
You'll be up against a guy with a mind gone rotten and a lust for killing!
That's the way I was and that's the way I like it!

I grabbed the phone and dialed Pat's home number. When I got him
I said hello and didn't give him a chance to interrupt me. "I need a favor
as fast as you can do it, kid. Find out where the phone with the number
Longacre 3-8099 is located and call me right back. Shake it because I
need it right away."

Pat let out a startled answer that I cut off by slamming the phone
back. Five minutes later the phone rang and I picked it up.

"What goes on with you, Mike? That number is a pay station in the
Times Square subway station."

"Fine," I answered, "that's all I need to know. See you later."

"Mike . . . hey . . ." I cut him off again and picked up my coat.

They thought they were smart but they forgot I had a fast brain and a
lot of connections. Maybe they thought I wouldn't take the chance.

I was downstairs and in the car like a shot. Going up Broadway I pulled
out all the stops and forgot there was such a thing as a red light. When I
turned off Broadway onto Times Square I saw a patrolman standing in
front of the subway entrance idly swinging his stick in his hands.

Tonight was my night and I was going to play it all the way to the hilt. I yanked out the wallet I had taken from that overturned car the other night, plucked the F.B.I. card from the pocket and fitted it into mine. The cop was coming out into the rain to tell me I couldn't park there when I stepped out and shoved the wallet under his nose.

I didn't let him have more than a peek at it, but it was enough. I said, "Stay here and watch that car. I don't want it gone when I come back."

He drew himself all the way up with a look that only public servants old in the service can get and passed me a snappy salute. With the headlines blaring from all the papers he didn't have to ask questions to know what was up. "I'll take care of it," he shot back.

I ran down the stairs and slipped a dime in the turnstile. I had fifteen minutes to find the right booth, fifteen short minutes. I made a tour of the place, poking my head into the empties hoping the one I was looking for wouldn't be occupied.

It wasn't. I found it over near the steps that led to the B.M.T. line, the last one on the end of five booths. I stepped into one and shut the door. The light above my head was too damn bright, but one crack with the nose of the .45 took care of that. I lifted the receiver off the hook without dropping a nickel in and started a conversation with an imaginary person on an imaginary phone.

At five minutes to nine he walked up to the end booth, obviously ignoring the others, and closed the door. I let the minutes tick off until the hands of my watch were at right angles to each other, then shoved a nickel in the slot and dialed LO 3-8099.

It rang just once. "Yes?"

I forced a bluff into my voice, keeping it low. "This is Mike Hammer. Who the hell are you and what's this business with the card?"

"Ah, yes, Mr. Hammer. You got our card. That is very fortunate indeed. Need I tell you who is speaking?"

"You damn well better, friend."

"No, certainly not a friend. Just the opposite, I would think. I'm calling about a matter of documents you have, Mr. Hammer. They're very important documents, you know. We have taken a hostage to insure their safe delivery to us."

"What. . . ?"

"Please, Mr. Hammer. I'm speaking about your very lovely secretary. A very obstinate woman. I think we can force her to talk if you refuse, you know."

"You bastard!"

"Well?"

My voice changed pitch and stuttered into the mouthpiece. "What can I say? I know when I'm licked. You . . . can have them."

"I was sure you'd see the light, Mr. Hammer. You will take those documents to the Pennsylvania Station on Thirty-fourth Street and deposit them in one of the pay lockers at the end of the waiting room. You will then take the key and walk about on the streets outside until someone says, 'Wonderful night, friend,' and give that person the key. Keep your hands in plain sight and be absolutely alone. I don't think I have to warn you that you will be under constant observation by certain people who will be armed."

"And the girl . . . Velda?" I asked.

"Provided you do as you are told, and we receive the documents, the girl shall be released, of course."

"Okay. What time do I do all this?"

"Midnight, Mr. Hammer. A fitting hour, don't you think?"

He hung up without waiting for an answer. I grinned and watched him squirm out of the booth, a guy who fitted his voice to perfection. Short, soft and fat, wearing clothes that tried without success to make him look tall, hard and slim.

I grinned again and gave him a good lead, then climbed out of the booth and stayed on his tail. He hesitated at the passages, settled on the route that led up the northwest corner of the block and started up the stairs. My grin like to have split my face open. The famous Hammer luck was riding high, wide and handsome. I could call his shots before he made them and I knew it.

When he reached the street I brushed by him and gave him the elbow for luck. He was so intent upon waving to a cab that he never gave me a tumble. I waited for him to get in then started my car. The cop waved me off with his night stick and I was on my way.

Three hours before the deadline.

How much time was that? Not much, yet plenty when it counted. The cab in front of me weaved around the traffic and I stayed right with it. I could see the back of his head in the rear window and I didn't give a hoot whether or not he turned around.

He didn't. He was so sure that I was on the end of the stick that it never occurred to him that he was being tailed. He was going to get that stick up the tail himself when the time came.

So the judge was right all while. I could feel the madness in my brain eating its way through my veins, chewing the edges of my nerves raw, leaving me something that resembled a man and that was all. *The judge had been right!* There *had* been too many of those dusks and dawns; there *had* been pleasure in all that killing, an obscene pleasure that froze your face in a grin even when you were charged with fear. Like when I cut down that Jap with his own machete and laughed like hell while I made slices of his scrawny body, then went on to do the same thing again because it got to be fun. The little bastards wanted my hide and I gave them a hard time when they tried to take it. Sure, my mind was going rotten even then. I remember the ways the guys used to look at me. You'd think I had fangs. *And it hung on and rotted even further!* How long had it been since I had taken my face out of the ground? How long had it been since they handed me the paper that said it was over and we could go back to being normal people again? And since . . . how many had died while I backed up the gun? Now who was I trying to fool— me? I enjoyed that killing, every bit of it. I killed because I had to and I killed things that needed killing. But that wasn't the point. *I enjoyed killing those things and I knew the judge was right!* I was rotten right through and I knew that at that moment my face was twisted out of shape into a grin that was half sneer and my heart beat fast because it was nice sitting back there with a rod under my arm and somebody was going to hurt pretty quick now, then die. And it might even be me and I didn't give a good damn one way or another.

I tried to figure out where the hell we were. We had passed over a viaduct and a few other things that were vague outlines, but I couldn't tell where we were. If I didn't see the name on the movie house I would have been screwed up, but I caught it in time along with the smell of the river and knew we were some place in Astoria heading down toward the water where the people gave way to the rats and the trash that littered the shore.

There wasn't much more to the block. I cut my lights and drifted in to the curb, snatching the keys out of the ignition as I opened the door. Ahead of me the tail light of the cab was a red dot getting smaller and for one second I thought I had been too soon.

The red dot stopped moving away from me.

Of all the fates who were out for my skin, only one backed me up. It was a lovely fate that turned over a heap and spilled the pair of studious-looking boys out, the ones who had the F.B.I. cards and that gorgeous black tommy gun that was still in the trunk of my car. I held the lid open and yanked it out, shucking the case on the pavement. It nestled in my hands like a woman, loaded and cocked, with two spare clips that made a pleasant weight in my pocket.

I got in close to the buildings and took off at a half-trot. A drunk watched me go by, then scurried back into his doorway. The dot up front disappeared, turned into two headlights on dim and came back and past me.

I ran faster. I ran like a guy with three feet and reached the corner in time to see the guy angling up the rutted street that paralleled the river.

How nice it is when it gets dark. It's all around you, a black coat that hides the good and the bad, and lets you stay shouting distance behind somebody else and never gives you away. My little man stepped right along as if he knew where he was going.

There weren't any houses now. There was a smell of decay, noises that didn't belong to a city. Far away the lights of cars snaked along a bridge happily unaware of this other part of New York.

Then the rain began again. The glorious rain of purity was nothing but light tears . . . the sky protesting because I was walking and thinking when I should be dead. Long dead. I spit on the ground to show what I thought of it.

My little man was gone. The constant, even grinding of his shoes in the gravel had stopped and now there was a silence that shut out all other noises, even the rain.

I was alone in the darkness and my time had come. It had to come, there was only an hour left and never time to undo it if it had all been a mistake! For about ten seconds I stood still, watching those cars in the distance. They wormed ahead, they disappeared as if going into a tunnel, emerging again many seconds later. I knew where my little man was now.

Not far off was a building. That was what stopped those lights. There was a building and I saw it when I took a dozen more steps. It was the remains of a building, anyway. Three floors staggered up from the ground in uneven rows of bricks. Only the windows on the top floors showed a few panes whole and unbroken, most likely because they were beyond a stone's throw. The rest were plastered with boards that seemed to be there to keep things in rather than out.

I was back in the jungle again. I had that feeling. There was a guy at my shoulder in deeper black than the night and he carried a scythe and a map to point out the long road. I didn't walk, I stalked and the guy stalked with me, waiting patiently for that one fatal misstep.

He was death and I knew him well. I had seen him plenty of times before and I laughed in his face because I was me, see? I was Mike Hammer and I could laugh because what did I give a damn about death? He could laugh back at me with his grisly, bony laugh, and even if we didn't make any sound at all my laugh was louder than his. Stick with me, man in black. Stick close because some customers are going to be made that should have been made a long time ago. You thought I was bad when there was a jungle around me for cover and I learned how to kill and kill and kill and walk away and remind myself that killing was nice. Yeah, you thought I was a wise guy. Stick around, old man, maybe you'll see me for the first time doing something I really enjoy. Maybe some day I'll pick on you and we'll have it out, a hot .45 against that blade of yours.

All the instincts came back. The chatter gun was slung just right for easy carrying and quick action. Without me telling it to, my hand had scooped up gobs of mud and daubed my face and hands, even blanking out the luminous dial of my watch.

The pleasure of the hunt, the wonderful knowledge that you're hot and right! The timing was there, that sense of alertness that gets bred into you when there's blood in the air. I liked it!

I stood in the shadow of the building, melting into the wall with the rain, watching the two men. One was there at the doorway, an invisible figure I sensed rather than saw. The other was coming toward me just as I planned it. It had taken a long while just to get this far. I knew without looking that the hands of my watch would be overlapping. Somewhere back in Manhattan a guy would be looking for me to call me friend. Somewhere inside Velda would be sitting, a hostage who would never talk.

The guy came nearer and I knew he had a gun in his hand. I let him come.

Now I could see him plainly. He stopped three feet away and looked back uncertainly. I had the tommy gun in one hand and the nose of the .45 in the other. I let him look back again and this time I let him see me.

No, it wasn't me he saw, it was the other guy, the one with the cowl and the scythe. I swung that gun butt so hard it made a wet smack and almost twisted out of my hand. The guy didn't have any forehead left. There was nothing but a black hole from his eyes to his hair and I was grinning. I eased him down without a sound and picked up the tommy gun. Then I started around the building.

It goes that way. One guy makes one lousy error and everybody falls into the trap. The guy at the door thought it was the other one when I walked out of the murk. He grunted the last sound he ever made because I wrapped my arm under his neck and started bending him over backwards. I had my knee in his spine, pulling him into a living bow that clawed at my hands to release the scream that sudden fear had driven into his throat.

The goddamn grin wouldn't come off my face even when I heard his spine snap and felt that sickening lurch that comes when the bow is bent too far. Two of them. A pair of bastards who had wanted to play in the Big Game. Slimy, squirmy worms who had visions of being on top where they could rule with the whip.

I went into the building with death at my shoulder and he was mad because I was giving the orders. He was waiting for the mistake he knew I'd have to make sooner or later.

My breath wasn't coming easy now. It was hot and coarse in my throat, rasping into my lungs. I stood inside the door, listening, waiting, letting my eyes use precious seconds to orient themselves to this new gloom. My watch made a mad ticking to remind me that now it had to be quick. Time, it had gone. There was nothing left!

I saw the empty packing boxes that had been smashed and left to rot. I saw the welter of machinery, glazed with rust, lying in heaps under the high, vaulted roof. Long ago it had been a factory of some sort. I wondered incongruously what had been made here. Then the smell of turpentine gave it to me. Paint. There was three hundred feet of length to it, almost that in width. I could make out the partitions of wood and brick separating it into compartments.

But I didn't have time to look through it all, not all three floors of it!

The sons-of-bitches had picked the best spot on earth, not a sound would penetrate these walls! In that maze of partitions and cubicles even the brightest beam of light that could escape would be dulled and unseen. I wanted to pull the trigger of the gun and blast the whole dump to bits and wade into the wreckage with my bare hands. I wanted to scream just like the guys outside wanted to scream and I couldn't.

Another minute to make myself cool off. Another minute to let instinct and training take over.

Another minute for my eyes to see and they picked out the path that led through the rubbish, a path I should have seen sooner because it had been deliberately made and often used. Old paint cans had been pushed aside and spilled their thick, gooey mess on the floor. The larger drums had been slop pails for left-over stuff and marked the turns in the trail.

My eyes saw it, my feet followed it. They took me around the bend and through a hall then up the stairs.

And the path that was cleared through the dirt on the floor led to the middle, then the top story. It led to rooms that reeked of turpentine so strong it almost took my breath away. It led to a corridor and another man who stepped out of the shadows to die. It led to a door that swung open easily and into a room that faced on other rooms where I was able to stand in my invisible cloak of blackness with barely the strength to hold the gun.

I stood there and looked at what I was, hearing myself say, "Good God, no, please . . . no!" I had to stand there for a moment of time that turned into eternity while I was helpless to intervene and see things my mind wanted to shut out . . . hear things my ears didn't want to hear.

For an eternal moment I had to look at them all, every one. General Osilov in a business suit leaning on his cane almost casually, an unholy leer lighting his face. My boy of the subway slobbering all over his chin, puking a little without noticing it, his hands pressed against his belly while his face was a study in obscene fascination.

And the guy in the pork-pie hat!

Velda.

She was stark naked.

She hung from the rafters overhead by a rope that chewed into her wrists, while her body twisted slowly in the single light of the electric lantern! The guy in the pork-pie hat waited until she turned to face him then brought the knotted rope around with all the strength of his arm and I heard it bite into her flesh with a sickening sound that brought her head up long enough for me to see that even the pain was dulling under the evil of this thing.

He said, "Where is it? You'll die if you don't tell me!"

She never opened her mouth. Her eyes came open, but she never opened her mouth!

Then there was only beauty to the nakedness of her body. A beauty of the flesh that was more than the sensuous curve of her hips, more than the sharp curve of breasts drawn high under the weight of her body, more than those long, full legs, more than the ebony of her hair. There was the beauty of the flesh that was the beauty of the soul and the guy in the pork-pie hat grimaced with hate and raised the rope to smash it down while the rest slobbered with the lust and pleasure of this example of what was yet to come, even drooled with the passion that was death made slow in the fulfillment of the philosophy that lived under a red flag!

And in that moment of eternity I heard the problem asked and knew the answer! I knew why I was allowed to live while others died! I knew why my rottenness was tolerated and kept alive and why the guy with the reaper couldn't catch me and I smashed through the door of the room with the tommy gun in my hands spitting out the answer at the same time my voice screamed it to the heavens!

I lived only to kill the scum and the lice that wanted to kill themselves. I lived to kill so that others could live. I lived to kill because my soul was a hardened thing that reveled in the thought of taking the blood of the bastards who made murder their business. I lived because I could laugh it off and others couldn't. I was the evil that opposed other evil, leaving the good and the meek in the middle to live and inherit the earth!

They heard my scream and the awful roar of the gun and the slugs tearing into bone and guts and it was the last they heard. They went down as they tried to run and felt their insides tear out and spray against the walls.

I saw the general's head splinter into shiny wet fragments and splatter over the floor. The guy from the subway tried to stop the bullets with his hands and dissolved into a nightmare of blue holes.

There was only the guy in the pork-pie hat who made a crazy try for a gun in his pocket. I aimed the tommy gun for the first time and took his arm off at the shoulder. It dropped on the floor next to him and I let him have a good look at it. He couldn't believe it happened. I proved it by shooting him in the belly. They were all so damned clever!

They were all so damned dead!

I laughed and laughed while I put the second clip in the gun. I knew the music in my head was going wild this time, but I was laughing too hard to enjoy it. I went around the room and kicked them over on their backs and if they had faces left I made sure they didn't. I saved the last burst for the bastard who was M.V.D. in a pork-pie hat and who looked like a kid. A college boy. He was still alive when he stared into the flame that spit out of the muzzle only an inch away from his nose.

I cut her down carefully, dressed her, cradled her in my arms like a baby and knew that I was crying. Me. I could still do that. I felt her fingers come up and touch one of the wet spots on my cheek, heard her say the three words that blessed everything I did, then I went back to the path that led out into the night that was still cold and rainy, but still free to be enjoyed. There was a soft spot on the ground where I laid her with my coat under her head while I went back to do what I had to do. I went back to the room where death had visited and walked under the rafters until I reached the pork-pie hat that lay next to the remains of the thing that wore it. I lifted his wallet out of his back pocket and flipped his coat open so I could rip the inside lining pocket out along with some shreds of the coat fabric. That was all. Except for one thing. When I went down the stairs once more I found a drum of paint whose spilled contents made a sticky flow into some empty cans. When I built up a mound of old papers around the stuff I touched a match to it, stood there until I was satisfied with its flame, then went back to Velda. Her eyes were closed and her breathing heavy. She came up in my arms and I fixed my coat around her.

I carried her that way to my car and drove her home, and stayed while a doctor hovered above her. I prayed. It was answered when the doctor came out of the room and smiled. I said another prayer of thankfulness and did the things that had to be done to make her comfortable. When the nurse came to sit by her side I picked up my hat and went downstairs.

The rain came down steadily. It was clear and pure. It swept by the curb carrying the filth into the sewer.

We know now, don't we, Judge? We know the answer.

There were only a few hours left of the night. I drove to the office and opened the lamp. I took out the two envelopes in there and spread them out on my desk. The beginning and the end. The complexities and the simplicities. It was all so clever and so rotten.

And to think that they might have gotten away with it!

It was over and done with now. Miles away an abandoned paint factory would be a purgatory of flame and explosions that would leave only the faintest trace of what had been there. It was a hell that wiped away all sins leaving only the good and the pure. The faintest trace that it left would be looked into and expounded upon. There would be nothing left but wonder and the two big words, WHY and HOW. There were no cars at the scene. They wouldn't have been foolish enough to get there that way. The flames would char and blacken. They would leave remains that would take months to straighten out, and in that straightening they would come across melted leaden slugs and a twisted gun that was the property of the investigating bureau in Washington. There would be cover-up and more wonder and more speculation, then, eventually, someone would stumble on part of the truth. Yet even then, it was a truth only half-known and too big to be told.

Only I knew the whole thing and it was too big for me. I was going to tell it to the only person who would understand what it meant.

I picked up the phone.

CHAPTER 11

The sixth time it rang I heard it come off the cradle. A sharp click was the light coming on then Lee Deamer's voice gave me a sleepy hello.

I said, "This is Mike Hammer, Lee." My voice had a tired drag too. "Hate to call you at this hour, but I have to speak to you."

"Well, that's all right, Mike. I was expecting you to call. My secretary told me you had called earlier."

"Can you get dressed?"

"Yes. Are you coming over here?"

"I'd rather not, Lee. I don't want to be cooped up right now. I need the smell of air. A hell of a lot has happened. It isn't anything I can broadcast and I can't keep it to myself. You're the only one I can talk to. I want to show you where it started and how it happened. I want you to see the works. I have something very special to show you."

"What Oscar left behind?"

"No, what somebody else did. Lee, you know those government documents that were copied?"

"Mike! It can't be!"

"It is."

"This is . . . why, it's. . . ."

"I know what you mean. I'll pick you up in a few minutes. Hurry up."

"I'll be ready by the time you get here. Really, Mike, I don't know what to say."

"Neither do I, that's why I want you to tell me what to do. I'll be right over."

I put the phone back slowly, then gathered the envelopes into a neat pack and stuck them in my pocket. I went downstairs and stood on the sidewalk with my face turned toward the sky.

It was still raining.

It was a night just like that first one.

The rain had a hint of snow in it.

Before I reached Lee's house I made a stop. The place was a rooming house that had a NO VACANCY sign in front and a row of rooms with private entrances. I went in and knocked on the second door. I knocked again and a bed squeaked. I knocked the third time and a muffled voice swore and feet shuffled across the floor.

The door went open an inch and I saw one eye and part of a crooked nose. "Hello, Archie," I said.

Archie threw the door open and I stepped in. Archie owed me a lot of favors and now I was collecting one. I told him to get dressed and it took him about two minutes to climb into his clothes.

He waited until we were in the car before he opened his yap. "Trouble?" That was all he said.

"Nope. All you're going to do is drive a car. No trouble."

We went over to Lee's place and I rang the bell. They have one of those speaking-tube gadgets there and Lee said he'd be right down. I saw him hurry through the lobby and open the door.

He grinned when we shook hands. I was too tired to grin back. "Is it pretty bad, Mike? You look like you're out on your feet."

"I am. I'm bushed but I can't go to bed with this on my mind. My car is out front."

The two of us went down the walk and I opened the door for him. We got in the back together and I told Archie to head for the bridge. Lee sat back and let his eyes ask me if we could talk with Archie in the car. I shook my head no so we just sat there watching the rain streak across the windows.

At the entrance to the bridge I passed Archie half a buck and he handed it to the cop on duty at the toll booth. We started up the incline when I tapped him on the shoulder.

"Stop here, Archie. We're going to walk the rest of the way. Go on over to Jersey and sop up some beer. Come back in a half-hour. We'll be at the top of the hump on the other side waiting for you." I dropped a fin on the seat beside him to pay for the beer and climbed out with Lee behind me.

It was colder now and the rain was giving birth to a snowflake here and there. The steel girders of the bridge towered into the sky and were lost, giant man-made trees that glistened at the top as the ice started to form.

Our feet made slow clicking sounds against the concrete of the walk and the boats on the river below called back to them. I could see the red and green eyes staring at me. They weren't faces this time.

"This is where it started, Lee," I said.

He glanced at me and his face was puzzled.

"No, I don't expect you to understand, because you don't know about it." We had our hands stuffed in our pockets against the cold, and our collars turned up to keep out the wet. The hump was ahead of us, rising high into the night.

"Right up there is where it happened. I thought I'd be alone that night, but there were two other people. One was a girl. The other was a little fat guy with a stainless-steel tooth. They both died."

I took the fat envelope out of my pocket and shook out the pages inside. "It's amazing, isn't it? Here the best minds in the country are looking for this and I fell right into it. It's the detailed plans of the greatest weapon ever made and I have it right here in my hand."

Lee's mouth fell open. He recovered and reached for it. "How, Mike? How could this come to you?"

There wasn't any doubting its authenticity. He shook his head, completely bewildered, and gave it back to me. "That's the story, Lee. That's what I wanted to tell you, but first I want to make sure this country has a secret that's safe."

I took my lighter out and spun the little wheel. There was a spark, then a blue flame that wavered in the wind. I touched it to the papers and watched them smolder and suddenly flame up. The yellow light reflected from our faces, dying down to a soft red glow. When there was nothing left but a corner that still held the remnants of the symbols and numbers, I flicked the papers over the edge and watched them go to the wind. That one corner I put in my pocket.

"If it had happened to anyone else, I wonder what the answer would have been?"

I shook my head and reached for a Lucky. "Nobody will ever know that, Lee." We reached the top of the hump and I stopped.

The winter was with us again. The girders were tall white fingers that grew from the floor of the bridge, scratching the sky open. Through the rift the snow sifted down and made wet patches on the ground.

I leaned on the handrail, looking out over the river. "It was the same kind of night: it was cold and wet and all alone. A girl came running up that ramp with a guy behind her who had a gun in his pocket. I shot the guy and the girl jumped over the railing. That's how simple it was. The only things they left behind were two green cards that identified them as members of the Communist Party.

"So I was interested. I was interested in anything that toted around a green card. That's how I got interested in Oscar. The guy he killed had a green card too. Hell, you know the rest of the story. There's a few things only I know and that's the main thing. I know how many people died tonight. I know what the papers will look like tomorrow and the month after. You know what, Lee, I killed more people tonight than I have fingers on my hands. I shot them in cold blood and enjoyed every minute of it. I pumped slugs in the nastiest bunch of bastards you ever saw and here I am calmer than I've ever been and happy too. They were Commies, Lee. They were Red sons-of-bitches who should have died long ago, and part of the gang who are going to be dying in the very near future unless they get smart and take the gas pipe. Pretty soon what's left of Russia and the slime that breeds there won't be worth mentioning and I'm glad because I had a part in the killing.

"God, but it was fun! It was the way I liked it. No arguing, no talking to the stupid peasants. I just walked into that room with a tommy gun and shot their guts out. They never thought that there were people like me in this country. They figured us all to be soft as horse manure and just as stupid."

It was too much for Lee. He held on to the rail and looked sick.

I said, "What's the matter, Oscar?"

His eyes were glazed and he coughed. "You mean . . . Lee."

"No I don't. I mean Oscar. Lee's dead."

It was all there, the night, the cold and the fear. The unholy fear. He was looking at my face and he had the same look of unholy fear as the girl had that other night so long ago.

I said it slow. I let him hear every word. "The girl that died here that night was Paula Riis. She was a nurse in an asylum for the insane. I had it wrong . . . she didn't help Oscar to escape . . . she just quit and Oscar escaped later by himself. Paula came to New York and got tied up with a lot of crappy propaganda the Commies handed out and went overboard for it. She thought it was great. She worked like hell and wound up in a good spot.

"Then it happened. Somehow she saw the records or was introduced to the big boy in this country. She knew it was you. What happened, did she approach you thinking you were Oscar's brother? *Whatever happened she recognized you as Oscar and all her illusions were shattered. She knew you were Oscar Deamer and demented as hell!*

"That's why you were a Commie, Oscar, because you were batty. It was the only philosophy that would appeal to your crazy mind. It justified everything you did and you saw a chance of getting back at the world. You escaped from that sanitarium, took Lee's private papers and made yourself a name in the world while Lee was off in the woods where he never saw a paper of any kind and never knew what you did. You must have had an expert dummy the fingerprints on that medical record . . . but then, you had access to that kind of expert, didn't you?

"It was rough when Paula recognized you. She lost her ideals and managed to contact Lee. She told him to come East and expose you, but she did something else first. She had a boy friend in the party. His name was Charlie Moffit and she told him the story hoping to drag him out of the Commie net.

"Charlie was the stupid one. He saw a play of his own and made it. He saw how he could line you up for some ready cash and gave you the story over the phone. It was right after the Legion Parade, the 13th, that you had a heart attack according to your secretary . . . not because your brother contacted you because his ticket was dated the 15th, a Friday, and he didn't arrive until the day after. *You had a heart attack when Charlie Moffit called you!*

"You contacted the torpedo that went under the M.V.D. title and you worried about it, but there was no out until Lee arrived himself and gave you a buzz. That was the best touch of all! Then you saw how you could kill Charlie yourself, have the blame shifted to your brother with a reasonable story that would make it look good. You knew you had a way to kill two birds with one stone . . . and get rid of a brother who could have stood in your way. There was only one thing you didn't foresee. Charlie Moffit was a courier in the chain that passed along those documents. During one of his more lucid moments he recognized that they were important and held on to them for life insurance. He mailed them to his girl friend, Paula, to take care of."

He was white. He hung on to the rail and shook. He was scared stiff.

"So you waited until Charlie called again and arranged to meet him. You had it all figured out beforehand and it looked good as gold. You got hold of an old actor and had him impersonate you while you went out and killed Charlie Moffit. The actor was good, too. He knew how to make speeches. You paid him off, but you didn't know then that he liked to drink. He never did before because he had no money. Later you found that he had a loose tongue when he drank and he had to go too. But that was an easy kill and it's getting ahead of the story.

"You killed Charlie, switched with the actor at the dinner meeting, and made yourself a wonderful alibi. It happened after the supper when you were going around speaking to the groups, a time when nobody would be conscious of the switch, especially since none of them knew you too well anyway.

"I don't know what the play was at your brother's place when Pat and I went after him, but I'll try to set it up. See if I'm right. Mr. M.V.D. went there first and got him running. He got him in the subway and shoved him under the train so his identity would be washed out."

As casually as I could I took Velda's envelope from my pocket and fingered out the sheet inside. He didn't bother to look at it.

I said, "My secretary dug up this story. She went back to your home state and went through the records. She found out that you and your brother were twins, all right, but you weren't identical twins. *You were fraternal twins and he didn't look like you at all!*

"But to get back to the beginning. You knew when Lee called you that there was more to it than you thought. You knew Charlie wasn't smart enough to dig up the stuff by himself, so you and fat boy did some fast snooping and found out about Paula. During that time she saw you or the other guy and got scared. She wanted to talk and called the police, asking them to meet her on the bridge where they could be alone.

"Your M.V.D. pal was a little shrewder. He tapped her phone line and moved in to intercept her, but she moved a little faster and got out of the house before he came around. She had just enough lead to make it to the top of the bridge right where we're standing when he arrived. It was pretty—you should have been here. You should have seen what I did to him. The sour note was Paula. She thought I was one of them looking for a cut of the loot or something, because she couldn't picture any decent person hauling out a rod just like that and blowing a guy's face off. She went over the bridge.

"It would have been so nice for you if I hadn't had a conscience and wanted to find out what the green card meant. You knew my reputation but never thought I could go that far. You hired me so you could keep tabs on me and now look what happened.

"Maybe nothing would have happened if those documents hadn't turned up missing. Those people would have died just to keep your identity a secret. But one of those dead men was a critical link connected with the missing documents, so you cooked up the story of your brother's having left something incriminating behind him, thinking that maybe I'd come across the documents and hand them over to you. Well,

Oscar, I did. You had your boys try to run them down first, but they didn't quite make it.

"I got to be a very dangerous guy in your little game. I was all over the picture with my nose picking up a lot of smells. You passed the orders to get me out of the way at any price and damn near succeeded. Too bad your new M.V.D. boy didn't get me instead of Ethel Brighton up in the cabin there. She was dangerous too. She finally got wise to how foolish she had been and talked to the right people. She was even going to turn me in, but your M.V.D. boy stopped that.

"You know, I thought Ethel put the finger on me when she saw my identification in my wallet. But it wasn't Ethel, it was you. You fingered me because I was getting in there. You thought that I had gone too far already and didn't want to take any more chances. So out come the strong-arm boys and the M.V.D. lad.

"He sure was a busy little beaver. He wanted to kill me in the worst way. When you guys discovered that I had those documents you must have gone nuts. Maybe it even occurred to you that in the process of getting them I would have uncovered all the angles to the thing. I did that, little man, I did just that.

"You got real gay at the end, though. You pulled a real smartie when you put the snatch on Velda. For that there was only one answer . . . I wanted to see you die. I saw them die. You should have seen what I saw and you would have died yourself even before a bullet reached you.

"But none of that is bad when you compare it to the big thing. That's you, Mr. Deamer. You, the little man whom the public loves and trusts . . . you who are to lead the people into the ways of justice . . . you who shouted against the diabolic policies of the Communists . . . you are the biggest Communist of them all!

"You know the theory . . . the ends justify the means. So you fought the Commie bastards and on the strength of that you hoped to be elected, and from there the Politburo took over. With you in where it counted you could appoint Party members to key positions, right in there where they could wreck this country without a bit of trouble. Brother, that was a scheme. I bet the boys in the Kremlin are proud of you."

I saw the gun snake out of his pocket and I reached over and plucked it out of his fingers. Just like that. He stared after it as it arched out and down into the river.

"Tomorrow," I said, "the boys in the Kremlin are going to be wondering what the hell happened. They'll wonder where their boys are and they'll put up a yell, but there will be fear behind that yell because when they learn what happened they'll have to revise their whole opinion of what kind of people are over here. They'll think it was a tough government that uncovered the thing secretly. They'll think it was one of Uncle's boys who chopped down that whole filthy mob, and they won't complain too much because they can't afford to admit those same boys who were here on diplomatic passes were actually spying. The Kremlin mob will really stand on their heads when they get my final touch. It's a beauty, Mr. Deamer. Do you know what I'm going to do?"

He was staring at my face. His eyes couldn't leave my eyes and his flesh was already dying with the fear inside him. He tried to talk and made only harsh breathing sounds. He raised his hands as if I were something evil and he had to keep me away. I was evil. I was evil for the good. I was evil and he knew it. I was worse than they were, so much worse that they couldn't stand the comparison. I had one, good, efficient, enjoyable way of getting rid of cancerous Commies. I killed them.

I said, "The touch is this, Oscar. You, the greatest Commie louse of them all, will be responsible for the destruction of your own party. You're going to die and the blame will go to the Kremlin. I'm going to stick a wallet and some shreds of cloth in your fist when you're dead. In your other hand will be the remains of those documents, enough to show what they were. Enough to make the coppers think that somehow you alone, in a burst of patriotic effort, managed to get hold of those important papers and destroyed them. It'll make them think that just as you were destroying them the killer came up and you fought it out. You came out second best, but in the struggle you managed to rip out the pocket that held his wallet and the cops will track it down thinking it came from your murderer, and what they find will be this . . . they'll find that it came from a guy who was an M.V.D. man. He'll be dead, but that won't matter. If they manage to tie it in with the bodies in the paint shop they'll think that the killer went back to report without the papers he was sent after and the Party, in their usual manner of not tolerating inefficiency, started to liquidate him and they smeared each other in the process. No, the Kremlin won't think that. They'll think it was all a very clever plan, an ingenious jumble that will never be straightened out, which it is. You're going to be a big hero. You saved the day and died in the saving. When the news is made public and the people know their favorite hero has been knocked off by the Reds they'll go on a hunt that won't stop until the issue is decided, and brother, when the people in this country finally do get around to moving, they move fast!"

The irony of it brought a scream to his lips. He made a sudden mad lurch and tried to run, but the snow that came down so white and pure tripped him and I only had to reach out to get his throat in my hand.

I turned him around to face me, to let him look at what I was and see how I enjoyed his dying. The man who had thrown a lot of people on the long road to nowhere was a gibbering idiot slobbering at the mouth. I had his neck in my one hand and I leaned on the railing while I did it. I squeezed and squeezed and squeezed until my fingers were buried in the flesh of his throat and his hands clawed at my arm frantically, trying to tear me away.

I laughed a little bit. It was the only sound in the night. I laughed while his tongue swelled up and bulged out with his eyes and his face turned black. I held him until he was down on his knees and dead as he was ever going to be, then I took my hand away and watched while he fell forward into the snow. I had to pry his fingers apart to get the wallet in them. I made sure he had a good hold on the thing then I laughed again.

Maybe Archie would guess, I thought. He could guess all he wanted to, but he couldn't talk. I was holding a murder over his head, too. A justified killing that only he and I knew about. I saw the headlights of my car coming from the other end of the bridge and I walked across the steel walk to be there when Archie drove up.

The snow was coming down harder now. Soon that dark mass over there would be just a mound. And when the sun shone again the thaw would provide the deluge that would sweep everything into the sewer where it belonged.

It was lonely standing there. But I wouldn't be here long now. The car had almost reached the top of the ramp. I saw Archie bent over the wheel and took a last look around.

No, nobody ever walked across the bridge, especially not on a night like this.

Well, hardly nobody.

THE BIG

KILL

CHAPTER 1

It was one of those nights when the sky came down and wrapped itself around the world. The rain clawed at the windows of the bar like an angry cat and tried to sneak in every time some drunk lurched in the door. The place reeked of stale beer and soggy men with enough cheap perfume thrown in to make you sick.

Two drunks with a nickel between them were arguing over what to play on the juke box until a tomato in a dress that was too tight a year ago pushed the key that started off something noisy and hot. One of the drunks wanted to dance and she gave him a shove. So he danced with the other drunk.

She saw me sitting there with my stool tipped back against the cigarette machine and change of a fin on the bar, decided I could afford a wet evening for two and walked over with her hips waving hello.

"You're new around here, ain't ya?"

"Nah. I've been here since six o'clock."

"Buy me a drink?" She crowded in next to me, seeing how much of herself she could plaster against my legs.

"No." It caught her by surprise and she quit rubbing.

"Don't gentlemen usually buy ladies a drink?" she said. She tried to lower her eyelids seductively but one came down farther than the other and made her look stupid.

"I'm not a gentleman, kid."

"I ain't a lady either so buy me a drink."

So I bought her a drink. A jerk in a discarded army overcoat down at the end of the bar was getting the eye from the bartender because he was nursing the last drop in his glass, hating to go outside in the rain, so I bought him a drink too.

The bartender took my change with a frown. "Them bums'll bleed you to death, feller."

"I don't have any blood left," I told him. The dame grinned and rubbed herself against my knees some more.

"I bet you got plenty of everything for me."

"Yeah, but what I got you ain't getting because you probably got more than me."

"What?"

"Forget it."

She looked at my face a second, then edged away. "You ain't very sociable, mister."

"I know it. I don't want to be sociable. I haven't been sociable the last six months and I won't be for the next six if I can help it."

"Say, what's eatin' you? You having dame trouble?"

"I never have dame trouble. I'm a misanthropist."

"You *are*?" Her eyes widened as if I had something contagious. She finished her drink and was going to stick it out anyway, no matter what I said.

I said, "Scram."

This time she scowled a little bit. "Say, what the hell's eatin' you? I never. . . ."

"I don't like people. I don't like any kind of people. When you get them together in a big lump they all get nasty and dirty and full of trouble. So I don't like people including you. That's what a misanthropist is."

"I coulda sworn you was a nice feller," she said.

"So could a lot of people. I'm not. Blow, sister."

She gave me a look she kept in reserve for special occasions and got the hell out of there so I could drink by myself. It was a stinking place to have to spend the night but that's all there was on the block. The East Side doesn't cater to the uptown trade. I sat there and watched the clock go around, waiting for the rain to stop, but it was as patient as I was. It was almost malicious the way it came down, a million fingers that drummed a constant, maddening tattoo on the windows until its steady insistence rose above the bawdy talk and raucous screams of the juke box.

It got to everybody after a while, that and the smell of the damp. A fight started down at the other end and spread along the bar. It quit when the bartender rapped one guy over the head with an ice stick. One bum dropped his glass and got tossed out. The tomato who liked to rub herself had enough of it and picked up a guy who had enough left of his change to make the evening profitable and took him home in the rain. The guy didn't like it, but biology got the better of common sense again.

And I got a little bit drunk. Not much, just a little bit.

But enough so that in about five minutes I knew damn well I was going to get sick of the whole mess and start tossing them the hell out the door. Maybe the bartender too if he tried to use the stick on me. Then I could drink in peace and the hell with the rain.

Oh, I felt swell, just great.

I kept looking around to see where I'd start first, then the door opened and shut behind a guy who stood there in his shirt sleeves, wet and shivering. He had a bundle in his arms with his coat over it, and when he quit looking around the place like a scared rabbit he shuffled over to one of the booths and dropped the bundle on the seat.

Nobody but me had paid any attention to him. He threw a buck on the bar, had a shot then brought the other shot over to his table. Still nobody paid any attention to him. Maybe they were used to seeing guys who could cry.

He set the drink down and took the coat off the bundle. It was quite a bundle, all right. It was a little kid about a year old who was sound asleep. I said something dirty to myself and felt my shoulders hunch up in disgust. The rain, the bar, a kid and a guy who cried. It made me sicker than I was.

I couldn't take my eyes off the guy. He was only a little squirt who looked as if he had never had enough to eat. His clothes were damp and ragged, clinging to him like skin. He couldn't have been any older than me, but his face was seamed around the mouth and eyes and his shoulders hung limply. Whatever had been his purpose in life, he had given up long ago.

But damn it, he kept crying. I could see the tears running down his cheeks as he patted the kid and talked too low to be heard. His chest heaved with a sob and his hands went up to cover his face. When they came away he bent his head and kissed the kid on top of his head.

All of a sudden my drink tasted lousy.

I turned around to put a quarter in the cigarette machine so I wouldn't have to look at him again when I heard his chair kick back and saw him run to the door. This time he had nothing in his arms.

For about ten seconds I stood there, my fingers curled around the deck of Luckies. Something crawled up my spine and made my teeth grind together, snapping off a sound that was a curse at the whole damn world. I knocked a drunk down getting around the corner of the bar and ripped the door open so the rain could lash at my face the way it had been wanting to. Behind me somebody yelled to shut the door.

I didn't have time to because I saw the guy halfway down the street, a vague silhouette under the overhead light, a dejected figure of a man too far gone to care any more. But he was worth caring about to somebody in the Buick sedan that pulled away from the curb. The car slithered out into the light with a roar and I heard the sharp cough of the gun over the slapping of my own feet on the sidewalk.

It only took two of them and the guy slammed forward on his face. The back door flew open and another shadow ran under the light and from where I was I could see him bend over and frisk the guy with a blurred motion of his hands.

I should have waited, damn it. I shouldn't have tried a shot from where I was. A .45 isn't built for range and the slug ripped a groove in the pavement and screamed off down the block. The guy let out a startled yell and tore back toward the car with the other guy yelling for him to hurry. He damn near made it, then one of the ricochets took him through the legs and he went down with a scream.

The other guy didn't wait. He jammed the gas down and wrenched the wheel over as hard as he could and the guy shrieking his lungs out in the gutter forgot the pain in his legs long enough to let out one final, terrified yell before the wheels of the car made a pulpy mess of his body. My hand kept squeezing the trigger until there were only the flat echoes of the blasts that were drowned out by the noise of the car's exhaust and the futile gesture as the gun held opened, empty.

And there I was standing over a dead little guy who had two holes in his back and the dried streaks of tears on his face. He didn't look tired any more. He seemed to be smiling. What was left of the one in the gutter was too sickening to look at.

I opened the cigarettes and stuck one in my mouth. I lit it and breathed out the smoke, watching it sift through the rain. The guy couldn't hear me, but I said, "It's a hell of a city, isn't it, feller?"

A jagged streak of lightning cut across the sky to answer me.

The police cars took two minutes getting to the spot. They converged from both ends of the street, howling to a stop under the light and the boys next to the drivers were out before the tires stopped whining.

One had a gun in his hand. He meant business with it too. It was pointed straight at my gut and he said, "Who're you?"

I pointed my butt at the thing on the sidewalk. "Eyewitness."

The other cop came behind me and ran his hand over my pockets.

He found the gun, yanked it out of the holster and smelled the barrel. For a second I thought he was going to clip me with it, but this cop had been around long enough to ask questions first. He asked them with his eyes.

"Look in my side pocket," I said.

He dipped his hand in my coat and brought out my wallet. The badge was pinned to the flap with my P.I. ticket and gun license inside the cardcase. He looks them both over carefully, scrutinizing my picture then my face. "Private Investigator, Michael Hammer."

"That's right."

He scowled again and handed the gun and wallet back. "What happened?"

"This guy came in the bar back there a few minutes ago. He looked scared as hell, had two drinks and ran out. I was curious so I tagged after him."

"In this rain you were curious," the cop with the gun said.

"I'm a curious guy."

The other cop looked annoyed. "Okay, go on."

I shrugged. "He ran out and a Buick came after him. There were two shots from the car, the guy fell and one punk hopped out of the car to frisk him. I let loose and got the guy in the legs and the driver of the car ran over him. Purposely."

"So you let loose!" The lad with the gun came in at me with a snarl.

The other cop shoved him back. "Put that thing away and call the chief. I know this guy."

It didn't go over big with the young blood. "Hell, the guy's dead, isn't he? This punk admits shooting, don't he? Hell, how do we know there was a Buick?"

"Go take a look at the corpse over there," the cop said patiently.

Laddie boy with the gun shoved it back on his hip and walked across the street. He started puking after his first look and crawled back in the prowl car.

So at one o'clock in the morning Pat got there with no more fanfare than the winking red light on the top of the police car. I watched him step out and yank his collar up against the rain. The cops looked smart when he passed because there wasn't anything else to do. A killing in this neighborhood was neither important nor interesting enough to drag out the local citizenry in a downpour, so the harness bulls just stood at attention until the brass had given his nod of recognition.

The cop who had frisked me said, "Good evening, Captain Chambers."

Pat said hello and was led out to look over the pair of corpses. I stayed back in the shadows smoking while he bent over to look at the one on the sidewalk. When he finished his inspection he straightened up, listened to the cop a minute and wrinkled up his forehead in a perplexed frown.

My cigarette arched through the night and fizzled out in the gutter. I said, "Hi, Pat."

"What are you doing here, Mike?" Two cops flanked him as he walked over to me. He waved them away.

"I'm the eyewitness."

"So I've heard." Behind Pat the eager beaver cop licked his lips, wondering who the hell I was and hoping I didn't sound off about his gun-waving. "What's the whole story, Mike?"

"That's it, every bit of it. I don't know any more about it than you do."

"Yeah." He made a sour face. "Look, don't screw me. Are you on a case?"

"Chum, if I was I'd say so then keep my trap closed. I'm not on a case and I don't know what the hell happened. This guy got shot, I nicked the other guy and the boy in the car finished him off."

Pat shook his head. "I hate coincidence. I hate it especially when you're involved. You smell out murder too well."

"Sure, and this one stinks. You know either one of them?"

"No. They're not carrying any identification around either."

The morgue wagon rolled up with the Medical Examiner about fifty feet in the rear. The boys hopped out and started cleaning up the mess after the verdict was given and the pictures taken. I ambled out to the middle of the street and took a look at the body that was squashed against the roadbed.

He looked like an hourglass.

Fright and pain had made a distorted death mask of his face, but the rain had scrubbed away the blood leaving him a ghostly white in contrast with the asphalt of the street. He was about forty-five and as medium as you can get. His clothes had an expensive look about them, but one shoe had a hole in the bottom and he needed a haircut bad.

The driver of the wagon splashed the light of a flash over him and gave me a toothy grin. "He's a goodie, ain't he?"

"Yeah, a real beaut."

"Not so much, though. You shoulda seen what we had last week.

Whole damn trailer truck rolled over that one and we had to scrape him away from between the tires. Coulda put him in a shoe box."

"Do you sleep good nights?" I gave him my best disgusted look.

"Sure, why?" He even sounded surprised.

"Forget it. Put that light on his face again."

The guy obliged and I had a close look this time. I walked around and had a squint from the other side then told him to knock off the light. Pat was a vague figure in a trench coat, watching me closely. He said, "Know him?"

"I've seen him before. Small-time hardcase, I think."

"The M.E. remembered him. He was a witness at a coroner's inquest about twelve years ago. The guy was one of Charlie Fallon's old outfit."

I glanced at Pat then back to the corpse again. The guy had some odd familiarity I couldn't place and it wasn't Fallon I was thinking of. Fallon died of natural causes about the same time I was opening up shop and what I knew of him came strictly from the papers.

"Nope, can't quite place him," I said.

"We'll get him tagged. Too bad they couldn't've had the decency to carry a lodge card or something. The one on the sidewalk there only had forty cents in change and a house key in his pocket. This guy had a fin and two ones and nothing else."

I nodded. "A buck must have been all that first lad had then. He bought two drinks in the bar before he left."

"Well, let's go back there and check. Maybe somebody'll know him there."

"Nobody will," I said.

"Never can tell."

"Nuts. They didn't know him when he came in, I'm telling you. He just had two drinks and left."

"Then what're you getting excited about?" He had his hands shoved down in his pockets and was watching me with eyes that were half shut.

"Skip it."

"The hell I'll skip it. Two guys are murdered and I want to know what the hell goes on. You got another wild hair up your tail, haven't you?"

"Yeah." The way I said it brought the scowl back to his face.

"Spill it, Mike."

"Let's go back to the bar. I'm getting so goddamn sick of the things that happen in this town I have to take a bath every time I even stick my head out the door."

The rain stopped momentarily as if something had amazed it, then slashed down with all the fury it could muster, damning me with its millions of pellets. I took a look around me at the two rows of tenements and the dark spots on the pavement where the dead men were a minute ago and wondered how many people behind the walls and windows were alive today who wouldn't be alive tomorrow.

Pat left a moment, said something to the M.E. and one of the cops, then joined me on the sidewalk. I nudged a brace of Luckies out of the pack, handed him one and watched his face in the light. He looked teed off like he always did when he came face to face with a corpse.

I said, "This must gripe the pants off you, Pat. There's not one blasted thing you can do to prevent trouble. Like those two back there. Alive one minute, dead the next. Nice, huh?" The cops get here in time to clear up the mess, but they can't move until it happens. Christ, what a place to live!"

He didn't say anything until we turned into the bar. By that time most of the customers were so helplessly drunk they couldn't remember anything anyway. The bartender said a guy was in for a few minutes awhile back, but he couldn't help out. Pat gave up after five minutes and came back to me. I was sitting at the booth with my back to the bundle in the corner ready to blow up.

Pat took a long look at my face. "What's eating you, Mike?"

I picked the bundle up and sat it on my knee. The coat came away and the kid's head lolled on my shoulder, his hair a tangled wet mop. Pat pushed his hat back on his head and tucked his lip under his teeth. "I don't get it."

"The dead guy . . . the one who was here first. He came in with the kid and he was crying. Oh, it was real touching. It damn near made me sick, it was so touching. A guy bawling his head off, then kissing his kid good-by and making a run for the street.

"This is why I was curious. I thought maybe the guy was so far gone he was deserting his kid. Now I know better, Pat. The guy knew he was going to die so he took his kid in here, said so long and walked right into it. Makes a nice picture, doesn't it?"

"You're drawing a lot of conclusions, aren't you?"

"Let's hear you draw some better ones. Goddamn it, this makes me mad! No matter what the hell the guy did it's the kid who has to pay through the nose for it. Of all the lousy, stinking things that happen. . . ."

"Ease off, Mike."

"Sure, ease off. It sounds real easy to do. But look, if this was his kid and he cared enough to cry about it, what happens to him?"

"I presume he has a mother."

"No doubt," I said sarcastically. "So far you don't know who the father is. Do we leave the kid here until something turns up?"

"Don't be stupid. There are agencies who will take care of him."

"Great. What a hell of a night this is for the kid. His old man gets shot and he gets adopted by an agency."

"You don't know it's his father, friend."

"Who else would cry over a kid?"

Pat gave me a thoughtful grimace. "If your theory holds about the guy knowing he was going to catch it, maybe he was bawling for himself instead of the kid."

"Balls. What kind of a kill you think this is?"

"From the neighborhood and the type of people involved I'd say it was pretty local."

"Maybe the killer hopes you'll think just that."

"Why?" He was getting sore now too.

"I told you he ran over his own boy deliberately, didn't I? Why the hell would he do that?"

Pat shook his head. "I don't think he did."

"Okay, pal, you were there and I wasn't. You saw it all."

"Damn it, Mike, maybe it looked deliberate to you but it sounds screwball to me! It doesn't make sense. If he did swerve like you said he did, maybe he was intending to pick the guy up out of the gutter and didn't judge his distance right. When he hit him it was too late to stop."

I said something dirty.

"All right, what's your angle?"

"The guy was shot in the legs. He might have talked and the guy in the car didn't want to be identified for murder so he put the wheels to him."

Suddenly he grinned at me and his breath hissed out in a chuckle. "You're on the ball. I was thinking the same thing myself and wanted to see if you were sure of yourself."

"Go to hell," I said.

"Yeah, right now. Let's get that kid out of here. I'll be up half the night again on this damn thing. Come on."

"No."

Pat stopped and turned around. "What do you mean . . . 'no'?"

"What I said. I'll keep the kid with me . . . for now anyway. He'll only sit down there at headquarters until morning waiting for those agency people to show up."

Maybe it's getting so I can't keep my face a blank any more, or maybe Pat had seen that same expression too often. His teeth clamped together and I knew his shoulders were bunching up under the coat. "Mike," he told me, "if you got ideas about going on a kill-hunt, just get rid of them right now. I'm not going to risk my neck and position because of a lot of wild ideas you dream up."

I said it low and slow so he had to listen hard to catch it. "I don't like what happened to the kid, Pat. Murder doesn't just happen. It's thought about and planned out all nice and neat, and any reason that involves murder and big fat Buicks has to be a damn good one. I don't know who the kid is, but he's going to grow up knowing that the guy who killed his old man died with a nice hot slug in the middle of his intestines. If it means anything to you, consider that I'm on a case. I have me a legal right to do a lot of things including shooting a goddamn killer if I can sucker him into drawing first so it'll look like self-defense.

"So go ahead and rave. Tell me how it won't do me any good. Tell me that I'm interfering in police work and I'll tell you how sick I am of what goes on in this town. I live here, see? I got a damn good right to keep it clean even if I have to kill a few bastards to do it. There's plenty who need killing bad and if I'm electing myself to do the job you shouldn't kick. Just take a look at the papers every day and see how hot the police are when politics can make or break a cop. Take a look at your open cases like who killed Scottoriggio . . . or Binnaggio and his pal in Kansas City . . . then look at me straight and say that this town isn't wide open and I'll call you a liar."

I had to stop and take a breath. The air in my lungs was so hot it choked me.

"It isn't nice to see guys cry, Pat. Not grown men. It's worse to see a little kid holding the bag. Somebody's going to get shot for it."

Pat knew better than to argue about it. He looked at me steadily a long minute, then down at the kid. He nodded and his face went tight. "There's not much I can do to stop you, Mike. Not now, anyway."

"Not ever. Think it's okay to keep the kid?"

"Guess so. I'll call you in the morning. As long as you're involved the D.A. is probably going to want a statement from you anyway. This time keep your mouth shut and you'll keep your license. He's got enough trouble on his hands trying to nail the big boys in the gambling racket and he's just as liable to take it out on you."

My laugh sounded like trees rubbing together. "He can go to hell for all I care. He got rough with me once and I bet it still hurts when he thinks about it. What's the matter with him now . . . can't he even close up a bookie joint?"

"It isn't funny, Mike."

"It's a scream. Even the papers are laughing."

A slow burn crept into his face. "They should. The same guys who do the laughing are probably some of the ones who keep the books open. It's the big shots like Ed Teen who laugh the loudest and they're not laughing at the D.A. or the cops . . . they're laughing at Joe Citizen, guys like you, who take the bouncing for it. It isn't a bit funny when Teen and Lou Grindle and Fallon can go on enjoying a life of luxury until the day they die while you pay for it."

He got it out of his system and remembered to hand me a good night before he left. I stared at the door swinging shut, my arms tight around the kid, hearing his words come back slowly with one of them getting louder every time it repeated itself.

Lou Grindle. The arm. Lou Grindle who was a flashy holdover from the old days and sold his services where they were needed. Lou Grindle, tough boy de luxe who was as much at home in the hot spots along the Stem as in a cellar club in Harlem.

Lou Grindle who was on his hands and knees in the back of Lake's joint a week ago shooting craps with the help while two of his own boys stood by holding his coat and his dough and the one who held his coat was the dead guy back in the gutter who looked like an hourglass.

I wrapped the coat around the kid and went out in the doorway where I whistled at cabs until one stopped and picked me up. The driver must have had kids of his own at home because he gave me a nasty sneer when he saw the boy in my arms.

I told him where to make his first stop and he waited until I came back. Then I had him make seven others before I got any results. A bartender with a half a bag on mistook me for one of the boys and told me I might find Lou Grindle on Fifty-seventh Street in a place called the Hop Scotch where a room was available for some heavy sugar card games once a week. I threw him a buck and went back to the cab.

I said, "Know where the Hop Scotch is on Fifty-seventh?"

"Yeah. You goin' there now?"

"Looks that way, doesn't it?"

"Don't you think you better take that kid home, buddy? It ain't no good fer kids to be up so late."

"Chum, there's nothing I'd like to do better, but first I got business to take care of."

If I was drunk the cabbie might have tossed me out. As it was, he turned around in his seat to make sure I wasn't, then rolled across to Fifty-seventh.

I left the kid in the cab with a fin to keep the driver quiet and got out. The Hop Scotch was a downstairs gin mill that catered to crowds who liked dirty floor shows and a lot of noise and didn't mind footing the bill. It was hopping with drunks and half drunks who ganged up around the dance floor where a stripper was being persuaded not to stay within the limits prescribed by New York law and when they started throwing rolled-up bills out she said to hell with the law, let go her snaps and braces and gave the customers a treat when she did a two-handed pickup of all the green persuaders.

A waiter was watching the show with a grin on his fat face and I grabbed him while he was still gone over the sight of flesh. I said, "Where's Lou?" just like we were real pals.

"Inside. Him and the others're playin'." His thumb made a vague motion toward the back.

I squeezed through the crowd to where a bus boy was clearing off an empty table and pulled out a chair. The boy looked at the five in my fingers and waited. "Lou Grindle's inside. Go tell him to come out."

He wanted the five, but he shook his head. "Brother, nobody tells Lou nothing. You tell 'im."

"Say it's important business and he'll come. He won't like it if he doesn't get to hear what I have to tell him."

The guy licked his lips and reached for the five. He left the tray on the table, disappeared around a bend that led to the service bar and kitchen, came back for his tray and told me Lou was on his way.

Out on the floor another stripper was trying to earn some persuasion dough herself so the outside of the room was nice and clear with no big ears around.

Lou came around the bend, looked at the bus boy who crooked a finger my way, then came over to see who the hell I was. Lou Grindle was a dapper punk in his forties with eyes like glass marbles and a head of hair that looked painted on. His tux ran in the three-figure class and if you didn't look for it you'd never know he was packing a gun low under his arm.

The edges of his eyes puckered up as he tried to place me and when he saw the same kind of a gun bulge on me as he had himself he made the mistake of taking me for a cop. His upper lip twitched in a sneer he didn't try to hide.

I kicked another chair out with my foot and said, "Sit down, Lou."

Lou sat down. His fingers were curled up like he wanted to take me apart at the seams. "Make it good and make it quick," he said. He hissed when he talked.

I made it good, all right. I said, "One of your butt boys got himself killed tonight."

His eyes unpuckered and got glassier. It was as close as he could come to looking normally surprised. "Who?"

"That's what I want to find out. He was holding your coat in a crap game the other night. Remember?"

If he remembered he didn't tell me so.

I leaned forward and leaned on the table, the ends of my hand inside the lapel of my coat just in case. "He was a medium-sized guy in expensive duds with holes in his shoes. A long time ago he worked for Charlie Fallon. Right now I'm wondering whether or not he was working for you tonight."

Lou remembered. His face went tight and the cords in his neck pressed tight against his collar. "Who the hell are you, Mac?"

"The name's Mike Hammer, Lou. Ask around and you'll find what it means."

A snake wore the same expression he got just then. His eyes went even glassier and under his coat his body started sucking inward. "A goddamn private cop!" He was looking at my fingers. They were farther inside my coat now and I could feel the cold butt of the .45.

The snake look faded and something else took its place. Something that said Lou Grindle wasn't taking chances on being as fast as he used to be. Not where he was alone, anyway. "So what?" he snarled.

I grinned at him. The one with all the teeth showing.

"That boy of yours, the one who died . . . I put a slug through his legs and the guy who drove the car didn't want to take a chance on him being picked up so he put the wheels to him. Right after the two of 'em got finished knocking off another guy too."

Lou's hand moved up to his pocket and plucked out a cigar. Slowly, so I could watch it happen. "Nobody was working for me tonight."

"Maybe not, Lou, maybe not. You better hope they weren't."

He stopped in the middle of lighting the cigar and threw those snake eyes at me again. "You got a few things to learn, shamus, I don't like for guys to talk tough to me."

"Lou . . ." His head came back an inch and I could see the hate he wore like a mask. ". . . if I find out you had a hand in this business tonight I'm going to come back here and take that slimy face of yours and rub it in the dirt. You just try playing rough with me and you'll see your guts lying on the floor before you die. Remember what I said, Lou. I'd as soon shoot your goddamn greasy head off as look at you."

His face went white right down to his collar. If he had lips they didn't show because they were rolled up against his teeth. The number on the floor ended and the people were coming back where they belonged, so I stood up and walked away. When I looked back he was gone and his chair was upside down against the wall.

The cab was still there with another two bucks chalked up on the meter. It was nearly three o'clock and I had told Velda I'd meet her at two-thirty. I said, "Penn Station," to the driver, held the kid against me to soften the jolts of the ride and paid off the driver a few minutes later.

Velda isn't the kind of woman you'd miss even in Penn Station. All you had to do was follow the eyes. She was standing by the information booth tall and cool-looking, in a light gray suit that made the black of her hair seem even deeper. Luscious. Clothes couldn't hide it. Seductive. They didn't try to hide it either. Nobody ever saw her without undressing her with their eyes, that's the kind of woman she was.

A nice partner to have in the firm. And someday. . . .

I came up behind her and said, "Hello, Velda. Sorry I'm late."

She swung around, dropped her cigarette and let me know she thought I was what I looked like right then, an unshaven bum wringing wet. "Can't you ever be on time, Mike?"

"Hell, you're big enough to carry your own suitcases to the platform. I got caught up in a piece of work."

She concentrated a funny stare on me so hard that she didn't realize what I had in my arms until it squirmed. Her breath caught in her throat sharply. "Mike . . . what . . ."

"He's a little boy, kitten. Cute, isn't he?"

Her fingers touched his face and he smiled sleepily. Velda didn't smile. She watched me with an intensity I had seen before and it was all I could do to make my face a blank. I flipped a butt out of my pack and lit it so my mouth would have a reason for being tight and screwed up on the side. "Is this the piece of work, Mike?"

"Yeah, yeah. Look, let's get moving."

"What are you doing with him?"

I made what was supposed to be a laugh. "I'm minding him for his father."

She didn't know whether to believe me or not. "Mike . . . this Florida business can wait if there's something important."

The speaker system was calling off that the Miami Limited was loading. For a second I debated whether or not I should tell her and decided not to. She was a hell of a woman but a woman just the same and thought too goddamn much of my skin to want to see me wrapped up in some kind of a crazy hate again. She'd been through that before. She'd be everything I ever wanted if she'd just quit making sure I stayed alive. So I said, "Come on, you got five minutes."

I put her on the train downstairs and made a kiss at her through the window. When she smiled with that lovely wide mouth and blew a kiss back at me I wanted to tell her to get off and forget going after a punk in Miami who had a hatful of stolen ice, but the train jerked and slipped away. I waved once more and went back upstairs and caught another cab home.

Up in the apartment I undressed the kid, stuffed the ragged overalls in the garbage pail and made him a sack on the couch. I backed up a couple of chairs to hold him in and picked him up. He didn't weigh very much. He was one of those little bundles that were probably scattered all over the city right then with nobody caring much about them. His pale hair was still limp and damp, yet still curly around the edges.

For a minute his head lolled on my shoulder, then his eyes came open. He said something in a tiny voice and I shook my head. "No, kid, I'm not your daddy. Maybe I'll do until we find you another one, though. But at least you've seen the last of old clothes and barrooms for a while."

I laid him on the couch and pulled a cover up over him.

Somebody sure as hell was going to pay for this.

CHAPTER 2

The sun was there in the morning. It was high above the apartments beaming in through the windows. My watch read a few minutes after ten and I unpiled out of bed in a hurry. The phone let loose with a startling jangle at the same time something smashed to the floor in the living room and I let out a string of curses you could have heard on the street.

If I yelled it got stuck in my throat because the kid was standing barefooted in the wreckage of a china-base table lamp reaching up for my rod on the edge of the end table. Even before I got to him he dragged it out of the clip by the trigger guard and was bringing his other hand up to it.

I must have scared the hell out of him the way I whisked him off the floor and disentangled his mitt from the gun. The safety was off and he had clamped down on the trigger while I was thanking the guy who invented the butt safety on the .45.

So with a gun in one hand and a yelling kid in the other I nudged the phone off the hook to stop the goddamn ringing and yelled hello loud enough so the yowls wouldn't drown me out.

Pat said, "Got trouble, Mike?" Then he laughed.

It wasn't funny. I told him to talk or hang up so I could get myself straightened out.

He laughed again, louder this time. "Look, get down as soon as you can, Mike. We have your little deal lined up for you."

"The kid's father?"

"Yeah, it was his father. Come on down and I'll tell you about it."

"An hour. Give me an hour. Want me to bring the kid along?"

"Well . . . to tell the truth I forgot all about him. Tell you what, park him somewhere until we can notify the proper agency, will you?"

"Sure, just like that I'll dump the kid. What's the matter with you? Oh, forget it, I'll figure something out."

I slammed the phone back and sat down with the kid on my knee. He kept reaching for the gun until I chucked it across the room in a chair. On second thought I called the doorman downstairs and told him to send up an errand boy. The kid got there about five minutes later and I told him to light out for the avenue and pick up something a year-old kid could wear and groceries he could handle.

The kid took the ten spot with a grin. "Leave it to me, mister. Me, I got more brudders than you got fingers. I know whatta get."

He did, too. For ten bucks you don't get much, but it was a change of clothes and between us we got the boy fed. I gave the kid five bucks and got dressed myself. On the floor downstairs was an elderly retired nurse who agreed to take the kid days as long as I kept him nights and for the service it would only cost me one arm and part of a leg.

When she took the kid over I patted his fanny while he tried to dig out one of my eyes with his thumb. "For a client," I said, "you're knocking the hell out of my bank roll." I looked at the nurse, but she had already started brushing his hair back and adjusting his coveralls. "Take good care of him, will you?"

"Don't you worry a bit now. As a matter of fact, I'm glad to have something to do with my time." The kid yelled and reached his hand inside my coat and when I pulled away he yelled again, this time with tears. "Do you have something he wants?" she asked me.

"Er . . . no. We were . . . er, playing a game with my coat before. Guess he remembered." I said so long and got out. She'd eat me out if she knew the kid wanted the rod for a toy.

Pat was at ease in his office with his feet up on the desk, comparing blown-up photos of prints in the light that filtered in the windows. When I came in he tossed them aside and waved me into a chair.

"It didn't take us long to get a line on what happened last night."

I sat back with a fresh cigarette in my fingers and waited. Pat slid a report sheet out of a stack and held it in front of him.

"The guy's name was William Decker," he said. "He was an ex-con who had been released four years ago after serving a term for breaking and entering. Before his arrest he had worked for a safe and lock company in a responsible position, then, probably because of his trade, was introduced to the wrong company. He quit his job and seemed to be pretty well off at the same time a wave of safe robberies were sweeping a section of the city. None of those crimes were pinned on him, but he was suspected of it. He was caught breaking into a place and convicted."

"Who was the bad company?" I cut in.

"Local boys. A bunch of petty gangsters, most of whom are now up the river. Anyway, after his release, he settled down and got married. His wife died less than a year after the baby was born. By the way, the kid's name is William too.

"Now . . . we might still be up in the air about this if something hadn't happened last night that turned the light on the whole thing. We put Decker's prints through at the same time another investigation was being made. A little before twelve o'clock last night we had a call to investigate a prowler seen on a fire escape of one of the better apartment buildings on Riverside Drive. The squad car that answered the call found no trace of the prowler, but when they investigated the fire escape they came across a broken window and heard a moan from inside.

"When they entered they found a woman sprawled on the floor in a pretty battered condition. Her wall safe was open and the contents gone. There was one print on the dial that the boys were able to lift and it was that of William Decker. When we pulled the card we had the answers."

"Great." My voice made a funny flat sound in the room.

Pat's head came up, his face expressionless. "Sometimes you *can't* do what you want to do, Mike. You were all steamed up to go looking for a killer and now you're getting sore because it's all so cut and dried."

"Okay, okay, finish reading. I want to hear it."

He went back to the report. "Like I said, his wife died and in all likelihood he started going bad again. He and two others planned a safe robbery with Decker opening the can while the others were lookouts and drove. It's our theory that Decker tried to get away with the entire haul without splitting and his partners overtook and killed him."

"Nice theory. How'd you reach it?"

"Because it was a safe job where Decker would have to handle the thing alone . . . because he went home long enough after the job to pick up his kid . . . and because you yourself saw the man you shot frisking him for the loot before you barged in on the scene."

"Now spell it backwards."

"What?"

"Christ, can't you see your own loopholes? They're big enough."

He saw them. He stuck his tongue in the corner of his cheek and squinted at the paper. "Yeah, the only catch is the loot. It wasn't."

"You hit it," I agreed. "And something else . . . if he was making a break for it he would have taken the dough along. This guy Decker knew he was damn well going to die. He walked right out into it like you'd snap your fingers."

Pat nodded. "I thought of that too, Mike. I think I can answer it. All Decker got in that haul was three hundred seventeen dollars and a string of cultured pearls worth about twenty bucks. I think that when he realized that was all there was to be had, he knew the others wouldn't believe him and took a powder. Tried to, at least."

"Then where's the dough?"

Pat tapped his fingernails against his teeth. "I think we'll find it in the same place we'll find the pearls . . . if anybody's honest enough to turn it in . . . and that's on top of a garbage pail somewhere."

"Aw, nuts. Even three hundred's dough these days. He wouldn't chuck it."

"Anger and disgust can make a person do a lot of things."

"Then why did he let himself get knocked off?"

Pat waited a moment then said, "I think because he realized that they might try to take out their revenge on the child."

I flipped the butt into the waste basket. "You sure got it wrapped up nice and tight. Who was the other guy?"

"His name was Arnold Basil. He used to work for Fallon and had a record of three stretches and fourteen arrests without convictions. We weren't able to get much of a line on him so far. We do know that after Fallon died he went to Los Angeles and while he was there got drunk and was picked up for disorderly conduct. Two of our stoolies reported having seen him around town the last month, but hadn't heard about him being mixed up in anything."

"Did they mention him sticking close to Lou Grindle?"

Pat scowled. "Where'd you get that?"

"Never mind. What about it?"

"They mentioned it."

"What're you doing about it?"

"Checking."

"That's nice."

He threw the pencil across the desk. "Don't get so damn sarcastic, Mike." He caught the stare I held on him and started tapping his teeth again. "As much as I'd like to pin something on that cheap crook, I doubt if it can be done. Lou doesn't play for peanuts and you know it. He has his protection racket and he manages to stay out of trouble."

"You could fix that," I said. "Breed 'im some trouble he can't get out of."

"Yeah, try it."

I stood up and slapped on my hat. "I think maybe I will just for the hell of it."

Pat's hands were flat on the desk. "Damn it, Mike, lay off. You're in a huff because the whole thing works out and you're not satisfied because you can't go gunning for somebody. One of these days you're going to dig up more trouble than you can handle!"

"Pat, I don't like orphan-makers. There's still the driver of that car and don't forget it."

"I haven't. He'll be in the line-up before the week is out."

"He'll be dead first. Mind if I look at this?" I picked up the report sheet and scanned it. When I finished remembering a couple of addresses I tossed it back.

He was looking at me carefully now, his eyes guarded. "Mike, did you leave something out of what you've told me?"

"Nope, not a thing."

"Then spill it."

I turned around and looked at him. I had to put my hand in my pocket to keep it still. "It just stinks, that's all. The guy was crying. You'd have to see him to know what he looked like and you didn't see him. Grown men don't cry like that. It stinks."

"You're a crazy bastard," Pat said.

"So I've been told. Does the D.A. want to see me?"

"No, you were lucky it broke so fast."

"See you around then, Pat. I'll keep in touch with you."

"Do that," he said. I think he was laughing at me inside. I wasn't laughing though. There wasn't a damn thing to laugh about when you saw a guy cry, kiss his kid, then go out and make him an orphan.

Like I said, the whole thing stunk.

To high heaven.

It took me a little while to get over to the East Side. I cruised up the block where the murder happened, reached the corner and swung down to the street where Decker had lived. It was one of those shabby blocks a few years away from condemnation. The sidewalks were littered with ancient baby buggies, a horde of kids playing in the garbage on the sidewalks and people on the stoops who didn't give a damn what the kids did so long as they could yap and slop beer.

The number I had picked from Pat's report was 164, a four-story brownstone that seemed to tilt out toward the street. I parked the car and climbed out, picking my way through the swarm of kids, then went up the steps in to the vestibule. There wasn't any door, so I didn't have to ring any bells. One mailbox had SUPT scratched into the metal case under the 1-C. I walked down the dark channel of the hallway until I counted off three doors and knocked.

A guy loomed out of the darkness. He was a big guy, all right, about two inches over me with a chest like a barrel. There might have been a lot of fat under his hairy skin, but there was a lot of muscle there too.

"Whatta ya want?" The way he said it you could tell he was used to scaring people right off.

I said, "Information, friend. What ya bet you give it to me?"

I watched his hands. They looked like they wanted to grab me. I stood balancing myself on my toes lightly so he'd get the idea that whatever he had I had enough to get away from him. Just like that he laughed. "You're a cocky little punk."

"You're the first guy who ever called me little, friend."

He laughed again. "Come on inside and have some coffee and keep your language where it belongs. I got all kinds of visitors today."

There was another long hallway with some light at the end that turned out to be a kitchen. The big guy stood in the doorway nodding me in and I saw the priest at the table nibbling at a hard roll. The big guy said, "Father, this is . . . uh, what's the name?"

"Mike Hammer. Hello, Father."

The priest held out a big hand and we shook. Then the super tapped his chest with a forefinger. "Forgot myself, I did. John Vileck's the name. Sit down and have a bite and let's hear what you got on your mind." He took another cup and saucer off the shelf and filled it up. "Sugar'n milk's on the table."

When I was sugared and stirred I put my cards on the table. "I'm a private investigator. Right now I'm trying to get a line on a guy who lived here until last night."

Both the priest and the super exchanged glances quickly. "You mean William Decker?" the priest asked.

"That's right."

"May I ask who is retaining you?"

"Nobody, Father. I'm just sore, that's all. I was there when Decker was knocked off and I didn't like it. I'm on my own time and my own capital." I tried the coffee. It was strong as acid and hot as hell.

Vileck stared at his cup, swirling it around to cool it off. "Decker was an all-right guy. Had a nice wife, too. The cops was here last night and then morning again."

"Today?"

He looked up at me, his teeth tight together. "Yeah, I called 'em in about an hour before you come alone. Couple cops in a patrol car. Me and the Father here went upstairs to look around and somebody'd already done a little looking on their own. The place's a wreck. Turned everything upside down."

The priest put his cup down and leaned back in his chair. "Perhaps you can make something of it, Mr. Hammer."

"Maybe I can. If the police have the right idea, whoever searched Decker's place was looking for a pile of dough that he was supposed to have clipped during a robbery last night. The reason he was bumped was because he never got that dough to start with and knew his pals wouldn't believe him. He tried to get out but they nailed him anyway. Apparently they thought that when he came back to get his kid he stashed the money figuring to pick it up later."

Vileck said, "The bastards!" then looked across the table. "Sorry, Father."

The priest smiled gently. "Mr. Hammer . . . do you know anything at all about William Decker?"

"I know he had a record. Did you?"

"Yes, he told me about that some time ago. You see, what puzzles me is the fact that William was such a straightforward fellow. He was doing his best to live a perfect life. It wasn't easy for him, but he seemed to be making a good job of it."

Vileck nodded agreement. "That's right, too. Me and the Father here was the only ones around here that knew he had a record. When he first moved here he made no bones about it, then he started having trouble keeping a job because guys don't like for ex-cons to be working for them. Tell you somethin' . . . Decker was as honest as they come. None of this wrong stuff for him, see? Wouldn't even cheat at cards and right on time with his rent and his bills. Never no trouble at all. What do you make of it?"

"Don't you know?"

There was genuine bewilderment in his eyes. "For the love of me, I sure don't see nothing. He was okay all the way. Always doing things fer his kid since his wife died of cancer."

"Then he had it tough, eh?"

"Yeah, real tough. Doctors come high and he couldn't afford much. She was supposed to have an operation and he finally got her lined up for it, but by that time it was too late and she died a few days after they cut her apart. Decker was in bad shape for a while."

"He drink much?" I asked.

"Nope. Never had a drop all that time. He didn't want to do nothin' that might hurt his kid. He sure was crazy about that boy. That's why he was strictly on the up and up."

The priest had been listening, nodding occasionally. When Vileck finished he said, "Mr. Hammer, a week ago William came to church to see me and asked me if I would keep his insurance policies. They are all made out to the child, of course, and he wanted to be sure that if ever anything happened to him the child would be well provided for."

That one stopped me for a second. I said, "Tell me, was he jumpy at the time? I mean, now that you look back, did he seem to have anything on his mind at all?"

"Yes, now that I look back I'd say that he *was* upset about something. At the time I believed it was due to his wife having died. However, his story was plausible enough. Being that he had to work, he wanted his important papers in safe hands. I never believed that he was intending to . . . to . . ."

Vileck balled his hands up and knocked his knuckles together. "Nuts. I don't believe he done it because he was going to rob a joint. The guy was straight as they come."

"Some things happen to make a guy go wrong," I said. "Did he need dough at all?"

"Sure he needed dough. He'd get in maybe two, three days a week on the docks . . . pier 51 it was, but that was just enough to cover his eats. He lived pretty close, but he got by."

"Any friends?"

The super shrugged. "Sometimes a guy from the docks would come up awhile. He played chess with the blind newsie down the block every Monday night. Both of 'em picked it up in the big house. Nope, can't say that he had any other friends 'cept me. I liked the guy pretty much."

"No reason why he needed money . . . nothing like that?"

"Hell, not now. Before the wife died, sure. Not now though."

I nodded, finished my coffee and turned to the priest. "Father, did Decker make any tentative plans concerning the boy at all?"

"Yes, he did. It was his intention that the boy be brought up by one of our church organizations. We discussed it and he went so far as to make a will. The insurance money will take care of the lad until he finishes school, and what else Decker had was to be held in trust for his boy. This whole affair is very distressing. If only he had come to me with his problem! Always before he came to the church for advice, but this time when he needed to most he failed. Really, I. . . ."

"Father, I have the boy. He's being well cared for at present and whenever you're ready I'll be glad to turn him over to you. That kid is the reason I'm in this and when I get the guy that made him an orphan they can get another grave ready in potter's field. This whole town needs its nose wiped bad. I'm sick of having to live with some of the scum that breeds here and in my own little way I'm going to do something about it."

"Please . . . my son! I . . ."

"Don't preach to me now, Father. Maybe when it's over, but not now."

"But surely you can't be serious."

Vileck studied my face a second, then said, "He is, Father. If I can help ya out, pal . . . lemme know, will ya?"

"I'll let you know," I said. "When you make arrangements for the boy, Father, look me up in the phone book. By the way, who was the friend of Decker's . . . the one on the docks?"

"Umm . . . think his name was Booker. No, Hooker, that's it. Hooker. Mel Hooker."

I pushed the cup back and shoved away from the table.

"That's all then. Any chance of taking a look around the apartment?"

"Sure, go on up. Top floor, first door off the landing. And it won't do no good to ask them old biddies nothin'. They was all doing the weekly wash when whoever took the place apart was there. Once a week they get hot water and their noses were all in the sinks."

"Thanks," I said. "For the coffee too."

"Don't mention it."

"So long, Father. You'll buzz me later?"

He nodded unhappily. "Yes, I will. Please . . . no violence."

I grinned at him so he'd feel better and walked down the tunnel to the hall.

Vileck hadn't been wrong about somebody taking the place apart. They had started at one end of the three tiny rooms and wound up at the other leaving a trail of wreckage behind them that could have been sifted through a window screen. It was one hell of a mess. The bag of garbage beside the door that had been waiting to get thrown out had been scattered with a kick and when I saw it I felt like laughing because whatever they were looking for they didn't get. There was no stopping place in the search to indicate that the great *It* had been located.

For a while I prowled through the ruin of poverty, picking up a kid's toy here and there, a woman's bauble, a few work-worn things that had belonged to Decker. I even did a little probing in a few spots myself, but there wasn't a damn thing of any value around. I finished my butt and flipped it into the sink, then closed the door and got out of there.

I had a nasty taste in my mouth because so far it looked like Pat was right all along the line. Decker had gotten himself loused up with a couple of boys and pulled a job that didn't pay off. The chances were that they had cased the joint so well they wouldn't have believed him when he gave them the story of the nearly empty safe.

I sat there in the car and thought about it. In fact, I gave it a hell of a lot of thought. I thought so much about it I got playing all the angles against each other until all I could see was Decker's face with the tears rolling down his cheeks as he bent over to kiss the kid.

So I said a lot of dirty words.

The goon who drove the car was still running around loose and if I had to go after somebody it might as well be him. I stepped on the starter, dragged away from the curb and started back across town.

It was more curiosity than anything else that put me on Riverside Drive. When I finally got there I decided that it might be a good idea to cruise around a little bit and see if anybody with a pair of sharp eyes might have spotted the boys who cased the joint before they pulled the job.

I didn't have any more luck than you could stuff in your eye. That section of town was a money district, and the people who lived there only had eyes for the dollar sign. They were all sheer-faced apartment buildings with fancy doormen doing the honors out front and big, bright Caddies hauled up close to the curb.

One of the janitors thought he remembered a Buick and a couple of men that hung around the neighborhood a week back but he couldn't be sure. For two bucks he took me through an underground alley to the back court and let me have a look around.

Hell, Decker had had it easy. Every one of the buildings had the same kind of passageway from front to back, and once you were in the rear court it was a snap to reach up and grab the bottom rung of the fire ladder. After I had my look I told the guy thanks and went back to the street.

Two doors down was the building where Decker had pulled the job so I loped in past the beefy doorman and went over the bellboard until I found LEE, MARSHA and gave the button a nudge. There was a phone set in a niche in the wall that gave the cliff dweller upstairs a chance to check the callers before unlocking the door and I had to stand with it at my ear a full minute before I heard it click.

Then heaven answered. What a voice she had. It made the kind of music song writers try to imitate and can't. All it said was, "Yes?" and I started getting mental images of LEE, MARSHA that couldn't be sent through the mail.

I tried hard to sound like a gentleman. "Miss Lee?"

She said it was.

"This is Mike Hammer. I'm a private investigator. Could I speak to you a few minutes?"

"Oh . . . about the robbery?"

"That's right," I said.

"Why . . . yes. I suppose you may. Come right up."

So I went up to heaven in a private elevator that let me out in a semi-private foyer where cloud 4D had a little brass hammer instead of a doorbell. I raised it, let it drop and a ponderous nurse with a mustache scowled me in.

And there was my angel in a big chair by the window. At least the right half of her was angel. The left half sported a very human mouse under the eye and a welt as big as a fist across her jaw.

My face must have been doing some pretty funny things trying to keep from laughing, because she tapped her fingers on the end of the chair and said, "You had better be properly sympathetic, Mr. Hammer, or out you go."

I couldn't hold it back and I laughed anyway, but I didn't go out. "Half of you is the most beautiful girl I ever saw," I grinned.

"I half thank you," she grinned back. "You can leave if you want to, Mrs. Ross. You'll be back at five?"

The nurse told her she would and picked up her coat. When she made sure her patient was all right she left. I was hoping she'd get herself a shave while she was out.

"Please sit down, Mr. Hammer. Can I get you a drink?"

"No, I'll get it myself. Just tell me where to find the makings."

My angel got up and pulled the filmy housecoat around her like a veil. "Hell, I'll get it myself. This leading the life of a cripple is a pain. Everybody treats me like an invalid. The nurse is the 'compliments of the management' hoping I don't sue them for neglecting to keep their property properly protected. She's a good cook, otherwise I would have told them to keep her."

She walked over to a sideboard and I couldn't take my eyes off her. None of this fancy hip-swinging business; just a nice plain walk that could do more than all the fancy wriggling a stripper could put out. Her legs brushing the sheer nylon of the housecoat made it crackle and cling to her body until every curve was outlined in white with pink undertones.

She had tawny brown hair that fell loosely about her shoulders, with eyes that matched perfectly, and a mouth that didn't have to go far to meet mine. Marsha must have just come from a bath, because she smelt fresh and soapy without any veneer of perfume.

When she turned around she had two glasses in her hands and she looked even prettier coming toward me than going away. Her breasts were precocious things that accentuated the width of her shoulders and the smooth contours of her stomach, rising jauntily against the nylon as though they were looking for a way out.

I thought she was too busy balancing the glasses to notice what I was doing, but I was wrong. She handed me a highball and said, "Do I pass?"

"What?"

"Inspection. Do I pass?"

"If I could get my mouth unpuckered I'd let out a long low whistle," I told her. "I'm getting tired of seeing dames in clothes that make them look like a tulip having a hard time coming up. With all the women wearing crew cuts with curled ends these days it's a pleasure to see one with hair for a change."

"That's a left-handed compliment if ever I heard one. What a lover you'd make."

I looked at her a long time. "Don't fool yourself."

She looked at me just as long. "I'm not."

We raised the glasses in a silent toast and sipped the top off them. "Now, Mr. Hammer . . ."

"Mike."

Her lips came apart in a smile. "Mike. It fits you perfectly. What was it you wanted to see me about?"

"First I want to know why you seem so damn familiar. Even with the shiner you remind me of somebody I've seen before."

Her hands smoothed the front of the housecoat. "Thank you for re-membering." She let her eyes drift to the piano that stood in the corner and the picture on top of it. I picked up my drink and walked over to it and this time I did let out a long low whistle.

It was a big shot of Marsha in a pre–Civil War dress that came up six inches above her waist before nature took over. The make-up artist had to do very little to make her the most beautiful woman I had ever seen. She had been younger when it was taken, but me . . . I'd take Marsha like she was now. Time had only improved her. Almost hidden by the frame was a line that said the photo was released by the Allerton Motion Picture Company.

Marsha was familiar because I had seen her plenty of times before. So have you. Ten years ago she was an up-and-coming star in Hollywood.

"Yesteryear, those were the days," she said.

I put the picture back and sat down opposite her so I could see her better. She was well worth looking at and she didn't have to cross her legs to attract attention, either. They were nice legs, too.

"It's a wonder I forgot you," I said.

"Most people do. The public has a short memory."

"How come you quit?"

"Oh, it's a sad but brief story. Perhaps you read about it. There was a man, a bit player but a charming heel if ever I saw one. He played up to me to further his own career by picking up a lot of publicity. I was madly in love with him until I found that he was making a play for my secretary in his spare time. In my foolishness I made an issue of it and he told me how he was using me. So, I became the woman scorned and said if he saw her again I'd see that he was blacklisted off every lot in Hollywood. At the time I carried enough potential importance to let me get away with it. Anyway, he told my secretary that he'd never see her after that and she promptly went out and drove her car off a cliff.

"You know Hollywood. It was bad publicity and it knocked me back plenty. Before they could tear my contract up I resigned and came back East where I stuck my savings in investments that allow me to live like I want to."

I made a motion with my head to take in the room. The place held a fortune in well-chosen furniture and the pictures on the wall weren't any cheap copies, either. Every one of them must have cost four figures. If this was plain living, I'd like to take a crack at it myself.

I pulled out a smoke and she snapped the catch on a table lighter, holding the flame out to me. "Now . . . you didn't come up here for the story of my life," she said. Her eyes danced for me.

"Nope, I want to know about the robbery."

"There's little to tell, Mike. I left here a few minutes before seven to pick up one of the Little Theater members who broke his arm in a fall, drove him home, stopped off at a friend's for a while then came in about a quarter to twelve. As I was about to turn on the lights I saw the beam of a flashlight inside here and like a fool ran right in. For a second I saw this man outlined against the window and the next thing I knew I was flat on my back. I got up and tried to scream, then he hit me again and the world turned upside down. I was still there on the floor when the police came."

"I got that much of the story from Captain Chambers. Did they tell you the guy is dead?"

"No, they haven't gotten in touch with me at all. What happened?"

"One of his partners killed him. Ran right over him with the car."

"Did they . . . recover the money?"

"Nope, I'm beginning to think they never will, either."

"But . . ."

I dragged on the butt and flipped the ashes off in the tray. "I'm willing to bet that the guy chucked the cash and your pearls on the top of some rubbish pile. He didn't come in here for any three hundred bucks. That kind of job isn't worth the trouble."

She bit her lips and frowned at me. "You know something, Mike, I was thinking the same thing."

I looked at her curiously. "Go on."

"I think this . . . this robber knew what he was doing, but got his floors mixed. Do you know Marvin Holmes?"

"The playboy who keeps a stable of blondes?"

"That's right. He has the apartment directly above me. The rooms are laid out exactly the same and even the wall safe is in the identical spot as mine. He always keeps a small fortune on hand and he wasn't home last night either. I met him just as I was going out and he mentioned something about a night club."

"You've been up there?"

"Several times. He's always throwing parties. I don't rate because I'm not a blonde," she added as an afterthought.

It made sense, all right. Just to see how much sense it did make I picked Marvin Holmes' number out of the phone book and dialed it. A butler with a German accent answered, told me yes, Mr. Holmes was at home and put him on. I lied and said I was from the insurance company and wanted to know if he kept a bundle at his fingertips. The sap sounded half looped and was only too happy to tell me there was better than ten grand in his safe and tacked on that he thought the guy who opened the safe on the floor below him had made a mistake. I thanked him and hung up.

Marsha said, "Did he . . ."

"The guy has the same idea as you, chick. He thinks there was a one-floor error and for my money you're both right."

Her shoulders made a faint gesture of resignation. "Well, I guess there's little that can be done then. I had hoped to recover the pearls for sentimental reasons. I wore them in my first picture."

If I grinned I couldn't have been nice to look at. My lips felt tight over my teeth and I shook my head. "It's a dirty mess, Marsha. Two guys are dead already and there'll be another on the way soon. The guy who robbed your place left a baby behind, then went right out to get chopped down. Hell, it isn't what he took, it's why he took it. He was on the level for a long time then just like that he went bad and no guy like him is going to pull something that'll let his own kid get tossed to the dogs.

"Damn it, I was there and saw it! I watched him cry and kiss his kid good-by and go out and cash in his chips. Now I have the kid and I know what he must have felt like. Goddamn it anyway, there's a reason why these things happen and that's what I want. Maybe it's only a little reason and maybe it's a big one, but by God, I'm going to get it."

Her eyes were square and steady on mine, a deep liquid brown that got deeper as she stared at me. "You're a strange kind of guy," she said. I picked up my hat and stood up. She came forward to meet me, holding her hand out. "Mike . . . about the child . . . if I can help out with it, well I'm pretty well set up financially . . ."

I squeezed her hand. "You know, you're a strange kind of guy yourself."

"Thanks, Mike."

"But I can take care of the kid okay." She gave me a lopsided smile that made her look good even with the shiner. "By the way . . . would you happen to have an extra picture around . . . like that one?" I nodded toward the piano.

For a long space of time she held on to my hand and ran her eyes over my face. "What for, won't I do in person?"

I let my hat drop and it stayed on the floor. My hands ran up her arms until my fingers were digging into her shoulders and I drew her in close. She was all woman, every bit of her. Her body was taut, her breasts high and firm with all the vitality of youth, and I could feel the warm outlines of her legs as I pressed her against me. She raised herself on her toes deliberately, tantalizing, a subtle motion that I knew was an invitation not lightly given.

I wanted to kiss her, but I knew that when I did I'd want to make it so good and so hard it would hurt long enough to be remembered and now wasn't the time. Later, when her mouth was smooth and soft again.

"You'll be back, Mike?" she whispered.

She knew the answer without being told. I pushed her away and picked up my hat.

There were things in this city that could be awfully nasty.

There were things in this city that could be awfully nice too.

I stopped by the office that afternoon. The only one in the building to say hello was the elevator operator and he had to look twice to recognize me. It was a hell of a feeling. You live in the city your whole life, take off for six months and you are unknown when you come back. I opened the door and felt a little better when I saw the same old furniture in the same old place. The only thing that was missing was Velda. Her desk was a lonely corner in the anteroom, dusted and ready for a new occupant.

I said something dirty. I was always saying something dirty these days.

She had left a folder of correspondence she thought I might want to see on my desk. It wasn't anything important. Just a record of bills paid, my bank statements and a few letters. I closed the folder and stowed it away in a drawer. There was a fifth of good whisky still there with the wrapper on. I stripped off the paper, uncorked the bottle and looked at it. I worked the top off and smelled it. Then I put it back and shut the drawer. I felt stinking and didn't like the feeling.

Outside on Velda's desk the phone started ringing. I went out in a hurry hoping it might be her, but a rough voice said, "You Mike Hammer?"

"Yeah, who's this?"

"Johnny Vileck. You know, the super down in Decker's building. I had a hell of a time tryin' to get you. Lucky I remembered your name."

"What's up?" I asked.

"I was thinking over what we was speaking about this morning. Remember you asked me about Decker needin' dough?"

"Uh-huh."

"When I went out to get the paper I got talking to the blind newsie on the corner. The old guy was pretty busted up about it. Him and Decker was pretty good friends. Anyway, one night after the old lady died, he was up there playing chess when this guy come around. He wanted to know when Decker was going to get the cash he owed. Decker paid him something and the guy left and after it he mentioned that he had to borrow a big chunk to cover the wife's operation. Mentioned three grand."

I let it jell in my head for a minute, twisting it around until it made sense. "Where could he get that kind of dough?"

Vileck grunted and made a shrug I couldn't see. "Beats me. He never borrowed nuthing and it's damn sure he didn't go to no bank."

"Anybody in the neighborhood got it?"

"Not in this neighborhood, pal. Once somebody'll hit a number or a horse, but he ain't lending it out, you can bet. There's plenty of tough guys around here who show up with a roll sometimes, but it's flash money and they're either gone or in jail the next day. Nope, he didn't get it around here."

"Thanks for the dope, John. If you ever need a favor, let me know."

"Sure, pal, glad to let you know about it."

"Look . . . did you mention this to the cops?"

"Naw. I found out after they left. Besides, they don't hear from me unless they ask. Cops is okay long as they stay outa my joint."

I told him so long and put the receiver back. There was the reason for murder and it was a good one. Three grand worth. Now it was coming out right. Decker went into somebody for three grand and he had to bail himself out by stealing it. So he made a mistake when he raided the wrong apartment and his pals didn't believe it. They thought he was holding out. So they bump him figuring to lift a jackpot and all they got was a measly three hundred bucks and a string of pearls.

Damn it, the whole thing made me boil over! Because a guy couldn't wait to get his dough back a kid is made an orphan. My city, yeah. How many places around town was the same thing going on?

I sat down on the edge of the desk to think about it and the whole thing hit me suddenly and sharply and way back in my head I could hear that crazy music start until it was beating through my brain with a maddening frenzy that tried to drive away any sanity I had left. I cursed to myself until it was gone then went back to my desk and pulled out the bottle. This time I had a drink.

It took me all afternoon to find what I wanted. I went down to the docks and let my P.I. ticket and my badge get me inside the gates until I reached the right paymaster who had handled William Decker's card. He was a little guy in his late fifties with an oversize nose built into a face that was streaked with little purple veins.

He made me wait until he finished tallying up his report, then stuck the clipboard on a nail in the wall and swung around in his chair. He said, "What's on your mind, buddy?"

I offered him a smoke and he waved it away to chew on a ratty cigar. "Remember a guy named Decker?"

He grunted a yes and waited.

"He have any close friends on the docks here?"

"Might have. What'cha want to know for?"

"I heard he died. I owed him a few bucks and I want to see that it goes to his estate."

The guy clucked and sucked his tongue a minute. He opened his desk drawer and riffled through a file of cards until he came to the one he wanted. "Well, here's his address and he's got a kid. Got him down for two dependents, but I think his wife died awhile back."

"I found that out. If I can dig up a pal of his maybe he'll know something more about him."

"Yeah. Well, seems like he always shaped in with a guy named Hooker. Mel Hooker. Tall thin guy with a scar on his face. They got paid off today so they'll be in the joints 'cross the way cashing their checks. Why don'tcha go over an' try?"

I stuffed the butt in the ash tray on the desk. "I'll do that. Give me his address in case I miss him."

He scratched something on a pad and handed it over. I said thanks and left.

It wasn't that easy. I thought I hit every saloon on the street until a guy told me about a couple I had missed and then I found him. The place was a rattrap where they'd take the drunks that had been kicked out of other places and make them spend their last buck. You had to go down a couple of steps to reach the door and before you reached it you could smell what you were walking into.

The place was a lot bigger than I expected. They were lined up two deep at the bar and when they couldn't stand any more they sat down at the bench along the wall. One guy had passed out and was propped up against a partition with his pockets turned inside out.

Mel Hooker was down the back watching a shuffleboard game. He had half a bag on and looked it. The yellow glare of the overhead lights brought out the scar that ran from his forehead to his chin in bold relief almost as if it was still an ugly gash. I walked over and pulled out the chair beside him.

He looked at me enough to say, "Beat it."

"You Mel Hooker?"

"Who wants to know?" His voice had a nasty drunken snarl to it.

"How'd you like to get the other side of your face opened up, feller?"

He dropped his glass like it was shot out of his hand and tried to get up off his chair. I shoved him back without any trouble. "Stay put, Mel. I want to talk to you."

His breathing was noisy. "I don't wanna talk to you," he said.

"Tough stuff, Mel. You'll talk if I tell you to. It's about a friend of yours. He's dead. His name was William Decker."

The flesh around the scar seemed to get whiter. Something changed in his eyes and he half twisted his head. One of the guys at the shuffle-board was taking a long time to make his play. Mel unfolded himself and nodded to an empty table over in the corner. "Over . . . here. Make it quick."

I got up and went back to the bar for a pair of drinks and brought them back to the table. When Mel took his his hand wasn't too steady. I let him take half of it down in one gulp before I asked, "Who'd he owe dough to, Mel?"

He almost dropped this glass, too. In time, he recovered it and set it down very deliberately and wiped his mouth with the back of his hand. "You a cop?"

"I'm a private investigator."

"You're gonna be a dead investigator if you don't get the hell outa here."

"I asked you a question."

"His tongue flicked out and whipped over his lips. "Get this, I don't know nothing about nothing. Bill was a friend of mine but his business was his own. Now lemme alone."

"He needed three grand, Mel. He borrowed it from somebody. He didn't get it around home so he must have got it someplace around here."

"You're nuts."

"You're a hell of a friend," I said, "one hell of a friend."

Hooker dropped his head and stared at his hands. When he looked up his mouth was drawn back tight. His voice came out barely a whisper. "Listen, Mac, you better quit asking questions. Bill was my friend and I'd help him if I could, but he's dead and that's that. You see this scar I got? I'd sooner have that than be dead. Now blow and lemme alone."

He wouldn't look back at me when he left. He staggered out to the bar and through the mob around it until he reached the door, then disappeared up the stairs. I polished my drink off and waved the waiter over with another. He gave me a frozen look and snatched the buck out of my hand.

The place got too damn quiet. The weights weren't slamming on the shuffleboard and everybody at the bar seemed to have taken a sudden interest in the television set over the bar. I sat there and waited for my change, but I had the drink gone without seeing it.

This I liked. This I was waiting for because the stupid bastards should have known better. My God, did I look like some flunkey from the sticks or did the wise boys lose their memories too?

I pushed the glass back and got up. I found the men's room in the back by the smell and did what I had to do and started to wash my hands. That's how long they gave me.

The guy in the double-breasted suit in the doorway spoke out of the corner of his mouth to somebody behind him. His little pig eyes looked like he was getting ready to enjoy himself. "He's a big one, ain't he?"

"Yeah." The other guy stepped in and seemed to fill up the doorway.

The little guy's hand came out of his pocket with a sap about a foot long and he swung it against his knee waiting to see if I was going to puke or start bawling. The big guy took his time about slipping on the knucks. Outside the volume on the television went up so loud it blasted its way all the way back there.

I dropped the paper towel and backed off until my shoulders were up against the doors of the pot. The little guy was leering. His mouth worked until the spit rolled down his chin and his shoulder started to draw back the sap. His pal closed in on the side, only his eyes showing that there might be some human intelligence behind that stupid expression.

The goddamn bastards played right into my hands. They thought they had me nice and cold and just as they were set to carve me into a raw mess of skin I dragged out the .45 and let them look down the hole so they could see where sudden death came from.

It was the only kind of talk they knew. The little guy stared too long. He should have been watching my face. I snapped the side of the rod across his jaw and laid the flesh open to the bone. He dropped the sap and staggered into the big boy with a scream starting to come up out of his throat only to get it cut off in the middle as I pounded his teeth back into his mouth with the end of the barrel. The big guy tried to shove him out of the way. He got so mad he came right at me with his head down and I took my own damn time about kicking him in the face. He smashed into the door and lay there bubbling. So I kicked him again and he stopped bubbling. I pulled the knucks off his hand then went over and picked up the sap. The punk was vomiting on the floor, trying to claw his way under the sink. For laughs I gave him a taste of his own sap on the back of his hand and felt the bones go into splinters. He wasn't going to be using any tools for a long time.

They moved aside and let me get in to the bar. They moved aside so far you'd think I was contaminated. The bartender looked at me and his thick lips rubbed together. I dropped the knucks and the sap on the bar and waved the bartender over with my forefinger. "I got some change coming," I said.

He turned around and rang up a NO SALE on the register and handed me fifty-five cents.

If somebody breathed before I left I didn't hear it. I got out of there feeling like myself again and went back to the car. I only had one thing to do before I saw Pat. I checked the slip the timekeeper gave me and saw that Mel Hooker lived not too far from where Decker had lived. I got snarled up in traffic halfway there and it was dark by the time I found his address.

The place was a rooming house with the usual sign outside advertising a lone vacancy and a landlady on the bottom floor using her window for a crow's nest. She was at the door before I got up the steps waiting to smile if I was a renter or glare if I was a visitor.

She glared when I asked her if Mel Hooker had come in yet. Her finger waved up the stairs. "Ten minutes ago and drunk. Don't you two raise no ruckus or out you both go."

If she had been nicer I would have soothed her feelings with a bill. All she got was a sharp thanks and I went upstairs. I heard him shuffling around the room and when I knocked all sound stopped. I knocked again and he dragged across the floor and snapped the lock back. I don't know who he expected to see. It sure wasn't me.

I didn't ask to come in; I gave the door a shove and he reeled back. His face had lost its tenseness and was dull, his mouth sagging. There was a table in the middle of the room and I perched on it, watching him close the door, then turn around until he faced me!

"Christ!" he said.

"What'd you expect, Mel?" I lit a Lucky and peered at him through the smoke. "You're a hell of a guy," I told him. "I guess you knew those boys would tag after me and you didn't want to stick around to see the blood."

"Wh . . . what happened?"

I grinned at him. "I've been messing around with bastards like that for a long time. They should have remembered my face. Now they're going to have trouble remembering what they used to look like before. Did you pull the same stunt on your friend Decker, Mel? Did you beat it when they went looking for him?"

He staggered over to a chair and collapsed in it. "I don't . . . know . . . whatcha talking about."

I leaned forward on the edge of the table and spit the words out. "I'm talking about the loan shark racket. I'm talking about a guy named William Decker who used to be your friend and needed dough bad. He couldn't get it from a legitimate source so he hit up a loan shark and got what he needed. When he couldn't pay off they put the pressure on him probably through his kid so he tries to cop a bank roll from a rich guy's safe. He miffed the job and they gave him the works. Now do you know what I'm talking about?"

Hooker said, "Christ!" again and grabbed the arms of the chair. "Friend, you gotta get outa here, see? You gotta leave me alone!"

"What's the matter, Mel? You were a tough guy when I met you tonight. What's getting you so soft?"

For a minute a crazy madness passed over his face, then he let out a gasp and buried his head in his hands. "Damn it, get outa here!"

"Yeah, I'll get out. When you tell me who's banking the soaks along the docks I'll get out."

"I . . . I can't. Oh, Lord, lemme alone, will ya!"

"They're tough, huh?" He read something in my words and his eyes came up in a series of little jerks until they were back on mine. "Are they tougher than the guys you pushed on me?"

Mel swallowed hard. "I didn't . . ."

"Don't crap me, friend. Those guys weren't there by accident. They weren't there just for me, either. Somebody's got a finger on you, haven't they?"

He didn't answer.

"They were there for you," I said, "only you saw a nice way to shake them loose on me. What gives?"

His finger moved by itself and traced the scar that lay along the side of his jaw. "Look, I got cut up once, I did. I don't want to fool around with them guys no more. Honest. I didn't do nothing! I don't know why they was there but they was!"

"So you're in a trap too," I said.

"No I ain't!" He shouted it. His face was a sickly white and he drooled a little bit. "I'm clean and I don't know why they're sticking around me. Why the hell did you came butting in for?"

"Because I want to know why your pal Decker needed dough."

"Christ, his wife was dying. He had to have it. How'd I know he couldn't pay it back!"

"Pay what back to who?"

His tongue flashed over his lips and his mouth clammed shut.

"You have a union and a welfare fund for that, don't you?"

This time he spit on the floor.

"Who'd you steer him to, Mel?"

He didn't answer me. I got up off the edge of the table and jerked him to his feet. "Who was it, Mel . . . or do you want to find out what happened to the tough boys back in the bar?"

The guy went limp in my hands. He didn't try to get away. He just hung there in my fist, his eyes dead. His words came out slow and flat. "He needed the dough. We . . . thought we had a good tip on the ponies and pooled our dough."

"So?"

"We won. It wasn't enough so we threw it back on another tip, only Bill hit up a loan shark for a few hundred to lay a bigger bet. We won that one too and I pulled out with my share. Bill thought he could get a big kill quick and right after he paid the shark back, knocked him down for another grand to add to his stake and this time he went under."

"Okay, so he owed a grand."

Mel's head shook sadly. "It was bigger. You pay back one for five every week. It didn't take long to run it up into big money."

I let him go and he sank back into the chair. "Now names, Mel. Who was the shark?"

I barely heard him say, "Dixie Cooper. He hangs out in the Glass Bar on Eighth Avenue."

I picked up my deck of smokes and stuffed them in my pocket. I walked out without closing the door and down past the landlady who still held down her post in the vestibule. She didn't say anything until Mel hobbled to the door, glanced down the stairs and shut it. Then the old biddy humphed and let me out.

The sky had clouded up again, shutting out the stars and there was a damp mist in the air. I called Pat from a candy store down the corner and nobody answered his phone at home, so I tried the office. He was there. I told him to stick around and got back in my car.

Headquarters building was like a beehive without any bees when I got there. A lone squad car stood at the curb and the elevator operator was reading a paper inside his cab. The boys on the night stand had that bored look already and half of them were piddling around trying to keep busy.

I got in the elevator and let him haul me up to Pat's floor. Down the corridor a typewriter was clicking busily and I heard Pat rummaging around the drawers of his file cabinet. When I pushed the door open he said, "Be right with you, Mike."

So I parked and watched him work for five minutes. When he got through at the cabinet I asked him, "How come you're working nights?"

"Don't you read the papers?"

"I didn't come up against any juicy murders."

"Murders, hell. The D.A. has me and everybody else he can scrape together working on that gambling probe."

"What's he struggling so hard for, it isn't an election year for him. Besides, the public's going to gamble anyway."

Pat pulled out his chair and slid into it. "The guy's got scruples. He has it in for Ed Teen and his outfit."

"He's not getting Teen," I said.

"Well, he's trying."

"Where do you come in?"

Pat shrugged and reached for a cigarette. "The D.A. tried to break up organized gambling in this town years ago. It flopped like all the other probes flopped . . . for lack of evidence. He's never made a successful raid on a syndicate establishment since he went after them."

"There's a hole in the boat?"

"A what?"

"A leak."

"Of course. Ed Teen has a pipeline right into the D.A.'s office somehow. That's why the D.A. is after his hide. It's a personal affront to him and he won't stand for it. Since he can't nail Teen down with something, he's conducting an investigation into his past. We know damn well that Teen and Grindle pulled a lot of rough stuff and if we can tie a murder on them they'll be easy to take."

"I bet. Why doesn't he patch that leak?"

Pat did funny things with his mouth. "He's surrounded by men he trusts and I trust and we can't find a single person who's talking out of turn. Everybody's been investigated. We even checked for dictaphones, that's how far we went. It seems impossible, but nevertheless, the leak's here. Hell, the D.A. pulls surprise raids that were cooked up an hour before and by the time he gets there not a soul's around. It's uncanny."

"Uncanny my foot. The D.A. is fooling with guys as smart as he is himself. They've been operating longer too. Look, any chance of breaking away early tonight?"

"With this here?" He pointed toward a pile of papers on his desk. "They all have to be classified, correlated and filed. Nope, not tonight, Mike. I'll be here for another three hours yet."

Outside the racket of the typewriter stopped and a stubby brunette came in with a wire basket of letters. Right behind her was another brunette, but far from stubby. What the first one didn't have she had everything of and she waved it around in front of you like a flag.

Pat saw my foolish grin and when the stubby one left said, "Miss Scobie, have you met Mike Hammer?"

I got one of those casual glances with a flicker of a smile. "No, but I've heard the District Attorney speak of him several times."

"Nothing good, I hope," I said.

"No, nothing good." She laughed at me and finished sorting out the papers on Pat's desk.

"Miss Scobie is one of the D.A.'s secretaries," Pat said. "For a change I have some help around here. He sent over three girls to do the manual labor."

"I'm pretty good at that myself." I think I was leering.

The Scobie babe gave me the full voltage from a pair of deep blue eyes. "I've heard that too."

"You should quit getting things secondhand."

She packed the last of the papers in a new pile and tacked them together with a clip. When she turned around she gave me a look Pat couldn't see but had a whole book written there in her face. "Perhaps I should," she said.

I could feel the skin crawl up my back just from the tone of her voice.

Pat said, "You're a bastard. Mike. You and the women."

"They're necessary." I stared at the door that closed behind her.

His mouth cracked in a grin. "Not Miss Scobie. She knows her way around the block without somebody holding her hand. Doesn't her name mean anything to you?"

"Should it?"

"Not unless you're a society follower. Her family is big stuff down in Texas. The old man had a ranch where he raised horses until they brought oil in. Then he sat back and enjoyed life. He raises racing nags now."

"The Scobie Stables?"

"Uh-huh. Ellen's his daughter. When she was eighteen she and the old boy had a row and she packed up and left. This department job is the first one she ever had. Been here better than fifteen years. She's the gal the track hates to see around. When she makes a bet she collects."

"What the hell's she working for then?"

"Ask her."

"I'm asking you."

Pat grinned again. "The old man disinherited her when she wouldn't marry the son of his friend. He swore she'd never see a penny of his dough, so now she'll only bet when a Scobie horse is running and with what she knows about horses, she's hard to fool. Every time she wins she sends a telegram to the old boy stating the amount and he burns up. Don't ask her to tip you off though. She won't do it."

"Why doesn't the D.A. use her to get an inside track on the wire rooms?"

"He did, but she's too well known now. A feature writer for one of the papers heard about the situation, and gave it a big play in a Sunday supplement a few years ago, so she's useless there."

I leaned back in my chair and stared at the ceiling. "Texas gal. I like the way they're built."

"Yeah, big." Pat grunted. "A big one gets you every time." His fingers rapped on the desk. "Let's come back to earth, Mike. What's new?"

"Decker."

"That's not new. We're still looking for the driver who ran down his buddy. They found the car, you know."

I sat up straight.

"You didn't miss everything that night. There were two bullet holes in the back. One hit the rear window and the other went through the gas tank. The car was abandoned over in Brooklyn."

"Stolen heap?"

"Sure, what'd you expect? The slugs came from your gun, the tires matched the imprints in the body and there wasn't a decent fingerprint anywhere."

"Great."

"We'll wrap it up soon. The word's out."

"Great."

Pat scowled at me in disgust. "Hell, you're never satisfied."

I shook a cigarette out and lit up. Pat pushed an ash tray over to me. I said, "Pat, you got holes in your head if you think that this was a plain, simple job. Decker was in hock to a loan shark for a few grand and was being pressured into paying up. The guy was nuts about his kid and they probably told him the kid would catch it if he didn't come across."

"So?"

"Christ, *you* aren't getting to be a cynic like the rest of the cops, are you? You want things like this to keep on happening? You like murder to dirty up the streets just because some greaseball wants his dirty money! Hell, who's to blame . . . a poor jerk like Decker or a torpedo who'll carve him up if he doesn't pay up? Answer me that."

"There's a law against loan sharks operating in this state."

"There's a law against gambling, too."

Pat's face was dark with anger.

"The law has been enforced," he snapped.

I put the emphasis on the past tense. "It *has*? That's nice to know. Who's running the racket now?"

"Damn it, Mike, that isn't my department."

"It should be; it caused the death of two men so far. What I want to know is, is the racket organized or not?"

"I've heard that it was," he replied sullenly. "Fallon used to bank it before he died. When the state cracked down on them somebody took the sharks under their wing. I don't know who."

"Fallon? Fallon, hell, the guy's been dead since 1940 and he's still making news."

"Well, you asked me."

I nodded. "Who's Dixie Cooper, Pat?"

His eyes went half shut. "Where do you get your information from? Goddamn, you have your nose in everywhere."

"Who is he?"

"The guy's a stoolie for the department. He has no known source of income, though he claims to be a promoter."

"Of what?"

"Of everything. He's a guy who knows where something is that somebody else wants and collects a percentage from the buyer and seller both. At least, that's what he says."

"Then he's full of you know what. The guy is a loan shark. He's the one Decker hit up for the money."

"Can you prove it?"

"Uh-huh."

"Show me and we'll take him into custody."

I stood up and slapped on my hat. "I'll show you," I said. "I'll have him screaming to talk to somebody in uniform just to keep from getting his damn arms twisted off."

"Go easy, Mike."

"Yeah, I'll do just that. I'll twist 'em nice and easy like he twisted Decker. I'll go easy, all right."

Pat gave me a long look with a frown behind it. When I said so long he only nodded, and he was reaching for the phone as I shut the door.

Down the hall another door slammed shut and the stubby brunette came by, smiled at me politely and kept on going to the elevator. After she got in I went back down the corridor to the office, pushed the door open and stuck my head in. Ellen Scobie had one foot on a chair with her dress hiked up as far as it would go, straightening her stocking.

"Pretty leg," I said.

She glanced back quickly without bothering to yank her dress down like most dames would. "I have another just like it," she told me. Her eyes were on full voltage again.

"Let's see."

So she stood up in one of those magazine poses and pulled the dress up slowly without stopping until it couldn't go any further and showed me. And she was right. The other was just as pretty if you wasted a sight like that trying to compare them.

I said, "I love brunettes."

"You love anything." She let the dress fall.

"Brunettes especially. Doing anything tonight?"

"Yes . . . I was going out with you, wasn't I? Something I should learn about manual labor?"

"Kid," I said, "I don't think you have anything to learn. Not a damn thing."

She laughed deep in her throat and came over and took my arm. "I'm crazy about heels," she said. "Let's go."

We passed by Pat's office again and I could still hear him on the phone. His voice had a low drone with a touch of urgency in it but I couldn't hear what he was saying. When we were downstairs in the car Ellen said, "I hope you realize that if we're seen together my boss will have you investigated from top to bottom."

"Then you do the investigating. I have some fine anatomy."

Her mouth clucked at me. "You know what I mean. He's afraid to trust himself these days."

"You can forget about me, honey. He's investigated me so often he knows how many moles I got. Who the hell's handing out the dope, anyway?"

"If I knew I'd get a promotion. Right now the office observes war-time security right down to burning everything in the wastebaskets in front of a policeman. You know what I think?"

"What?"

"Somebody sits in another building with a telescope and reads lips."

I laughed at her. "Did you tell the D.A. that?"

She grinned devilishly. "Uh-huh. I said it jokingly and damned if he didn't go and pull down the blinds. Everybody hates me now." She stopped and glanced out the windows, then looked back at me curiously. "Where're we going?"

"To see a guy about a guy," I said.

She leaned back against the cushions and closed her eyes. When she opened them again I was pulling into a parking lot in Fifty-second Street. The attendant took my keys and handed me a ticket. The evening was just starting to pick up and the gin mills lining the street were starting to get a play.

Ellen tugged at my hand. "We aren't drinking very fancy tonight, are we?"

"You come down here much?"

"Oh, occasionally. I don't go much for these places. Where are we going?"

"A place called the Glass Bar. It's right down the block."

"That fag joint," she said with disgust. "The last time I was there I had three women trying to paw me and a guy with me who thought it was funny."

"Hell, I'd like to paw you myself," I laughed.

"Oh, you will, you will." She was real matter-of-fact about it, but not casual, not a bit. I started to get that feeling up my back again.

The Glass Bar was a phony name for a phonier place. It was all chrome and plastic, and glass was only the thing you drank out of. The bar was a circular affair up front near the door with the back half of the place given over to tables and a bandstand. A drummer was warming up his traps with a pair of cuties squirming to his jungle rhythm while a handful of queers watched with their eyes oozing lust.

Ellen said, "The bar or back room?"

I tossed my hat at the redhead behind the check booth. "Don't know yet." The redhead handed me a pasteboard with a number on it and I asked her, "Dixie Cooper been in yet?"

She leaned halfway out of the booth and looked across the room. "Don't see him. Guess he must be in back. He came in about a half hour ago."

I said thanks and took Ellen's arm. We had a quick one at the bar, then pushed through the crowd to the back room where the babes were still squirming with the drummer showing no signs of tiring. He was all eyes for the wriggling hips and the table with the queers had been abandoned for one closer to the bandstand.

Only four other tables were occupied and the kind of people sitting there weren't the kind I was looking for. Over against the wall a guy was slouched in a chair reading a late tabloid while he sipped a beer. He had a hairline that came down damn near to his eyebrows and when his mouth moved as he read his top teeth stuck out at an angle. On the other side of the table a patsy was trying to drag him into a conversation and all he was getting was a grunt now and then.

The guy with the bleached hair looked up and smiled when I edged over, then the smile froze into a disgusted grimace when he saw Ellen. I said, "Blow, Josephine," and he arched his eyebrows and minced off.

Buck teeth didn't even bother to look at me.

Ellen didn't wait to be invited. She plunked herself in a chair with a grin and leaned on the table waiting for the fun to start.

Buck teeth interrupted his reading long enough to say, "Whatta you want?"

So I took the .45 out and slid it down between his eyes and the paper and let him stare at it until he went white all the way back of his ears. Then I sat down too. "You Dixie Cooper?"

His head came around like somebody had a string on it. "Yeah." It was almost a whisper and his eyes wouldn't come away from the bulge under my coat.

"There was a man," I said. "His name was William Decker and he hit you up for a loan not long ago and he's dead now."

Cooper licked his lips twice and tried to shake his head. "Look . . . I . . ."

"Shut up."

His eyes seemed to get a waxy film over them.

"Who killed him," I said.

"Honest to God, Mac, I . . . Christ . . . I didn't kill 'im. I swear . . ."

"You little son-of-a-bitch you, when you put the squeeze on him for your lousy dough he had to pull a robbery to pay off!"

This time his eyes came away from my coat and jerked up to mine. His upper lip pared back from his teeth while his head made funny shaking motions. "I . . . don't get it. He . . . didn't get squeezed. He paid up. I give 'im a grand and two days later he pays it back. Honest to God, I . . ."

"Wait a minute. He paid you back all that dough?"

His head bobbed. "Yeah, yeah. All of it."

"You know what he used it for?"

"I . . . I think he was playing the ponies."

"He lost. That means he paid you back and his losses too. Where'd he get it?"

"How should I know? He paid me back like I told you."

Dixie started to shake when I grinned at him. "You know what'll happen to you if I find out you're lying?"

He must have known, all right. His buck teeth started showing gums and all. Somehow he got his lips together enough to say, "Christ, I can prove it! He . . . he paid me off right in Bernie Herman's bar. Ask Bernie, he was there. He saw him pay me and he'll remember because I bought the house a drink. You ask him."

I grinned again and pulled out the .45 and handed it to Ellen under the table. Dixie couldn't seem to swallow his own spit any more. I said, "I will, pal. You better be right. If he tries to scram, put one in his leg, Ellen."

She was a beautiful actress. She never changed her smile except to give it the deadly female touch and it wasn't because she meant it, but because she was having herself a time and was enjoying every minute of it.

I went out to the phone and looked up Bernie Herman's number and got the guy after a minute or so and he told me the same thing Dixie had. When I got back to the table they were still in the same position only Dixie had run out of spit altogether.

Ellen handed me the rod and I slipped it back under my coat. I nodded for her to get up just as a waiter decided it was about time to take our order. "Your friend cleared you, Dixie. You better stay cleared or you'll get a slug right in those buck teeth of yours. You know that, don't you?"

A drop of sweat rolled down in his eye and he blinked, but that was all. I said, "Come on, kitten," and we left him sitting there. When I passed the waiter I jerked my thumb back to the table. "You better bring him a whiskey. Straight. Make it a double."

He jotted it down and went over to the service bar.

Outside a colored pianist was trying hard to play loud enough to be heard over the racket of the crowd that was four deep around the bar. I pushed Ellen behind me and started elbowing a path between the mob and the booths along the side and if I didn't almost trip over a foot stuck out in the aisle I wouldn't have seen Lou Grindle parked in the booth across from a guy who looked like a Wall Street banker.

Only he wasn't a banker, but the biggest bookie in the business and his name was Ed Teen.

Lou just stopped talking and stared at me with those snake eyes of his. I said, "Your boy's still in the morgue, Lou. Don't you guys go in for big funerals these days?"

Ed Teen smiled and the creases around his mouth turned into deep hollows. "Friends of yours, Lou?"

"Sure, we're real old buddies, we are," I said. "Some day I'm gonna kick his teeth in."

Lou didn't scare a bit. The bastard looked almost anxious for me to try it. Ellen gave me a little push from behind and we got through the crowd to the checkroom where I got my hat, then went outside to the night.

Her face was different this time. The humor had gone out of it and she watched me as though I'd bite her. "Lord, Mike, a joke's a joke, but don't go too far. Do you know who they were?"

"Yeah, scum. You want to hear some dirty words that fit 'em perfectly?"

"But . . . they're dangerous."

"So I've heard. That makes it more fun. You know them?"

"Of course. My boss would give ten years off his life to get either one of them in court. Please, Mike, just go a little easy on me. I don't mind holding your gun to frighten someone like that little man back here, but those two . . ."

I slipped my arm around her shoulders and squeezed. "Kitten, when a couple of punks like that give me the cold shivers I'll hang up. They're big because they have money and the power and guns that money can buy, but when you take their clothes off and there's no pockets to hold the money or the guns they're just two worms looking for holes to hide in."

"Have it your way, but I need a drink. A big one and right now. My stomach is all squirmy."

She must have been talking about the inside. I felt her stomach and it was nice and flat. She poked me with her elbow for the liberty and made me take her in a bar.

Only this one was nearly empty and the only dangerous character was a drunk arguing with the bartender about who was going to win the series. When we had our drink I asked her if she wanted another and she shook her head. "One's enough on top of what happened tonight. I think I'd like to go home, Mike."

She lived in the upper Sixties on the top floor of the only new building in the block. About a half-dozen brownstones had been razed to clear an area for the new structure and it stood out like a dame in a French bathing suit at an old maids' convention. It was still a pretty good neighborhood, but most of the new convertibles and sleek black sedans were lumped together in front of her place.

I got in line behind the cars at the curb and opened the door for her. "Aren't you coming up for a midnight snack, Mike?"

"I thought I was supposed to ask that," I laughed.

"Times have changed. Especially when you get my age."

So I went up.

There was an automatic elevator, marble-lined corridors under the thick maroon rugs, expensive knickknacks and antique furniture all for free before you even hit the apartment itself. The layout wasn't much different inside, either. For apartment-hungry New York, this was luxury. There were six rooms with the best of everything in each as far as I could see. The living room was one of these ultra modern places with angular furniture that looked like hell until you sat in it. All along the mantel of the imitation fireplace was a collection of genuine Paul Revere pieces that ran into big dough, while the biggest of the pieces, each with its own copper label of historical data, was used beside the front windows as flowerpots.

I kind of squinted at Ellen as I glanced around. "How much do they pay you to do secretarial work?"

Her laugh made a tinkling sound in the room. "Not this much, I'll tell you. Three of us share this apartment, so it's not too hard to manage.

The copper work you seem to admire belongs to Patty. She was working for Captain Chambers with me tonight."

"Oh, short and fat."

"She has certain virtues that attract men."

"Money?"

Ellen nodded.

"Then why does she work?"

"So she can meet men, naturally."

"Cripes, are all the babes after all the men?"

"It seems so. Now, if you'll just stay put I'll whip up a couple of sandwiches. Want something to drink?"

"Beer if you have it."

She said she had it and went back to the kitchen. She fooled around out there for about five minutes and finally managed to get an inch of ham to stay between the bread. A lanky towheaded job in one of these shortie nightgowns must have heard the raid on the icebox, because she came out of the bedroom as Ellen came in and snatched the extra sandwich off the plate. Just as she was going to pop it in her mouth she saw me and said, "Hi."

I said "Hi" back.

She said, "Ummm," but that was before she bit into the sandwich.

Moving her arms jerked the shortie up too far. Ellen blocked the view by handing me my beer and called back over her shoulder, "Either go put some more clothes on or get back in bed."

The towhead took another bite and mumbled, "With you around I need a handicap." She took another bite and shuffled back to the bedroom.

"See what I have to put up with?"

"I wish I had to put up with it."

"You would."

So we sat and finished the snack and dawdled over a beer until I said it was time to scram and she looked painfully unhappy with an expression that said I could stay if I wanted to badly enough. I told her about the kid and the arrangements I had made with the nurse, tacking on that I should have tucked him into bed long ago.

The same look she had in the office stole into her face. "Tuck me into bed too, Mike," she said. With the lithe grace of an animal she slid out of the chair past me and in the brief second that our eyes met I felt the heat of the passion that burned behind those deep blue irises.

Not much more than a minute could have passed. Her voice was a husky whisper calling, "Mike . . ." and I went to her.

There was no light except that which seeped in from the other room, a faint glow that made a bulky shadow of the bed with lesser shadows outlining the furniture against the deeper blackness of the room itself. I could hear the rhythmic sigh of her breathing, too heavy to be normal, and my hands shook when I stuck a cigarette in my mouth.

She said, "Mike . . ." again and struck the match.

Her hair was a smooth mass of bronze on the pillow, her mouth full and rich, showing the shiny white edges of her teeth. There was only the sheet over her that rose and dipped between the inviting hollows of her breasts. Ellen was beautiful as only a mature woman can be beautiful. She was lustful as only a mature woman can be lustful.

"Tuck me in, Mike."

The match burned closer to my fingers. I reached down and got the corner of the sheet in my fingers and flipped it all the way back. She lay there beautiful and naked and waiting.

"I love brunettes," I said.

The tone of my voice told her no, not tonight, but her smile didn't fade. She just grinned impishly because she knew I'd never be able to look at her again and say no. "You're a heel, Mike."

The match went out. "You told me that once tonight."

"You're a bigger heel than I thought." Then she laughed. When I backed out of the room she was still chuckling, but that thing was running up my back again.

I was thinking of her all the way back to my apartment and thinking of her when I put my car away. I was thinking too damn much to be careful. When I stabbed my key in the lock and turned it there was a momentary catch in the tumblers before it went all the way around and I swore out loud as I rammed the door with my shoulder and hit the floor. Something swished through the air over my head and I caught an arm and pulled a squirming, fighting bundle of muscle down on top of me.

If I could have reached my rod I would have blown his guts out. His breath was in my face and I brought my knee up, but he jerked out of the way bringing his hand down again and my shoulder went numb after a split second of blinding pain. He tried again with one hand going for my throat, but I got one foot loose and kicked out and up and felt my toe smash into his groin. The cramp of the pain doubled him over on top of me, his breath sucking in like a leaky tire.

Then I got cocky. I thought I had him. I went to get up and he moved. Just once. That thing in his hand smashed against the side of my head and I started to crumple up piece by piece until there wasn't anything left except the sense to see and hear enough to know that he had crawled out of the room and was falling down the stairs outside. Then I thought about the lock on my door and how I had a guy fix it so I could tell if it had been jimmied open so I wouldn't step into any blind alleys without a gun in my hand, but because of a dame who lay naked and smiling on a bed I wouldn't share I had forgotten all about it.

And that was all.

CHAPTER 4

I thought I was in a boat that was sinking and I tried to get over the side before it turned over on me. I clawed for the railing that wouldn't stand still while the screaming of the bells and mechanical pounding of laboring engines blasted the air with frantic insistence.

Somehow I got my eyes open and saw that I wasn't in a boat, but on the floor of my own apartment trying to grab the edge of the table. My head felt like a huge swollen thing that throbbed with a terrible fury, sending the pain shooting down to the balls of my feet. I choked on my tongue and muttered thickly, "God . . . my head . . . my head!"

The phone didn't let up and whoever was pounding on the door wouldn't go away because they could hear me inside.

I staggered to the door first and cursed. It was still unlocked; nobody had to pound like that. The damn thing was almost too heavy for me to open with one hand.

I guess I must have looked pretty bad. The elderly nurse took one look at me and her arms tightened protectively around the kid. He didn't scare so easily though, or maybe he was used to seeing a bloated, unshaven face. He laughed.

"Come on in," I said.

The old lady didn't like the idea, but she came in. Mad, too. "Mr. Hammer . . ." she started.

"Look, get off my back. I wasn't drunk or disorderly. I damn near got my skull smashed in. . . ." I looked at the light streaming in the windows, "last night. Right here. I'm sorry you were inconvenienced, but I'll pay for it. Goddamn that phone . . . hello, hello!"

"Mike?"

I recognized Pat's voice. "Yeah, it's me. What's left of me."

"What happened?" He sounded sharp and impatient.

"Nothing. I just got jumped in my own joint and nearly brained, that's all. The bastard got away."

"Look, you get down here as fast as you can, understand? On the double."

"Now what's up?"

"Trouble, and it's all yours, friend. Damn it, Mike, how many times do I have to remind you to keep your nose out of police business!"

"Wait a minute . . ."

"Wait my foot. Get down here before the D.A. sends somebody after you. There's another murder and it's got your name on it."

I hung up and told my head to go right ahead and explode if it wanted to.

Then the old lady let out a short scream and nearly broke her neck running for the kid. He was on his hands and knees reaching for my gun that lay under the table on the floor. She kicked it away and snapped him back on her lap.

Lord, what a day this was going to be!

Somebody else was at the door this time and all they had to do was rap just once more before I got it opened and they'd get a rap right in the teeth. The guy in the uniform said, "You Michael Hammer?"

Nodding my head hurt, so I grunted that I was.

He handed me a box about two feet long and held out a pad. "Package from the Uptown Kiddie Shop. Sign here, please."

I scrawled my name, handed him a quarter and took the package inside. There was a stack of new baby clothes under the wrappings with a note on top addressed to me. It said,

Dear Mike:
   Men are never much good at these things, so I picked up some clothes for the little boy. Let me know if they fit all right.

Marsha

The nurse was still eyeing me suspiciously. I handed her the boy and edged back to a nice soft chair. "Before you say anything, let me explain one thing. The kid's old man was bumped. Murdered. He's an orphan and I'm trying to find out who made him that way. Somebody doesn't like the idea and they got funny ways of telling me so, but that isn't stopping me any. Maybe this'll happen again and maybe it won't, but you'd be doing me and the kid a big favor if you'll put up with it until this mess is cleaned up. Will you?"

Her face was expressionless a moment, then broke into a smile. "I . . . think I understand."

"Good. Arrangements are being made now so the kid'll be taken care of permanently. It won't be long." I patted the back of my head and winced.

"You'd better let me take a look at your scalp," she said.

She let me hold the kid while she probed around the lump awhile. If she had found a hole to stick her finger in, I wouldn't have been at all surprised. Finally she stood back satisfied and picked the kid up. "There doesn't seem to be anything wrong, but if I were you I'd see a doctor anyway."

I told her I would.

"You know, Mr. Hammer, in my time I've seen a great deal of suffering. It isn't new to me, not by a long sight. All I ask is that you don't bring any of it home to the child."

"Nothing will bother the kid. I'll see to that. He'll be all right with you then?"

"I'll take perfect care of him." She paused and her face creased in a frown. "This town is full of rabid dogs and there's not a dogcatcher in sight."

"I kill mad dogs," I said.

"Yes, I've heard that you do. Good morning, Mr. Hammer." I handed her the box of clothes, picked the rod up from the floor and ushered her out.

My head was still booming away and I tried to fix it up with a hot shower. That helped, but a mess of bacon and eggs helped even more. It woke me up enough to remember Pat said my name was on a murder and I didn't have the sense to ask who he was talking about.

I gave it a try on the phone anyway, but they couldn't locate Pat in the building anywhere. I held the receiver down for a second, long enough to check Marsha's number in the book, then punched out her call. The nurse with the mustache answered and told me that Miss Lee had just left for a morning rehearsal of the Little Theater Group and wasn't expected back until later that afternoon.

Nuts. So now I had to go down to police headquarters and face an inquisition. My legs had more life in them by the time I reached the street, and when I had pulled up in front of the building downtown I was back to normal in a sense. At least I felt like having a beer and a butt without choking over the thought.

They were real happy to see me, they were. They looked like they hoped I wouldn't come so they could go drag me down by the neck, but now that I was there everything was malicious, tight smiles and short, sharp sentences that steered me into a little room where I was supposed to sit and sweat so I'd blab my head off when they asked me questions.

I spit on the floor, right in the middle, to be exact, and had the Lucky I wanted. The college boy with the pointed face who rated as the D.A.'s assistant glared at me but didn't have the guts to back it up with any words. He parked behind a desk and tried to look important and tough. It was a lousy act.

When I started wondering how long they were going to let me cool my heels the corridor got noisy and I picked out Pat's voice raising Cain with somebody. The door slammed open and he stalked in with his face tight in anger.

I said, " 'lo, Pal," but he didn't answer.

He walked up to the desk and leaned on it until his face wasn't an inch away from the D.A.'s boy and he did a good job of keeping his hands off the guy's neck. "Since when do you take over the duties of the Police Department? I'm still Captain of Homicide around here and when there's murder I'll handle it myself, personally, understand? I ought to knock your ears off for pulling a stunt like that!"

The boy got a blustery red and started to get up. "See here, the District Attorney gave me full permission . . ."

"To butt into my business because a friend of mine is suspected of murder!"

"Exactly!"

Pat's voice got dangerously low. "Get your ass out of this office before I kick hell out of you. Go on, get out. And you tell the D.A. that I'll see him in a few minutes."

He practically ran to the door. I could see the D.A. getting a sweet version of the story, all right. I said, "What'd he do to you, kid?"

"Crazy little bastard. He thinks because I'm a friend of yours I'll do a little whitewashing. He got me out of the building on a phony call right after I spoke to you."

"You're not going to be very popular with the D.A. for that."

"I'm sick of that guy walking all over this office. They pulled a raid on a wire room last night and all they got was an empty apartment with a lot of holes in the walls and a blackboard that still showed track results and a snotty little character who said he was thinking of opening a school for handicappers. The guy was clean and there wasn't a thing the D.A. could do."

"Sounds like a good business. Whose wire room was it?"

"Hell, who else has wire rooms in this town? The place was run by one of Ed Teen's outfit."

"Or so your information said."

"Yeah. So now the D.A. gets in a rile and raises hell with everyone from the mayor down. He's pulled his last rough sketch on me with this deal though. Let him try getting rough just once and the news boys are going to get a lot of fancy stuff that won't do a thing for him when election time comes."

"Where is he now?"

"Inside waiting for you."

"Let's see the guy then."

"Just a minute. Tell me something straight. Did you kill a guy named Mel Hooker?" he asked.

"Oh, God!"

Pat's eyes got that squinty look. "What's the matter?"

"Your corpse was the friend of William Decker . . . That beautiful local-type kill the police seem to be ignoring so well."

"The police aren't ignoring anything."

"Then they're not looking very hard. Mel and Decker were playing the ponies and Mel introduced him to a loan shark that financed his little escapades. There was a catch in it. Mel said Decker lost his shirt, but the loan shark, that Dixie Cooper guy, said Decker paid him off in full and was able to prove it."

Pat muttered something under his breath. He nodded for me to follow him and started for the door. This time the tight smiles loosened up and nobody seemed to want to get in our way. From the way Pat was glowering it looked like he was ready to take me and anybody else apart and had already started.

Pat knocked on the door and I heard the D.A. call out for somebody to see who it was. The door opened, a pair of thick-lensed glasses did a quick focus on the two of us and the D.A. said, "Show them in, Mr. Mertig."

It was quite a gathering. The D.A. straddled his throne with two assistant D.A.'s flanking him, a pair of plainclothes men in the background and two more over by the window huddled together for mutual protection apparently.

"Sit down, Hammer," the D.A. said.

Everybody watched me with the annoyed look you see when the king isn't obeyed pronto. I walked up to his desk, planted my hands on the top and leaned right down in his face. I didn't like the guy and he didn't like me, but he wasn't getting snooty now or any other time. I said, "You call me *Mister* when you use my name. I don't want any crap from you or your boys and if you think you can make it tough for me just go ahead and try it. I came in here myself to save you the trouble of getting a false arrest charge slapped against your office and right now I'm not above walking out just to see what you'd do. It's about time you learned to be polite to your public when you're not sure of your facts."

The D.A. started to get purple. In fact, a lot of people started to get purple. When they all got a nice livid tinge I sat down.

He made a good job of keeping his voice under control. "We are sure of the facts . . . *Mister* Hammer."

"Go on."

"A certain Mel Hooker has been found dead. He was shot to death with a .45."

"I suppose the bullet came from my gun?" I tried to make it sound as sarcastic as possible.

The purple started to fade into an unhealthy red. Unhealthy for me, I mean. "Unfortunately, no. The bullet passed through the man and out the window. So far we haven't been able to locate it."

I started to interrupt, but he held up his hand. "However, you were very generous with your fingerprints. They're all over the place. The landlady identified your picture and vouched that she heard threats before you left, so it is quite a simple matter to see what followed."

"Yeah, I went back later and shot him. I'm really that stupid."

"Yes, you really are." His eyes were narrow slits in his face.

"And you got rocks in your head," I said. He started to get up but I beat him to it. I stood there looking down at him so he could see what I thought of him. "You're a real bright boy, you are. Brother, the voters sure must be **proud** of you! Christ, you're ready to kick anything around because your vice racket business is getting the works. It's got you so far down you're all set to slap me in the clink without having the foresight to ask me if I got an alibi or not for the time of the shooting. So it happened last night and I don't know what time and without bothering to find out I'll hand you my alibi on a platter and you can choke on it."

I pointed to the intercom on his desk. "Get Ellen Scobie in here."

The D.A.'s face was wet with an angry sweat. His finger triggered the gadget and when Ellen answered he told her to come in.

Before the door opened I had a chance to look at Pat and he was shaking his head slowly trying to tell me not to go overboard so far I couldn't get back. Ellen came in, smiled at me through a puzzled frown and stood there waiting to see what was going on. From the look that passed between us, the D.A. caught on fast, but he wasn't letting me get in any prompting first. He said, "Miss Scobie, were you with this . . . with *Mister* Hammer last night at, say eleven-thirty?"

She didn't have to think to answer that one. "Yes, I did happen to be with him."

"Where were you?"

"I should say that we were sitting in a bar about then. A place on Fifty-second Street."

"That's all, Miss Scobie."

Everybody ushered her out of the room with their eyes. When the door clicked shut the D.A.'s voice twanged like a flat banjo string. "You may go too, *Mister* Hammer. I'm getting a little tired of your impertinence." His face had turned a deadly white and he was speaking through his teeth. "I wouldn't be a bit surprised if your license was revoked very shortly."

My voice came out a hiss more than anything else. "I'd be," I said. "You tried that once before and remember what happened?"

That's all I had to say and for a few seconds I was the only one who didn't stop breathing in the room. Nobody bothered to open the door for me this time. I went out myself and started down the corridor, then Pat caught up with me.

We must have been thinking the same things, because neither one of us bothered to speak until we were two blocks away in Louie's place where a quick beer cooled things down to a boil.

Pat grinned at me in the mirror behind the bar. "You're a lucky bastard, Mike. If the press wasn't so hot on the D.A.'s heels you'd be out of business if he lost the election over it."

"Aw, he gives me a pain. Okay, he's got it in for me, but does he have to be so goddamn stupid about it? Why didn't he do some checking first. Christ, him and his investigators are making the police look ridiculous. I'm no chump. I got as much on the ball as any of his stooges and in my own way maybe I got as many scruples too."

"Ease off, Mike. I'm on your side."

"I know, but you're tied down too. Who has to get murdered before the boob will put some time in on the case? Right now you got three corpses locked together as nicely as you please and what's being done?"

"More than you think."

I sipped the top of my beer and watched his eyes in the mirror. "It wasn't any news that Decker and Hooker were tied up. The lab boys lifted a few prints out of his apartment. Some of them were Hooker's."

"He have a record?"

Pat shook his head. "During the war he had a job that required security and he was printed. We picked up the blind newspaper dealer's prints too. He had a record."

"I know. They graduated from the same Alma Mater up the river."

Pat grinned again. "You know too damn much."

"Yeah, but you do it the easy way. What else do you know?"

"You tell me, Mike."

"What?"

"The things you have in that mind of yours, chum. I want your angle first."

I ordered another round and lit a cigarette to go with it. "Decker needed dough. His wife was undergoing an operation that cost heavy sugar and he had to get it from someplace. He and Hooker got some hot tips on the nags and they pooled their dough to make some fast money. When they found out the tips were solid ones they went in deeper. Hooker pulled out while he was ahead, but Decker wanted to make the big kill so he borrowed a grand from Dixie Cooper. According to Hooker, he lost everything and was in hock to Cooper for plenty, but when I braced the guy he proved that Decker had paid him back.

"Okay, he had to get the dough from somebody. He sure as hell didn't work for it because the docks have been too slow the past month. He had to do one of two things . . . either steal it or borrow it. It could be that when he went back to his old trade he found it so profitable he couldn't or didn't want to give it up. If that was the case then he made a mistake and broke into the wrong apartment. He and his partners were expecting a juicy haul and if Decker spent a lot of time casing the joint a gimmick like breaking into the wrong apartment would have looked like a sorry excuse to the other two who were expecting part of the proceeds. In that case he would have tried to take a flyer and they caught up with him."

Pat looked down into his glass. "Then where does Hooker come in?"

"They were friends, weren't they? First Decker gets bumped for pulling a funny stunt, the driver of the car gives the second guy the works so he won't be captured and squeal, then he goes and gets Hooker because he's afraid Decker might have spilled the works to his friend."

"I'll buy that," Pat said. "It's exactly the way I've had it figured."

"You buy it and you'll be stuck," I told him. I finished my beer and let the bartender fill it up again. Pat was making wry faces now. He was waiting for the rest of it.

I gave it to him. "William Decker hadn't been pulling any jobs before that one. He was going straight all along the line. He must have known what might happen and got his affairs in order right down to making provisions for his kid. If Decker paid off Cooper then he borrowed the dough from somebody else and the somebody put on the squeeze play. For my money they even knew where the dough could be had and laid it out so all Decker had to do was go up the fire escape and open up the safe.

"That's where he made his mistake. He got into the wrong place and after all the briefing he had who the hell would believe his story. No, Decker knew he jimmied the wrong can and didn't dare take a chance on correcting the error because Marsha Lee could have come to at any time and called the cops. In the league where he was playing they only allow you one mistake. Decker knew they would believe that he had stashed the money thinking to come back later and get it, so he took off by himself.

"What happened was this . . . he had to go home for his kid. When they knew he had taken a powder they put it together and beat it back to his place. By that time he was gone, but they picked him up fast enough. When he knew he was trapped he kissed his kid good-by and walked out into a bullet. That boy of Grindle's searched him for the dough and when he didn't find it, the logical thought was that he hid it in his apartment. He didn't have much chance to do anything else. So, the driver of the car scooted back there and got into the place and messed it up."

Pat's teeth were making harsh grating noises and his fingers rasped against the woodwork of the bar. "So you're all for nailing the driver of the murder car, right?"

The way I grinned wasn't human. It tied my face up into a bunch of hard knots. "Nope," I said, "that's your job. You can have him. I want the son-of-a-bitch who put the pressure on him. I want the guy who made somebody decent revert back to a filthy crime and I want him right between my hands so I can squeeze the juice out of him."

"Where is he, Mike?"

"If I knew I wouldn't tell you, friend. I want him for myself. Someday I want to be able to tell that kid what his face looked like when he was dying."

"Damn it anyway, Mike, you can stretch friendship too far sometimes."

"No, I'll never stretch it, Pat. Just remember that I live in this town too. Besides having what few police powers the state chooses to hand me, I'm still a citizen and responsible in some small way for what happens in the city. And by God, if I'm partly responsible then I have a right to take care of an obligation like removing a lousy orphan-maker."

"Who is he, Mike?"

"I said I didn't know."

"But you know where to find out."

"That's right. It isn't too hard if you want to take a chance on getting your head smashed in."

"Like you did last night?"

"Yeah. That's something else I have to even up. I don't know why or how it happened, but I got a beaut of an idea, I have."

"Something like looking for a guy named Lou Grindle whom you called all sorts of names and threatened to shoot on sight if you found out he was responsible for Decker's death?"

My mouth fell open. "How the hell did you get that?"

"Now you're taking me for the chump, Mike. I checked the tie-up Arnold Basil had with Grindle thoroughly, and from the way Lou acted I knew somebody had been there before me. It didn't take long to guess who it was. Lou was steamed up to beat hell and told me what happened. Let me tell you something. Don't try anything with that boy. The D.A. has men covering him every minute he's awake trying to get something on him."

"Where was he last night then?"

A thundercloud rolled over Pat's face. "The bastard skipped out. He pulled a fastie and skipped his apartment and never got back until eleven. In case you're thinking he had anything to do with Hooker's death, forget it. He couldn't have gotten back at that time."

"I'm not thinking anything. I was just going to tell you he was in a place called the Glass Bar on Eighth Avenue with Ed Teen somewhere around ten. The D.A. ought to get new eyes. The old ones are going bad."

Pat swore under his breath.

I said, "What made you say that, Pat?"

"Say what?"

"Oh, connect Lou and Hooker."

"Hell, I didn't connect anything. I just said . . ."

"You said something that ought to make you think a lot more, boy. Grindle and Decker and Hooker don't go together at all. They're miles apart. In fact, they're so far apart they're backing into each other from the ends."

He set his glass down with a thump. "Wait a minute. Don't go getting this thing screwed up with a lot of wacky ideas. Lou Grindle isn't playing with anything worth a few grand and if he is, he doesn't send out blockheads to do the job. You're way the hell out of line."

"Okay, don't get excited."

"Good Lord, who's getting excited? Damn it, Mike . . ."

My face was as flat as I could make it. I just sat there with the beer in my hand and stared at myself in the mirror because I started thinking of something that was like a shadow hovering in the background. I thought about it for a long time and it was still a shadow when I finished and it had a shape that was so curious I wanted to go up closer for another look.

I didn't hear Pat because his voice was so low it was almost a whisper, but he repeated it loud enough so I could hear it and he made me look at him so I wouldn't forget it. His hands were a nervous bunch of fingers that opened and shut with every word and his mouth was all teeth with sharp biting edges.

"Mike, you try pulling a smart frame that will pull Grindle into that damn murder case of yours and you and I are finished! We've worked too damn long and hard to nail that punk and his boss to have you slip over a cutie that will stink up the whole works. Don't give me the business, friend. I know you and the way you work. Anything appeals to you just as long as you can point a gun at somebody. For my money Lou Grindle is as far away from this as I am and because one of his boys tried to pick up some extra change you can't fix him for it. All right, I'll give you the benefit of the doubt and say that if you tried hard enough and lived through it you'd do it, but Lou's got Teen and a lot more behind him. He'd get out of that charge easy as pie and only leave the department open for another big laugh. When we get those two, we want them so it'll stick, and no frame is going to do it. You lay off, hear?"

I didn't answer him for a long minute, then: "I wasn't thinking of any frame, Pat."

Pat's hands were still jerking on the bar. "The hell you weren't. Remember what I told you, that's all." He swilled his beer down and fiddled with the empty glass until the bartender moved in and filled it up again. I didn't say a damn thing. I just sat. Pat's fingernails were little firecrackers going off against the wood while his coat rippled as the muscles bunched underneath the fabric.

It lasted about five minutes, then he drained the glass and shoved it back. He muttered, "Goddamn!"

I said, "Relax, chum."

Then he repeated what he said the first time, told me to take it easy, and swung off the stool. I waited until he was out the door, then started to laugh. It wasn't so easy to be a cop. At least not a city cop. Or maybe it was the years that were getting him down. Six years ago you couldn't get him excited about anything, not even a murder or a naked dame with daisies in her hair.

The bartender came over and asked me if I wanted another. I said no and shoved him a quarter to make into change, then picked up a dime and walked back to the phone booth. The book listed the Little Theater as being on the edge of Greenwich Village and a babe with a low-down voice told me that Miss Lee was there and rehearsing and if I was a friend I could certainly come up.

The Little Theater was an old warehouse with a poster-decorated front that was a lousy disguise. The day had warped into a hot afternoon and the air inside the place was even hotter, wetter and bedded down with the perfumed smell of make-up. A sawed-off babe in a Roman toga let me in, locked the door to keep out the spies, then wiggled her fanny in the direction of all the noise to show me where to go. A pair of swinging doors opened and two more dames in togas came through for a smoke. They stood right in the glare of the only light in the place look-ing too cool to be real and lit up the smokes without seeing me there in the shadows.

Then I saw why they were so cool. One of them flipped the damn thing open and stood with her hands on her hips and she didn't have a thing on underneath it. Sawed-off said, "Helen, we have a visitor."

And Helen finally saw me, smiled, and said, "How nice."

But she didn't bother to do anything about the toga. I said, "The play's the thing," and sawed-off grinned a little like she wished she had thought of the open-toga deal first herself and sort of pushed me into the swinging doors.

Inside, a pair of floor fans moved the air around enough to make you think you were cool, at least. I opened my shirt and tie, then stood there for a moment getting used to the artificial dusk. All around the place were stacks of funeral-parlor chairs with clothes draped over them. Up front a rickety stage held up some more togas and a few centurians in uniform while a hairy-legged little squirt in tennis shorts screamed at them in a high falsetto as he pounded a script against an old upright piano.

It wasn't hard to find Marsha. There was a baby spot behind her outlining a hundred handfuls of lovely curves through the white cotton toga. She was the most beautiful woman in the place even with a touched-up shiner, and from where I stood I could see that there was plenty of competition.

The squirt with the hairy legs called for a ten-minute break and sawed-off called something up to Marsha I didn't catch. She tried to peer past the glare of the footlights, didn't make out too well, so came off the stage in a jump and ran all the way back to where I was.

Her hands were warm, friendly things that grabbed mine and held on. "Did you get my package, Mike?"

"Yup. Came down to think you personally."

"How is the boy?"

"Fine, just fine. Don't ask me how I feel because I'll give you a stinking answer. Somebody tried to break my head open last night."

"Mike!"

"I got a hard head."

She moved up close and ran her hand over my hair to where the bump was and wrinkled her nose at me. "Do you know who it was?"

"No. If I did the bastard'd be in the hospital."

Marsha took my arm and nodded over to the side of the wall. "Let's sit down a few minutes. I can worry better about you that way."

"Why worry about me at all?"

The eye with the shiner was closed just enough to give it the damnedest look you ever saw. "I could be a fool and tell you why, Mike," she said. "Shall I be a fool?"

If ever I had wanted to kiss a woman it was then, only she had too much make-up on and there were too many people for an audience. "Later. Tonight, maybe," I told her. "Be a fool then." I was grinning and her lips went into a smile that said a lot of things, but mostly was a promise of tonight.

When we had a pair of cigarettes going I tipped my chair back against the wall and stared at her. "We have another murder on our hands, kitten."

The cigarette stopped halfway to her lips and her head came around slowly. "Another? Oh, no!"

I nodded. "Guy named Mel Hooker. He was Decker's best friend.

You know, Marsha, I think there's a hell of a lot more behind this than we thought."

"Chain reaction," she softly.

"Sort of. It didn't take much to start it going. Three hundred bucks and a necklace, to be exact."

Marsha nodded, her lips between her teeth. "My playboy friend in the other apartment was coerced into keeping his money in a bank instead of the wall safe. The management threatened to break his lease unless he co-operated. Everybody in the building knows what happened and raised a fuss about it. Apparently the idea of being beaten up by a burglar doesn't sound very appealing, especially when the burglar is wild over having made a mistake in safes."

"You got off easy. He might have killed you."

Her shoulders twitched convulsively. "What are you going to do, Mike?"

"Keep looking. Make enough stink so trouble'll come looking for me. Sometimes it's easier that way."

"Do you . . . have to?" Her eyes were soft, and her hand on my arm squeezed me gently.

"I have to, kid. I'm made that way. I hate killers."

"But do you have to be so . . . so damned reckless about it?"

"Yeah. Yeah, I do. I don't have to be but that's the way I like it. Then I can cut them down and enjoy it."

"Oh, Lord! Mike, please . . ."

"Look, kid, when you play with mugs you can't be coy. At first this looked all cut-and-dried-out and all there was to it was nailing a bimbo who drove a car with a hot rod in the back seat. That's the way it looked at first. Now we got names creeping into this thing, names and faces that don't belong to any cheap bimbos. There's Teen and Grindle and a guy who died a long time ago but who won't stay buried . . . his name was Charlie Fallon and I keep hearing it every time I turn around."

Somebody said, "Charlie Fallon?" in a voice that ended with a chuckle and I turned around, chewing on my words.

The place was getting to look like backstage of a burlesque house. The woman in the dress toga did a trick with the oversize cigarette holder and stood there smiling at us. She was medium in height only. The rest of her was over-done, but that's the way they liked them in Hollywood. Her name was Kay Cutler and she was right in there among the top movie stars and it wasn't hard to see why.

Marsha introduced us and I stood there like an idiot with one of those nobody-meets-celebrity grins all over my pan. She held my hand longer than was necessary and said, "Surprised?"

"Hell, yes. How come all the talent in this dump?"

The two of them laughed together. Kay did another trick with the holder. "It's a hobby that gets a lot of exciting publicity. Actually we don't play the parts for the audience. Instead we portray them so the others can use our interpretation as a model, then coach them into giving some sort of a performance. You wouldn't believe it, but the theater group makes quite a bit of money for itself. Enough to cover expenses, at least."

"You come for free?"

She laughed and let her eyes drift to one of the centurians who was giving me some dark looks. "Well, not exactly."

Marsha poked me in the back so I'd quit leering. I said, "You mentioned Charlie Fallon before. Where'd you hear of him?"

"If he's the one I'm thinking of a lot of people knew him. Was he the gangster?"

"That's right."

"He was a fan-letter writer. God, how that man turned them out! Even the extras used to get notes and flowers from the old goat. I bet I've had twenty or more."

"That was a long time ago," I reminded her.

She smiled until the dimples showed in her cheeks. "You aren't supposed to mention the passage of time so lightly. I still claim to be in my early thirties."

"What are you?"

I got the dimples again. "I'm a liar," she said. "Marsha, didn't you ever get mail from that character?"

"Perhaps. At the time I didn't handle my own correspondence and it was all sorted out for me." She paused and squinted a little. "Come to think of it, yes. I did. I remember talking about it to someone one day."

I pulled on the butt and let the smoke out slowly. "He was like that. The guy made plenty and didn't know how to spend it, so he threw it away on the girlies. I wonder if he ever followed it up?"

"Never," Kay stated flatly. "When he was still news some of the columnists kept up with his latest crushes and slipped in a publicity line now and then, but nobody ever saw him around the Coast. By the way, what's so important about him now?"

"I wish I knew. For a dead man he's sure not forgotten."

"Mike is a detective, Kay," Marsha said bluntly. "There have been a couple of murders and Mike's conducting an investigation."

"And not getting far," I added.

"Really?" Her eyebrows went up and she cocked the holder between her teeth and gave me a look that was sexy right down to her sandals. "A detective. You sound exciting."

"You're not going to sound at all if you don't get back to your warrior, lady," Marsha cut in. "Now scram."

Kay faked a pout at her and said so long to me after another long hand-clasp. When she was across the room Marsha slipped her arm through mine. "Kay's a wonderful gal, but if you have it and it wears pants she wants it."

"Good old Kay," I said.

"Luckily, I know her too well."

"Any more around like that?"

"Well, if it's a celebrity you'd like to meet, I can take you backstage and introduce you to a pair of Hollywood starlets, a television sensation, the country's biggest comic and . . ."

"Never mind," I said. "You're enough for me."

She gave me another one of those squeezes with a laugh thrown in and I wanted to kiss her again. The kid with an arm in a sling who tapped her on the shoulder as he murmured, "Two minutes more, Marsha," must have read my mind, because his eyes went limp and sad.

Marsha nodded as he walked off and I pointed my cigarette at his back. "The kid's got a crush on you."

She watched him a moment, then glanced at me. "I know it. He's only nineteen and I'm afraid he has stars in his eyes. A month ago he was in love with Helen O'Roark and was so far down in the dumps when he found out she was married he almost starved himself to death. He's the one I took to the hospital the night the Decker fellow broke into my apartment."

"What happened to him?"

"He was setting up props and fell off the ladder."

Down at the end of the hall hairy legs in short pants was banging on the piano again screaming for everyone to get back on the stage. Togas started to unravel from the floor, chairs and the scenery and if I had a dozen more pairs of eyes I could have enjoyed myself. Those babes didn't give a damn what they showed and I seemed to be the only one there who appreciated the view. The overhead lights went out and the stage spots came on and I was doing good watching the silhouettes until Marsha said, "I'm getting jealous, Mike."

It wasn't so much what she said as the way she said it that made me jerk around. And there she was leaning on the stack of chairs like a nymph under a waterfall with her own toga wide open down the middle and an impish little grin playing with her mouth. She was barely a reflection of light and shadow, a vague white statue of warm, live flesh that moved with her breathing, then the toga came shut slowly before I could move and she was out of reach.

"You don't have to be jealous of anybody," I said.

She smiled again, and in the darkness her hand touched mine briefly and the cigarette fell out of my fingers to the floor where it lay like a hot red eye. Then she was gone and all I could think about was tonight.

CHAPTER 5

After the Little Theater the glare of the sun was almost blinding. I fired up another butt and climbed back into the car where I finished smoking it before I had myself in line again. All the while I kept seeing Marsha in that white toga until it was branded into my brain so deeply that it blotted out everything else. Marsha and Kay and Helen of Troy or something in a lot of white togas drifting through the haze like beautiful ghosts.

Like the ghost of a killer I was after. I threw the butt out the window and hit the starter.

I let my hands and my eyes drive me through traffic while the rest of me sat and thought. It should have been so damn easy. Three guys dead and a killer running loose looking for his lousy split of a robbery that didn't happen. Decker dead on the sidewalk. Arnold Basil dead in the gutter. Hooker dead in his own room and me damn near dead on the floor. Sure it was easy, just like an illiterate doing acrostics.

Then where the hell was the big puzzle? Was it because Basil had been Lou Grindle's boy, or because Fallon's name kept cropping up? I jammed the horn down at the guy in front of me and yelled as I pulled around him. He gave me a scared grimace and plenty of room and I shot by him swearing at the little things that piled up one after the other.

Then I grinned because that was where the puzzle was. In all the little things.

Like the boys who tried to take me when I was putting the buzz on Hooker.

Like the money that Decker had picked up from somewhere to pay off Dixie Cooper.

Like Decker putting his affairs in order before he walked out and got himself bumped.

Now I knew where I was going and what I wanted to do, so I got off the avenue onto a street and headed west until I could smell the river and see the trucks pulling into their docks for the night and hear the mixture of tongues as the longshoremen streamed out of the yards.

The nearest of them were still ten minutes away when I pulled up outside the hole-in-the-wall saloon and there weren't any early birds inside when I pushed the door open. The bartender was perched on a stool watching the television and his hand automatically went out for a glass as he heard me slide up to the bar.

I didn't let him waste his beer. I said, "Remember me, buddy?"

He had a frown all set and his mouth shaped to tell me off when his memory came back with a jolt. "Yeah." His frown had a twisted look now.

I leaned on the bar so my coat hung loose enough for him to see the leather of the gun sling and he knew I wasn't kidding around. "Who were they, buddy?"

"Look, I . . ."

"Maybe I ought to ask it different. Maybe I ought to ask it with the nose of a gun shoved down your throat. You can get it that way if you want."

He choked up a little and his eyes kept darting toward the door hoping someone would come in. He licked his lips to bring the words out and said, "I . . . don't know . . . who the hell they were."

"You like it the hard way, don't you? Now just once I'm going to tell you something and I want an answer. Scarface Hooker is dead. He was shot last night and because you know who they were you might be sitting on top of a powder keg. In case you're not sure, let me tell you that you are right now . . . with me. I'm going to bust you wide open or leave you for those babies to handle."

The guy started to sweat. It formed in little cold drops along the ridges of his forehead and rolled down his cheeks. He made a swipe with the back of his hand across his mouth and swallowed hard. "They was private detectives."

"They were like hell."

"Look, I'm telling ya, I saw their badges."

"Tell me some more."

"They come in here looking for Hooker. They said he was working against the union and pulling a lot of rough stuff. Hell, how'd I know? I'm a union man myself. If that's what he was doing he shoulda got beat up. They showed me their badges and said they was working for the union so I played along."

"Ever see them before?"

"No."

"Anybody else see them?"

"Yeah."

"Goddamn it, say something! Don't give me one word."

"One guy says they was uptown boys. They was roughs . . . strong-arm boys. The little guy . . . I heard the other one call him Nocky."

"What else?"

"That's all. I swear to God I don't know no more."

I slid my elbows off the bar and gave him a tight grin. "Okay, friend, you did fine. Let me give you a word of advice. If either of those boys come in here again you pick up the phone and call the nearest precinct station."

"Sure. I'll ask 'em to blow my crazy head off, too."

"They might do it before you reach the phone, mister. Those lads were after Hooker and it might have been them who got to him. They won't like anybody who can put the finger on 'em. Remember what I told you."

He started to sweat again. All along his neck the cords were standing out against the layer of fat. He didn't look a bit happy. A couple of longshoremen pushed in through the door and lined up at the rail and he had one hell of a time trying to keep the glasses under the beer tap. He didn't want to look up when I left, but he had to and I could feel his eyes on my back.

So they were private dicks and one's name was Nocky. Anybody could pick up a badge to flash if he wanted to, but there was just the chance that they were the real thing, so the first pay station I came to I changed two bucks into nickels and started dialing all the agencies I knew of.

None of them picked up the description, but one of them did hear of a Nocky something-or-other but was sure it was a nickname. He couldn't give me any further information so I tried a couple of precincts uptown where I had an in at the desk. A Sergeant Bellew came on and told me the name was familiar, but that was all. He had the idea that the guy was a private dick too but couldn't be sure.

On the off-chance that Pat might know, I called his office. He picked up his phone on the first ring and his voice had a snap to it that wasn't too nice. I said, "It's Mike, Pat. What's eating you now?"

"Plenty. Listen, I'm pretty busy now and . . ."

"Nuts. You're not that busy."

"Damn it, Mike, what is it now?"

"Ever hear of a private cop called Nocky? It's a nickname."

"No."

"Can you check on it for me?"

"Hell no!" His voice had an explosive crack to it. "I can't do a damn thing except obey orders. The D.A.'s working up another stink ever since this afternoon and he's got us nuts up here."

"What happened, another raid go sour?"

"Ah, they all go sour. He closed down a wire room and pulled in a couple of punks when he was looking for something big. Ed Teen came down with a lawyer and a bondsman and got them both out within the hour."

"No kidding? So Ed's taking a personal interest in what goes on now."

"Yeah. He doesn't want 'em to talk before he does a little coaching first. You know, I think we're on to something this time. We had to pull a Gestapo act and check on our own men, but I think we have that leak located."

"How does it look?"

"Lousy. He's a first-grade detective and up to his ears in hock. He's one of three who have been in on every deal so far and money might be a powerful persuader to get him to pass a sign along somehow."

"Have you picked up the tip-off yet?"

"Nope. If he's doing it he's got a damn good system. Keep shut about this. The only reason I mentioned it is because I may need you soon. The guy knows all the other cops and I may have to stick a plant along the line to see who's picking up the flash from him."

"Okay, I'll be around any time you need me. If you run into any-thing on that Nocky character, let me know."

"Sure, Mike. Wish I could help you out now, but we're all tied up."

I said so long and hung up. I still had a handful of nickels to go so I made a blind stab at a barroom number downtown and asked if Cookie Harkin was there. I had to wait while the guy looked and after a minute or so a voice said, "Cookie speaking."

"Mike Hammer."

"Hey, boy. Long time no see. How's tricks?"

"Good enough. You still got wide-open ears?"

"Sure. See all, hear all and say plenty if the pay's right. Why?"

"Ever hear of a private dick named Nocky? He's a wise runt who has an oversize partner. Supposedly a couple of tough boys from somewhere uptown."

I didn't get any answer for a minute, so I said, "Well?"

"Wait a minute, Mike. You know what you're asking about, don't you?" He spoke in next to a whisper. I heard him pull the door of the booth closed before he said anything else. "What're you working on?"

"Murder, friend."

"Brother!"

"Who is he?"

"I'll have to do a little checking around first. I think I know who you mean, all right. I'll see what I can do, but if it's the guy I think it is, I'm not sticking my neck out too far, understand?"

"Sure, do what you can. I'll pay you for it."

"Forget the pay. All I want is some inside stuff I can pass along for what it's worth. You know my angle."

"How long will it take?"

"Gimme a coupla hours. Suppose I meet you at the Tucker Bar. It's a dive, but you can get away with anything in there."

It was good enough. I told him I'd be there and put the rest of the nickels back in my pocket. They make a big lump and a lot of noise so I went across town to an Automat and spent them all on a supper I needed bad.

It was dark when I finished and had started to rain again.

The Tucker Bar was built under a neon sign that put out more light in advertising than was used up inside. It was off on a side street in a place nobody smart went to even on a slumming party, but it was a place where people who knew people could be found and gotten drunk enough to spill over a little excess information if the questions were put right.

I saw Cookie in the back room edging through the tables with a drink in his hand, stopping at a table here and there to say hello. He was small and skinny with a big nose, bigger ears and loose pockets that could spill out the right kind of dough when he needed it. The guy looked and acted like a cheap hood when he was the head legman for one of the biggest of the syndicated columnists. I waited at the bar nursing a beer until the act on the dance floor was finished. A couple of strippers were trying to see how fast they could shed their clothes in time to the same music. They got down to bare facts in a minute's time and there was a lot of noise around the ringside. The rest of the crowd was having a hard time trying to see what they were paying for.

There was a singer and a solo pianist after that before the management decided to let the customers go back to drinking. I picked up my glass and squeezed through the bunch standing under the arch that let to the back room and worked my way to the table where Cookie was sitting.

He had two chicks with him, a pair of phony blondes with big bosoms and painted faces and he was showing them a coin trick so they had to lean forward to see what he was doing and he could leer down their necklines. He was having himself a great time. The blondes were drinking champagne. They were having a great time too.

I said, "Hello, ape man."

He looked up and grinned from one big ear to another until he looked like a clam just opened. "How do ya like that, my old pal, Mike Hammer! What're you doin' down here where people are?"

"Looking for people."

"Well, sit right down, sit right down. Here's one all made to order for you. Meet Tolly and Joan."

I said, "Hi," and pulled out the fourth chair.

"Mike's a friend of mine from way back, kids. A real good skate." He nodded at the blonde who was giving me the eye already. "You take Tolly, Mike. Joan and me's already struck up a conversation. She's a French maid from Brooklyn who works for the Devoe family. Wait'll you catch her accent. She sure fooled them. Gawd, what a family of jerks they are!"

I caught his expression and the slight wink that went with it. Tomorrow the stuff Joan was handing out would turn up in print and hell would get raised in the Devoe household. She gave us a demonstration of her accent with giggles and launched into a spiel of how the old man had tried to make her and how she refused and I almost wanted to ask her how she got the mink cape that was draped over the back of her chair on a maid's salary.

Tolly turned out to be the better of the two. She was a juicy eyeful with a lot of skin showing and nothing on under the dress she wore just to be conventional. She told me she had been posing for an artist down in the Village until she caught him using a camera instead of a paintbrush. She found he was peddling the prints and made him kick in with a fifty-fifty cut or get the pants knocked off him by an ex-boy friend in the Bronx, and now she was living off the cream of the land.

"Your artist friend sure mixes pleasure with business, honey," I told her. "Hell, I wouldn't mind seeing you undraped a bit."

She snapped open her purse and tossed me a wallet-sized print with a laugh. "Get right to it." She had a body that would make a statue drool, and with the poses the artist got her into it was easy to see why she wasn't hurting for dough. She let me look at it a little while, asked me if I wanted to dance and laughed when I said maybe later, but not right then.

Finally we got up and danced while Cookie sat and yapped with the French maid from Brooklyn. Tolly didn't have any trouble giving me the business because the mob on the dance floor had us pressed together like the ham in a sandwich.

Every bit of her was pressed against every bit of me and her mouth was right next to my ear. Every once in a while she'd stick her tongue out and send something chasing down my spine. "I like you, Mike," she said.

I gave her a little squeeze until her eyes half closed and she said something through her teeth. I slapped her fanny for it. We got back to the table and played kneesies while we talked until the girls decided to hit the powder room.

As they walked away Cookie said, "Cute kids, hey?"

"Real cute. Where the devil do you find them?"

"I get around. I don't look like much, but I get around. With a pair like them on my arms it's a ticket to anyplace I want to go so long as a guy's taking up the tickets."

I picked a smoke out of my pack and handed one to him. "What about our deal?"

His eyes crawled up my arm to my face. "I know them. The boys are hurting right now. You do that?"

"Uh-huh."

"What a mess. The little one wants your guts."

"Who are they?"

"Private dicks. That's what the little piece of paper says in their wallets. They're hoods who'll do anything for some cash."

"If they're cops they aren't making any money unless they're hired to protect somebody."

"They are. You know anything about the rackets, Mike?"

"A little."

"The town's divided into sections, see. Like the bookies. They pay off to the local big boy who pays off to Ed Teen."

The cigarette froze in my fingers. "Where's Teen in this?"

"He's not, but one of his local boys is the mug who uses your two playmates for a bodyguard. His name is Toady Link. Ever hear of him?"

"Yeah."

"Then you didn't hear much. He keeps his nose clean. The body-guards are to keep the small-timers moving and not to protect him. As bookies go, the guy's okay. Now how about coming across with something I can sell."

I squashed the butt out and started on another. Cookie's ears were pinned and he leaned across the table with a grin like we were telling dirty stories. I said, "There was a little murder the other night. Then there was another. In the beginning they looked little, but now they're starting to look pretty big. I haven't got a damn thing I can tell you . . . yet. When it happens you'll get it quick. How's that?"

"Fair enough. Who got killed?"

"A guy named William Decker, Arnold Basil, then the next day Decker's friend Mel Hooker."

"I read about that." .

"You'll be reading more about it. Where'll I find this Toady Link?"

Cookie rattled off a couple of addresses where I might pick him up and I let them soak in so I wouldn't forget them. "Just one thing, Mike," he added, "you don't know from nothing, see? Keep me out of it. I stay away from them boys. My racket takes dough but no rough stuff, and when it comes to rods or brass knucks you can count me out. I don't want none of them hoods after my hide."

"Don't worry," I said. I stood up and threw a fin on the table to cover some of Tolly's champagne.

Cookie's eyebrows went up to his hairline. "You aren't going now, are you? Hell, what about Tolly? She's got a yen for you already and I can't make out with two dames."

"Sure you can. Nothing to it."

"Aw, Mike, what a guy you are, and after I hand you such a sweet dish too."

My mouth twisted into a lopsided smile. "I can get all the dishes I want without having them handed to me. Tell Tolly that maybe I'll look her up someday. She interests me strangely."

He didn't say anything, but he looked disappointed. He sat there wiggling those big ears and I cleared out of the place before the blonde came back and twisted my arm into staying.

Dames.

It was turning into a night just like that first one. The sidewalks and pavements were one big wet splash reflecting the garish lights of the streets and throwing them back at you. I pulled my raincoat out of the back and slipped into it, then climbed behind the wheel.

My watch read a few minutes after nine and it was tonight. Marsha said tonight. But there were other things first and Marsha could wait. It would be all the better for the waiting.

So I got in line behind the other cars and headed uptown. On the edge of the Bronx I turned off and looked for the bar that was one of the addresses Cookie had given me and found it in the middle of the block. I left the engine going while I asked around inside, but neither the bartender nor the manager had seen the eminent Mr. Link so far that night. They obliged with his home address and I thanked them politely even though I already had it.

Toady Link was at home.

Maybe it would be better to say he was occupying his Bronx residence. That's the kind of a place it was. All fieldstone and picture windows on a walled-in half-acre of land that would have brought a quarter-million at auction. There were lights on all three floors of the joint and nobody to be seen inside. If it weren't for the new Packard squatting on the drive I would have figured the lights to be burglar protection.

I slid my own heap in at the curb and walked up the gravel to the house and punched the bell. Inside there was a faraway sound of chimes and about a minute later the door opened on a chain and a face looked at me waiting to see what I wanted.

You could see why he was called Toady. It was a big face, bigger around the jowls than it was on top with a pair of protruding eyes that seemed to have trouble staying in their sockets.

I said, "Hello, Toady. Do I get asked in?"

Even his voice was like a damned frog. "What do you want?"

"You maybe."

The frog face cracked into a wide-mouthed smile, a real nasty smile and the chain came off the lock. He had a gun in his hand, a big fat revolver with a hole in the end big enough to get your finger into. "Who the hell are you, bub?"

I took it easy getting my wallet out and flipped it back so he could see the tin. I shouldn't have bothered. His eyes never came off mine at all. I said, "Mike Hammer. Private Investigator, Toady. I think you ought to know me."

"I should?"

"Two of your boys should. They tried to take me."

"If you're looking for them . . ."

"I'm not. I'm looking for you. About a murder."

The smile got fatter and wider and the hole in the gun looked even bigger when he pointed it at my head. "Get in here," he said.

I did like he said. I stood there in the hall while he locked the door behind me and I could feel the muzzle of that rod about an inch behind my spine. Then he used it to steer me through the foyer into an outsized living room.

That much I didn't mind. But when he lowered the pile of fat he called a body into a chair and left me standing there on the carpet I got a little bit sore. "Let's put the heater away, Toady.

"Let's hear more about this murder first. I don't like people to throw murder in my face, Mr. Investigator. Not even lousy private cops."

Goddamn, that fat face of his was making me madder every second I had to look at it.

"You ever been shot, fat boy?" I asked him.

His face got red up to his hairline.

"I've been shot, fat boy," I said. "Not just once, either. Put that rod away or I'm going to give you a chance to use it. You'll have time to pump out just one slug and if it misses you're going to hear the nastiest noise you ever heard."

I let my hand come up so my fingertips were inside my coat. When he didn't make a move to stop me I knew I had him and he knew it too. Fat boy didn't like the idea of hearing a nasty noise a bit. He let the gun drop on the chair beside him and cursed me with those bug eyes of his for finding out he was as yellow as they come.

It was better that way. Now I liked standing in the middle of the room. I could look down at the fat slob and poke at him with a spear until he told me what I wanted to hear. I said, "Remember William Decker?"

His eyelids closed slowly and opened the same way. His head nodded once, squeezing the fat out under his chin.

"Do you know he's dead?"

"You son-of-a-bitch, don't try tagging me with that!" Now he was a real frog with a real croak.

"He played the ponies, Toady. You were the guy who picked up his bets."

"So what! I pick up a lot of bets."

"I thought you didn't fool around with small-time stuff."

"Balls, he wasn't small-time. He laid 'em big as anybody else. How'd I know how he was operating? Look, you . . ."

"Shut up and answer questions. You're lucky I'm not a city cop or you'd be doing your talking with a light in your face. Where'd Decker get the dough to lay?"

He relaxed into a sullen frown, his pudgy hands balled into tight fists. "He borrowed it, that's where."

"From Dixie Cooper if you've forgotten." He looked at me and if the name meant anything I couldn't read it in his face. "How much did Decker drop to you?"

"Hell, he went in the hole for a few grand, but don't go trying to prove it. I don't keep books."

"So you killed him."

"Goddamn you!" He came out of the chair and stood there shaking from head to foot. "I gave him that dough back so he could pay off his loan! Understand that? I hate them creeps who can't stand a loss. The guy was ready to pull the dutch act so I gave him back his dough so's he could pay off!"

He stood there staring at me with his eyes hanging out of that livid face of his sucking in his breath with a wheezy rasp. "You're lying, Toady," I said. "You're lying through your teeth." My hands twisted in the lapels of his coat and I pulled him in close so I could spit on him if I felt like it. "Where were you when Decker was killed?"

His hands fought with mine to keep me from choking him. "Here! I was . . . right here! Let go of me!"

"What about your boys . . . Nocky and that other gorilla?"

"I don't know where they were. I . . . didn't have anything to do with that! Goddamn, that's what I get for being a sucker! I should've let them work on the bastard. I should've kept his dough and kicked him out!"

"Maybe they did work over somebody. They had Decker's buddy all lined up for a shellacking until he shook 'em off on me. I thought I taught 'em to keep their noses out of trouble, but I guess I didn't teach 'em hard enough. The guy they were going to give the business to died with a bullet in him the same night. I hear tell those boys work for you, and they weren't out after the guy on their own."

"You . . . you're crazy!"

"Am I? Who put them on Hooker . . . you?"

"Hooker?" He worked his head into a frown that wouldn't stick.

"Don't play innocent, damn it. You know who I'm talking about. Mel Hooker. The guy who teamed up with Decker to play the nags."

An oversize tongue made a quick pass over his lips. "He . . . yeah, I know. Hooker. Nocky and him got in a fight. It was when he picked up his dough and cleared out. He was drunk, see? He started shooting off his mouth about how it was all crooked and he talked enough to keep some dough from coming across the board. That's how it was. Nocky tried to throw him out and he nearly brained him."

"So your boy picked him off?"

"No, no. He wouldn't do that. He was plenty mad, that's why he was laying for him. He didn't knock anybody off. I don't go for that. Ask anybody, they'll tell you I don't go for rough stuff."

I gave him a shove to get him away from me. "For a bookie you're a big-hearted son-of-a-bitch. You're one in a million and, brother, you better be telling the truth, because if you aren't you're going to get a lot of that fat sweated off you. Where's these two mugs?"

"How the hell do I know?"

I didn't play with him this time. I backhanded him across the mouth and did it again when he stumbled away and tried to grab the gun on the chair. His big belly shook so hard he swayed off balance and I gave it to him again. Then he just about fell into the chair and with the rod right under his hand he didn't have the guts to make a play for it.

I asked him again. "Where are they, Toady?"

"They . . . have rooms over the . . . Rialto Restaurant."

"Names, Pal."

"Nocky . . . he's Arthur Cole. The other one's Glenn Fisher." He had to squeeze the words out between lips that were no more than a thin red gash in his face. The marks of my fingers were across his cheek, making it puff out even farther. I could tell that he was hoping I'd turn my back, even for a second. The crazy madness in his eyes made them bulge so far his eyelids couldn't cover them.

I turned my back. I did it when I picked up the phone, but there was a mirror right in front of me and I could stand there and watch him hate me while I thumbed through the directory until I found the number listed under "Cole" and dialed it.

The phone rang, all right, but nobody answered it. Then I called the Rialto Restaurant and went through two waiters before the manager came on and told me that the boys didn't live there any more. They had packed their bags about an hour before, climbed into a cab and scrammed. Yeah, they were all paid up and the management was glad to be rid of them.

I hung up and turned around. "They beat it, Toady."

Link just sat.

"Where'd they go?"

His shoulders hunched into a shrug.

"I have a feeling you're going to die pretty soon, Toady," I said. And after I said it I looked at him until it sank all the way in and put his eyes back in place so the eyelids could get over them. I picked up the gun that lay beside him, flipped out the cylinder and punched the shells into my hand. They were .44's with copper-covered noses that could rip a guy in half. I tossed the empty rod back on the chair beside him and walked out of the room.

Somehow the night smelled cleaner after Toady. The rain was a light mist washing the stink of the swamp away. It shaded part of the monstrous castle the ugly frog sat in as though it were ashamed of it. I looked back at the lights and I could see why they were all on. They were the guy's only friends.

When I got back in my car I drove down to the corner, swung around and came back up the street. Before I got as far as the house the Packard came roaring out of the drive and skidded halfway across the road before it straightened out and went tearing off down the street. I had to laugh because Toady wasn't going anyplace at all. Not driving like that he wasn't. Toady was so goddamn mad he had to take it out on something and tonight the car took the beating.

I would have kept right on going myself if he hadn't left the door wide open so that the light made a streaming yellow invitation down the gravel. I jammed on the brakes and left the car sitting, the motor turning over and picked up the invitation.

The house was Toady's attempt at respectability, but it was only an attempt. The upstairs lights were turned on from switches at the foot of the stairs and only one set of prints showed in the dust that lay over the staircase. There were three bedrooms, two baths and a sitting room on the top floor, a full apartment-sized layout on the second and the only places that had been used were one bedroom and a shower stall. Everything else was neat and dormant, with the dust-mop marks last week's cleaning woman had left. Downstairs the kitchen was a mess of dirty dishes and littered newspapers. The pantry was stocked to take care of a hundred people who never came and the only things in the guest closet were Toady's hat and coat that he hadn't bothered to wear when he dashed out.

I rummaged around in the library and the study without touching anything then went down the cellar and had a drink of private stock at his bar. It was a big place with knotty pine walls rimmed with a couple hundred beer steins that were supposed to give it the atmosphere of a beer garden. Off to one side was the poolroom with the balls neatly racked and gathering more dust. He even had a cigarette machine down there. The butts were on the house and all you had to do was yank the lever, so I had a pack of Luckies on Toady too.

There were two other doors that led off the poolroom. One went into the furnace room and I stepped into a goddamned rattrap that nearly took my toes off. The other was a storeroom and I almost backed out of it when the white cloths that shrouded the stockpile of junk took shape. I found the light switch and turned it on. Instead of an overhead going on, a red light blossomed out over a sink on the end of the wall, turning everything a deep crimson.

The place was a darkroom. Or at least it had been. The stuff hadn't been touched since it was stored here. A big professional camera was folded up under wraps with a lot of movie-screen-type backdrops and a couple of wrought-iron benches. The processing chemicals and film plates had rotted away on a shelf next to a box that held the gummy remains of tubes of retouching paints. Off in the corner was a screwy machine of some sort that had its seams all carefully dustproofed with masking tape.

I put the covers back in place and turned the light off. When I closed the door I couldn't help thinking that Toady certainly tried hard to work up a hobby. In a way I couldn't blame him a bit. For friends all that repulsive bastard had was a lot of toys and dust. The louse was rich as sin with nobody to spend his money on.

I left the door open like I found it and climbed in under the wheel of my heap. I sat there feeling a little finger probing at my mind, trying to jar something into it that should already be there and the finger was still probing away when I got back to Manhattan and started down Riverside Drive.

So damn many little things and none of them added up. Some place between a tenement slum that had belonged to Decker and Toady's dismal swamp castle a killer was whistling his way along the street while I sat trying to figure out what a finger nudging my mind meant.

Lord, I was tired. The smoke in the car stung my eyes and I had to open the window to let it out. What I needed was a long, natural sleep without anything at all to think and dream about, but up there in the man-built cliffs of steel and stone was Marsha and she said she'd wait for me. The back of my head started to hurt again and even the thought of maybe sleeping with somebody who had been a movie star didn't make it go away.

But I went up.

And she was still waiting, too.

Marsha said, "You're late, Mike."

"I know, I'm sorry." She picked the hat out of my hand and waited while I peeled off my coat. When she had them stowed in the closet she hooked her arm under mine and took me inside.

There were drinks all set up and waiting beside a bowl that had held ice but was now all water. The tall red candles had been lit, burned down a few inches, then had been blown out.

"I thought you would have been here earlier. For supper perhaps."

She handed me a cigarette from a long narrow box and followed it with a lighter. When I had my lungs full of smoke I leaned back with my head pillowed against the chair and looked at her close up. She had on a light green dress that swirled up her body, over her shoulder and came down again to a thin leather belt at her waist. The swelling around her eye had gone down and in the soft light of the room the slight purple discoloration almost looked good.

I watched her a second and grinned. "Now I'm nearly sorry I didn't. You're nice to look at, kitten."

"Just half?"

"No. All this time. From top to bottom too."

Her eyes burned softly under long lashes. "I like it when you say it, Mike. You're used to saying it too, aren't you?"

"Only to beautiful women."

"And you've seen plenty of them." The laugh was in her voice now.

I said, "You've got the wrong slant, kid. Pretty is what you mean. Pretty and beautiful are two different things. Only a few women are pretty, but even one who's not so hot to look at can be beautiful. A lot of guys make mistakes when they turn down a beautiful woman for one who's just pretty."

Her eyebrows went up in the slightest show of surprise, letting the fires of her irises leap into plain view. "I didn't know you were a philosopher, Mike."

"There're a lot of things you don't know about me."

She uncurled from the chair and picked up the glasses from the table. "Should I?"

"Uh-uh. They're all bad." I got that look again, the one with the smile around the edges, then she brought in some fresh ice from the kitchen and made a pair of highballs. The one she gave me went down cold and easy, nestling there at the bottom of my stomach with a pleasant, creeping kind of warmth that tiptoed silently throughout my body until it was the nicest thing in the world to just sit there with my eyes half shut and listen to the rain drum against the windows.

Marsha's hand went to the switch on the record player, flooding the room with the soft tones of the "Blue Danube." She filled the glasses again, then drifted to the floor at my feet, laying her head back against my knees. "Nice?" she asked me.

"Wonderful. I'm right in the mood to enjoy it."

"You still . . ."

"That's right. Still." I closed my eyes all the way for a minute. "Sometimes I think I'm standing still too. It's never been like this before."

Her hand found mine and pulled it down to her cheek. I thought I felt her lips brush my fingers, but I wasn't sure. "Do you have the boy yet?"

"Yeah, he's in good hands. Tomorrow or maybe the next day they'll come for him. He'll be all right."

"I wish there was something I could do. Are you sure there isn't? Could I keep him for you?"

"He'd be too much for you. Hell, he's only a little over a year old. I have a nurse for him. She's old, but reliable."

"Then let me take him out for a walk or something. I really do want to help, Mike, honest."

I ran my fingers through the sheen of her hair and across the soft lines of her face. This time I knew it when her lips parted in a kiss on my palm.

"I wish you could, Marsha. I need help. I need something. This whole thing is getting away from me."

"Would it help to tell me about it?"

"Maybe."

"Then tell me."

So I told her. I sat there staring at the ceiling with Marsha on the floor and her head on my knees and I told her about it. I lined up everything from beginning to end and tried to put them together in the right order.

When you strung them out like that it didn't take long to tell. They made a nice neat pile of facts, one on top of the other, but there was nothing there to hold them together. One little push scattered them all over the place. Before I finished my jaws ached from holding my teeth together so tightly.

"Being so mad won't help you think," Marsha said.

"I gotta be mad. Goddamn, you can't go at a thing like this unless you are mad. I never knew much about kids, but when I held the Decker boy in my hands I could see why a guy would give his insides to keep his kid alive. Right there is the thing that screws everything up. Decker knew he was going to die and didn't try to do a single thing about it. Three days before, he knew it was going to happen too. He got all his affairs put right and waited. God knows what he thought about in those three days."

"It couldn't have been nice."

"Oh, I don't know. I don't get it at all." I rubbed my face disgustedly. "Decker and Hooker tie in with Toady Link and he ties in with Grindle and Teen and it was one of Grindle's boys who shot Decker. There's a connection there if you want to look for one."

"I'm sorry, Mike."

"You don't have to be."

"But I am. In a way it started with me. I keep thinking of the boy."

"It would have been the same if Decker had broken into the other apartment. The guy knew he was going to die . . . but why? Whether or not he got what he was after he was still planning to die!"

Marsha lifted her face and turned around. "Couldn't it have been . . . a precaution? Perhaps he *was* planning to run out with the money. In that case he would know there *was* a possibility that they might catch up with him. As it was, it turned out to be the same thing. He knew they'd never believe his story about the wrong apartment so he ran anyway, bringing about the same results."

My eyes felt hot and heavy. "It's crazy as hell. It's a mess no matter how I look at it, but someplace there's an answer and it's lost in my head. I keep trying to work it loose and it won't come. Every time I stop to think about it I can feel it sitting here and if the damn thing was human it would laugh at me. Now I can't even think any more."

"Tired, darling?"

"Yeah."

I looked at her and she looked at me and we were both thinking the same thing. Then her head dropped slowly and her smile had a touch of sadness in it.

"I'm a fool, aren't I?" she said.

"You're no fool, Marsha."

"Mike . . . have you ever been in love?"

I didn't know how to answer that so I just nodded.

"Was it nice?"

"I thought so." I was hoping she wouldn't ask me any more. Even after five years it hurt to think about it.

"Are you . . . now?" Her voice was low, almost inaudible. I caught the brief flicker of her eyes as she glanced at my face.

I shrugged. I didn't know what to tell her.

She smiled at her hands and I smiled with her. "That's good," she laughed. Her eyes went bright and happy and she tossed her head so that her hair fell in a glittering dark halo around her shoulders. "I had tonight all planned. I was going to be a fool anyway and make you want me so that you'd keep wanting me."

"It's been like that."

She came up off the floor slowly, gracefully, reaching for my hand to pull me out of the chair. Her mouth was warmer than it should have been. Her body was supple and lovely, like a fluid filling in the gaps between us. I ran my fingers through her hair, pulling her face away while still wanting to keep her crushed against me.

"Why, Marsha?" I asked. "Why me? You know what I'm like. I'm not fancy and I'm not famous and I work for my dough. I'm not in your class at all."

She looked up at me with an expression you don't try to describe. A sleepy expression that wasn't a bit tired. Her hands slid up my back and tightened as she leaned against me. "Let me be a woman, Mike. I don't want those things you say you're not. I've had them. I want all the things you are. You're big and not so handsome, but there's a devil inside you that makes you exciting and tough, yet enough of an angel to make you tender when you have to be."

My hands wanted to squeeze right through her waist until they met and I had to let her go or she would have felt the way they were shaking. I turned around and reached for the bottle and glass on the table and while I was pouring one there was a click and the light dimmed to a pale glow.

Behind me I heard her say softly, "Mike . . . you never told me whether I was . . . just pretty or beautiful."

I turned around and was going to tell her that she was the most lovely thing I had ever seen, but her hands did something to her belt and the fold of the dress that came up over one shoulder dropped away leaving her standing there with one hand on the lamp like a half-nude vision and the words got stuck in my throat.

Then the light disappeared altogether and I could only drink the drink quickly, because although the vision was gone it was walking toward me across the night and somewhere on the path there was another whisper of fabric and she was there in my hands without anything to keep her from being a woman now, an invisible, naked dream throwing a mantle of desire around us both that had too great a strength to break and must be burned through by a fire that leaped and danced and towered in a blazing crescendo that could only be dampened and never extinguished.

And when the mantle was thrown back I left the dream there in the dark, warm and soft, breathing quickly to tell me that it was a dream that would come back on other nights too, disturbing and at the same time satisfying.

She was beautiful. She was pretty, too.

She was in my mind all the way home.

At a quarter past ten I got up, dressed and made myself some breakfast. Right in the middle of it the phone rang and when I answered it the operator told me to hold on for a call from Miami. Velda's husky voice was a pleasure to hear again. She said, "Mike?"

And I said, "Hello, sweetheart. How's everything?"

"Fine. At least it's partly fine. Our boy got out on a plane, but he left all the stuff behind. The insurance investigator is here making an inventory of the stuff now."

"Great, great. Try to promote yourself a bonus if you can."

"That wouldn't be hard," she laughed. "He's already made a pass. Mike, miss me?"

I felt like a heel, but I wasn't lying when I said, "Hell yes, I miss you."

"I don't mean as a business partner."

"Neither do I, kitten."

"You won't have to miss me long. I'm taking the afternoon train out."

My fingers started batting out dots and dashes on the table. I wanted her back but not too soon. I didn't want anybody else climbing all over me. "You stay there," I told her. "Stay on that guy's tail. You're still on salary from the company and if you can get a line on him now they'll cut us in for more business later. They're as interested in him as they are in recovering the stuff."

"But, Mike, the Miami police are doing all they can."

"Where'd he hop to?"

"Some place in Cuba. That's where they lost him."

"Okay, get over to Cuba then. Take a week and if it's no dice forget it and come on home."

She didn't say anything for a few seconds. "Mike . . . is something wrong up there?"

"Don't be silly."

"You sound like it. If you're sending me off . . ."

"Look, kid," I cut her off, "you'd know about it if anything was wrong. I just got up and I'm kind of sleepy yet. Be a good girl and stay on that case, will you?"

"All right. Love me?"

"You'll never know," I said.

She laughed again and hung up. She knew. Women always know.

I went back and finished my breakfast, had a smoke then turned on the faucet in the bathroom sink to bring the hot water up. While I shaved I turned on the radio and picked up the commentator who was just dropping affairs in Washington to get back to New York and as far as he was concerned the only major problem of the day was the District Attorney's newest successes in the gambling probe. At some time last night a series of raids had been carried out successfully and the police dragnet had brought in some twenty-five persons charged with book-making. He gave no details, but hinted that the police were expecting to nail the kingpins in the near future.

When I finished shaving I opened my door and took the tabloid out of the knob to see what the press had to say about it. The front page carried the pictures of those gathered in the roundup with appropriate captions while the inside double spread had a layout showing where the bookies had been operating.

The editorial was the only column that mentioned Ed Teen at all. It brought out the fact that Teen's personal staff of lawyers were going to bat for the bookies. At the same time the police were finding that a lot of witnesses were reluctant to speak up when it came to identifying the boys who took their money or paid off on wins, places and shows. At the end of the column the writer came right out with the charge that Lou Grindle had an organization specially adept at keeping witnesses from talking and demanded that the police throw some light on the subject.

I went through the paper again to make sure I didn't miss anything, then folded it up and stuck it in the bottom of my chair until I got around to reading it. Then I went downstairs and knocked on the door of the other apartment and stood there with my hat in my hands until the door opened and the nurse said, "Good morning, Mr. Hammer. Come on in."

"I can only stay a minute. I want to see how the kid is."

"Oh, he's a regular boy. Right now he's trying to see what's inside the radio."

I walked in behind her to the living room where the kid was doing just that. He had the extension cord in his fists and the set teetered on the edge of the table a hair away from complete ruin. I got there first and grabbed the both of them.

The kid knew me, all right. His face was sunny with a big smile and he shoved his hand inside my coat and then chattered indignantly when I pulled it out. "How's the breakage charge coming?"

"We won't count that," the nurse said. "As a matter of fact, he's been much better than I expected."

I held the kid out where I could look at him better. "There's something different about him."

"There ought to be. I gave him a haircut." I put him back on the floor where he hung on my leg and jabbered at me. "He certainly likes you," she said.

"I guess I'm all he's got. Need anything?"

"No, we're getting along fine."

"Okay, anything you want just get." I bent down and ruffled the kid's hair and he tried to climb up my leg. He yelled to come with me so I had to hand him back and wave good-by from the door. He was so damn small and pathetic-looking I felt like a heel for stranding him, but I promised myself I'd see that he got a lot of attention before he was dropped into some home for orphans.

The first lunch shift was just hitting the streets when I got to Pat's office. The desk man called ahead to see if he was still in and told me to go right up. A couple of reporters were coming out of the room still jotting down notes and Pat was perched on the edge of a desk fingering a thick manila folder.

I closed the door behind me and he said, "Hi, Mike."

"Making news?"

"Today we're heroes. Tomorrow we'll be something else again."

"So the D.A.'s making out. Did you find the hole?"

He turned around slowly, his face expressionless. "No, if that cop is passing out the word then he wised up. Nothing went out on this deal at all."

"How could he catch on?"

"He's been a cop a long time. He's been staked out often enough to spot it when he's being watched himself."

"Did he mention it?"

"No, but his attitude has changed. He resents the implication apparently."

"That's going to make pretty reading. Now the papers'll call for the D.A. to make a full-scale investigation of the whole department, I suppose."

"The D.A. doesn't know a damn thing about it. You keep it to yourself too. I'm handling the matter myself. If it is the guy there's no sense smearing the whole department. We still aren't sure of it, you know."

He tossed the folder on top of the filing cabinet and sat down behind the desk with a sigh. There were tired lines around his eyes and mouth, little lines that had been showing up a lot lately.

I said, "What came of the roundup?"

"Oh, hell, Mike." He glanced at me with open disgust, then realized that I wasn't handing him a dig. "Nothing came of it. So we closed down a couple of rooms. We got a hatful of small-timers who will probably walk right out of it or draw minimum sentences. Teen's a smart operator. His lawyers are even smarter. Those boys know all the angles there are to know and if there are any new ones they think them up."

"Teen's a real cutie. You know what I think? He's letting us take some of his boys just to keep the D.A. happy and get a chance to put in a bigger fix."

"I don't get it," I said.

"Look, Teen pays for protection. That is, if it takes money to keep his racket covered. If it takes muscle he uses Lou Grindle. But supposing it does take dough . . . then all the chiselers, petty politicians and maybe even the big shots who are taking his dough are going to want more to keep his personal fix in because things are getting tougher. Okay, he pays off, and the more those guys rake in the deeper in they are too. Suddenly they realize that they can't afford to let Teen get taken or they'll go along with him, so they work overtime to keep the louse clean."

"Nice."

"Isn't it though?" he sat there tapping his fingers on the desk, then: "Mike, for all you've heard, read and seen of Ed Teen, do you know what we actually have on him?"

"Tell me."

"Nothing. Not one damn thing. Plenty of suspicions, but you don't take suspicions to court. We know everything he's hooked up with and we can't prove a single part of it. I've been upside down for a month backtracking over his life trying to tie him into something that happened a long time ago and for all I've found you could stuff it in your ear." Pat buried his face in his hands and rubbed his eyes.

"Have you had time to do anything about Decker and Hooker?"

At least it made him smile a little. "I haven't been upside down *that* long, Pal," he said. "I was going to call you on that. Routine investigation turned up something on Hooker. For the last four months he made bank deposits of close to a thousand bucks each time. They apparently came in on the same date and were all for the same amount, though he spent a little of each wad before he deposited it. That sort of ties in with your story about him hitting the winning ponies."

I rolled a cigarette between my fingers slowly then stuck it in my mouth. "How often were the deposits made?"

"Weekly. Regular as pie."

"And Decker?"

"Clean. I had four men cover every minute of his time as far back as they could go. As far as we could find out he didn't even associate with any shady characters. The kind of people who vouched for him were the kind who knew what they were talking about too. Incidentally, I talked to his parish priest personally. He's made all the arrangements for the boy and cleared them with the authorities, so he'll pick him up at the end of the week."

He stopped and watched my face a moment. The silence was so thick you could slice it with a knife. "All right, now what are you thinking, Mike?"

I let a lazy cloud of smoke sift up toward the ceiling. "It might scare you," I said.

The tired lines got deeper when his mouth clamped shut. "Yeah? Scare me then."

"Maybe you've been closer to nailing Teen than you thought, chum."

His fingers stopped their incessant tapping.

"After Decker was killed a lot of awfully funny things started to happen. Before they didn't seem to make much sense, but just because you can't actually see what's holding them together doesn't mean that they're not there. Wouldn't it be a scream if the guy who killed Decker could lead you to Teen?"

"Yeah, I'd laugh myself sick." Now Pat's eyes were just thin shiny slits in his head.

I said, "Those bank deposits of Hooker's weren't wins. Hooker was being paid off to do something. You got any idea what it was?"

"No," sullenly.

"I'd say he was being paid to see that a certain guy was put in a certain spot where he was up the creek."

"Damn it, Mike, quit talking in riddles!"

"Pat, I can't. It's still a puzzle to me, too, but I can tell you this. You've been routine on this case all along. It's been too small-time to open up on but I think you'd damn well better open up on it right now because you're sitting on top of the thing that can blow Teen and his racket all to hell. I don't know how or why . . . yet. But I know it's there and before very long I'm going to find the string that's holding it together. As far as Ed Teen's concerned I don't care what happens to him, only someplace in there is the guy who made an orphan out of a nice little kid and he's the one I want. You can take it for what it's worth or I can go it alone. Just don't shove the Decker kill down at the bottom of the page and hope something turns up on it because you think grabbing Teen is more important."

He started to come up out of his chair and his face was strictly cop without tired lines any more. He got all set to give me the business, then, like turning on the light, the scowl and the tired lines went away and he sat back smiling a little with that excited, happy look I hadn't seen him wear for so long.

"What's it about, Mike?"

"I think the Decker murder got away from somebody. It was supposed to be nice and clean and didn't happen that way."

"What else?"

"A lot of scrambled facts that are going to get put right fast if you help out. Then I'll give it to you so there's sense to it."

"You know, you're damn lucky I know what makes you tick, Mike. If you were anybody else I'd hammer out every last bit of information you have. I'm only sorry you didn't get on the force while you were still young enough."

"I don't like the hours. The pay either."

"No," he grinned, "you'd sooner work for free and get me all hopped up whenever you feel like it. You and the D.A. Okay, spill it. What do you need?"

"A pair of private detectives named Arthur Cole and Glenn Fisher."

He jotted the names down and stared at them blankly a second. "Nocky . . . ?"

"That's Cole."

"You should have given me their names before."

"I didn't know them before."

He reached out and flipped the switch on the intercom. "Tell Sergeant McMillan to come in a moment, please."

A voice rasped that it would and while we waited Pat went to the filing cabinet and pawed through the drawers until he had what he wanted. He tossed the stuff in my lap as a thick-set plain-clothesman came in chewing on a dead cigar.

Pat said, "Sergeant, this is Mike Hammer."

The cop shifted his cigar and held out his hand. I said, "Glad to know you."

"Same here. Heard lots about you, Mike."

"Sergeant McMillan has the inside information on the uptown boys," Pat said. He turned to the plain-clothesman with, "What do you know about two supposedly private detectives named Cole and Fisher?"

"Plenty. Fisher lost his license about a month ago. What do you want to know?"

Pat raised his eyebrows at me. "Background stuff," I said.

"The guys are hoods, plain and simple. Especially Fisher. You ever see them?"

I nodded. Pat pointed to the folder in my lap and I pulled out a couple of candid shots taken during a strike-breaking melee on the docks. My boys were right there in the foreground swinging billies.

The cop said, "They're troublemakers. About a year ago somebody with a little pull had them tagged with badges so what they did would be a little bit legal. Neither one of 'em have records, but they've been pulled in a few times for minor offenses. Brawling mostly. They'll work for anybody who pays off. You want me to put out a call for 'em, Captain?"

"What about it, Mike?" Pat asked.

"It wouldn't be a bad idea, but you won't find them in New York. Stick them on the teletype and see if they aren't holing up in another city. You might try alerting the railroad dicks to keep an eye out for them. They skipped out last night and might still be traveling. Cole has a broken hand and Fisher's face is a mess. They ought to be easy to identify."

"You want to do that, sergeant?"

He nodded at Pat. "I have everything I need. They shouldn't be too hard to trace." He said so long to me and went back the way he came.

Pat picked the photo up and studied it. "What's with these two?"

"They worked for Toady Link." Pat's head came up quickly. "They were on to Hooker for some reason until I started buzzing the guy, then they went into me. I didn't get the pitch in time or Hooker might still be alive. Last night I paid a visit to our friend Link and he was happy to tell me who the boys were."

"Mike, damn it . . ."

"If you're wondering how I found out who they were when the cops didn't know . . . I have a friend who gets around. With blondes."

"I'm not wondering that at all! I'm wondering how the hell I could have been so negligent or stupid, whatever you want to call it." He grinned wryly. "I used to be a bright boy. A year ago I would have seen the connection or let you talk me into something a lot sooner. Everything you do is tying right in with this Teen affair. Did you know that we had Link slated to go through the mill this week?"

"No."

"Well, we had. He and four others. While the D.A.'s been getting pushed around he's been doing one hell of a job on the organization's working men. Toady's about a month away from a man-sized stretch up the river. Every move you make you step on my toes."

"Why didn't you pick it up sooner?"

"Because it's no novelty to be tied up with Teen or Grindle, especially when there's money or murder concerned. Some of the help those two employ have turned up on more than one offense. It wasn't too difficult to suppose that Basil was just out for extra cash when he went in on that robbery and shot Decker afterward."

"Are you positive that he's the one who did the shooting?"

"As positive as the paraffin test. Of course, he may have discharged the bullet prior to the killing, but if he did I don't know where. If this Decker thing has even the slightest tie-up with the boys we want then we'll get to it."

"Hang on, Pat. I'm not saying that it has."

"I'll damn soon find out."

I tried to be unconcerned as I pulled on my smoke. "How about letting me find out for you. So far Decker has been my party."

"Nix, Mike. I know what you want. All you have in your head is the idea that you want to tangle with that killer. Not this time. Taking that one guy out of play could screw up this whole thing so nicely we'll be left with nothing at all."

"Okay, pal," I grinned, "go right to it. Just try to get an identification out of me. Just try it."

"Mike . . ."

"Aw, nuts, Pat. I'm as critical to this thing as those two mugs are. It was me who saw them and me who pushed them around. Without my say-so you don't have a thing to haul them in on. You're taking all the gravy for yourself . . . or at least you're trying to."

"What do you want, Mike?"

"I want three or four days to make my own play. Things are just beginning to look up. I'd like a file on Toady Link too."

"That's impossible. The D.A. has it classified top secret. That's out."

"Can't *you* get it, kid?"

"Nope. That would mean an explanation and I'm not giving blue boy a chance to climb up my back again."

"Well, hell . . . do you know anything about the guy at all?"

He leaned back in the chair and shook his head slowly. "Probably no more than you know, Mike. I haven't done anything more than listen in and supply a little information I had when Toady's name came up. The D.A. had his own men doing the legwork."

I looked out the window and while I watched the people on the roofs across the street Pat studied my face and studied it hard. I could feel his eyes crawl across me and make everything I was thinking into thoughts and words of his own.

He said, "You're thinking Toady Link's the last step in the chain, aren't you?"

I nodded.

"Spell it out for me."

So I spelled it out. I said, "Big-money boys like to splurge. They say they go for wine, women and song but whoever said it forgot to add the ponies too. Go out to the races and take a look around. Take a peek at the limousines and convertibles and the bank rolls that own them."

"So?"

"So there was a big-money boy named Marvin Holmes who likes his blondes fast and furious and very much on hand. He spends his dough like water and keeps plenty of it locked up in a safe on his wall. He plays the nags through a bookie named Toady Link and doesn't like the way the ponies run so he won't pay off his bet. He's too big to push around, but Link can't take a welch so he looks around for a way to get his dough. Somebody tips him about a former safe expert named Decker, but the guy is honest and wants to stay that way. Okay, so Toady waits until the guy needs dough. He finds out who his friend is . . . a guy named Mel Hooker, and pays him to steer Decker his way. They use a rigged-up deal to make it look like they're winning a pot and everybody is happy. Then Decker goes in over his head. He borrows from a loan shark to make the big kill and loses everything. That's where the pressure starts. He's not a big shot and he's got a kid and he's an easy mark to push around. He knows what happens on this loan-shark deal and he's scared, so when Toady comes up with the proposition of opening a safe . . . a simple little thing like that . . . Decker grabs it, takes a pay-off from Link to keep the shark off his neck and goes to it.

"It would have been fine if Decker had hit the right apartment, but he made a mistake he couldn't afford. He had to take a powder. Maybe he had even planned on taking a powder and arranged for his kid to be taken care of if things didn't go right. I don't know about that. He had something planned anyway. The only trouble was that he didn't plan well enough, or the guys who went out with him in the job were too sharp. They had him cold. Basil shot him then went over him for the dough. He must have yelled out that Decker was clean just before I started shooting. When he went down the driver couldn't afford to let him be taken alive and ran over him.

"Just take it from there . . . he already knew where Decker lived and thought that maybe when he went back for his kid he stashed the dough he was supposed to have. The guy searched the place and couldn't find it. Then he got the idea that maybe Basil had been too hurried when he searched Decker's corpse . . . but I had been right there and figured that I wouldn't overlook picking up a pile from a corpse if I got the chance. So while I was out my apartment was searched and I came back in time to catch the guy at it. I was in too damn much of a hurry and he beat the hell out of me.

"Now let's suppose it *was* Toady. Two guys are dead and he can be right in line for the hot seat if somebody gets panicky and talks. After all, Hooker didn't know the details of the kill so he could have thought that Toady was getting him out of the way to keep him from talking. That puts him in the same spot and he's scared stiff. Evidently he did have one run-in with the tough boys before and carried the scar around on his face to prove it.

"So Hooker spots two of Toady's boys and gets the jumps. They're sticking around waiting for the right spot to stick him. When Hooker got confidential with me they must have thought that Mel was asking for protection or trying to get rid of what I knew so they tried to take me. They muffed that one and went back to get Hooker. They didn't muff that one.

"Up to there Toady didn't have too much to worry about, but when I showed my face he got scared. Just before that he packed his boys out of town because he couldn't afford to have them around, so if we can get them back we ought to finger Toady without any trouble at all. Not the least little bit of trouble."

There was a silence that lasted for a full minute and I could hear Pat breathing and my own watch ticking. Pat said, "That's supposing you got all this dealt out right."

"Uh-huh."

"We can find out soon enough." He picked up the phone and said, "Give me an outside line, please," and while he waited riffled through the phone book. I heard the dial tone come on and Pat fingered out a number. The phone ringing on the other end made a faraway hum. Then it stopped. "I'd like to speak to Mr. Holmes," Pat said. "This is Captain Chambers, Homicide, speaking."

He sat there and frowned at the wall while he listened, then put the receiver back too carefully. "He's gone, Mike. He left for South America with one of his blondes yesterday morning."

"That's great," I said. My voice didn't sound like me at all.

Pat's mouth got tight around the corners. "That's perfect. It proves your point. The guy isn't too big to push around after all. Somebody's scared him right out of the city. You called every goddamn move right on the nose."

"I hope so."

I guess he didn't like the way I said it.

"It looks good to me."

"It looks too good. I wish we had the murder weapons to back it up."

"Metal doesn't rot out that fast. If we get those two we'll get the gun and we'll get Toady too. It doesn't matter which one we get him for."

"Maybe. I'd like to know who drove the car that night."

"Toady certainly wouldn't do it himself."

I stopped watching the people on the roof across the way and turned my face toward Pat. "I'm thinking that he did, Pat. If it was the kind of haul he expected he wasn't going to let it go through a few hands before it got back to him. Yeah, feller, I think I'll tag Toady with this one."

"Not you, Mike . . . *we'll* tag him for it. The police. The public. Justice. You know."

"Want to bet?"

Suddenly he wasn't my friend any more. His eyes were too gray and his face was too bland and I was the guy in the chair who was going to keep answering questions until he was done with me. Or that's what he thought.

I said, "A few minutes ago I asked you if you'd like to nail the whole batch of them at once."

"So there's more to it?"

"There could be. Lots more. Only if I get a couple extra days first."

Something you might call a smile threw a shadow around his mouth. "You know what will happen to me if you mess things up?"

"Do you know what might happen to me?"

"You might get yourself killed."

"Yeah."

"Okay, Mike, you got your three days. God help you if you get in a jam because I won't."

He was lying both times and I knew it. I'd no more get three days than he'd give me a boot when I needed a hand, but I played it like I didn't catch the drift and got up out of my chair. He was sitting there with the same expression when I closed the door, but his hand had already started to reach for the phone.

I went down the corridor to where a bunch of typewriters were banging out a madhouse symphony and asked one of the stenos where I could find Ellen Scobie. She told me that she had gone out to lunch at noon and was expected back that afternoon, but I might still find her in the Nelson Steak House if I got over there right away.

It took me about ten minutes to make the four blocks and there was Ellen in the back looking more luscious than the oversize T-bone steak she was gnawing on.

She saw me and waved and I wondered what it was going to cost to get hold of that file on Toady Link.

It made nice wondering.

She was all in black, but without Ellen inside it the dress would have been nothing. The sun had kissed her skin into a light toast color, dotting the corner of her eyes with freckles. Her hair swept back and down, caressing her bare shoulders whenever she moved her head.

She said, "Hello, man."

I slid in across the table. "Did you eat yourself out of company?"

"Long ago. My poor working friends had to get back to the office."

"What about you?"

"You are enjoying the sight of a woman enjoying the benefits of working overtime when the city budget doesn't allow for unauthorized pay. They had to give me the time off. Want something to eat?"

A waitress sneaked up behind me and poised her pencil over her pad. "I'll have a beer and a sandwich. Ham. Plenty of mustard and anything else you can squeeze on."

Ellen made a motion for another coffee and went back to the remains of the steak. I had my sandwich and beer without benefit of small talk until we were both finished and relaxing over a smoke.

She was nice to look at. Not because she was pretty all over, but because there was something alive about everything she did. Now she was propped in the corner of the booth with one leg half up on the bench grinning because the girl across the way was talking her head off to keep her partner's attention. The guy was trying, but his eyes kept sliding over to Ellen every few seconds.

I said, "Give the kid a break, will you?"

She laughed lightly, way down in her throat, then leaned on the table and cupped her chin in her hands. "I feel real wicked when I do things like that."

"Your friends must love you."

"Ooh," her mouth made a pouty little circle, ". . . they do. The men, I mean. Like you, Mike. You came in here especially to see me. You find me so attractive that you can't stay away." She laughed again.

"Yeah," I said. "I even dream about you."

"Like hell."

"No kidding, I mean it."

"I can picture you going out of your way for a woman. I'd give my right arm to hear you say that in a different tone of voice, though. There's something about you that fascinates me. Now that we have the love-making over with, what do I have that you want?"

I shouldn't have let my eyes do what they did.

"Besides that, I mean," she said.

"Your boss has a certain file on Toady Link. I want a look at it."

Her hands came together to cover her eyes. "I should have known. I spend every waking hour making myself pretty for you, hoping that you'll pop in on me and when you do you ask me to climb up a cloud."

"Well?"

"It's . . . well, it's almost impossible, Mike."

"Why?"

Her eyes drifted away from mine reluctantly. "Mike, I . . ."

"It isn't exactly secret information with me, Ellen. Pat told me about the D.A. getting ready to wrap Link up in a gray suit."

"Then he should have told you that those files are locked and under guard. He doesn't trust anybody."

"He trusts you."

"And if I get caught doing a thing like that I'll not only lose this job and never be able to get another one, but I'll get a gray suit too. I don't like the color." She reached out and plucked a Lucky from my pack and toyed with it before accepting the light I held out.

"I only want a look at it, kid. I don't want to steal the stuff and I won't pass the information along to anybody."

"Please, Mike."

I bent the match in my fingers and threw it on my plate. "Okay, okay. Maybe I'm asking too damn much. You know what the score is as well as I do. Everything is so almighty secret with the D.A. that he doesn't know what he has himself. If he'd open up on what he knows he'd get a little more action out of the public. Right now he's trying to squelch the big-time gambling in the city and what happens? Everybody thinks it's funny. By God, if they had a look behind the scenes at what's been going on because of the same gambling they condone they'd think twice about it. They ought to take a look at a corpse with some holes punched in it. They ought to take a look at some widows crying at a funeral or a kid who was made an orphan crying for his father who's one of the corpses."

The cigarette had burned down in her fingers without being touched, the long ash drooping wearily, ready to fall. Ellen's eyes were bright and smoky at the same time—languid eyes that hid the thoughts behind them.

"I'll get it for you, Mike."

I waited and saw the richness of her lips grow richer with a smile.

"But it'll cost you," she said.

I didn't get it for a second. "Cost me what?"

"You."

And that thing on my spine started crawling around again.

She reached out for my hand and covered it with hers. "Mike . . . you're only incidental in the picture this time. It's the only way I'll ever be able to get you and it's worth it even if I have to buy you. But it's because of what you said that I'm doing it."

There was something new about her, something I hadn't noticed before. I said, "You'll never have to buy me, Ellen."

It was a long minute before I could take my eyes off her face and get rid of the thing chasing up my back. The waitress dropped the check on the table and I put down a bill to cover them both and told her to keep the change. When we came out of the booth together the guy across the room looked at me enviously and Ellen longingly. His lunch date looked relieved.

We went back to the street and got as far as the bar on the corner. Ellen stopped me and nodded toward the door. "Wait here for me. I can't go back upstairs or somebody's likely to think it peculiar."

"Then how are you going to get the file out?"

"Patty—my short and stout roommate, if you remember—is on this afternoon. I'll call her and have her take them when she leaves this evening. The way my luck runs, if I took them any earlier he'd pick just this day to want to see them."

"That's smart," I agreed. "You know her well enough so there won't be a hitch, don't you?"

She made an impatient gesture with her hand. "Patty owes me more favors than I can count. I've never asked her for anything before and I might as well start now. I'll be back in about ten minutes. Stay at the bar and wait for me, will you?"

"Sure. Then what?"

"Then you're going to take me to the races. Little Ellen cleans up today."

I gave her my fattest smile and jingled a pocketful of coins. "Pat told me about that. You're not going to be selfish about the thing, are you?"

"I think we're both going to have a profitable day, Mike," she said impishly. She wasn't talking about money, either. I watched her cross the street and admired her legs until she was out of sight, then went into the bar and ordered a beer.

The television was tuned to the game in Brooklyn and the bets were flowing heavy and fast. I stayed out of the general argument and put my beer away. A tall skinny guy came in and stood next to me and did the same thing himself. A kid came in peddling papers and I bought one before the bartender told him to scram and quit annoying the customers.

But it didn't do any good. The guys on my left were arguing batting averages and one poked me to get my opinion. I said he was right and the other guy started jawing again and appealed to the tall skinny guy. He shrugged and tapped his ear, then took a hearing aid out of his shirt pocket and made indications that it wasn't working. He was lucky. They turned back to me again, spotted my paper and I handed it over to settle the argument. The one guy still wouldn't give in and I was about to become the backstop of a beautiful brawl.

But Ellen walked in just then and baseball switched to sex in whispers. I got her out so they could see her going away and really have something to talk about.

She cuddled up under my arm all the way back to the car and climbed in next to me looking cool and lovely and very pleased with herself. When I had about as much silence as I could take I asked, "Did it work out?"

"Patty was glad to help out. She was a little nervous about it, but she said she'd wait until everyone had cleared out and put it in her brief case. She's taking some work home with her tonight and it shouldn't be hard to do at all."

"Good girl."

"Don't I deserve a kiss for effort?" She timed it as the light turned red.

Her mouth wasn't as cool as it looked. It was warm, a nice soft, live warmth with a delicate spicy sweetness that was excited into a heady wine by the tip of her tongue.

Then the car behind me blasted that the light was green again and I had to put my cup of wine down not fully tasted.

★ ★ ★

I hit three winners that afternoon. The two of us crowded the railing and yelled our heads off to push the nags home and when the last one slowed up in the stretch my heart slowed up with it because I had a parlay riding on his nose that was up in four figures. Fifty yards from the finish the jock laid on the whip and he crossed the line leading by a nostril.

Ellen shook my arm. "You can open your eyes now. He won."

I checked the board to make sure and there it was in big square print. I looked at the tickets that had gotten rolled up in the palm of my hand. "I'll never do that again! How the hell do the guys who bet all their lives stand this stuff! You know what I just won?"

"About four thousand dollars, didn't you?"

"Yeah, and before this I worked for a living." I smoothed out the pasteboards with my thumb and forefinger. "You ought to be a millionaire, kitten."

"I'm afraid not."

"Why? You cleaned up today, didn't you?"

"Oh, I did very well."

"So?"

"I don't like the color of the money."

"It's green, isn't it? You got a better color than that?"

"I have a cleaner kind of green," she said. Her body seemed to stiffen with a tension of some sort, drawing her hands into tight little fists. "You know why I like to see the Scobie horses win. It's the only way and the best way I can get back at my father. Just because of me he tries to run them under other colors, but I always learn about it before the races. He pays me a living whether he wants to or not and it hurts him right where he should be hurt. However, it's still money that came from him, even if it was indirectly given, and I don't want any part of it."

"Well, if you're going to throw it away, I'll take it."

"It doesn't get thrown away. You'll see where it goes."

We walked back to the ticket window and picked up a neat little pile of brand-new bills. They felt crisp as new lettuce and smelled even better. I folded mine into my wallet and stowed it away with a fond pat on the leather and started thinking of a lot of things that needed buying bad. Ellen threw hers in the wallet as if it happened every day. Thinking about it like that put a nasty buzz in my head.

"Why can't somebody follow you play for play? If anybody used your system and put a really big bundle down the odds would go skittering all over the place."

She gave me a faint smile and took my hand going up the ramp to the gate. "It doesn't work that way, Mike. All Scobie horses don't win by a long sight. It just happens that I know the ones that will win. It isn't that I'm a clever handicapper either. Dad has a trainer working for him who taught me all I know about horses. Whenever a winner is coming up I'm notified about it and place my bets."

"That's all there is to it?"

"That's all. Once the papers did a piece about it and according to them I did all the picking and choosing. I let them get the idea just to infuriate the old boy. It worked out fine."

"You're a screwball," I said. She looked hurt. "But you're nice," I added. She squeezed my arm and rubbed her face against my shoulder.

On the way back to the city the four G's in my pocket started burning through and it was all I could do to keep it there and let it burn. I wanted to stop off at the fanciest place we could find and celebrate with a drink, but Ellen shook her head and made me drive over to the East Side, pointing out the directions every few minutes.

Everything was going fine until we got stuck behind a truck and I had a chance to see where we were. Then everything wasn't so fine at all. There was a run-down bar with the glass cracked across the center facing the sidewalk. The door opened and a guy walked out, and before it shut again the familiarity of it came back with a rush and I could smell the rain and the beer-soaked sawdust and almost see a soggy little guy kissing his kid good-by.

My throat went dry all of a sudden and I breathed a curse before I wrenched the wheel and sent the heap screaming around the truck to get the hell out of the neighborhood.

We went straight ahead for six blocks, then Ellen said, "Turn right at the next street and stop near the corner."

I did as I was told and parked between a beer truck and a dilapidated sedan. She opened the door and stepped out, looking back at me expectantly. "Coming, Mike?"

I said okay and got out myself.

Then she walked me into a settlement house that was a resurrected barn or something. The whole business took about five minutes. I got introduced to a pair of nice old ladies, a clergyman and a cop who was having a cup of tea with the old ladies. Everybody was all smiles and joy and when Ellen gave one of the women a juicy wad of bills I thought they were going to cry.

Ellen, it seemed, practically supported the establishment.

I had a chance to look through the door at a mob of raggedy kids playing in the gym and I got rid of a quarter of the bundle of my wallet. I avoided a lot of thanks and got back to the car as fast as I could and looked at Ellen like I hadn't seen her before.

"Boy, am I a big-hearted slob," I said.

She laughed once and leaned over and kissed me. This time I had a long sip of the wine before she took my cup away. "It was worth it at that," I mused.

"You know something, Mike . . . you're not such a heel. I mean, such a *very* big heel."

I told her not to come to any hasty conclusions and backed the car out. It was a quarter to six and both of us were pretty hungry, so I drove up Broadway to a lot, left the car and walked back to a place that put out good food as well as good dinner music. While we waited for our orders Ellen bummed a nickel from me and went back to the phone booth to call Patty.

I could hardly wait for her to sit down again. "Get her?"

"Uh-huh. Everything's all set. Most of the office crew have left already. She'll leave the stuff at the house for us."

"Could we meet her somewhere? It would save time."

"Too risky. I'd rather not. Patty seemed a little jittery on the phone and I doubt if she'd like it either. I only hope they can be put back as easily as they're taken out."

"You won't have any trouble." Maybe I didn't put enough conviction in my voice, because she just looked at me and bent down to her salad. I said, "Now quit worrying. There won't be anything there that I couldn't find out if I had the time to look for it."

"All right, Mike, it's just that I've never done anything like that before. I won't worry."

She wrinkled her nose at me and dug into her supper.

It was eight-ten when we left the place. A thunderhead was moving up over Jersey blotting out the stars, replacing them with the dull glow of sheet lightning. I let Ellen pick up a couple quarts of beer while I rolled the car out and met her on the corner. She hopped in as the first sprinkle of rain tapped on the roof.

Sidewalks that were just damp a moment before took on a black sheen of water and drained it off into the gutter. Even with the wipers swatting furiously like a batter gone mad I could hardly see out. The car in front of me was a wavering shadow with one sick red eye, the neon signs and window fronts on either side just a ghostly parade of colors.

It was another night like that first one. The kind that made you run anywhere just to get away from it. You could see the vague shapes that were people huddled under marquees and jammed into doorways, the braver making the short dash to waiting cabs and wishing they hadn't.

By the time we reached Ellen's apartment it had slacked off into a steady downpour without the electrical fury that turned the night into a noisy, deafening day.

A doorman with an oversize umbrella led Ellen into the foyer and came back for me. Once we were out of it we could laugh. I was only making sloshing noises with my shoes but Ellen had gotten rained on down the back and her dress was plastered against her skin like a postage stamp. Going up in the elevator she stood with her back against the wall and edged sidewise after making me walk ahead of her.

I was going to knock first, but she poked her key in the lock and waved me inside.

"Nobody home?"

"Don't be silly. Tonight's date night . . . or haven't you noticed the couples arm in arm dashing for shelter."

"Yeah." I kicked my shoes off and carried them out to the kitchen. Ellen dumped the beer on the table and showed me where the glasses were.

"Pour me, Mike. I'll be back as soon as I get these wet things off."

"Hurry up."

She grinned at me and waltzed out while I was uncorking the bottles. I just finished topping the glasses off when she waltzed right back in again wrapped up in a huge terrycloth bathrobe, rubbing the rain out of her hair with a towel.

I handed her a glass and we clinked them in a toast we didn't speak. I drank without taking my eyes from hers, watching the deep blue swirl into a smoky gray that seemed to come up from the depths of a fire.

It got to be a little more than I could take. She knew it when I said, "Let's look at the files, Ellen."

"All right." She tucked the bottle under her arm and I trailed after her into the living room. A large console set took up a corner of the room and she pulled it away from the wall and worked her hand into the opening.

"Your private safe?"

"For intimate letters, precious nylons and anything else a nosy cleaning woman might take home with her."

She pulled out another of those manila folders held together with a thick rubber band and handed it to me. My hand started to shake when I worked the band off it. The thing snapped and flew across the room.

I took it sitting down. I reached in and pulled out a stack of official reports, four photographs and more affidavits than I could count. I spread them out across the coffee table and scanned them to see what I could pick up, laying the discards on top of the empty folder. When I tried to do it carefully I got impatient, and when I went faster I got clumsy and knocked the whole batch on the floor. Ellen picked them up and sorted them out again and I went on from there.

I was cursing myself and the whole damn mess long before I was finished because it was ending in a blank, a goddamn stone wall with nothing there but a fat ha-ha and to hell with you, bub. My hand went out of its own accord and spilled everything all across the room while Ellen let out a little scream and stepped back with her hand to her mouth.

"Mike!"

"I'm sorry, kid. It's a dud. Goddamn it, there's not a thing in there!"

"Oh, Mike . . . it can't be! The D.A. has been working on that a month!"

"Sure, trying to tangle Link up in that lousy gambling probe of his. So he proves he's a bookie. Hell, anybody can tell you that. All he had to do was go in and lay a bet with the guy himself. I'll say he's worked a month on it. Link doesn't stand a chance of getting out of this little web, but for all the time he'll draw for it, it will be worth it."

I scooped up a couple of the reports and slammed them with my fingers. "Look at this stuff. Two official reports that give any kind of background on the guy at all and those were turned in while Roberts was the D.A. What was going on in all the years until a month ago?"

Ellen glanced at the reports curiously and took them out of my hand, tapping the rubber-stamped number in the upper right-hand corner with her finger. "This is a code number, Mike. These reports are part of a series."

"Where are the rest of them then?"

"Either in the archives or destroyed. I won't say so for certain, but it's more likely that they were discarded. I've been with the department long enough to have seen more than one new office holder make a clean sweep of everything including what was in the files."

"Damn!"

"I'll check on it the first thing in the morning, Mike. There's a possibility that they're stored away someplace."

"Nuts on tomorrow morning. There isn't that much time to waste. There has to be another way."

She folded the sheets up carefully, running her nail along the edges. "I can't think of anything else unless you want to contact Roberts. He might remember something about the man."

"That's an idea. Where does he live?"

"I don't know . . . but I can find out." She looked at me pensively. "Does it have to be tonight?"

"Tonight."

I caught up with her before she reached the phone. I put my arms around her and breathed the fragrance that was her hair. "I'm sorry, kitten."

Ellen let her head fall back on my shoulder and looked up at me. "It's all right, Mike, I understand."

She had to make three separate calls to locate Roberts' number. It was an address in Flushing and when she had it she handed me the phone to do the calling. It was a toll call, so I put it through the operator and listened to it ring on the other end. When I was about ready to hang up a woman came on and said, "Hello, this is Mrs. Roberts."

"Can I speak to Mr. Roberts, please?"

"I'm sorry, but he isn't home right now. Can I take a message?"

Somebody had bottled up all my luck and thrown it down the drain. I said, "No, but can you tell me when he'll be back?"

"Not until tomorrow sometime. I expect him about noon."

"Well, thanks. I'll call him then. 'By."

I tried not to slam the receiver back in its cradle. I tried to sit on myself to keep from exploding and if it hadn't been for Ellen chuckling to herself from the depths of the couch I would have kicked something across the room. I spun around to tell her to shut up, but when a woman looks at you the way she was doing you don't say anything at all. You just stand there and look back because a toast-colored body that is all soft, molded curves and smooth hollows makes a picture to take your breath away, especially when it is framed against the thick texture of white terrycloth.

She laughed again and said, "You're trapped, Mike."

I wanted to tell her that I wasn't trapped at all, but there wasn't any room for words in my throat. I walked across the room and stood there staring at her, watching her come up off the couch into my arms to prove that she was real and not just a picture after all.

The cup was full this time, the wine mellow and sweet, and she was writhing in my arms fighting to breathe, yet not wanting me to stop holding her. I heard her say, "Mike . . . I'm sorry you're trapped, but I'm glad . . . glad." And I kissed her mouth shut again letting the rain slashing against the window pitch the tempo, hearing it rise and rise in a crescendo of fury, shrieking at me because the minutes were things not to be wasted.

It took all I had to shove her away. "Texas gal, don't make it rough for me. Not now."

She opened her eyes slowly, her fingers kneading my back. "I can't even buy you, can I?"

"You know better than that, sugar. Let me finish what I have to do first."

"If I let you get away you'll never come back, Mike. There are too many others waiting for you. Every week, every month there will be someone new."

"You know too much."

"I know I'm a Texas gal who likes a Texas man."

My grin was a little flat. "I'm a city boy, kid."

"An accident of birth. Everything else about you is Texas. Even a woman doesn't come first with you."

She stretched up on her toes, not far because she didn't have to go far, and kissed me lightly. "Sometimes Texas men do come back. That's why there are always more Texas men." She smiled.

"Don't forget to take those files in," I reminded her. Then there was nothing more to say.

I went back to the rain and the night, looking up just once to see her silhouetted against the window waving to me. She didn't see me, but I waved back to her. She would have liked it if she'd known what I was thinking.

On the way back I stopped off for a drink and a sandwich and tried to think it out. I wanted to be sure of what I was doing before I stuck my neck out. I spent an hour going over the whole thing, tying it into Toady Link and no matter how I looked at it the picture was complete.

At least I tried to tell myself that it was.

I said it over and over to myself the same way I told Pat, but I couldn't get it out of my mind that some place something didn't fit. It was only a little thing, but it's the little things that hold bigger things together. I sat there and told myself that it was Toady who drove the murder car and Toady who gave the orders to Arnold Basil because he couldn't afford to trust anybody else to do the job right. I told myself that it was Toady who engineered Hooker's death and tried to engineer mine.

Yet the more I told myself the more that little voice inside my head would laugh and poke its finger into some forgotten recess and try to jar loose one fact that would make me see what the picture was really like.

I gave up in disgust, paid my bill and walked out.

I walked right into trouble, too. Pat was slouched up against the wall outside my apartment with the friendliness gone completely from his face.

He didn't even give me a chance to say hello. He held out his hand with an abruptness I wasn't used to. "Let's have your gun, Mike."

I didn't argue with him. He packed it open, checked the chamber and the slide, then smelled the barrel.

"You already know when I shot it last," I said.

"I do?" It didn't sound like a question at all.

It started down low around my belly, that squeamish feeling when something is right there ready to pop in your face. "Quit being a jerk. What's the act for?"

He came away from the door frame with a scowl. "Goddamn it, Mike, play it straight if you have to play it at all!"

I said a couple of words.

"You've had it, Mike," he told me. He put it flat and simple as if I knew just what he meant.

"You could tell me about it."

"Look, Mike, I'm a cop. You were my friend and all that, but I'm not getting down on my knees to anybody. I did everything but threaten you to lay off and what happened? You did it your way anyhow. It doesn't go, feller. It's finished, washed up. I hated to see it happen, but it was just a matter of time. I thought you were smart enough to understand. I was wrong."

"That isn't telling me about it."

"Cut it, Mike. Toady's dead. He was shot with a .45," he said.

"And I'm tagged."

"That's right," Pat nodded. "You're tagged."

CHAPTER 8

Sometimes you get mad and sometimes you don't. If there was any of that crazy anger in me it had all been drained out up there in Ellen's apartment. Now it's making sense, I thought. Now it's where it should be.

Pat dropped my gun in his pocket. "Let's go, Mike."

So I went as far as the front door and watched the rain wash through under the sill. Before Pat opened the door I said, "You're sure about this, aren't you?"

He *was* sure. Two minutes ago he had been as sure of it as the day he was born and now he wasn't sure of it at all. His mouth hardened into a gash that pushed his eyes halfway shut with some uncontrollable emotion until they seemed to focus on something right behind me.

I didn't want him to answer me before he knew. "I didn't kill him, Pat. I was hoping I would, but somebody beat me to it."

"The M.E. sets the time of death around four o'clock last night." His voice asked for an explanation.

I said, "You should have told me, Pat. I was real busy then. Real busy."

His hand came away from the door. "You mean you can prove it?"

"I mean just that."

"Mike . . . if you're lying . . ."

"I've never been that stupid. You ought to know that."

"I ought to know a lot of things. I ought to know where you were every minute of last night."

"You know how to find out."

"Show me."

I didn't like the way he was looking at me at all. Maybe I'm not so good at lying any more, and I was lying my head off. Last night I was busy as hell sleeping and there wasn't one single way I could prove it. If I tried to tell him the truth it would take a month to talk my way clear.

I said, "Come on," and headed for the phone in the lobby. I shoved a dime in the slot and dialed a number, hoping that I could put enough across with a few words to say what I wanted. He stood right there at my elbow ready to take the phone away as soon as I got my party and ask the question himself.

I couldn't mistake her voice. It was like seeing her again with the lava green of her dress flowing from her waist.

"This is Mike, Marsha. A policeman . . . wants to ask you something. Mind?"

That was as far as I could get. Pat had the phone while she was still trying to figure it out. He gave me a hard smile and turned to the phone. "Captain Chambers speaking. I understand you can account for Mr. Hammer's whereabouts last night. Is that correct?"

Her voice was music pouring out of the receiver. Pat glanced at me sharply, curiously, then muttered his thanks and hung up. He still didn't quite know what to make of it. "So you spent the night with the lady."

I said a beautiful thanks to Marsha under my breath. "That's not for publication, Pat."

"You better stop tomcatting around when Velda gets back, friend."

"It makes a good alibi."

"Yeah, I'd like to see the guy who'd sooner kill Toady than sleep with a chick like that. Okay, Mike, you got yourself an alibi. I have a screwy notion that I shouldn't believe it, but Link isn't Decker and if you're in this there'll be hell to pay and I'll find out about it soon enough."

I handed him a butt and flipped a light with my thumbnail. "Can I hear about the deal or is it secret info like everything else?"

"There's not much to it. Somebody walked in and killed him."

"Just like that?"

"He was in bed asleep. He got it right through the head and whoever killed him went through the place like a cyclone. I'm going back there now if you want to come along."

"Blue boy there?"

"The D.A. doesn't know about it yet. He's out with the vice squad again," Pat said tiredly.

"You checked the bullet, didn't you?"

Pat squirmed a little. "I didn't wait for the report. I was so god-damned positive it was you that I came right over. Besides, you could have switched barrels if you felt like it. I've seen the extras you have."

"Thanks. I'm a real great guy."

"Quit rubbing it in."

"Who found the body?"

"As far as we know, the police were the first on the scene. A tele-graph boy with a message for Toady saw the door open and went to shut it. Enough stuff was kicked around inside to give him the idea there was a robbery. He was sure of it when he rang the bell and nobody answered. He called the police and they found the body."

"Got any idea what they were looking for . . . or if they found it?"

Pat threw the butt at the floor. "No. Come on, take a look at it your-self. Maybe it'll make you feel better."

What was left of Toady wouldn't make anybody feel better. Death had taken the roundness from his body and made an oblong slab of it. He lay there on his back with his eyes closed and his mouth open, a huge, fat frog as unlovely dead as he was alive. Right in the center of his forehead was the hole. It was a purplish-black hole with scorched edges flecked by powder burns. Whoever held the gun held it mighty close. If there was a back to his head it was smashed into the pillow.

Outside on the street a couple more prowl cars screamed to a stop and feet came pounding into the house. A lone newshawk was sound-ing off about the rights of the press and being told to shut up. Pat left me there with a plain-clothesman while he got things organized and started the cops going through the rooms in a methodical search for any-thing that might be a lead.

When I had enough of Toady I went downstairs and followed Pat around, watching him paw through the wreckage of the living room. "Somebody didn't make a lot of noise, did they?"

I got a sharp grin. "Brother, this place was really searched."

I picked up a maple armchair and looked at it closely. There wasn't a scratch on it. There weren't any scratches on anything for that matter. For all the jumble that it seemed to be, the room had been carefully and methodically torn apart and the pieces put down nice and gently. You could even see some order in the way it was done. The slits in the seat cushions were evenly cut all in the same place. Anything that could be unscrewed or pulled out was unscrewed or pulled out. Books were scat-tered all over the floor, some with the back linings ripped right out of them.

Pat had one in his hand and waved it at me. "It wasn't very big if they went looking for it here."

I thought I said something to myself, but I said it out loud and Pat's head swiveled around at me. "What?"

I didn't tell him the second time. I shook my head, knowing the leer

I was wearing had pulled my face out of shape and if Pat had good eyes he could read what I was thinking without looking any farther than my eyes. He might have done it if a cop hadn't come up to tell him about the junk in the basement, and he left me standing in the middle of the room right where Toady had made me stand, only this time I wasn't after Toady's hide any more because he wasn't the end at all.

Another cop came in looking for Pat. I told him he was downstairs and would be right back. The cop spread out the stuff in his hand and flashed it at me. "Look at the pin-ups I found." He gave a short laugh. "I guess he didn't go for this new stuff. Don't blame him. I like the pre-war crop better myself."

"Let's see them."

He handed them over to me as he looked through them.

Half of them were regular studio stills and the rest were enlargements of snapshots taken during stage shows. Every one of them was personally autographed to Charlie Fallon with love and sometimes kisses from some of the biggest stars in Hollywood.

When he was done with the pictures the cop let me look at a couple of loose-leaf pads that had scrawled notations of appointments to be made for more photos of more lovelies and the list of private phone numbers he had accumulated would have made any Broadway columnist drool. Every so often there was a reminder after a name . . . *introduction to F.*

And there it was again. Fallon. No matter where I turned the name came up. Fallon, Fallon, Fallon. Arnold Basil was an old Fallon boy. All the dames knew Fallon, Toady had some connection with Fallon. Damn it, the guy was supposed to be dead!

I didn't wait for Pat to come back. I told the cop to tell him I'd left and would call up tomorrow. Before I got to the door the reporter who was trying to make the most of being first on the scene tried to corner me for a story and I shook my head no. He dropped me for the cop and got the same story.

Something had gentled the rain, taking the madness out of it. The curious were there in a tight knot at the gate shrinking together under umbrellas and raincoats to gape at the death place and speculate among themselves. I managed to push myself through to the outer fringes of the crowd with about a minute to spare. Just as I broke clear the D.A. came in from the other side with his boys doing the blocking. His face was blacker than the night itself and I knew right away that somebody had crossed him up on another deal. His boat still had a hole in the bottom and if it leaked any more he was going to get swamped.

If it hadn't been so late I would have called Marsha to kiss her hand for pulling me out of a spot, but tonight I didn't want to see anybody or speak to anybody. I wanted to stretch out in bed and think. I wanted to start at the beginning and chew my way through it slowly until I found the tough hunk that didn't chew so easily and put it through the grinder.

Then I'd have my killer.

Two blocks down a hackie tooted his horn at me and I ran for the door he held open. I gave him my address and settled back into the seat. The guy was one of those Dodger fans who couldn't keep quiet about how the bums were doing and talked my ear off until I climbed out in front of my apartment and handed over a couple of bucks.

I got all the way upstairs and there they were again. Two of them this time. One was big as a house and the other wasn't much smaller. The little guy closed in with a badge flashing in his palm while the other one stood by ready to take me if I didn't act right. Both of them kept one hand in their pockets just to let me know that the play was theirs all the way.

The guy said, "Police, buddy," and stowed the badge back in his pants.

"What do you want with me?"

"You'll find out. Get moving."

The other one said, "Wait a minute," and yanked my gun out of the holster. Under his flat smile his teeth were yellowed from too much smoking. "You're supposed to have a bad temper. Guns and guys with bad tempers don't go together."

"Neither do badges without those leather wallets a cop keeps them in."

I caught the quick look that passed between them, but I caught the nose of a gun in my back at the same time. The big guy smiled again. "Wise guy. You wanta do it the hard way."

"That rod'll make a big boom in here. A nice quiet joint like this people'll want to know what all the noise is about."

The gun pressed in a little deeper. "Maybe. You won't hear it, buddy. Move."

Those two were real pros. Not the kind of hoods who pick up some extra change with nickel-plated rods either. These were delivery boys, the real McCoy. They knew just where to stand so I couldn't move in and just how to look so nobody would get the pitch. One had a pint bottle of whisky outlined in his inside jacket pocket to pour over me so

I'd smell like a drunk in case they had to carry me out. And they had that look. Somebody had given the orders to bump me fast if I tried to get rough.

That look was enough for me. Besides, I was curious myself.

We got downstairs and big boy said, "Where's your car?"

I pointed it out. He snapped his fingers for my keys and got them. The other one did something with his hand and a car down the block pulled away from the curb and shot by us without looking over.

It didn't take much to see what was going to happen. I was getting a one-way ride in my own car. After I was delivered someplace first. I wasn't supposed to know about it. I was supposed to be a real good boy and act nice and polite so they wouldn't have any trouble with me. I was supposed to be a goddamn fool and let myself get killed with no fuss at all while a couple of pros congratulated themselves on their technique.

My head started banging with that insane music that was all kettle-drums and shrill flutes blended together in wild discord until my hands shook with the madness of it. What kind of a simple jerk did they take me for? Maybe they thought they were the only ones who were pros in this game. Maybe they thought this had never happened before and if it had I wouldn't be ready for it to happen again.

By God, if they played this the way a pro would play it they were going to get one hell of a jolt. I had a .32 hammerless automatic in a boot between the seat and the door right where I could get at it if I had to.

They played it that way too. Big boy said, "You drive, shamus. Take it nice and easy or we'll take it for you." He held the door open so I could get in and was right there beside me when I slid under the wheel. He didn't crowd me. Not him, he was an old-timer. He kept plenty of room between us, sitting jammed into the corner with his arm on the sill. His other arm was in his lap pointing my own gun at me. The little guy didn't say much. He climbed in back and leaned on the seat behind my head like he was talking to me confidentially. But it was the gun he had pressed against my neck that was doing all the talking.

We took a long ride that night. We were three happy people taking a cruise out to the shore. To keep everybody happy I switched on the radio and picked up a disk jockey and made a habit of lighting my cigarettes from the dashboard lighter so they'd get used to seeing my arms move around.

My pal beside me was calling the turns and someplace before we came to Islip he said, "Slow down." Up ahead a macadam road intersected the highway. "Go right until I tell you to turn."

I swung around the corner and followed the black strip of road. It lasted a half-mile, butting against an oiled-top dirt road that went the rest of the way. We made a few more turns after that and I started to smell the ocean coming in strong with the wind. The houses had thinned out until they were only black shapes on spindly legs every quarter-mile or so. The road curved gently away from the shore line, threading its way through the knee-high sawgrass that bent with the breeze and whisked against the fender of the car with an insidious hissing sound.

Nobody had to tell me to stop. I saw the shaded lights of the house and the bulk of the sedan against its side and I eased on the brakes. Big boy looked pleased with himself and the pressure of the gun on my neck relaxed. The guy behind me got out and stood by the door while the other one tucked the keys in his pocket and came up stepping on my shadow.

"You got the idea good," he told me. "Let's keep it that way. Inside and take it slow."

I practically crawled. The boys stayed behind me and to the right and left, beautiful spots in case I tried to run for it. Either one of them could have cut me down before I got two feet. I picked the last smoke out of my pack and dropped the empty wrapper. Shortie was even smart enough to pick that up. I didn't have a match and nobody offered me one, so I let it droop there between my lips. It was a little too soon to start worrying. This wasn't the time nor the place. A body doesn't hide so easy and neither does a car. When we went we'd go together. I could almost draw a picture of the way it would happen.

The door opened and the guy was a thin dark shadow against the light. I said, "Hello, scrimey."

I should have kept my mouth shut. Lou Grindle backhanded me across the mouth so that my teeth went right through my lips. Two guns hit me in the spine at the same time ramming me right into him and I couldn't have gotten away with it in a million years but I tried anyway. I hooked him down as low as I could then felt my knuckles rip open when I got him in the mouth.

Neither of the guys behind me dared risk a shot, but they did just as well. One of them brought a gun barrel around as hard as he could. There wasn't even any pain to it, just a loud click that grew into a thunderous wave of sound that threw me flat on the floor and rolled over me.

The pain didn't come until later. It wasn't there in my head where I thought it would be. It was all over, a hundred agonizing points of torture where the toe of a shoe had ripped through my clothes and torn into the skin. Something dripped slowly and steadily like a leaky faucet. Every movement sent the pain shooting up from my feet and if screaming wouldn't have only made it worse I would have screamed. I got one eye open. The other was covered by a puffy mass of flesh on my cheekbone that kept it shut.

Somebody said, "He's awake."

"He'll get it worse this time."

"I'll tell you when." The voice was so decisive that nobody gave it to me worse.

I managed to focus the one good eye then. It was pointed at the floor looking at my feet. They were together at attention strapped to the rungs of a chair. My arms weren't there at all so I guess that they were tied someplace behind the same chair. And the drip wasn't from the faucet at all.

It was from something on my face that used to be a nose.

Somehow, I dragged myself straight up. It didn't hurt so bad then. When the fuzziness went away I squinted my one good eye against the light and saw them sitting around like vultures waiting for the victim to die. The two boys with the rods over by the door and Lou Grindle holding a bloody towel to his mouth.

And Ed Teen perched on the edge of the leather armchair with his chin propped on a cane. He still looked like a banker, even to the gray homburg.

He stared at me very thoughtfully for a minute. "Feel pretty bad?"

"Guess." The one word almost choked me.

"It wasn't necessary, you know. We just wanted to talk to you. Everything would have been quite friendly." He smiled "Now we have to tie you down until we're finished talking."

Lou threw the towel at me. "Christ, quit stalling around with him. I'll make him talk in a hurry."

"Shut up." Ed didn't even stop smiling. "You're lucky I'm here. Lou is rather impulsive."

I didn't answer him.

He said, "It was too bad you had to kill Toady, Mr. Hammer. He was very valuable to me."

I got the words out. "You're nuts."

He pushed himself up off the cane and leaned back in the chair. "Don't bother with explanations. I'm not the police. If you killed him that's your business. What I want is what's my business. Where is it?"

My lips felt too thick to put any conviction in my voice. "I don't know what the hell you're talking about."

"Remind him, Lou."

Then he sat back chewing on a cigar and watched it. Lou didn't use his foot this time. The wet towel around his fist was enough. He was good at the job, but I had taken so much the first time that even the half-consciousness I had left went fast.

I tried to stay that way and couldn't. My head twitched and Teen said metallically, "Now do you remember?"

I only had to shake my head once and that fist clubbed it again. It went on and on and on until there was no pain at all and I could laugh when he talked to me and try to smile when the delivery boy in the corner got sick and turned his head away to puke.

Ed rapped the cane on the floor. "Enough. That's enough. He can't feel it any more. Let him sit and think about it a few minutes."

Lou was glad to do that. He was breathing hard through his mouth and his chin was covered with blood. He went over and sat down at the table to massage his hand. Lou was very happy.

The cane kept up a rhythm on the floor. "This is only the beginning you know. There's absolutely no necessity for it."

I managed to say, "I didn't . . . kill Link."

"It doesn't matter whether you did or not. I want what you took from his apartment."

Lou started to cough and spat blood on the floor. He gagged, put his hand to his mouth and pushed a couple of teeth into his palm with his tongue. When he brought his head up his eyes bored into mine like deadly little black bullets. "I'm going to kill that son-of-a-bitch!"

"You sit there and shut up. You'll do what I say."

He was on his feet with his hands apart fighting to keep himself from tearing Teen's throat out with his fingers. Ed wasn't so easy to scare. The snub-nosed gun in his hand said so.

Lou's face was livid with rage. "Damn you anyway. Damn you and Fallon and Link and the whole stinking mess of you!"

"You're lisping, Lou. Sit down." Lou sat down and stared at his teeth some more. He was proud of those teeth. They were so nice and shiny.

They lay where they were dropped on the table and seemed to fascinate him. He kept feeling his gums as though he couldn't believe it, cursing his heart out in black rage. Ed's gun never left him for a second. Right then Lou was in a killing rage and ready to take it out on anybody.

He kept saying over and over, "Goddamn every one of 'em! Goddamn 'em all!" His mouth drew back baring the gap in his teeth and he slammed the table with his fist. "Goddamn, this wouldn't've happened if you'd let me do it my way! I would've killed Fallon and that lousy whore he kept and Link and this wouldn't've happened!" I got the eyes this time. They came around slow and evilly. "I'll kill you for it, too."

"You'll get new teeth, Lou," Ed said pleasantly. Everything he said was pleasant.

Grindle gagged again and walked out of the room. Water started to run in a bowl somewhere and he made sloshing noises as he washed out his mouth. Ed smiled gently. "You hit him where he hurts the most . . . in his vanity."

"Where does it hurt you the most, Ed?"

"A lot of people would like to know that."

"I know." I tried to grin at him. My face wouldn't wrinkle. "It's going to hurt you in two places. Especially when they shave the hair off your head and leg."

"I think," he told me, "that when Lou comes back I'll let him do you up right."

"You mean . . . like old times when Fallon pulled the strings . . . with cigar butts and pliers?"

His nostrils flared briefly. "If you have to say something at all, tell me where it is."

"Where what is?"

The water was still running inside. Without turning his head Ed called, "Johnny. Give it to him."

The big guy came over. Under his shirt his stomach made peculiar rolling motions. His techniques stunk. His fist made a solid chunk against my chin and I went out like a light. They poured cold water over me so I'd wake up and watch it happen all over again.

It started to get longer between rounds. I would come only partially back out of that jet-black land of nowhere and hang there limply. The big guy's voice was a hoarse croak. "He's done, Ed. I don't think he knows what you're talking about."

"He knows." His cane tapped the floor again. "Give him another dousing."

I got the water treatment again. It washed the blood out of my eyes so I could see again and the shock of it cleared my mind enough to think.

Ed knew when I was awake. He had a cigar lit and gazed at the cherry-red end of it speculatively. "You can hear me?"

I nodded that I could.

"Then understand something. I shall ask you just once more. Remember this, if you're dead you can't use what you have."

"Tell . . . me what the hell . . . you want."

Only for a second did his eyes go to the pair leaning on the window sill. If they weren't there I would have had it, but whatever I was supposed to know was too much for their big ears. "You know very well what I mean. You've been trouble from the very first moment. I know you too well, Mr. Hammer. You're only a private investigator, but you've killed people before. In your own way you're quite as ruthless as I am . . . but not quite as smart. That's why I'm sitting here and you're sitting there. Keep what you have. I've no doubt that it's hidden some place you alone can get it, and after you're dead nobody else will find it. Not in my time at least. Johnny . . . go see what's keeping Lou."

The guy walked inside and came right back. "He's lying down. He puked on the bed."

"Let him stay there then. Untie this man."

The straps came off my hands and legs, but I couldn't get up. They let me sit there until the circulation came back, and with it the flame that licked at my body. When I could move Johnny hauled me to my feet.

"What'll I do with him, Ed?"

"That's entirely up to you. Martin, drive me back to the city. I've had enough of this."

The little guy saluted with his two fingers and waited until Ed had picked up his topper. He made a beautiful flunky. He opened the door and probably even helped him down the steps. I heard the car purr into life and drag back on the road.

Johnny let go my coat collar and jammed the gun in my back. "You heard what the man said." He started me off with a push to the door.

The long walk. The last ride. The boys call it a lot of things. You sit there in the car with your head spinning around and around thinking of all the ways to get out and every time you think of one there's a gun staring you in the face. You sweat and try to swallow. All your joints feel shaky and though you want a cigarette more than anything in the world you know you'll never be able to hold one in your mouth. You sweat some more. Your mouth wants to scream for help when you see somebody walking along the street. A gun pokes you to keep quiet. There's a cop on the corner under the arc light. A prayer gets stuck in your throat. He'll recognize them . . . he'll see the glint of their guns . . . his hand will go up and stop the car and you'll be safe. But he looks the other way when the car passes by and you wonder what happened to your prayer. Then you stop sweating because your body is dried out and your tongue is a thick rasp working across your lips. You think of a lot of things, but mostly you think of how fast you're going to stop living.

I remembered how I thought of all those things the first time. Now it was different. I was beat to hell and too far gone to fight. I had the strength to drive and that was all. Johnny sat there in his corner watching me and he still had my own gun.

This time I wanted a cigarette and he gave me one. I used the dash lighter again. I finished that and he gave me another while he laughed at the way my hand shook when I tried to get it in my mouth. He laughed at the way I kept rolling the window up first to get warm then down to get cooled off. He laughed at the way I made the turns he told me to take, creeping around them so I'd have seconds longer to live.

When he told me to stop he laughed again because my arms seemed to relax and hang limply at my sides.

He took his eyes off me for one second while he searched for the door handle and he never laughed again.

I shot him through the head five times with the .32 I had pulled out of the boot and kicked him out in the road after I took my gun from his hand. When I backed around the lights of the car swept over him in time to catch one final involuntary twitch and Johnny was getting his first taste of hell.

The gray haze of morning was beginning to show in the sky behind me when I reached the shack again. It was barely enough to show me the road through the grass and outline the car against the house. I killed the engine, backed into the sand and opened the door.

This time the car wasn't any big sedan. It was the same coupé that had brought the boys to get me then pulled away at their signal. I knew who was in there. The little guy Ed called Martin had come back for Lou.

I made a circuit of the house and stopped under the bedroom window. Lou was cursing the guy, telling him to stop shaking him. I straightened up to look in, but there was no light and the curtains made an effective blind. Somebody started running the water and there was more talk I couldn't catch. It faded away until it was in the back of the house and I grabbed at the chance.

I hugged the wall climbing up on the porch, squeezing myself into the shadows. The wood had rotted too soft to have any squeak left in it but I wasn't taking any chances. I got down low with the gun in one hand and reached up for the knob with the other.

Somebody had oiled it not so long ago. It turned noiselessly and I gave the door a shove. The guy with the oilcan was nice people. He had oiled the hinges too.

My breath stuck in my lungs until I was inside with the door closed behind me, then I let it out in a low hiss and tried to breathe normally. The blood was pounding through my body making noise enough to be heard throughout the house. My legs wanted to drag me down instead of pushing me forward and the .45 became too heavy to hold steadily.

I had to fight against the letdown that was sweeping over my body. It couldn't come now! The answer was there in Lou's bloody mouth waiting to be squeezed out. I started to weave a little bit and reached out to grab the wall and hang on. My hand hit the door of a closet and slammed it shut.

Silence.

A cold, black silence.

A tentative voice calling, "Johnny?"

I couldn't fake an answer. My knees started to go.

Again, "Johnny, damn it!"

Lou cursed and a tongue of flame lashed out of a doorway.

There was no faking about the way I hit the floor. Lou had heard too many men fall like that before. It was real, but only because my legs wouldn't hold me any longer. I still had the .45 in my mitt and I let the feet come my way just so far before I squeezed the trigger.

The blasting roar of the gun echoed and shattered on the walls. I rolled until I hit something and stopped, my free hand clawing my one good eye to keep it open. The remnants of a scream were still in the air and the pin points of light were two guns punching holes in the wood-work searching for me. I got my hand around the leg of an end table and let it go. The thing bounced on the floor and split under the impact of the bullets. They were shouting at each other now, calling each other fools for wasting shots. So they stopped wasting shots. They thought I was hit and waited me out.

Somebody was breathing awfully funny. It made a peculiar racket when you took time to listen to it. I could hear them changing position, getting set. I went as quietly as I could and changed position myself.

It had to come soon. A few more minutes and the light would come through the curtains and they could see better than I could. It went on like a kid's game, that incessant crawling, the fear that you'd be caught, the deliberate motions of stealth that were so hard to make.

The funny breathing was real close. I could reach out and touch it. It was there on the other side of the chair. It heard me too, but it didn't change its tone. From across the room came the slightest sound and a whisper from only five feet away. "He's over there."

Orange flame streaked across the room and the sound jolted my ears even before the scream and the hoarse curse. The answer was two shots that pounded into the floor and a heavy thud as a body toppled over.

Lou's voice said, "I got the son-of-a-bitch." He still lisped.

He moved out past the chair and I saw him framed in the window.

I said, "You got your own man, Lou."

Lou did too many things at once. He tried to drop, shoot and curse me at the same time. He got two of them done. He dropped because I shot him. His gun went off because a dead hand pulled the trigger. He didn't curse because my bullet went up through his mouth into his brain taking the big answer with it.

There was nothing left there for me at all.

Outside the gray haze had brightened into morning, very early morning. It took me a long time to get back to the car, and much, much longer to get to the highway.

Fate allowed me a little bit of luck. It gave me a hitchhiker stranded between towns. I picked him up and told him I'd been in a fight and that he could drive.

The hiker was glad to. He felt sorry for me.

I felt sorry for myself too.

CHAPTER 9

We were on a side street just off Ninth Avenue and the guy beside me was pulling my arm to wake me up. He tugged and twisted until I thought the damn thing would come off. I got the one eye open and looked at him.

"You sure were dead to the world, brother. Took me a half-hour to get you out of it."

"What time is it?"

"Eight-thirty. Feel pretty rotten?"

"Lousy."

"Want me to call somebody?"

"No."

"Well, look, I have to catch a bus. You think you're going to be all right? If you're not I'll stick around awhile."

"Thanks . . . I'll make out."

"Okay, it's up to you. Sure appreciate the ride. Wish I could do something for you."

"You can. Go get me a pack of butts. Luckies."

He waved away the quarter I handed him and walked down to the corner to the newsstand. He came back with the pack opened, stuck one in my mouth and lit it. "You take care now. Better go home and sleep it off."

I said I would and sat there smoking the butt until a cop came along slapping tickets on car windows. I edged over behind the wheel, kicked the starter in and got out of there.

Traffic wasn't a problem like it usually was. I was glad to get behind a slow-paced truck and stay there. Every bone and muscle in my body ached and I couldn't have given the wheel a hard wrench if I wanted to. I got around the corner somehow and the truck crossed over to get in the lane going through the Holland Tunnel. I dropped out of position, squeezed through the intersection as the light changed and got on the street that led up to police headquarters.

Both sides of the street were lined with people going to work. They all seemed so happy. They walked alone or in couples, thousands of feet and legs making a blur of motion. I envied them the sleep they had had. I envied their normal unswollen faces. I envied a lot of things until I took time to think about it. At least I was alive. That was something.

The street in front of the red brick building was a parade ground of uniformed patrolmen. Some were walking off to their beats and others were climbing in squad cars. The plain-clothesmen went off in pairs, separating at the corner with loud so longs. Right in front of the main entrance three black sedans with official markings were drawn up at the curb with their drivers reading tabloids behind the wheel. Directly across from them a pair of squad cars pulled out and the tan coupé in front of me nosed into the space they left. I followed in behind him, did a better job of parking than he did and was up against the bumper of the car behind me so the guy would have room to maneuver.

I guess the jerk got his license wholesale. He tried to saw his way in without looking behind him and I had to lean on the horn to warn him off. Maybe I should have planted a red flag or something. He ignored the horn completely and slammed into me so hard I wrapped my chest around the wheel.

That did it. That was as much as I could take. I opened the door with my elbow and got out to give him hell. You'd think with all the cops around one of them would have jumped him, but that's how it goes. The guy was getting out of his heap with a startled apology written all over him. He took a look at my face and forgot what he was going to say. His mouth hung open and he just looked.

I said, "You deaf or something? What the devil do you think a horn's for?"

His mouth started to say something, but he was too confused to get it out. I took another good look at him and I could see why. He was the guy who stood next to me in the bar the afternoon before with the busted headset. He was making motions at his ears and tapping the microphone or whatever it was. I was too disgusted to pay any attention to him and waved him off. He still smacked the bumper twice again before he got himself parked.

This was starting off to be a beautiful day too.

When I got in the building I started to attract a little attention. A cop

I know pretty well passed right by me with no more than a cursory glance. One asked me if I was there to register a complaint and looked surprised when I shook my head no. The place was a jumble of activity with men going in and out of the line-up room, getting their orders at the desk or scrambling to get off on a case.

Too much was popping in the morning to hope Pat would be in his office, so I waited my turn at the information desk and told the cop at the switchboard that I wanted to see Captain Chambers.

He said, "Name?"

And I said, "Hammer, Michael Hammer."

Then his hand paused with the plug in it and he said, "Well, I'll be damned."

He tried about ten extensions before he got Pat, said Yes, sir a few times and yanked the plug out. "He'll be right down. Wait here for him."

By the clock I waited exactly one minute and ten seconds. Pat came out of the elevator at a half-run and when he saw me his face did tricks until it settled down in a frown.

"What happened to you?"

"I got took, pal. Took good, too."

He didn't ask me any more questions. He looked down at his shoes a second then put it to me hard and fast. "You're under arrest, Mike."

"What?"

"Come on upstairs."

The elevator was waiting. We got on and went up. We got off at the right floor and I started to walk toward his office automatically, but he put out his hand and stopped me.

"This way, Mike."

"Say, what's going on?"

He wouldn't look at me. "We've had men covering your apartment, your office and all your known places of entertainment since six this morning. The D.A. has a warrant out for your arrest and there's not a damn thing you can do about it."

"Sorry. I should have stayed home. What's the charge?"

We paused outside a stained-oak door. "Guess."

"I give up."

"The D.A. looked for Link's personal file last night and found it missing. He was here when Ellen Scobie tried to put it back this morning. You have two girls on the carpet right this minute who are going to lose their jobs and probably have charges preferred against them too. You're going in there yourself and take one hell of a rap and this time there's no way out. You finished yourself, Mike. You'll never learn, but you're finished."

I dropped my hands in my pockets and made like I was grinning at him.

"You're getting old, son. You're getting set in your ways. For the last two years all you've done is warn me about this, that, and the next thing. We used to play a pretty good game, you and me, now you're starting to play it cautious and for a cop who handles homicide that's no damn good at all."

Then just for the hell of it that little finger that was probing my brain deliberately knocked a couple of pieces together that made lovely, beautiful sense and I remembered something Ellen had told me not so long ago. I twisted it around, revamped it a little and I was holding something the D.A. was going to pay for in a lot of pride. Yep, a whole lot of pride.

I reached for the knob myself. "Let's go, chum. Me and the D.A. have some business to transact."

"Wait a minute. What are you pulling?"

"I'm not pulling a thing, Pat. Not a thing. I'm just going to trade him a little bit."

Everything was just like it was the last time. Almost.

There was the D.A. behind his desk with his boys on either side. There were the detectives in the background, the cop at the door, the little guy taking notes and me walking across the room.

Ellen and her roommate were the exceptions this time. They sat side by side in straight-back chairs at the side of the big desk and they were crying their eyes out.

If my face hadn't been what it was there would have been a formal announcement made. As it was, everybody gave me a kind of horrified stare and Ellen turned around in her seat. She stopped crying abruptly and put her hand to her mouth to stifle a scream.

I said, "Take it easy, kid."

Her teeth went into her lip and she buried her face in her hands.

The District Attorney was very sarcastic this time. "Good morning, *Mister* Hammer."

"I'm glad you remembered," I told him.

Any other time his face would have changed color. Not now. He liked this cat-and-mouse stuff. He had waited a long time for it and now he was going to enjoy every minute of it while he had an audience to appreciate it. "I suppose you know why you're here?" He leaned back in his chair and folded his arms across his chest. The two assistants did the same thing.

"I've heard about it."

"Shall I read the charges?"

"Don't bother." My legs were starting to go again. I pulled a chair across the floor and sat down. "Start reading me off any time you feel like it," I said. "Get it all off your chest at once so you'll be able to listen to somebody else except your yes-men for a change."

The two assistants came to indignant attention in their seats.

It was so funny I actually got a grin through.

The D.A. didn't think it was so funny. "I don't intend to take any of your nonsense, *Mister* Hammer. I've had about all I can stand of it."

"Okay, you know what you can do. Charge me with conspiracy and theft, toss me in the pokey and I catch hell at the trial. So I'll go up."

"You won't be alone." He glanced meaningly at the two women. There were no tears left in Ellen any more, but her friend was sobbing bitterly.

I said, "Did you stop to think why the three of us bothered to take a worthless file out of here?"

"Does it matter?"

Ellen had nudged her companion and the crying stopped. I took the deck of cigarettes out of my pocket and fiddled with it to keep my hands busy. The white of the wrapper flashed the light back at the sun until attention seemed to be focused on it rather than me.

"It matters," I said. "As the charge will state, it was a deliberate conspiracy all right, perpetrated by three citizens in good standing who saw a way to accomplish something that an elected official couldn't manage. The papers will have a field day burying you."

He smiled. The damn fool smiled at me! "Don't bother going through that song and dance again."

He was getting ready to throw the book in my face when Pat spoke from the back of the room. His voice held a strained note, but it had a lot of power behind it. "Maybe you better hear what he has to say."

"Say it then." The smile faded into a grimace of anger. "It had better be good, because the next time you say anything will be to a judge and jury."

"It's good. You'll enjoy hearing about it. We," and I emphasized that "we," "found the hole in the boat."

I heard Pat gasp and take a step nearer.

"Ellen suggested it to you at one time and the full possibilities of the thing never occurred to you. We know how information is getting out of this office."

The D.A.'s eyes were bright little beads searching my face for the lie. They crinkled up around the edges when he knew I was telling the truth and sought out Pat for advice. None came so he said, "How?"

Now I had the ball on his goal line and I wasn't giving it up. "I won't bother you with the details of how we did it, but I can tell you how it was being done."

"Damn it . . . How!"

I gave him his smile back. On me it must have looked good. "Uh-uh. We trade. You're talking to three clams unless you drop all those charges. Not only drop 'em, but forget about 'em."

What else could he do? I caught Pat's reflection in the window glass behind the D.A.'s head and he was grinning like an idiot. The D.A. tapped his fingers on the desk-top, his cheeks working. When he looked up he took in the room with one quick glance. "We'll finish this privately if you gentlemen don't mind. You may stay, Captain Chambers."

As far as the two assistants were concerned, it was the supreme insult. They hid their tempers nicely though and followed the others out. I laughed behind their backs and the thing that was working at the D.A.'s cheeks turned into a short laugh. "You know, there are times when I hate your guts. It happens that it's all the time. However, I admire your precocity in a way. You're a thorn in my skin, but even a thorn can be used to advantage at times. If what you have to say is true, consider the charges dropped completely."

"Thanks," I said. The women couldn't say anything. They were too stunned. "I understand you have a man in the department who is suspected of carrying information outside."

He frowned at Pat. "That is correct. We're quite sure of it. What we don't know is his method of notifying anyone else."

"It isn't hard. There's a guy with a tin ear who stands across the street. He wears a hearing aid that doesn't work. He reads lips. A good dummy can read lips at thirty feet without any trouble at all. Your man gets to the street, moves his mouth silently like he's chewing gum or something, but actually calls off a time and place, gets in a car and goes off on a raid. Meanwhile the guy had time to reach a phone and pass the word. Those places are set up for a quick scramble and are moved out before you get there. It's all really very simple."

"Is he there now?"

"He was when I came in."

The D.A. muttered a damn and grabbed the phone.

You know how long it took? About three minutes. He started to blab the second they had him inside the building. The voice on the phone got real excited and the D.A. slammed the phone back. His face had happy, happy smeared all over it and he barely had time to say thanks again and tell the women that their efforts were appreciated before he was out the door.

I got to Ellen and tried to put my arms around her. She put her hands on my chest and pushed me away. "Please, Mike, not now. I . . . I'm much too upset. It was . . . horrible before you came."

"Can I call you later?"

"Yes . . . all right."

I let go of her and she hurried out, dabbing at her mouth with a damp handkerchief.

"Well," Pat said, "you're a smart bastard anyway. You certainly made life miserable for them for a while even if you did get them off the hook in the end."

He held the door open and came out behind me. We walked down the corridor to his office without saying anything and when we were inside he waved me into a chair I needed worse than ever and slumped into his own in back of the desk.

Pat let me get a smoke going. He let me have one long drag, then: "I'm not the D.A., Mike. You don't have anything to trade with me so let's have it straight. That business with the dummy outside was strictly an accident. If the D.A. wasn't so damn eager to grab Teen and Grindle he would have seen it. Two good questions would have put you right back on the spot again."

"And I still would have had something to trade."

"Like what?"

"Lou Grindle is dead. I killed him a few hours before I walked in here. Not only that, but two of his boys are dead. I got one and Lou bumped the other by mistake thinking he was me."

"Mike . . ." Pat was drumming his fists on the arms of the chair.

"Shut up and listen. Teen had me picked up. He thought I killed Link and took something from the apartment. It was kidnaping and I was within the law when I shot them so don't worry about it. There's a body in the road out near Islip someplace and the local police ought to have it by now. The other two are in a house I can locate for you on a map and you better hop to it before they get turned up.

"Ed Teen gave the orders to bump me but you can bet your tail you aren't picking him up for it. He probably had an alibi all set for an emergency anyway, and now that he no doubt knows what happened he'll insure it."

"Why the hell didn't you tell me this earlier? Good Lord, we can break any alibi he has if he's involved!"

"You're talking simple again, friend. I'd like to see you break his alibi. Whoever stands up for him has a chance of being dead if he talks. All you can offer is a jail cell. Nope, you won't put anything down on Teen. He's been through this mill before."

Pat slammed his head with his open palm. "So you waste an hour playing games with the D.A. Damn, you should have said something."

"Yeah, I had plenty of time to talk. You would have heard all about it if you didn't give me that under arrest business."

"I wish I knew what was going on, Mike."

"That makes two of us."

He dragged out a map of the Island and handed it to me. I penciled in the roads and marked the approximate spot where the house was and handed it back. Pat had the thing on the wires immediately. Downstairs somebody checked with the police in Islip and verified the finding of the body on the road.

I said, "Pat . . ."

He covered up the mouthpiece of the phone and looked at me.

"Go through the motions of finding Lou's body before you hand the story to the D.A., will you?"

The phone went back into its cradle slowly. "What's the score, Mike?"

"I think I know how we can get Teen."

"That's not a good reason at all." His voice was soft, dangerous.

"You tell him now and I'll get the treatment again, Pat. Look . . . you've been working this from the wrong angle. You would have gotten there, but it would have taken longer. I'm hot now. I can't stop while I'm hot. You said I could have three days."

"The picture's changed."

"Nix . . . it's just hanging a little crooked, that's all. With all your cops and all your equipment, you're still chasing after shadows."

"You know it all, is that it?"

"No . . . but I got the shadows chasing me now. I know something I shouldn't know. I wish to God I knew where and how I picked it up. I've been wandering through this thing picking up a piece here and there and it should have ended when Toady died. I thought he was the one I was after."

"He was."

Pat said it so flatly that I almost missed it.

"What'd you say?"

"He drove the car when Decker was killed."

It was like a wave washing up the beach, then receding back into itself, the way my body was suddenly flushed before it was drained completely dry. I couldn't get my hands unclenched. They were the only live part of me, balled up in my lap doing the cursing my throat wanted to do. The killer was supposed to be mine, goddamn it. I promised the kid and I promised myself. He wasn't supposed to die in bed never knowing why he died. He should have gone with his tongue hanging out and turning black while I choked the guts out of him!

"How do you know?"

"Cole and Fisher were apprehended in Philadelphia. They decided to shoot it out and lost. Cole lived long enough to say a few things."

"What things?"

"You were right about Hooker and Decker. Toady gave the orders to get Mel. He was going to put Cole and Fisher out with Decker, changed his mind and went himself instead. That was all they knew."

"You mean they were supposed to bump Decker?"

"No . . . just go with him when they pulled the job."

I got up slowly. I put my hat back on and dropped my butt in the ash tray on the desk. "Okay, Pat, get Teen your own way. I still want you to give me a break with the D.A. I want to get some sleep. I need it bad."

"If Grindle's dead he'll stay dead. Make yourself scarce. When you wake up give me a ring. I'll hold things as long as I can."

"Thanks."

"And Mike . . ."

"Yeah?"

"Do something about your face. You look like hell."

"I'll cut it off at the neck and get a new one," I said.

Pat said seriously, "I wish you would."

I had company again. I had a whole hall full of company. Everybody was coming to see me. I was the most popular guy in town and everybody was standing in front of my door dying to get a look at me. One of my company gasped in a huge breath of air before she said, "Oh . . . oh, thank heavens, there he is."

The super's wife was a big fat woman no corset could contain properly and with all that air in her she looked ready to burst. But she was smiling as she recognized my walk and then the smile froze on her face. The super stopped poking a key in the lock on my door, pushed through the small knot and he froze too.

Then there was Marsha. She shoved them all out of the way. The laugh she had ready for me twisted to dismay and she said, "Mike!"

"Hello, sugar."

"Oh, Mike, I knew something happened to you!" She ran into my arms and the tears welled into her eyes. Her fingers touched my cheek gently and I felt them tremble. "Darling, darling . . . what was it . . ."

"Oh, I'll tell you about it sometime. What's all the excitement about?"

She choked and gasped the words out. "I kept calling you and calling you all last night and this morning. I . . . thought something happened . . . like that last time in your apartment. Oh, Mike . . ."

"It's all right now, honey. I'll be back to normal soon."

"I . . . came up and you didn't answer. I told the superintendent you might be hurt . . . and he . . . he was going to look. Mike, you scared me so."

The super was nodding, licking his lips. The others crowded in for a last look at me before going back to their apartments. His wife said, "You scared us all, Mr. Hammer. We were sure you were dead or something."

"I almost was. Anyway, thanks for thinking of me. Now if you don't mind, I'd just like to be left alone for a while. I'm not feeling any too hot."

"Is there anything . . ."

"No, nothing, thanks." I took out my key and opened the door. I had to prop myself against the jamb for a minute before I could go in. Marsha grabbed my arm and held me steady, then guided me inside to a chair and helped me down.

The day had been too long . . . too much to it. A guy can't take days like that one and stay on his feet. I let my head fall back and closed my eyes. Marsha sobbed softly as she untied my shoes and slid them off. The aches and pains came back, a muted throbbing at first, taking hold slowly and biting deeper with each pulse beat.

Marsha had my tie off and was unbuttoning my shirt when the knock came. It didn't make any difference any more who it was. I heard her open the door, heard the murmur of voices and the high babble of a child's voice in the background.

"Mike . . . it's a nurse."

"The superintendent asked me to look in on you," the other voice said.

"I'm all right."

Her voice became very efficient. "I doubt it. Will you watch the child, please? Thank you." Her hand slipped under my arm. "You'll do better lying down."

I couldn't argue with her. She had an answer for everything. Marsha was on the couch still crying, playing with the kid. I got up and went to the bedroom. She had me undressed and in bed before I realized it. The sting of the iodine and the cold compresses on my face jerked me out of immediate sleep and I heard her telling Marsha to call a doctor. It seemed like only seconds before he was there, squeezing with hands that had forgotten how to be gentle, then gone as quickly as he had come. I could hear the two women discussing me quietly, deciding to stay until I had awakened. The kid squealed at something and it was the last thing I heard.

There were only snatches of dreams after that, vague faces that had an odd familiarity and incomprehensible mutterings about things I didn't understand. It took me away from the painful present and threw me into a timeless zone of light and warmth where my body healed itself immediately. It was like being inside a huge beautiful compound where there was no trouble, no misery and no death. All that was outside the transparent walls of the compound where you could see it happen to everyone else without being touched yourself.

They were all there, Decker with his child, listening intently to what Mel Hooker had to say, and Toady Link in the background watching and nodding to make sure he said it right, his boys ready to move in if he said the wrong thing. Lou and Teen were there too, standing over the body of a man who had to be Fallon, their heads turned speculatively toward Toady. A play was going on not far away. Everybody was dressed in Roman togas. Marsha and Pat held the center of the stage with the D.A. and Ellen was standing in the open wings waiting to come on. They turned and made motions to be quiet to the dozens of others behind them . . . the women. Beautiful women. Lovely women with faces you could recognize. Women whose faces I had seen before in photographs.

When the players moved it was with deliberate slowness so you could watch every move. I stood there in the center of the compound and realized that it was all being done for my benefit without understanding why. It was a scene of impending action, the evil of it symbolized by the lone shadow of the vulture wheeling high above in a gray, dismal sky.

I waited and watched, knowing that it had all happened before and was going to happen again and this time I would see every move and understand each individual action. I tried to concentrate on the players until I realized that I wasn't the only audience they had. Someone else was there in the compound with me. She was a woman. She had no face. She was a woman in black hovering behind me. I called to her and received no answer. I tried to walk to her, but she was always the same distance away without seeming to move at all. I ran on leaden feet without getting any closer, and tiring of the chase turned back to the play.

It was over and I had missed it again.

I said something vile to the woman because she had caused me to miss it and she shrank back, disappearing into the mist.

But the play wasn't over, not quite. At first I thought they were taking a curtain call, then I realized that their faces were hideous things and in unreal voices of pure silence they were all screaming for me to stop her and bring her back. Teen and Grindle and Link were slavering in their fury as they tried to break through the transparent wall and were thrown back to the ground. Their faces were contorted and their hands curved into talons. I laughed at them and they stopped, stunned, then withdrew out of sight.

The gray and noiseless compound dissolved into sound and yellow light. I was rocked gently from side to side and a voice said, "Mike . . . please wake up."

I opened my one eye and the other came open with it a little bit. "Marsha?"

"You were talking in your sleep. Are you awake, Mike?"

She looked tired. The nurse behind her looked tired too. The boy in her arms was smiling at me. "I'm awake, honey." I made a motion for her to pull down the shade. "Same day?"

"No, you slept all through yesterday, all night and most of today."

I rubbed my face. Some of the puffiness had gone down. "Lord. What time is it?"

"Almost four-thirty. Mike . . . that Captain Chambers is on the phone. Can you answer him?"

"Yeah, I'll get it. Let me get something on."

I struggled into my pants, swearing when I hit a raw spot. I was covered with adhesive tape and iodine, but the agony of moving was only a soreness now. I padded outside and picked up the phone. "Hello . . ."

"Where've you been, Mike? I told you to call me."

"Oh, shut up. I've been asleep."

"I hope you're awake now. The D.A. found Grindle."

"Good."

"Now he wants you."

"What's it this time, a homicide charge?"

"There's no charge. I explained that away. He wants Teen and he thinks you're pulling a fast one again."

"What's the matter with that guy?"

"Put yourself in his shoes and you'll see. The guy is fighting to hang on to his job."

"Christ, I gave him enough. What does he want . . . blood? Did he expect me to get Teen the hard way for him?"

"Don't be a jerk, Mike. He doesn't want Teen dead. He doesn't want a simple obit in the papers. He wants Teen in court so he can blow the whole thing wide open before the public. That's the only thing that will keep him in office."

"What happened to the tin ear?"

"All the guy had was the telephone number of a booth in Grand Central Station. If he didn't call in every hour it meant there was trouble. We traced the number and there was nobody around. The guy worked through an intermediary who passed the information on to the right people. Both of them got paid off the same way . . . a bundle of cash by mail on the first of every month."

"I suppose Ed Teen's laughing his head off."

"Not exactly, but he's grinning broadly. We checked his alibi for the night before last and it's perfect. You know and I know that it's phony as hell, but nobody is breaking it down in court. According to Teen the entire thing is preposterous. He was playing cards with a group of friends right through the night."

"Nuts. His story is as old as his racket. One good session under the lights and he'll talk."

"You don't put him under lights."

"There're other things you can do," I suggested.

"You don't do that either, Mike. Teen's going around under the watchful eye of a battery of lawyers well protected by a gang of licensed strong-arm boys. You try anything smart and it'll be your neck."

"Great. Now what's with the D.A.?"

It was a moment before he said anything. "Mike . . . are you on the level with me?"

"You know everything I know, Pat. Why?"

"You're going to be tied up with our boy for a long time if you don't get a move on," he said. "And by the way, call Ellen when you have time. She wants to talk to you."

"She there now?"

"No, she left a little while ago. I got something else for you. The playboy is back."

"Marvin Holmes?"

"Yeah. Customs passed the word on to us but it was too late to stop him. We traced him as far as New York and lost him here. The last lead we had said he was with a foreign-looking blonde and was doing his damnedest to stay under cover."

I let it run through my mind a minute. "He's still scared of something."

"It looks that way. I'm hoping to pick him up some time today. He's too well known to stay hidden long. Look, you give me a call when you have time. I have to get going now. This place is a madhouse. I wish the D.A. would operate out of his own office for a change."

I heard the click of his receiver cutting off the connection. Good old Pat. We still played on the same ball team. He was still worrying about me enough to want me to pick my own time and place when I had a long talk with the District Attorney.

Marsha was propped against the corner of the couch yawning. "We have to scram, kid."

Her mouth came shut. "Something wrong?"

"People want to talk to me and I can't afford the time. I want to go someplace and think. I want to be where nobody'll bother me for a week if I don't feel like seeing them."

"Well . . . we can go to my place. I won't bother you, Mike. I just want to crawl in bed and sleep forever."

"Okay. Get your things on. I'll get dressed."

I went back to the bedroom and finished putting on my clothes. There was a light tap on the door and I yelled come on in. The nurse opened the door and stood there holding the boy's hand. He would have been content to stay there, only he spotted the sling of the shoulder holster dangling from the dresser and made a dash for it.

This time she grabbed him before he was halfway there and dragged him back.

"I wish he liked his toys that way," she said.

"Maybe he'll grow up to be a cop."

I got a disapproving look for that. "I hope not!" she paused. "Miss Lee tells me you have to leave again."

"That's right."

"Then perhaps you'll do me a favor."

"Sure."

"They came to repaint my apartment this morning. I was wondering if you'd mind my staying here tonight."

"Go right ahead. You'll be doing me the favor if you stay. If anybody calls tell them I'm out, you don't know where I am, nor when I'll be back. Okay?"

A frown creased her forehead. "You . . . expect callers?" There was a tremulous note in her voice.

I laughed at her and shook my head. "Not that kind. They'll be respectable enough."

She sighed uncertainly and took the kid back to the living room with her. I finished tying my shoes, strapped the gun around my chest and picked my jacket off a coat hanger in the closet. My other suit was draped over the back of the chair and a quick inspection said that it wasn't worth wearing any more. I emptied out the pockets on the dresser, rolled them up in a tight ball and carried them out to the kitchen. I stuffed them into the garbage can on top of the kid's old clothes, pressed the lid down tight and shoved the can back into the corner.

Marsha was waiting for me inside trying to hide her red-rimmed eyes with some mascara. We said good-by to the nurse and the kid and picked up the elevator going down. She fell asleep almost immediately and I had a hell of a time trying to wake her up when we got to her place.

I tried shaking her, pinching her and when that didn't work I bent over and kissed her.

That worked.

She wrinkled her nose and fought her eyes open. I said, "We're here. Come on, snap out of it."

"You did this to me," she smiled.

"That mustached bodyguard you got upstairs will wring my neck for it."

Her lips crinkled in a grin. "So that's why you came so readily. You thought you were going to be chaperoned. I'm sorry, Mike, but I'm all alone. The nurse is gone."

I gave her a playful rap on the chin and scooted her out of the car. She took my hand and we went up together. The guy on the elevator gaped at me until I said, "Up," twice, then he swallowed hard and slid the door shut. It was too bad he didn't see me yesterday.

We were so far away from everything up there. The evening filtered through the blinds, the late, slanting rays of the sun forming a crosshatch pattern on the rug. She settled me back in a big chair and disappeared in the kitchen where she made all the pleasant sounds of a woman in her element. I smelled the coffee and heard the bacon and eggs sizzling in the pan. My stomach remembered how long it was since it had been filled, and churned in anticipation.

I was out there before she called me, trying to be helpful by making the toast. She said, "Hungry?"

"Starving."

"Me too, I finished a box of stale crackers in your place and haven't eaten since."

That was all we said. You just don't talk when you don't leave room between bites. The coffee was hot and strong the way I like it and I finished it before I picked up a smoke.

Marsha turned the small radio on to a local station and picked up a supper orchestra and everything was perfect. It stayed that way until the band went off on the hour and a news commentator came on. It was the same boy who got all worked up over affairs in the city and this time he was really running over.

He gushed through his usual routine of introducing himself to the public and said, "Tonight has seen the end of an era. The man known to the police, the press, and the underworld as Lou Grindle has been found dead in a summer cottage near Islip, Long Island. Two men known to have been Grindle's associates were found shot to death, one in the same house and another twenty miles east of the spot. The house was the scene of violent gunplay and according to police ballistics experts, it was a bullet from Grindle's own gun that killed one of his men. An early reporter on the scene claims that the house had been used as some sort of inquisition chamber by Grindle and his men, but when questioned on the point the police refused to comment. Because of the significance of Grindle's death, the District Attorney has issued a No comment statement, but it is hinted that he is in full possession of the facts.

"Lou Grindle was a product of the racketeering of the early Twenties. Since the repeal of Prohibition he has been suspected of being a key figure in . . ."

I reached out and tuned in another station. I got a rhumba band that was all drums filling in behind a piano and let it beat through the room. But Marsha wasn't listening to it. Her mouth held a fixed position of surprise that matched the startled intensity of her eyes.

"Mike . . . that was . . . you?"

So I grinned at her. My mouth twisted up on the side and I said, "They were going to kill me. They worked me over then took me for a ride."

Her hands were flat on the table, pushing her up from her chair. "Good heavens, Mike, no!" She trembled all over.

"They won't do it again, kid."

"But . . . why, Mike?"

"I don't know. Honest to God, I don't know."

She sat down limply and pushed her hair back from her face. "All this . . . all this started . . . from that night . . ."

"That's right. From a loused-up robbery. You got beat to hell, I got beat to hell. A kid's an orphan. A big-shot racketeer and two of his boys are dead. Arnold Basil's dead. Toady Link is dead and so are a pair of phony private investigators who tried to shoot it out with the cops. Mel Hooker's dead. Goddamn, there won't be anybody alive before you know it!"

"Supposing they come back?"

"They won't. I'm not going to give them the chance. If anybody goes after anybody else I'll do the going." I snubbed the butt out in my saucer. "Mind if I use your phone?"

She told me to go ahead and came inside with me. I checked the directory again and dialed Marvin Holmes' number. It buzzed at steady intervals and just as somebody picked it up there was a knock at the door and Marsha grabbed my arm. It rattled me for a second too. Then I picked the .45 out of the holster, thumbed the safety off and handed it to her while I answered the hellos that were making a racket in my ear.

She opened the door with the gun pointed straight ahead, stared a moment then began to shake in a soft hysterical laugh. I said, "Is Mr. Holmes there?"

It was the butler with the accent. "If this is the police again may I say that he has not come in during the last five minutes. You are being very annoying. He is not expected back, but if he comes I will give him your message."

I slammed the phone back the same time he did and walked over to Marsha who was still laughing crazily. The kid with his arm in a sling was trying to comfort her and shake the gun loose at the same time. I picked it out of her fingers, put it back where it belonged and shook her until she snapped out of it.

The laughing left her and she leaned against my shoulder. "I . . . I'm sorry, Mike. I thought . . ."

The kid said, "Gee, Marsha . . ."

"Come on in, Jerry." He stepped inside and shut the door. "This is Mr. Hammer . . . Jerry O'Neill."

Jerry said "Hi," but didn't make any effort to shake hands. Jerry didn't like me very much. It was easy to see why.

Marsha gave my hand a little squeeze. "Mike, I need a drink. Do you mind?"

"Not a bit, kitten. How about you, Jerry?"

"No. No, thanks. I gotta go right away. I . . ." he looked at Marsha hoping for some sign of jealousy, ". . . gotta date tonight."

She disappointed him. The stars in his eyes blinked out when she said, "Why, that's fine, Jerry. Is there something you wanted to see me about?"

"Well," he hesitated and shot me a look that was pure disgust, "we were all kind of worried when you didn't show up today. We called and all that and I kinda thought, well, they didn't want me to, but I came up anyway. To make sure. Nobody was home then."

"Oh, Jerry, I'm sorry. I was with Mr. Hammer all day."

"I see."

"You tell them they can stop worrying."

"I'll do that." He reached for the knob. "By, Marsha."

"Good-by, Jerry."

He didn't say anything to me. I handed Marsha the drink. "You shouldn't have done that. He's crazy mad in love with you."

She sipped and stared at the amber liquid thoughtfully. "That's why I have to do it, Mike. He's got to learn sometime."

I raised my glass and toasted her. "Well, I don't blame the kid much at that."

"I wish you felt the same way," she said.

It was a statement that needed an answer, but she didn't let me give it. She smiled, her face reflecting the fatigue of her body, finished her drink in a long draught and walked away to the bedroom. I sat down on the arm of the chair swirling the ice around in the glass. I was thinking of the kid with the busted wing, knowing how he must have felt. Some guys got everything, I thought. Others have nothing at all. I was one of the lucky ones.

Then I knew how lucky I was because she was standing in the doorway bathed in the last of the light as the sun went down into the river outside. The soft pink tones of her body softened the metallic glitter of the nylon gown that outlined her in bronze, flowing smoothly up the roundness of her thighs, melting into the curve of her stomach, then rising higher into rich contours to meet the dagger point of the neckline that dropped into the softly shaded well between her breasts.

She said simply, "Good night, Mike," and smiled at me because she knew she was being kissed right then better than she had ever been kissed before. The sun said good night too and drowned in the river, leaving just indistinct shadows in the room and the sound of a door closing.

I waited to hear a lock click into place.

There wasn't any.

I thought it would be easy to sit there with a drink in my hand and think, staring into the darkness that was a barrier against any intrusion. It wasn't easy at all. It was comfortable and restful, but it wasn't easy. I tried to tell myself that it was dark like this when Decker had come through the window and gone to the wall directly opposite me and opened the safe. I tried like hell to picture the way it started and see it through to the way it ended, but my mind wouldn't accept the continuity and kept throwing it back in jumbled heaps that made no sense. The ice in my glass clinked against the bottom four times and that didn't help either.

Someplace, and I knew it was there, was an error in the thought picture. It was a key that could unlock the whole thing and I couldn't pick it out. It was the probing finger in my brain and the voice that nagged at me constantly. It made me light one butt after another and throw them away after one drag. It got to me until I couldn't think or sit still. It made my hands want to grab something and break it into a million fragments and I would have let myself go ahead and do it if it weren't for Marsha asleep in the room, her breathing a gentle monotone coming through the door.

I wasn't the kind of guy who could sit still and wait for something to happen. I'd had enough of the darkness and myself. Maybe later I'd want it that way, but not now.

I snapped the latch on the lock that kept it open and closed the door after me as quietly as I could. Rather than go through another routine with the elevator operator I took the stairs down and got out to the street to my car without scaring anybody. I rolled down the window and let the breeze blow in my face, feeling better for it. I sat there watching the people and the cars go by, then remembered that Pat had told me Ellen had wanted me to call her.

Hell, I could do better than that. I shoved the key in the lock and hit the starter.

My finger found the bell sunk in the framework of the door and pushed. Inside a chair scraped faintly and heels clicked on the woodwork. A chain rattled on metal and the door opened.

"Hello, Texas."

She was all bundled up in that white terrycloth robe again and she couldn't have been lovelier. Her mouth was a ripe red apple waiting to be bitten, a luscious curve of surprise over the edges of her teeth. "I . . . didn't expect you, Mike."

"Aren't you glad to see me?"

It was supposed to be a joke. It went flat on its face because those eyes that seemed to run through the full colors of the spectrum at times suddenly got cloudy with tears and she shook her head.

"Please come in."

I didn't get it at all. She walked ahead of me into the living room and nodded to a chair. I sat down. She sat down in another chair, but not close. She wouldn't look directly at me either.

I said, "What's the matter, Ellen?"

"Let's not talk about it, Mike."

"Wait a minute . . . you *did* tell Pat that you wanted me to call, didn't you?"

"Yes, but I meant . . . oh, never mind. Please, don't say anything more about it." Her mouth worked and she turned her head away.

That made me feel great. Like I kicked her cat or something.

"Okay, let's hear about it," I said.

She twisted out of the chair and walked over to the radio. It was already pulled out so she didn't have to fool with it. Then she handed me another one of those manila folders.

This one had seen a lot of years. It was dirty and crisp with years. The string that held it together had rotted off leaving two stringy ends dangling from a staple. Ellen went back to her chair and sat down again. "It's the file on Toady Link. I found it buried under tons of other stuff in the archives."

I looked at her blankly. "Does the D.A. know you have this?"

"No."

"Ellen . . ."

"See if it's what you want, Mike." Her voice held no emotion at all.

I turned up the flap only to have it come off in my hand, then reached in for the sheets of paper that were clipped together. I leaned back and took my time with these. There wasn't any hurry now. Toady was dead and his file was dead with him, but I could look in and see what his life had been like.

It was quite a life.

Toady Link had been a photographer. Apparently he had been a good one because most of the professional actresses had come to him to have their publicity pictures made. Roberts hadn't missed a trick. His reports were full of marginal notes speculating on each and every possibility and it was there that the real story came out.

Because of Toady's professional contacts he had been contacted by Charlie Fallon. The guy was a bug on good-looking female celebrities and had paid well for pictures of them and paid better when an introduction accompanied the photographs.

But it wasn't until right after Fallon died that Toady became news in police circles. After that time there was no mention made of photography at all. Toady went right from his studio into big-time bookmaking and though he had little personal contact with Ed Teen it was known that, like the others, he paid homage and taxes to the king and whenever he took a step it was always up.

There was a lot of detail stuff there that I didn't pay any attention to, stuff that would have wrapped Toady up at any time if it had been put to use. Roberts would have used it, that much was evident by the work put in on collecting the data for the dossier. But like Ellen had said, a new broom had come in and swept everything out including months and miles of legwork.

Ellen had to speak twice before I heard her. "Does it . . . solve anything?"

I threw them on the coffee table in disgust. "Fallon. It solves him. He's still dead and so is Toady. Goddamn it anyway."

"I'm sorry. I thought it would help."

"You tried, kid. That was enough. You can throw these things away now. What the D.A. never saw he won't miss." I picked up my cigarettes from the table and stuffed them in my pocket. She still watched me blankly. "I'd better be going," I told her.

She didn't make any motion to see me out. I started to pass her and stopped. "Texas . . . what the hell goes on? Tell me that at least, will you? It wasn't so long ago that you were doing all the passing and I thought you were a woman who knew what was going on. All right, I asked you to do me a favor and I put you in a spot. It wasn't so bad that I couldn't get you off it."

"That's not it, Mike." She still wouldn't look at me.

"So you're a Texas gal who likes guys that look like Texas men. Maybe I should learn to ride a horse."

She finally looked up at me from the depths of the couch. Her eyes were blue again and not clouded. They were blue and hurt and angry all at once. "You're a Texas man, Mike. You're the kind I dreamed of and the kind I want and the kind I'll never have, because your kind are never around long enough. They have to go out and play with guns and hurt people and get themselves killed.

"I was wrong in wanting what I did. I read too many stories and listened to too many old men telling big tales. I dreamed too hard, I guess. It isn't so nice to wake up suddenly and know somebody you're all gone over is coming closer to dying every day because he likes it that way.

"No, Mike. You're exactly what I want. You're big and strong and exciting. While you're alive you're fun to be with but you won't be any fun dead. You're trouble and you'll always be that way until somebody comes along who can make bigger trouble than you.

"I'm afraid of a Texas man now. I'm going to forget all about you and stop looking for a dream. I'll wait until somebody nice and safe comes along, somebody peaceful and quiet and shy and I'll get all those foolish romanticisms out of my head and live a bored and relatively normal life."

I planted my feet apart and looked down at her with a laugh that came up from my chest. "And you'll always wonder what a Texas man would have been like," I said.

The change stole over her face slowly, wiping out the bitterness. Her eyes half closed and the blue of her irises was gray again. The smile and the frown blended together like a pleasant hurt. She leaned back with a fluid animal motion, her head resting languidly against the couch. The pink tip of her tongue touched her lips that were parted in a ghost of a smile making them glisten in the light of the single lamp. Then she stretched back slowly and reached out her arms to me, and in reaching the entire front of the robe came open and she made no move to close it.

"No," she said "I'll find out about that first."

We said good-by in the dim light of morning. She said good-by, Texas man, and I said so long, Texas gal, and I left without looking back because everything she had said was right and I didn't want to hear it again by looking back at her eyes. I got in the car, drove over to Central Park West and cruised along until I found a parking place. It was right near an entrance so I left it there and walked off the pavements to the grass and sat on a hill where I could see the sun coming up over the tops of the buildings in the background.

The ground still held the night dampness, letting it go slowly in a thin film of haze that was suspended in mid-air, rising higher as the sun warmed it. The whole park had a chilled eerie appearance of something make-believe. An early stroller went by on the walk, only the top half of him visible, the leash in his hand disappearing into the fog yet making all the frantic motions of having some unseen creature on its end.

When the wind blew it raised the gray curtain and separated it into angry segments that towered momentarily before filtering back into the gaps. There were other people too, half-shapes wandering through a dream world, players who didn't know they had an audience. Players buried in their own thoughts and acts on the other side of a transparent wall that shut off all sound.

I sat there scowling at it until I remembered that it was just like my dream even to the colors and the synthetic silence. It made me so uncomfortable that I turned around expecting to see the woman in black who had no face.

She was there.

She wasn't in black and she had a face, but she stopped when she saw me and turned away hurriedly just like the other one did. This one seemed a little annoyed because I blocked her favorite path.

And I knew who the woman was in the compound with me that night. She had a name and a face I hadn't seen yet. She was there in the compound trying to tell me something I should have thought of myself.

I waited until the sun had burned off the mist and made it a real world again. I went back to the daylight and searched through it looking for a little guy with big ears and a brace of dyed blondes on his arms. The sun made an arc through the sky and was on its way down without me finding him.

At three-thirty I made a call. It went through three private secretaries and a guy who rumbled when he talked. He was the last man in front of Harry Bailen, the columnist, and about as high as I was going to get.

I said, "This is a friend of Cookie Harkin's. I got something for him that won't keep and I can't find the guy. I want his address if you have it."

He had it, but he wasn't giving it out. "I'm sorry, but that's private information around here."

"So is what I got. Cookie can have it for your boss free or I can sell it to somebody else. Take your pick."

"If you have anything newsworthy I'll be glad to pass it on to Mr. Bailen for you."

"I bet you would, feller, only it happens that Cookie's a friend of mine and either he gets it or the boss'll get scooped and he isn't gonna like that a bit."

The phone dimmed out a second as he covered up the mouthpiece. The rumble of his voice still came through as he talked to somebody there in the office and when he came back to me he was more sharp than before.

"Cookie Harkin lives in the Mapuah Hotel. That's M-A-P-U-A-H. Know where it is?"

"I'll find it," I told him. "And thanks."

He thanked me by slamming the phone back.

I looked up the Mapuah Hotel in the directory and found it listed in a crummy neighborhood off Eighth Avenue in the upper Sixties. It was as bad as I expected, but just about the kind of a place a guy like Cookie would go for. The only rule it had was to pay the rent on time. There was a lobby with a couple of old leather chairs and a set of wicker furniture that didn't match. The clerk was a baldheaded guy who was shy a lower plate and he was bent over the desk reading a magazine.

"Where'll I find Cookie Harkin?"

"309." He didn't look up and made no attempt at announcing me.

The only concession to modernization the place made was the automatic elevator. Probably they couldn't get anybody to run a manual job anyway. I closed the door, pushed the third button in the row and stood there counting bricks until the car stopped.

Cookie had a good spot. His room took up the southwest corner facing the rear court where there was a reasonable amount of quiet and enough of a breeze that wasn't contaminated by the dust and exhaust gases on the street side.

I knocked twice, heard the bedsprings creak inside, then Cookie yelled, "Yeah?"

"Mike, Cookie. Get out of the sack."

"Okay, just a minute."

The key rattled in the lock and Cookie stood there in the top half of his pajamas rubbing the sleep out of his eyes. "This is a hell of an hour to get up," I said.

"I was up late."

I looked at the second pillow on his bed that still had the fresh imprint of a head, then at the closed door that led off the room. "Yeah, I'll bet. Can she hear anything in there?"

He came awake in a hurry. "Nah. Whatcha got, Mike?"

"What would you like to have?"

"Plenty. Did you see the papers?" I said no. "I'm not so dumb, Mike. The D.A.'s giving out a song and dance about that triple kill in Islip. Me, I know what happened. The rags gotta clam up because no names are mentioned, but you let me spill it and I'll clean up."

I sat down and pulled out a butt. "I'll swap," I said.

"Now wait a sec, Mike . . ."

"There aren't any rough boys this time. Do something for me and you'll get the story. Right from the beginning."

"You got a deal."

So I told him straight without leaving anything out and he was on the phone before I was finished talking. Dollar bills were drooling out of his eyes and the thing was big enough to get a direct line to Harry Bailen himself. I told him not to play the cops down and when he passed it down with the hint that more was yet to come if it was played right, the big shot agreed and his voice crackled excitedly until he hung up.

Cookie came back rubbing his hands and grinning at me. "Just ask me, Mike. I'll see that you get it."

I dragged in on the smoke. "Go back a ways, Cookie. Remember when Charlie Fallon died?"

"Sure. He kicked off in a movie house on Broadway, didn't he? Had a heart attack."

"That's right."

"He practically lived in them movies. Couldn't tell if he was in the classiest playhouse or the lousiest theater if you wanted to go looking for him."

I nodded that I knew about it and went on, "At the time he was either married or living with a woman. Which was it?"

"Umm . . ." he tugged at one ear and perched on the edge of the bed. "Nope, he wasn't married. Guess he was shacking with somebody."

"Who?"

"Hell, how'd I know? That was years ago. The guy was woman-happy."

"This one must have been special if he was living with her."

His eyes grew shrewd. "You want her?"

"Yep."

"When?"

"As soon as you can."

"I dunno, Mike. Maybe she ain't around no more."

"She'll be around. That kind never leaves the city."

Cookie made a face like a weasel and started to grin a little bit. "I'll give it a spin. Supposing I gotta lay out cash?"

"Go ahead. I'll back it up. Spend what you have to." I stood up and scrawled a number on the back of a match-book cover. "I'll be waiting for you to call. You can reach me here anytime and if anybody starts buzzing you about that story your boss is going to print, tell them you picked it up as a rumor and as far as I'm concerned, you haven't seen me in a month of Sundays."

"I got it, Mike. You'll hear from me."

He was reaching for his shorts when I closed the door and I knew that if she was still there he'd find her. All I had to do was wait.

I went back to Marsha's apartment, went in and made myself a drink. She was still asleep. I knew how she felt.

It wasn't so bad this time because somebody else was doing the work. At least something was in motion. I picked up the phone, tried to get Pat and missed him by a few minutes. I didn't bother looking for him. The liquor was warm in my stomach and light in my head; the radio was humming softly and I lay there stretched out watching the smoke curl up to the ceiling.

At a quarter to eight I opened the door to the bedroom and switched on the light. She had thrown back the covers and lay there with her head pillowed on her arm, a dream in copper-colored nylon who smiled in her sleep and wrinkled her nose at an imaginary somebody.

She didn't wake up until I kissed her, and when she saw me I knew who it was she had been dreaming of. "Don't ever talk about me, girl, you just slept the clock around too."

"Oh . . . I couldn't have, Mike!"

"You did. It's almost eight P.M."

"I was supposed to have gone to the theater this afternoon. What will they think?"

"I guess we're two of a kind, kid."

"You think so?" Her hands met behind my head and she pulled my face down to hers, searching for my mouth with lips that were soft and full and just a little bit demanding. I could feel my fingers biting into her shoulders and she groaned softly asking and wanting me to hold her closer.

Then I held her away and looked at her closely, wondering if she would be afraid like Ellen too. She wrinkled her nose at me this time as if she knew what I had been thinking and I knew that she wouldn't be afraid of anything. Not anything at all.

I said, "Get up," and she squirmed until her feet were on the floor. I backed out of the room and made us something to eat while she showered, and after we ate there was an hour of sitting comfortably watching the sun go back down again, completing its daily cycle.

At five minutes to ten it started to rain again.

I sat in the dark watching it slant against the lights of the city. Something in my chest hammered out that this, too, was the end of a cycle. It had started in the rain and was going to end in the rain. It was a deadly cycle that could start from nothing, and nothing could stop it until it completed its full revolution.

The Big Kill. That's what Decker had wanted to make.

He made it. Then he became part of it himself.

The rain tapped on the window affectionately, a kitten scratching playfully to be let in. A jagged streak of lightning cut across the west, a sign that soon that playful kitten would become a howling, screaming demon.

At seven minutes after ten Cookie called.

There was a tenseness in my body, an overabundance of energy that had been stored away waiting for this moment before coming forward. I felt it flow through me, making the skin tighten around my jaws before it seeped into my shoulders, bunching the muscles in hard knots.

I picked up the phone and said hello.

"This is Cookie, Mike." He must have had his face pressed into the mouthpiece. His voice had a hoarse uncertain quality.

"Go ahead."

"I found her. Her name is Georgia Lucas and right now she's going under the name of Dolly Smith."

"Yeah. What else?"

"Mike . . . somebody else is after her too. All day I've been crossing tracks with somebody. I don't like it. She's hot, Mike."

The excitement came back, all of it, a hot flush of pleasure because the chase was till on and I was part of it. I asked him, "Who, Cookie? Who is it?"

"I dunno, but somebody's there. I've seen signs like these before. I'm telling you she's hot and if you want her you better do something quick."

"Where is she?"

"Not twenty-five feet away from where I'm standing. She's got on a red and white dress and hair to match. Right now she's doing a crummy job of singing a torch song."

"Where, dammit!"

"It's a place in the Village, a little night club. Harvey's."

"I know where it is."

"Okay. The floor show goes off in about ten minutes and won't come on for an hour again. In between times she's doubling as a cigarette girl. I don't like some of the characters around this place, Mike. If I can I'll get to her in the dressing room. And look, you can't get in the back room where she is if you're stag, so I better call up Tolly and have her meet us."

"Forget Tolly. I'll bring my own company. You stick close to her." I slapped the phone back, holding it in place for a minute. I was thinking of what her face would be like. She was the woman in the compound with me, the other one watching the play. She was the woman Lou Grindle found worth cursing in the same breath with Fallon and Link and me. She was the woman somebody was after and the woman who could supply the answers.

From the darkness Marsha said, "Mike . . ."

My hands were sweating. It ran down my back and plastered my shirt to my skin. I said, "Get your coat on, Marsha. We have to go out."

She did me the favor of not asking any questions. She snapped on the lights and took her coat and mine out of the closet. I helped her into it, hardly knowing what I was doing, then opened the door and walked out behind her.

We got on Broadway and drove south while the windshield wipers ticked off the seconds.

The rain had grown. The kitten was gone and an ugly black panther was lashing its tail in our faces.

The bars were filling up, and across town on the East Side an over-painted redhead in last year's clothes would be rubbing herself up against somebody else.

A guy would be nursing a beer down at the end of the bar while a pair of drunks argued over what to play on the juke box.

The bartender would club somebody who got out of line. The floor would get damper and stink of stale beer and sawdust.

Maybe the door would open and another guy would be standing there with a bundle in his arms. A little wet bundle with a wet, tousled head.

Maybe more people would die.

"You're quiet, Mike."

"I know. I was remembering another night like this."

"Where are we going?"

I didn't hear the question. I said, "All the way it's been Fallon. Whenever anything happened it was his name that came up. He was there when Decker was killed. He was there when Toady died. He was there when Grindle died. He was there at the beginning and he's right here at the end. There was a woman in it. She disappeared after Fallon died and she's the one we're going to see. She's going to tell us why she disappeared and why Toady Link got so important and when she tells that I'll know why Decker made his own plans to die and kissed his kid good-by. I'll know why Teen sat there and watched me being cut up and know what was so important in Toady's apartment. I'll know all that and I'll be able to live with myself again. I went out hunting a killer and I missed him. I never missed one before. Somebody else had a bigger grudge and cut him down before I had a chance, but at least I have the satisfaction of knowing he's dead. Now I want to know why it happened. I want to make sure I did miss. I've been thinking and thinking . . . and every once in a while when I think real hard I can see a hole no bigger than a pinhead and I begin to wonder if it was really Toady I was after at all."

Her hand tightened over mine on the wheel. "We'll find out soon," she told me.

A rain-drenched canopy sagging on its frame braced itself against the storm. Lettered on the side was HARVEY'S. The wind had torn a hole in the top and the doorman in the maroon uniform huddled in the entrance to stay dry. I parked around the corner and locked the car, then dragged my raincoat over the two of us for the run back to the joint.

The doorman said it was a bad night and I agreed with him.

The girl in the cloakroom said the same thing and I agreed with her too.

The headwaiter who was the head bouncer with a carnation didn't say anything. I saw Cookie over at a corner table with another bleach job and let muscles make a path through the crowd for us until we reached him.

Somewhere, Cookie had lost his grin. We went through the introductions and ordered a drink. He looked at me, then at Marsha and I said, "You can talk. She's part of it."

The blonde who looked like a two-bit twist caught my attention.

"Don't mind my getup. I can get around better when I act like a floozie. I've been on this thing with Cookie ever since he started."

"Arlene's one of Harry's stenos. We use her once in a while. She's the one who dug up the dame."

"Where is she, Cookie?"

His head made a motion toward the back of the bandstand. "Probably changing. The act goes on again in a few minutes." He was scowling.

The blonde had a single sheet of paper rolled up in her hand. She spread it out and started checking off items with her fingernail.

"Georgia . . . or Dolly . . . is forty-eight and looks like it. She was Fallon's girl friend and then his mistress. At one time she was a looker and a good singer, but the years changed all that. After Fallon died she went from one job to another and wound up being a prostitute. We got a line on her through a guy who knows the houses pretty well. She took to the street for a while and spent some time in the workhouse. Right after the war she was picked up on a shoplifting charge and given six months. Not two weeks after she got out she broke into an apartment and was caught at it. She got a couple years that time. She got back in the houses after that to get eating money, broke loose and got this job. She's been here a month."

"You got all that without seeing her?"

The blonde nodded.

"I thought you were going to speak to her, Cookie."

"I was," he said. "I changed my mind."

He was staring across the room to where Ed Teen was sitting talking to four men. Only two of them were lawyers. The other two were big and hard-looking. One chewed on a match-stick and leered at the dames.

My drink slopped over on the table.

Cookie said, "I thought you told me there wouldn't be any rough stuff."

"I changed my mind too." I had to let go of the glass before I spilled the rest of it. "They see me come in?"

"No."

"They know you or why you're here?"

Cookie's ears went back, startled. "Do I look like a dope?" His tongue licked his lips nervously. "You think . . . that's who I been crossing all day."

I was grinning again. Goddamn it, I felt good! "I think so, Cookie," I said.

And while I was saying it the lights turned dim and a blue spot hit the bandstand where a guy in a white tux started to play. A girl with coal-black hair stepped out from behind the curtains and paused dramatically, waiting for a round of applause before going into her number.

I couldn't wait any longer. It was coming to a head too fast. I said, "I'm going back there. Cookie, you get over to the phone and call the police. Ask for Captain Chambers and tell him to get down here as fast as he can move. Tell him why. I don't know what's going to happen, but stick around and you'll get your story."

I could see Cookie's face going white. "Look, Mike, I don't want no part of this. I . . ."

"You won't get any part of it unless you do as you're told. Get moving."

I started to get up and Marsha said, "I'm going with you, Mike."

All the hate and excitement died away and there was a little piece of time that was all ours. I shook my head. "You can't, kid. This is my party. You're not part of the trouble any more." I leaned over and kissed her. There were tears in her eyes.

"Please, Mike . . . wait for the police. I don't want you . . . to be hurt again."

"Nobody's going to hurt me now. Go home and wait for me."

There was something final in her voice. "You won't . . . come back to me. Mike."

"I promise you," I said. "I'll be back."

A sob tore into her throat and stayed there, crushed against her lips by the back of her hand. Part of it got loose and I didn't want to stay to see the pain in her face.

I nudged the .45 in the holster to kick it free of the leather and tried to see across the room. It was much too dark to see anything. I started back and heard Marsha sob again as Cookie led her toward the front. The blonde had disappeared somewhere too.

A curtain covered the arch. It led into a narrow, low-ceilinged alcove with another curtain at the far end. The edges of it overlapped and the bottom turned up along the floor, successfully cutting out the backstage light that could spoil an effective entrance.

I stepped through and pulled it back to place behind me. The guy tilted back in the chair, put his paper down and peered at me over his glasses. "Guests ain't allowed back here, buddy."

I let him see the corner of a sawbuck. "Could be that I'm not a guest."

"Could be." He took the sawbuck and made it vanish. "You look like a fire inspector to me."

"That'll do if anybody asks. Where's Dolly's room?"

"Dolly? That bag? What you want with her?" He took his glasses off and waved them down the hall. "She ain't got no room. Under the stairs is a supply closet and she usually changes in there." The glasses went back on and he squinted through them at me. "She's no good, Mac. Only fills in on an empty spot."

"Don't worry about it."

"I won't." He tilted the chair back again and picked up the paper. His eyes stayed on me curiously, then he shrugged and started reading.

There was a single light hanging from the ceiling halfway down and a red exit bulb over a door at the end. A pair of dressing rooms with doors side by side opened off my right and I could hear the women behind them getting ready for their act. In one of them a man was complaining about the pay and a woman told him to shut up. She said something else and he cracked her one.

The other side was a blank beaverboard wall painted green that ran down to the iron staircase before meeting a cement-block wall. It must have partitioned off the kitchen from the racket that was going on in back of it.

I found the closet where the guy said it would be. It had a riveted steel door with an oversize latch and SUPPLIES stenciled across the top. I stepped back in the shadows under the staircase and waited.

From far off came the singer's voice rising to the pitch of the piano. Down the hall the guy was still tilted back reading. I knocked on the door.

A muffled voice asked who it was. I knocked again.

This time the door opened a crack. I had my foot in the opening before she could close it. She looked like she was trying hard to scream. I said, "I'm a friend, Georgia."

Stark terror showed in her eyes at the mention of her name. She backed away until the fear reached her legs, then collapsed on a box. I went all the way in and shut the door.

Now the figure from the mist had a face. It wasn't a nice face. Up close it showed every year and experience in the tiny lines that crisscrossed her skin. At one time it had been pretty. Misery and fear had wiped all that out without leaving more than a semblance of a former beauty. She was small and fighting to hold her figure. None of the artifices were any good. The red hair, the overly mascaraed eyes, the tightly corseted waist were too plainly visible. I wondered why the management even bothered with her. Maybe she sang dirty songs. That always made a hit with the customers who were more interested in lyrics than music.

The kind of terror that held her was too intense to last very long. She managed to say, "Who . . . are you?"

"I told you I was a friend." There was another box near the door and I pulled it over. I wanted this to be fast. I sat down facing the door, a little behind it. "Ed Teen's outside."

If I thought that would do something to her I was wrong. Long-suffering resignation made a new mask on her face. "You're afraid of him, aren't you?"

"Not any more," she replied simply. The mascara on her lashes, suddenly wet, made dark patches under her eyes. Her smile was a wry, twisted thing that had no humor in it. "It had to come sometime," she said. "It took years to catch up with me and running never put it behind me."

"Would you like to stop running?"

"Oh, God!" Her face went down into her hands.

I leaned on my knees and made her look at me. "Georgia . . . you know what's happened, don't you?"

"I read about it."

"Now listen carefully. The police will be here shortly. They're your friends too if you'd only realize it. You won't be hurt, understand! Nobody is going to hurt you." She nodded dumbly, the dark circles under her eyes growing bigger. I said, "I want to know about Charlie Fallon. Everything. Tell me about Fallon and Grindle and Teen and Link and anybody else that matters. Can you do that?"

I lit a cigarette and held it out to her. She took it, holding her eyes on the tip while she passed her finger through the thin column of smoke. "Charlie . . . he and I lived together. He was running the rackets at the time. He and Lou and Ed worked together, but Charlie was the top man.

"It . . . it started when Charlie got sick. His heart was bad. Lou and Ed didn't like the idea of doing all the work so they . . . they looked for a way to get rid of him. Charlie was much too smart for them. He found out about it. At the time, the District Attorney was trying his best to break up the organization and Charlie saw a way to . . . to keep the two of them in line. He was afraid they'd kill him . . . so he took everything he had that would incriminate Ed and Lou, things that would put them right in the chair, and brought them to Toady Link to be photographed. Toady put them on microfilms.

"Charlie told me about it that night. We sat out in the kitchen and laughed about it. He thought . . . he had his partners where they could never bother him again. He said he was going to put the microfilms in a letter addressed to the District Attorney and send it to a personal friend of his to mail if anything ever happened to him.

"He did it, too. He did it that same night. I remember him sitting there doing all his correspondence. It was the last letter he ever wrote. He intended to wait awhile, then tell Lou and Ed about it, but something else happened he didn't foresee. Toady Link saw a way to work himself into the organization. He went to Ed and told him what Charlie had done.

"That's . . . where I came into it. Lou came for me. He threatened me. I was afraid. Honest, it wasn't my fault . . . I couldn't help myself. Lou . . . would have killed me if I didn't do what he said! They wanted to kill Charlie so they wouldn't be suspected at all. They knew he had frequent attacks and had to take nitroglycerin tablets and they made me steal the tablets from his pockets. God, I couldn't help myself! They made me do it! Charlie had an attack the next day and died in the theater. God, I didn't mean it, I had to do it to stay alive!"

"The bastards!" The word cut into her sobbing. "The lousy miserable bastards. Toady pulled a double-cross as long as your arm. He must have made two prints of those films. He kept one himself and let the boys know about it, otherwise they would have knocked him off long ago. That was his protection. That's what Teen thought I took out of his apartment!"

Georgia shook her head, not knowing what I was talking about, but it made sense to me. It made a damn lot of sense now.

I said, "After Fallon died . . . what happened? What did the District Attorney do?"

"Nothing. Nothing happened."

The evil of it was like the needle-point of a dagger digging into my brain. The incredible evil of it was right there in front of my face and needed nothing more than a phone call to make it a fact.

All along I had tripped over that one stumbling block that threw me on my face. I had missed it because it had been so goddamn small, but now it stuck out like a huge white rock with a spotlight on it.

I grabbed Georgia by the arm and lifted her off the box. "Come on, we're getting out of here. Anything you want to take with you?"

She reached out automatically for her hat and purse, then I shoved her out the door. The hallway was empty. There was no guy in the chair down under the light. A pair of tom-toms made the air pulsate with a harsh jungle rhythm that seemed to enjoy echoing through the corridor as if it were in its natural element.

I didn't like it a bit.

The red exit light pointed the way out. If Ed Teen was waiting to see Georgia he was going to have a long wait. Maybe he thought he was the only one looking for her and he didn't have to hurry. I pulled the door open and stepped out ahead of her, feeling for the step.

The voice behind the gun said, "This the one, Ed?"

And Ed said, "That's the one. Take him."

I was keyed up for it. There was no surprise to it except for them. A gun is a gun and when one is rammed in your ribs you aren't supposed to scream your guts out while you slam into a woman in the darkness and hit the pavement as the flame blasts out above your head.

The .45 was a living thing in my hand cutting its own lightning and thunder in the rain. I rolled, scrambled to my feet and ran in a crouch only to roll again. They were shouting at each other, running for the light that framed the end of the alley. The bright flashes of gunfire at close range made everything blacker than before. I saw the legs go past my face and grabbed at them, slashing at a head with the barrel of my gun. Back in the shadows Georgia's voice was a wail of terror. There was the sound of other feet hugging the wall and for an instant a shape was there in the frame. I had time to get in one shot that sparked off the brick wall then a body slammed into mine that was all feet and something heavy that pounded at my head.

The cursing turned into a hoarse wheeze when my fingers raked across a throat and held on. But a foot found my stomach and my fingers slid off. They had me down on my back; an arm was under my chin wrenching my head to the side and the guy was telling the other one to give it to me.

Before he could a siren moaned and wheels screamed on the pavement. There was only that one way out. They ran for it and I saw them stop completely when the beams of three torches drenched them. Georgia was still a shrill voice buried under the shadows and Pat was calling to me. His light picked me out of the rubble and he jerked me to my feet.

I said, "She's back there. Go find her."

"Who?"

"Fallon's old girl friend."

He said something I couldn't catch and went back for her, letting me lean up against the wall until my breath came back. I heard him in there behind the garbage can, then he came back with her in his arms. She hung there limply, completely relaxed.

I didn't want to ask it. "Is she . . . dead?"

"She's all right. Passed out, I think."

"That's good, Pat. You don't want anything to happen to her. Right now she's the most precious thing you have. The D.A. is going to love her."

"Mike, what the hell is this about?"

"She'll tell you, Pat. Treat her nice and she'll tell you all about it. When you hear her story you're going to have Ed Teen just a step away from the chair. He was an accomplice before the fact of Fallon's murder and she's the girl who's going to prove it."

I followed him back to the street, my feet dragging. The two boys were trying to explain things to a cop who didn't want to listen. Pat passed Georgia into a car and told the driver to get her down to headquarters. He looked at the big boys and they started to sweat. The rain was beating in their faces, but you could still tell they were sweating.

I said, "They're Teen's men, Pat. Ed was here to supervise things himself. He was real smart about it too. I had a man trying to run down the woman while Ed was doing the same thing. He guessed who was doing it. He came to make sure I didn't get away with it. He's gone now, but you won't have any trouble picking him up. An hour ought to do it."

The crowd had gathered. They fought for a look, standing on their toes to peer over shoulders and ask each other what had happened. Cookie was on the edge and I waved him over. He had my coat in his hand and I put it on. "Here's the guy I was telling you about, Pat. I'd appreciate it if you'd let him in on the story before it gets out to the papers. Think you can?"

"Who's going to tell the story . . . you?"

"No . . . I'm finished, kid. It's all over now. Let Georgia tell it. She had to live with it long enough; she ought to be glad to get it off her chest. I'm going home. When you get done come on up and we'll talk about it."

Pat made a study of my face. "All this . . . it had something to do with Decker?"

"It had a lot to do with Decker. We just couldn't see it at first."

"And it's finished now?"

"It's finished."

I turned around and walked through the crowd back to my car. The rain didn't matter now. It could spend its fury on me if it wanted to. The city was a little bit cleaner than it was before, but there was still some dirt under the carpet.

Back uptown I found a drugstore that was open all night and went into the phone booth. I dialed the operator and got a number out on the Island. It rang for a few minutes and the voice that answered was that of a tired man too rudely awakened. "Mr. Roberts?"

"Speaking."

"This is Mike Hammer. I was going to call you earlier but something came up. If you don't mind, there's something I'd like to ask you. It's pretty important."

His voice was alert now. "I don't mind a bit. What is it?"

"During your term in office you conducted a campaign to get rid of Fallon and his gang. Is that right?"

"Yes, quite right. I wasn't very successful."

"Tell me, did you ever have any communication from Fallon about that?"

"Communication?"

"A letter."

He thought a moment, then: "No . . . no, I didn't." Then he thought again. "Now that you mention it . . . yes, there was a peculiar incident at one time. An envelope was in my waste basket. It was addressed to me and had Fallon's home address on it. I recognized the address, of course, but since he lived in an apartment hotel that was fairly prominent I didn't give it another thought. Besides, Fallon was dead at that time."

"I see. Well, thanks for your trouble, Mr. Roberts. Sorry I had to bother you." It was a lie. I wasn't a bit sorry at all.

"Perfectly all right," he said, and hung up.

And I had the answer.

I mean I had all of it and not just part of it like I had a minute before and my brain screamed a warning for me to hurry before it was too late even though it knew that it was already too late.

I cursed the widow-makers and the orphan-makers and every goddamn one of the scum that found it so necessary to kill because their god was a paper one printed in green. But I didn't curse the night and the rain any more. It kept the cars off the street and gave me the city for my own where red lights and whistles didn't mean a thing.

It gave me a crazy feeling in my head that pushed me faster and faster until the car was a mad dervish screaming around corners in a race with time. I left it double-parked outside my apartment and ran for the door. I took the stairs two at a time, came out on my floor with the keys in my hand reaching out for the lock.

I didn't stop to feel the gimmick on the lock. I turned the key, shoved the door open and pushed in with my gun in my fist and she was there like I knew she'd be there and it wasn't too late after all. The nurse was face down on the floor with her scalp cut open, but she was breathing and the kid was crying and pulling at her dress.

"Marsha," I said, "you're the rottenest thing that ever lived and you're not going to live long."

There was never any hate like hers before. It blazed out of those beautiful eyes trying to reach my throat and if ever a maniac had lived she was it. She dropped the knife that was cutting so neatly into the sofa cushion and got up from her crouch like the lovely deadly animal she was.

I looked at the partial wreckage of the room and the guts of the chairs that were spread over the floor. "I should have known, kid. God knows it slapped me in the face often enough. No man would cut up a cushion as neat as that. You're doing almost as nice a job here as you did in Toady's place. You're not going to find what you're looking for, Marsha. They were never hidden. You couldn't believe that everybody's not like yourself, could you? You had to think that anybody who saw those films would try to make them pay off like you did."

She started to tremble. Not from fear. It was an involuntary spasm of hate suffusing her entire body at once. I laughed at her. Now I could laugh.

Her mouth wasn't soft and rich now. It was slitted until it bared her teeth to the gums. "You don't like me to laugh, do you? Hell, you must have laughed at me plenty of times. Woman, when you were alone you must have laughed your damned head off. You know, it *was* funny the way this thing went. I based everything I had on a false premise yet I wound up with the right answers in the long run. You had me talked into it as nicely as you please.

"*All this time I thought Decker had made a mistake in apartments.* Like hell! Decker knew what he was doing. They had your place cased too well to make any mistake.

"But just to see if I'm right, let's go back to the beginning. I haven't got a damn thing to stand on but speculation, yet I bet I can call every turn right on the button. What I have got will hold you until we can dig up the real stuff though. We may have to go back a way, but we'll get it and you'll burn for it.

"You were even nice enough to give me a lot of hints. There you were out in Hollywood in a spot most girls would give their right arms to be in and there was only one drawback. You weren't big time. You weren't going to get to be big time, either. You were one of that big middle class of actors who were okay, but not for the feature films. Then a man came along who gave you a hard time and you got sour on the world.

"Right then you were ripe for the kicker. You were shaking hands with the devil and didn't know it. Back in New York a guy named Charlie Fallon was writing a batch of letters. One was a fan letter to you. The other was to the District Attorney with enough evidence on microfilms to put a couple of racketeers where they belonged. Old Charlie was feeling good that night. He felt so good that he got his envelopes mixed and those films came to you.

"That was just before your secretary died, wasn't it? Yeah, I can tell that much by your face. She was all for turning them in to the authorities and you put the kibosh on that. You saw a way to get yourself a lot of easy dough. That man came in handy too. When you knocked off that secretary you made it look like a suicide and it wasn't hard to explain away at all.

"Now let me speculate on what happened right here in New York. The D.A. got a letter, all right. It was from Fallon, but it contained a fan letter to you. Teen and Grindle put out a lot of cash to have a pipeline in where it counted and they had a slick cop watching the mail for that letter. When they got it they must have turned green because it didn't take much thought to figure out what had happened. All they could do was to sit back and see what you would do.

"You did it. You came around with your hand out and they greased it to whatever tune you called. For ten years that went on. Even the time checks. It's a lot of years, too. Hell, you know what blackmail is like. It grows and grows like a damned fungus. Ed and Lou had two of you on their necks. When Toady Link made those films for Fallon he made a copy for himself. But at least he added something to the outfit. Then one day one of you put too much pressure on the boys. One of you had to go. Toady probably pulled the squeeze play. Since he knew all about it anyway they told him that if he could lift those copies you had he'd make out better himself.

"That's where Decker came in. Good safe men are hard to get for those jobs. Toady located Decker somehow and had Mel Hooker steer him right into a trap where he had to play ball with Toady or else. They figured it out nice as you please and never stopped to figure out what can go in inside a guy's mind.

"Decker had been through the mill and he wasn't setting his kid up to have any part of it. In his own way he was a martyr. He knew what he was going to do and knew he'd die for it. When he lifted that stuff from your place I think he planned to take it straight to the police. He didn't move fast enough though. So he did the next best thing. He stuck those films where they'd probably be found and went out and died.

"You know the rest of it from there, Marsha. I don't have to tell you any more, do I? I shot my mouth off to you and spilled it about Toady, so you went up there to see him yourself. You did a nice job of bumping him. Nice and clean. Maybe in those ten years you figured it all out for yourself, and if you didn't think Toady had those films you were going to get his copy. Yeah, me and my big mouth. You hung on like a leech and kept giving me the old sex treatment just to know where you stood. And I fell for it. You sure learned how to act these last ten years, all right. I thought it was pretty real.

"What gets me is the way you thought that I had them all this time. You couldn't get that out of your head. You thought I had them and Teen thought I had them. They were worth a million bucks on the open market and I didn't look like a guy who'd throw it away. You even went to the trouble of getting a copy made of my keys while I was asleep, didn't you? Tonight you used them. Tonight you had to take a look to be sure because you knew that when I talked to Fallon's old girl I was going to know the truth!

"Yeah, everybody was looking for those pictures. That's what should have tipped me off. Toady searched Decker's apartment and I thought Toady or his boys searched mine. That was where I kept tripping up. That was the one fault in the whole picture. *When Toady drove that car he never had time to see who I was at all, so how could he know where I lived? You, Marsha, were the only other person at the time who knew I had gone over Decker's body right after he was shot because I told you that myself.*

"That was a nice set-to up here that night. Want me to guess who it was? It was that jerk from the theater . . . the kid with the broken arm who's so much in love with you that he'd do anything you ask. He got me with that damn cast.

"Where is he tonight? He'd like to be in on this, wouldn't he?"

All that pent-up hate on her face turned into a cunning sneer and she said, "He's here, Mike."

I started to move the same time she started to talk and I wasn't fast enough. I had a glimpse of something white streaking toward my head just before it smashed the consciousness from my body.

Long before my eyes could see again I knew what would be there when I opened them. I heard the kid crying, a series of terror-stricken gasps because the world was too much for him. I pushed up from the floor, forced my eyes open and saw him huddled there in the corner, his thin body shivering. Whatever I did with my face made him stop, and with the quick switch of emotions a child is capable of, he laughed. He climbed to his feet and held on to the arm of the chair babbling non-sense at the wall.

I raised my head and caught her looking at me, a spiteful smile creasing her face. She was a big beautiful evil goddess with a gun in her hand ready to take a victim and there wasn't a thing I could do about it. My .45 was over there on the table and I didn't have the strength to go for it.

Jerry was in a chair holding his broken arm to his chest, rocking back and forth from the pain in it. One side of the cast was split halfway.

Then I saw the junk on the floor. The suit I had thrown away and the kid's overalls that had been stuffed in the bottom of the can. And Marsha smiled. She opened her palm and there were the films, four thin strips of them. "They were in the pocket of the overalls." She seemed amazed at the simplicity of it.

"They won't do you any good, Marsha. Teen's finished and so are they. Your little racket's over." I had to stop for breath. Something sticky ran down my neck.

"They'll serve their purpose," she said. "Somebody else might guess like you did, but they'll never know now. Those Toady had I destroyed. These will go too and only you will be left, Mike. I really hate having to kill you, but it's necessary, you know."

There was none of the actress in her voice now. There was only death. She had finished acting. The play was over and she could put away the smiles and tears until the next time.

I swung my head around until my eyes were fixed on Jerry. He stopped rocking. I said, "Then I guess you'll have to marry Jerry, won't you? He'll have you trapped like you had Ed and Lou trapped. He'll have something you'll pay dearly for, won't he?"

I think she laughed again. It was a cold laugh. "No, Mike. Poor Jerry will have to go too. You see, he's my alibi." Her hand went out and picked up my gun. "Everyone knows how crazy he is about me. And he's so jealous he's liable to do anything . . . especially if he came up here and caught us together . . . like tonight. There would have been gunplay. Unfortunately, you killed each other. The nurse was in the way and she died too. Doesn't that make a good story, Mike?"

Jerry came out of his chair slowly. He had time to whisper incredulously, "Marsha!" The .45 slammed in her hand and blasted the night to bits. She watched the guy jerking on the floor and threw the gun back on the table. The rod she held on me was a long-barreled revolver and it didn't tremble in her hand at all. She held it at her hip slanting it down enough to catch me in the chest.

She was going to get that shot off fast for the benefit of the people who were listening. She was killing again because murder breeds murder and when she had killed she was going to put the guns in dead hands and go into her act. She'd be all faints and tears and everyone would console her and tell her how brave she was and damn it all to hell, her story would stand up! There wouldn't be a hole in it because everything was working in her favor just like when she killed her secretary! It would be a splash in the papers and she could afford that.

The hate was all there in my face now and she must have known what I was thinking. She gave me a full extra second to see her smile for the last time, but I didn't waste it on the face of evil.

I saw the kid grab the edge of the table and reach up for the thing he had wanted for so long, and in that extra second of time she gave me his fingers closed around the butt safety and trigger at the same instant and the tongue of flame that blasted from the muzzle seemed to lick out across the room with a horrible vengeance that ripped all the evil from her face, turning it into a ghastly wet red mask that was really no face at all.

KISS ME, DEADLY

CHAPTER 1

All I saw was the dame standing there in the glare of the headlights waving her arms like a huge puppet and the curse I spit out filled the car and my own ears. I wrenched the wheel over, felt the rear end start to slide, brought it out with a splash of power and almost ran up the side of the cliff as the car fishtailed. The brakes bit in, gouging a furrow in the shoulder, then jumped to the pavement and held.

Somehow I had managed a sweeping curve around the babe. For a few seconds she had been living on stolen time because instead of getting out of the way she had tried to stay in the beam of the headlights. I sat there and let myself shake. The butt that had fallen out of my mouth had burned a hole in the leg of my pants and I flipped it out the window. The stink of burned rubber and brake lining hung in the air like smoke and I was thinking of every damn thing I ever wanted to say to a harebrained woman so I could have it ready when I got my hands on her.

That was as far as I got. She was there in the car beside me, the door slammed shut and she said, "Thanks, mister."

Easy, feller, easy. She's a fruitcake. Don't plow her. Not yet. Hold your breath a minute, let it out easy, then maybe bend her over the fender and paddle her tail until she gets some sense in her head. Then boot her the hell out and make her walk the rest of the way home.

I fumbled out another cigarette, but she reached it before I did. For the first time I noticed her hands shaking as hard as mine were. I lit hers, got one out for me and lit that one too. "How stupid can you get?" I said.

She bit the words off. "Pretty stupid."

Behind me the lights of another car were reaching around a curve.

Her eyes flicked back momentarily, fear pulling their corners tight. "You going to sit here all night, mister?"

"I don't know what I'm going to do. I'm thinking of throwing you over that cliff over there."

The headlights shone in the car through the rear window, bathed the roadway in light then swept on past. In the second that I had a good look at her she was rigid, her face frozen expressionlessly. When only the red dot of the taillight showed in front of us she let out her breath and leaned back against the seat.

In a way she was good-looking, but her face was more interesting than pretty. Wide-set eyes, large mouth, tawny hair that spilled onto her shoulders like melted butter. The rest of her was wrapped into a tailored trench coat that was belted around her waist and I remembered her standing there in the road like something conjured up too quickly in a dream. A Viking. A damn-fool crazy Viking dame with holes in her head.

I kicked the stalled engine over, crawled through the gears and held on tight to the wheel until my brain started working right. An accident you don't mind. Those you halfway expect when you're holding seventy on a mountain road. But you don't expect a Viking dame to jump out of the dark at you while you're coming around a turn. I opened the window all the way down and drank in some of the air. "How'd you get up here?"

"What does it look like?"

"Like you got dumped." I looked at her quickly and saw her tongue snake out over her lips. "You picked the wrong guy to go out with."

"I'll know better the next time."

"Pull a trick like that last one and there won't be any next time. You damn near became a painting on the face of that rockslide."

"Thanks for the advice," she said sarcastically, "I'll be more careful."

"I don't give a hoot what you do as long as you don't get strained through my radiator."

She plucked the cigarette from her lips and blew a stream of smoke at the windshield. "Look, I'm grateful for the ride. I'm sorry I scared hell out of you. But if you don't mind just shut up and take me somewhere or let me out."

My mouth pulled back in a grin. A dame with nerve like that sure could've made a mess out of a guy before he gave her the boot. "Okay, girl," I said, "now it's my turn to be sorry. It's a hell of a place for anybody to be stranded and I guess I would have done the same thing. Almost. Where do you want to go?"

"Where're you going?"

"New York."

"All right, I'll go there."

"It's a big city, kid. Name the spot and I'll take you there."

Her eyes got cold. The frozen expression came back in her face. "Make it a subway station. The first one you come to will do."

Her tone wiped my grin away. I eased the car around another turn and settled down to a straightway, jamming hard on the gas. "Damn rape-happy dame. You think all guys are the same?"

"I . . ."

"Shut up."

I could feel her watching me. I knew when she dropped her eyes in her lap and knew when she looked back at me again. She started to say something and closed her mouth over the words. She turned to stare out of the window into the blackness of the night and one hand wiped her eyes. Let her bawl. Maybe she'd learn how to be a little polite.

Another car was coming up behind us. She saw it first and pressed back into the seat until it was past. It went on down the long incline ahead of us until its taillights merged and disappeared into the maze of neons that were part of the town below.

The tires whined on a turn and the force of it made her lean across the seat until our shoulders touched. She pulled away at the contact, braced herself until the car rocked back to level and edged into the corner. I looked at her, but she was staring out of the window, her face still cold.

I slowed to fifty coming into the town, then to thirty-five and held it. The sign along the road said HANAFIELD, POP. 3600, SPEED LIMIT 25. A quarter mile up the highway a flashing red light winked in our direction and I got on the brakes. There was a police car in the middle of the road and two uniformed cops stood alongside it checking the cars as they came by. The car that had passed us further back was just getting the okay to go on through and the flashlight was waving at me to make a full stop.

Trouble. Like the smoke over a cake of dry ice. You can't smell it but you can see it and watch it boil and seep around things and know that soon something's going to crack and shatter under the force of the horrible contraction. I looked at the dame and she was stiffly immobile, her lips held so tight her teeth showed, a scream held in her throat ready to let go.

I leaned out the car before I reached the cop and took the beam of his flash in the face before he lowered it. "Trouble, officer?"

His hat was pushed back on his head and a cigarette drooped from his mouth. The gun he wore hung cowboy style and for effect he draped his hand on its butt. "Where'd you come from, bud?"

A real cop, this guy. I wondered how much he paid for his appointment. "Coming down from Albany, officer. What's up?"

"See anybody along the road? Anybody hitchhiking?"

I felt her hand close over mine before I answered him. It closed and squeezed with a sudden warmth and urgency and in a quick movement she had taken my hand in hers and slid it under the trench coat and I felt the bare flesh of her thigh there, smooth and round, and when my fingers stiffened at the touch she thought I was hesitating and with a fluid motion moved her grip up my forearm and pulled my hand against her body where there was no doubting her meaning, then amplified it by squeezing her legs together gently to keep it there.

I said, "Not a thing, officer. My wife or me have been awake all the way and if anybody was there we sure would know about it. Maybe they came on ahead."

"Nobody came ahead, bud."

"Who were you looking for?"

"A dame. She escaped from some sanitarium upstate and hitched a ride down to a diner with a truck. When they started broadcasting a description she beat it outside and disappeared."

"Say, that's pretty serious. I wouldn't want to be the guy who picks her up. Is she dangerous?"

"All loonies are dangerous."

"What does she look like?"

"Tall blonde. That's about all we got on her. Nobody seems to remember what she was wearing."

"Oh. Well, okay for me to go?"

"Yeah, go on, beat it."

He walked back to the patrol car and I let out the clutch. I took my hand away slowly, keeping my eyes on the road. The town went by in a hurry, and on the other side I stepped on it again.

This time her hand crept up my arm and she slid across the seat until she was beside me. I said, "Get back where you came from sister. You didn't have to pull a stunt like that."

"I meant it."

"Thanks. It just wasn't necessary."

"You don't have to drop me at a subway station if you don't want to."

"I want to."

Her foot nudged mine off the gas pedal and the car lost headway. "Look," she said, and I turned my head. She had the coat wide open and was smiling at me. The coat, that's all, all the rest was sleekly naked. A Viking in satin skin. An invitation to explore the curves and valleys that lay nestled in the shadows and moved with her breathing. She squirmed in the seat and her legs made a beautifully obscene gesture and she smiled again.

She was familiar then. Not so much the person, but the smile. It was a forced, professional smile that looks warm as fire and really isn't anything at all. I reached over and flipped the coat closed. "You'll get cold," I said.

The smile twisted crookedly on her mouth. "Or is it that you're afraid because you think I'm not quite sane?"

"That doesn't bother me. Now shut up."

"No. Why didn't you tell him then?"

"Once when I was a kid I saw a dogcatcher about to net a dog. I kicked him in the shins, grabbed the pup and ran. The damn mutt bit me and got away, but I was still glad I did it."

"I see. But you believed what the man said."

"Anybody who jumps in front of a car isn't too bright. Now shut up."

The smile twisted a little more as if it weren't being forced. I looked at her, grinned at what had happened and shook my head. "I sure get some dillies," I said.

"What?"

"Nothing." I pulled the car off the road into the dull glare of the service-station sign and coasted up to the pumps. A guy came out of the building wiping his eyes and I told him to fill it up. I had to get out to unlock the gas cap and I heard the door open, then slam shut. The blonde went up to the building, walked inside and didn't come back until I was counting the money into the guy's hand.

When she got back in the car there was something there that hadn't been there before. Her face had softened and the frost had thawed until she seemed almost relaxed. Another car came by as we rolled off the gravel to the road only this time she didn't pay any attention to it at all. The coat was belted again, the flicker of a smile she gave me was real, and she put her head back against the seat and closed her eyes.

I didn't get it at all. All I knew was that when I hit the city I was going to pull up to the first subway station I saw, open the door, say goodby, then check on the papers until I found where somebody had put her back on the shelf again. I thought that. I wished I could mean it. All I felt was the trouble like the smoke over dry ice and it was seeping all over me.

For five minutes she sat and watched the edge of the road, then said, "Cigarette?" I shook one into her hand and shoved the dashboard lighter in. When it was lit she dragged in deeply and watched the gray haze swirl off the windows. "Are you wondering what it's all about?" she asked me.

"Not particularly."

"I was . . ." she hesitated, "in a sanitarium." The second pull on the butt nearly dragged the lit end down to her fingers. "They forced me to go there. They took away my clothes to make me stay there."

I nodded as if I understood.

She shook her head slowly, getting the meaning of my gesture. "Maybe I'll find somebody who will understand. I thought maybe . . . you would."

I went to say something. It never came out. The moon that had been hidden behind the clouds came out long enough to bathe the earth in a quick shower of pale yellow light that threw startlingly long shadows across the road and among those dark fingers was one that seemed darker still and moved with a series of jerks and a roar of sound that evolved into a dark sedan cutting in front of us. For the second time I heard the scream of tires on pavement and with it another scream not from the tires as metal tore into metal with a nasty tearing sound as splintering glass made little incongruous musical highlights above it all.

I kicked the door open and came out of the car in time to see the men piling out of the sedan. The trouble was all around us and you couldn't walk away from it. But I didn't expect it to be as bad as that. The gun in the guy's hand spit out a tongue of flame that lanced into the night and the bullet's banshee scream matched the one that was still going on behind me.

He never got another shot out because my fist split his face open. I went into the one behind him as something hissed through the air behind my head then hissed again and thudded against my shoulders. My arm went on that one and I spun around to get him with my foot. It was just a little too late. There was another hiss of something whipping through the air and whatever it was, it caught me across the forehead and for a second before all time and distance went I thought I was going to be sick and the hate for those bastards oozed out of my skin like sweat.

I didn't lie there for long. The pain that pounded across my head was too sharp, too damn deep. It was a hard, biting pain that burst in my ears with every heartbeat, sending a blinding white light flashing into my eyes even though they were squeezed shut.

In back of it all was the muffled screaming, the choked-off sobs, the cadence of harsh, angry voices biting out words that were indistinguishable at first. The motor of a car chewed into the sounds and there was more jangling of metal against metal. I tried to get up, but it was only my mind that could move. The rest of me was limp and dead. When the sense of movement did happen it wasn't by command but because arms had me around the waist and my feet and hands scraped cold concrete. Somewhere during those seconds the screaming had been chopped off, the voices had ceased and a certain pattern of action had begun to form.

You don't think at a time like that. You try to remember first, to collect events that led up to the end, to get things relatively assorted in their proper places so you can look at and study them with a bewildered sort of wonder that is saturated with pain, to find a beginning and an end. But nothing makes sense, all you feel is a madness and hate that rises and grows into a terrible frenzy that even wipes out the pain and you want to kill something so bad your brain is on fire. Then you realize that you can't even do that and the fire explodes into consciousness because of it and you can see once more.

They had left me on the floor. There were my feet and my hands, immobile lumps jutting in front of my body. The backs of the hands and the sleeves were red and sticky. The taste of the stickiness was in my mouth too. Something moved and a pair of shoes shuffled into sight so I knew I wasn't alone. The floor in front of my feet stretched out into other shoes and the lower halves of legs. Shiny shoes marred with a film of dust. One with a jagged scratch across the toe. Four separate pairs of feet all pointing toward the same direction and when my eyes followed them I saw her in the chair and saw what they were doing to her.

She had no coat on now and her skin had an unholy whiteness about it, splotched with deeper colors. She was sprawled in the chair, her mouth making uncontrollable mewing sounds. The hand with the pliers did something horrible to her and the mouth opened without screaming.

A voice said, "Enough. That's enough."

"She can still talk," the other one answered.

"No, she's past it. I've seen it happen before. We were silly to go this far, but we had no choice."

"Listen . . ."

"I'll give the orders. You listen."

The feet moved back a little. "All right, go ahead. But so far we don't know any more than we did before."

"That's satisfactory. What we do know is still more than anyone else. There are other ways and at least she won't be talking to the wrong ones. She'll have to go now. Everything is ready?"

"Yeah." It was a disgusted acknowledgment. "The guy too?"

"Naturally. Take them out to the road."

"It's a shame to dress her."

"You pig. Do what you're told. You two, help carry them out. We've spent enough time on this operation."

I could feel my mouth working to get some words out. Every filthy name I could think of for them was stuck in my throat. I couldn't even raise my eyes above their knees to see their faces and all I could do was hear them, hear everything they said and keep the sound of their voices spilling over in my ears so that when I heard them again I wouldn't need to look at their faces to know I was killing the right ones. The bastards, the dirty lousy bastards!

Hands went under my knees and shoulders and for a second I thought I would see what I wanted to see, but the hate inside me sent the blood beating to my head, bringing back the pain, and it was like a black curtain being pulled closed across my mind. Once it drew back hesitatingly and I saw my car on the side of the road, the rear end lifted with a jack and red flares set in front and in back of it.

Clever, I thought. Very clever of them. If anybody passed they'd see a car in trouble with warning signals properly placed and the driver obviously gone into town for help. Nobody would stop to investigate. Then the thought passed into the darkness as quickly as it came.

It was like a sleep that you awaken from because you had been sleeping cramped up. It was a forced awakening that hurts and you hear yourself groan as you try to straighten out. *Then suddenly there's an immediate sharpness to the awakening as you realize that it hadn't been a bad dream after all, but something alive and terrifying instead.*

She was there beside me in the car, the open coat framing her nakedness. Her head lolled against the window, the eyes staring sightlessly at the ceiling. She jerked and fell against me.

But not because she was alive! The car was moving ahead as something rammed into the rear of it!

Somehow I got myself up, looked over the wheel into the splash of light ahead of me and saw the edge of the cliff a few short feet away and even as I reached for the door the wheels went over the edge through the ready-made gap in the retaining wall and the nose dipped down into an incredible void.

CHAPTER 2

"Mike . . ."

I turned my head toward the sound. The motion brought a wave of silent thunder with it like the surf crashing on a beach. I heard my name again, a little clearer this time.

"Mike . . ."

My eyes opened. The light hurt, but I kept them open. For a minute she was just a dark blur, then the fuzzy edges went away and the blue became beautiful. "Hello, kitten," I said.

Velda's mouth parted in a slow smile that had all the happiness in the world wrapped up in it. "Glad to see you back, Mike."

"It's . . . good to be back. I'm surprised . . . I got here."

"So are a lot of people."

"I . . ."

"Don't talk. The doctor said to keep you quiet if you woke up. Otherwise he'd chase me away."

I tried to grin at her and she dropped her hand over mine. It was warm and soft with a gentle pressure that said everything was okay. I held it for a long time and if she took it away I never knew about it because when I awoke again it was still there.

The doctor was an efficient little man who poked and prodded with stiff fingers while he watched the expression on my face. He seemed to reel off yards of tape and gauze to dress me in and went away looking satisfied as though he had made me to start with.

Before he closed the door he turned around, glanced at his watch and said, "Thirty minutes, miss. I want him to sleep again."

Velda nodded and squeezed my hand. "Feel better?"

"Somewhat."

"Pat's outside. Shall I ask him to come in?"

". . . Yeah."

She got up and went to the door. I heard her speak to somebody, then there he was grinning at me foolishly, shaking his head while he looked me over.

"Like my outfit?" I said.

"Great. On you white looks good. Three days ago I was figuring I'd have to finance a new tux to bury the corpse in."

Nice guy, Pat. A swell cop, but he was getting one hell of a sense of humor. When his words sank in I felt my forehead wrinkling under the turban. "Three days?"

He nodded and draped himself in the big chair beside the bed. "You got it Monday. This is Thursday."

"Brother!"

"I know what you mean."

He glanced at Velda. A quick look that had something behind it I didn't get. She bit her lip, her teeth glistening against the magenta ripeness of her mouth, then nodded in assent.

Pat said, "Can you remember what happened, Mike?"

I knew the tone. He tried to cover it but he didn't make out. It was the soft trouble tone, falsely light yet direct and insistent. He knew I had caught it and his eyes dropped while he fiddled with his coat. "I remember."

"Care to tell me about it?"

"Why?"

This time he tried to look surprised. That didn't work either. "No reason."

"I had an accident, that's all."

"That's all?"

I got the grin out again and turned it on Velda. She was worried, but not too worried to smile back. "Maybe you can tell me what's cooking, kid. He won't."

"I'll let Pat tell you. He's been pretty obscure with me too."

"It's your ball, Pat," I said.

He stared at me a minute, then: "Right now I wish you weren't so sick. I'm the cop and you're the one who's supposed to answer questions."

"Sure, but I'm standing on my constitutional rights. It's very legal. Go ahead."

"All right, just keep your voice down or that medic will be hustling me out of here. If we weren't buddies I couldn't get within a mile of you with that watchdog around."

"What's the pitch?"

"You're not to be questioned . . . yet."

"Who wants to question me?"

"Among other law enforcement agencies, some government men. That accident of yours occurred in New York State, but right now you happen to be just over the state line in a Jersey hospital. The New York State Troopers will be looking forward to seeing you, plus some county cops from upstate a ways."

"I think I'll stay in Jersey a while."

"Those government men don't care what state you're in."

And there was that tone again.

"Suppose you explain," I said.

I watched the play of expression across his face to see what he was trying to hide. He looked down at his fingers and pared his nails absently. "You were lucky to get out of the car alive. The door sprung when it hit the side of the drop and you were thrown clear. They found you wrapped around some bushes. If the car hadn't sprayed the place with burning gas you might still be there. Fortunately, it attracted some motorists who went down to see what happened. Not much was left of the car at all."

"There was a dame in there," I told him.

"I'm coming to that." His head came up and his eyes searched my face. "She was dead. She's been identified."

"As an escapee from a sanitarium," I finished.

It didn't catch him a bit off base. "Those county cops were pretty sore about it when they found out. Why did you pass them up?"

"I didn't like their attitude."

He nodded as if that explained it. Hell, it did.

"You better start thinking before you pull stunts like that, Mike."

"Why?"

"The woman didn't die in the crash."

"I figured as much."

Maybe I shouldn't have been so calm about it. His lips got tight all of a sudden and the fingernails he had been tending disappeared into balled-up fists. "Damn it, Mike, what are you into? Do you realize what kind of a mess you've been fooling around with?"

"No. I'm waiting for you to tell me."

"That woman was under surveillance by the feds. She was part of something big that I don't know about myself and she was committed to the institution to recover so she could do some tall talking to a closed session of Congress. There was a police guard outside her door and on the grounds of the place. Right now the Washington boys are hopping and it looks like the finger is pointed at you. As far as they're concerned you got her out of there and knocked her off."

I lay there and looked at the ceiling. A crack in the plaster zigzagged across the room and disappeared under the molding. "What do *you* think, Pat?"

"I'm waiting to hear you say it."

"I already said it."

"An accident?" His smile was too damn sarcastic. "It was an accident to have a practically naked woman in your car? It was an accident to lie your way through a police roadblock? It was an accident to have her dead before your car went through the wall? You'll have to do better than that, pal. I know you too well. If accidents happen they go the way you want them to."

"It was an accident."

"Mike, look . . . you can call it what you like. I'm a cop and I'm in a position to help you out if there's trouble, but if you don't square away with me I'm not going to do a thing. When those Federal boys move in you're going to have to do better than that accident story."

Velda moved her hand up to my chin and turned my head so she could look at me. "It's big, Mike," she said. "Can you fill in the details?" She was so completely serious it was almost funny. I felt like kissing the tip of her nose and sending her out to play, but her eyes were pleading with me.

I said, "It was an accident. I picked her up on the way down from Albany. I don't know a thing about her, but she seemed like a nervy kid in a jam and I didn't like the snotty way that cop acted when he stopped the car. So I went on through. We got down maybe ten miles when a sedan pulled out from the side of the road and nudged me to a stop. Now here's the part you won't believe. I got out sore as hell and some-body took a shot at me. It missed, but I got sapped and sapped so beau-tifully I never came completely out of it. I don't know where the hell they took us, but wherever it was they tried to force something out of the dame. She never came across. Those lads were anxious to get rid of her and me too so they piled us in the car and gave it a shove over the cliff."

"Who are they?" Pat asked.

"Damned if I know. Five or six guys."

"Can you identify them?"

"Not by their faces. Maybe if I heard them speak."

I didn't mean maybe at all. I could still hear every syllable they spoke and those voices would talk in my mind until I died. Or they did.

The silence was pretty deep. The puzzle was on Velda's face. "Is that all?" she asked me.

Pat spoke out of the stillness, his voice soft again. "That's all he's going to tell anybody." He got up and stood by the bed. "If that's the way you want it, I'll play along. I hope like hell you're telling me the truth."

"But you're afraid I'm not, is that it?"

"Uh-huh. I'll check on it. I can still see some holes in it."

"For instance?"

"The gap in the guard rail. No slow-moving car did that. It was a fresh break, too."

"Then they did it with their car purposely."

"Maybe. Where was your heap while they were working the woman over?"

"Nicely parked off the road with a jack under it and flares set out."

"Clever thought."

"I thought so too," I said.

"Who could ever find anybody who noticed the flares? They'd just breeze right on by."

"That's right."

Pat hesitated, glanced at Velda, then back to me again. "You're going to stick with that story?"

"What else?"

"Okay, I'll check on it. I hope you aren't making any mistakes. Good night now. Take it easy." He started to the door.

I said, "I'll do my own checking when I'm up, Pat."

He stopped with his hand on the knob. "Don't keep asking for trouble, kid. You have enough right now."

"I don't like to get sapped and tossed over a cliff."

"Mike . . ."

"See you around, Pat." He shot me a wry grin and left. I picked up Velda's hand and looked at her watch. "You have five minutes left out of the thirty. How do you want to spend it?"

The seriousness washed away all at once. She was a big, luscious woman smiling at me with a mouth that was only inches away and coming closer each second. Velda. Tall, with hair like midnight. Beautiful, so it hurt to look at her.

Her hands were soft on my face and her mouth a hot, hungry thing that tried to drink me down. Even through the covers I could feel the firm pressure of her breasts, live things that caressed me of their own accord. She took her mouth away reluctantly so I could kiss her neck and run my lips across her shoulders.

"I love you, Mike," she said. "I love everything about you even when you're all fouled up with trouble." She traced a path down my cheek with her finger. "Now what do you want me to do?"

"Get your nose to the ground, kitten," I told her. "Find out what the hell this is all about. Take a check on that sanitarium and get a line into Washington if you can."

"That won't be easy."

"They can't keep secrets in the Capitol, baby. There will be rumors."

"And what will you do?"

"Try to make those feds believe that accident yarn."

Her eyes widened a little. "You mean . . . it didn't happen that way?"

"Uh-uh. I mean it did. It's just that nobody's going to believe it."

I patted her hand and she straightened up from the bed. I watched her walk toward the door, taking in every feline motion of her body. There was something lithe and animal-like in the way she swung her hips, a jungle tautness to her shoulders. Cleopatra might have had it. Josephine might have had it. But they never had it like she had it.

I said, "Velda . . ." and she turned around, knowing damn well what I was going to say. "Show me your legs."

She grinned impishly, her eyes dancing, standing in a pose no calendar artist could duplicate. She was a Circe, a lusty temptress, a piece of living statuary on display, that only one guy would be able to see. The hem of the dress came up quickly, letting the roundness under the nylon evolve into a magical symmetry, then the nylon ended in the quick whiteness of her thigh and I said, "Enough, kitten. Quit it."

Before I could say anything else she laughed down deep, threw me a kiss and grinned, "Now you know how Ulysses felt."

Now I knew. The guy was a sucker. He should have jumped ship.

CHAPTER 3

It was Monday again, a rainy, dreary Monday that was a huge wet muffler draped over the land. I watched it through the window and felt the taste of it in my mouth. The door opened and the doctor said, "Ready?"

I turned away from the window and squashed out the cigarette. "Yeah. Are they waiting for me downstairs?"

His tongue showed pink through his lips for a moment and he nodded. "I'm afraid so."

I picked my hat up from the chair and walked across the room. "Thanks for keeping them off my back so long, doc."

"It was a necessary thing. You had quite a blow, young man. There still may be complications." He held the door open for me, waved toward the elevator down the hall and waited silently beside me for it to crawl up to the floor. He took his place beside me on the way down, once letting his eyes edge over so he could watch me.

We got out in the lobby, shook hands briefly and I went to the cashier's window. She checked my name, told me everything had been paid for by my secretary, then handed me a receipted bill.

When I turned around they were all standing there politely, hats in their hands. Young guys with old eyes. Sharp. Junior executive types. Maybe you could pick them out of a crowd but most likely you couldn't. No gun bulges under the suit jackets, no high-top shoes with arch supports. Not too fat, not too lean. Faces you wouldn't want to lie past. Junior executives all right, but in J. Edgar Hoover's organization.

The tall guy in the blue pin stripe said, "Our car is out front, Mr. Hammer." I fell in beside him with the others bringing up on the flank and went out to get driven home. We took the Lincoln Tunnel across into

New York, cut east on Forty-first then took Ninth Avenue downtown to the modern gray building they used for operational headquarters.

They were real nice, those boys. They took my hat and coat, shoved up a chair for me to sit in, asked if I felt well enough to talk and when I told them sure, suggested that maybe I'd like a lawyer present.

I grinned at that one. "Nope, just ask questions and I'll do what I can to answer them. But thanks anyway."

The tall one nodded and looked over my head at someone else. "Bring in the file," he said. In back of me a door opened and closed. He leaned forward on the desk, his fingers laced together. "Now, Mr. Hammer, we'll get down to cases. You're completely aware of the situation?"

"I'm aware that no situation exists," I said bluntly.

"Really?"

I said, "Look, friend. You may be the F.B.I. and I may be up to my ears in something you're interested in, but let's get something straight. I don't get bluffed. Not even by the feds. I came here of my own free will. I'm fairly well acquainted with the law. The reason I didn't squawk about coming down here was because I wanted to get straightened out all the way around and quick because I have things to do when I leave and I don't want any cops tagging me around. That much understood?"

He didn't answer me right away. The door opened and closed again and a hand passed a folder over my shoulder. He took it, flipped it open and glanced through it. But he wasn't reading it. He knew the damn thing by heart. "It says here you're pretty tough, Mr. Hammer."

"Some people seem to think so."

"Several close brushes with the law, I notice."

"Notice the result."

"I have. I imagine your license can be waivered if we want to press the issue."

I dragged out my deck of Luckies and flipped one loose. "I said I'd cooperate. You can quit trying to bluff me."

His eyes came over the edge of the folder. "We're not bluffing. The police in upstate New York want you. Would you sooner talk to them?"

It was getting a little tiresome. "If you want. They can't do anything more than talk either."

"You ran a roadblock."

"Wrong, chum, I stopped for it."

"But you did lie to the officer who questioned you?"

"Certainly. Hell, I wasn't under oath. If he had any sense he would have looked at the dame and questioned her." I let the smoke drift out of my mouth toward the ceiling.

"The dead woman in your car . . ."

"You're getting lame," I said. "You know damn well I didn't kill her."

His smile was a lazy thing. "How do we know?"

"Because I didn't. I don't know how she died, but if she was shot you've already checked my apartment and found my gun there. You've already taken a paraffin test on me and it came out negative. If she was choked the marks on her neck didn't match the spread of my hands. If she was stabbed . . ."

"Her skull was crushed by a blunt instrument," he put in quietly.

And I said just as quietly, "It matched the indentation in my own skull then and you know it."

If I thought he was going to get sore I was wrong. He twisted his smile in a little deeper and leaned back in the chair with his head cradled in his hands. Behind me someone coughed to cover up a laugh.

"Okay, Mr. Hammer, you seem to know everything. Sometimes we can break even the tough ones down without much trouble. We did all the things you mentioned before you regained consciousness. Were you guessing?"

I shook my head. "Hell, no. I don't underestimate cops. I've made a pretty good living in the racket myself. Now if there's anything you'd really like to know I'd be glad to give it to you."

His mouth pursed in thought a minute. "Captain Chambers gave us a complete report on things. The details checked . . . and your part in it seems to fit your nature. Please understand something, Mr. Hammer. We're not after you. If your part was innocent enough that's as far as we need to go. It's just that we can't afford to pass up any angles."

"Good. Then I'm clear?"

"As far as we're concerned."

"I suppose they have a warrant out for me upstate."

"We'll take care of it."

"Thanks."

"There's just one thing . . ."

"Yeah?"

"From your record you seem to be a pretty astute sort of person. What's your opinion on this thing?"

"Since when do you guys deal in guesswork?"

"When that's all we have to go on."

I dropped the cigarette into the ash tray on the desk and looked at him. "The dame knew something she shouldn't have. Whoever pulled it were smart cookies. I think the sedan that waited for us was one that passed us up right after I took her aboard. It was a bad spot to try anything so they went ahead and picked the right one. She wouldn't talk so they bumped her. I imagine it was supposed to look like an accident."

"That's right, it was."

"Now do you mind if I ask one?"

"No. Go right ahead."

"Who was she?"

"Berga Torn." My eyes told him to finish it and he shrugged his shoulder. "She was a taxi dancer, night-club entertainer, friend of boys on the loose and anything else you can mention where sex is concerned."

A frown pulled at my forehead. "I don't get it."

"You're not supposed to, Mr. Hammer." A freeze clouded up his eyes. It told me that was as much as he was about to say and I was all through. I could go now and thanks. Thanks a lot.

I got up and pulled my hat on. One of the boys held the door open for me. I turned around and grinned at him. "I will, feller," I said.

"What?"

"Get it." My grin got bigger. "Then somebody else is going to get it."

I pulled the door closed and got out in the hall. I stood there a minute leaning up against the wall until the pounding in my forehead stopped and the lights left my eyes. There was a dry sour taste in my mouth that made me want to spit, a nasty hate buzzing around my head that pulled my lips tight across my teeth and brought the voices back in my ears and then I felt better because I knew that I'd never forget them and that some day I'd hear them again only this time they'd choke out the last sound they'd ever make.

I took the elevator downstairs, called a cab and gave him Pat's office address. The cop on the desk told me to go ahead up and when I walked in Pat was sitting there waiting for me, trying on a friendly smile for size.

He said, "How did it go, Mike?"

"It was a rotten pitch." I hooked a chair over with my foot and sat down. "I don't know what the act was for, but they sure wasted time."

"They *never* waste time."

"Then why the ride?"

"Checking. I gave them the facts they hadn't already picked up."

"They didn't seem to do anything about it."

"I didn't expect them to." He dropped the chair forward on all four legs. "I suppose you asked them some things too."

"Yeah, I know the kid's name. Berga Torn."

"That all?"

"Part of her history. What's the rest?"

Pat dropped his eyes and stared at his hands. When he was ready to speak he looked up at me, his face a study in caution. "Mike . . . I'm going to give you some information. The reason I'm doing it is because you're likely to fish around and find it yourself if I don't and interference is one thing we can't have."

"Go ahead."

"You've heard of Carl Evello?"

I nodded.

"Evello is the boy behind the powers. The last senatorial investigations turned up a lot of big names in the criminal world, but they never turned up his. That's how big he is. The others are pretty big too, but not like him."

I felt my eyebrows go up. "I didn't know he was that big. Where does it come from?"

"Nobody seems to know. A lot is suspected, but until there's plenty of concrete evidence, no charges are going to be passed around even by me. Just take my word for it that the guy is big. Now . . . they want him. They want him bad and when they get him all the other big boys are going to fall too."

"So what."

"Berga Torn was his mistress for a while."

It started to make sense now. I said, "So she had something on the guy?"

Pat shrugged disgustedly. "Who knows? She was supposed to have had something. She can't talk. When they were giving her the business as you said they were trying to get it out of her."

"You figure they were Carl's men then."

"Evidently."

"What about the sanitarium she was in?"

"She was there under the advice of her doctor," Pat said. "She was going to testify to the committee and under the strain almost had a nervous breakdown. All the committee hearings were tied up until she was released."

I said, "That's a pretty picture, kid. Where do I come in?"

Little light lines seemed to grow around his eyes. "You don't. You stay out of it."

"Nuts."

"Okay, hero, then let's break it down. There's no reason for you to mess around. It was just an accident that got you into it anyway. There's nothing much you can do and anything you *try* to do is damn well going to be resented by all the agencies concerned."

I gave him my best big grin. All the teeth. Even the eyes. "You flatter me."

"Don't get smart, Mike."

"I'm not."

"All right, you're a bright boy and I know how you work. I'm just trying to stop any trouble before it starts."

"Pal, you got it wrong," I said, "it's already started, remember? I got patted between the eyes, a dame got bumped and my car is wrecked." I stood up and looked down at him feeling things changing in my smile. "Maybe I have too much pride, but I don't let anybody get away with that kind of stuff. I'm going to knock the crap out of somebody for all that and if it gets up to Evello it's okay with me."

Pat's hand came down on the edge of the desk. "Damn it, Mike, why don't you get a little sense in your head? You . . ."

"Look . . . suppose somebody took you for a patsy. What would you do?"

"That didn't happen."

"No . . . but it happened to me. Those boys aren't that tough that they can get away with it. Damn it, Pat, you ought to know me better than that."

"I do, that's why I'm asking you to lay off. What do I have to do, appeal to your patriotism?"

"Patriotism, my back. I don't give a damn if Congress, the President and the Supreme Court told me to lay off. They're only men and they didn't get sapped and dumped over a cliff. You don't play games with guys who pull that kind of stuff. The feds can be as cagey as they like, but when they wrap the bunch up what happens? So they testify. Great. Costello testified and I can show you where he committed perjury in the minutes of the hearing. What happened? Yeah . . . you know what happened as well as I do. They're too big to do anything with. They got too much dough and too much power and if they talk too many people are going to go under. Well, the hell with 'em. There are a bunch of guys who drove a sedan I want to see again. I don't know what they look like, but I'll know them when I see them. If the feds beat me to 'em it's okay by me, but I'll wait, pal. If I don't reach them first I'll wait until they get through testifying or serving that short sentence those babies seem to draw and when I do you won't be having much trouble from them again ever."

"You have it all figured?"

"Uh-huh. Right down to the self-defense plea."

"You won't get far."

I grinned at him again. "You know better than that, don't you?"

For a moment the seriousness left his face. His mouth cracked in a grin. "Yeah," he said, "that's what I'm afraid of."

"That wasn't any ordinary kill."

"No."

"They were a bunch of cold-blooded bastards. You should have seen what they did to that kid before they killed her."

"Nothing showed on her body . . . or what was left of it after the fire."

"It was there. It wasn't very pretty." I stared at him hard. "It changes something in the way you were thinking."

His eyes came up speculatively.

"They didn't give her the works to see how much she knew. They were after something she knew and they didn't. She was the key to something."

Pat's face was grave. "And you're going after it?"

"What did you expect?"

"I don't know, Mike." He wiped his hand across his eyes. "I guess I didn't expect you to take it lying down." He turned his head and glanced out of the window at the rain. "But since it's going to be that way you might as well know this much. Those government boys are shrewd apples. They know your record and how you work. They even know how you think. Don't expect any help from this end. If you cross those boys you're going to wind up in the can."

"You have your orders?" I asked him.

"In writing. From pretty high authority." His eyes met mine. "I was told to pass the news on to you if you acted up."

I stood up and fiddled with my pack of butts. "Great guys. They want to do it all alone. They're too smart to need help."

"They have the equipment and manpower," Pat said defensively.

"Yeah, sure, but they don't have the attitude." A grimace pulled at my mouth. "They want to make a public example out of those big boys.

They want to see them sweat it out behind bars. Nuts to that. Those lads in the sedan don't give a hoot for authority. They don't give a damn for you, me or anybody besides themselves. They only respect one thing."

"Say it."

"A gun in their bellies that's going off and splashing their guts around the room. That kind of attitude they respect." I stuck my hat on my head, keeping it back off the blue lump between my eyes. "See you around, Pat," I said.

"Maybe, maybe not," he said to my back.

I went downstairs into the rain and waited there until a cab came along.

Unless you knew they were there you'd never notice it. Just little things out of place here and there. A streak through the dust where a coat sleeve dragged, an ash tray not quite in place, the rubber seal around the refrigerator door hanging because they didn't know it was loose and had to be stuffed back by hand.

The .45 was still hanging in the closet, but this time there was a thumbprint on the side where I knew I had wiped it before I stuck it away. I picked the rig off the hook and laid it on the table. The Washington boys were pretty good at that sort of thing. I started to whistle a tuneless song as I climbed out of my jacket when I noticed the wastebasket beside the dresser. There was a cigarette butt in the bottom with the brand showing and it wasn't my brand. I picked it up, stared at it, threw it back and went on whistling. I stopped when the thought of it jelled, picked up the phone and dialed the super's number downstairs.

I said, "This is Mike Hammer, John. Did you let some men in up here?"

He hedged with, "Men? You know, Mr. Hammer, I . . ."

"It's okay, I had a talk with them. I just wanted to check on it."

"Well, in that case . . . they had a warrant. You know what they were? They were F.B.I. men."

"Yeah, I know."

"They said I shouldn't mention it."

"You're sure about it?"

"Sure as anything. They had a city cop along too."

"What about anybody else?"

"Nobody else, Mr. Hammer. I wouldn't let a soul in up there, you know that."

"Okay, John. Thanks." I hung up the phone and looked around again.

Somebody else had gone through the apartment. They had done a good job too. But not quite as good as the feds. They had left their trademark around.

The smoke that was trouble started to boil up around me again. You couldn't see it and you couldn't smell it, but it was there. I started whistling again and picked up the .45.

CHAPTER 4

She came in at half-past eleven. She used the key I had given her a long time ago and walked into the living room bringing with her the warmth and love for life that was like turning on the light.

I said, "Hello, beautiful," and I didn't have to say anything more because there was more in the words than the sound of my voice and she knew it.

She started to smile slowly and her mouth made a kiss. Our lips didn't have to touch. She flung that warmth across the room and I caught it. Velda said, "Ugly face. You're uglier now than you were but I love you more than ever."

"So I'm ugly. Underneath I'm beautiful."

"Who can dig down that deep?" she grinned. Then added, "Except me, maybe."

"*Just* you, honey," I said.

The smile that played around her mouth softened a moment, then she slipped out of the coat and threw it across the back of a chair.

I could never get tired of looking at her, I thought. She was everything you needed just when you needed it, a bundle of woman whose emotions could be hard or soft or terrifying, but whatever they were it was what you wanted. She was the lush beauty of the jungle, the sleek sophisticate of the city. Like I said, to me she was everything, and the dull light of the room was reflected in the ring on her finger that I had given her.

I watched her go to the kitchen and open a pair of beer cans. I watched while she sat down, took the frosted can from her and watched while she sipped the top off hers and felt a sudden stirring when her tongue flicked the foam from her lips.

Then she said what I knew she was going to say. "This one's too big, Mike."

"It is?"

Her eyes drew a line across the floor and up my body until they were staring hard into mine. "I was busy while you were in the hospital, Mike. I didn't just let things wait until you got well. This isn't murder as you've known it before. It was planned, organizational killing and it's so big that even the city authorities are afraid of it. The thing has ballooned up to a point where it's Federal and even then it's touching such high places that the feds have to move carefully."

"So?" I let it hang there and pulled on the can of beer.

"It doesn't make any difference what I think?"

I set the can on the end table and made the three-ring pattern on the label. "What you think makes a lot of difference, kitten, but when it comes to making the decisions I'll make them on what I think. I'm a man. So I'm just one man, but as long as I have a brain of my own to use and experience and knowledge to draw on to form a decision I'll keep on making them myself."

"And you're going after them?"

"Would you like me better if I didn't?"

The grin crept back through the seriousness on her face. "No." Then her eyes laughed at me too. "Ten million dollars' worth of men and equipment bucking another multi-million outfit and you elect yourself to step in and clean up. But then, you're a man." She sipped from the beer can again, then said, "But what a man. I'll be glad when you step off that bachelorhood pedestal and move over to where I have a little control over you."

"Think you ever will?"

"No, but at least I'll have something to bargain with," she laughed. "I'd like to have you around for a long time without worrying about you."

"I feel the same way myself, Velda. It's just that some things come first."

"I know, but let me warn you. From now on you're going to be up against a scheming woman."

"That's been tried before."

"Not like this."

"Yeah," I said, and finished the beer. I waited until she put hers down too, then shook out a Lucky and tossed the pack over to her. "What did you pick up?"

"A few details. I found a trucker who passed your car where they had it parked with the flares fore and aft. The guy stopped, and when he saw nobody around he went on. The nearest phone was three miles down the road in a diner and he was surprised when nobody had shown up there because he hadn't seen anyone walking. The girl in the diner knew about an abandoned shack a few hundred yards from the spot and I went there. The place was alive with feds."

"Great."

"That's hardly the word for it." She squirmed in the chair and ran her fingers through her hair, the deep ebony of it rubbed to a soft glow in the pale lamplight. "They held me for a while, questioned me, and re-leased me with a warning that had teeth in it."

"They find anything?"

"From what I could see, nothing. They backtracked the same way that I did and anything they found just supported what you had already told them.

"There's a catch in it though," she said. "The shack was a good fifty yards in from the highway and covered with brush. You could light the place up and it wouldn't be seen, and unless you knew where to look you'd never find it."

"It was too convenient to be coincidental, you mean?"

"Much too convenient."

I spit out a stream of smoke and watched it flow around the empty beer can. "That doesn't make sense. The kid was running away. How'd they know which direction she'd pick out?"

"They wouldn't, but how would they know where that shack was?"

"Who'd the shack belong to?"

A frown creased her forehead and she shook her head. "That's an-other catch. The place is on state property. It's been there for twenty years. One thing I did learn while I was being questioned was that aside from its recent use the place had no signs of occupancy at all. There were dates carved in the doorpost and the last one was 1937."

"Anything else?"

Velda shook her head slowly. "I saw your car. Or what's left of it."

"Poor old baby. The last of the original hot rods."

"Mike . . ."

I finished the beer and put the empty down on the table. "Yeah?"

"What are you going to do?"

"Guess."

"Tell me."

I had a long pull on the smoke and dropped the butt into the can.

"They killed a dame and tried to frame me for it. They wrecked my heap and put me in the hospital. They're figuring us all for suckers and don't give a hang who gets hurt. The slobs, the miserable slobs." I rammed my fist against my palm until it stung. "I'm going to find out what the score is, kid. Then a lot of heads are going to roll."

"One of them might be yours, Mike."

"Yeah, one of 'em might, but it sure won't be the first to go. And you know something? They're worried, whoever they are. They read the papers and things didn't quite happen like they wanted them to. The law of averages bucked 'em for a change and instead of getting a sucker to frame they got me. Me. That they didn't like because I'm not just the average joe and they're smart enough to figure out an angle."

Her face pulled tight and the question was in her eyes. "They were up here looking around," I said.

"Mike!"

"Oh, I don't know what they were after, but I don't think they knew either. But you can bet on this, they went through this place because they thought I had something they wanted and just because they didn't find it doesn't mean they think I haven't got it. They'll be back. The next time I won't be in an emergency ward."

"But what could it be?"

"Beats me, but they tried to kill two people to find out. Whether I like it or not I'm in this thing as deep as that dame was." I grinned at Velda sitting there. "And I like it, too. I hate the guts of those people. I hate them so bad it's coming out of my skin. I'm going to find out who 'they' are and why and then they've had it."

A note of sarcasm crept into her voice. "Just like always, isn't that right?"

"No," I said, "Maybe not. Maybe this time I'll do it differently. Just for the fun of it."

Velda's hands were drawn tight on the arms of the chair. "I don't like you this way, Mike."

"Neither do a lot of people. They know something just like their own names. They know I'm not going to sit on my fanny and wait for something to happen. They know from now on they're going to have to be so careful they won't even be able to spit because I'm going to get closer and closer until I have them on the dirty end of a stick. They know it and I know it too."

"It makes you a target."

"Kitten, it sure does and that I go for. If that's one way of pulling 'em inside shooting range I'm plenty glad to be a target."

Her face relaxed and she sat back. For a long minute neither one of us spoke. She sat there with her head against the cushion staring at the ceiling, then, "Mike, I have news for you."

The way she said it made me look up. "Give."

"Any shooting that's to be done won't be done by you."

A muscle in my face twitched.

Velda reached in her jacket pocket and came out with an envelope. She flipped it across the room and I caught it. "Pat brought it in this morning. He couldn't do a thing about it, so don't get teed off at him."

I pulled the flap out and fingered the sheet loose. It was very brief and to the point. No quibbling. No doubting the source. The letterhead was all very official and I was willing to bet that for the one sheet they sent me a hundred more made up the details of why the thing should be sent.

It was a very simple order telling me I no longer had a license to carry a gun and temporarily my state-granted right to conduct private investigations was suspended. There was no mention of a full or partial refund of my two-hundred-buck fee for said license to said state.

So I laughed. I folded the sheet back into the envelope and laid it on the table. "They want me to do it the hard way," I said.

"They don't want you to do it at all. From now on you're a private citizen and nothing else and if they catch you with a gun you get it under the Sullivan law."

"This happened once before, remember?"

Velda nodded slowly. There was no expression at all on her face. "That's right, but they forgot about me. Then I had a P.I. ticket and a license for a gun too. This time they didn't forget."

"Smart boys."

"Very." She closed her eyes again and let her head drop back. "We're going to have it rough."

"Not we, girl. Me."

"We."

"Look . . ."

Only the slight reflection of the light from her pupils showed that her eyes were open and looking at me. "Who do you belong to, Mike?"

"You tell me."

She didn't answer. Her eyes opened halfway and there was something sad in the way her lips tried to curve into a smile. I said, "All right, kid, you know the answer. It's we and if I stick my neck out you can be there to help me get back in time." I picked the .45 up off the floor beside the chair, slid the clip out and thumbed the shells into my palm. "Your boy Mike is getting on in years, pal. Soft maybe?"

There was laughter in the sad smile now. "Not soft. Smarter. We're up against something that's so big pure muscle won't even dent it. We're up against a big brain and being smart is the only thing that's going to move it. At least you have the sense to change your style."

"Yeah."

"It won't be so easy."

"I know. I'm not built that way." I grinned at her. "Let's not worry about it. Everybody's trying to step on me because they don't want me around. Some of 'em got different reasons, but the big one is they're afraid I'll spoil their play. That happened before too. Let's make it happen again."

Velda said, "But let's not try so hard, huh? Seven years is a long time to wait for a guy." Her teeth were a white flash in the middle of her smile. "I'd like him in good shape when he gets ready to take the jump."

I said, "Yeah," but not so loud that she heard me.

"Where do we take it from here, Mike?"

I let the shells dribble from my fingers into the ash tray. They lay there, deadly and gleaming, but helpless without the mother that could give them birth.

"Berga Torn," I said. "We'll start with her. I want those sanitarium records. I want her life history and the history of anybody she was associated with. That's your job."

"And you?" she asked.

"Evello. Carl Evello. Someplace he comes into this thing and he's my job."

Velda nodded, drummed her fingernails against the arm of the chair and stared across the room. "He won't be easy."

"Nobody's easy."

"Especially Evello. He's organized. While you were under wraps in the hospital I saw a few people who had a little inside information on Evello. There wasn't much and what there was of it was mostly speculation, but it put the finger on a theme you might be interested in."

"Such as?"

She looked at me with a half smile, a beautiful jungle animal sizing up her mate before telling him what was outside the mouth of the den. "Mafia," she said.

I could feel it starting way down at my toes, a cold, burning flush that crept up my body and left in its wake a tingling sensation of rage and fear that was pure emotion and nothing else. It pounded in my ears and dried my throat until the words that came out were scratchy, raspy sounds that didn't seem to be part of me at all.

"How did they know?"

"They don't. They suspect, that's all. The Federal agencies are interested in the angle."

"Yeah," I said. "They *would* be interested. They'd go in on their toes, too. No wonder they don't want me fishing around."

"You make too much noise."

"Things happen, don't they?"

Velda didn't answer that one either.

"So now it makes sense," I told her. "They have the idea I'm in the deal someplace but they can't come out and say it. They play twenty questions hoping I do have a share of it so they'll have someplace to start. They won't give up until the day they die or I do because once the finger touches you it never comes away. There's no such thing as innocence, just innocence touched with guilt is as good a deal as you can get."

Velda's mouth moved slowly. "Maybe it's a good thing, Mike. It's a funny world. Pure innocence as such doesn't enter in much nowadays. There's always at least one thing people try to hide." She paused and ran her finger along the side of her cheek. "If a murderer is hung for the wrong killing, who is wrong?"

"That's a new twist for you, kid."

"I got it from you."

"Then finish it."

Her fingers reached out and plucked a cigarette from the pack. It was a graceful, feminine motion that spoke of soft girlishness, the texture of her skin satiny and amber in the light. You could follow the fingers into the hand and the hand into the arm, watching the curves melt into each other like a beautiful painting. Just watching like that and you could forget the two times that same hand held a snarling, spitting rod that chewed a guy's guts out. "Now innocence touched with guilt pays off," she said. "You'll be one of the baited hooks they'll use until something bites."

"And in the end the public will benefit."

"That's right." She grinned, the corner of her mouth twisting upward a little. "But don't feel badly about it, Mike. They're stealing your stuff. You taught them that trick a long time ago."

My fingers went out and began to play with the slugs that squatted in the bottom of the ash tray where I had dropped them. She watched me from across the room, her eyes half closed in speculation. Then she uncurled, tossed my deck of smokes into the chair beside me and reached for her coat.

I didn't watch her walk away. I sat there dreaming of the things I'd like to do and how maybe if nobody was there to see me I'd do anyway. I was dreaming of a lot of fat faces with jowls that got big and loose on other people's meat and how they'd look with that smashed, sticky expression that comes with catching the butt end of a .45 across their noses. I was dreaming of a slimy foreign secret army that held a parade of terror under the Mafia label and laughed at us with our laws and regulations and how fast their damned smug expressions would change when they saw the fresh corpses of their own kind day after day.

She didn't have to go far to read my mind. She had seen me look like this before. She didn't have to go far to get me back on the track, either. "Isn't it about time you taught them some fresh tricks, Mike?" Velda said softly.

Then she left and the room got a little darker.

CHAPTER 5

I sat there for a while, staring at the multicolored reflections of the city that made my window a living, moving kaleidoscope. The voice of the monster outside the glass was a constant drone, but when you listened long enough it became a flat, sarcastic sneer that pushed ten million people into bigger and better troubles, and then the sneer was heard for what it was, a derisive laugh that thought blood running from an open wound was funny, and death was the biggest joke of all.

Yeah, it laughed at people like me and you. It was the voice of the guy with the whip who laughed at each stroke to drown out the screams of the victim. A subtle voice that hid small cries, a louder voice that covered the anguished moans.

I sat and heard it and thought about it while the statistics ran through my head. So many a minute killed by cars, so many injured. So many dead an hour by out-and-out violence. So many this and so many that. It made a long impressive list that was recited at board meetings and assemblies.

There was only one thing left out. How many were scared stiff? How many lay awake nights worrying about things they shouldn't have to worry about at all? How many wondered where their kids were and what they were doing. *How many knew the army of silent men who made their whispered demands and either got them or extracted payment according to the code?*

Then I knew the voice outside for what it was. Not some intangible monster after all. Not some gigantic mechanical contrivance that could act of its own accord. Not a separate living being with its own rules and decrees. Not one of those things.

People, that's all.

Just soft, pulpy people, most of them nice. And some of them filthy and twisted who gorged themselves on flesh and puffed up with the power they had so that when they got stuck they popped like ripe melons and splashed their guts all over the ground.

The Mafia. The stinking, slimy Mafia. An oversize mob of ignorant, lunkheaded jerks who ruled with fear and got away with it because they had money to back themselves up.

The Black Hand? You think you can laugh it off? You think all that stuff went out with Prohibition? There's a lot of widows around who can tell you differently. Widowers, too.

Like Velda said, it wasn't going to be easy at all. You don't just ask around where you can find the top boy.

First you find somebody to ask and if you're not dead by then, or he's not dead, you ask. Then you ask and look some more, each time coming closer to the second when a bullet or a knife reaches across space and spears you.

There's a code they work by, a fixed unbreakable code. Once the Mafia touches you it never takes its hand away. And if you make one move, just one single, hesitant move to get out from under, it's all over. Sometimes it takes a day or two, even a year maybe, but it was all over from then.

You get dead.

In a sense though, it was funny. Someplace at the top of the heap was a person. From him the fear radiated like from the center of a spiderweb. He sat on his throne and made a motion of his hand and somebody died. He made another motion and somebody was twisted until they screamed. A nod of his head did something that sent a guy leaping from a roof because he couldn't take it any more.

Just one person did that. One soft, pulpy person.

I started to grin a little bit thinking how he'd act stripped of weapons and his power for a minute or so in a closed room with someone who didn't like him. I could almost see his face behind the glass and my grin got bigger because I was pretty sure of what I was going to do now.

It was late, but only by the clock. The city was yawning and stretching after its supper, waking up to start living. The rain had died, leaving a low grumble in the skies overhead to announce its passing. The air was fresher now, the light a little brighter, and the parade of cabs had slowed down enough so I could whistle one down and hop a ride over to Pat's apartment.

He let me in with a grin and muttered something between the folder of papers he had clamped in his teeth, waved me into the living room and took my coat. His eyes made a casual sweep over my chest and he didn't have to look a second time to tell I wasn't wearing a rig under my arm.

Pat said, "Drink?"

"Not now."

"It's only ginger ale."

I shook my head and sat down. He filled his glass, relaxed into a wing chair and shoved all the papers into an envelope. "Glad to see you traveling light."

"Didn't you expect me to?"

His mouth crooked up at the corner. "I figured you'd know better than not to. Just don't blame me for the deal, that's all."

"You're not too sorry about it, are you?"

"As a matter of fact, no." His fingers tapped the envelope, then his eyes came up to mine. "It puts you on the spot as far as business is concerned, but I don't imagine you'll starve."

"I don't imagine I will either," I grinned back at him. "How long am I supposed to be in solitary for?"

He didn't like the grin at all. He got those wrinkles around his eyes that showed when something was getting under his hide and took a long drag on the drink to muffle what he knew I saw. "When they're ready to lift it they'll lift it and not before."

"They won't have it that soft," I told him.

"No?"

I flicked a butt into my mouth and lit it. "Tomorrow you can remind 'em I'm an incorporated business, a taxpayer and a boy with connections. My lawyer has a judge probably getting up a show cause right now and until they settle the case in court they aren't pulling any bill-of-attainder stuff on me."

"You got a mouthful of words on that one, Mike."

"Uh-huh. And you know what I'm talking about. Nobody, not even a Federal agency is going to pull my tail and not get chewed a little bit."

His hands got too tight around the glass. "Mike . . . this isn't just murder."

"I know."

"How much?"

"No more than before. I've been thinking around it though."

"Any conclusions?"

"One." I looked at him, hard. "Mafia."

Nothing changed in his face. "So?"

"I can be useful if you'd quit booting me around." I took a drag on the smoke and let it curl out into the light. "I don't have to pull my record out. You know it as well as I do. Maybe I have shot up a few guys, but the public doesn't seem to miss them any. If your buddies think I'm stupid enough to go busting in on something over my head without knowing what I'm doing then it's time they took a refresher course. They haven't got one guy in Washington that's smarter than I am . . . not one guy. If they had they'd be making more moolah than I am and don't fool yourself thinking they're in there for love of the job. It's about the limit they can do."

"You sure think a lot of yourself."

"I have to, friend. Nobody else does. Besides, I'm still around when a lot of others have taken their last car ride."

Pat finished off the glass and swirled the last few drops around the bottom. "Mike," he said, "if I had my way I'd have you and ten thousand more in on this thing. That's about how many we'd need to fight it. As it is, I'm a city cop and I take orders. What do you want from me?"

"You say it, Pat."

He laughed this time. It was like the old days when neither one of us gave a damn about anything and if we had to hate it was the same thing. "Okay, you want me for your third arm. You're going to dive into this thing no matter who says what and as long as you are we'd might as well use your talents instead of tripping over them."

The grin was real. It was six years ago and not now any longer. The light was back in his eyes again and we were a team riding over anything that stood in our way. "Now I'll tell you something, Mike," he said, "I don't like the way the gold-badge boys do business either. I don't like political meddling in crime and I'm sick of the stuff that's been going on for so long. Everybody is afraid to move and it's about time something jolted them. For so damn long I've been listening to people say that this racket is over our heads that I almost began to believe it myself. Okay, I'll lay my job on the line. Let's give it a spin and see what happens. Tell me what you want and I'll feed it to you. Just don't hash up the play . . . at least not for a while yet. If something good comes of it I'll have a talking point and maybe I can keep my job."

"I can always use a partner."

"Thanks. Now let's hear your angle."

"Information. Detailed."

He didn't have to go far for it. The stuff was right there in his lap. He pulled it all out of the envelope and thumbed the sheets apart. The light behind his head made the sheets translucent enough so the lines of type stood out and there weren't very many lines.

"Known criminals with Mafia connections," he drawled. "Case histories of Mafia efficiency and police negligence. Twenty pages of arrests with hardly enough convictions to bother about. Twenty pages of murder, theft, dope pushing, and assorted felonies and all we're working with are the bottom rungs of the ladder. We can name some of the big ones but don't fool yourself and think they are the top joes. The boys up high don't have names we know about."

"Is Carl Evello there?"

Pat looked at the sheets again and threw them on the floor in disgust. "Evello isn't anywhere. He's got one of those investigatable incomes but it looks like he'll be able to talk his way out of it."

"Berga Torn?"

"Now we're back to murder. One of many."

"We don't think alike there, Pat."

"No?"

"Berga was special. She was so special they put a crew of boys on her who knew their business. They don't do that for everybody. Why did the committee want her?"

I could see him hesitate a moment, shrug and make up his mind. "There wasn't much to the Torn dame. She was a good-looking head with a respectable mind but engaged in a mucky racket, if you get what I mean."

"I know."

"There was a rumor that Evello was keeping her for a while. It was during the time he was raking in a pile. The same rumor had he gave her the boot and the committee figured she'd be mad enough to spill what she knew about him."

"Evello wouldn't be that dumb," I said.

"When it comes to dames, guys can be awfully dumb," he grinned at me knowingly.

"Finish it."

"The feds approached her. She was scared stiff, but she indicated that there was something she could give out, but she wanted time to collect her information and protection after she let it out."

"Great." I snuffed the butt out and leaned back in the chair. "I can see Washington assigning her a permanent bodyguard."

"She was going to appear before the committee masked."

"No good. Evello could still spot her from the info she handed them."

Pat confirmed the thought with a nod. "In the meantime," he went on, "she got the jitters. Twice she got away from the men assigned to cover her. Before the month was out she was practically hysterical and went to a doctor. He had her committed to a sanitarium and she was supposed to stay there for three weeks. The investigation was held up, there were agents assigned to guard the sanitarium, she got away and was killed."

"Just like that."

"Just like that only you were there when it happened."

"Nice of me."

"That's what those Washington boys thought."

"Coincidence is out," I said.

"Naturally." His mouth twitched again. "They don't know that you're the guy things happen to. Some people are accident prone. You're coincidence prone."

"I've thought of it that way," I told him. "Now what about the details of her escape?"

He shrugged and shook his head slightly. "Utter simplicity. The kind of thing you can't beat. Precautions were taken for every inconceivable thing and she does the conceivable. She picked up a raincoat and shoes from the nurses' quarters and walked out the main entrance with two female attendants. It was raining at the time and one of them had an umbrella and they stayed together under it the way women will who try to keep their hair dry or something. They went as far as the corner together, the other two got in a bus while she kept on walking."

"Wasn't a pass required at the gate?"

He nodded deeply, a motion touched with sarcasm. "Sure, there was a pass all right, each of the two had a pass and showed it. Maybe the guy thought he saw the third one. At least he said he thought so."

"I suppose somebody was outside the gate too?"

"That's right. Two men, one on foot and one in a car. Neither had seen the Torn girl and were there to stop anyone making an unauthorized exit."

I let out a short grunt.

Pat said, "They thought it *was* authorized, Mike."

I laughed again. "That's what I mean. *They thought.* Those guys are supposed to think right or not at all. Those are the guys who had my ticket lifted. Those are the guys who want no interference. Nuts."

"Anyway, she got away. That's it."

"Okay, we'll leave it there. What attitude are the cops taking?"

"It's murder so they're working it from that end."

"And getting nowhere," I added.

"So far," Pat said belligerently. I grinned at him and the scowl that creased his forehead disappeared. "Lay off. How do you plan to work it?"

"Where's Evello?"

"Right here in the city."

"And the known Mafia connections?"

Pat looked thoughtful a moment. "Other big cities, but their operational center is here too." He bared his teeth in a tight grimace. His eyes went hard and nasty as he said, "Which brings us to the end of our informative little discussion about the Mafia. We know who some of them are and how they operate, but that's as far as it goes."

"Washington doesn't have anything?"

"Sure, but what good does it do. Nobody fingers the Mafia. There's that small but important little item known as evidence."

"We'll get it," I told him, ". . . one way or another. It's still a big organization. They need capital to operate."

Pat stared at me like he would a kid. "Sure, just like that. You know how they raise that capital? They squeeze it out of the little guy. It's an extra tax he has to pay. They put the bite on guys who are afraid to talk or who can't talk. They run an import business that drives the Narcotics Division nuts. They got their hand in every racket that exists with a political cover so heavy you can't bust through it with a sledge hammer."

He didn't have to remind me. I knew how they operated. I said, "Maybe, chum, maybe. Could be that nobody's really tried hard enough yet."

He grunted something under his breath, then, "You still didn't say how you were going to work it."

I pushed myself out of the chair, wiping my hand across my face. "First Berga Torn. I want to find out more about her."

Pat reached down and picked the top sheet off the pile he had dropped on the floor beside him. "You might as well have this then. It's as much as anyone has to start with."

I folded it up and stuck it in my pocket without looking at it. "You'll let me know if anything comes up?"

"I'll let you know." I picked up my coat and started for the door.

"And Mike . . ."

"Yeah?"

"This is a two-way deal, remember?"

"Yeah, I remember."

Downstairs, I stood in front of the building a minute. I took the time to stick a Lucky in my mouth and even more time lighting it. I let the flare of the match bounce off my face for a good ten seconds, then dragged in deeply on the smoke and whipped it back into the night air. The guy in the doorway of the apartment across the street stirred and made a hesitant motion of having come out of the door and not know-ing which way to walk. I turned east and he made up his mind. He turned east too.

Halfway down the block I crossed over to make it a little easier on him. Washington didn't discount shoe leather as expenses so there was no sense giving the boy a hard time. I went three more blocks closer to the subway station and pulled a few gimmicks that had him practically climbing up my back.

This time I had a good look at him and was going to say hello to add insult to injury when I caught the end of a gun muzzle in my ribs and knew he wasn't Washington at all.

He was young and good-looking until he smiled, then the crooked march of short, stained teeth across his mouth made him an expensively dressed punk on a high-class job. There was no hop behind his pupils so he was a classy workman being paid by an employer who knew what the score was. The teeth smiled bigger and he started to tell me something when I ripped his coat open and the gun in the pocket wasn't pointing at me any more. He was half spun around fighting to get the rod loose as the side of my hand caught him across the neck and he sat down on the sidewalk with his feet out in front of him, plenty alive, plenty awake, but not even a little bit active.

I picked the Banker's Special out of his hand, broke it, dumped the shells into the gutter and tossed the rod back into his lap. His eyes were hurting. They were all watered up like he was ashamed of himself.

"Tell your boss to send a man out on the job the next time," I said.

I walked on down the street and turned into the subway kiosk won-dering what the deuce had happened to Washington. Little boy blue back on the sidewalk would have a good story to take home to papa this time. Most likely he wouldn't get his allowance. At least they'd know a pro was in the game for a change.

I shoved a dime in the turnstile, went through, pulled the sheet out of my pocket, glanced at it once and walked over to the downtown platform.

CHAPTER 6

Something happens to Brooklyn at night. It isn't a sister borough any more. She withdraws to herself and pulls the shades down, then begins a life that might seem foreign to an outsider. She's strange, exciting, tinted with bright lights, yet elusive somehow.

I got off the Brighton Line at De Kalb and went up to the street. A guy on the corner pointed the way to the address I wanted and I walked the few blocks to it.

What I was looking for was an old-fashioned brownstone, a hangover from a half-century past that had the number painted on the door and looked at the street with dull, blank eyes. I went up the four sandstone steps, held a match to the mailboxes and found what I wanted.

The names CARVER and TORN were there, but somebody had drawn a pencil through the two of them and had written in BERNSTEIN underneath. All I could do was mutter a little under my breath and punch the end button on the line, the one labeled SUPER. I leaned on it until the door started clicking then I opened it and went in.

He came to the door and I could almost see his face. Part of it stuck out behind the fleshy shoulder of a woman who towered all around him and glared at me as if I had crawled up out of a hole. Her hair was a gray mop gathered into tiny knots and clamped in place with metal curlers. She bulged through the bathrobe, trying to slow down her breathing enough so she could say something. Her hands were big and red, the knuckles showing as they bit into her hips.

Dames. The guy behind her looked scared to death. She said, "What the hell do you want! You know what time it is? You think . . ."

"Shut up." Her mouth stopped. I leaned against the door jamb. "I'm looking for the super."

"I'm the . . ."

"You're not anything to me, lady. Tell your boy to come out." I thought her face would fall apart. "Tell him," I repeated.

When men learn to be men maybe they can handle dames. There was something simpering in the way she forced a smile and stepped aside.

The boy didn't want to come out, but he did. He made himself as big as he could without it helping much. "Yes?"

I showed him the badge I still had. It didn't mean a thing any more, but it still shined in the light and wasn't something everybody carried. "Get your keys."

"Yessir, yessir." He reached up beside the door, unhooked a ring and stepped back into the hall.

The dame said. "You wait a minute, I'll be right . . ."

He seemed to stand on his toes. "*You* wait right there until I come *back*," he told her. "*I'm* the super." He turned and grinned at me. Behind him his wife's face puffed out and the door slammed.

"Yessir?" he said.

"Berga Torn's place. I want to go through it."

"But the police have already been through there."

"I know."

"Today I rented it already."

"Anybody there now?"

"Not yet. Tomorrow they're supposed to come."

"Then let's go."

First he hesitated, then he shrugged and started up the stairs. Two flights up he fitted a key into the lock of a door and threw it open. He felt around for the light switch, flipped it and stood aside for me.

I don't know what I expected to find. Maybe it was more curiosity than anything that dragged me up there. The place had been gone over by experts and if anything had been worth taking it was gone by now. It was what you might call a functional apartment and nothing more. The kitchen and living room were combined with a bathroom sandwiched between two bedrooms that jutted off the one wall. There was enough furniture to be comfortable, nothing gaudy and nothing out of place.

"Whose stuff is this?"

"We rent furnished. What you see belongs to the landlord."

I walked into the bedroom and opened the door of the closet. A half dozen dresses and a suit hung there. The floor was lined with shoes. The dresser was the same way, filled to the brim. The clothes were good, fairly new, but not the type that came out of exclusive shops.

Stockings were neatly rolled up and packed into a top drawer. Beside them were four envelopes, two with paid-up receipts, one a letter from the Millburn Steamship Line saying that there were no available berths on the liner *Cedric* and how sorry they were, and the other a heavier envelope holding about a dozen Indianhead pennies.

The other small drawer was cluttered with half-used lipsticks and all the usual junk a dame can collect in hardly any time at all.

It was the other bedroom that gave me the surprise. There was nothing there at all. Just a made-up bed, a cleaned-out closet and dresser drawers lined with old sheets of newspaper.

The super watched me until I backed out into the living room, saying nothing.

"Whose room?" I jerked my thumb at the empty place.

"Miss Carver's."

"Where is she?"

"Two days ago . . . she moved out."

"The police see her?"

He nodded, a fast snap of the head. "Maybe that's why she moved out."

"You going to empty this place out?"

"Guess I got to. The lease is up next month, but it was paid in advance. Hope I don't get in trouble renting so soon."

"Who paid it?"

"Torn's name is on the lease." He looked at me pointedly.

"I didn't ask that."

"She handed me the dough." I stared at him hard and he fumbled with his pajamas again. "How many times do I have to tell you guys. I don't know where she got the dough. Far as I know she didn't do any messing around. This place sure wasn't no office or that nosy old lady of mine would've known about it."

"Did she have any men here to see her?"

"Mister," he said, "there's twelve apartments in this rat-trap and I can't keep track of who comes in and who goes out so long as they're paid up. If you ask me right off I'd say she wasn't no tramp. She was a dame splitting her quarters with another dame who paid her dough and didn't make trouble. If a guy was keeping her he sure didn't get his money's worth. If you want to know what I think then I'd say yes, she was being kept. Maybe the both of 'em. The old lady never thought so or she would've given them the boot, that's for sure."

"Okay then," I said, "that's it."

He held the door open for me. "You think anything's going to come of this?"

"Plenty."

The guy was another lip licker. "There won't be . . ."

"Don't worry about it. You know how I can reach the Carver girl?"

The look he gave me was quick and worried. "She didn't leave no address."

I made it sound very flat and businesslike. "You know . . . when you step in front of the law there's charges that can be pressed."

"Aw, look, mister, if I knew . . ." His tongue came out and passed over his mouth again. He thought about it, shrugged, then said, "Okay. Just don't let my wife know. She called today. She's expecting some mail from her boy friend and asked me to send it to her." He pulled in a deep breath and let it out in a sigh. "She don't want anybody to know where she is. Got a pencil?"

I handed him one with the remains of an envelope and he jotted it down.

"Wish I could do something right for a change. The kid sounded pretty worried."

"You don't want to buck the law, do you friend?"

"Guess not."

"Okay, then you did right. Tell you what though . . . don't bother giving it out to anyone else. I'll see her, but she won't know how I reached her. How's that?"

His face showed some relief. "Swell."

"By the way," I said, "what was she like?"

"Carver?"

"Yeah."

"Kind of a pretty blonde. Hair like snow."

"I'll find her," I said.

The number was on Atlantic Avenue. It was the third floor over a secondhand store and there was nothing to guide you in but the smell. All the doorbells had names that had been there long enough to get dirtied up, but the newest one said TRENTEN when it didn't mean that at all.

I punched the button three times while I stood there in the dark, heard nothing ringing so I eased myself into the smell. It wasn't just an odor. It was something that moved, something warm and fluid that came down the stairs, tumbling over slowly, merging with other smells until it leaked out into the street.

In each flight there were fourteen steps, a landing, a short corridor that took you to the next flight and at the top of the last one, a door. Up there the smell was different. It wasn't any fresher; it just smelled better. A pencil line of light marked the sill and for a change there was no bag of garbage to trip over.

I rapped on the door and waited. I did it again and springs creaked inside. A quiet little voice said, "Yes?"

"Carver?"

Again, "Yes." A bit tired-sounding this time.

"I'd like to speak to you. I'm pushing my card through under the door."

"Never mind. Just come right in."

I felt for the knob, twisted it and pushed the door open.

She was sitting there swallowed up in a big chair facing me, the gun in her hand resting on her knee in a lazy fashion and there wasn't even the slightest bit of doubt that it would start going off the second I breathed too hard.

Carver wasn't pretty. She was small and full bodied, but she wasn't pretty. Maybe no dame can be pretty with a rod in her mitt, even one with bleached white hair and a scarlet mouth. A black velvet robe outlined her against the chair, seeming like the space of nighttime between the white of her hair and that of the fur-lined slippers she wore.

For a minute she looked at me, her eyes wandering over me slowly. I let her look and pushed the door shut. Maybe she was satisfied by what she saw, maybe not. She didn't say anything, but she didn't put the gun away either. I said, "Expecting someone else?"

What she did with her mouth didn't make up a smile. "I don't know. What have you to say?"

"I'll say what it takes to make you point that heater someplace else."

"You can't talk that loud or that long, friend."

"Do I reach in my pocket for a smoke?"

"There's some on the table beside you. Use those."

I picked one up, almost went for my lighter in my pocket, thought better of it and took the matches that went with the cigarettes. "You're sure not good company, kid." I blew a stream of smoke at the floor and rocked on my toes. That little round hole in the tip of the automatic never came off my stomach.

"The name is Mike Hammer," I told her. "I'm a private investigator. I was with Berga Torn when she got knocked off."

This time the rod moved. I was looking right down the barrel.

"More," her mouth said.

"She was trying to hitch a ride to the city. I picked her up, ran a roadblock that was checking for her, got edged off the road by a car and damn near brained by a pack of hoods who were playing for keeps. I was there with my head dented in when they worked her over and behind the wheel of the car they pushed over the cliff. To them I was a handy, class-A red herring that was supposed to cover the real cause of her death only it didn't quite happen that way."

"How did it happen?"

"I was thrown clear. If you want I'll show you my scars."

"Never mind."

So we stared at each other for a longer minute and I was still looking down the barrel and the hole kept getting bigger and bigger.

"You loaded?"

"The cops lifted my rod and P.I. ticket."

"Why?"

"Because they knew I'd bust into this thing and they wanted to keep me out."

"How did you find me?"

"It's not hard to find people when you know how. Anybody could do it." Her eyes widened momentarily, seemed to deepen, then narrowed sharply.

"Suppose I don't believe you," she said.

I sucked in a lungful of smoke and dropped the butt to the floor. I didn't bother to squash it out. I let it lie there until you could smell the stink of burned wool in the room and felt my face start to tighten around the edges. I said, "Kid, I'm sick of answering questions. I'm sick of having guns pointed at me. You make the second tonight and if you don't stow that thing I'm going to beat the hell out of you. What'll it be?"

I didn't scare her. The gun came down until it rested in her lap and for the first time the stiffness left her face. Carver just looked tired. Tired and resigned. The scarlet slash of her mouth made a wry grimace of sadness. "All right," she said, "sit down."

So I sat down. No matter what else I could have done, nothing would have been more effective. The bewilderment showed on her face, the way her body arched before sinking back again. Her leg moved and the gun dropped to the floor and stayed there.

"Aren't you . . ."

"Who were you expecting, Carver?"

"The name is Lily." Her tongue was a lighter pink against the scarlet as it swept across her lips.

"Who, Lily?"

"Just . . . men." Her eyes were hopeful now. "You . . . told me the truth?"

"I'm not one of them if that's what you mean. Why did they come?"

The hardness left her face. It seemed to melt away like a film that should never have been there and now she was pretty. Her hair was a pile of snow that reflected the loveliness of her face. She breathed heavily, the robe drawing tight at regular intervals.

"They wanted Berga."

"Let's start at the beginning. With you and Berga. How's that?"

Lily paused and stared into the past. "Before the war, that's when we met. We were dance-hall hostesses. It was the first night for the both of us and we both sort of stuck together. A week later we found an apartment and shared it."

"How long?"

"About a year. When the war came I was pretty sick of things and went into a defense plant. Berga quit too . . . but what she did for a living was her business. She was a pretty good kid. When I was sick she moved back in and took care of me. After the war I lost my job when the plant closed down and she got a friend of hers to get me a job in a night club in Jersey."

"Did she work there too?" I asked.

The white hair made a negative. "She was . . . doing a lot of things."

"Anybody special?"

"I don't know. I didn't ask. We went back to living in the same apartment for a while, though she was paying most of the bills. She seemed to have a pretty good income."

Lily's eyes came off the wall behind my head and fastened on mine. "That's when I noticed her starting to change."

"How?"

"She was . . . scared."

"Did she say why?"

"No. She laughed it off. Twice she booked passage to Europe, but couldn't get the ship she wanted and didn't go."

"She was that scared."

Lily shrugged, saying nothing, saying much. "It seemed to grow on her. Finally she wouldn't even leave the house at all. She said she didn't feel well, but I knew she was lying."

"When was this?"

"Not so very long ago. I don't remember just when."

"It doesn't matter."

"She went out once in a while after that. Like to the movies or for groceries. Never very far. Then the police came around."

"What did they want?"

"Her."

"Questions or an arrest?"

"Questions, mostly. They asked me some things too. Nothing I knew about. That night I saw someone following me home." Her face had a curious strained look about it. "It's been that way every night since. I don't know if they've found me here yet or not."

"Cops?"

"Not cops." She said it very simply, very calmly, but couldn't quite hide the terror that tried to scream the answer out.

She begged me to say something, but I let her squeeze it out herself. "The police came again, but Berga wouldn't tell them anything." The tongue moistened the lips again. The scarlet was starting to wash away and I could see the natural tones of the wet flesh. "The other men came . . . they were different from the police. Federal men, I think. They took her away. Before she came back . . . *Those* men came."

She put something into the last three words that wasn't in the others, some breathless, nameless fear. Her hands were tight balls with the nails biting into the palms. A glassiness had passed over her eyes while she thought about it, then vanished as if afraid it had been seen.

"They said I'd die if I talked to anyone." Her hand moved up and covered her mouth. "I'm tired of being scared," she said. Her head drooped forward, nodding gently to the soft sobs that seemed to stick in her chest.

What's the answer? How do you tell them they won't die when they know you're lying about it because they're marked already?

I got up and walked to her chair, looked at her a second and sat down on the arm of it. I took her hand away from her face, tilted her chin up and ran my fingers through the snow piled on top of her head. It was as soft and as fine as it looked in the light and when my fingers touched her cheek she smiled, dropped her eyes and let that beauty come through all the way, every bit of it that she had kept hidden so long. There was a faint smell of rubbing alcohol about her, a clean, pungent odor that seemed to separate itself from the perfume she wore.

Her eyes were big and dark, soft ovals under the delicate brows, her mouth full and pink, parted in the beginning of a smile. My fingers squeezed her shoulder easily and her head went back, the mouth parting even further and I bent down slowly.

"You won't die," I said.

And it was the wrong thing to say because the mouth that was so close to mine pulled back and everything had changed. I just sat there next to her for a little while until the dry sobs had stopped. There were no tears to be wiped away. Terror doesn't leave any tears. Not that kind of terror.

"What did they want to know about Berga?"

"I don't know," she whispered. "They made me tell everything I knew about her. They made me sit there while they went through her things."

"Did they find anything?"

"No. I . . . I don't think so. They were horribly mad about it."

"Did they hurt you?" I asked.

An almost imperceptible shudder went through her whole body. "I've been hurt worse." Her eyes drifted up to mine. "They were disgusting men. They'll kill me now, won't they?"

"If they do they've had it."

"But it would still be too late for me."

I nodded. It was all I could do. I got up, took the last smoke out of my old pack and tapped the butt against my knuckle. "Can I take a look at that suitcase of hers?"

"It's in the bedroom." She pushed her hair back with a tired motion. "The closet."

I walked in, snapped on the light and found the closet. The suitcase was there where she said it was, a brown leather gladstone that had seen a lot of knocking around. I tossed it on the bed, unfastened the straps and opened it up.

But nothing was in there that could kill a person. Not unless a motive for murder was in a couple old picture albums, three yearbooks from high school, a collection of underwear, extra-short bathing suits, a stripper's outfit and a batch of old mail.

I thought maybe the mail would do it, but most of them were trivial answers from some friend to letters she had written and were postmarked from a hick town in Idaho. The rest were steamship folders and a tour guide of southern Europe. I shoved everything back in the suitcase, closed it up and dropped it in the closet.

When I turned around Lily was standing there in the doorway, a fresh cigarette in her mouth, one hand holding the robe closed around her waist, her hair a white cloud that seemed to hover above her. When she spoke the voice didn't sound as though it belonged to her at all.

"What am I to do now?"

I reached out and folded my hand over hers and drew her closer to me. The fingers were cold, her body was a warm thing that wanted to search for something.

"Got any place to go?"

"No," faintly.

"Money?"

"Just a little."

"Get dressed. How long will it take?"

"A . . . a few minutes."

For the briefest interval her face brightened with a new hope, then she smiled and shook her head. "It . . . won't do any good, I've seen men like that before. They're not like other people. They'd find me."

My laugh was short and hard. "We'll make it tough for them just the same. And don't kid yourself about them being too different. They're just like anybody else in most ways. They're afraid of things too. I'm not kidding you or me. You know what the score is so all we can do is give it a try."

I stopped for a second and let a thought run through my head again. I grinned down at her and said, "You know . . . don't be a bit surprised if you live a lot longer than you think you should."

"Why?"

"I have an idea the outfit who worked you over don't really know what they're after and they're not going to kill any leads until they get it."

"But I . . . don't have any idea . . ."

"Let them find that out for themselves," I interrupted. "Let's get you out of here as fast as we can."

I dropped her hand and pushed her into the bedroom. She looked at me, her face happy, then her body went tight and it showed in the way her eyes lit up, that crazy desire to say thanks somehow; but I pulled the door shut before she could do what she wanted to do and went inside opening a fresh deck of Luckies.

The gun was still there on the floor, a metallic glitter asleep on a bed of faded green wool. The safety was off and the hammer was still back. All that time in the beginning I was about a literal ounce away from being nice and dead. Lily Carver hadn't been fooling a bit.

She took almost five minutes. I heard the door open and turned around. It wasn't the same Lily. It was a new woman, a fresh and lovely woman who was a taller, graceful woman. It was one for whom the green gabardine suit had been intended, exquisitely molding every feature of her body. Her legs were silken things, their curves flashing enough to take your eyes away from the luxury of her hair that poked out under the hat.

It wasn't a worried or a scared Lily this time. It was a Lily who took my arm and held it tightly, smiling a smile that was real. "Where are we going, Mike?"

It was the first time she had said my name and I liked the way she said it.

"To my place." I told her.

We went downstairs and out on Atlantic Avenue. We played a game of not being seen in case there were watchers and if there were they weren't good enough to keep up with us. We used the subway to go home and took a cab to the door. When I was sure nobody was in the lobby I took her in.

It was all very simple.

When we got upstairs I told her to hop into the sack and showed her the spare bedroom. She smiled, reached out and patted my cheek and said, "It's been a long time since I met a nice guy, Mike."

That strange excitement seemed to be inside her like a coiled spring. I squeezed her wrist and she knew what I was saying without having to use words and her mouth started to part.

I stopped it there.

Or maybe she stopped it.

The spring wound tighter and tighter, then I let her go and walked away.

Behind me the door closed softly and I thought I heard a whispered "Good night, Mike."

I started it that night. At three-thirty the word went out in the back room of a gin mill off Forty-second and Third. Before morning it would yell and before the night came again it would pay off. One way or another.

Wherever they were, whoever they were, they would hear about it. They'd know me and know what the word meant. They'd sit and think for a little while and if they knew me well enough maybe they'd feel a little bit sweaty and not so sure of themselves any more. They couldn't laugh it off. With anybody else, perhaps, but not with me.

Wise guys, A pack of conniving slobs with the world in their hands and the power and money to buck a government while they sat on their fat tails, yet before morning there wouldn't be one of them who didn't have a funny feeling around his gut.

This time they had to move.

The word was out.

I went back to the apartment and listened at the door of Lily's room. I could hear her regular, heavy breathing. I stood there a minute, took a final drag on the butt, put it out and headed for my sack.

CHAPTER 7

She was up when the phone rang in the morning. I heard the dishes rattling and smelt the coffee. She called out, "Any time you're ready, come eat."

I said okay and picked up the phone.

The voice was low and soft, the kind you'd never miss in a million years. It was the best way to wake up and it showed in my voice when I said, "Hi Velda, what's doing?"

"Plenty is doing, but nothing I want to talk about over the phone."

"Get something?"

"Yes."

"Where are you now?"

"Down at the office. A place you ought to try to get to once a week, at least."

"You know how things are, honey," I said.

Lily looked in the door, waved and pointed toward the kitchen. I nodded, glad that Velda didn't know how things were right then.

"Where were *you* last night? I called until I was too tired to stay awake and tried again this morning."

"I was busy."

"Oh, Pat called." She tried to keep her voice its natural huskiness but it wanted to get away.

"I suppose he said too much."

"He said enough." She stopped and I could hear her breathing into the phone. "Mike, I'm scared."

"Well don't be, kitten. I know what I'm doing. You ought to know that."

"I'm still scared. I think somebody tried to break into my apartment last night."

That one got a low whistle out of me. "What happened?"

"Nothing. I heard a noise in the lock for a while but whoever was trying it gave up. I'm glad I got that special job now. Are you coming over?"

"Not right away."

"You ought to. A lot of mail is piling up. I paid all the bills, but you have a sackful of personal stuff."

"I'll get to it later. Look, did you make out on that info?"

"Somewhat. Do you want it now?"

"*Right* now, kitten. I'll meet you in the Texan Bar in an hour."

"All right, Mike."

"And kitten . . . you got that little heater of yours handy?"

"Well . . ."

"Then keep it handy but don't let it show."

"It's handy."

"Good. Grab a cab and get over there."

"I'll be there in an hour."

I slapped the phone back, hopped up and took a fast shower. Lily had everything on the table when I got there, a hopeful smile on her face. The table was spread with enough for a couple of lumberjacks and I ate until I made a dent in the mess, then went for seconds on the coffee.

Lily handed me a fresh pack of Luckies, held out a match and smiled again when I slumped back in my chair. "Have enough?"

"Are you kidding? I'm a city boy, remember?"

"You don't look like a city boy."

"What do I look like?"

Her eyes did it slow. Up and down twice, then a steady scrutiny of my face. For a minute it was supposed to be funny, but the second time there was no humor in it. The eyes seemed to get bigger and deeper with some far-away hungry quality that was past defining. Then almost as quickly as it had come there was a crazy, fearful expression there in its place that lasted the blink of an eye and she forced a laugh out.

"You look like a nice guy, Mike. I haven't seen many nice guys. I'm afraid they make an impression."

"Don't get the wrong impression, Lily," I told her. "I used to think I wasn't much of a sentimentalist, but sometimes I wonder. Right now you're pretty important to me so I may look like a good egg to you. Just don't go walking off with anything while you're here or I'll look different to you."

Her smile got bigger. "You're not fooling me."

I tossed the butt in my empty cup and it fizzled out. "So I'm getting old. You don't stay young in this racket very long."

"Mike . . ."

I knew what she was going to say before she said it. "I'll be gone for awhile. I don't know how long. The chances are nobody will be up here, but just to keep from sticking our necks out, don't answer that door. If a key goes in the lock it'll be me. Keep the chain on the door until I open it, look for yourself then to make sure and then open up."

"Supposing the phone rings?"

"Let it ring. If I want you I'll call the janitor, have him push the doorbell twice, then I'll call you. Got it?"

"I got it."

"Good. Now take it easy until I get back."

She gave me a slow, friendly wink and a grin, then followed it up with a soft kiss that formed on her lips and crossed the room to me. She was all dressed up with no place to go and didn't care, a beautiful white-headed doll with funny eyes that said she had been around too long and seen too many things. But now she looked happy.

I went downstairs, waited until a cab cruised by and grabbed it. We made the Texan Bar with ten minutes left out of the hour so I loafed around outside until a cab pulled into the curb and Velda got out.

Getting out of a cab is one of the things most women don't do right. But most women aren't Velda. Without half trying she made a production out of it. When you saw her do it you knew she wasn't getting out of a cab so much as making an entrance onto the street. Nothing showed, but there was so much to show that you had to watch to see if it would happen or not and even when it didn't you weren't a bit disappointed.

She turned around, gave me that impish grin and took my arm with a tight squeeze that said she was happy as all get out to see me and the guy with the packages beside me sighed and muttered something about some guys having all the luck.

Inside the Texan we picked a booth as far back as we could get, ordered up lunch for Velda, a beer for me and then she handed me the envelope from her handbag. "As much as I could get. It cost two hundred and a promise of favors to be repaid . . . if necessary."

"By you?"

Her face darkened, then twisted into a smile. "By you."

I slipped my finger under the flap and drew out the sheets. One was a handwritten copy of the sanitarium report with the rest filling in Berga

Torn's life history. Velda had carried out instructions. At the bottom of the last page was a list of names.

Evello's was there. So was Congressman Geyfey's. At the tail end was Billy Mist and when I held my finger on it Velda said, "She went out with him periodically. She was seen with him, but whenever it was, the spotlight was on him . . . not her."

"No," I said softly, "the spotlight is always on Billy. The picture's starting to get dirty."

"Mike . . ." She was tapping her nails against the table. "Who is Billy Mist?"

I grunted, picked up a Lucky and lit it. "It's a picture that goes back pretty far. He used to be known as Billy the Kid and he had as many notches on his rod as the original, if they still notch rods. Just before the war he went legit. At least on the outside he looked clean. He's been tied into a lot of messy stuff but nothing's been proven against him."

"So?"

"He's a known Mafia connection," I said. "He sits pretty high, too."

Velda's face paled a little. "Brother!"

"Why?"

"Eddie Connely gave me the lead this morning in Toscio's Restaurant. He and another reporter seemed to have a pretty good inside track on the Torn gal, both of them being on the police beat. Trouble was, they had to suppress most of it and they were pretty disgusted. Anyway, Eddie mentioned Billy Mist and pointed him out. He was over at the bar and I turned around to look at him. About then he happened to turn around too, caught me watching him and got the wrong slant on things. He left his drink, came over and handed me the slimiest proposition I ever heard right out in the open. What I told him no lady should repeat, but Eddie and his pal got a little green and I thought the Mist character would pop his buttons. Eddie didn't say much after that. He finished his coffee, paid the check and out they went."

I could feel my teeth showing through the grin. My chest was tight and things were happening in my head. Velda said, "Easy, chum."

I spit the cigarette out and didn't say anything for a minute. Billy Mist, the jerk with the duck's-tail haircut held down with a pound of grease. The tough guy who took what he wanted whenever he wanted. The uptown kid with the big money and the heavy connections.

When I got rid of the things in my head I squinted at her across the table. "Kitten, don't ever say I'm the guy who goes looking for trouble."

"Bad, Mike?"

"Bad enough. Mist isn't the type to forget. He can take anything except a slam at his manhood."

"I can take care of myself."

"Honey . . . *no* dame can take care of herself, including you. Be careful, will you?"

She seemed to smile all over. "Worried, Mike?"

"Certainly."

"Love me?"

"Yeah," I said, "I love you, but I go for the way you are and not the way you could look if Mist started working you over." I grinned at her and slapped my hand down over hers. "Okay, I'm not the romantic type this early and in this place."

"I don't care."

She sat there, tall and straight, the black page-boy hair swirling around her shoulders like a waterfall at night with the moon glinting on it. Broad-shouldered, smooth and soft-looking, but firm underneath. She always had that hungry animal quality about her, eyes that drank everything in and when they looked at me seemed to drain me dry. Her mouth was expressive, with full, ripe lips that shone wetly, a crimson blossom that hid even white teeth.

I said it again and this time it sounded different and her fingers curled up over mine and squeezed.

A guy like me doesn't take the kind of look she was giving me very long. I shook my head, got my hand loose and went back to the report she had compiled.

"Let's not get off the track." Her laugh was a silent thing, but I knew she felt the same way I did. "We have three names here. What about the other three?"

Velda leaned across the table to see where I was pointing and I had to keep my eyes down. "Nicholas Raymond was an old flame apparently. She went with him before the war. He was killed in an auto accident."

It wasn't much, but to pick up details like that takes time. "Who said?"

"Pat. The police know that much about her."

"He's really going all out, isn't he?"

"The next one came from him too. Walter McGrath seemed to be another steady she was heavy on. He kept her for about a year during the war. She had an apartment on Riverside Drive then."

"He local?"

"No, from out of state, but he was in the city often."

"Business?"

"Lumber. Gray-market operations on steel too. He has a police record." She saw my eyebrows go up. "One income-tax evasion, two arrests for disorderly conduct, one conviction and suspended sentence for carrying concealed weapons."

"Where is he now?"

"He's been in the city here for about a month taking orders for lumber."

"Nice." She nodded agreement.

"Who's this Leopold Kawolsky?"

Velda frowned, her eyes turning a little darker. "I can't figure that one out. Eddie tapped him for me. Right after the war Berga was doing a number in a night club and when the place closed down there was a street brawl that seemed to center around her. This guy knocked off a couple of men giving her a hard time and a photog happened along who grabbed a pic for the front page of his tabloid. It was pure sensationalism, but the picture and the name stuck in Eddie's mind. The same thing happened about a month later and one of those kids who snap photos in the night clubs caught the action and submitted it for the usual pay-on-acceptance deals. That's how Eddie remembered who the girl was so well."

"The guy, honey . . . what about him?"

"I'm coming to him. From the pictures he looked like an ex-fighter. I called the sports editor of a magazine and he picked the name out for me. Kawolsky fought under the name Lee Kawolsky for a year and was looking pretty good until he broke his hand in training. After that he dropped out of the picture. Now, about a month and a half after the last public brawl Lee was hit by a truck and killed. Since there were two deaths by cars in the picture I went into the insurance records and went over them carefully. As far as I could tell, or anybody else for that matter, they were accidents, pure and simple."

"Pure and simple," I repeated. "The way it would have to look."

"I don't think so, Mike."

"Positive."

"Good enough."

I ran my eyes over the copy of the medical report, folded it before I finished it and tucked it back into the envelope. "Brief me on this thing," I said.

"There really isn't much. She appeared before Dr. Martin Soberin for an examination, he diagnosed her case as extreme nervousness and suggested a rest cure. They mutually agreed on the sanitarium she was admitted to, an examination there confirmed Dr. Soberin's diagnosis and that was that. She was to stay there approximately four weeks. She paid in advance for her treatment."

If ever there was a mess, this was it. Everything out of place and out of focus. The ends didn't even try to meet. Meet? Hell, they were snarled up so completely nothing made any sense.

"How about this Congressman Geyfey?"

"Nothing special. He was seen with her at a couple of political rallies. The man isn't married so he's clean that way. Frankly, I don't think he knew anything about her."

"This keeps getting worse."

"Don't get impatient. We're only getting started. What did Pat have to say about her?"

"It's all in writing. Probably the best parts they're not telling. Except for her connection with Evello she didn't seem to be out of the ordinary for a kid with her tastes. She was born in Pittsburgh in 1920. Her father was Swedish, her mother Italian. She made two trips to Europe, one when she was eight to Sweden, the next one in 1940 to Italy. The jobs she held didn't pay the kind of money she spent, but that's easy to arrange for a babe like that."

"Then Evello's the connection?"

"Evello's the one," I said. She looked at my face and her breathing seemed to get heavier. "He's here in New York. Pat'll give you the address."

"He's mine then?"

"Until I get around to him."

"What's the angle?"

"An approach. Better arrange for a regular introduction and let him do the rest. Find out who his friends are."

Only her eyes smiled. "Think I can pull it off?"

"You can't miss, baby, you can't miss."

The smile in her eyes got bigger.

"Where are you carrying the heater, kitten?"

The smile faded then. It got a little bit cold and deadly. "The shoulder rig. Left side and low down."

"Nobody'd ever notice, kitten."

"They're not supposed to," she said.

We finished eating and went back into the daylight. I watched her get into the cab the way she had got out and when the hack turned the corner I could feel the skin on my shoulder crawl thinking about where she was going. The next cab that came along I flagged down, gave him a Brooklyn address with instructions to stop by the Atlantic Avenue apartment first. The answer came fast enough when we reached the joint. The name was still on the wall but the neighbors said she had moved out during the night and the apartment was empty. A small truck with the trunks of a new customer started backing into the curb as we drove away.

The second Brooklyn address belonged to a newspaperman who had retired ten years ago. He was forty-nine years old but looked seventy. One side of his face had a scar that ran from the corner of his eye to his ear and down to his mouth. If he took off his shirt he could show you the three dimples in his stomach and the three larger angry pink scars in his back. One arm couldn't move at the elbow. He hadn't retired because he had wanted to. Seems like he had written an exposé about the Mafia one time.

When I came out it was two hours later and I had a folio of stuff under my arm that would have been worth ten grand to any good slick magazine. I got it free. I took another cab back uptown, sat in the back room of a drug store a buddy of mine ran, went through it twice, then wrapped it and mailed it back to the guy I got it from. I went into a bar and had a beer while the facts settled down in my mind. While I sat there I tried to keep from looking at myself in the mirror behind the back bar but it didn't work. My face wasn't pretty at all. Not at all. So I moved to a booth in the back that had no mirrors.

Evello's name was there. Billy Mist's name was there. In the very beginning. They were punks then but they showed promise. The guy in Brooklyn said you didn't pick up the connections any more because most likely the boys had new assignments. They had been promoted. That was a long time ago so by now they should be kings. There were other names that I didn't know, but before long I'd know. There were empty spaces where names should be but couldn't be supplied and those were in the throne room. Nobody knew who the royalty was. They couldn't even suspect.

Big? Sure, they were big. But then even the big ones would hear the word and their bigness would start to leak out all the holes. I was thinking about it and wondering if they had heard it yet when Mousie Basso came in.

Guys like Mousie you see around when there's not too much light and never see around when the heat's on. Guys like Mousie you see in the papers when the police pull in their dragnet at a time when there were no holes in the walls for them to duck into. In the faces of guys like Mousie you can tell the temperature of the underworld cauldron or read your popularity with the wrong people by the way they shy away or hang on to you.

From Mousie's face I knew I was hot.

I knew, too, I wasn't very popular.

Mousie took one look at me sitting there, shot a quick look at the door and would have been out if I hadn't been reaching inside my coat for a smoke at the time. Mousie got white past the point of being pale when he saw where my hand was and when I gave him the nod to come over, he didn't walk, he slunk.

I said, "Hello, Mousie," and the corner of his mouth made a fast, fake smile and he slid into the booth hoping nobody had seen him.

He grabbed a nervous cigarette that didn't do him a bit of good, shook out the match and flicked it under the table. "Look, Mr. Hammer, you and me ain't got a thing to talk about. I . . ."

"Maybe I like your company, Mousie."

His lips got tight and he tried hard to keep from watching my hands. Half under his breath he said, "You ain't good company to be seen with."

"Who says?"

"Lots of people. You're nuts, Mr. Hammer . . ." He waited to see what would happen and when nothing did, said, "you go blowing off your stack like you been doing and you'll be wearing a D.O.A. tag on your toe."

"I thought we were friends, kid." I bit into my sandwich and watched him squirm. Mousie wasn't happy. Not even a little bit.

"Okay, so you did me a favor. That doesn't make us that kind of buddies. If you want trouble you go find it by yourself. Me, I'm a peace-loving guy, I am."

"Yeah."

Mousie's face sagged under the sarcasm. "So I'm a chiseler. So what? I don't want shooting trouble. If I'm small potatoes that's all I want to be. Nobody gets bumped for being small potatoes."

"Unless somebody sees them talking to big potatoes," I grinned at him.

It scared him, right down to his shoes. "Don't . . . don't kid around with me, will you? You don't need me for nothing. Besides which if you do I ain't giving or selling. Lay off."

"What did you hear, Mousie?"

His eyes were quick things that swept the whole room twice before they came back to me. "You know."

"What?"

"You're going to scramble some people."

"What people." I didn't ask him. I told him to say it.

He whispered the word. "Mafia." Then as if it had been a key he swallowed he spilled over with the things he had been holding down while his eyes bulged in his head. His hands grabbed the edge of the table and hung on while the butt he had started to smoke burned through the tablecloth. "You're nuts. You went and got everybody hopped up. Wherever you go you'll be poison. Is it true you got something on the wheels? You better clam if you have. That kind of stuff is sure to lead to trouble. Charlie Max and Sugar . . ." The mouth stopped and stayed open.

"Say it, Mousie."

Maybe he didn't like the way I had edged forward. Maybe he saw the things that should have been written across my face.

The bulging eyes flattened out, sick. "They're spending advance money along the Stem."

"Moving fast?"

I could hardly hear his voice. "Covering the bars and making phone calls."

"Are they in a hurry?"

"Bonus, probably."

Mousie wasn't the same guy who came in. He was the mouse, but a mouse who didn't care any more. He was the mouse who spilled his guts to the cat about where the dog was and if the dog found out, he was dead. He reached for the remains of the cigarette, tried to drag some life into it and couldn't make it. I shook a new one out of my pack and handed it to him. The light I held out was steady, but he couldn't keep the tip of the butt in it. He got it going after a few seconds and stared into the flame of the lighter.

"You ain't scared a bit, are you?" He looked at his own hands, hating himself. "I wish I was that way. What makes a guy like me, Mr. Hammer?"

I could hate myself too. "Guys like me," I said.

The laugh came out his nose like he didn't believe me. "One guy," he said, "just one big guy and everybody gets hopped up. For anybody else, even the mayor, they wouldn't even blink, but for you they get hopped up. You say you're going to scramble and they make like a hillbilly feud. The word goes out and money starts passing hands. Two of the hottest rods in town combing the joints looking for you and you don't even get bothered enough to stop eating. They know you, Mr. Hammer. Guess maybe everybody knows something about you. That's why Charlie Max and Sugar Smallhouse got the job. They don't know nothing about you. They're Miami boys. You say you're going to do something, you do it and always there's somebody dead and it ain't you. Now the word has it you're going to scramble the top potatoes. Maybe you will and maybe you won't. With anybody else I'd take bets on your side, only this time it's different."

He stopped and waited to see what I'd say. "It's not so different."

"You'll find out."

He saw my teeth through the smile and shuddered. It does funny things to some people. "The world still goes," I said. "From now on to the end they'll have to stay away from windows and doors. They'll never be able to go out alone. Every one of the pack will have to keep a rod in his fist and wait. They'll have to double check everything to make sure I won't find out who they are and no matter how hard they try I'll reach them. Their office boys'll try to check me off but they're like flies on the wall. I'm going to the top. Straight up. I'm finding out who they are and when I do they're dead. I know how they operate . . . they're bad, but they know me and I'm worse. No matter where I find them, or when . . . any time, any place . . . that's it. The top dogs, those are the ones I want. The slime who pull the strings in the Mafia. The kings, you understand? I want them."

My grin got bigger all the time. "They've killed hundreds of people, see, but they finally killed the wrong dame. They tried to kill me and they wrecked my car. That last part I especially didn't like. That car was hand built and could do over a hundred. And for all of that a lot of those top dogs are paying through the kiester starting now. That's the word."

Mousie didn't say anything. He stood up slowly, his teeth holding his bottom lip to keep it up. He jerked his head in what was supposed to be a so long and slid out from behind the table. I watched him walk to the door, forgetting the sandwich that lay on top of the counter. He opened the door slowly, walked out to the sidewalk and turned east, not looking to either side of himself. When he had gone I got up myself, paid my bill and took the change to a phone booth.

Pat was home and still up. I said, "It's me, pal. Velda told me you heard the news."

He sounded a little far away. "You don't have much sense, do you?"

"They're looking for me. Two boys by the name of Charlie Max and Sugar Smallhouse."

"They have reps."

"So I hear. What kind?"

"Teamwork. Max is the one to watch. They're killers, but Smallhouse likes to do it slow."

"I'll watch Max then. What else?"

"Charlie Max is an ex-cop. He'll probably have a preference for a hip holster."

"Thanks."

"Don't mention it."

I slapped the receiver back on the hook. The dime plinked into the box and the gaping mouth of the thing laughed at me silently. Well, in a way it was a pretty big joke. The army of silent men couldn't stay silent. I didn't know them but they knew me. They were just like the rest: crumbs who knew how to play a one-sided game—but when they were playing somebody who could be twice as silent, twice as dirty and twice as quick they broke in the middle and started begging. Someplace in the city were people with names and some without names. They were organized. They had big money in back of them. They had political connections. They had everything it took to stay where they were except one thing and that was me with my own slab in a morgue. They knew what to expect from the cops and what to expect from the vast machine that squatted on the Potomac but they didn't know what to expect from me. Already one guy had told them, a punk with crooked yellow teeth who had had a gun on me and lost it. Then they'd ask around if they didn't already know and the stories they'd hear wouldn't be pretty. The fear they handed out so freely to others they'd taste themselves, knowing that before long, if I was still alive, they'd have to chew the whole lump and swallow it.

At the cigarette counter I picked up a fresh deck of Luckies, went out into the air and headed for the Stem. Out there were the hunters spending advance money. Cold boys with reps who didn't know the whole score. They knew the word was out and wanted to cut it off.

But they didn't hear the whole word. Before the night was over they'd hear a lot of things that might make them want to change their minds. One of the things was the rest of the word. They'd find out the hunters were being hunted.

Just for the fun of it.

CHAPTER 8

The *Globe* gave me the information on Nicholas Raymond. It was an old clipping that Ray Diker dragged out for me and which wouldn't have been printed at all if there hadn't been an editorial tie-up. The press was hot on hit-and-run drivers and used his case to point up their arguments about certain light conditions along the bridge approaches.

Nicholas Raymond got it as he stepped into the street as the light changed and his body was flung through a store window. Nobody saw the accident except a drunk halfway down the block and the car was never tracked down. The only details about him were that he was forty-two years old, a small-time importer and lived in an apartment hotel in the lower Fifties.

I told Ray Diker thanks and used his phone to call Raymond's old address. The manager told me in a thick accent that yes, he remembered Mr. Nick-o-las Raymondo, he was the fine man who always paid his bills and tipped like a gentleman extreme. It was too bad he should die. I agreed with him, poked around for some personal information and found that he was the kind nothing can be said about. Apparently he was clean.

Finding something on McGrath was easy. The papers carried the same stuff Velda had passed to me without adding anything to it. Ray made a couple calls downstairs and supplied the rest. Walter McGrath was a pretty frequent visitor to some of the gaudier night clubs around town and generally had a pretty chick in tow. A little persuasion and Ray managed to get his address. A big hotel on Madison Avenue. The guy was really living.

We sat there a few minutes and Ray asked, "Anything else?"

"Lee Kawolsky. Remember him?"

Ray didn't have to go to his files for that. "Good boy, Mike. It was a shame he couldn't follow through. Broke his hand in training and it never healed properly. He could have been a champ."

"What did he do for a living after that?"

"Let's see." Ray's face wrinkled in thought. "Seems like he bartended for Ed Rooney a bit, then he was doing a little training work with some of the other fighters. Wait a sec." He picked up the phone again, called Sports and listened for a minute to the droning voice on the other end. When he hung up he had a question in his eyes.

"What's the pitch, Mike?"

"Like what?"

His eyes sharpened a bit as they watched me. "Lee went to work for a private detective agency that specialized in supplying bodyguards for society brawls and stuff. One of his first assignments was sticking with a kid who was killed across the river a few days ago."

"Interesting," I said.

"Very. How about the story angle?"

"If I knew that I wouldn't be here now. How did he die?"

"It wasn't murder."

"Who says?"

He picked up a pipe, cradled it in his hand and began to scrape the bowl with a penknife. "Killers don't drive the same beer truck for ten years. They aren't married with five kids and don't break down and cry on the street when they've had their first accident."

"You got a good memory, kid."

"I was at the funeral, Mike. I was interested enough to find out what happened."

"Any witnesses?"

"Not a one."

I stood up and slapped my hat on. "Thanks for the stuff, Ray. If I get anything I'll let you know."

"Need any help?"

"Plenty. There's three names you can work on. Dig up anything good and I'll make it worth your while."

"All I want is an exclusive."

"Maybe you'll get one."

He grinned at me and stuck the pipe in his mouth. Ray wasn't much of a guy. He was little and skinny and tight as hell with a buck, but he could get places fast when he wanted to. I grinned back, waved and took the elevator to the street.

Dr. Martin Soberin had his office facing Central Park. It wasn't the world's best location, but it came close. It took in a corner, was blocked in white masonry with Venetian shuttered windows and a very discreet sign that announced his residency. The sign said he was in so I pushed open the door while the chimes inside toned my arrival.

Inside it was better than I thought it would be. There was a neat, precise air about the place that said here was a prominent medical man suited to the needs of the upper crust, yet certainly within the financial and confidential range of absolutely anybody. Books lined the walls, professional journals were neatly stacked on the table and the furniture had been chosen and arranged to put any patient at ease. I sat down, started to light a cigarette and stopped in the middle of it when the nurse walked in.

Some women are just pretty. Some are just beautiful. Some are just gorgeous. Some are like her. For a minute you think somebody slammed one to your belly then your breath comes back with a rush and you hope she doesn't move out of the light that makes a translucent screen out of the white nylon uniform.

But she does and she says hello and you feel all gone all over.

She's got light chestnut hair and her voice is just right. She's got eyes to go with the hair and they sweep over you and laugh because she knows how you feel. And only for a moment do the eyes show disappointment because somehow the cigarette gets lit as if she hadn't been there at all and the smoke from my mouth smooths out any expression I might have let show through.

"The doctor in?"

"Yes, but he's with a patient right now. He'll be finished shortly."

"I'll wait," I said.

"Would you care to step inside while I make out a card for you?"

I took a pull on the Lucky and let it out in a fast, steady stream. I stood up so I could look down at her, grinning a little bit. "Right now that would be the nicest thing I could think of, but I'm not exactly a patient."

She didn't change her expression. Her eyebrows went up slightly and she said, "Oh?"

"Let's say I'll pay the regular rates if it's necessary."

The eyebrows came down again. "I don't think that will be necessary." Her smile was a quick, friendly one. "Is there any way I can help you?"

I grinned bigger and the smile changed to a short laugh.

"Please," she said.

"How long will the doctor be?"

"Another half hour perhaps."

"Okay, then maybe you can do it. I'm an investigator. The name is Michael Hammer, if it means anything to you. Right now I'd like to get some information on a girl named Berga Torn. A short while back Dr. Soberin okayed her for a rest cure at a sanitarium."

"Yes. Yes, I remember her. Perhaps you'd better come inside after all."

Her smile was a challenge no man could put up with. She opened the door, walked into the light again and over to a desk in the corner. She turned around, saw me standing there in the doorway and smoothed out her skirt with a motion of her hands. I could hear the static jump all the way across the room and the fabric clung even closer than it had.

"You'd be surprised how fast a person decides he really isn't sick after all," she said.

"What about the women patients?"

"They get sicker." Her mouth pursed in a repressed laugh. "What are you thinking?"

I walked over to the desk and pulled up the straight-backed chair. "Why a dish like you takes a job like this."

"If you must know, fame and fortune." She pulled out a file case and began to thumb through the cards.

"Try it again," I said.

She looked up quickly. "Truly interested?"

I nodded.

"I studied to be a nurse right after high school. I graduated, and quite unfortunately, won a beauty contest before I could start practicing. A week later I was in Hollywood sitting on my . . . sitting around posing for stills and nothing more. Six months later I was car-hopping at a drive-in diner and it took me another year to get wise. So I came home and became a nurse."

"So you were a lousy actress?"

She smiled and shook her head.

"It couldn't have been that you didn't have a figure after all?"

Her cheeks sucked in poutingly and her eyes looked up at me with a you-should-know-better expression. "Funny enough," she said, "I wasn't photogenic. Imagine that?"

"No, I can't."

She sat up with three typewritten cards in her hand. "Thank you, Mr. Hammer." Her voice was a song of some hidden forest bird that made you stop whatever you were doing to listen. She laid the cards out in front of her, the smile fading away. "I believe this is what you came for. Now can I see your insurance credentials, and if you have your forms I'll . . ."

"I'm not an insurance investigator."

She gave me a quizzical look and automatically gathered the cards together. "Oh . . . I'm sorry. You know, of course, that this information is always confidential and . . ."

"The girl is dead. She was murdered."

She went to say something and stopped short. Then: "Police?"

I nodded and hoped she didn't say anything more.

"I see." Her teeth pinched her lower lip and she looked sideways at the door to her left. "If I remember I believe the doctor had another policeman in to see him not long ago."

"That's right. I'm following up on the case. I'd like to go over everything personally instead of from reports. If you'd rather wait for the doctor . . ."

"Oh, no, I think it will be all right. Shall I read these off to you?"

"Shoot."

"To be brief, she was in an extremely nervous condition. Overwork, apparently. She was hysterical here in the office and the doctor had to administer a sedative. Complete rest was the answer and the doctor arranged for her to be admitted to the sanitarium." Her eyebrows pulled together slightly. "Frankly, I can't possibly see what there is here to interest the police. There was no physical disorder except symptoms brought on by her mental condition."

"Could I see the cards?"

"Certainly." She handed them to me and leaned forward on the desk, thought better of it when my head turned, smiled and sat back again.

I didn't bother with the card she had read from. The first gave the patient's name, address, previous medical history and down at the bottom along the left side was the notation RECOMMENDED BY and next to it was the name William Wieton. The other card gave the diagnosis, suggested treatment and corroboration from the sanitarium that the diagnosis was correct.

I looked at the cards again, made a face at the complete lack of information they gave me, then handed them back.

"They help any?"

"Oh, you can never tell."

"Would you still like to see the doctor?"

"Not specially. Maybe I'll be back."

Something happened to her face. "Please do."

She didn't get up this time. I walked to the door, looked back and she was sitting there with her chin in her hands watching me. "You ought to give Hollywood another try," I said.

"I meet more interesting people here," she told me. Then added, "Though it's hard to tell on such short acquaintance."

I winked, she winked back and I went out on the street.

Broadway had bloomed again. It was there in all its colorful glory, stretching wide-open arms to the sucker, crying out with a voice that was never still. I walked toward the lights trying to think, trying to put bits together and add pieces where the holes were.

I found a delicatessen, went in and had a sandwich. I came out and headed up Broadway, making the stops as I came to them. Two hours went by in a hurry and nothing had happened. No, I didn't stay on the Stem because nobody would be looking for me on the Stem. Later maybe, but not now.

So I got off the Stem and went east where the people talked different and dressed different and were my kind of people. They didn't have dough and they didn't have flash, but behind their eyes was the knowledge of the city and the way it thought and ran. They were people who were afraid of the monster that grew up around them and showed it, yet they couldn't help liking it.

I made my stops and worked my way down to the Twenties.

I had caught the looks, seen the nods and heard the whispers.

At any time now I could have picked the boys out of a line-up by sight from the descriptions that came to me in an undertone.

In one place something else was added. There were others to watch for too.

Two-thirty and I had missed them by ten minutes.

The next half hour and they seemed to have lost themselves.

I got back to the Stem before all of the joints started closing down. The cabbie dropped me on a corner and I started the rounds on foot. In two places they were glad to see me and in the third the bartender who had pushed a lot of them my way tried to shut the door in my face, mumbling excuses that he was through for the night. I wedged it open, shoved him back inside and leaned against it until it clicked shut.

"The boys were here, Andy?"

"Mike, I don't like this."

"I don't either. When?"

"About an hour ago."

"You know them?"

His head bobbed and he glanced past me out the side window. "They were pointed out to me."

"Sober?"

"Two drinks. They barely touched 'em." I waited while he looked past me again. "The little guy was nervous. Edgy. He wanted a drink but the other one squashed it."

Andy ran his hands down under his fat waistband to keep them still. "Mike . . . nobody's to say a word to you. This is rough stuff. Do you . . . well, sort of stay clear of here until things blow over."

"Nothing's blowing over, friend. I want you to pass it around where it'll get heard. Tell the boys to stay put. I'll find them. They don't have to go looking for me any more."

"Jeepers, Mike."

"Tell it where it'll get heard."

My fingers found the door and pulled it open. The street outside was empty and a cop was standing on the corner. A squad car went by and he saluted it. Two drunks turned the corner behind his back and mimicked him with thumbs to their noses.

I turned my key in the lock. I knew the chain should be on so I opened the door a couple of inches and said, "It's me, Lily."

There was no sound at first, then only that of a deeply drawn breath being let out slowly. The light from the corner lamp was on, giving the room an empty appearance. She drifted into it silently and the glow from her hair seemed to brighten it a little.

Something was tight and strange in the smile she gave me through the opening in the door. Strange, faraway, curious. Something I couldn't put my finger on. It was there, then it was gone and she had the door unhooked and I stepped inside.

It was my turn to haul in my breath. She stood there almost breathlessly, looking up at me. "Her mouth was partly open and I could see her tongue working behind her teeth. For some reason her eyes seemed to float there, two separate dark wells that could knead your flesh until it crawled.

Then she smiled, and the light that gilded her hair made shadows across the flat of her stomach and I could see the lush contours harden with an eager anticipation that was like her first expression . . . there, then suddenly gone like a frightened bird.

I said, "You didn't have to wait up."

"I . . . couldn't sleep."

"Anybody call?"

"Two. I didn't answer." Her fingers felt for the buttons on the robe, satisfied themselves that they were all there from her chin down to her knees, an unconscious gesture that must have been a habit. "Someone was here." The thought of it widened her eyes.

"Who?"

"They knocked. They tried the door." Her voice was almost a whisper. I could see the tremor in her chin and from someplace in the past I could feel the hate pounding into my head and my fingers wanted to squeeze something bad.

Her eyes drifted away from mine slowly. "How scared can a person get, Mike?" she asked. "How . . . scared?"

I reached out for her, took her face in my hands and tilted it up. Her eyes were warm and misty and her mouth a hungry animal that wanted to bite or be bitten, a questioning thing waiting to be tasted and I wanted to tell her she never had to be scared again. Not ever.

But I couldn't because my own mouth was too close and she pulled away with a short, frenzied jerk that had a touch of horror in it and she was out of reach.

It didn't last long. She smiled and I remembered her telling me I was a nice guy and nice guys have to be careful even when the lady has been around. Especially a lady who has just stepped out of the tub to open the door for you and had nothing to put on but a very sheer silk robe and you know what happens when those things get wet. The smile deepened and sparkled at me, then she drifted to the bedroom and the door closed.

I heard her moving around in there, heard her get into the bed, then I sat down in the chair facing the window and turned out the light. I switched the radio on to a late station, sitting there, seeing nothing at all, my mind miles away up in the mountains. I was coming around a curve and then there was that Viking girl standing there waving at me. She was in the beams of the lights, the tires shrieking to a stop, and she got closer and closer until there was no hope of stopping the car at all. She let out one final scream that had all the terror in the world in it and I could feel the sweat running down the back of my neck. Even when she was dead under the wheels the screaming didn't stop, then my eyes came open and my ears heard again and I picked up the phone and her cry stopped entirely.

I said a short hello into it, said it again and then a voice, a nice gentle voice asked me if this was Mike Hammer.

"That's right," I said. "Who's this?"

"It really doesn't matter, Mr. Hammer. I merely wanted to call your attention to the fact that as you go out today please notice the new car in front of your building. It belongs to you. The papers are on the seat and all you have to do is sign them and transfer your plates."

It was a long foul smell that seeped right through the receiver. "What's the rest of it, friend?"

The voice, the nice gentle voice, stopped purring and took on an insidious growl. "The rest of it is that we're sorry about your other car. Very sorry. It was too bad, but since things happened as they did, other things must change."

"Finish it."

"You can have the car, Mr. Hammer. I suggest that if you take it you use it to go on a long vacation. Say about three or four months?"

"If I don't?"

"Then leave it where it is. We'll see that it is returned to the buyer."

I laughed into the phone. I made it a mean, low kind of laugh that didn't need any words to go with it. I said. "Buddy . . . I'll take the car, but I won't take the vacation. Someday I'll take you too."

"However you wish."

I said. "That's the way it always is," but I was talking to a dead phone. The guy had hung up.

They were at me from both ends now. The boys walking around the Stem on a commission basis. One eye out for me, the other for the cops that Pat would have scouting. Now they were being generous.

Like Lily had said, how scared could a person get? They didn't like the way it was going at all. I sat there grinning at the darkness outside thinking about the big boys whose faces nobody knew. Maybe if I had boiled over like the old days they would have had me. The waiting they didn't go for.

I shook a Lucky out of the pack and lit it up. I smoked it down to the end, put it out, then went in and flopped down on the bed. The alarm was set for eight, too early even at that hour, but I set it back to seven and knew I'd be hating myself for it.

The heap was a beauty. It was a maroon Ford convertible with a black top and sat there gleaming in the early morning sunlight like a dew drop. Bob Gellie walked around it once, grinning into the chrome and came back and stood by me on the sidewalk.

"Some job, Mike. Got twin pipes in back." He wiped his hands on his cover-alls and waited to see what came next.

"She's gimmicked. Bob. Think you can reach it?"

"Come again?" He stared at me curiously.

"The job is a gift . . . from somebody who doesn't like me. They're hoping I step into it. Then goes the big boom. They're probably even smart enough to figure I'd put a mechanic on the job to find the gimmick so it'll be well hidden. Go ahead and dig it out."

He wiped the back of his hands across his mouth and shoved the hat back further on his head. "Best thing to do is run it in the river for a couple of hours."

"Hop to it, Bob, I need transportation."

"Look, for a hundred I can do a lot of things, but . . ."

"So I'll double it. Find the gimmick."

The two C's got him. For that many pieces of paper he could take his chances with a gallon of soup. He wiped his mouth clean again and nodded. The sun wasn't up over the apartments yet and it was still cool, but it didn't do much for the beads of sweat that started to shape up along Bob's forehead. I went down to a restaurant, filled up with breakfast, spent an hour looking in store windows and came back.

Bob was sitting behind the wheel looking thoughtful, the hood in front of him raised up like a kid with his thumb to his nose. He got out when he saw me, lit a cigarette and pointed to the engine. "She's hot, Mike. A real conversion."

I could see what he meant. The heads were finned aluminum jobs flanking dual carburetors and the headers that came off the manifold poked back in a graceful sweep.

"Wonder what she's like inside?"

"Probably complete. Think your old heap could take this baby?"

"I haven't even driven this one yet. Find the stuff?"

His mouth tightened and he looked around him once, fast. "Yeah. Six sticks wired to the ignition."

"It stinks."

"That's what I thought too," he told me. "Couldn't find a thing anyplace else though. Checked the whole assembly inside and out and if there's more of it the guy who placed it sure knew his business."

"He does, Bob. He's an expert at it."

I stood there while he finished his butt. He walked around the hood, got down under the car and poked around there, then came back and looked at the engine again.

Then his face changed, went back a half dozen years into the past, got tight, relaxed into a puzzled grin, then he looked at me and snorted. "Bet I got it, Mike."

"How much?"

"Another hundred?"

"You're on."

"I remember a booby trap they set on a Heinie general's car once. A real cutie." He grinned again. "Missed the general but got his driver a couple of days later."

He slid into the car, bent down under the dash and worked at something with his screwdriver. He got out looking satisfied, shoved his tools under the car and crawled in with them. The job took another twenty minutes and when he came out he was moving slowly, balancing something in his hand. It looked like a section of pipe cut lengthwise and from one end protruded a detonation cap.

"There she is," he said. "Nice, huh?"

"Yeah."

"Rigged to the speedometer. A few hundred miles from now a contact would have been made and you'd be dust. Had the thing wrapped around the top section of the muffler. What'll I do with it?"

"Drop it in the river, Bob. Keep the deal to yourself. Drop up to my place tonight and I'll write you a check."

He looked at the thing in his hand, shuddered and held it even tighter. "Er . . . if it doesn't mean anything to you, Mike . . . I'd like to have the dough now."

"I'm good for it. What're you worried . . ."

"I know, I know, but if anybody's after you this bad you might not live to tonight. Understand?"

I understood. I went up and wrote him out a check, gave him an extra buck for the cab fare to the river and got in the car. It wasn't a bad buy at all for three C's. And one buck. Then I started it up, felt good when I heard the low, throaty growl that poured out of the twin pipes and eased the shift into gear for the short haul north.

Pat had been wrong about Carl Evello being in the city. In one week he had gone through two addresses and the last was the best. Carl Evello lived in Yonkers, a very exclusive section of Yonkers.

At first the place seemed modest, then you noticed the meticulous care somebody gave the garden, and saw the Cadillac convertible and new Buick sedan that made love together in a garage that would have looked well as a wing on the Taj Mahal. The house must have gone to twenty rooms at the least and nothing was left out.

I rolled up the hard-topped driveway and stopped. From someplace behind the house I could hear the pleasant laughter of women and the faint strains of a radio. A man laughed and another joined him.

I cut the engine and climbed out, trying to decide whether I should crash the party or go through the regular channels. I started around the car when I heard tires turn into the driveway and while I stood there a light-green Merc drove up behind me, honked a short note of hello, revved up fast and stopped.

Beauty is a funny thing. Like all babies are beautiful no matter how they're shaped. Like how there are times when any woman is beautiful as long as she's the color you want. It's not something that only shows in a picture. It's a composite something that you can't quite describe, but can recognize the second you see it and that's the way this woman was.

Her hair was a pale brown ocean that swirled with motion and threw off the sunlight that bounced into it. She smiled at me, her mouth a gorgeous curve that had a peculiar attraction so that you almost missed the body that bore it. Her mouth was full and wet as if it had just been licked, a lush mouth with a will of its own and always hungry.

She walked up with a long stride, pressing against the breeze, smiling a little. And when she smiled her mouth twisted a bit in the corner with an even hungrier look and she said, "Hi. Going to the social?"

"I wasn't," I said. "Business. Now I'm sorry."

Her teeth came out from under the soft curves and the laugh filled her throat. For the barest second she gave me a critical glance, frowned with a mixture of perplexed curiosity and the smile got a shade bigger. "You're a little different, anyway," she said.

I didn't answer and she stuck out her hand. "Michael Friday."

I grinned back and took it. "Mike Hammer."

"Two Mikes."

"Looks like it. You'll have to change your name."

"Uh-uh. You do it."

"You were right the first time . . . I'm different. I tell, not get told."

Her hand squeezed in mine and the laugh blotted out all the sounds that were around us. "Then I'll stay Michael . . . for a time, anyway." I dropped her hand and she said, "Looking for Carl?"

"That's right."

"Well, whatever your business is, maybe I can help you out. The butler will tell you he isn't in so let's not ask him, okay?"

"Okay," I said.

This, I thought, is the way they should be. Friendly and uncomplicated. Let the good breeding show. Let it stick out all over for anybody to see. That was beauty. The kind that took your hand as if you were lovers and had known each other a lifetime, picking up a conversation as if you had merely been interrupted in one already started.

We took the flagstone path that led around the house through the beds of flowers, not hurrying a bit, but taking in the fresh loveliness of the place.

I handed her a cigarette, lit it, then did mine.

As she let the smoke filter through her lips she said, "What *is* your business, by the way? Do I introduce you as a friend or what?"

Her mouth was too close and too hungry looking. It wasn't trying to be that way. It just was, like a steak being grilled over an open fire when you're starved. I took a drag on my own butt and found her eyes. "I don't sell anything, Michael . . . not unless it's trouble. I could be wrong, but I doubt if I'll need much of an introduction to Carl."

"I don't understand."

"Sometime look up my history. Any paper will supply the dope."

I got looked at then like a prize specimen in a cage. "I think I will, Mike," she smiled, "but I don't think anything I find will surprise me." The smile went into that deep laugh again as we turned the corner of the building.

And there was Carl Evello.

He wasn't anything special. You could pass him on the street and figure him for a businessman, but nothing more. He was in his late forties, an average-looking joe starting to come out at the middle a bit but careful enough to dress right so it didn't show. He mixed drinks at a table shaded by a beach umbrella, laughing at the three girls who relaxed in steamer chairs around him.

The two men with him could have been other businessmen if you didn't know that one pulled the strings in a racket along the waterfront that made him a front-page item every few months.

The other one didn't peddle forced labor, hot merchandise or tailor-made misery, but his racket was just as dirty. He had an office in Washington somewhere and peddled influence. He shook hands with presidents and ex-cons alike and got rich on the proceeds of his introductions.

I would have felt better if the conversation had stopped when I walked over. Then I would have known. But nothing stopped. The girls smiled pleasantly and said hello. Carl studied me during the name swapping, his expression one of trying to recall an image of something that should have been familiar.

Then he said, "Hammer, Mike Hammer. Well, of course. Private detective, aren't you?"

"I was."

"Certainly. I've read about you quite often. Leave it to my sister to find someone unusual for an escort." He smiled broadly, his whole face beaming with pleasure. "I'd like you to meet Al Affia, Mr. Hammer. Mr. Affia is a business representative of a Brooklyn outfit."

The boy from the waterfront pulled his face into a crooked smile and stuck out his hand. I felt like whacking him in the mouth.

I said, "Hello," instead and laughed into his eyes like he was laughing in mine because we had met a long time ago and both knew it.

Leo Harmody didn't seem to do anything. His hand was sticky with sweat and a little too limp. He repeated my name once, nodded and went back to his girl.

Carl said, "Drink?"

"No thanks. If you got a few minutes I'd like to speak to you."

"Sure, sure."

"This isn't a social visit."

"Hell, hardly anybody comes to see me socially. Don't feel out of place. This a private talk?"

"Yeah."

"Let's go inside." He didn't bother to excuse himself. He picked up a fresh drink, nodded to me and started across the lawn toward the house. The two goons sitting on the steps got up respectfully, held the door open and followed us in.

The house was just what I expected it to be. A million bucks properly framed and hung. A fortune in good taste that didn't come from the mouth of a guy who started life on the outer fringe of a mob. We went through a long hall, stepped into a study dominated by a grand piano at one end and Carl waved me to a chair.

The two goons closed the door and stood with their backs to it. I said, "This is a private talk."

Carl waved unconcernedly. "They don't hear anything," then sipped his drink. Only his eyes showed over the lip of the glass. They were almond shaped and beady. They were the kind of eyes I had seen too many times before, hard little diamonds nestling in their soft cushions of fat.

I looked at the goons and one grinned, rising on his toes and rocking back and forth. Both of them had a bulge on the right hip that meant just one thing. They were loaded. "They still have ears."

"They still don't hear anything. Only what I want them to hear." His face beamed into a smile. "They're necessary luxuries, you might say. There seem to be people who constantly make demands on me, if you know what I mean."

"I know what you mean." I pulled a cigarette out and tapped thoughtfully against the arm of the chair. Then I let him watch me make a smile, turning a little so the two goons could see it too. "But they're not worth a damn, Carl, not a damn. I could kill you and the both of them before any one of you could get a rod in his fist."

Carl half rose and the big goon stopped rocking. For a second he stood that way and it looked like he'd try it. I let my smile tighten up at the edges and he didn't try it after all. Carl said, "Outside, boys."

They went outside.

"Now we can talk," I said.

"I don't like that kind of stuff, Mr. Hammer."

"Yeah. It spoils 'em. They know they're not the hot rods they're paid off for being. It's kind of funny when you think of it. Put a guy real close to dying and he changes. I mean real close. They're only tough because they're different from ordinary people. They have little consciences and nothing bothers them. They can shoot a guy and laugh because they know they probably won't get shot back at, but like I said, let 'em get real close to dying and they change. They found out something right away. I got a little conscience too."

All the time I was speaking he was half out of his chair. Now he slid back into it again and picked up his drink. "Your business, Mr. Hammer."

"A girl. Her name was Berga Torn."

His nostrils seemed to flare out a little. "I understand she died."

"Was killed."

"And your interest in it?"

"Let's not waste time, you and me," I said. "You can talk to me now or I can do it the hard way. Take your pick."

"Listen, Mr. Hammer . . ."

"Shut up. You listen. I want to hear you tell me about your connection with the dame. Nothing else. No crap. You play games with somebody else, but not me. I'm not the law, but plenty of times there were guys who wished the law was around instead of me."

It was hard to tell what he was thinking. His eyes seemed to harden, then melted into the smile that creased his mouth. "All right, Mr. Hammer, there's no need to get nasty about anything. I've told the police exactly what the score was and it isn't important enough to keep back from you if you're genuinely interested. Berga Torn was a girl I liked. For a while back there I . . . well, kept her, you might say."

"Why?"

"Don't be ridiculous. If you knew her then you know why."

"She didn't have much to offer that you couldn't get someplace else."

"She had enough. Now, what else is there?"

"Why did you break it off?"

"Because I felt like it. She was getting in my hair. I thought you had a reputation with women. You should know what it's like."

"I didn't know you checked up on me that close, Carl."

The eyes went hard again. "I thought we weren't playing games now."

I lit the cigarette I was fooling with, taking my time with that first drag. "How do you stand with the Mafia, Carl?"

He played it nice. Nothing showed at all, not even a little bit. "That's going pretty far."

"Yeah, I guess it is." I stuck the cigarette in my mouth and stood up. "But it's not nearly as far as it's going to go. I started for the door.

His glass hit the desk top and he came forward in his seat again. "You sure put up a big stink for a lot of small talk, Mr. Hammer."

I turned around and smiled at him, a nice dead kind of smile that had no laugh behind it and I could see him go tight from where I stood. I said, "I wasn't after talk, Carl. I wanted to see your face. I wanted to know it so I'd never forget it. Someday I'm going to watch it turn blue or maybe bleed to death. Your eyes'll get all wide and sticky and your tongue will hang out and I won't be making any mistake about it being the wrong joe. Think about it Carl, especially when you go to bed at night."

I turned the knob and opened the door.

The two boys were standing there. All they did was look at me and it wasn't with much affection. I was going to have to remember them too.

When I got back outside Michael Friday spotted me and waved. I didn't wave back so she came over, a mock frown across her face. I couldn't get my eyes off her mouth, even when she faked a pout. "Bum steer," she said, "no business?"

She looked like a kid, a very beautiful kid and all grown up where it counted, but with the grin and impishness of a kid nevertheless. And you don't get sore at kids. "I hear you're his sister."

"Not quite. We had the same mother but came from different hatches."

"Oh."

"Going to join the party?"

I looked over at the group still downing the drinks. "No thanks. I don't like the company."

"Neither do I for that matter. Let's both leave."

"Now you got something," I said.

We didn't even bother with good-bys. She just grabbed my arm and steered me around the building talking a blue streak about nothing at all. We made the front as a car was coming up the driveway and as I was opening the door of my new heap it stopped and a guy got out in a hurry, trotted around the side and opened the door.

I started wondering what the eminent Congressman Geyfey was doing up this way when he was supposed to be serving on a committee in Washington. Then I stopped wondering when he took the woman's arm and helped her out and Velda smiled politely in our direction a moment before going up the path.

Michael said, "Stunning, isn't she?"

"Very. Who is she?"

She stayed deadpan because she meant it. Her head moved slightly as she said, "I don't know. Most likely one of Bob's protégés. He seems to do very well for himself."

"He doesn't if he overlooked you."

Her laugh was quick and fresh. "Thank you, but he didn't overlook me, I overlooked him."

"Nice for me," I grinned. "What's a congressman doing with Carl? He may be your brother, but his reputation's got spots on it."

Her grin didn't fade a bit. "My brother certainly isn't the most ethical man I've known, but he is big business, and in case you haven't known about it, big business and government go hand in hand sometimes."

"Uh-uh. Not Carl's kind of business."

This time her frown wasn't put on. She studied me while she slid into the car and waited until I was behind the wheel. "Before Bob was elected he was Carl's lawyer. He handled some corporation account Carl had out West." She stopped and looked into my eyes. "It's wrong someplace, isn't it?"

"Frankly, Friday gal, it stinks."

I started the engine, sat and listened to it purr a minute then eased the gearshift in. All that power under the hood was dying to let go and I sat on it. I took the heap down the drive, rolled out to the street and swung toward the center of town. We didn't talk. We sat and rode for a while and watched the houses drift past. The sun was high overhead, a warm ball that smiled at the world, a big warm thing that made everything seem all right when everything was so damned wrong.

Pretty soon it would come. I thought about how she'd put it and how I'd answer it. It could come guarded, veiled or in a roundabout way, but it would come.

When it did come it was right out in the open and she asked, "What did you want with Carl?" Her voice sounded sleepy and relaxed. I glanced at her lying back there so lazily against the cushions, her hair spilling down the back of the seat. Her mouth was still a wet thing, deliciously red, firm, yet ready to vibrate like the strings on a fiddle the moment they were touched.

I answered her the same way she asked it; right out in the open. "He had a girl once. She's dead now and he may be involved in her murder. Your big-business brother may have a Mafia tie-up."

Her head rolled on the seat until she was looking at me. "And you?"

"When I get interested in people like your brother they usually wind up dead."

"Oh." That's all. Just "Oh" and she turned and looked out the window, staring straight ahead.

"You want me to take you back?"

"No."

"Want to talk about it?"

Her hand reached over and took the deck of Luckies from the seat beside me. She lit two at the same time and stuck one in my mouth. It tasted of lipstick, a nice taste. The kind that makes you want to taste it again, this time from the source.

"I'm surprised it took this long," she said. "He used to try to fool me, but now he doesn't bother. I've often wondered when it would happen." She breathed in deeply on the smoke, then watched it whip out the half-opened ventilator. "Do you mind if I cry a little bit?"

"Go ahead."

"Is it serious trouble?"

"You don't get more serious than killing somebody."

"But was it Carl?"

Her eyes were wet when they turned in my direction. "I don't know," I said.

"Then you're not sure?"

"That's right. But then again, I don't have to be sure."

"But . . . you're the police?"

"Nope. Not anybody. Just such an important nobody that a whole lot of people would like to see me knocked off. The only trouble is they can't make the grade."

I pulled the car to the curb, backed it into the slot in front of a gin mill and cut the engine. "You were talking about your brother."

She didn't look at me. She worked the cigarette down to a stub and flipped it into the gutter. "There isn't much to tell, really. I know what he's been and I know the people he's associated with. They aren't what you would call the best people, though he mixes with them too. Generally he has something they want."

"Ever hear of Berga Torn?"

"Yes, I remember her well. I thought Carl had quite a crush on her. He . . . kept her for a long time."

"Why did he dump her?"

"I . . . I don't know." There was a catch in her voice. "She was a peculiar sort of girl. All I remember is that they had an argument one night and Carl never bothered with her much after that. Somebody new came along."

"That all?"

Michael nodded.

"Ever hear of the Mafia?"

She nodded again. "Mike . . . Carl isn't . . . one of those people. I know he isn't."

"You wouldn't know about it if he was."

"And if he is?"

I shrugged. There was only one answer to a question like that.

Her fingers were a little unsteady when they picked up another cigarette. "Mike . . . I'd like to go back now."

I lit the butt for her and kicked the motor over. She sat there, smoked it out and had another. Never talking. Not seeming to do anything at all. Her bottom lip was puffed up from chewing on it and every few minutes her shoulders would twitch as she repressed a sob. I drove up to the gateway of the house, leaned across her and opened the door.

"Friday . . ."

"Yes, Mike?"

"If you think you know an answer to it . . . call me."

"All right, Mike." She started to get out, stopped and turned her head. "You looked like fun, Mike. For both of us, I'm honestly sorry."

Her mouth was too close and too soft to just look at. My fingers seemed to get caught in her hair and suddenly those lovely, wet lips were only inches away, and just as suddenly there was no distance at all.

The bubbling warmth was just what I expected. The fire and the cushiony softness and the vibrancy made a living bed of her mouth. I leaned into it, barely touched it and came away before there was too much hunger. The edges of her teeth showed in a faint smile and she touched my face with the tips of her fingers, then she climbed out of the car.

All the way back to Manhattan I could taste it. The warmth and the wetness and a tantalizing flavor.

The garage was filled so I parked at the curb, gassed up for an excuse to stay there and walked into the office. Bob Gellie was busy putting a distributor together, but he dropped it when I came in.

I said, "How did it go, kid?"

"Hi, Mike. You gave me a job, all right."

"Get it?"

"Yeah, I got it. I checked two dozen outlets before I found where those heads came from. A place out in Queens sold 'em. The rest of the stuff I couldn't get a line on at all. Most of it's done directly from California or Chicago."

"So?"

"They were ordered by phone and picked up and paid for by a messenger."

"Great."

"Want me to keep trying?"

"Never mind. Those boys have their own mechanics. What about the car?"

"Another cutie. It came out of the Bronx. The guy who bought it said it was a surprise for his partner. He paid cash. Like a jerk the dealer let him borrow his plates and it got driven down, the plates were taken off and handed back to the dealer again." He opened the drawer and slid an envelope across to me. "Here's your registration. I don't know how the hell they worked it but they did. Them guys left themselves wide open."

"Who bought the car?"

"Guess."

"Smith, Jones, Robinson. Who?"

"O'Brien. Clancy O'Brien. He was medium. Mr. Average Man. Nobody could describe him worth a hoot. You know the kind?"

"I know the kind. Okay, Bob, call it quits. It isn't worth pushing."

He nodded and squinted up his face at me. "Things pretty bad, Mike?"

"Not so bad they can't get worse."

"Gee."

I left him there fiddling with his distributor. Outside the traffic was thick and fast. Women with bundles were crowding the sidewalks and baby carriages were parked alongside the buildings.

Normal, I thought, a nice normal day. I hauled my heap away from the curb, cut back to Broadway and headed home. It took thirty minutes to get there, another thirty for a quick lunch at the corner and I went into the building fishing my keys out of my pocket.

Any other time I would have seen them. Any other time it would have been dark outside and light inside and my eyes wouldn't have been blanked out. Any other time I would have had a rod on me and it wouldn't have happened so easy. But this was now and not some other time.

They came out of the corners of the lobby, the two of them, each one with a long-nosed revolver in his fist and a yen to use it. They were bright boys who had been around a long time and who knew all the angles. I got in the elevator, leaned against the wall while they patted me down, turned around and faced the door as they pushed the LOBBY button instead of getting off, and walked out in front of them to my car.

Only the short one seemed surprised that I was clean. He didn't like it at all. He felt around the seat while his buddy kept his gun against my neck, then got in beside me.

You don't say much at a time like that. You wait and keep hoping for a break knowing that if it came at all it would be against you. You keep thinking that they wouldn't pop you out in broad daylight, but you don't move because you know they will. New York. This is New York. Something exciting happening every minute. After a while you get used to it and don't pay any attention to it. A gunshot, a backfire, who can tell the difference or who cares. A drunk and a dead man, they both look the same.

The boy next to me said, "Sit on your hands."

I sat on my hands. He reached over, found my keys in my pocket and started the car. "You're a sucker, mac," he said.

The one in the back said, "Shut up and drive." We pulled out into the street and his voice came again. This time it was closer to my ear. "I don't have to warn you about nothing, do I?"

The muzzle of the gun was a cold circle against my skin. "I know the score," I said.

"You only think you do," he told me.

CHAPTER 9

I could feel the sweat starting down the back of my neck. My insides were all bottled up tight. My hands got tired and I tried to slide them out and the side of the gun smashed into my head over my ear and I could feel the blood start its slow trickle downward to join the sweat.

The guy at the wheel threaded through Manhattan traffic, hit the Queens Midtown Tunnel and took the main drag out toward the airport. He did it all nice and easy so there wouldn't be any trouble along the way, deliberately driving slowly until I wanted to tell him to get it rolling and quit fooling around. They must have known how I felt because the guy in the back bored the rod into me every time I tightened up and laughed when he did it.

Overhead an occasional plane droned in for a landing and I thought we were going into the field. Instead he passed right by it, hit a stretch where no cars showed ahead and started to let the Ford out.

I said, "Where we going?"

"You'll find out."

The gun tapped my neck. "Too bad you took the car."

"You had a nice package under the hood for me."

The twitch on the wheel was so slight the car never moved, but I caught the motion. For a second even the pressure against my neck stopped.

"Like it?" the driver asked.

He shouldn't have licked his lips. They should have taught him better.

The pitch was right there in my lap and I swung on it hard. "It stunk. I figured the angle and had a mechanic pull it."

"Yeah?"

"So I punch the starter and blooie. It stunk."

This time his head came around and his eyes were little and black, eyes so packed with a crazy terror that they watered. His foot slammed into the brake and the tires screamed on the pavement.

It wasn't quite the way I wanted it but it was just as good. Buster in the back seat came pitching over my shoulder and I had his throat in my hands before he could do a thing about it. I saw the driver's gun come out as the car careened across the road and when it slapped the curbing the blast caught me in the face.

There wasn't any sense holding the guy's neck any more, not with the hole he had under his chin. I shoved as hard as I could, felt the driver trying to reach around the body to get at me while he spit out a string of curses that blended together in an incoherent babble.

I had to reach across the corpse to grab him and he slid down under the wheel still fighting, the rod in his hand. Then he had it out from the tangle of clothes and was getting up at me.

But by then it was too late. Much too late. I had my hand clamped over his, snapped it back and he screamed the same time the muzzle rocketed a bullet into his eyeball and in the second before he died the other eye that was still there glared at me balefully before it filmed over.

They happen fast, those things. They happen, yet time seems to drag by when there's only a matter of seconds and the first thing you wonder is why nobody has come up to see what was going on, then you look down the road and the car you saw in the distance when it all started still hasn't reached you yet, and although two kids across the street are pointing in your direction, nobody else is.

So I got in the driver's side, sat the two things next to me in an upright position and drove back the way we came. I found a cutoff near the airport, turned into it and followed the road until it became a one-lane drive and when I reached its limit there was a sign that read DEAD END.

I was real cute this time. I sat them both under the sign in a nice, natural position and drove back home. All the way back to the apartment I thought of the slobs who gave me credit for finding both gimmicks in the heap and then suddenly realized I was dumber than they figured and the big one was still there ready to go off any second.

Night had seeped in by the time I reached the apartment. I parked and went up to the apartment, opened the door enough to call in for her to take the chain off, but it wasn't necessary at all.

There was no chain.

There was no Lily either and I could feel that cold feeling crawl up my back again. I walked through the rooms to be sure, hoping I was wrong when I was right. She was gone and everything she owned was gone. There wasn't even a hairpin left to show that she had been there and I was so damned mad my eyes squinted almost shut and I was cursing them, the whole stinking pack of them under my breath, cursing the efficiency of their organization and the power they held in reserve, swearing at the way they were able to do things nobody else could do.

I grabbed the phone and dialed Pat's number. Headquarters told me he had left for the day and I put the call through to his apartment. He said hello and knew something was up the minute he heard my voice. "Lily Carver, Pat, you know her?"

"Carver? Damn, Mike . . ."

"I had her here at the apartment and she's gone."

"Where?"

"How am I supposed to know where! She didn't leave here by herself. Look . . ."

"Wait up, friend. You have some explaining to do. Did you know she had been investigated?"

"I know the whole story, that's why I pulled her out of Brooklyn. She had the city boys, the feds and another outfit on her back. The last bunch pulled a fast one today and got her out of here somehow."

"You stuck your neck out on that one."

"Ah, shut up," I said. "If you have a description, pass it around. She might know what it was the Torn kid was bumped for."

His breathing came in heavy over the receiver. "A pickup went out on her yesterday, Mike. As far as we knew she disappeared completely. I wish to hell you'd let me in on the deal."

"What have you got on her?" I asked him.

"Nothing. At least not now. A stoolie broke the news that she was to be fingered for a kill."

"Mafia?"

"It checks."

"Damn," I said.

"Yeah, I know how you feel." He paused, then, "I'll keep looking around. There's big trouble winding up, Mike."

"That's right."

"Stuff has been pouring in here."

"Like what?"

"Like more tough guys seen on the prowl. We picked up one on a Sullivan rap already."

I grunted. "That law finally did some good."

"The word is pretty strong. You know what?"

"What?"

"You keep getting mentioned in the wrong places."

"Yeah." I lit up a smoke and pulled in a deep drag. "This rumble strictly on the quiet between you and me?"

"I told you yes once."

"Good. Anybody find a pair of bodies propped up against a sign in Queens?"

He didn't say anything right away. Then he whispered huskily, "I should've figured it. I sure as blazes should've figured it."

"Well, just don't figure me for your boy. I checked my rod in a few days ago."

"How'd it happen?"

"It was real cute," I said. "Remind me to tell you someday."

"No wonder the boys are out for you."

"Yeah," I said, then I laughed and hung up.

Tonight there'd be more. Maybe a whole lot more.

I stood there and listened and outside the window there was another laugh. The city. The monster. It laughed back at me, but it was the kind of a laugh that didn't sound too sure of itself any more.

Then the phone jangled and the laugh became the muted hum once more as I said hello. The voice I half expected wasn't there. This one was low and soft and just a little bit sad. It said, "Mike?"

"Speaking."

"Michael Friday, Mike."

I could visualize her mouth making the words. A ripe, red mouth, moistly bright, close to the phone and close to mine. I didn't know what to answer her with, except, "Hi, where are you?"

"Downtown." She paused for a moment. "Mike . . . I'd like to see you again."

"Really?"

"Really."

"Why?"

"Maybe to talk, Mike. Would you mind?"

"At one time I would. Not any more."

Her smile must have had the same touch of sadness her voice had just then. "Perhaps I'm using that for an excuse."

"I'd like that better," I said.

"Will you see me then?"

"Just say where and when."

"Well . . . one of Carl's friends is giving a party this evening. I'm supposed to be there and if you don't mind . . . could we go together? We don't have to stay very long."

I thought about it a minute. I let a lot of things run through my mind, then I said, "Okay, I don't have anything else on the fire. I'll meet you in the Astor lobby at ten. How's that?"

"Fine, Mike. Shall I wear a red carnation or something so you'll know me?"

"No . . . just smile, kid. Your mouth is one thing I'll never forget."

"You've never really got close enough to tell."

"I can remember how I said good-by the last time."

"That isn't *really* close," she said as she hung up.

I looked at the phone when I put it down. It was black, symmetrical and efficient. Just to talk to somebody put a thousand little things into operation and the final force of it all culminated in a minor miracle. You never knew or thought about how it happened until it was all over. Black, symmetrical, efficient. It could be a picture of a hand outlined in ink. Their organization was the same and you never knew the details until it was too late.

That's when they'd like me to see the picture.

When it was too late.

How many tries were there now? The first one they spilled me over the cliff. Then there was laughing boy who kept his gun in his pocket. And don't forget the DEAD END sign. That one really must have scared them.

The jerks.

And someplace in the city were two others. Charlie Max and Sugar Smallhouse. For a couple of grand they'd fill a guy's belly with lead and laugh about it. They'd buck the biggest organization in the country because theirs was even bigger. They wouldn't give a damn where they scrammed to because wherever they went their protection went too. The name of the Mafia was magic. The color of cash was even bigger magic.

My lips peeled back over my teeth when I thought of them. Maybe now that they knew about the DEAD END sign they'd do a little drinking to calm themselves down. Maybe they'd be thinking if they really were good enough after all. Then they'd decide that they were and wait around until it happened and if it came out right in a penthouse somewhere, or in a crummy dive someplace else one of the kings would swallow hard and make other plans and begin to get curious about footsteps behind him and the people around him. Curiosity that would put knots in their stomach first, tiny lumps that would harden into balls of terror before too long.

Ten o'clock. It was still a few hours off.

Ten o'clock, an exquisite, desirable mouth. Eyes that tried to eat you. Ten o'clock Michael Friday, but I had another appointment first.

I started in the low Forties and picked the spots. They were short stops because I wasn't after a good time. I could tell when I was getting ripe by the sidewise looks that came my way. In one place they started to move away from me so I knew I was nearing the end. A little pigeon I knew shook his head just enough so I knew they weren't there and when his mouth pulled down in a tight smile I could tell he wasn't giving me much of a chance.

Nine-fifteen. I walked into Harvey Pullen's place in the Thirties. Harvey didn't want to serve me but I waited him out. He went for the tap and I shook my head and said, "Coke."

He poured it in a hurry, walked away and left me by the faded redhead to drink it. A plain-clothes man I recognized walked in, had a fast beer at the bar, took in the crowd through the back mirror, finished his butt and walked out. In a way I hoped he had spotted me, but if he did he was better at spotting than I was at keeping from being spotted.

She didn't move her mouth at all. Sometimes the things they pick up in stir pay off and this was one of them. She said, "Hammer, ain'tcha?"

"Uh-huh."

"Long John's place. They're settin' you up."

I sipped my Coke. "Why you?"

"Take a look, buster. Them creeps gimme the business a long time ago. I coulda had a career."

"Who saw them?"

"I just came from there."

"What else?"

"The little guy's a snowbird and he's hopped."

"Coppers?"

"Nobody. Just them. The gang in the dump ain't wise yet."

I laid the Coke down, swirled the ice around in the glass and rubbed out my cigarette. The redhead had a sawbuck on her lap when I left.

Long John's. The name over the door didn't say so, but that's what everybody called it. The bartender had a patch over one eye and a peg leg. No parrot.

A drunk sat on the curb puking into the gutter between his legs. The door was open and you could smell the beer and hear a pair of shrill voices. Background music supplied by a jukebox. Maybe a dozen were lined up at the bar talking loud and fast. The curses and filth sifted out of the conversation like minor highlights and the women's voices shrilled again.

The boys were pros playing it cute.

Sugar Smallhouse was sitting at the corner of the bar, his back facing the door so anybody coming in wouldn't recognize him.

Charlie Max was in the back corner facing the door so anybody coming in he'd recognize.

They played it cute but they didn't play it right and Charlie Max took time out to bend his head into the match he held up to light his cigarette and that's when I came in and stood behind his partner.

I said, "Hello, Sugar," and thought the glass he held would crumple under his fingers. The little hairs on the back of his neck went up straight like happens to a dog when he meets another dog, only on this mutt the skin under the hair happened to be a pale, pale yellow.

Sugar had heard the word. He had heard other people talk. He knew about the sign marked DEAD END and about me and how things hadn't happened as they were planned. I could feel the things churning through his head as I reached under his arm for a rod and all the while Sugar never moved a muscle. It was a little rod with a big bore. I flipped the shells out of the cylinder, dropped them in my pocket and put the gun back in its nest. Sugar didn't get it. He sweated until it soaked through the collar of his shirt but he still didn't get it.

Long John came up, saw me half hidden behind Sugar and said, "What'll it be, feller?" Then Sugar got it while Long John's eye got big and round. I had my hands around his middle in just the right spot, jerked hard and fast with my locked thumbs going into flesh under the breastbone like a kid snapping worms. Hard and fast . . . just once, and Sugar Smallhouse was another drunk who was sleeping it off at the bar.

And Charlie Max was a guy suddenly alive and sober coming up out of his chair trying to clear a gun from a hip holster to collect his bonus. Eternity took place right then in the space of about five seconds of screaming confusion. Somebody saw the gun and the scream triggered the action. Charlie's gun never got quite cleared because the dame beside him pushed too hard getting away and his chair caught him behind the knees. They were all over the joint, cursing, pushing, falling out of the way and fighting to make the door. Then the noise stopped and it was just a tableau of silent panic because the crowd was behind me and there was nothing more to do except stand there with fascinated terror as Charlie Max scrambled for his rod and I closed in with a couple of quick steps.

The gun was there in his fist, coming up and around as I brought my foot up and the things that were in Charlie's face splashed all over the floor. His face looked soft and squashy a second, became something not at all human and he tried once more with the gun.

Nobody heard that kick because his arm made too much noise.

Somehow his eyes were still there, swelling fast, yet still bright. They were eyes that should have been filled with excruciating pain, but horror pushed it out as he saw what was going to happen to him.

"The job was too big, buddy. Somebody should have told you how many guys I put on their backs with skulls split apart because they were gunning for me." I said it real easy and reached for the gun.

The voice behind me said, "Don't touch it, Hammer."

I looked up at the tall guy in the blue pin-striped suit, straightened and grunted my surprise. His face stayed the way it was. There were two more of them standing in the back of the room. One was trying to wake up Sugar Smallhouse. The other came forward, ran his hands over me, looked at his partner with a startled expression that was almost funny before giving me a stare that you might see coming from a kid watching a ballplayer hit a homer.

There wasn't a damn thing they could do and they knew it, so I turned around, walked back outside and started crosstown to the Astor.

Washington had finally showed up.

She was waiting there in a corner of the lobby. There were others who were waiting too and used the time just to watch her. Some had even taken up positions where they could move in if the one she was waiting for didn't show up. She wasn't wearing a red carnation, but she did smile and I could almost feel that mouth on me across the room.

Her hair was the same swirly mass that was as buoyant as she was. There aren't many words to describe a woman like Michael Friday as she was just then. You have to look at the covers of books and pick out the parts here and there that you like best, then put them all together and you have it. There was nothing slim about her. Maybe a sleekness like a well-fed, muscular cat, an athletic squareness to her shoulders, a sensual curve to her hips, an antagonizing play of motion across her stomach that seemed unconsciously deliberate. She stood there lazily, flexing one smoothly rounded leg that tightened the skirt across her thigh.

I grinned at her and she held out her hand. My own folded around it, stayed there and we walked out together. "Waiting long?" I asked her.

She squeezed my arm under hers. "Longer than I usually wait for anyone. Ten minutes."

"I hope I'm worth it."

"You aren't."

"But you can't help yourself," I finished.

Her elbow poked me. "How did you know?"

"I don't," I said. "I'm just bragging."

There wasn't any smile there now. "Damn you," she whispered. I could feel her go all tight against me, saw her do that trick with her tongue that left her mouth damp and waiting. I pulled my eyes away and opened the door of the cab that sat at the curb, helped her in and climbed in after her.

"Where to?"

She leaned forward, gave an address on Riverside Drive and eased back into the cushions.

It seemed to come slowly, the way sleep does when you're too tired, the gradual coming together of two people. Slow, then faster and all of a sudden her arms were around me and my hands were pressing into her back and my fingers curled in her hair. I looked at that mouth that wasn't just damp now, but wet and she said, "Mike, damn you," softly and I tasted the hunger in her until the fury of it was too much and I let her go.

Some shake and some cry, some even demand right then, but all she did was close her eyes, smile, open them again and relax beside me. I held out a cigarette, lit it for her, did mine and sat there without saying anything until the cab stopped by the building.

When we were in the lobby I said, "What are we supposed to be doing here, gal?"

"It's a party. Out-of-town friends of Carl and his business associates get together."

"I see. Where do you come in?"

"You might call me a greeter. I've always been the go-between for my big brother. You might say . . . he takes advantage of my good looks."

"It's an angle." I stopped her and nodded toward one of the love seats in the corner. She frowned, then went over and sat down. I parked next to her and turned out the light on the table beside me. "You said you wanted to talk. We'll never make it upstairs."

Her fingers made nervous little motions in her lap. "I know," she said softly. "It was about Carl."

"What about him?"

She looked at me appealingly. "Mike . . . I did what you told me to. I . . . found out all about you."

"So?"

"I . . . it's no use trying to be clever or anything. Carl is mixed up in something. I've always known that." She dropped her eyes to her hands, twining her fingers together. "A lot of people are . . . and it didn't seem to matter much, really. He has all sorts of important friends in government and business. They seem to know what he does so I never complained."

"You just took whatever he gave you without asking," I stated.

"That's right. Without asking."

"Sort of what you don't know won't hurt you."

Michael stared blankly at her lap for a few seconds. "Yes."

"Now you're worried."

"Yes."

"Why?"

The worry seemed to film her eyes over. "Because . . . before it was only legal things that gave him trouble. Carl . . . had lawyers for that. Good ones. They always took care of things." She laid her hand over mine. It shook a little. "You're different."

"Say it."

"I . . . can't."

"All right. You're a killer, Mike. You're dirty, nasty and you don't care how you do it as long as you do it. You've killed and you'll keep killing until you get killed yourself."

I said, "Just tell me one thing, kid. Are you afraid for me or Carl?"

"It isn't for you. Nothing will ever touch you." She said it with a touch of bitterness that was soft and sad at the same time.

I looked at her wonderingly. "You're not making sense now."

"Mike . . . look at me closely and you'll see. I . . . love Carl. He's always taken care of me. I love him, don't you see? If he's in trouble . . . there are other ways, but not you, Mike, not you. I . . . wouldn't want that."

I took my hand away gently, lit a cigarette and watched the smoke sift out into the room. Michael smiled crookedly as she watched me. "It happened fast, Mike," she said. "It sounds very bad and very inadequate. I'm a very lovely phony, you're thinking and I can't blame you a bit. No matter what I ever say, you'll never believe me. I could try to prove it but no matter how hard I tried or what I did, it would only make it look worse so I won't try any more at all. I'd just like to say this, Mike. I'm sorry it had to be this way. You . . . hit me awfully hard. It never happened to me before. Shall we go up now?"

I got up, let her take my arm and walked to the elevator. She hit the top button and stood there facing the door without speaking, but when I squeezed her arm her hand closed tighter around mine and she tossed her hair back to start the smile she'd have when we got out.

Carl's two boys were by the door in the foyer. They wore monkey suits and on them the term was absolutely descriptive. They started their smiling when they saw Michael and stopped when they saw me. You could see them exchange looks trying to figure the next move and they weren't up to it. We were through the door and a girl was taking my hat while they stood there watching us foolishly.

The place was packed. It was loud with laughs and conversation to the point where the music from the grand piano in the corner barely penetrated. Quiet little men with trays passed through the huddled groups handing out drinks and as heads turned to take them I could spot faces you see in the paper often. Some you saw in the movies too, and there were a few you heard making political speeches over the air.

Important people. So damn important you wondered about the company they kept because in each group were one or two not so important unless you looked at police records or knew what they did for a living.

There were hellos from a dozen different directions. Michael smiled, waved back and started to steer me toward the closest group. Leo Harmody was there in all of his self-assuming importance ready to introduce her to the others. I took my arm away and said, "You go to it, baby. I'll find the bar and get a drink."

She nodded, a trace of a frown shadowing the corner of her mouth.

So I went to the bar.

Where Affia was holding Velda's hand and Billy Mist was giving her a snow job while Carl Evello watched cheerfully.

Velda was good. She showed pleasant curiosity and smiled. Carl wasn't so good. He got a little white.

Billy Mist was even worse. He got color in his greasy face but most of it was deep red and his lips tightened so much his teeth showed. I said, "If you're wondering, Carl, your little sister invited me along."

"Oh?"

"Charming girl," I said. "You'd never know she was your sister."

Then I looked at Billy. I was hating his guts inside and out so hard I could hardly stand still. I looked him over real slow like I was trying to find a spot in the garbage pail for the latest load and said, "Hello, stupid."

They can't take it. You can tear their heart out with one word and they can't take it. Billy's face was something ready to blow up like a land-mine and he wasn't even thinking of the consequences. He was all alone in the room with me for that brief second and his hand tightened, got ready to grab something under his coat and right at the top of every-thing he felt I just stood there lazy-like and said, "Go ahead."

And he thought and thought about the dead men and watched his bubble bust wide open because his mind was telling him he'd never make it while he faced me and he got like Carl. White.

But I wasn't watching Billy Mist any more. I was watching Al Affia, plodding Al Affia who had the waterfront sewed up. Ignorant, thick-headed, slow Al who kept stroking Velda's hand all the while and who didn't turn color or go tight or do anything at all except say, "What's the matter with you guys?"

Velda repeated it. "What *is* the matter? After all . . ."

"Forget it, honey," Billy told her. "Just kidding around. You know how it is."

"Sure you know how it is," Al said.

I looked at the Brooklyn boy and watched him carve his face into a grin, muscle by muscle. Somebody should have mentioned Al's eyes to the boys. They weren't a bit stupid. They were small and close together, but they were bright with a lot of things nobody ever knew about. Someday they'd know.

"Nobody introduced me to the lady," I said.

Carl put his drink down on the bar, afraid to let go of it. "Hammer, I believe it is." He looked at me questioningly and I grinned. "Yes, Mike Hammer. This is Miss Lewis. Candy Lewis."

"Hello Candy," I said.

"Hello, Mike."

"Neat. Very neat. Model?"

"I do fashions for newspaper advertising."

Good mind, that secretary of mine. Nice and easy to explain to Billy how come she was shooting it with a couple of newshawks. I wondered how she had smoothed out his feelings.

She knew what I was thinking and went me one better. "What do you do, Mr. Hammer?"

They were watching me now. I said, "I hunt."

"Big game?"

"People," I said, and grinned at Billy Mist.

His nostrils seemed to flare out a little. "Interesting."

"You'll never know, chum. It gets to be real sport after a while." His mouth pressed together, a nasty smirk starting, "Like tonight. I got me two more. You ever hunt?"

His face wasn't red any more. It was calm and deadly. "Yeah, I hunt."

"We ought to try it together sometime. I'll show you a few tricks."

A low rumble came from Al's chest. "I'd like to see that," he laughed. "I sure would."

"Some people haven't got the guts for it," I told him. "It looks easy when you're always on the right side of a gun." I took them all in with one sweep of my eyes. "When you're on the wrong end it gives you the squirms. You know what I mean?"

Carl was on the verge of saying something. I would like to have heard it, but Leo Harmody came up, bowed himself into our little clique with a deep laugh and spoke to Velda. "Could I borrow you long enough to meet a friend of mine, my dear?"

"No, certainly not. You don't care, do you, Billy?"

"Go ahead. Bring her back," he told Leo. "We was talking."

She smiled at the four of us, got down off the stool and walked away. Billy wasn't looking at me when he said, "You better stay home nights from now on, wise guy."

I didn't look at him either. I kept watching Velda passing through the crowd. I said, "Any time, any place," and left them there together. A waiter came by with a tray, offered me a drink and I picked one up. It was a lousy drink but I threw it down anyway.

People kept saying hello just to be polite and I said hello back. I picked Michael out of the crowd and saw that she was looking around for me too. Just as I started toward her I heard a whispered, "Mike!"

I stood there, took another drink from a passing waiter and sipped it. Velda said, "Meet me on the corner in an hour. The drug store."

It was enough. I walked off, waved to Michael and waited while she made excuses to her friends.

Her smile looked tired, her face worried, but she swung across the room and held her hands out to me. "Enjoying yourself?"

"Oh, somewhat."

"I saw you talking to my brother."

"And friends. He sure has great friends."

"Is everything . . . all right?"

"For now."

She sucked her lip between her teeth and frowned. "Take me home, Mike."

"Not tonight, kid." Her face came up, hurt. "I've been read off," I said. "I'm unhealthier than ever to be seen with. When it happens I don't want you around."

"Carl?"

"He's part of it."

"And you think I am too."

"Michael, you're a nice kid. You're lovely as hell and you have everything to go with it. If you're trying to get something across to me I don't get it. Even if I did I wouldn't trust you a bit. I could go crazy nuts about you but I still wouldn't trust you. I told you a word the last time I saw you. It was Mafia. It's a word you don't speak right out because it means trouble. It's a word that has all the conniving and murder in the world behind it and as long as it touches you I'm not trusting you."

"You . . . didn't feel that way . . . when you kissed me."

There was no answer to it. I ran my hand along her cheek and squeezed her ear while I grinned at her. "A lot of things don't make much sense. They just happen."

"Will I see you again?"

"Maybe."

She walked to the door with me, said good-by and let her tongue run over her mouth slowly like she was enjoying the taste of something. I grabbed my hat and got out of there fast before she talked me into something I wasn't going to get talked into.

The two goons were still outside. There was something set in their faces and they didn't move when I went past them. When the elevator came up I stepped in, hit the button marked B and had a smoke on the way down. The door opened, I hit the main-floor buzzer as I got out and the elevator went back up a floor.

It wasn't hard to get out of there the back way. I went past the furnaces, angled around closed storerooms and found the door. There was a concrete yard in back bordered by a fence with a door that swung into the same arrangement on the other side. This time I met a young kid firing one of the furnaces, held out a bill as I went by and said, "Dames. You know how it is." He nodded wisely, speared the bill and went back to his work whistling.

I found the drug store and went in for a soda. They sold magazines up front so I brought one back with me while I waited. It was five minutes past the hour when Velda came in, saw me and slipped into the booth.

"You get around, Mike."

"I was thinking of saying the same to you. How come you tangled with Mist?"

"Later. Now listen, I haven't too much time. Earlier this evening two names came up. One of Carl's men turned in a report and I was close enough to hear it. The report was that somebody had double checked on Nicholas Raymond and Walter McGrath. Carl got all excited about it.

"At the time I was talking to Al and Billy and had my back to Carl. He sent the guy off, called Billy off and I could tell from Billy's face that he passed the news on to him. He looked like a dead fish when he came back to the bar with us. He was so mad his hands were shaking."

I said, "Did Affia get the news?"

"Most likely. I excused myself for a few minutes to give him a chance to pass it politely."

"I wonder about something, kitten."

"What?"

"I made a few phone calls."

"It sounded more important than that."

"Maybe Washington is getting hot."

"They'll have to get hotter," Velda grinned. "Billy said he had to talk a little business tonight." She reached in her handbag and brought out something. "He gave me a key to his apartment and told me to go ahead up and wait for him there."

I whistled between my teeth and picked the key out of her fingers. "Let's go then. This is hot."

"Not me, Mike. You go." There was a deadly seriousness about her face.

"What's the rest of it, Velda?"

"This is a duplicate key I dragged Carlo Barnes out of bed to make up for me. It took some fast and fancy working to get it so quickly."

"Yeah."

"Al Affia caught the pitch and invited me up to his place for awhile *before* I went to Billy's," Velda said softly.

"The lousy little . . ."

"Don't worry about it, Mike."

"I'm not. I'm just going to smash his face in for him, that's all." I sat there with my hands making fists and the hate pumping through my veins so hard it hurt.

Velda squeezed my hand and dumped a small aspirin bottle out of her bag and showed it to me. There weren't any pills in it, only a white powder. "Chloral," she said. "Don't worry."

I didn't like it. I knew what she figured to do and I didn't go for the play. "He's no tourist. The guy's been around."

"He's still a man."

My mouth felt dry. "He's a cagey guy."

Her elbow nudged her side meaningly. "I still have that, Mike."

You have to do things you don't want to do sometimes. You hate your-self for it but you still have to do it. I nodded, said, "Where's his place?"

"Not Brooklyn. He has a special little apartment under the name of Tony Todd on Forty-seventh between Eighth and Ninth Avenues." She pulled a note pad out, jotted down the number with the phone to go with it and handed it over. "Just in case, Mike."

I looked at it, memorized every detail there, then let the flame of my lighter wipe it out of existence. My beautiful, sleek animal was smiling at me, her eyes full of excitement and when you looked hard you could see the same thing there that you could see in mine. She stood up, winked and said, "Good hunting, Mike."

Then she was gone.

I gave her five minutes. I followed the shadows further uptown along the Drive to the building Billy Mist owned.

For the first time I was glad he was such a big man. He was so damn big he didn't have to stake anybody out around his place. He could relax in the luxury of security knowing that just one word could bring in an army if anybody tried to take the first step across the line.

It was another one of those things that came easy. You go in like you belonged there. You get on the elevator and nobody notices. You get off and go down the hall then stick the key in the lock and the door opens. You get treated to the best that money can buy even if the taste is crummy.

There were eight rooms in all. They were spotlessly clean and treated with all the care a well-paid maid could give them. I took forty-five minutes going through seven of them without finding one thing worth looking at until I came to the eighth.

It was a little room off the living room. At one time it must have been intended for a storeroom, but now it had a TV set, a tilt-back chair with an ottoman in place facing it, a desk and a bookcase loaded with pulps. Out of eight rooms here was the place where Billy Mist spent his solo time.

The desk was locked, but it didn't take more than a minute to get it open. Right in the middle section was a dimestore scrapbook fat with clippings and photos and he was in all of them. My greasy little friend was one hell of an egotist from the looks of the thumbmarks on the pages.

Another ten minutes went by going through the book and then I came to Berga's picture. There was no caption. It was just a rotogravure cutout and Billy was grinning at the camera. Berga was supposed to be background but she outsmiled Billy. Two pages later she came up again only this time she was with Carl Evello and it was Billy who was in the background talking to somebody hidden by Carl's back. I found two more like that, first with Billy, then with Carl, and topping it all was a close-up glossy of Berga at her best with *"love to my Handsome Man"* penned in white across the bottom.

Nothing else unless you wanted to count the medicine bottles in the pigeonholes. It looked like the cabinet in the bathroom. Billy must have had a pretty nervous stomach.

I closed the desk, locked it and wiped it clean. I went back to the living room, checked my watch and knew the time was getting close. I picked up the phone and dialed Pat's home number. Nobody answered so I called headquarters and that's where he was. It was a tired, disgusted Pat that said hello.

"Busy, Pat?"

"Yeah, up to my ears. Where have you been? I've been calling between your office and your house all night."

"If I told you you'd never believe it. What's up?"

"Plenty. Sugar Smallhouse talked."

I could feel the chills crawl up my legs until the hairs on the backs of my hands stood straight out.

"Give, Pat. What's the score?"

He lowered his voice deliberately and didn't sound like himself at all. "Sugar was on the deal when Berga got bumped. Charlie Max was called in on the job but didn't make it."

"Come on, come on. Who did he finger?"

"He didn't. The other faces were all new to him."

"Damn it," I exploded, "can't you get something out of him?"

"Not any more, pal. Nobody can. They were taking the two downtown to the D.A.'s and somebody chopped them."

"What're you talking about?"

"Sugar and Charlie are dead. One Federal man and one city cop are shot up pretty bad. They were sprayed by a tommy gun from the back seat of a passing car."

"Capone stuff. Hell, this isn't Prohibition. For Pete's sake, Pat, how big are these guys? How far can they go?"

"Pretty far, it looks like. Sugar gave us one hot lead to a person with a Miami residence. He's big, too."

I could taste something sour in my mouth. "Yeah," I said, "so now he'll be asked polite questions and whatever answers he gives will satisfy them. I'd like to talk to the guy. Just him and me and a leather-covered sap. I'd love to hear his answers."

"It doesn't work that way, Mike."

"For me it does. Any trace of the car?"

"Sure, we found it." He sounded very tired. "A stolen job and the gun was still in it. We traced it to a group heisted from an armory in Illinois. No prints. Nothing. The lab is working on other things."

"Great. A year from now we'll get the report. I'd like to do it my way."

"That's why I was calling you."

"Now what."

"That screwball play of yours with Sugar and Max. The feds are pretty sore about it."

"You know what to tell them," I said.

"I did. They don't want to waste time pulling you out of jams."

"Why, those apple heads! Who are they supposed to be kidding? They must have had a tail on me all night to run me down in that joint and they sure waited until it was finished before they came in to get their suits dirty."

"Mike . . ."

"Nuts to them, brother. They can stick their heads . . ."

"Shut up for a minute, will you!" Pat's voice was a low growl. "You didn't have a tail . . . those two hoods did. They lost the boys and didn't get picked up again until they reached Long John's."

"So what?"

"So they needed a charge to drag them in on. The boys caught the tail, ditched their rods someplace and when one of our plain-clothes men braced them they were clean. They had a second tail and didn't know it, but they didn't take any chances and pulled some pretty fancy footwork just in case. If they could have been pulled in on a Sullivan rap we would have squeezed something out of them. You didn't leave them in condition to talk."

"Tell 'em thanks," I grunted. "I don't like to be gunned for. I'll try not to break up their next play."

"Yeah," Pat said sourly.

"Anything on Carver yet?" I asked him.

"Not a thing. We have two freshly killed blondes, more or less. One's been in the river at least three days and the other was shot by an irate lover just tonight. They interest you?"

"Quit being funny." I looked at my watch. Time was getting too damn short. I said, "I'll buzz you if anything turns up, otherwise I'll see you in the morning."

"Okay. Where are you now?"

"In the apartment of a guy named Billy Mist and he's due in any second."

His breath made a sharp hissing sound over the phone as I hung up.

I had almost timed it too close. The elevator marker was climbing toward the floor when I reached it and just in case I stepped around the corner of the stairs, went up to the first landing and waited.

Billy Mist and a heavyset muscleman came off the elevator, opened the apartment door and went in. There wasn't anything I wanted to talk to him about so I took the stairs back down instead of the elevator and got out the front door in one piece.

I got halfway down the block when some elusive little thing flashed across my mind and my eyes twisted into a squint as I tried to catch it. Something little. Something trivial. Something in the apartment I should have noticed and didn't. Something that screamed out to be seen and I had passed it by. I tried to bring it into focus and it wouldn't come and after a minute or so it passed out of sight altogether.

I stood there on the corner waiting for the light and a taxi swung by. I had the briefest glimpse inside the back and I saw Velda sitting there with somebody else. I couldn't stop it and I couldn't chase it. I had to stand there and think about it until I was all mixed up and I wasn't going to feel right until I knew the score. An empty cab came along and I told him to take me down to Forty-seventh Street.

The house was in the middle of the block. It was a beat-up affair fifty years old bearing the scars only a neighborhood like that can give it. The doorbell position said Todd lived on the ground floor in back. I didn't have to do any ringing because the front door was open. The hall was littered with junk I had to push aside until I came to the door that had TODD written on the card in the square metal holder.

I didn't have to ring any bells here either. This door was open too. I shoved it open and the light streamed out around me, light that glistened off the fetid pools of vomit on the floor, shining even more ominously from the drops of blood between the pools. The blood was in the hall too, and the light picked it up. It made sticky sounds on the soles of my shoes.

With a rod in my hand I would have felt better. It's company that can do your talking for you and a voice they listen to. I missed the rod, but I went in anyway but on my toes ready to move if I had to.

Nothing happened.

But I saw what had happened.

The glasses were there on the table with a half-empty bottle of mixer and an almost empty fifth of whisky. Ice had melted in the bowl with a few small pieces floating on top of the water.

On the floor was the remains of a milk bottle and there was blood all over one piece. Velda had given him the chloral treatment and he went out, but somehow he had spilled it out of his system and made a play for her. He would have killed her if he could have but she got him with the milk bottle.

Then it hit me all at once and I felt like adding to the pools on the floor. She had gone about in her search, left for Billy's and Al snapped out of it. He didn't stay cold as she had expected him to and Al would have got the news to him by now.

I made a grab for the phone in the corner, spun the dial to Pat's number again and sweated until he answered. I said, "Listen fast, Pat and no questions. They got Velda. She went up to Billy Mist's place and walked into a trap. Get a squad car up there as fast as you can. Got that? Get her the hell out of there no matter what happens and be damn fast about it because they may be working her over." I shot my number to him and told him to call back as soon as word came through.

When I hung up I was cold with sweat and tasting the cotton in my mouth. I closed the door and hoped Al would come back so I could do things to him myself. I didn't move out of the room until I got impatient waiting for the phone to ring, then I prowled through the place.

There was a full cabinet of liquor I was going to try but the smell of it sickened me when I got the bottle near my mouth so I shoved it back again. *Damn it, I thought, why doesn't he call!*

I started a butt going, spit it out after a second drag and went around the place some more. To keep my mind still and the buzzing out of my ears I used my eyes and saw why Al kept the place at all. For what he wanted it was a pretty good base of operation. There were souvenirs all over the place. It was a sloppy hovel, but sloppiness was part of the setup and probably nobody complained.

Al must have even done a little work there when he was finished with his parties. There were work sheets and union reports spread out on the table and a batch of company check stubs in the drawer held together by a rubber band. Like a sap he left a pair of empty checkbooks in the same drawer and the hundred and fifty he made a week from the company wouldn't have backed up the withdrawals shown in the books.

So he had a sideline. He cheated the government most likely. Try to find whose name the checking account was in and there'd be fun.

The phone still didn't ring so I rolled a stack of blueprints that showed dock layouts. At least two of them did. Nine of the others were ships' plans that were blown up in detail until they centered around one mass of lines I couldn't make out. I threw them all back on the table and started to walk away as the phone rang.

I caught it before the ring was finished and Pat said, "You Mike?"

"Speaking."

"What're you pulling, kid?"

"Cut the funny stuff, Pat, what happened?"

"Nothing, except a pair of my men are highly squiffed off. Mist was in bed alone. He let the cops in, let them look around, then chewed the hell out of them for pulling a search. He made one phone call and I've been catching it ever since."

I wasn't hearing him. I laid the phone back on its rack and stared at it dumbly. It started to ring again. It went through the motions four times, then stopped.

Outside it had started to rain. It tapped the windows in the back of the room, cutting streaks through the dust. When I looked again the dust was gone completely and the window seemed to have a live wavy motion about it. I pulled the Luckies out of my pocket, lit one and watched the smoke. It floated lazily in the dead air, then slowly followed a draft that crossed the room.

I was thinking things that scared me.

My watch counted off the seconds and each tick was louder and more demanding, screaming not to be wasted.

I went back to the table, unfolded the blueprints, pushed the first two aside and looked at the legend on the bottom of the nine others.

The ship's name was there. Same ship. The name was *Cedric.*

It was starting to hang together now. When it was too late it was starting to hang together.

They wouldn't kill her yet, I thought. They'd do a lot of things, but they wouldn't kill her until they were sure. They couldn't afford the chance.

Then when they were sure they'd kill her.

CHAPTER 10

I slept hard. The rain on the windows kept me asleep and I went through the morning and the rest of the day with all the things I pictured going through my mind and when they came together in one final, horrible ending I woke up. It was nearly six in the evening but I felt better. Time was too important to waste but I couldn't afford to let it pass while I was half out on my feet.

There was a box of frozen shrimp in the refrigerator I put on the fire and while it cooked up I put through a call. It took two more to locate Ray Diker and his voice sounded as sharp and pinched as his face. He said, "Glad you called, Mike. I was going to buzz you."

"Got something?"

"Maybe. I followed up on Kawolsky. The office he worked for pulled out the records and I got the details. He was hired to cover the Torn kid. She complained that someone was following her and she was a pretty scared baby. She paid the fee in cash and they put Lee on permanent duty. He picked her up in the morning and took her home at night."

"You told me that already, Ray."

"I know, but here's the good part. Lee Kawolsky quit reporting to the office in person after a week of it. He started checking in by phone. The office got ideas about it and put another man outside the apartment and found out Lee was pulling a voluntary twenty-four-hour duty. He was staying with the dame all the time."

"The office complain?"

"What for? It was his business and if she wanted it that way why sound off on it. Her checks still rolled in."

"Did they leave it that way?"

"There wasn't much they could do. The report the other investigator sent in said Lee was doing a fairly serious job of bodyguarding. He had already got into a couple of scrapes over her and she seemed to like it."

It was another thread being woven into place. The rope was getting longer and stronger.

Ray said, "You still there?"

"I'm still here."

"What did you call me for then?"

"The driver of the truck who killed Lee. Got that too?"

"Sure. Harvey Wallace. He lives upstairs over Pascale's saloon on Canal Street. You know where the place is."

"I know," I said.

"Might have something here on Nick Raymond."

"What?"

"He retailed imported tobacco through a concern in Italy. He had his name changed from Raymondo to Raymond before the war. Made a few trips back and forth every year. One of his old customers I ran down said he didn't look like much, but he spent the winters in Miami and dropped a wad of cabbage at the tables there. He was quite a ladies' man too."

"Okay, Ray. Thanks a lot."

"Got a story yet?"

"Not yet. I'll tell you when."

I hung up and turned the shrimp over in the pan. When they were done I ate, finished my coffee and got dressed.

Just as I was going out the front-door buzzer went off and when I opened it the super was standing there with his face twisted up into one big worry and he said, "You better come downstairs, Mr. Hammer."

Whatever it was he didn't want to speak about in the hall and I didn't ask him. I followed him down, got into his apartment and he motioned with his thumb and said, "In there."

She was sitting on the couch with the super's wife wiping the tears away from her face, filthy dirty and her clothes torn and dust streaked.

I said, "Lily!" and she looked up. Her eyes were red things that stared back at me like a rabbit cornered in its hole.

"You know her, Mr. Hammer?"

"Hell yes, I know her." I sat on the couch beside her and felt her hair. It was greasy with dirt, its luster completely gone. "What happened, kid?"

The eyes filled with tears again and her breath came in short, jerky sobs.

"Let her alone a little bit, Mr. Hammer. She'll be all right."

"Where'd you find her?"

"In the cellar. She was holed up in one of the bins. I never would've seen her if I didn't see the milk bottles. First-floor tenants were squawking about somebody stealing their milk. I seen those two bottles and looked inside the bin and there she was. She said to call you."

I took her hand and squeezed it in mine. "You all right? You hurt or anything?"

She licked her lips, sobbed again and shook her head slowly.

The super's wife said, "She's just scared. Supposing I get her cleaned up and into some fresh clothes. She had a bag with her."

White outlined the red of Lily's eyes. She pulled back, her face tight. "No . . . I . . . I'm all right. Let me alone, please let me alone!" Then there was something fierce about the way she looked at me and bit out, "Mike . . . take me with you. Please. Take me with you!"

"She in trouble, Mr. Hammer?"

I looked at him steadily. "Not the kind of trouble you know about."

He saw what I meant, spoke rapidly to his wife in that language of his and her wise little eyes agreed.

"Help me get her upstairs."

The super took her bag, hooked one arm under hers and she came up from the couch. We used the service elevator in the rear, made my floor without meeting anybody and got her inside the apartment.

He said. "Anything I can do to help, just let me know."

"Right. Clam up about this. Tell your wife the same."

"Sure, Mr. Hammer."

"One other thing. Get me a damn big barrel bolt and slap it on my door."

"First thing tomorrow." He closed the door and I locked it after him.

She sat there in the chair like a kid waiting to be slapped. Her face was drawn and the eyes in it were as big as saucers. I fixed her a drink, made her take it all and filled it up again.

"Feel better?"

"A . . . little."

"Want to talk?"

Her teeth were a startling contrast to her skin when she bit her lip and nodded.

"From the beginning," I said.

"They came back," she said. Her voice was so low I could barely hear it. "They tried the door and one of them did something with the lock.

It . . . opened. I sat there and I couldn't even scream. I couldn't move. The . . . the chain on the door stopped them." A shudder went through her whole body.

"They were arguing in whispers outside about the chain, then they closed the door and went away. One of them said they'd need a saw. I . . . couldn't stay here, Mike. I was terrified. I threw my clothes in the bag and ran out but when I got to the street I was afraid they might still be watching and I went down the cellar! Mike . . . I'm . . . I'm sorry."

"That's all right, Lily. I know how it is. Did you see them?"

"No. No, Mike."

The shudder racked her body again and she bit into her finger.

"When . . . that man found me . . . I thought he was . . . one of them."

"You don't have to worry any more, Lily. I'm not going to leave you here alone again. Look, go in and clean up. Take a nice hot bath and fix your hair. Then get something in your stomach."

"Mike . . . are you . . . going out?"

"For a little while. I'll have the super's wife stay with you until I get back. Would you mind that?"

"You'll hurry back?"

I nodded that I would and picked up the phone. The super's wife said she'd be more than glad to help out and would come right up.

From in back of me Lily said, "I'm so dirty. Ask her to bring some rubbing alcohol, Mike."

She said she'd do that too and hung up. Lily had finished her drink and lay with her head against the back of the chair watching me sleepily. The tautness had left her cheeks and color had come back to her mouth. She looked like a dog who had just been lost in the swamp then suddenly found his way home.

I started the water in the tub, filled it and lifted her out of the chair. She was light in my arms, completely relaxed, her breathing soft against my face. There was something too big in her eyes while she was so close to me and the strain of it showed in the corner of her mouth. She dug her fingers into my arms with a repressed hunger of a sort, sucked in her breath in a series of almost soundless staccato jerks and before I could kiss her she twisted her head and buried it against my shoulder.

The super's wife came in while she was still splashing around in the tub. She made clucking noises like a mother hen and wanted to go right to her, but the door was locked so she started scrounging some chow up in the kitchen. The bottle of alcohol was on the table and before I left I knocked on the door.

"You want a rub-down, Lily?"

The water stopped splashing.

"Glad to give you a hand if you want," I said.

She laughed from inside and I felt better. I left the bottle by the door, told the mother hen I was leaving and got out.

Seven thirty-two. The gray overcast brought a premature dusk to the city, a gloomy wet shroud that came down and poured itself inside your clothes. It was the kind of night that made the city withdraw into itself, leaving the sidewalks empty and people inside the glass-fronted stores staring aimlessly into the wet.

I left my car where it was and hopped a cab down to Canal. He let me out at Pascale's and I went in the door on the right of the place. Here the hall was clean, clear and well lit. You could hear the hum of voices from the gin mill through the walls, but it diminished as I went up the stairs.

She was a short woman, her hair neatly in place and a ready smile that said hello.

"Mrs. Wallace?"

"Yes."

"My name is Hammer. I'd like to talk to your husband if he's home."

"Certainly. Won't you come in?"

She stepped aside, closed the door and called out, "Harv, there's a gentleman here to see you."

From inside a paper rustled and kids' voices piped up. He said something to them and they quieted down. He came out to the kitchen with that expression one stranger has for another stranger, nodded to his wife, then to me and stuck out his hand.

"Mr. Hammer," his wife said and smiled again. "I'll go in with the children if you'll excuse me."

"Sit down, Mr. Hammer." He pulled a chair out by the table, waved me into it and took one himself. He was one of those big guys with beefy shoulders and thinning hair. There was Irish in his face and a trace of Scandinavian.

"This'll be quick," I told him. "I'm an investigator. I'm not digging up anything unpleasant just for the fun of it and what you say won't go any further."

His tongue rolled around his cheek and he nodded.

"Sometime ago you drove the truck that killed a man named Lee Kawolsky."

The side of his face moved.

"I explained . . ."

"You don't get the angle yet," I said. "Wait. As far as you were concerned it was an out-and-out accident. Your first. It was one of those things that couldn't be helped so you weren't touched for it."

"That's right."

"Okay. Like I said, it's been a long time since it happened. Nobody else but you saw it. Tell me, have you ever gone over the thing in your mind since?"

Harvey said very quietly, "Mr. Hammer . . . there are some nights when I never get to sleep at all."

"You could see the thing happen. Sometimes the details would be sharp, then they'd fade?"

He squinted his eyes at me. "Something like that."

"What are you uncertain about?"

"You know something, Mr. Hammer?"

"Maybe."

This time he leaned forward, his face set in a puzzled grimace. "It's not clear. I see the guy coming out from behind the L pillar and I'm yelling at him while I slam on the brakes. The load in the truck lets go and rams the wall back of the cab and I can feel the wheels . . ." He stopped and looked down at his hands. "He came out too fast. He didn't come out walking."

Harvey looked at me, his eyes beseeching. "You know what I mean? I'm not making up excuses."

"I know," I said.

"I came out of the cab fast and he was under the axle. I know I yelled for somebody to help me. Sometimes . . . I think I remember a guy running. Away, though. Sometimes I think I remember that and I can't be sure."

I stood up and put my hat on. "You can stop worrying then. It wasn't an accident." His eyes came wide open. "It was murder. Kawolsky was pushed. You were the sucker."

I opened a door, waved a finger at him. "Thanks for the help."

"Thank . . . you, Mr. Hammer."

"It's over with so there's no use fooling with the report," I said.

"No . . . but it's good to know. I won't be waking up in the middle of the night any more now."

Ten minutes after nine. In the lobby of the hotel a row of empty telephone booths gaped at me. Two people were sitting in the far corner holding hands. One other, not looking as though he belonged there, was reading the paper and dripping water all over the floor.

The girl at the magazine counter changed a buck into dimes for me and I took the end booth on the row.

Thirty cents got me my party. His voice was deep and fat and it never sounded right coming out of the skinny little neck. He'd need a shave and his suit pressed but he didn't give a damn for either. He was strictly a nobody up until the squash was put on bookie operations then all of a sudden he was a somebody. He had a mind like a recording machine and was making hay in the new deal of black-market betting operations.

"I said, "Dave?""

"Right here."

"Mike Hammer."

The voice got closer to the phone and almost too casual. I could see him with his hand cupped around the mouthpiece and his eyes watching everybody in the place. "Sure, boy, whatcha doin'?"

"They're saying things along the row, Dave?"

"Piling up, big boy. Everybody got it."

"How do you feel about it?"

"Come on, mister, you know better'n that." The meaning sifted out of his words and I grinned. There was no humor in the grin.

I said, "I got what they want, kid. You tell it in the right places."

"You're killing me. Try again."

"So you saw me. I was in the bag and let it slip."

His voice dropped an octave. "Look, I'll do a lot of things, but you don't mess with them monkeys. They make a guy talk. Me, I got a big mouth when I get hurt up."

"It'll set, Dave. This is a big one. If it was a little one I'd ask some-body else. They got Velda. Understand that?"

He said three sharp, nasty curses at the same time. "You're trading."

"I'm willing. If it don't come off I'll blow the thing apart."

"Okay, Mike. I'll spin it. Don't bother calling me again, okay?"

"Okay," I said and hung up.

I walked over to the desk and the clerk smiled, "Room, sir?"

"Not now, thanks. I'd like to see the manager."

"I'm afraid you can't. He's gone for the evening. You see . . ."

"He live here?"

"Why, er . . . why, yes, but . . ."

I let a bill do the talking. The guy was well-dressed but underpaid and the ten looked big. "No trouble. I have to speak to him. He won't know."

The bill left my fingers magically. "Suite 101." He pointed a long forefinger across the room. "Take the stairs past the mezzanine. It's quicker."

There was a buzzer beside the door. I leaned on it until I heard the knob turn and a middle-aged, sensitive Latin face was peering out at me. The professional smile creased his lower jaw pulling the thin mustache tighter and he cocked his head in an attentive attitude ready to hear my complaint. His eyes were telling me that he trusted it would be a good one because Mr. Carmen Trivago was preparing to leave in a moment for a very important engagement.

I gave him a shove that wiped the smile clean off his face and he stumbled back inside while I closed the door. There was an instantaneous flash of mingled terror and hatred in his expression that dissolved into indignation as he drew himself up stiffly and said, "What is the meaning of this?"

"Get back inside."

"I . . ."

My hand cracked him across the mouth so hard he hit the wall, flattened against it making unintelligible noises in his throat. He wasn't so stiff when I gave him a shove into the living room. He was all loose and jelly-like as if his bolts were ready to come apart.

I said, "Turn around and look at me." He did. "I'm going to ask you things and you answer them right. If you think you'd do better by lying look at my face and you won't lie. Let me catch you in one and I'll mangle you so damn bad you won't even crawl out of this dump for a month. Just for the hell of it I ought to do something to you now so you know I'm not kidding about it."

Carmen Trivago couldn't stand up any more. His knees went as watery as his eyes and he slumped crookedly on the edge of a chair.

"No . . . don't . . ."

"His right name was Nicholas Raymondo. With an 'O.' You were the only one who knew that. I thought it was your accent, but you knew his name, didn't you?"

His mouth opened to speak but the words wouldn't come out. He nodded dumbly.

"Where'd he get his dough?"

The spread of his hands said he didn't know and before he could shake his head to go with it I rocked him with another open-handed slap that left the prints of my fingers across his jaw.

He couldn't take anything at all and tried to burrow into the chair while he moaned, "Please. No . . . I'll tell you . . . anything. Please."

"When, then?"

"He had . . . the business. From abroad he . . ."

"I know about that. Business didn't give him the kind of money he spent."

"Yes, yes. It is true. But he never said. He spoke of big things but he never said . . ."

"He liked dames."

Carmen's eyes told me he didn't get what I was driving at.

I said slowly, "So do you. Two of a kind, you guys. Lady killers. You knew his right name. Those things only come when you know a person. You know that much and you know a lot more. Think about it. I'll give you a minute. Just one."

His neck seemed to stretch out of shape as he held his head up. The longer he looked at me the more he curled up inside and his mouth started to move. "It is true . . . he had the money. It was enough. He was . . . satisfied to spend it all on much foolishness. There would be more soon, he told me, much more. At first . . . I thought he was making a boast. But no. He was serious. Never would he tell me more than that."

I took a slow step a little closer to him.

His hands went up to hold me off. "It is true, I swear it! This other money . . . several times when he was feeling, how you say it, high? he would ask me how I would like to have two million dollars. It was always the same. Two million dollars. I would ask how to get it and would smile. Raymondo . . . he had it, I know he had it. I tell you, this money was no good. I knew it would happen someday. I knew . . ."

"How?"

This time his eyes made passes around me, looking for something that wasn't there yet. "Before he . . . died . . . there were men. I knew of these men."

"Say the word."

It almost stuck in his throat, but he managed it. "Mafia," he said hoarsely.

"Did Raymondo know he was being followed?"

"I do not think so."

"You didn't tell him?"

He looked at me as if I was crazy.

"You never thought he was killed accidentally either, did you?" The fear showed in his face so plain it was a voice by itself. "You knew the score right along," I said.

"Please . . ."

"You're a crummy little bastard, Trivago. There's a lot of dead people lying around because you made them that way."

"No, I . . ."

"Shut up. You could have sounded off."

"No!" He stood up, his hands claws that dangled at his sides. "I know them! From Europe I know them and who am I to speak against them. You do not understand what they do to people. You . . ."

My knuckles cracked across his jaw so hard he went back over the arm of the chair and spilled in a heap on the floor. He lay there with his eyes wide open and the spit dribbling out of his open mouth started to turn pink. He was the bug caught in the web trying to hide from the spider and he'd backed into the hornet's nest.

Carmen Trivago would never be the same again.

I used the phone in the lobby again. I buzzed my apartment and the super's wife answered it. I hadn't told her not to do so, she was doing me a favor. I told her it was me, asked if everything was okay and she said it was. Lily was asleep with the door locked but she could hear her breathing and talking in there. Her husband was making doubly sure things stayed quiet by pretending to do some work in the hall outside.

There were three other phone calls. A Captain Chambers had called and wanted to see me right away. I thanked her and hung up.

I turned up the collar of my trench coat and stepped out into the rain. The wind was lashing it up the street in waves now, pounding it against the buildings and as the cars went by you had a quick look at the drivers as the wipers ripped it aside before the faces muddled into a liquid haze.

The cab didn't wait to be called. He pulled into the curb and I hopped in, gave him the address and stuck a smoke in my mouth.

Someplace Velda was looking at the rain. It wouldn't be a pleasant sound, not this time. She'd be crazy with fear, scared so hard she wouldn't be able to think. They weren't the kind you could stall. She could only wait. And hope.

And someplace the people who had her were thinking too. They were thinking of a long string of kills and two fresh ones propped up against a DEAD END sign. They were thinking of the word that went out and before they'd do anything at all they'd think harder still and it wouldn't be until I was dead that they'd feel right to do what they wanted to her.

I wasn't the cops and I wasn't the feds. I was one guy by himself but I was one who could add to the score without giving a damn at all. I was the one guy they were afraid of because the trail of dead men hadn't stopped yet. It was a trail that had to be walked and they were afraid of stepping on it.

Pat was in his office. You had to look twice to make sure he wasn't asleep, then you saw the light glinting off his almost-closed eyes and saw the movement of his mouth as he sucked on the dry pipe.

I threw my hat on the desk and sat down. He didn't say anything. I got out my next-to-last Lucky, held a light to it and let the smoke go. He still didn't say anything. I didn't have the time to trade thoughts. "Okay, chum, what is it?"

The pipe came out of his mouth slowly. "You conned me, Mike."

I started to get warm all over, an angry flush that burned into my chest. "Great. Just like that I gave you the business! You don't say anything . . . you sit there like a dummy then pull the cork. Say what's eating you or I'll get the hell out of here."

What distrust was in his face turned uncertain. "Mike, this thing is a bombshell. The biggest staff that ever operated on one case is out there working. They're going night and day looking for the answer then you come up with it ready to trade off for something."

I sat back in the chair. I took a deep, relieved pull on the smoke and grinned. "Thanks for the compliment. I didn't know it would get back so fast. Where'd you pick it up?"

"Every stoolie we know has his ears open. What are you trading for?"

My grin pulled tight at the edges, flattened across my teeth and stayed that way. "Velda. The bastards have Velda. She suckered Al Affia into a trap that didn't work and got caught in one herself. She played it too smart and now they have her."

It was quiet in the room. The clock on the wall hummed over the drone of the rain outside, but that was all.

"You don't look too worked up about it," Pat said. Then he saw my eyes and took it back without saying so out loud.

"They'll want to be sure. They'll want to know if I have it or not before they cut loose on her. They'll have to be sure. Right in the beginning they thought Berga Torn passed it on to me, went through my apartment. If it was anybody else they could have taken it easy, but not with me. They knew what was going to happen."

"Let's have it, Mike."

"The answer?" I said. I shook my head. "I don't have it. Not where I can reach out and touch it yet. I need more details."

"So do we. I thought we were sharing this thing."

"I didn't forget. What have you got?"

Pat stared at me a long time, reached out and fanned a few papers across his desk. "Berga didn't escape from the sanitarium. She had it planned for her. She had a guest early that evening, a woman. The name and address were phony and we got no description except that she had brown hair. An attendant stated that she was pretty nervous after the guest left."

I cut in with, "How come you're just finding this stuff out?"

"It's a private sanitarium and they were afraid of ruining their reputation. They held off until we scared them. Anyway, we checked everybody in the place that night and came up with a spot from a couple of female visitors in the next room.

"When the closing bell ran they stood outside in the hall a few minutes talking. They were close to Berga's door and overheard a voice saying . . ." He glanced down at the sheet and read from it. ". . . 'they're after you. They were at the house today.' " The rest of it we had to put together and when we had it the dame was telling her something about the main gate, to be as casual as possible, and there would be a car waiting for her at the northwest corner."

Pat stopped and tapped the sheet. He tapped the stem of the pipe against his teeth and said, "On that corner was an F.B.I. wagon so whoever was waiting had to take up another spot. She got scared out of the deal and started hitchhiking when she didn't see the person she was expecting."

I said, "She saw the person, all right. He was in another car. She knew damn well she was being followed."

"There's something wrong," Pat said.

"Yeah. Like murders on the books as accidents."

Pat's jaw worked. "Proof?"

"No, but that's the way it happened." I couldn't see his face, but I knew what he was thinking. In his own way he had covered every detail I had. "The first one was Nicholas Raymond. That's where the answer is, Pat."

His eyes peered out at me. "Nicholas Raymond was a Mafia agent. He ran an import business as an excuse to make frequent overseas trips."

I didn't answer so he said, ". . . He was the guy who ran the stuff into this country that was turned into cash for Mafia operations."

He was watching me so closely that you couldn't see anything but the black pupils of his eyes. His face was all screwed up with the intensity of watching me and it was all I could do to hold still in the chair. I covered by dragging in another lungful of smoke and letting it go toward the ceiling so I could do something with my mouth except feel it try to stretch out of shape.

The picture was perfect now. It was the most beautiful piece of art work I had ever seen. The only trouble was I couldn't make out what it was all about nor who drew it.

I said, "How much would two million in narcotics before the war be worth now, Pat?"

"About double."

I got up and put on my hat. "That's what you're looking for, friend. A couple of shoe boxes that big. If I find them I'll tell you about it."

"Do *you* know where it is?"

"No. I have a great big fat idea, but if it's stayed buried this long it won't hurt anybody staying buried a while longer. All I want is the person who is after it because that person has Velda. If I have to I'll dig it up and trade for her."

"Where are you going now?"

"I think I'm going out and kill somebody, Pat," I said.

The cop at the switchboard told me to go ahead and use the phone. He plugged in an outside line and I dialed the number that got me Michael Friday. I said, "Your line clear? This is Mike."

"Mike! Yes . . . There's no one here."

"Good. Now listen. There's a place called the Texan Bar on Fifty-sixth Street. Get down there as fast as you can. I'll be waiting. You got that?"

"Yes, but . . ."

I hung up on her. It was the best thing you could do with a woman when you wanted her to move fast. She'd be a good hour getting there which was just what I needed.

They were changing shifts outside the building and the flow of cops was getting thicker. I stepped outside, flagged down a cab and gave him the address of Al Affia's place. The rain had thinned traffic down to a minimum and he didn't take long getting there.

Nothing had changed. The blood was still there on the floor, dried into a crusty maroon. Close to the door the air was a little foul and inside it was worse. I shoved the door open, snapped on the light and there was Al grinning at me from the corner of the room, but it was a horrible kind of grin because somebody had broken him into pieces with the whisky bottle. He wasn't killed plain. He was killed fancy as a person could be killed. He was killed so that he couldn't make any sound as he died and whoever did it must have had a great time laughing because Al died slow.

What I came for was gone. There were still two of the blueprints on the table but they showed the layout of the docks. The rest were missing. I picked the phone up, dialed the operator and said very quietly, "Operator . . . get me the local office of the F.B.I."

Somebody said briskly, "Federal Bureau of Investigation, Moffat speaking."

"You better get down here, Moffat," I said. I laid the phone down gently alongside the base and walked out.

They'd know. They were lads you never noticed in the crowd, but they were all eyes and ears and brains. They worked quietly and you never read about them in the papers, but they got things done and they'd know. Maybe they knew a lot more than I thought they'd know.

She was waiting for me at the bar. She was a lusty, beautiful woman with a mouth that made you hungry when she smiled at you as you came in. There was humor in her eyes, but the wonder and curiosity showed below in the little lines that radiated from the corners of her lips.

There was nothing in mine. I could feel them flat and dull in their sockets. I nudged my chin to the booths in the back and she followed me. We sat down and she waited for me to say something and all I could think of was the last time I had sat here it was with Velda and now time was getting short.

I took the cigarette she held out from the case, lit it and leaned on the table. "How much do you love your brother, kid?"

"Mike . . ."

"I'm asking the questions."

"He's my brother."

"Partially."

"That doesn't matter."

"He's mixed up in one of the dirtiest rackets you'll ever find. He has a part in it someplace and is paid off in the blood and terror you'll find wherever you find the Mafia operating. He's part of a chain of killers and thieves, yet you like what his money can buy. Your love doesn't stop anyplace, does it?"

She sat away from me as if I held a snake out at her.

"Stop, Mike, please stop!"

"You can stay on his side or mine, kid. The choice is up to you."

The hysteria was caught in her chest. Her mouth wasn't pretty any more. One little sob got loose and that was all. "Al Affia is dead. So far he's the latest. He isn't the last. Where do you stand?"

It came out slowly. She fought it all the way and won it. "With you, Mike."

"I need some information. About Berga Torn." She dropped her head and toyed with the ash tray. "Your brother played around with her some time ago. Why?"

"He . . . hated that woman. She was a tramp. He hated tramps."

"Did she know it?"

Michael shook her head. "In public he seemed fond of her. When we were alone . . . he said awful things about her."

"How far did he go?"

She looked up helplessly. "He kept her. I don't know why he did it . . . he didn't like her at all. The woman he did care for at the time left him because he spent all his time . . . nights . . . with Berga. Carl . . . was upset about it. One night he had an argument with someone about her in his study. He was so mad afterward he went out and got drunk, but he never saw Berga after that. He had an argument with her, too."

"You know about Carl's testifying before a congressional committee?"

"Yes. It . . . didn't seem to bother him. Not until . . . he heard that . . . she was going to speak against him."

"That was never made public."

"Carl has friends in Washington," she said simply.

"Yet he never worried about it?"

"No."

"Let's go back further, sugar. Let's go back before the war. Was there any time you can remember when something bothered Carl so much it damn near drove him nuts?"

The shadows around her eyes deepened, her hands pressed together tightly and she said, "How did you know? Yes, there was . . . a time."

"Now go over it slowly. Think about it. What did he do?"

Something panicky crossed her face. "I . . . nothing. He was hardly ever home. He wouldn't let me talk to him at all. When he was at home all he did was make long-distance calls. I remember because the phone bill was almost a thousand dollars for the month."

My breath was coming in hot. It hissed in between my teeth with a whisper and burned into my lungs. I said, "Can you get that bill? Can you get the itemized list that went with it?"

"I . . . might. Carl keeps everything . . . in the safe at home. Once I saw the combination on the back of the desk blotter."

I wrote down an address. Pat's. But all I gave her was the address and the apartment number. "Find it. When you do, bring it here." I folded the paper into her hand and she dropped it into her bag after looking at it long enough to etch it into her memory.

He'd get it. He'd pass it on and the boys in the blue suits would tie into it. They had the men and the time and the means. They'd do in a day what it would take me a year to do.

I snubbed out my butt, pulled the belt tight on the trench coat and stood up. "You'll spend the rest of your life hating yourself for doing this. Hating me too. If it gets too much I'll take you around and show you a lot of dirty little kids who are orphans and some widows your own age. I can show you pictures of bodies so cut up you'll get sick. I'll show you reports of kids who have killed and are condemned to death because they were sky-high on dope when they decided to see what it was like to burn a man down. You won't be stopping it all. You'll slow it down a little, maybe, but a few people who would have died will go on living because of you."

For a few seconds she seemed completely empty. If there was any emotion in her it had drained out and all she was left with were her thoughts. They showed on her face, every one of them. They showed when she looked back into the past and brought to life what she had known all along but had refused to acknowledge. They showed when the life came back to her eyes and her mouth. She tilted one eyebrow at me, did something to her head that shook her hair loose down her back.

"I won't hate you, Mike. Myself, perhaps, but not you."

I think she knew it then. The thought of it hung in the air like a charged cloud. Michael said, "They'll finally kill me, won't they, Mike." It wasn't a question.

"What's left of them . . . if they ever find out . . . would like to think they will. They'd like to kill me too. You can always remember one thing because they'll be remembering it too. They're not as big as they think they are."

She smiled, a wan, drawn smile. "Mike . . ."

I took the hand she held out to me.

"Kiss me again. Just in case."

The wetness glistened on her lips. They were firm lips, large, ripe, parted slightly over the even lines of her teeth. There was fire there that grew hotter as I came closer. I could see her mouth open even more, the tip of her tongue impatiently waiting, then the impatience broke and it met me before the lips did.

I held her face in my hands, heard the soft moan she made, felt her nails biting into my arms through the coat, then I let her go. She trembled so violently she had to press her hands against the booth and the fiery liquid of her mouth passed on into her eyes.

"Please go, Mike," she said.

And I went. The rain took me back again, put its arms around me and held tight. I became part of the night, part of the wet, part of the noise and life that was the city. I could hear it laughing at me, a low, dull rumble with a sneer in it.

I walked down the side streets, crossed the avenues and got back to my kind of people again. I drifted through the night while my mind was days away and I was saying it off to myself and wondering how many other people were doing the same things. I was looking at a picture through the rain, knowing what was going on and not being able to make out the details.

It was a picture of a grim organization that stretched out its tentacles all over the world with the tips reaching into the highest places possible. It was an organization fed on the money of destruction and one tentacle was starving. The two million that was sent to feed it never arrived. No, that was wrong. It did arrive, but someplace it sat and was still there. In its sitting it had doubled its worth and the tentacle wanted it bad. It had to feast now to live. It was after the food with all the fury of its hunger, ready to do anything in the final, convulsive gesture of survival.

You could say it started with Berga. She wasn't the girl in the head-lights any longer. She was younger now, a tall luscious Viking with eyes that could draw a man. She was a blonde snare with a body full of play-ful curves that held out triple challenges, a body full of dares waiting to be taken up. She was coming home from a visit to Italy and in the hid-den hours on board that ship she had found a person who was ready to call the dare. He wasn't a special kind of a man. He was a guy with a small export business who could pass unnoticed in the crowd. He was a guy with a legitimate excuse to travel at certain times. He was a guy who was part of a great plan, a guy named Nicholas Raymond who really wasn't anything at all and because of it was the one they used as a messenger to bring in the vital food for the tentacle over here.

But he had a fault and because of it a lot of people died and the ten-tacle was starving. He liked the women. And Berga was special. He liked her so much he never followed the plan of delivery through and made plans to use the stuff himself. He and Berga. Two million bucks after conversion. Tax free. Someplace the stuff was still there. Maybe it took them a long time to find him again, or maybe they wanted the stuff first and were afraid the secret would die with him. However it was it took him a while to die. Maybe they thought Berga had it then. And she died. That put it on me.

I was thinking of something then. Horror, terror, fear . . . all of it that was there in her face for a little while, a confusion of emotions that stopped too suddenly.

I cursed to myself as the minute details started to fall into place, spun around and yelled at a cab. He jammed on the brakes, swerved slightly and was hardly stopped before I had the door opened. I told him where to take me and sat on the edge of the seat until we got there.

The elevator took me up to my office. I got out jangling my keys from my hand, stuck one in the lock and turned it. The outer office was empty, her typewriter a forlorn thing under its cover. Velda's desk was covered with mail separated into classified piles of bills, personals and miscellaneous. I went through them twice, didn't find what I was look-ing for, then spotted the pile that had come through the door slot I had pushed aside when I came in. There wasn't anything there, either. I went back to the desk, the curse still in my mouth when I saw it. The sheet lay under the stapler with the top under the flap of the envelope. I turned it over and saw the trade name of a gasoline company.

It was simple statement. One line. *"The way to a man's heart—"* and under it the initials, *"B.T."* Velda would have known, but Velda never saw it. Berga must have scribbled it at the service station after lifting the address from the registration tacked to the steering post of my heap, but it was the old address. The new one was on the back out of sight and she hadn't seen the lines drawn through the words that voided it.

I looked at it, remembered her face again and knew what she was thinking when she wrote it. I felt the thing crumple in my hand as I squashed it in my fingers and never heard the door open behind me.

He stood in the doorway of my inner office and said, "I trust you can make something out of it. We couldn't."

I knew he had a gun without looking. I knew there were more of them without seeing them and I didn't give a damn in the world because I knew the voice. *I knew the voice and it was the one I said I'd never forget!* The last time it spoke I was supposed to die and before it could speak again I let out a crazy sound of hate that filled the room and was at them in a crouch with the bullets spitting over my head. I had the guy in my hands feeling my fingers tear his eyes loose while he screamed his lungs out and even the gun butt pounding on the back of my skull didn't stop me. I had enough left to lash out with my foot and hear it bite into flesh and bone and enough left to do something to one of them that turned his stomach inside out in my face. The horrible, choked scream of an-guish one was letting out on the floor diminished to a whimper before disappearing altogether in the blackness that was closing in around me. Far in the distance I thought I heard sharp, flat sounds and a voice swear-ing hoarsely. Then I heard nothing at all.

It was a room. It had one window high off the floor and you could see the pinpoints that were stars through the film of dirt on the glass. I was spread-eagled on the bed with my hands and legs pulled tight to the frame and when I tried to twist the ropes bit into my skin and burned like acid. The muscles in my side had knotted in pain over ribs that were torturous hands gripping my chest.

There was a taste of blood in my mouth and as I came awake my stomach turned over and dragged long, agonized retches up my throat. I tried to breathe as deeply as I could, draw the air down to stop the retching. It seemed to take a long time before it stopped. I lifted my head and felt my hair stick to the bed. The back of it throbbed and felt like it was coming off so I let it ease back until the giddiness passed.

The room took shape, a square empty thing with a musty odor of disuse filling it. I could see the single chair in one corner, the door in the wall and the foot of the bed. I tried to move, but there wasn't an inch of play in the ropes and the knots that tied them only seemed to get tighter.

I wondered how long I had been there. I listened for sounds I could place but all I got was the steady drip of water outside the window. It was still raining. I listened even more intently, straining my ears into the silence and then I knew about how long I had been there.

My watch had stopped. I could see the luminous hands and number so it hadn't broken . . . it just stopped. This wasn't the same night it had happened. Everything I felt seemed to pour out of my mouth and I fought those damned ropes with every ounce of strength in me. They bit in, cut deeper and held like they were meant to and when I knew it wasn't any use fighting them I slumped back cursing myself for being so jackassed stupid as to walk into the deal without a rod and let them take me. I cursed myself for letting Velda do what she wanted to and cursed myself for not playing it right with Pat. No, I had to be a damned hero. I had to make it by myself. I had to take on the whole organization at once knowing what they were like and how they operated. I passed out advice all around then forgot to give some of it to myself.

There were footsteps in the other room that padded up to the door. It opened into an oblong of yellow light framing the man and the one behind him who stood there. They were opaque forms without faces but it didn't matter any more. One said, "He awake?"

"Yeah, he's out of it."

They came in and stood over me. Two of them and I could see the billies in their hands.

"Tough guy. You were hard to take, mister. You know what you did?

You pulled the eyes right out of Foreman. He screamed so loud my friend here had to tap him one and he tapped too hard and now Foreman's lying in a Jersey swamp dead. They don't come like Foreman any more. You know something else? You ruptured Duke, you bastard. You fixed him good, you did."

"Go to hell," I said.

"Still tough. Sure, you got to keep up the act. You know it won't do any good even if you got down on your knees and begged." He grunted out a laugh. "Pretty soon the boss is coming in here. He's going to ask you some questions and to make sure you answer we're going to soften you up a little bit. Not much . . . just a little bit."

The billy went up slowly. I couldn't keep my eyes off it. The thing reached his shoulder then snapped down with a blur of motion and smashed into my ribs. They both did it then, a pair of sadistic bastards trying to kill me by inches, then one made the mistake of cutting for my neck and got the side of my head instead and that wonderful, sweet darkness came back again where there was no more pain or sound and I tumbled headlong into the pool.

But the same incredible pain that had brought the sleep brought the awakening. It was a pain that turned my whole body into a mass of broken nerve ends that shrieked their messages to my brain. I lay there with my mouth open sucking in air, wishing I could die, but knowing at the same time I couldn't yet.

The body doesn't stand for that kind of torture very long. It shocks itself into forgetting it and soon the pain goes away. It isn't gone for good, but the temporary relief is a kiss of love. It lies there in that state of extreme emergency, caring for its own, and when the realization of another emergency penetrates it readies itself to act again.

I had to think. There had to be a gimmick somewhere and I had to find it. I could see the outlines of the bed and feel the ropes that tied me to the steel frame. It was one of those fold-away things with a heavy innerspring mattress and I was laced down so tightly my hands dented the rolled edges of it. I looked down at my toes, over my head at my hands and took the only way out.

There was noise to it, time involved, and pressures that started the blood flowing down my wrists again. I rocked the bed sideways until it teetered on edge, then held my breath as it tipped. I hit the floor and the thing came halfway over on top of me before it slithered back on its side. The mattress had pulled out from under my feet and when I kicked around I got the lower half entirely free of the springs. I had to stop and get my breath, then when I tried the second time it came away from under my hands too and I had the play in the ropes that I needed. They were wet and slippery with my own blood. My fingernails broke tugging at them, but it was the blood that did it. I felt one come free, the next one and my hand was loose. It only took a few minutes longer to get the other one off and my feet off the end of the bed and I was standing up with my heart trying to pound the shock away and the pain back in place.

I didn't let it get that far. I was half drugged with exertion but I knew what I had to do. I put the bed back on its legs, spread the mattress out and got back the way I had been. I was able to dummy the ropes around both feet and one hand and hoped they wouldn't see the one I couldn't get to.

Time. Now I could use a little time. Every second of it put strength back in my body. I lay there completely relaxed, my eyes closed. I tried to bring the picture back in focus and got part of it. I got Berga and Nicholas Raymond and a guy pushing him into the path of a truck. I was thinking that if they had pulled an autopsy on the body they would have found a jugful of stuff in his veins that made him a walking automaton.

The picture got just a little bit clearer and I could see the work they did on Berga. Oh, it had to be easy. With two million bucks in the bag you don't barge around until you're sure what you're doing. First they tried to scare her, then came the big con job. Carl Evello, the man-about-town putting on the heavy rush act, trying to get close enough to the babe to see what she knew.

I thought about it while I lay there, trying to figure the mind of one little guy who thought he could beat the Mafia out of a fortune and pretty soon I was reading his thoughts as if they were my own. Raymond had planned pretty well. In some way he had planted the secret of his cache with Berga so that she'd have to do some tall thinking to get to it. It had taken her a long time, but she had finally caught on and the Mafia knew when she did. She had hired a bodyguard that didn't work but she still wouldn't let go of what she knew because as soon as she did she'd take the long road too. Maybe she saw her way out of it when Uncle Sam put the squeeze on Evello. Maybe she thought with him away she'd have a chance. If she did she thought wrong. They still got to her.

My eyes opened and squinted at the ceiling. A couple more details were looking for a place to crawl into and I was just about to shove them there when I heard the voices outside.

They didn't try to be quiet. Two of them were bragging that I'd be ready to spill my guts and the other one said I had better be. It was a quiet voice that wasn't a bit new to me. It said, "Wait here and I'll see."

"You want us to come in, boss? He might need more softening."

"I'll call you if he does."

"Okay, boss."

Chairs rasped against the floor as the door opened. I could see the two of them there starting to open a bottle on the table, then the door closed and he was feeling for a light switch. He swore at the blackness, struck a match and held it out in front of him. There was no light, but a candle in a bottle was on the chair and he lit it. He put the bottle down beside me, drew up the chair and lit a cigarette.

The smoke tasted sweet in my nostrils. I licked my lips as I watched the butt glow a deep red and he grinned as he blew the cloud across my face.

I said, "Hello, Carl." I made it good and snotty, but he didn't lose the grin.

"The infamous Mike Hammer. I hope the boys did a good job. They can do a better one if I let them."

"They did a good job."

I rolled my head and took a good look at him. "So you're . . . the boss."

The grin changed shape this time. One side of it dropped caustically. "Not quite . . . yet." The evil in his eyes danced in the candlelight. "Perhaps by tomorrow I will be. I'm only the boss locally . . . now."

"You louse," I said. The words seemed to have an effort to them. My breathing was labored, coming through my teeth. I closed my eyes, stiffened and heard him laugh.

"You did a lot of legwork for us. I hear you blundered right on what we have been looking for."

I didn't say anything.

"You wanted to trade. Where is it?"

I let my eyes come open. "Let her go first."

He gave me that twisted grin again. "I'm not trading for her. Funny enough, I don't even know where she is. You see, she wasn't part of my department."

It took everything I could do to hold still. I could feel the nervous tremors creeping up my arms and I made fists of my hands to keep from shaking.

"It's you I'm trading for. You can tell me or I can walk out of here and say something to the boys. You'll want to talk then."

"The hell with you."

He leaned a little closer. "One of the boys is a knife man. He likes to do things with a knife. Maybe you can remember what he did to Berga Torn." I could see the smile on his face get ugly. "That isn't even a little bit what he'll do to you."

The side of his hand traced horrible gestures across my body, meaningful, cutting gestures with the nastiest implications imaginable in them. Then the gestures ended as the side of his palm sliced into my groin for emphasis and the yell that started in my throat choked off in a welter of pain and I mumbled something Carl seemed to want to hear and he bent forward saying, "What? What?"

And that repeated question was the last Carl Evello ever spoke again because he got too close and there were my hands around his throat squeezing so hard his flesh buried my fingers while his eyes were hard little marbles trying to roll out of their sockets. I squeezed and pushed him on his knees and there wasn't even any sound at all. His fingernails bit into my wrists with an insane fury that lived only a few seconds, then relaxed as his head went back with his tongue swelling in the gaping opening that was his mouth. Things in his throat stretched and popped and when I let go there was only the slightest wheeze of air that trickled back into lungs that were almost at the bursting point.

I got him on the bed. I spread him out the way I had been and let him lie there. The joke was too good to pass up so Carl lived a minute longer than he should have. I tried to make my voice as close to his as I could and I called to the door, "He talked. Now put him away."

Outside a chair scraped back. There was a single spoken word, silence, and the slow shuffle of footsteps coming toward the door. He didn't even look at me. He walked up to the bed and I could hear the *snick* as the knife opened. The boy was good. He didn't drive it in. He put it in position and pushed. Carl's body ached, trembled and as I stepped away from the candle the boy saw the mistake and knew he had made his last one. I put everything I could find into the swing that caught the side of his neck and mashed his vertebrae into his spinal cord and he was dead before I eased him to the floor.

Cute. Getting cuter all the time.

I came out of the door with a yell I couldn't keep inside me and dived at the guy at the table. His frenzied stare of hesitation cost him the second he needed to clear his rod and while he was still digging for it my fingers were ripping into his face and my body smashed him right out of the chair. The gun hit the floor and bounced across the room. My knees slammed into him, brought a scream bubbling out of his mouth that snapped off when my fist twisted his jaw out of shape. He didn't try for the gun any more. He just reached for his face and tried to cover it but I didn't let him have the pleasure out of not seeing what was happening. His eyes had to watch everything I did to him until they filmed over and blanked out when the back of his head cracked against the floor. The blood trickled out his nose and ears when I stood over him, a bright red that seemed to match the fire burning in my lungs. I pulled him inside to the other two, tangled his arms around the boy who still held the knife and left them that way.

Then I left. I got out on the street and let the rain wash me clean. I breathed the air until the fire went out, until some of the life I had left back inside crawled into my system again.

The guy sitting in the doorway ten feet away heard me laugh. His head jerked up out of the drunken stupor and he looked at me. Maybe he could see the way my face was and understand what was behind the laugh. The eyes bleary with cheap whisky lost their glassiness and he trembled a little bit, trying to draw back into his doorway. My laugh got louder and he couldn't stand it, so he stood up and lurched away, looking back twice to make sure I was still there.

I knew where I was. Once you put in time on Second Avenue you never forget it. The store front I came out of was dirty and deserted. At one time it had been a lunch counter, but now all that was left was the grease stains and the FOR RENT sign in the window. The gin mill on the corner was just closing up, the last of the human rubble that inhabited the place drifting across the street until he dissolved into the mist.

I walked slow and easy, another one of the dozens you could see sprawled out away from the rain. Another joe looking for a place to park, another joe who couldn't find one. I made the police call box on the second corner down, got it open and said hello when I heard the voice answer. I didn't have to try hard to put a rasp into my voice, I said, "Cooper, you better get somebody down this way fast. Somebody screaming his head off in that empty dog wagon two blocks south."

Two minutes were all they took. The siren whined through the rain and the squad car passed me with its tires spitting spray. They'd find a nice little mess, all right. The one guy left could talk his head off, but he was still going to cook in the hot squat up the river.

I pulled my wallet out and went through it. Everything was there except money. Even my change was gone. I needed a dime like I never needed one before and there wasn't even a character around to bum one from. Down the street lights of a diner threw a yellow blob on the sidewalks. I walked toward it, stood outside the door a second looking at the two drunks and the guy with the trombone case perched on the stools.

There wasn't any more I could lose so I walked in, called the counterman over and tossed my watch on the counter. "I need a dime. You can hold my watch."

"For a dime? Mac, you nuts? Look, if you need some coffee say so."

"I don't need coffee. I want to make a phone call."

His eyes went up and down me and his mouth rounded into a silent "oh." "You been rolled, huh?" He fished in his pocket, tossed a dime on the counter and pushed my watch back to me. "Go ahead, mac, I know how it is."

Pat wasn't at home. My dime clinked back and I tried his office. I asked for Captain Chambers and he wasn't there either. The cop on the board wanted to take a message and the captain would take care of it when he came in. I said, "Pal, this kind of message won't wait. It's something he's been working on and if I can't get word to him right away he's going to hit the roof."

The phone dimmed out as the operator spoke away from it. I could hear the hurried exchange of murmurs, then: "We'll try to contact the captain by radio. Can you leave your phone number?"

I read it off the dial, told him I'd wait and hung up. The counterman was still watching me. There was a steaming hot cup of coffee by an empty stool with a half pack of butts lying alongside it. The guy grinned, nodded to the coffee and made himself a friend. Coffee was about all my stomach would hold, but it sat there inside me like a million bucks in my hand. It took the shakes out of my legs and the ache from my body.

I lit a smoke, relaxed and watched the window. The wind in the street whipped the rain against the plate glass until it rattled. The door opened, a damp blast momentarily freshening the air. Another musician with a fiddle case under his coat sat down tiredly and ordered coffee. Someplace off in the distance a siren moaned, and a minute later another crossed its fading echo. Two more came on top of it, not close, but distant voices racing to a sore spot in the great sprawling sick body of the city.

Corpuscles, I thought. That's what they were like. White corpuscles getting to the site of the infection. They'd close in and wipe out the parasites and if they were too late they'd call for the carpenter corpuscles to come and rebuild broken tissue around the wound.

I was thinking about it when Pat walked in, tired lines around his eyes, his face set in a frozen expression. There was a twitch in the corner of his mouth he tried to wipe away with the back of his hand.

He came over and sat down. "Who kicked the crap out of you, Mike?"

"I look that bad?"

"You're a mess."

I could grin then. Tomorrow, the next day, the day after, maybe, I'd be too sore to move, but right then I could grin. "They reached me but they didn't hold on to me, chum."

His eyes got narrow and very, very bright. "There was a dirty little mess not too far from here. That wouldn't be it, would it?"

"How good is it like it stands?"

Pat's lips came apart over his teeth. "The one guy left is wanted for three different kills. This one finishes him."

"The coroner say that?"

"Yeah, the coroner says that. I say that. We have two experts on the spot who say that too but the guy doesn't say that. The guy doesn't know what to say. He's still half out and he says things about a girl named Berga Torn he worked over and when he knew what he did it woke him up and now he won't say anything. He's the scaredest clam you ever saw in your life."

"So it stands?"

"Nobody'll break it. Now what do you say about it?"

I took a big pull on the butt and stamped it out in the ash tray. "It's a detail. Right now it doesn't mean a damn one way or the other to you or me. Someday over a beer I'll make it into a good story."

"It better be good," Pat said, "I have all hell breaking loose around my ears. Evello's sister came to us with a list of phone calls yesterday and we tracked down the names into the damnedest places you ever saw. We have some of the wheels in the Mafia dangling by their you-know-whats and they're scramming for cover. They're going nuts down in Florida and on the Coast the police have pulled in people big enough to make your hair stand on end. Some of 'em are talking and the thing's opening wider."

He passed his hand over his eyes and drew it away slowly. "Damn it, we're up as far as Washington itself. It makes me sick."

The shake was back in my legs again. "Talk names, Pat."

"Names you don't know and some you do. We have the connections down pat but the ones up top are sitting tight. The Miami police pulled a quick raid on a local big shot and turned up a filing case of information that gives us a line into half the narcotics outlets in the States. Right now the Federal boys have assigned extra men to pick up the stuff and they're coming home loaded."

"How about Billy Mist?" I asked him.

"Nothing doing. Not a word on him so far. He can't be located, anyway."

"Leo Harmody?"

"You got another case? He's howling police persecution and threatening to take things up with Congress. He can yell because there's nothing we can slap him with."

"And Al Affia's dead," I said.

Pat's head turned toward me, his eyes a sleepy gray. "You wouldn't know anything about that, would you?"

"It couldn't've happened to a better guy."

"He was chopped up good. Somebody had a little fun."

I looked at him, lit another smoke and flipped the match in the ash tray where it turned into a charred arc. "How far did you get with him?"

"Not a thing. There wasn't a recognizable print on that bottle."

"What's the word on it, Pat?"

His eyes got sleepier. "His waterfront racket is going sky-high. There's been two killings down there already. The king is dead, but somebody is ready to take his place."

The rain had the sound of a rolling snare drum. It was working up in tempo, backed by the duller, more resonant peals of thunder that cracked the sky open. The three drunks stared at the window miserably, hugging their cups as an anchor to keep from drifting out into the night. The fiddle player shrugged, paid his bill and tucked the case back under his coat and left. At least he was lucky enough to grab an empty cab going by.

I said, "Do you have the picture yet, Pat?"

"Yeah, I have a picture," he said. "It's the biggest one I ever saw."

"You're lost, kid."

The sleepiness left his eyes. His fingers turned the ash tray around slowly, then he gave me that wry grin of his. "Play it out, Mike."

I shrugged. "Everything's coming your way. Now you're having fun. What started it?"

"Okay, so it began with Berga."

"Let's not forget it. Let's tie it all up together so when you're out there having fun you'll know why. I'll make it short and sweet and you can check on it. Ten, twelve, maybe fifteen years ago a guy was bringing a package of dope into the country for delivery to the Mafia. He tangled with a dame on board and fell for her. That's where Berga came into it. Instead of handing over the package he decided to keep it for his sweetie and himself even though he ran the risk of being knocked off."

"Nicholas Raymond," Pat said.

I knew the surprise showed on my face when I nodded. "Nicholas had them on the spot. They couldn't bump him until they located the stuff and he wasn't stupid enough to lead them to it. There was two million bucks' worth in that consignment and they needed it badly. So Nick goes on living with this gal and one day he dies accidentally. It's a tricky pitch but it isn't a hard one. They figured that by this time he would have passed the secret along to her or she would have found out herself somehow.

"But it didn't happen that way. Nick was trickier than they thought. He got the word to her in case something happened to him, but even she didn't know where it was or what it was that keyed it. I guess they must have tried to scare it out of her for a while because she hired herself a bodyguard. He played it too good and moved in. The Mafia didn't like that. If he came across the stuff they'd be out of luck, so he went too."

Pat was watching me closely. There was an expression on his face like I wasn't telling him anything new, but he wasn't saying a word.

"Now we come to Evello. He gets a proper knockdown to her somehow and off he goes on the big pitch. He gave her the whole treatment and probably winds it up with a proposal of marriage to make it sound good. Maybe he over-played his hand. Maybe he just wasn't smart enough to fool her. Something slipped and Berga got wise that he was one of the mob. But she got wise to something else too. *About then she suddenly discovered what it was they were all after and when she had the chance to get Evello creamed before that congressional committee she put in her bid figuring to get the stuff on her own hook later.*"

Now Pat's face was showing that he didn't know it all. There were sharp lines streaking out from the corners of his eyes and he waited, his tongue wetting down his lips from time to time.

I said, "She pulled out all the stops and so did they. The boys with the black hands get around. They scared her silly and by that time it didn't take much. She went to pieces and tried to fight it out in that sanitarium."

"That was her biggest mistake," Pat said.

"You mentioned a woman who came to see her."

He gave a slow nod, his hands opening and closing slowly. "We still can't make her."

"Could it have been a man dressed like a dame?"

"It could have been anything. There was no accurate description and no record of it."

"It was somebody she knew."

"Great."

"Now the stuff is still missing."

"I know where it is."

Pat's head came around faster this time.

"The two million turned into four by just sitting there," I said. "Inflation."

"Damn it, Mike, where?" His voice was all tight.

"On the good ship *Cedric*. Our friend Al Affia was working on the deal. He had given all the plans to her in his dive back there and whoever killed him walked off with them."

"Now you tell me," he said hoarsely. "Now you spill it when somebody has had time to dig it loose."

I took a deep breath, grunted when the sting of pain stabbed across my chest and shook my head. "It's not that easy, Pat. Al had those plans a long time. I'm even beginning to think I know why he was bumped."

Pat waited me out.

"He tried to sucker Velda into his dump for a fast play at her. She slipped him a dose of chloral and while he was out started turning the place upside down. Al didn't stay out very long. He got sick, his stomach dumped the stuff overboard and he saw what she was doing. Velda used the bottle on him then."

His eyes snapped wide open. "Velda!"

"She didn't kill him. She bopped him one and it cut his head open. He staggered out after her and got word to somebody. That somebody caught the deal in a hurry and someplace she's still sweating." All at once every bit of pain in my body flooded back and trapped me in its agony before fading away. I finished with, "I hope."

"Okay, Mike, let it loose! Damn it, what else have you got? So the kid's sweating, you hope . . . and I hope too. You know them well enough to realize what's liable to happen to her now."

"She was on her way to see Billy Mist." My grin turned sour and my teeth came out from under my lips again. "The cops didn't find her."

"Supposing she never reached there?"

"It's a possibility I've been considering, friend. I saw her pass in a cab and she wasn't alone."

I was going warm again. The coffee didn't sit so well in my gut any more. I thought about it as long as I could then shut out the picture when I buried my face in my hands.

Pat kept saying, "The bastards, the bastards!" His nails made a tattoo of sound on the counter and his breathing was almost as hard as mine was. "It's breaking fast, but it's not wide open yet, Mike. We'll get to Billy. One way or another."

I felt a little better. I took my hands away and reached for the last butt in the pack. "It won't break until you get the stuff. You and the whole staff up in Washington can work from now until ten years later and you won't make a hole in the organization big enough to stop it. You'll knock it kicking but you won't kill it. Slowing it down a little is all we can hope for. They're going to hang on to Velda until somebody has that four million bucks lined up.

"I'm the target, chum. Me personally. I've scared the crap out of those guys as individuals . . . not as an organization. They know I don't give a damn what happens to the outfit, the dough or anything that goes with it. All I want is a raft of hides nailed to the barn door. That's where I come in. I'm the little guy with a grudge. I'm the guy so damn burned up he's after a man, not an organization. I'm the guy who wants to stand there and see him die and he knows it. He wants that consignment of narcotics in the worst way but before it does him any good I have to die first.

"So they're holding Velda. She's the bait and she's something else besides. I've been getting closer to this than anybody else and they've known something I never got wise to. Berga passed the clue to me before she died and I've been sitting on it all this time. For a little while they had it, but they couldn't make it out. They expect me to. When I do I'll have to use it to ransom Velda with it."

"They're not that dumb, Mike," Pat told me.

"Neither am I. Someplace the answer slapped me in the teeth and I was in such a hurry I missed it. I can feel the damn thing crawling around in my head and can't lay my finger on it. The damn arrogant bastards . . ."

Pat said, "The head is pretty far from the body."

"What?"

He looked out the window and watched the rain. "They can afford to be arrogant. The entire structure of the Mafia is built on arrogance.

They flout the laws of every country in the world, they violate the integrity of the individual, they're a power in themselves backed by ruthlessness, violence and some of the shrewdest brains in existence."

"About the head and the body, I mean."

"We can smash the body of this thing, Mike, but in this country the head and the body aren't connected except by the very thin thread of a neck. The top man, men, or group is a separate caste. The organization is built so that the head can function without the body if it comes to it. The body parts can be assembled any time, but it's an assembly for the benefit of the head, never forget that. It's a government. The little people in it don't count. It's the rulers who are important and the government is run solely for their benefit and to satisfy their appetites. They're never known and they're not going to be known."

"Unless they make one stinking little mistake," I said.

Pat stopped looking at the rain.

I rubbed the ache out of my side. "The stuff is on the *Cedric*. All you have to do is find the ship. The records will carry the stateroom Raymond used. When you find it call Ray Diker at the *Globe* and give him first crack at the details of the yarn. Tell him to hold the story until I call you. By then I'll have Velda."

"Where are you going?"

"The last time you asked that I said I was going out to kill somebody." I held out my hand. "Gimme a fin."

He looked puzzled, scowled, then pulled five ones out of his pocket. I laid two of them on the counter and nodded to the counterman to come get it. He was all smiles.

"Where's Michael Friday?"

"She said she was going to your place to see you."

"I wasn't home."

"Well, she's not reporting to me on the hour."

"No police guard?"

His frown got bigger this time. "I tried to but she said no. One of the feds pulled out after her anyway. He lost her when she got in a cab."

"Sloppy."

"Lay off. Everybody's up to their ears in this thing."

"Yeah. You going to trace the *Cedric*?"

"What do you think. Where are you going?"

I let a laugh out that sounded hollow as hell. "I'm going out in the rain and think some more. Then maybe I'll go kill somebody else."

I could see Pat remembering the other years. Younger years when the dirt seemed to be only on the surface. When being a cop looked good and the law was for protection and guidance. When there weren't so many strings and sticky red tape and corruption in high places.

His hand went into his pocket and brought out the blued .38. He handed it to me under the shelf of the hanger. "Here, use this for a change."

And I remembered what Velda had said and I shook my head. "Some other time. I like it better this way."

I went out and walked down the street and let the rain hit me in the face. Someplace there was a gimmick and that was what I had to find. I reached the subway kiosk, bought a pack of Luckies and dropped them in my pocket. I waited for the uptown local and got aboard when it came in.

With every jolt the train took I could feel the shock wear off a little bit more. It got worse and when it was too bad I stood up and leaned against the door watching the walls of the tunnel go by in a dirty blur.

A gimmick. One lousy little gimmick and I could have it. It was there trying to come out and whenever I thought I had it my stomach would retch and I'd lose it.

The train pulled into the station, opened its multitude of mouths but I was the only one who stepped out. I had the platform all to myself then, so I let go and the coffee came up.

There weren't any cabs outside. I didn't waste time waiting for one. I walked toward my apartment not conscious of the rain any more, hardly conscious of the protest my body was setting up. I felt my legs starting to go when I reached the door and the super and his wife took a startled look at me and helped me inside.

Lily Carver came up out of the chair holding back the sharp intake of her breath with the back of her hand. Her eyes went soft, reflected the hurt mine were showing, then she had my hand and helped me into the bedroom.

I flopped on the bed and closed my eyes. Hands loosened my collar and pulled at my shoes. I could hear the super telling his wife to stay out, and hear her frightened sobs. I could hear Lily and feel her hands on my forehead. For a second I glimpsed the white halo of her hair and saw the sensuous curves of her body in hazy detail hovering over me.

The super said, "You want me to call a doctor, Mr. Hammer?"

I shook my head.

"I'll call a cop. Maybe . . ."

I shook my head again. "I'll be okay."

"You feel good enough to talk a minute?"

"What?" I could feel the sleep closing in as I said it.

"A woman was here. Friday, her name was. She left you a note in an envelope and said it was pretty important. She wanted you to see it as soon as you came in."

"What was in it?"

"I didn't look. Should I open it?"

"Go ahead."

The bed jounced as he got up. It left me rocking gently, a soothing motion of pure comfort and there was a heaviness under my closed eyes too great to fight. Then the bed jounced again as he sat down and I heard the tearing of paper.

"Here it is." His voice paused. "Not much in it though."

"Read it," I said.

"Sure. *'Dear Mike . . . I found the list. Your friend has it. I found something much more important too and must see you at once. Call me. Please call me at once. Love Michael.'* That's all there is to it, Mr. Hammer."

"Thanks," I said, "thanks a lot."

From the other room his wife set up a nervous twittering. His fingers touched me. "Think it'll be all right if I go back?"

Before I could nod Lily said, "Go ahead. I'll take care of him. Thank you so much for everything."

"Well . . . if you need me, just call down."

"I'll do that."

I got my eyes open one last time. I saw the smooth beauty of her face unmarred by anything now. She was smiling, her hands doing things to my clothes. The strange softness was back in her eyes and she whispered, "Darling, darling . . ."

The sleep came. There was a face in it. The face had a rich, wet mouth, full and soft. It kept coming closer, opening slowly. It was Michael and in my dream I grinned at her, fascinated by her lips.

CHAPTER 12

You hurt too much to sleep. You wake up and it hurts more so you try to go back to sleep. There's a physical ache, a gnawing your body tries vainly to beat down and might have if the pain in your mind wasn't even worse. Processions of thoughts hammer at you, gouge and scrape until the brain is a wild thing seeking some kind of release. But there isn't any release. There's fire all around you, the tongues of it licking closer, needling the skin. The brain screams for you to awaken, but if you do you know the other things . . . the thoughts, will be a more searing pain so you fight and fight until the mind conquers and you feel the awakening coming on.

I thought I heard voices and one was Velda's. She kept calling to me and I couldn't answer back. Somebody was hurting her and I mouthed silent curses while I fought invisible bonds that held me tied to the ground. She was screaming, her voice tortured, screaming for me and I couldn't help her. I strained and kicked and fought but the ropes held until I was breathless and I had to lie there and listen to her die.

I opened my eyes and looked into the darkness, knowing it was only a dream but going nuts because I knew it could be real. My breathing was harsh, laboring, drying my mouth into leathery tissue.

The covers were pulled up to my neck, but under them there was nothing. The skin over my bruised muscles felt cool and pliable, then I found the answer with the tips of my fingers as they slid along flesh that had been gently oiled with some aromatic unguent. From somewhere the faint clean odor of rubbing alcohol crossed my nostrils, disturbing because of its unusual pungent purity. It was the raw smell of fine chemistry, the sharp, natural smell you might expect, but don't find in fresh, virgin forests.

Slowly, waiting for the ache to begin, I pulled my arm free, laid it across the bed, felt the warmth of a body under the back of my hand, then jerked it away as she almost screamed and pulled out of reach to sit there bolt upright with eyes still dumb with sleep reflecting some emotion nobody in the world would be able to put his finger on.

"Easy, Lily . . . It's only me."

She let her breath out with more of a gasp than a sigh, trying to wipe the sleep from her eyes. "You . . . scared me, Mike. I'm sorry." She smiled, sat on the edge of the bed and put her shoes on.

Her dreams must have been pretty rough too. She had taken care of me, lay there while I slept until her eyes closed too. She was a good kid who had been through the mill and was scared to death of a return trip. She wasn't going to get it from me.

I said, "What time is it?"

Lily checked her watch. "A little after nine. Can I get you something to eat?"

"What happened to the day?"

"You slept through. You groaned and talked . . . I didn't want to wake you up, Mike. Can I get you some coffee?"

"I can eat. I need something in my gut."

"All right. I'll call you." Her mouth creased in a smile, one corner of it pulling up with an odd motion. I let my eyes drift over her slowly. As they moved her hands tightened at her throat and the strangeness came back in her face. The smile disappeared into a tight grimace and she twisted around to go out the door.

Some of them are funny, I thought. Beautiful kids who would do anything one minute and scared stiff of doing it the next.

I heard her in the kitchen, got up, showered, managed to get the brush off my face and climbed into some clean clothes. I could hear things frying when I got on the phone and dialed Michael Friday's number.

The voice that answered was deep and guarded. It said, "Mr. Evello's residence," but the touch of Brooklyn in the tone was as plain as the badge it wore.

"Mike Hammer. I'm looking for Michael Friday, Carl's sister. She there?"

"I'm afraid . . ."

"Is Captain Chambers there?"

It caught the voice off base a second. "Who'd you say this was?"

"Hammer. Mike Hammer."

There was a muffled consultation, then: "This is the police, Hammer, what did you want?"

"I told you. I want Friday."

"So do we. She isn't around."

"Damn!" It exploded out of me. "You staked out there?"

"That's right. We're covering the place. You know where the girl is?"

"All I know is that she wants to see me bad, feller. How can I reach Chambers?"

"Wait a minute." The phone blanked out again and there was more talk behind a palm stretched over the mouthpiece. "You gonna be where you are a while?"

"I'll be here."

"Okay, the sergeant here says he'll try to get him for you. What's your number?"

"He knows it. Tell him to call me at home."

"Yeah. You get anything on that Friday dame, you pass it this way."

"No leads?"

"No nothing. She disappeared. She came back here after she left headquarters the other day, stayed a couple of hours and grabbed a cab into Manhattan."

"She was coming to see me," I said.

"She was what!"

"I was out. She left a note and took off again. That's why I called her place."

"I'll be damned. We checked all over the city to find out where she went to."

"If she's using cabs maybe you can pick her up from when she left here."

"Sure, sure. I'll pass it along."

The phone went dead and I socked it back in its hanger. Lily called me from the kitchen and I went out and sat down. She had it ready on the table, that same spread like she thought I was two more guys and instead of it looking good my stomach tried to sour at the sight of it. All I could think of was another one gone. Another kid cut down by a pack of scrimy hoods who wanted that two million bucks' worth of hell so bad they'd kill and kill and kill until they had every bit of it.

I smashed my fist into the table saying the same dirty words over and over until Lily's face went a pasty white and she backed against the wall. I was staring into space, but she was occupying the space ahead of me and whatever she saw going across my face made her shrink back even further.

How stupid were they? How far did they have to go? Wasn't their organization big enough to know every damn detail inside and out? They wouldn't be reaching the stuff now, not with the cops going over every inch of the *Cedric.* The whole shebang was coming apart at the edges and instead of piling up the counts against them they ought to be on the run.

Lily slid out of sight. She came up against me and reached out her hand until it was on my shoulder. "Mike . . ."

I looked at her without seeing her.

"What is it, Mike?"

The words started out of me. They came slow at first, then turned into a boiling current that was taking in the whole picture. I was almost finished with it when I could feel the sharp points of the gimmicks sticking out and ran my mind back to pick them up. Then I sat and cursed myself because I wasn't fast enough. They weren't there any more.

There was just one minor little detail. Just a little one I should have thought of long ago. I said to Lily, "Did you go to see Berga Torn in the sanitarium at all?"

Her eyebrows knit, puzzled. "No, I didn't." She pinched her lower lip between her teeth. "I called her twice and the second time she mentioned that someone had been to see her."

I was half out of my chair. "Who? Did she say who?"

She tried hard for it, reaching back through the days. "I think she did. I honestly didn't pay any attention at the time. I was so worried about what was happening it didn't register."

I had her by the shoulders, squeezing my fingers into her skin. "The name's important, kid. That somebody tipped the whole thing. Right then was the beginning of murder that hasn't ended yet. As long as you got that name in your head a killer is going to be prowling around loose and if he ever knows you might have it you're going the same way Berga did."

"Mike!"

"Don't worry about it. I'm not letting you out of my sight for a minute any more. Damn it, you got to dig that name out. You understand that?"

"I . . . think I do. Mike, please . . . you're hurting me."

I took my hands down and she rubbed the places where they had bitten in. There were tears in the corners of her eyes, little drops of crystal that swelled and I took a step closer to her. I reached out again, more gently this time, close enough for a second to taste the faint crispness of rubbing alcohol.

Lily smiled again. It was like the first time. The kind of smile you see on the face of a person waiting for death and ready to receive him almost gratefully. "Please eat something, Mike," she whispered.

"I can't, kid. Not now."

"You have to have something in your stomach."

Her words sent something racing up my back. It was a feeling you get when you know you have something and you can't wait to get it out of you. You stand there and wait for the final answer, waiting, waiting, waiting.

It was there in my hand when the phone set up a jangling that wouldn't stop. I grabbed the extension and Pat barked a short hello. I asked him, "Did you find Friday?"

He held his voice down. He sat on it all the way but the roughness showed through anyway. "We didn't find a damn thing. Nothing, got that? No Friday, no jug of hop, no nothing. This town's a madhouse. The feds are cutting a swath through the racket a mile wide and we still haven't come up with the stuff. Mike, if that stuff sits there . . ."

"I know what it means."

"Okay then, are you holding anything back?"

"You know better."

"Then what about Friday? If she was up there . . ."

"She wanted to see me. That's all I know."

"You know what I think?"

"I know what you think," I repeated softly. "Billy Mist . . . where's he?"

"You'd never guess."

"Tell me."

"Right now he's having supper at the Terrace. He's got an alibi for everything we can throw at him and nobody's going to break it for a damn long while. He's got people in Washington batting for him and boys with influence pulling strings so hard they're knocking us silly . . . Mike . . ."

"Yeah?"

"Find Velda?"

"Not yet, Pat. Soon."

"You're not saying it right, friend."

"I know."

"In case it makes you feel better, I put men on it."

"Thanks."

"Figured it might not be holing out like you expected."

"Yeah."

"Something else you better know. Your joint's been covered. Three guys were stationed around waiting for you. The feds picked them up. One of the muscle lads is in the morgue."

"So?"

"There may be more. Keep your eyes open. You may have a tail or two if you leave. At least one'll be our man."

"They're sticking close to me." I said the words through my teeth.

"You're primed for the kill, Mike. You know why? I'll tell you. News has it you were part of the thing from the beginning. You've been fooling me and everybody else, but they got the pitch. Tell me one thing . . . *have* you been shoving it in me?"

"No."

"Good enough. We'll keep playing it this way then."

"What about the *Cedric*?"

He cursed under his breath. "It's screwballed, Mike. It's the whole, lousy, stinking reason behind all this. The ship is in a Jersey port right now undergoing repairs. She was a small liner before the war and was revamped to carry troops. All the staterooms were torn out of her and junked to make it over into a transport. The stuff might have been there once, but it's been gone a long time now. None of this should've happened at all."

I let a few seconds pass before I spoke. I was feeling cold and dead all over. "You got a lot of people you've been wanting to get."

"Yeah, a lot of them." His voice was caustic. "A lot of punks. A lot of middle-sized boys. A few big ones. Hydra even lost a few of her heads." He laughed sarcastically. "But Hydra is still alive, buddy. She's one big head who doesn't care how many of her little heads she loses. We can chop all the little ones off and in a few months or years she'll grow a whole new crop as vicious as ever. Yeah, we're doing fine. I thought we did good when I had a look at the shiv hole in Carl. I felt great when I saw Affia's face. They were nothing, Mike. You know how I feel now?"

I didn't answer him. I put the phone back while he was still talking. I was thinking of Michael Friday's wet, wet mouth and the way Al Affia *had* looked and what Carl Evello had told me. I was thinking of undercurrents that could even work through an organization like the Mafia and I knew why Michael Friday had tried to see me.

Lily was a drawn figure slumped in the chair. Her fingers kept pushing the silken strands away from her eyes while she watched me. I said, "Get your coat."

"They'll be waiting for us outside?"

"That's right, they'll be waiting."

Even the last shred of hope she had nursed so long left her face. There was a dullness in her eyes and in the way she walked.

"We'll let them wait," I said, and she turned around and grinned with some of the life back in her.

While I waited for her I turned out the light and stood in front of the window watching the city. The monster squirmed, its bright-colored lights marking the threshing of its limbs, a sprawling octopus whose mouth was hidden under a horribly carved beak. The mouth was open, the beak ready to rip and tear anything that stood in its way. It made sounds out there, incomprehensible sounds that were the muted whinings of deadly terror. There were no spoken words, but the sounds were enough. The meaning was clear.

"I'm ready, Mike."

She had on the green suit again, trimly beautiful, her hair gone now under a pert little hat with a feather in it. The expression on her face said that if she must die it would be quick and clean. And dressed. She was ready. We both were ready. Two very marked people stepping out to look for the mouth of the octopus.

We didn't go down the stairs. We went up to the roof and crossed the abutments between the apartments. We found the door we wanted through the roof of a building a hundred yards down and used that. We took the elevator to the basement and went out through the back. The yard there was an empty place, too steeped in darkness to reflect any of the window lights above. The wall was head-high brick, easy to get over. I pushed Lily up, got over myself and helped her down. We felt our way around the wall until we reached the other basement door but the luck we had had bent a little around a lock under the knob.

I was ready to start working on it when I heard the muffled talk inside and the luck unbent a little bit. I whispered to Lily to keep quiet and pushed her against the side of the building. The talk got louder, the lock clicked and somebody shoved the door open.

The stream of light that flooded the yard didn't catch us. We stayed behind the door and waited. The kid with the wispy mustache backed out swearing under his breath while he tugged at a leash and for a second I was ready to jump him before the racket started. Lily saw it too and grabbed my hand so hard her nails punched holes into my skin. Then the kid was out and walking toward the wall in back with so much to say about people who have cats taken for a walk on a leash that he never saw us go through the door at all.

We got out the other end of the building and circled around the block to the garage. Sammy was just coming on duty and waved my way when he saw us. It was a funny kind of a wave with a motion of the other hand under it. I pushed Lily in ahead of me and closed the door.

Sammy didn't know whether to laugh or not. He decided not to, wrinkled up his face in a serious expression and said, "You hot, Mike?"

"In a way I'm boiling. Why?"

"People been around asking about your new heap. One of the boys tipped me that there's eyes watching for it."

"I heard the story."

"Hear what happened to Bob Gellie?" His face grew pretty serious.

"No."

"He got worked over. Something to do with you."

"Bad?"

"He's in the hospital. Whatever it was he wouldn't talk."

The bastards knew everything. What they didn't know they could find out and when they did the blood ran. The organization. The syndicate. The Mafia. It was filthy, rotten right through but the iron glove it wore was so heavy and so sharp it could work with incredible, terrible efficiency. You worked as they'd tell you to work or draw the penalty. There was no in-between. There was only one penalty. It could be slow or fast, but the result was the same. You died. Until they died, until every damn one of them was nothing but decaying flesh in a pile on the ground the killings would go on and on.

"I'll take care of him. You tell him that for me. How is he?"

"Bob'll come through it. He won't ever look the same, but he'll be okay."

"How do you feel, Sammy?"

"Lousy, if you gotta know. I got me a .32 in the drawer there that's gonna stay right handy all night and maybe afterward."

"Can you get me a car?"

"Take mine. I figured you'd be asking so I have it by the door nosing out. It's a good load and I like it, so bring it back in one piece."

He waved to the door, pulled down the blind over the window and followed us into the garage. He hauled the door up, grinned unhappily when we pulled out and let it slam back in place. I told Lily to get down until I was sure we were clear, made a few turns around one-way streets, parked for a few minutes watching for lights, then pulled out again and cut into traffic.

Lily said, "Where are we going, Mike?"

"You'll see."

"Mike . . . please. I'm awfully scared."

Her lower lip matched the flutter of her voice. She sat there pinching her hands together, her arms making jerky movements against her sides to control the shudder that was trying to take over her body.

"Sorry, kid," I told her. "You're as much a part of this as I am. You ought to know about it. We're going to see what made a woman want to see me pretty badly. We're going to find out what she knew that put her on the missing list. There isn't much you can do except sit tight, but while you're sitting there's plenty you can do. Remember that name. Dig up every detail of that talk you had with Berga and bring that name out."

She looked straight ahead, her face set, and nodded. "All right, Mike. I'll . . . try." Then her head came around and I could feel the challenge of her stare but couldn't match it while I was weaving through the traffic. "I'd do *anything* for you, Mike," she finished softly. There was a newness in her voice I'd never heard before. A controlled excitement that made me remember how I had awakened and what she was thinking of. Before I could answer she turned her head with the same suddenness and stared straight ahead again, but this time with an excited expression of anticipation.

There were only two men assigned to the place when we got there. One sat in the car and the other was parked in a chair by the door looking like he wanted a cigarette pretty bad. He gave me that frozen look all cops keep in reserve and waited for me to speak my piece.

"I'm Mike Hammer. I've been cooperating with Captain Chambers on the deal here and would like to take a look around. Who do I see?"

The freeze melted loose and he nodded. "The boys were talking about you before. The captain say it's okay?"

"Not yet. He will if you want to go get a call in to him."

"Ah, guess it's okay. Don't touch anything, that's all."

"Anybody around inside?"

"Nope. Joint's empty. The butler took an inventory of liquor before he left though."

"Careful guy. I'll be right out."

"Take your time."

So I went in and stood in the long hallway. I held a light up to the Lucky between my lips and blew a thin overcast into the air. There were lights on along the walls, dim things that gave the place the atmosphere of a funeral parlor and hardly any light.

In the back of my mind I had an idea but I didn't know how to start it going. You don't walk in and pick up important things after the cops have been through a place. Not unless they don't want what you're looking for.

I made the rounds of the rooms downstairs, finished the butt and snubbed it, then tried upstairs. The layout was equally as elaborate, as well appointed as the other rooms, a chain of bedrooms, a study, a small music room and a miniature hobby shop on the south side. There was one room that smelled of life and living. It had that woman smell I couldn't miss. It had the jaunty, carefree quality that was Michael Friday and when I snapped the lights on I saw I was right.

There was an orderly disarray of things scattered around that said the woman who belonged to the room would be back. The creams, the perfumes, the open box of pins on the dresser. The bed was large with a fluffy-haired poodle doll propped against the pillows. There were pictures of men on the dresser and a couple of enlarged snapshots of Michael in a sailboat with a batch of college boys in attendance.

Scattered, but neat.

Other signs too, professional signs. A cigar ash in the tray. Indentations in the rolled stockings in the box where a thumb had squeezed them. I sat on the edge of the bed and smoked another cigarette. When I had it halfway down I reached over to the night table for an ash tray and laid it on the cover beside me. The tray made an oval in the center of the square there, a boxy outline in dust. I picked it up, looked at the smudge on the cover and wiped at it with my fingertip.

The other details were there too, the thin line of grit and tiny edges of brownish paper that marked the lip of a box somebody had spilled out in emptying it on the bed. With my fingers held together the flat of my hand filled the width of the square and two hands made the length. I finished the butt, put it out and went back downstairs.

The cop on the porch said, "Make out?"

"Nothing special. You find any safes around?"

"Three of 'em. One upstairs, two downstairs. Nothing there we could use. Maybe a few hundred in bills. Take a look yourself. There's a pair in his study."

They were a pair, all right. One was built into the wall behind a framed old map of New York harbor, but the other was a trick job in the window sill. Carl was kicking his psychology around when he had them built. Two safes in a house a person could expect, but rarely two in the same room. Anyone poking around couldn't miss the one behind the map, but it would take some inside dope to find the other. The dial was pretty badly beaten up and there were fresh scratches in the wood around the thing. I swung the door open, held my lighter in front of it and squinted around. The dust marked the outline of the box that had been there.

The cop had moved to the steps this time. He grinned and jerked his head at the house. "Not much to see."

"Who opened the safes?"

"The city boys brought Delaney in. He's the factory representative of the outfit who makes the safes. Good man. He could make a living working lofts."

"He's doing all right now," I said. I told him so long and went back to the car. Lily was waiting, her face a pale glow behind the window.

I slid under the wheel, sat there fiddling with the gearshift letting the thought I had jell. Lily put her hand on my arm, held it still and waited. "I wonder if Pat found it," I muttered.

"What?"

"Michael Friday stooled on her brother. She went back home and found something else but this time she was afraid to give it to the police."

"Mike . . ."

"Let me talk, kid. You don't have to listen. I'm just getting it in order. There was trouble in the outfit. Carl was expecting to take over somehow. In that outfit you don't work your way up. Carl was expecting to move up a slot so somebody else had to go. That boy knew what he was doing. He spent some time getting something on the one he was after and was going to smear him with it."

I put it through my mind again, nodded, and said, "Carl was close enough to start the thing going so the other one knew about it. He went after what Carl had and found it gone. By that time the cops were having a field day with the labor department of the organization so he had a good idea who was responsible. He must have tailed her. He knew she had it and what she was going to do with it so he nailed her."

"But . . . who, Mike? Who?"

My teeth came apart in the kind of a smile nobody seemed to like. I was feeling good all over because I had my finger on it now and I wasn't letting go. "Friend Billy," I said. "Billy Mist. Now he sits quiet and enjoys his supper. Someplace he's got a dame on the hook and enjoying life because whatever it was Carl had isn't any more. Billy's free as a bird but he hasn't got two million in the bush to play with. He's got an ace in the hole with Velda in case the two million shows up and a deuce he can discard anytime if it doesn't. The greasy little punk is sitting pretty where he can't be touched."

The laugh started out of my chest and ripped through my throat. It was the biggest joke I ever laughed at because the whole play was made to block me out and I wasn't being mousetrapped. I was going back a couple of hours to the kitchen and what Lily had said and back even further to a note left in my office. Then, so I wouldn't forget how I felt right there at the beginning when I wanted to kill something with my hands, I went back to Berga and the way she had looked coming out of that gas station.

I kicked the engine over, pulled around the squad car and pointed the hood toward the bright eyes of Manhattan. I stayed with the lights watching the streets click by, cut over a few blocks to the building with the efficient look and antiseptic smell and pulled in behind the city hearse unloading a double cargo.

It was a little after one but you could still find dead people around.

The attendant in the morgue called me into his office and wanted to know if I wanted coffee. I shook my head. "It takes the smell away," he said. "What can I do for you?"

"You had a body here. Girl named Berga Torn."

"Still have it."

"Slated for autopsy?"

"Nope. At least I haven't heard about it. They don't usually in those cases."

"There will be one in this case. Can I use the phone?"

"Go ahead."

I picked it up and dialed headquarters. Pat wasn't around so I tried his apartment. He wasn't there, either. I buzzed a few of the places he spent time in but they hadn't seen him. I looked at my watch and the hand had spun another quarter. I swore at the phone and at myself and double cursed the red tape if I had to go through channels. I was thinking so hard I wasn't really thinking at all and while I was in the middle of it the door of the office opened and the little guy with the pot belly came in, dropped his bag on the floor and said, "Damn it, Charlie, why can't people wait until morning to die?"

I said, "Hi, doc," and the coroner gave me a surprised glance that wasn't any too pleased.

"Hello, Hammer, what are you doing here? Should I add 'again'?"

"Yeah, add it, doc. I always seem to come home, don't I?"

"I'd like it better if you stayed out of my sight."

He went to go past me. I grabbed his arm, turned him around and looked at a guy with a safe but disgusting job. He went up on his toes, tried to pull his arm away, but I held on. "Listen, doc. You and I can play games some other time. Right now I need you for a job that can't wait. I have to chop corners and it has to be quick."

"Let go of me!"

I let go of him. "Maybe you like to see those bodies stretched out in the gutter."

He turned around slowly. "What are you talking about?"

"Suppose you had a chance to do something except listen for a heartbeat that isn't there for a change. Supposing you had it in your hand to kick a few killers right into the chair. Supposing you're the guy who stands between a few more people living or dying in the next few hours . . . how would you pitch it, doc?"

The puzzle twisted his nose into a ridge of wrinkles. "See here . . . you're talking like . . ."

"I'm talking plain. I've been trying to get some official backing for what I have in mind but nobody's home. Even then it might take up time we can't spare. That chance I was talking about is in your hand, doc."

"But . . ."

"I need a stomach autopsy on a corpse. Now. Can do?"

"I think you're serious," he said in a flat tone.

"You'll never know how serious. There may be trouble later. Trouble isn't as bad as somebody having to die."

I could see the protest coming out of the attendant. It started but never got there. The coroner squared his shoulders, let a little of the excitement that was in my voice trickle into his eyes and he nodded.

"Berga Torn," I told the attendant. "Let's go see her."

He did it the fast, easy way you do when you cut corners. He did it right there in the carrier she lay on and the light overhead winked on the steel in his hand. I didn't get past the first glimpse because fire does horrible things to a person and it was nicer to remember Berga in the headlights of the car.

I could hear him, though.

I could even tell when he found it.

He did me the favor of cleaning it before he handed it to me and I stood there looking at the dull glitter of the brass key wondering where the lock to it was. The coroner said, "Well?"

"Thanks."

"I don't mean that."

"I know . . . only where it goes nobody knows. I thought it would be something else."

He sensed the disappointment and held out his hand. I dropped the key in it and he held it up to the light, turning it over to see both sides. For a minute he concentrated on one side, held it closer to the bulb, then nodded for me to follow him across the room. From a closet he pulled out a bottle of some acrid liquid, poured it into a shallow glass container, then dropped the key in. He let it stay there about twenty seconds before dipping it out with a glass rod. This time the dullness was gone. It was a gleaming thing with a new look and no coating to dull the details. This time when he held it in the light you could see CITY ATHLETIC CLUB, 529 scratched into the surface and I squeezed his arm so hard he winced through his grin.

I said, "Listen, get on the phone out there and find Captain Chambers. Tell him I found what we were looking for and I'm going after it. I'm not going to take any chances on this getting away so he can hop up to my office for a print of this thing."

"He doesn't know?"

"Uh-uh. I'm afraid somebody else might find out the same way I did. I'll call you back to see how you made out. If there's any trouble about . . . back there . . . Chambers'll clear things. Someday I'll let you know just how much of a boost up you gave the department."

The excitement in his eyes sparkled brighter and he was holding his jaw like a guy who's just done the impossible. The morgue attendant was on his way over for an explanation and apparently he wanted it in writing. He tried to stop me for some talk on the way out but I was in too much of a rush.

Lily knew I had it when I came bouncing down the stairs, opened the door for me and said, "Mike?"

"I know almost all the answers now, chicken." I held up the key. "Here's the big baby. Look at it, a chunk of metal people have died for and all this time it was in the stomach of a girl who was ready to do anything to beat them out of it. The key to the deal. For the first time in my life a real one. I know who had it and what's behind the door it opens."

As if the words I had said were a formula that split open Valhalla to let a pack of vicious, false gods spill through, a jagged streak of lightning cut across the sky with the thunder rolling in its wake. The first crashing wave of it was so sudden Lily tightened against it, her eyes closed tight.

I said, "Relax."

"I . . . can't, Mike. I hate thunderstorms."

You could feel the dampness in the air, the fresh coolness of the new wind. She shuddered again and turned up the little collar of her jacket around her neck. "Close the window, Mike."

I rolled it up, got the heap going and turned into traffic heading east. The voice of the city was starting to go quiet now. The last few figures on the streets were starting to run for cover and the cabs picked up their aimless cruising.

The first big drops of rain splattered on the hood and brought the scum flooding down the windshield. I started the wipers, but still had to hunch forward over the wheel to see where I was going. I could feel time going by. The race of the minutes. They never went any faster or any slower, but they always beat you. I turned south on Ninth Avenue, staying in tempo with the lights until I reached the gray-brick building with the small neon sign that read CITY ATHLETIC CLUB.

I cut the engine in front of the door and went to get out. Lily said, "Mike, will you be long?"

"Couple of minutes." Her face seemed to be all pinched up.

"What's the matter, kid?"

"Cold, I guess."

I pulled the blanket from the seat in the back and draped it over her shoulders. "You're catching something sure as hell. Keep it around you. I'll be right back."

She shivered and nodded, holding the edges of the blanket together under her chin.

The guy at the reception desk was a sleepy-eyed tall guy who sat there hating everybody who bothered him. He watched me cross the hall and didn't make any polite sounds until I got to him.

He asked one question. "You a member?"

"No, but . . ."

"Then the place is closed. Scram."

I pulled a fin out of my wallet and laid it on the desk.

He said, "Scram."

I took it back, stuffed it away and leaned across the chair and belted him right on his back. I picked him up by his skinny arms and popped him a little one in the gut before I threw him back in his chair again. "The next time be nice," I said. I held out the key and he looked at it with eyes that were wide awake now.

"You bastard."

"Shut up. What's the key for?"

"Locker room."

"See who has 529."

He curled his lip at me, ran his hand across his stomach under his belt and pulled a ledger out of the desk drawer. "Raymond. Ten-year membership."

"Let's go."

"You're nuts. I can't leave the desk. I . . ."

"Let's go."

"Lousy coppers," I heard him say. I grinned behind his back and followed him down the stairs. There was a sticky dampness in the air, an acrid smell of disinfectant. We passed a steam room and the entrance to the pool, then turned into the alcove that held the lockers.

They were tall affairs with hasps that allowed you to install your own lock. Raymondo had slapped on a beauty. It was an oversized brass padlock with a snap so big it barely passed through the hasp. I stuck the key in, turned it and the lock came apart.

Death, crime and corruption were lying on the floor in two metal containers the size of lunch pails. The seams were welded shut and the units painted a deep green. Attached to each was the cutest little rig you ever saw, a small CO_2 bottle with a heavy rubber ball attached to the nozzle. The rubber was rotted in the folds and the hose connection had cracked dry, but it didn't spoil the picture any. All you had to do was toss the unit out a porthole, the bottle stopper opened after a time interval and the stuff floated to the top where the rubber ball buoyed it until it was picked up.

The answer to the *Cedric* was there too, a short story composed of sales slips stapled together, a yarn that said Raymondo had taken good care of his investment and was on hand to pick up the junk when they stripped the ship. There was one special item marked *"wall ventilators— 12.50 ea. 25.00."*

I squatted down to pull them out and the guy down the end came away from the wall showing too much curiosity. The stuff had to be dumped someplace but I couldn't be carrying it to the dumping ground.

Pat had to see it, the Washington boys would want a look at it. I couldn't take any kind of a chance at all on losing it. Not now.

So I shut the door and closed the lock through the hasp. It had been there a lot of years . . . a few more hours wouldn't hurt it any. But now I had something I could talk a trade with. I could describe the stuff so they'd be sure and it would be my way all the way.

The guy followed me back upstairs and got behind his desk again. He was snottier looking than ever but when I stood close the artificial toughness faded into blankness and he had to lick his lips.

I said, "Remember my face, buddy. Take a good look and keep it in your mind. If anybody who isn't a cop comes in here wanting to know about that locker and you kick through with the information I'm going to break your face into a dozen pieces. No matter what they do I'll do worse, so keep your trap shut." I turned to go, stopped a second and looked back over my shoulder. "The next time be polite. You could have made dough on the deal."

My watch read five minutes to three. Time, time, time. The rain was a solid sheet blasting the sidewalks and spraying back into the air again. I yelled for Lily to open the door, made a dash for it and slid aboard. She trembled under the gust of cold air that got in with me, her face set tighter than it was before.

I reached over and put my arm around her shoulders. She was pulled tight as a drumhead, a muscular stiffness that made her whole body almost immobile. "Cripes, Lily, I got to get you to a doctor."

"No . . . just get me where it's warm, Mike."

"I haven't got much sense."

She forced a smile. "I . . . really don't mind . . . as long as you . . ."

"No more chasing around, kid. I found it. I can take you back now."

There was a catch in the sob that came out of her. Her eyes glistened and the smile didn't have to be forced.

I sat there looking into the rain, pulling on a Lucky while I figured it out. I said, "You'll go back to my apartment, kid. Dry off and sit tight."

"Alone?"

"Don't worry about it. There are cops stationed around the building. I'll tip them to keep the place well covered. We have to move fast now and I can't waste time. I have a key to a couple of million bucks in my pocket and I can't put all my eggs in one basket. I'm getting a duplicate of that key made and you're hanging on to it until Captain Chambers picks it up. I don't want you to move out of that place until I get back and don't pull a stunt like you did before. Let's go, I still have a fast stop to make that won't take more than five minutes."

That was all it did take. My friend turned out the key while he swore at the world for getting him out of bed so I left him to buy a good night in a gin mill for his trouble.

We reached my block at a quarter to four with the rain still lashing at the car in frenzied bursts. There was a patrol wagon at each end and two plain-clothes men were standing in the doorway. When they saw us they looked so mad they could bust and one spit disgustedly and shook his head.

I didn't give them a chance to ask questions. "Sorry you were standing guard over a hole, friend. One of those things. We got this business breaking over our heads and I can't go explaining every move I make. I've been putting in calls all over the lot for Pat Chambers and if one of you guys feels like expediting things you'll get on the line too."

I pointed to Lily. "This is Lily Carver. They're after her as bad as they are me. She's got a message for Pat that can't wait and if anything happens to her between now and when he sees her he'll have your hides. One of you better take her up and stick outside in the hall."

"Johnston'll go."

"Good. You'll call around for Pat."

"We'll locate the captain somehow."

I got Lily inside, saw her through the front door with the cop beside her and felt the load go lighter.

"You got something, Hammer?" The cop was watching me closely.

"Yeah. It's almost over."

His grunt was a sarcastic denial. "You know better, buddy. It never ends. This thing is stretched all over the states. Wait till you see the morning papers."

"Good?"

"Lovely. The voters'll go nuts when they see the score. This town is going to see a reform cleanup like it never happened before. We had to book four of our own boys this evening." His hand turned into a fist. "They were playing along with them."

"The little guys," I said. "They pay through the nose. The wheels keep rolling right along. They string the dead out and walk over them. The little guy pays the price."

"We got wheels too. Evello's dead."

"Yeah," I said.

"How far did they get with his step-sister?"

"As far as here, buddy. People are thinking about that."

I looked across the lobby at him. "They would. They'll try to put the finger anyplace."

Michael Friday and her wet, lovely mouth. The mouth that never did get close enough, really close. Michael Friday with the ready smile and the laugh in her walk, Michael Friday who got tired of the dirt herself and put herself on my side of the fence. Coming to me with the thing I wanted even more than the stuff in the locker. She should have known. Damn it, those things had been happening under her nose. She should have known the kind of people she was messing around with. They're fast and smart and know the angles and they're ready to follow through. She should have thought it out and got herself a cordon of cops instead of cutting loose herself to get the stuff to me. Maybe she knew they'd be after her. Maybe she thought she was as smart as they were. Berga thought those things too.

Lovely Michael Friday. She steps outside and they have her. She could have been standing right where I was that minute. The door behind her locks shut. There's only one person outside and that's the one she's afraid of. Maybe she knew she only had a minute more to live and her insides must have been tumbling around loose.

Like Berga. But Berga did something in that minute.

I got that creepy feeling again, an indescribable tingling sensation that burned up my spine and touched my brain with thoughts that seemed improbable. I looked down at my feet, my teeth shut tight, squinting at the floor. The cop's breathing seemed the loudest thing in the room, even drowning out the thunder and the rain outside. I walked to the mailbox and opened it with my key.

Michael had thought too. She had left an empty envelope in there telling me exactly what she meant. It didn't have my name on it, but I read the message. It said, "William Mist," but it was enough.

It was more than enough. It was something else. The gimmick I was looking for, the one I knew I had come across someplace else but I couldn't put my finger on. But for a little while it was enough.

I crumpled the thing up into a little ball and dropped it. I could feel the hate welling up in me until I couldn't stand it any more. My head was filled with a crazy overture of sound that beat and beat and beat.

I ran out of the place. I left the cop standing there and ran out. I forgot everything I was doing except for one thing when I got in the car. Light, traffic? Hell, nothing mattered. There was only one thing. I was going to see that greaseball die between my fingers and he was going to talk before he did. The car screamed at the corners, the tail end whipping around violently. I could smell the rubber and brake lining and hear the whining protest of the engine and occasionally the hoarse curses that followed my path. The stops were all out this time and nothing else counted.

When I reached the apartment building I didn't push any bells to be let in. I kicked out a pane of glass on the inside door, reached through the hole and turned the knob. I went up the stairs to the same spot I had been before and this time I did hit the bell.

Billy Mist was expecting somebody, all right, but it wasn't me. He was all dressed except for his jacket and he had a gun slung in a harness under his shoulder. I rammed the door so hard it kicked him back in the room and while he was reaching for his rod I smashed his nose into a mess of bloody tissue. He made a second try while he was on the floor and this time I kicked the gun out of his hand under the table and picked him up to go over him good. I held him out where I wanted him and put one into his ribs that brought a scream choking up his throat and had the next one ready when Billy Mist died.

I didn't want to believe it. I wanted him alive so bad I shook him like a rag doll and when the mouth lolled open under those blank eyes I threw him away from me into the door and his head and shoulders slammed it shut. His broken face leered at me from the carpet, the eyes seeing nothing. They were filmy already. I let it go then. I let that raspy yell out of me and began to break things until I was out of breath.

But Billy still leered.

Billy Mist, who knew where Velda was. Billy Mist who was going to talk before he died. Billy Mist who was going to give me the pleasure of killing him slowly.

It was thinking of Velda that smoothed it. My hands stopped shaking and my mind started thinking again. I looked around the mess I had made of the place, avoiding the eyes on the floor.

Billy had been packing. He had been five minutes away from being killed and he was taking a quick-acting powder. The one suitcase had a week's supply of clothes in it but he could afford to buy more when he got there because the rest of the space was taken up by packets of new bills.

I was picking the stuff apart when I heard them at the door. They weren't cops. Not these boys. They wanted in because I was there and nothing was stopping them.

How long ago was it that I asked Berga how stupid could she get?

Now I was the one. Sammy had told me. They were waiting for me. Now in squad cars on the corner of my block. Not for the Ford because by now they'd have figured the switch. So I go busting loose with the pack on my back and now I was up the tree.

Shoulders slammed into the door and a vertical crack showed in it. I walked to the overturned chair, picked up Billy's rod and kicked the safety off. They were a little stupid too. They knew I was traveling clean but forgot Billy would be loaded. I pumped five fast ones through the wood belly-high and the screams outside made a deafening cacophony that brought more screams from others in the building.

The curses and screams didn't stop the others. The door cracked again, started to buckle and I turned and ran into the bathroom. There was a barrel bolt on the door made for decency purposes only and wouldn't hold anything longer than a minute or two. I slid it in place, took my time about opening the bathroom window and sighting along the ledge outside.

I got my feet on the sill, started to go through when my arm swept the bottles from the shelf. Dozens of bottles. A sick man's paradise and Billy had been a very sick man after all. There was one left my arm didn't touch and I picked it up. I stared at it, swore lightly and dropped it in my pocket.

The door inside let loose. There was more letting loose too. Shots and shrieks that didn't belong there and I crawled through the window before I could find out why. I felt along the ledge with my toes, leaning forward at an angle with my hands resting on the building on the other side of the airway. I made the end where the building joined, found handholds on the other sills and went up.

For a change I was glad of the rain. It covered the noises I made, washed clean places for my fingers and toes and when I reached the roof bathed me in its coolness. I lay there on the graveled top breathing the fire out of my lungs, barely conscious of the fury going on in the streets. When I could make it I got across the building, got on the fire escape and crawled down.

Somebody in a dark window was screaming her lungs out telling the world where I was. Shouts answered her from someplace else and two shots whined off into the night. They never found me. I hit the yard and got out of there. Sirens were converging on the place and a hundred yards off the rapid belch of a tommy gun spit a skinful of sudden destruction into the airway.

I laughed my fool head off while I stood there on the sidewalk and felt good about it. In a way it paid to be stupid as long as you overdid it. I was too stupid to figure the boys planted around my apartment would follow me and too stupid to remember there were the Washington boys who would run behind them. It must have made a pretty picture when they joined forces. It was something that had to come. The Mafia wasn't a gang, it was a government. And governments have armies and armies fight.

The trouble was that while the war raged the leader got away and had time to cover his tracks. I pulled the bottle out of my pocket, looked at it and threw it away.

Not this leader. He wasn't going anywhere except a hole in the ground.

CHAPTER 13

The office was dark. Water leaked through the hole I had made in the glass and the pieces winked back at me. Nobody at the desk. No beautiful smile, challenging eyes. I knew where to look and pulled the file out. I held a match to it and the pieces clicked in place. I put the card back and went through the rooms.

Off the inner office a door led to stairs that ran up, thickly carpeted stairs that didn't betray the passage of a person. There was another door at the top and an apartment off it. I kicked my shoes off, laid the change in my pocket on the floor and walked away from the one that showed the light.

There was only one room that was locked, but those kinds of locks never gave me any trouble at all. I stepped inside, eased the door shut and flicked my lighter.

She was laced into an easy chair with a straitjacket, her legs tied down. A strip of adhesive tape was across her mouth and around it were red marks where other tapes had been ripped off to feed her or hear what she had to say. There was a sallowness about her face, a fearful, shrunken look, but the eyes were alive. They couldn't see me behind the lighter, but they cursed me just the same.

I said, "Hello, Velda," and the cursing stopped. The eyes didn't believe until I moved the lighter and the tears wiped out her vision. I took the ropes off, unlaced the jacket and lifted her up easily. The hurt sounds she wanted to make but couldn't came out in the convulsions of her body. She pressed against me, the tears wetting my face. I squeezed her, ran my hands across her back while I whispered things to her and told her not to be afraid any more. I found her mouth and tasted her, deeply, loving the way she held me and the things she said without really saying anything.

When I could I said, "You all right?"

"I was going to die tonight."

"Somebody'll take your place."

"Now?"

"You won't be here to see it." I found the key in my pocket and pressed it in her hand. I gave her my wallet to go with it and pulled her to the door. "Take a cab and find yourself a cop. Find Pat if you can. There's an address on that key. Go hold what's in the locker it opens. Can you do that much?"

"Can't I . . ."

"I said get a cop. The bastards know everything there is to know. We can't lose any time at all . . . and most of all I can't lose you at all. Tomorrow we'll talk."

"Tomorrow, Mike."

"It's crazy this way. Everything's crazy. I find you and I'm sending you off again. Damn it, move before I don't let you go."

"Tomorrow, Mike," she said and reached for me again. She wasn't tired now, she was brand-new again. She was a woman I was never going to let go again ever. She didn't know it yet, but tomorrow there would be more than talk. I wanted her since I had first seen her. Tomorrow I'd get her. The way she wanted it. Tomorrow she was going to belong to me all the way.

"Say it, Mike."

"I love you, kitten. I love you more than I've ever thought I could love anything."

"I love you too, Mike." I could feel her grin. "Tomorrow."

I nodded and opened the door. I waited until she had gone down the steps and this time walked the other way. To where the light showed.

I pushed it open, leaned against the jamb and when the gray-haired man writing at the table across the room spun around I said, "Doctor Soberin, I presume."

It caught him so far off base I had time to get halfway across to him before he dipped his hand in the drawer and I had his wrist before he could get the thing leveled. I let him keep the gun in his hand so I could bend it back and hear his fingers break and when he tried to yell I bottled the sound up by smashing my elbow into his mouth. The shattered teeth tore my arm and his mouth became a great hole welling blood. His fingers were broken stubs sticking at odd angles. I shoved him away from me, slashed the butt end of the rod across the side of his head and watched him drop into his chair.

"I got me a wheel," I said. "The boy at the top."

Dr. Soberin opened his mouth to speak and I shook my head.

"You're dead, mister. Starting from now you're dead. It took me a long time. It didn't really have to." I let out a dry laugh at myself. "I'm getting too old for the game. I'm not as fast as I used to be. One time I would have had it made as soon as I rolled it around a little bit.

"The gimmick, doc, there's always that damned gimmick. The kind you can't kick out of sight. This time the gimmick was on the bottom of that card your secretary made out on Berga Torn. She asked who sent her and she said William Mist. She signed the card, too. You pulled a cutie on that one. You couldn't afford to let a respectable dame know your business, and you knew she wouldn't put her name on a switch. You knew there might be an investigation and didn't want any suspicious erasures on the card so you simply dug up a name that you could type over Mist to make the letters fit. Wieton comes out pretty well. Unless you looked hard you'd never pick it up."

He had gone a deathly pale. His hand was up to his mouth trying to stop the blood. It was sickening him and he retched. All that came up was more blood. The hand with the broken fingers looked unreal on the end of his arm. Unreal and painful.

"You took a lot of trouble to get the information Berga had under her hat. A lot of clever thinking went into that deal at the sanitarium. You had it rigged pretty nicely, even to a spot where she could be worked over without anybody getting wise. Sorry I spoiled your plans. You shouldn't have wrecked my heap."

Something childish crept into his face. "You . . . got . . . another one."

"I'll keep it too. I didn't go for the booby trap, doc. That was kid stuff."

If his face screwed up any tighter he was going to cry. He sat there moaning softly, the complete certainty of it all making him rock in his chair.

I said, "This time I do it your way. I was the only one you were ever afraid of because I was like the men you give orders to. I'm not going to talk to you. Later I'll go over the details. Later I'll give my explanations and excuses to the police. Later I'll get raked over the coals for what I'm going to do now, but what the hell, doc. Like I said, I'm getting old in the game. I don't care any more."

He was quiet in his chair. The quiet that terror brings and for once he was knowing the hand of terror himself.

I said, "Doc . . ." and he looked at me. No, not me, the gun. The big hole in the end of the gun.

And while he was looking I let him see what came out of the gun.

Doctor Soberin only had one eye left.

I stepped across the body and picked up the phone. I called headquarters and tried to get Pat. He was still out. I had the call transferred to another department and the man I wanted said hello. I asked him for the identification on a dead blonde and he told me to wait.

A minute later he picked up the phone. "Think I got it. Death by drowning. Age, about . . ."

"Skip the details. Just the name."

"Sure, Lily Carver. Prints just came in from Washington. She had 'em taken while she worked at a war plant."

I said thanks, held the button down on the phone, let it go and when I heard the dial tone started working on my home number.

She said, "Don't bother, Mike. I'm right here."

And she was.

Beautiful Lily with hair as white as snow. Her mouth a scarlet curve that smiled. Differently, now, but still smiling. Her body a tight bundle of lush curves that swelled and moved under a light white terrycloth robe. Lovely Lily who brought the sharpness of an alcohol bath in with her so that it wet her robe until there was nothing there, no hill or valley, no shadow that didn't come out.

Gorgeous Lily with my .45 in her hand from where she had found it on the dresser.

"You forgot about me, Mike."

"I almost did, didn't I."

There was cold hate coming into her eyes now. Hate that grew as she looked again at the one eye in the body beside the table. "You shouldn't have done that, Mike."

"No?"

"He was the only one who knew about me." The smile left her mouth. "I loved him. He knew about me and didn't care. I loved him, you crumb you!" The words hissed out of her teeth.

I looked at her the way I did when she first held a gun on me. "Sure. You loved him so much you killed Lily Carver and took her place. You loved him so much you made sure there were no slips in his plan. You loved him so much you set Berga Torn up for the kill and damn near made sure Velda died. You loved him so much you never saw that all he loved was power and money and you were only something he could use.

"You fitted right into the racket. You were lucky once and smart the rest of the time. You reached Al after Velda left but you had time to catch up with her. By the way, did you ever find out why Al died? He was giving friend Billy Mist the needle. Billy knew what had happened when you called him down to tell him his girl friend wasn't what she was cracked up to be. With Billy that didn't go and he carved up his playmate. Nice people to have around."

"Shut up."

"Shut up hell. You stuck with me all the way. You ducked out because you thought the boys had me once, then came back when you found out I propped them up against a DEAD END sign. You passed the word right under my nose and had Billy packing to blow town. What a deal that was. I even showed you how to get out of my apartment without a tail picking you up. That's why you're here now. So what was supposed to happen? You go back to your real identity? Nuts. You're part of it and you'll die with it. You played me for a sucker up and down Broadway but it's over. This isn't the first time you've pointed a rod at me, sugar. The last time was a game, but I didn't know it. I'm still going to take it away from you. What kind of a guy do you think I am anyway?"

Her face changed as if I had slapped her. For an instant the strangeness was back again. "You're a deadly man, Mike."

Then I saw it in her face and she was faster than I was. The rod belched flame and the slug tore into my side and spun me around. There was a crazy spinning sensation, a feeling of tumbling end over end through space, an urge to vomit, but no strength left to vomit with.

My eyes cleared and I pushed myself up on an elbow. There was a loose, empty feeling in my joints. The end was right there ahead of me and nothing I could do about it.

Lily smiled again, the end of the .45 drifting down to my stomach. She laughed at me, knowing I could raise myself to reach for it. My mouth was dry. I wanted a cigarette. It was all I could think about. It was something a guy about to die always got. My fingers found the deck of Luckies, fumbled one loose and got it into my mouth. I could barely feel it laying there on my lips.

"You shouldn't have killed him," Lily said again.

I reached for the lighter. It wasn't going to be long now. I could feel things start to loosen up. My mind was having trouble hearing her. One more shot. It would be quick.

"Mike . . ."

I got my eyes open. She was a strong, pungent smell. Very strong. Still lovely though.

"I thought I almost loved you once. More than . . . him. But I didn't Mike. He would take me like I was. He was the one who gave me life, at least, after . . . it happened. He was the doctor. I was the patient. I loved him. You would have been disgusted with me. I can see your eyes now, Mike. They would have been revolted.

"He was deadly too, Mike . . . but not like you. You're even worse. You're the deadly one, but you would have been revolted. Look at me, Mike. How would you like to kiss me now? You wanted to before. Would you like to now? I wanted you to . . . you know that, don't you? I was afraid to even let you touch me. You wanted to kiss me . . . so kiss me."

Her fingers slipped through the belt of the robe, opened it. Her hands parted it slowly . . . until I could see what she was really like. I wanted to vomit worse than before. I wanted to let my guts come up and felt my belly retching.

She was a horrible caricature of a human! There was no skin, just a disgusting mass of twisted, puckered flesh from her knees to her neck making a picture of gruesome freakishness that made you want to shut your eyes against it.

The cigarette almost fell out of my mouth. The lighter shook in my hand, but I got it open.

"Fire did it, Mike. Do you think I'm pretty now?"

She laughed and I heard the insanity in it. The gun pressed into my belt as she kneeled forward, bringing the revulsion with her. "You're going to die now . . . but first you can do it. Deadly . . . deadly . . . kiss me."

The smile never left her mouth and before it was on me I thumbed the lighter and in the moment of time before the scream blossoms into the wild cry of terror she was a mass of flame tumbling on the floor with the blue flames of alcohol turning the white of her hair into black char and her body convulsing under the agony of it. The flames were teeth that ate, ripping and tearing, into scars of other flames and her voice the shrill sound of death on the loose.

I looked, looked away. The door was closed and maybe I had enough left to make it.

About the Author

A bartender's son, **Mickey Spillane** was born in Brooklyn, New York, on March 9, 1918. An only child who swam and played football as a youth, Spillane got a taste for storytelling by scaring other kids around the campfire. After a truncated college career, Spillane—already selling stories to pulps and slicks under pseudonyms—became a writer in the burgeoning comic-book field, a career cut short by World War II. Spillane, who had learned to fly at air strips as a boy, became an instructor of fighter pilots.

After the war, Spillane converted an unsold comic-book project—"Mike Danger, Private Eye"—into a hard-hitting, sexy novel. The thousand-dollar advance was just what the writer needed to buy materials for a house he wanted to build for himself and his young wife on a patch of land in New Jersey.

The 1948 Signet reprint of his 1947 E.P. Dutton hardcover novel *I, the Jury* sold in the millions, as did the six tough mysteries that soon followed; all but one featured hard-as-nails P.I. Mike Hammer. The Hammer thriller *Kiss Me, Deadly* (1952) was the first private eye novel to make the *New York Times* bestseller list.

Mike Hammer's creator claims only to write when he needs the money, and in periods of little or no publishing, Spillane has been occupied with other pursuits: flying, traveling with the circus, appearing in motion pictures, and nearly twenty years spoofing himself and Hammer in a lucrative series of Miller Lite beer commercials.

The controversial Hammer has been the subject of a radio show, a comic strip, two television series, and numerous gritty movies, notably director Robert Aldrich's seminal film noir *Kiss Me Deadly* (1955) and *The Girl Hunters* (1963), starring Spillane as his famous hero.

Spillane has been honored by the Mystery Writers of America with the Grand Master Award, and with the Private Eye Writers of America "Eye" Lifetime Achievement Award; he is also a Shamus Award winner. A major motion picture is in development of the science-fiction revival of his comic book character "Mike Danger" (cocreated by Max Allan Collins). Spillane lives with his wife, Jane, in South Carolina.